select
editions

Reader's
Digest

Reader's Digest

The condensations in this volume
are published with the consent of the authors
and the publishers © 2012 Reader's Digest, Inc.

www.readersdigest.co.uk

Published in the United Kingdom by Vivat Direct Limited
(t/a Reader's Digest), 157 Edgware Road,
London W2 2HR

For information as to ownership of
copyright in the material of this book,
and acknowledgments, see last page.

Printed in Germany
ISBN 978 1 78020 106 1

select
editions

contents

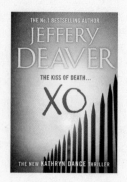

To Country singer Kayleigh Towne her song 'Your Shadow' is simply her latest hit. But to one obsessed fan, it holds a hidden message especially for him. Then people start dying, and the verses in the song are the only clues. A tense, taut thriller.

Our memories define us, but in one catastrophic moment Jack Vaughan loses all of his. As he reconstructs his past, he doesn't much care for the man he finds. Is it too late to change? A funny, moving and poignant story.

a most peculiar malaysian murder
shamini flint

315

Unlike Hercule Poirot, Inspector Singh is dishevelled, overweight and sweaty. But like Agatha Christie's Poirot, Singh has an instinct for solving crimes that might just foil the local police. And now he's in Kuala Lumpur to save a mother from death row.

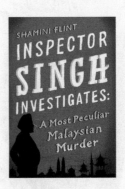

now you see her
joy fielding

453

A tale of courage, determination, and the power of a mother's love. Marcy Taggart cannot accept that her beloved, but troubled, daughter is dead. Then she sees her on the streets of Cork, and so begins her riveting quest for the truth.

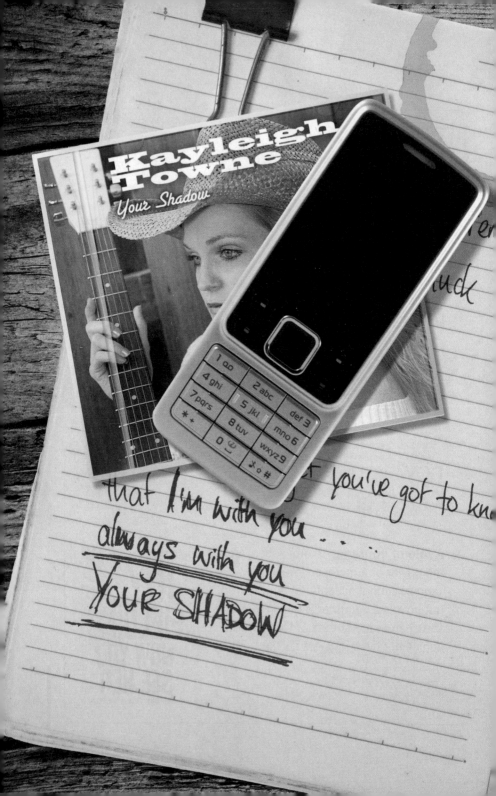

XO
JEFFERY
DEAVER

Kayleigh Towne is gorgeous, with a voice that has
taken her to the top of the Country music charts.
But being in the spotlight has its downsides—and one
particular fan won't leave the singer alone.
Then, Kayleigh's phone rings. When she answers, she
hears a verse from her latest hit, 'Your Shadow':

'You walk out onstage and sing folks your songs.
You make them all smile. What could go wrong?
But soon you discover, the job takes its toll,
And everyone's wanting a piece of your soul.'

Is this a warning? Is Kayleigh herself in peril?
For Special Investigator Kathryn Dance, the song
holds the only immediate clues . . .

Subject: Re: You're the Best!!!
From: noreply@kayleightownemusic.com
To: EdwinSharp18474@anon.com

January 2, 10:32 a.m.
Edwin:
Thanks for your email! I'm so glad you liked my latest album! Your support means the world to me. Be sure to go to my web site and sign up to get my newsletter and learn about new releases and upcoming concerts.

   And keep an eye out for the mail. I sent you that autographed photo you requested!
   XO, Kayleigh

Subject: Unbelievable!!!!!
From: EdwinSharp26535@anon.com
To: ktowne7788@compserve.com

September 3, 5:10 a.m.
Hi, Kayleigh:
I am totally blown away. I downloaded your new album last night and listened to 'Your Shadow'. Whoahhh! It's without a doubt the best song I have ever heard. I've told you nobody's ever expressed how I feel about loneliness and life and well everything better than you. And that song does that totally. But more important I can see what you're saying, your plea for help. It's all clear now. Don't worry. You're not alone, Kayleigh!! I'll be *your* shadow. Forever.
   XO, Edwin

Subject: Fwd: Unbelievable!!!!!
From: Samuel.King@CrowellSmithWendall.com
To: EdwinSharp26535@anon.com

September 3, 10:34 a.m.

Mr Sharp:

Ms Alicia Sessions, personal assistant to our clients Kayleigh Towne and her father, Bishop Towne, forwarded us your email of this morning. You have sent more than fifty emails and letters since we contacted you two months ago, urging you not to have any contact with Ms Towne or any of her friends and family. We are extremely troubled that you have found her private email address (which has been changed), and are looking into possible violations of state and federal laws regarding how you obtained such address.

Once again, we must tell you that we feel your behaviour is completely inappropriate and possibly actionable. We urge you in the strongest terms possible to heed this warning. As we've said repeatedly, Ms Towne's security staff and local law-enforcement officials have been notified of your intrusive attempts to contact her and we are fully prepared to take whatever steps are necessary to put an end to this alarming behaviour.

Samuel King, Esq., Crowell, Smith & Wendall, Attorneys At Law

Subject: See you soon!!!
From: EdwinSharp26535@anon.com
To: KST33486@westerninternet.com

September 5, 11:43 p.m.

Hi, Kayleigh:

Got your new email address. I know what they're up to but DON'T worry, it'll be all right.

I'm lying in bed, listening to you right now. I feel like I'm literally your shadow . . . And you're mine. You are so wonderful!

I don't know if you had a chance to think about it—you're sooooo busy, I know!—but I'll ask again—if you wanted to send me some of your hair that'd be so cool. I know you haven't cut it for ten years and four months. Maybe there's one from your brush. Or better yet your pillow. I'll treasure it forever.

Can't WAIT for the concert next Friday. C U soon.

Yours forever,

XO, Edwin

SUNDAY

1

The heart of a concert hall is people.

And when the vast space is dim and empty, as this one was at the moment, a venue can bristle with indifference. Even hostility.

OK, rein in that imagination, Kayleigh Towne told herself. Standing on the wide, scuffed stage of the Fresno Conference Center's main hall, she surveyed the place. She was preparing for Friday's concert, considering lighting and stage movements and where the members of the band should stand and sit.

There were a hundred other details to think about. She believed that every performance should be perfect and that every audience deserved the best. More than perfect. One hundred and ten per cent. She had, after all, grown up in Bishop Towne's shadow. An unfortunate choice of word, Kayleigh now reflected.

I'll be your *shadow. Forever . . .*

Back to the planning. This show had to be different from the previous one here, eight months ago. Many of the fans regularly attended her home-town concerts and she wanted to make sure they got something unexpected. Kayleigh's audiences were as loyal as golden retrievers. They knew her lyrics, knew her guitar licks, knew her moves onstage and laughed at her shtick before she finished the lines. They lived and breathed her perfor-mances, hung on her words, knew her bio and likes and dislikes. And some wanted to know much more . . .

With that thought, her heart and gut clenched. Thinking about *him*, of course. Then she froze, gasping. Someone was watching her from the far end of the hall! Where none of the crew would be.

Shadows were moving.

Or was it her imagination? Or her eyesight? Kayleigh had been given an angelic voice but God had skimped big-time on the vision. She squinted, adjusted her glasses. She was sure that someone was hiding in the doorway that led to the concession stands.

Then the movement stopped. She decided it wasn't movement at all. Just a hint of light, a suggestion of shading.

Though still, she heard a series of troubling clicks and snaps and groans—from where, she couldn't tell—and felt a chill of panic bubble up her spine. *Him* . . .

The man who had written her hundreds of emails and letters, intimate, delusional, speaking of the life they could share together, asking for a strand of hair, a fingernail clipping. The man who had somehow got near enough at a dozen shows to take close-up pictures of Kayleigh, without anyone ever seeing him.

The man who had sent her dozens of pictures of himself: shaggy hair, fat, in clothing that looked unwashed.

Her father had recently hired a personal bodyguard, a huge man with a round, bullet-shaped head. But Darthur Morgan was outside at the moment, making the rounds and checking cars.

She scanned the recesses of the hall again. Then, gritting her teeth in anger at her fear, she thought, What're you worried about? You're not alone. The band wasn't in town yet—they were finishing some studio work in Nashville—but Bobby Prescott was at the huge mixing console at the back of the hall, 200 feet away. Alicia was getting the rehearsal rooms in order. A couple of beefy guys in Bobby's road crew were unpacking the truck in the back, assembling and organising the hundreds of tools and props and ply-wood sheets and stands and amps and instruments and computers that even modest touring bands like Kayleigh's needed.

She supposed one of them could get to her in a hurry if the source of the shadow had been *him*. Dammit, quit making *him* more than *he* is! *Him, him, him,* like you're even afraid to say his name.

She'd had other obsessed fans—what gorgeous singer with a voice from heaven wouldn't collect a few inappropriate admirers? She'd had twelve marriage proposals from men she'd never met, a dozen couples wanted to adopt her, thirty teen girls wanted to be her best friend, a thousand men wanted to buy her dinner.

Usually she was cautiously amused by the attention. But not now. Kayleigh snagged her denim jacket from a nearby chair and pulled it on to cover her T-shirt, providing another barrier to any prying eyes. This, despite the characteristic September heat in Fresno, which filled the murky venue like thin stew.

And more of those clicks and taps from nowhere.

'Kayleigh?'

She turned quickly, trying to hide her slight jump, even though she recognised the voice.

A solidly built woman of around thirty paused halfway across the stage. She had cropped red hair and some subdued inking on her arms, shoulders and spine, partly visible thanks to her trim tank top and tight black jeans. Fancy cowboy boots. 'Didn't mean to scare you.'

'You didn't. What's up?' she asked Alicia Sessions.

A nod towards the iPad she carried. 'These just came in. Proofs for the new posters. If we get them to the printer today we'll definitely have them by the show. They look OK to you?'

Kayleigh examined them on the screen. Music nowadays is only partly about music, of course, and the business side of her career took up a lot more time than it used to. She didn't have much interest in these matters, but she didn't need to. Her father was her manager, Alicia handled the day-to-day paperwork, the lawyers read the contracts, the record company made arrangements with the recording studios, the CD production companies, the retail and download outlets; her long-time producer at BHRC Records, Barry Zeigler, handled the technical side of arranging and production, and Bobby and the crew set up and ran the shows. All so that Kayleigh could do what she did best: write songs and sing them.

Still, one business matter of interest to her was making sure fans—many of them young or without much money—could buy cheap but decent memorabilia to make the night of the concert that much more special. Posters like this one, T-shirts, key chains, bracelets, charms, guitar chord books, headbands and backpacks.

She studied the proofs. The image was of Kayleigh and her favourite Martin guitar. The photo was the inside picture from her latest album *Your Shadow*.

Him . . .

No, don't. Eyes scanning the doors again.

'You sure you're OK?' Alicia asked, voice buzzing with a faint Texas twang.

'Yeah.' Kayleigh returned to the proofs, which all featured the same photo though with different type, messages and background. Her picture depicted her much as she saw herself: at five foot two inches, her face a bit long, but with stunning blue eyes, lashes that wouldn't quit and lips that had some reporters talking collagen. Her trademark golden hair, four feet long, flowed in the fake gentle breeze from the photographer's electric fan. Designer jeans and high-collared dark red blouse. A diamond crucifix.

'You gotta give the fans the visual package,' Bishop Towne always said. 'And the standards're different 'tween men and women.' He meant that in the Country music world a man could get away with a look like Bishop's own: jutting belly, cigarette, a lined, craggy face riddled with stubble, wrinkled shirt, scuffed boots and faded jeans. A woman singer, he lectured—though he really intended to say 'girl'—had to be put together for date night. In Kayleigh's case that meant a church social: the good girl next door was the image on which she'd built her career. Sure, the jeans could be a little tight, the blouses could closely hug her round chest, but the necklines were high. The make-up was subtle and pink.

'Go with them.'

'Great.' Alicia shut off the device. A slight pause. 'I haven't got your father's OK yet.'

'They're good,' the singer reassured, nodding at the iPad.

'Sure. I'll just run it by him. You know.'

Now Kayleigh paused. Then, 'OK.'

'Acoustics good here?' asked Alicia, who had been a performer herself; she had quite a voice and a love of music, which was undoubtedly why she'd taken a job for Kayleigh Towne. She'd signed on last spring and had never heard the band perform here.

'Oh, the sound is great,' Kayleigh said, glancing at the ugly concrete walls. 'You wouldn't think it.' She explained that too many concert halls had been built by people without the confidence in the natural ability of musical instruments and voices to reach the farthest seats with the sound emanating from the stage. Architects would add angular surfaces and free-standing shapes to boost the volume of the music, which did that but also sent the vibrations in a hundred directions. This resulted in every performer's acoustic nightmare, reverberation: in effect, echoes upon echoes that yielded muddy, sometimes off-key, sounds.

Here, in modest Fresno, Kayleigh explained to Alicia, the designers had trusted in the power and purity of the voice and drum skin and reed and string. She was about to ask the assistant to join her in a chorus of one of her songs to prove her point—Alicia did great harmonies—when she noticed her looking towards the back of the hall, frowning.

'What?' Kayleigh asked.

'Isn't it just us and Bobby up front?'

'What do you mean?'

'I thought I saw somebody.' She lifted a finger tipped in a black-painted nail. 'That doorway. There.'

Just where Kayleigh had thought she'd seen the shadow ten minutes before. Palms sweating, Kayleigh stared at the changing shapes in the back of the hall. Yes . . . no. She just couldn't tell.

Shrugging her shoulders, Alicia said, 'Hm. Guess not. Whatever it was it's gone now . . . OK, see you at the restaurant at one?'

'Yeah, sure.'

Kayleigh listened to the thumping of boots as she left and continued to stare at the black doorways. Angrily, she whispered, 'Edwin Sharp.' There. I've said *his* name. Now that I've conjured you up, listen here: get out of my concert hall! I've got work to do.

She turned from the inky, gaping doorway, stepped to centre stage, looking over the masking tape on the dusty wood, blocking out where she would stand at different points during the concert.

It was then that she heard a man's voice crying from the back of the hall, 'Kayleigh!' It was Bobby, now rising from behind the mixing console, ripping his hardshell earphones off. He pointed to a spot over her head. 'Look out! . . . No, Kayleigh!'

She glanced up fast and saw one of the strip lights—a seven-foot Colortran unit—falling free of its mounting and swinging towards the stage by its thick electric cable.

Stepping back instinctively, she tripped over a guitar stand.

Tumbling, arms flailing, gasping . . .

The young woman hit the stage hard, on her tailbone. The massive light plummeted towards her, a deadly pendulum, growing bigger and bigger. She tried desperately to rise but fell back, blinded as the searing beams from the thousand-watt bulbs turned her way.

Then everything went black.

KATHRYN DANCE had several lives.

Widowed mother of two children approaching their teen years.

Agent with the California Bureau of Investigation, her speciality interrogation and kinesics—body language analysis.

Dutiful daughter to parents who lived nearby.

Then there was life number four, which was nearly as vital to her well-being as the first three: music. Dance was a folklorist. Occasionally she'd climb into her SUV, sometimes with kids and dogs, sometimes, like now, solo, and go in search of music.

Dance was now piloting her Pathfinder along Highway 152 from the Monterey Peninsula through a largely barren stretch of California to Fresno in the San Joaquin Valley, three hours away. This was the agricultural heart of the country and open double-trailer trucks, piled high with tomatoes, garlic and other fruits and vegetables, rolled endlessly towards the massive food-processing plants in the hazy distance. The working fields were verdant or, if harvested already, rich black, but everything else was dry and dun as forgotten toast.

Dance's mission over the next few days was to record the homemade tunes of a local group of Mexican musicians, all of whom lived in or near Fresno. Most of them picked in the fields so they'd adopted the name *Los Trabajadores*, the Workers. Dance would record them on her digital sound recorder, then edit and post the songs on her web site, 'American Tunes'.

People could download them for a small fee, of which she would send most to the musicians, and would keep enough to cover the cost of the site and to take herself and the kids out to dinner occasionally. No one got rich from the downloads but some groups she had discovered had come to regional or even national attention.

She'd just come off a tough case in Monterey, the CBI office she was assigned to, and had decided to take some time off. The children were at their music and sports camps and spending the nights, along with the dogs, with their grandparents. And Dance would be free to record *Los Trabajadores* and look for other talent in this musically rich area. Not only Latino but a unique strain of Country could be found here. In fact, the Bakersfield sound, originating in that city a few hours south of Fresno, had been a major Country music movement in the Fifties and it had enjoyed a recent resurgence.

Dance had considered making this trip a romantic getaway and inviting Jon Boling to come with her. But he'd just been given a consulting assignment for a computer start-up and would be tied up for several days.

Dance turned up the air conditioning. This time of year the Monterey Peninsula was comfortable, even chilly occasionally, and she'd dressed according to her port of embarkation. In a long-sleeved grey cotton shirt and blue jeans, she was hot. The Pathfinder's thermometer reported ninety-six degrees outside. September. Right.

Dance was looking forward to the trip for another reason—to see her only celebrity friend, Kayleigh Towne, the now-famous singer-songwriter. Kayleigh had been a long-time supporter of Dance's web site. The singer had invited Dance to her big concert on Friday night in Fresno. Though a dozen years younger than Dance, Kayleigh had been a performer since she was nine or ten years old and a pro since her late teens. Funny, sophisticated and one hell of a writer and entertainer, with no ego whatsoever, the woman was mature beyond her years. Dance enjoyed her company very much.

She was the daughter of Country music legend Bishop Towne. On two or three occasions when Dance had come to Kayleigh's concerts, or visited her in Fresno, Bishop had lumbered into the room with his thousand-pound ego and the intensity of somebody as addicted to recovery as he had been to cocaine and liquor. He was brash, crude and overtly theatrical. His voice had deserted him, but he was in bold control of Kayleigh's career.

Dance now entered Fresno proper. The city was a nondescript working town of about half a million. The satellite got her easily to the Mountain View Motel off Highway 41. Stepping into the brittle heat, Dance felt light-headed. Breakfast with the kids and dogs had been a long time ago.

The hotel room wasn't ready yet but that didn't matter, since she was meeting Kayleigh and some friends in a half-hour—at one. She checked her bags with the front desk, got back into the Pathfinder and punched another address into the GPS satellite navigation system. At a stop light she picked up her phone, glanced at the incoming call list. Empty.

Odd that there was nothing from Kayleigh, who was going to call that morning to confirm their get-together.

Dance called Kayleigh, but it went straight to voicemail.

KATHRYN DANCE had to laugh. The owners of the Cowboy Saloon had a sense of humour. The dark, woody place, giddily cool, had not one cowboy artefact in the whole place. But life in the saddle was well represented—by the *women* who rode the range, roped, branded and punched cattle.

At the bar Kathryn ordered an iced tea. She sat at one of the round tables, over-varnished and nicked, looking at the clientele. A trio of jump-suited utility workers, a slim young man in jeans and plaid shirt studying the old-fashioned jukebox, several businessmen in white shirts and dark ties.

She was looking forward to seeing Kayleigh, but she was concerned. It was now one twenty. Where was her friend?

Music from the jukebox filled the place. Dance gave a faint laugh. It was a Kayleigh Towne song—a good choice, considering this venue: 'Me, I'm Not a Cowgirl'. It was about a suburban soccer mom, who seems to live a life very different from that of a cowgirl but in the end realises that maybe she's one in spirit. Typical of Kayleigh's songs, it was light-hearted and yet spoke meaningfully to people.

It was then that the front door opened and a slab of powerful sunlight fell onto the scuffed linoleum floor, on which danced geometric shapes, the shadows of the people entering.

Dance rose. 'Kayleigh!'

Surrounded by four others, the young singer stepped into the restaurant, smiling but also looking around quickly. She was troubled, Dance noted. No, more than that, Kayleigh was scared.

But whatever she'd been concerned about finding here was absent and she relaxed, then stepped forward, hugging Dance firmly. 'Kathryn, hey. This is so great!'

'I couldn't wait to get here.'

The singer was in jeans and, oddly, a thick denim jacket, despite the heat. Her lovely hair flowed free, nearly as long as she was tall.

Dance added, 'I called a couple of times.'

'There was . . . well, there was a little problem at the concert hall. It's all right. Hey, everybody, this's my bud, Kathryn Dance.'

Dance greeted Bobby Prescott, whom she'd met a few years ago. Almost thirty, an actor's looks belied by a shy smile, curly brown hair. There was pudgy and terminally shy Tye Slocum, with long red hair, the band's guitar technician and repairman. Unsmiling, athletic Alicia Sessions, looking to Dance like she belonged in a Manhattan punk-rock club, was Kayleigh's personal assistant.

And someone else was in the entourage. An African-American man, over six feet tall, well into the 250-pound range.

Security. The fact that Kayleigh had a bodyguard wasn't surprising, though Dance was troubled to note that he was intent on the job, even here. He carefully examined everyone in the bar, then he turned his attention back to Kayleigh. 'Looks OK to me.'

His name was Darthur Morgan and when he shook Dance's hand he examined her closely and his eyes gave a flicker of recognition. Dance, as an expert in kinesics and body language, knew that she gave off 'cop' vibrations, even when not intending to.

'Join us for lunch,' Kayleigh said to the big man.

'No, thank you, ma'am. I'll be outside.' He steamed slowly through the restaurant and stepped outside.

A skinny bartender came over, carrying menus.

Kayleigh glanced at the jukebox, embarrassed that it was her voice serenading them.

'So,' Dance asked, 'what happened?'

'OK, I'll tell you.' Kayleigh explained that as she was doing some prep work, for the concert on Friday, a strip light—one of the long ones above the stage—came loose and fell.

'Good heavens. You're all right?'

'Yeah, fine. Aside from a sore butt.'

Bobby, sitting next to Kayleigh, gripped her arm. He looked at her protectively. 'I don't know how it happened,' he said in a low voice. 'I mean, it was a strip light. You don't mount or dismount it for a show. It was there permanently.'

Eyes avoiding everyone's, big Tye Slocum offered, 'And you checked it, Bobby. I saw you. Twice. All the lights.'

'If it'd hit her,' Alicia said, angrily, 'it could've killed her.'

Bobby added, 'Could've also set the place on fire, if the lamps had shattered. I'm going to check it out better tonight. I've got to go to Bakersfield first, to pick up a new amplifier and speaker bank.'

Then the incident was tucked away and they ordered lunch. The conversation turned to Dance's musical web site and she talked about her own failed attempts at being a singer in San Francisco.

A man's voice interrupted. 'Excuse me. Hey, there, Kayleigh.'

It was the young man from the jukebox.

'Hello.' The singer's tone was bright but guarded.

'Didn't mean to be eavesdropping. I heard there was some problem. You all right?'

'Just fine, thanks.'

Silence for a moment.

Kayleigh said, 'You're a fan?'

'Sure am.'

'Thanks for your support. You going to the concert on Friday?'

'Oh, you bet. I'll be there. You sure you're OK?'

A pause, bordering on the awkward. 'Sure am.'

Bobby said, 'OK, friend. We're going to get back to lunch.'

As if the roadie hadn't even spoken, the man said with a breathy laugh, 'You don't recognise me, do you?'

'Sorry,' the singer offered.

Alicia said, 'Ms Towne'd like some privacy, you don't mind.'

'Hey, Alicia,' the young man said to her.

The personal assistant blinked. Obviously she hadn't recognised the man and would be wondering how he knew her name.

Then he ignored her too and laughed again, his voice high, eerie. 'It's me, Kayleigh! Edwin Sharp. Your shadow.'

A LOUD BANG echoed in the restaurant as Kayleigh's iced tea glass slipped from her grip and slammed into the floor.

The big glass produced a sound so like a gunshot that Dance found her hand moving to the place where her Glock pistol—presently locked away in her bedside safe at home—normally rested.

Eyes wide, Kayleigh said, 'You're . . . you're . . . Edwin.'

Her reaction approached panic but, with a brow furrowed in sympathy, he said, 'Kayleigh, it's OK. Don't you worry.'

'But . . .' Her eyes were zipping to the door, on the other side of which was Darthur Morgan and, if Dance was right, his own pistol.

Dance tried to piece it together. Couldn't be a former boyfriend; she'd have recognised him earlier. Must be an inappropriate fan.

'No embarrassment you didn't recognise me,' Edwin said. 'Since I sent you that last picture of me I lost some weight. Yep, seventy-three pounds. I read *Country Week* and *EW*, see the pictures of you with those boys. I know you like slimmer builds. And I got myself a twenty-five-dollar haircut! Like your song. I wasn't going to give you a Mr Tomorrow. I'm a Mr Today.'

Kayleigh was speechless. Nearly hyperventilating.

From some angles Edwin would be good-looking—hair trimmed conservatively, deep brown eyes, smooth complexion. But that face was also very long, angular, with heavy, protruding eyebrows. He was trim, but big—easily six foot three inches and despite the weight loss he was probably 200 pounds. His arms were long and hands massive but curiously pink.

Instantly Bobby Prescott was on his feet and stepping in front of the man. Bobby was large too but wide, not tall, and Edwin towered over him.

'Hey,' Edwin said cheerfully, 'Bobby. The roadie. Excuse me, chief of the road crew.' And then his eyes returned to Kayleigh, staring at her adoringly. 'I'd be honoured if you'd have some iced tea with me. Just over there in the corner. I've got a few things to show you.'

'How did you—'

'Know you'd be here? Everybody knows this is your favourite place. Just look at the blogs. It's where you wrote "Me, I'm Not a Cowgirl".' He nodded at the jukebox, from which that very song was playing at the moment—for the second time, Dance noted.

'I really . . .' Kayleigh was a deer in the middle of the road.

Bobby put his hand on Edwin's shoulder. Edwin stepped back a few inches, ignoring Bobby. 'Come on, let's get that iced tea. Hey, your hair's really beautiful. Ten years, four months.'

Dance had no idea what that meant but the comment clearly upset Kayleigh even more. Her jaw trembled.

'Kayleigh'd like to be left alone,' Alicia said firmly.

'You enjoying working for the band, Alicia?' he asked her. 'You've been with 'em about, five, six months, right? You're talented too. I've seen you on YouTube. You can sing. Wow.'

Alicia leaned forward ominously. 'How do you know me?'

'Listen, friend,' Bobby muttered. 'Time for you to leave.'

Then Tye Slocum pushed back in his chair and strode to the door. Edwin's eyes followed. 'Kayleigh, I didn't want to bother you here but you never got back to me on email. I just want to visit for a bit.'

'I really can't.'

There was a blinding flash of light as the door opened. Darthur Morgan moved in fast. He looked at Edwin, and Dance could see the muscles around the mouth tighten. 'You're Edwin Sharp?'

'That's right, Mr Morgan.'

It wasn't hard to get information about people nowadays. But learning the name of Kayleigh Towne's security guard?

'I'm going to ask you to leave Ms Towne alone now. She wants you to leave. You're becoming a security threat.'

'Well, under *Giles v. Lohan*, I'm really not, Mr Morgan. There's not even an implied threat. I'm just here offering my friend some sympathy over something traumatic that happened to her. And seeing if she'd like some tea. Happy to buy you some too.'

'I think that's about it now,' Morgan said firmly.

Edwin continued, 'You're private. You can make a citizen's arrest but only if you see me committing a crime. I haven't done that. If you were a police officer, that'd be different but you're—'

Well, it's come to that, Dance thought. Guess I knew it would. And she rose, displaying her CBI identification card.

'Ah.' Edwin stared at it. 'Had a feeling you were law.'

'Could I see some ID?'

'You bet.' He handed over his Washington state driver's licence. Edwin Stanton Sharp. Address in Seattle. The picture was of somebody who was much heavier and with long, stringy hair.

'Where are you staying in Fresno?' Dance asked.

'A house by Woodward Park. One of those new developments.'

'You moved here?' Alicia asked in a surprised whisper.

'Nope, just renting. I'm in town for the concert.'

'No, you wanted to stalk Kayleigh,' Bobby blurted. 'The lawyers warned you about that.'

Lawyers? Dance wondered.

Edwin looked round the table. 'I think you all know the way you're acting is upsetting Kayleigh.' He said to her, 'I'm sorry about that. I know what you're up against. But it'll all work out.' He walked to the door.

WHEN DANCE SAID, 'Tell me,' they did. All of them. At once.

And only after she'd reined in the intersecting narratives did she grasp the whole picture. Last winter a fan had become convinced that Kayleigh's automated form letters and emails, which had ended '*XO, Kayleigh*', were to be taken literally. Because the songs had meant so much to him, he'd decided that they were soul mates. He began a barrage of correspondence and he'd sent her presents.

Advised to ignore him, Kayleigh and her assistants stopped responding, except to send back the gifts, but Edwin persisted.

He was told to stop, dozens of times. The law firm representing Kayleigh and her father threatened him with civil action and referral to the police if he didn't cease and desist.

But he hadn't.

'It's been so creepy,' Kayleigh said, her voice breaking. 'He'd want a strand of hair, a fingernail clipping. He'd get photos of me in places where I'd never seen anybody, backstage or in parking lots.'

Dance said, 'That's the thing. You never quite know where a stalker is. Maybe miles away. Maybe outside your window.'

Kayleigh continued, 'And the mail! Hundreds of letters and emails. I'd change my email address and a few hours later he'd have the new one.'

'Do you think he had anything to do with the light that fell?' Dance asked.

Kayleigh said she thought she'd seen some shadow moving at the convention centre, but she hadn't seen an actual person.

Alicia Sessions was more certain. 'I saw something too, I'm sure.' She shrugged her broad shoulders, offering hints of tattoos largely hidden under the cloth. 'Nothing specific, though. No face or body.'

Dance asked, 'Do the local deputies know about him?'

The singer answered, 'Oh, yeah, they do. They knew he was planning to come to the concert on Friday. But the sheriff was going to keep an eye on him if he showed up.'

'I'll call the sheriff's office,' Alicia said. 'And tell them he's here. And where he's staying. He sure didn't hide it.'

Kayleigh looked around, troubled. 'This used to be my favourite restaurant. Now it's all spoiled. I'm not hungry any more. I'd like to leave. I'm sorry.' She waved for and settled up the bill.

Alicia suggested that they go out the back. Tye went outside and asked Morgan to drive around to that lot and Dance accompanied the entourage through a beer-pungent storeroom, past a grim toilet. They stepped into a parking lot of dusty cars and crumbling asphalt.

Dance noticed Kayleigh glance to her right and gasp.

Twenty feet away a huge old red car was parked. Sitting in the car was Edwin. Through the open window, he called, 'Kayleigh, check out my wheels! It's not a Cadillac; it's just a Buick. Like it?' He didn't seem to expect an answer. He added, 'Don't worry, I'll never put my car ahead of you!'

'My Red Cadillac' was one of Kayleigh's smash hits. It was about a girl who loves her old car . . . and dumps any man who doesn't care for the big, battered vehicle.

Bobby stormed forward and raged, 'Get out of here. And don't even think about following us to find out where Kayleigh lives.'

Edwin nodded, smiling, and drove off.

Dance couldn't be positive but her impression was that the stalker's face had registered a hint of confusion when Bobby spoke—as if of *course* he knew where Kayleigh lived. Why wouldn't he?

CALIFORNIA HAS ALWAYS been home to Latino music, but the bulk of the sounds are *Mexicana*: traditional *mariachi*, *banda*, *ranchera*, and even South of the Border's own brand of ska and hip-hop.

It was close to 9 p.m. and Dance was now getting a first-hand taste of this musical sound in the sweltering garage of Jose Villalobos, on the outskirts of Fresno. The six musicians of *Los Trabajadores* were just finishing up the last number for Dance's digital recorder.

The recording had gone well, though the men hadn't been too focused at first—largely because of whom Dance had brought with her: Kayleigh Towne in faded jeans, T-shirt and denim waistcoat.

The musicians had been awed and two had scurried into the house to return with wives and children for autographs. One of the women had tearfully said, 'God bless you for writing "Leaving Home". We all love it.'

This was a ballad about an older woman who's packing up her belongings and leaving the house where she and her husband raised their children. The listener wonders if she's just become a widow, or if the house has been foreclosed on. Only at the end is it revealed that she's undocumented and is being deported, though she's spent her whole life in the United States. It was Kayleigh's most controversial song, earning her the anger of those taking a hard line on immigration reform. But it had become an anthem among Latino workers and those preaching a more open-border policy.

As they were packing up, Dance explained how the songs would be uploaded on to her web site. Given that the band was so good, they'd probably sell a fair number of downloads. It was possible that they might draw some producers' or ad agencies' attention.

Curiously, becoming successful didn't interest them. Oh, they wouldn't mind making some money with their music but with the downloads only. Villalobos explained, 'We don't want that kind of life—on the road. We won't travel. We have jobs, families, *bebés*.'

They said goodbye and Dance and Kayleigh climbed into her dark green Suburban. Dance had left her Pathfinder at the Mountain View and had ridden here with Kayleigh in her SUV. Darthur Morgan nodded silently and began the drive back to Dance's motel.

Kayleigh was looking out of the window. 'I envy those musicians. They play at night and on weekends for their friends and families. Sometimes I wish I wasn't so successful. I never really wanted to be a star. I wanted to have a husband and babies and sing to *them*.'

Dance could see Kayleigh's reflection. There were possibly tears in her eyes. Then Kayleigh shoved her troubled thoughts away, and said slyly, 'So. Tell me. Dish. You mentioned Jon somebody?'

'The greatest guy in the world,' Dance said. 'Used to be in Silicon Valley, now he teaches and consults. The most important thing is that Wes and Maggie like him. It's working out well. But I've only been a widow a few years. I'm in no hurry.'

'Sure.' Kayleigh didn't exactly believe the lame explanation.

And Dance reflected: yes, she liked Jon Boling a lot. She probably loved him. He was kind, easy-going, good-looking, with a great sense of humour.

In ten minutes they'd arrived at the Mountain View and Darthur Morgan steered the Suburban to the front of the motel. Dance said good night to them both.

It was then that Kayleigh's phone buzzed and she looked down at the screen, frowning. She hit answer, 'Hello? . . . Hello? Who is this?'

Hand on the door lever, Dance paused and looked back at her.

Kayleigh disconnected, regarding the screen once more. 'Weird. Somebody just played a verse from "Your Shadow".'

The title track of her latest album and already a huge hit.

'They didn't say anything. They just played the first verse.'

Dance had downloaded the track and she recalled the words.

> *You walk out onstage and sing folks your songs.*
> *You make them all smile. What could go wrong?*
> *But soon you discover the job takes its toll,*
> *And everyone's wanting a piece of your soul.*

'The thing is it was a recording from a concert.'

'You don't do live albums,' Dance said.

Kayleigh was still staring at the screen. 'Right. It'd be a bootleg. But it was really high quality—almost like a voice, not a recording. But who was playing it, why?'

'You recognise the phone number?'

'No. Not a local area code. You think it was Edwin?' she asked, her voice tense with stress. 'But, wait, only my friends and family have this number. How could he get it?'

'Give me the number,' Dance said. 'I'll make some calls. And I'll check out Edwin. What's his last name?'

'Sharp. No E. Would you, Kathryn?'

'You bet.' Dance wrote down the number of the call and climbed out of the Suburban. As it pulled away, Dance headed inside.

She walked to her room and stepped inside. She showered, pulled on a robe and plopped down on the bed and made a call.

'Hey, Boss,' TJ Scanlon said cheerfully.

TJ was the most alternative of the agents in the Monterey office of the CBI. He was the go-to man when it came to demanding assignments, undercover work and any trivia regarding the Sixties, Bob Dylan and lava lamps.

'Need you to check out something, TJ.'

She gave him what she knew on Edwin Sharp. She then recited the number of the caller who'd played the song for Kayleigh.

TJ asked, 'Anything in particular? On Sharp?'

'The usual. But civil too. Stalking, lawsuits, restraining orders. Here and Washington state. Throw in Oregon for good measure.'

'Will do. So long, Boss.'

Dance disconnected. It was time for bed. She brushed her teeth, ditched the robe and pulled on boxers and a T-shirt. She turned off the light, then walked to the window, about to draw the drapes shut. And froze.

It was eleven thirty and the park across the highway was empty . . . But, no. Someone was in the shadows. She couldn't make out a specific person but she saw the tiny orange glow of a cigarette.

She remembered Edwin's slow scan of her ID card in the restaurant. Stalkers, she knew, were experts at getting information on the objects of their obsession and those who threatened to impede their access.

Dance made sure all the windows were locked and the chain securely fixed to the door and she conducted one more examination of the park, through a crack in the curtains. It was too dark and hazy to see much. The orange glow of the cigarette flared as the smoker inhaled deeply. Then the dot dropped to the ground and vanished under a shoe or boot. She saw no other motion. Had he left?

Dance waited a moment more then climbed into bed. She closed her eyes, but sleep, she knew, would be a long, long time coming.

IT WAS CLOSE to midnight. Bobby Prescott parked near the convention centre, climbed out of the band's van, stretching after the drive to and from Bakersfield to pick up the custom-built amp.

Bobby unlocked the stage door at the convention centre and wheeled the big unit inside. He also had a box of light mounts and safety cables.

Thinking again of the strip light falling that morning.

Performing could be a dangerous business. His father had been a recording engineer in London in the Sixties and Seventies. Back then, the serious-minded professionals Robert Senior worked with—the Beatles and Stones, for instance—were outnumbered by crazy, self-destructive musicians, who managed to kill themselves pretty frequently with drugs, liquor, cars and poor judgment. But even taking bad behaviour out of the picture, performing could be dangerous. Electricity was the biggest risk—he'd known of three performers electrocuted onstage. But a light coming unfixed? That was weird and had never happened in his years as a roadie.

And endangering Kayleigh? He shivered, thinking about that.

Tonight the cavernous hall was filled with shadows cast by the exit lights. As Bobby approached the strip light that had fallen he noticed that someone had moved it. He had left instructions that the heavy black fixture shouldn't be touched, after he'd lowered it to the stage. But now it sat on the very edge, above the orchestra pit, a good thirty feet from where it had stopped swinging after it fell. He'd reprimand someone for that. Crouching down, Bobby examined the unit. What the hell had gone wrong?

Bobby Prescott never heard the footsteps of whoever came up behind him. He simply felt the hands slam into his back and he went forward, barking a brief scream as the concrete floor of the orchestra pit, twenty feet below, raced up to break his jaw and arm.

Oh God . . . He lay on his belly, staring at the bone, starkly white and flecked with blood, that poked through his forearm skin.

Bobby moaned and screamed and cried out for help.

Who? Who did it? Edwin? He might've heard me tell Kayleigh in the café that I was going to be here late.

'Help me!'

Silence.

Then he heard a faint sound above him, a scraping. He twisted his head and looked up. Gasping, he watched the strip light, above him, easing towards the edge of the stage.

'No! Who is that? No!'

Bobby struggled to crawl away, clawing at the concrete floor with the fingers of his unbroken arm. But his legs weren't working either.

One inch, two . . . Move, roll aside! But too late.

The light slammed into his back, going a hundred miles an hour. He felt another snap high in his body and all the pain went away.

My back . . . my back . . . His vision crinkled.

When Bobby came to, the room was bathed in astonishing light; the spotlight sitting on his back had been turned on. All thousand watts, pouring from the massive lamps.

He then saw on the wall the flicker of flames. At first he didn't know what was on fire—he felt no heat whatsoever. But then the repulsive scent of burning hair, burning flesh filled the small space.

And he understood.

MONDAY

2

At the braying of the phone Kathryn Dance awoke. She fumbled for her mobile and hit the green button. 'Yes?'

'Woke you up, Boss. Sorry.'

'Sorry what do you mean sorry is everyone all right there?' One sentence made of many. Dance was remembering, as she did all too often, the call from the state trooper about her husband Bill—a brief, sympathetic but emotionless call explaining to her that the life she'd planned on with her husband would not happen.

'Not here, there.'

Was it that she was exhausted? She blinked. What time was it? Five a.m.? Four? She struggled upright.

TJ Scanlon said, 'I didn't know if you needed me.'

'Start at the beginning.'

'Oh, you didn't hear?'

'No, I didn't hear.'

'Got a notice on the wire about a homicide in Fresno. Happened late last night. Somebody connected with Kayleigh Towne's band.'

'Who?' Brushing her dark blonde hair from her face. The worse the news, the calmer Kathryn Dance became.

'Somebody named Robert Prescott.'

Bobby? Yes, that was his last name, Prescott. This was bad . . . She'd noted from their interaction yesterday that he and Kayleigh were close friends, in addition to being work associates.

'Details?'

'Nothing yet.'

Dance also thought back to Edwin's unnatural smile, his leering eyes, his icily calm demeanour, which she believed might conceal bundled rage.

TJ said, 'It was just a one-paragraph notice on the wire. Information only, not a request for assistance. The vic died at the convention centre. It's being handled by the Fresno-Madera Consolidated Sheriff's Office. The sheriff is Anita Gonzalez. The head detective is P. K. Madigan. Been on the force a long time.'

'I'll get over there now. You have anything on Sharp yet? The stalker?'

'No warrants or court orders came up in California. Still waiting to hear from Washington and Oregon. The phone number you gave me? That somebody called Kayleigh on? It was bought with cash three days ago from a drugstore in Burlingame, south of San Francisco, near the airport. No video and no record of the transaction. The clerks have no idea who it was.'

'Keep on it. Email Sharp's full bio. Anything you can get.'

'Your command is what I wish for, Boss.'

They disconnected. What time *was* it? The room was still dark but light showed behind the curtains.

Glasses on. Oh, eight thirty. The crack of midmorning.

She walked into the bathroom for a brief, hot shower. In twenty minutes she was dressed in black jeans, a black T-shirt and a silk navy business jacket. The heat would be challenging with these clothes but the possibility of duty loomed. She left the hotel room.

HAD THERE REALLY been just one victim?

Pulling into the convention centre lot in her Pathfinder, Dance noted more emergency and public safety personnel than seemed necessary. Two dozen, easily. Four fire trucks, two ambulances, eight police cruisers and several unmarked. She drove forward to a Dodge, unmarked but obvious, parked and climbed out. A woman dressed in a deputy's uniform glanced

Dance's way, C. STANNING stamped on a plate above her breast. 'Help you?'

Dance displayed her CBI card and the woman didn't seem to know what to make of it. 'You . . . Is Sacramento involved?'

Dance said, 'Not yet. I happened to be nearby.'

Stanning juggled these words, perhaps factoring in her own instructions from on high, and said, 'OK.'

Dance continued on towards the convention centre. The air was dead and stifling. She stepped inside and the relief of the air conditioning was utterly negated by the stench.

Dance had been a law enforcer for some years and had attended hundreds of crime scenes. She was rarely a first responder and didn't do forensics; much of the horror had been tamed by the time she arrived. So the odour of burnt flesh and hair was unexpected. She steeled herself, keeping the nausea under control, and walked into the massive arena. On the stage and main floor were a dozen people in the uniforms of law enforcement, fire and EMS.

Onstage, she joined a cluster at the edge, looking into the orchestra pit, where a faint trail of smoke rose. What had happened? she wondered. She recalled the falling light from yesterday.

Dance noted immediately, from their posture and the sweep of their eyes, that two of the law officers, who all wore tan uniforms, were senior to the others. One was a stocky Latina woman.

The man she was speaking to was a tanned Caucasian. He was also stocky. A large, round face crisscrossed with sun wrinkles. His posture—leaning forward, shoulders up—and still, squinting grey eyes suggested an arrogant and difficult man. His hair was black and thick. He wore a revolver, a long-barrelled Colt, while on the hips of everyone else here were the semi-auto Glocks that were de rigueur among law enforcers in California.

She guessed he was P. K. Madigan, the head of detectives.

Conversation slowed as they turned to see the slim woman in jeans stride towards them.

Madigan asked brusquely, 'And you are . . .?' And he looked over her shoulder darkly towards who might have let her breach his outer perimeter.

She noted the woman was named Gonzalez, the sheriff, and so Dance addressed her and displayed her ID, which they both examined carefully.

'I'm Sheriff Gonzales. This is Chief Detective Madigan.' The decision not to offer first names in an introduction is often an attempt to assert power. Dance merely noted the choice. She wasn't here to flex muscles.

'My office called me about a homicide. I happened to be in the area on another matter.'

Could be official, might not be. Let the sheriff and chief detective guess.

Dance added, 'I'm also a friend of Kayleigh Towne's. When I heard the vic was in her crew I came right over.'

'Well, thanks, Kathryn,' Madigan said.

The use of first names is an attempt to disempower.

The flicker in Gonzalez's eyes at this faint affront—but absence of any look Madigan's way—told Dance reams about the chief detective. He'd carved out a major fiefdom at the FMCSO.

The detective continued, 'But we don't need any CBI involvement at this point. Wouldn't you say, Sheriff?'

'I'd think not,' Gonzalez said, staring Dance in the eyes.

Madigan continued, 'You said you were here on another matter? I look over the interagencies every morning. Didn't see any Bureau activity here. They—you—don't always tell us, of course.'

He'd called her bluff. 'A personal matter.' Dance steamed ahead. 'The victim was Bobby Prescott, the head of the road crew?'

'That's right.'

'Anyone else hurt?'

Sheriff Gonzalez offered, 'Only Bobby.'

'And what happened?'

Gonzalez said, 'He was doing some work on the stage last night. It seems he slipped and fell, a spotlight landed on him. It was on. He caught fire. Cause of death was blood loss and the burns.'

'Must've burned for a while. The alarms didn't go off?'

'The smoke detectors down there, in the pit, weren't working. We don't know why.'

The first thing in her mind was the image of Edwin Sharp, glancing towards Bobby Prescott, with that fake smile and with eyes that could easily reflect a desire to turn the roadie into a bag of dust.

'You ought to be aware—'

''Bout Mr Sharp, our stalker?' Madigan asked.

'Well, yes.'

'One of the boys with the crew, Tye Slocum, told me that there was an incident yesterday at the Cowboy Saloon.'

Dance described what she had seen and heard. 'Bobby confronted him a couple of times,' she said. 'And Edwin probably overheard Bobby say he was going to come back here later last night and check out some equipment malfunction.'

Madigan added, 'Edwin's on our radar. We know he's renting a house near Woodward Park, north part of town. For a month.'

Dance recalled that Edwin had been forthcoming about his residence. She was still curious why he'd rented for that length of time. She noted too that both she and Madigan were referring to him by his first name; this often happened when dealing with suspects who were potentially ED, emotionally disturbed.

The chief detective took a phone call. Then he was back to Dance, though only for the briefest of times. And with the briefest of smiles—just as phoney as Edwin's, she reflected. 'Appreciate you stopping by. We'll give CBI a call if there's anything we need.'

Gonzalez offered, 'So long now.'

Despite the double-barrelled goodbye, Dance didn't feel like leaving just yet. 'How did the light fall on him?'

'Maybe tugged it after him when he fell. The cord, you know.'

'Was it a strip light?' Dance asked.

Madigan muttered, 'Dunno what that is. Take a look.'

Dance did. It was indeed a hard thing to see: the scorched body. And, yes, the unit was a four-lamp strip.

'That might've been the one that fell yesterday. How did it come undone?'

'Wing nuts worked loose.' He regarded the scaffolding.

'And I wonder why Bobby fell. Not like it isn't marked.' Yellow warning tape clearly indicated the edge of the stage.

Then a woman's loud, haunting voice from the back of the hall: 'No . . . no, *no!*' The last time that word was repeated it became a scream.

Kayleigh Towne sprinted down the aisle to the stage where her friend had died so horribly.

Dance had seen the young singer a half-dozen times and she'd always been carefully, if not perfectly, assembled. But today she was dishevelled. No make-up, long hair askew, eyes puffy from crying.

P. K. Madigan became a different person. He stepped down the stairs and intercepted the young woman on the floor before she could get to the stage. 'Kayleigh, you shouldn't be here.'

'Bobby?'

'I'm afraid it is.'

'They told me . . . but I was praying it was a mistake.'

Then Sheriff Gonzalez joined them on the main floor and put her arm round the girl. Dance wondered if all friends and next of kin got this treatment, or only celebrities, then decided the cynical thought was unkind.

'I'm sorry, Kayleigh,' Gonzalez said. 'I'm so sorry.'

'It was him! Edwin. I know it! Go arrest him. He's parked in front of my house. Right now!'

'He's *what?*' Madigan asked.

'He's parked in the lot of the nature reserve across the street. He's just sitting there in that damn red car of his.'

Frowning, Madigan made a call and told a deputy to check it out.

Dance returned to the edge of the stage and looked down. The strip light, six feet long, lay atop the scorched remains of Bobby. Dance assessed the broken bones, the claw shape of the hands, partly due to the typical fire victim's contractions, but also because he'd been trying to drag his body out from underneath the edge of the stage. He was headed away from the stairs— not the logical direction in which he'd crawl if he was just seeking help.

'He fell first *before* the lamp hit him,' Dance said to the deputy standing next to her, softly so Kayleigh would not hear.

'What's that, ma'am?' The man, in his mid-thirties, of rectangular build, with a black moustache, stepped closer. He was tanned, like Madigan. The name on his tag said, DET. D. HARUTYUN.

She nodded down into the hole. 'His legs, the way they're angled, his hands. He fell first. Then the light landed on him.'

The deputy examined the scene silently. 'The light teetered and fell. He knew it was coming 'cause he tugged on the cord.'

But the wire was plugged into an outlet on the stage, not in the pit. Both she and the detective noticed this simultaneously. Bobby couldn't have pulled it down on himself. She asked, 'And why's it plugged into the wall there? A light like that's mounted on the rigging *above* the stage. That's where the power source is. And why was it plugged in at all? That'd be worth mentioning too.'

'I'll do that.'

Which he now did, walking down the stairs, pulling Madigan aside, whispering to him. The detective nodded. His face folded into a frown. 'OK,' he called, 'we're treating the stage as a crime scene. And the scaffolding where the light fell from yesterday. Clear everybody off. And get Charlie's folks searching there.'

Dance now joined Kayleigh, who was in a frantic state. Looking in many different directions, she began talking rapidly, gesturing. Dance was reminded of her own unhinged behaviour after she'd learned of the death of her husband, an FBI agent—not a victim of criminal activity but of a careless driver on Highway 1.

Dance hugged her hard and asked how she could help, phone calls to be made. Kayleigh thanked her and said no, she'd make the calls herself. 'Oh, Kathryn, can you believe it? I . . . I can't believe it. Bobby.' Her eyes strayed to the orchestra pit and then she turned to Madigan and Gonzalez and said that she was sure somebody had been watching her here yesterday.

'Where?'

Pointing. 'In those corridors there. Alicia—my assistant—saw something too. But we didn't see anyone clearly.'

Dance said, 'Tell the sheriff and detective about the phone call last night.'

Kayleigh explained about the call she'd received the evening before, someone playing part of her song 'Your Shadow'. Kayleigh added, 'The recording was very high quality. With your eyes closed, you couldn't tell the difference between someone singing or the digital replay. Only a pro would have a recorder like that.'

'Or a fanatical fan,' Dance suggested. She then mentioned what she'd learned from TJ about the mobile phone. Madigan didn't seem pleased that a law enforcer from another jurisdiction had started to investigate his case, though he wrote down the details.

At that moment Deputy C. Stanning joined them from out front.

'Crystal,' Madigan said coolly.

She said, 'Reporters're showing up. They'll want a press—'

'You keeping people out of the crime scene, Deputy?'

Her oblique apology: 'Big area to keep track of. Lot of onlookers, you know, curious folks. I'm keeping them back, best I can.'

Sheriff Gonzalez took a call, had a brief conversation then disconnected. 'I'm going to have to leave now. I'm sorry for your loss, Kayleigh.' This was offered sincerely. 'Anything I can do, let me know.'

The sheriff said goodbye to Dance. She left, along with two of the other deputies.

Dance said to Madigan, 'My speciality's interrogation and interviewing,

Detective. If you have a suspect or witness you'd like me to talk to just give me a call.' She handed him her card.

'I do a bit of that myself,' Madigan offered. 'Well, all righty then, Kathryn.' He pocketed the card like a used tissue.

'Oh, wait, that seminar,' Harutyun said, frowning. 'In Salinas. Body language, right? Kinetics. That was you.'

'Kinesics, yes.'

He turned to Madigan. 'Alberto and I went last year. It was helpful. You were funny too.'

'Seminar,' Madigan repeated. 'Funny. That's good to know. Here's a thought. Kayleigh, you saw somebody here yesterday?'

'Just a shadow,' the girl said.

He smiled. 'Shadows're left by somethin'. Or someone. Why don't you talk to people in the crew who were here, Kathryn? Any convention centre workers too. See what they have to say.'

'I could do that, Detective. But that's more along the lines of canvassing. I'm usually involved if there's reason for a witness or suspect to be deceptive or if they can't remember important facts.'

'And I hope we get somebody you can use those seminar skills of yours on, Kathryn. But until then, it'd be a big help if you'd see what the others have to say. Of course, don't feel you have to.'

Seminar skills . . .

She'd been outmanoeuvred. The dog had been sniffing around for juicy scraps at the picnic and got tossed a dry bone instead.

'Be glad to.' Dance pulled out her iPhone and got the names of the people with the crew and convention-centre employees who were here yesterday from Kayleigh, inputting them one by one.

She then said to Kayleigh, 'See you later.' Dance started up the aisle when the thought slammed her. She turned back. 'Kayleigh, last night? The caller played only one verse, right?'

'The first verse. And the chorus.'

'And it's about a concert hall,' Dance said.

'It's about being a public person. But it mentions a venue.'

'I don't know who's behind this,' Dance said, 'but if it's a stalker, like Edwin, I think he's going to keep killing.'

'Oh, Kathryn,' Kayleigh whispered. 'He might hurt somebody else?'

Committing murder was rare among stalkers but in her years as a reporter, a jury consultant and a cop, Dance had learned that when it came to violent crime, an outlier could kill you just as dead as a perp who fell smack in the middle of the bell curve. 'The basis for stalking is repetitive, obsessive behaviour. I think we should assume he may make more calls and more people will be at risk. I'd get a wire on Kayleigh's phone. Let's look at the other verses of that song to see who or where he might attack again.'

Madigan asked, 'But why would the perp do that? What's in it for him?'

Dance replied, 'I don't know. Some stalkers are simply psychotic.'

'Sounds kinda far-fetched,' Madigan said.

'I think it's important.'

'Seems you do.' The chief detective took a call, listened and said to Kayleigh. 'That was one of the patrols. They cruised past your house and didn't see him or his car.'

'Where *is* he, where did he *go?*' Kayleigh sounded panicked.

'They don't know.' Madigan looked at his watch. He told Harutyun to go outside, make a statement to the reporters. 'Don't give 'em anything specific, only Bobby's name. Being investigated, apparent accident. You know the drill.' He dismissed Dance too. 'If you could get to that interviewing, I'd appreciate it, Kathryn.'

Dance hugged Kayleigh once more. She then accompanied Harutyun towards the exit.

'Thanks for talking to him about the light, Detective Harutyun.'

'Made some sense. Call me Dennis.'

'Kathryn.'

'I heard.' Deadpan delivery.

As the two passed a sombre Darthur Morgan and pushed out of the front door, Harutyun's square face registered distress. He was looking at the reporters. Dance understood he'd rather be chasing a perp in a dark alley than handling this duty.

Dance slowed, typing an email into her phone. 'Detective, I just downloaded the lyrics to Kayleigh's song that she heard on her phone last night. I've forwarded a copy to the Detective Division. For your attention. I'd really appreciate it if you'd look over the second verse and let me know if you can think of any places it could mean, where a perp might decide to kill somebody else, based on the words. Like the concert hall in the first verse.'

A hesitation. 'I could check with Chief Madigan about that.'

Dance said slowly, 'You *could*, sure.'

Harutyun surveyed the reporters: 'The Chief's got the best forensic outfit in the Valley, better than Bakersfield's. And his arrest and conviction rate's in the top ten per cent in the state.'

'I can tell he's good,' she said.

Eyes still on the voracious journalists. 'I know he'd appreciate you getting him statements from those witnesses.'

Dance said firmly, 'Look over the lyrics. Please.'

Swallowing, the big detective didn't respond but stepped forward reluctantly to meet the pack of hungry wolves.

BOBBY PRESCOTT'S TRAILER was a double-wide, about fifty feet by twenty-five, Kathryn Dance guessed. Tan exterior, white trim.

Only law enforcers, some curious children and a few older spectators were present. There were no other residents in the trailer; TJ had reported that Bobby had lived here alone. It was 1 p.m., the sun at a September angle, but the air was still hot as July.

Two Fresno-Madera Consolidated cruisers were parked in the front and Dance nosed past them to the carport and climbed out of the Pathfinder. Detective Madigan and Dennis Harutyun were talking to the kids.

The mustachioed detective nodded noncommittally.

His boss said, 'Ah, Kathryn.' Not even a faux smile from Madigan. Beneath the leaf-thin veneer was anger—at her and probably at himself for having to play the politics game and not being able simply to kick the CBI agent out altogether.

Dennis Harutyun regarded her solemnly and she wondered if he'd bothered to download and review the lyrics to 'Your Shadow'. Probably not. He returned to interviewing locals.

P. K. Madigan continued, 'So. You talk to those witnesses?'

'I did, yes. I talked to Alicia Sessions, Kayleigh's PA, Tye Slocum and Darthur Morgan, Kayleigh's security guard. The facility also had a security guard and an electrician and a carpenter to help out the band. I interviewed them too. Their security man said three of the doors were unlocked. But that wasn't unusual. During the day, if there's no show, it's a pain to keep finding him and unlocking the doors, so they usually just leave them open. Nobody spotted anyone inside they didn't recognise.'

'You got all that in three hours?'

Eighty minutes, actually. The rest had been devoted to learning where

Bobby spent time—hiking in a state park nearby (no leads there) and hanging out in a guitar store with friends (ditto, lack of leads).

And discovering where he lived. Hence, her presence here. She asked, 'How'd your crime scene team do at the convention centre?'

A pause. 'Collected a lot of stuff. Don't know the results yet.'

Another FMC cruiser arrived—Crystal Stanning was at the wheel. She parked behind Dance's Nissan, climbed out and joined the others. Stanning, it seemed, wanted to report to her boss about whatever her mission had been but would say nothing until Dance was elsewhere or she had the OK.

The sweating Madigan was impatient. He snapped, 'The phone?'

'Service Plus Drugs in Burlingame. Cash. They don't have any videos. Maybe that's why he went there.'

Dance had told them all of this information.

But then Stanning continued, 'And you were right, Chief, he bought three other phones at the same time.'

A question Dance had *not* thought to have TJ Scanlon ask.

Madigan sighed. 'So this boy *may* have more on his plate.'

Which was, she guessed, a backhanded acknowledgment of her 'far-fetched' concern.

Four verses in 'Your Shadow', Dance reflected. Four victims? And that song might not be the only template for murder. Kayleigh had written lots of tunes.

'I got the numbers and the ESNs,' Crystal said.

You needed both the phone number and the electronic serial number of a mobile in order to trace it.

'We should get 'em shut off,' Madigan said. 'So Edwin'll have to buy one here. Easier to trace.'

We don't know it's Edwin, Dance thought. She said, 'I'd keep them active, like we haven't figured out what he's up to, but put a locator notice on them. If the perp calls again we can triangulate.'

Madigan paused, then glanced at Crystal Stanning. 'Do that.'

Motion from across the street, where a trailer squatted in sad grass. A round woman stood on the concrete stoop, smoking a cigarette. She wore a tight white strapless sundress with purple and red stains at toddler level.

Madigan told Stanning to help Harutyun canvas and he crossed the road, making for the woman, Dance following. The detective glanced back at her but she didn't slow down.

The neighbour walked forward uncertainly to greet them. She said, 'I heard the news about Bobby. I couldn't believe it.' She repeated fast, 'It was on the news. That's I how heard.'

'I'm Deputy Madigan, this is Officer Dancer.'

She didn't correct him.

'Your name?'

'Tabby Nysmith. Tabatha. Bobby never caused any trouble. Can't believe he's dead. What happened? The news didn't say.'

'We aren't sure what happened, ma'am. Not yet.'

'The nicest guy, really. He'd show my oldest these fancy guitars he had. He had one that Mick Jagger played, he said. Bobby's daddy worked with them and the Beatles. Or that's what he said.'

'Did you see anybody here recent you never saw before?'

'No, sir.'

'Anybody he had a fight with, loud voices, drug activity?'

'Nope. Didn't see anybody here last night or this morning.'

'You're sure?'

'Yessir.' She pressed out her cigarette and lit another one. She continued, 'It's hard for me to see his place.' She gestured at the windows in the front of her trailer, obscured by bushes. 'I'm after Tony Senior to trim the bushes but he never gets around to it.'

'Would your *husband* have seen anything?'

'He's on the road. Truck driver. Been away for three days.'

'All right then, ma'am. Thank you for your time.'

Madigan was loping back towards the trailer but Dance turned the other way, followed the woman back to the trailer and her brood.

'Excuse me. If I could ask a few more things?'

'I'm sorry. I really have to get back to the kids. I don't know much else than what I told that man.' The woman kept walking.

'Just one or two questions.'

They were at the screen door of her trailer. Tabatha peered through the dusty, rusted mesh. The TV was on. A soap opera.

'Just a few more details about Bobby.'

Dance was continuing the discussion with Tabatha because of an important rule in kinesic analysis: the volunteering principle. When one gives an answer then immediately offers what he or she anticipates will be the next question, that person is often trying to deflect a line of inquiry. Dance had noted that Tabatha had said she hadn't seen anybody here last night—or *this morning*. Why had she felt it important to mention that?

Dance removed her sunglasses.

'Tabatha, what did you see this morning at Bobby's trailer?'

'Nothing,' she said quickly.

Effective kinesic analysis of witnesses and suspects involves conversing with the individual for a long period of time. Initially nothing is said about the crime at all; the interviewer asks questions that relate to the subject's life, all topics about which the truth is known. This establishes the suspect's baseline behaviour—how the person speaks and acts when responding honestly. It's then that the interviewer segues into inquiries about the crime and compares the subject's behaviour when answering *those* questions to the baseline. Any variation suggests stress and therefore possible deception.

However, even without establishing a baseline, there are a few mannerisms that suggest lying. Tabatha's voice was now slightly higher in pitch than earlier—a sign of stress.

A glance towards Bobby's trailer, in front of which Madigan and his deputies were staring back at Dance. She said, 'It would be good for everybody if you could give us a little more information.'

Tabatha furrowed her eyebrows as she considered the risk to her children if she was honest.

'We'll make sure you're looked out for,' Dance said.

A low voice, woman to woman. 'It's easy to say that.'

'I give you my word.'

A long ten seconds passed. 'There *was* somebody in the trailer this morning. I couldn't see the face. 'Causa the angle, you know. Just the body, chest and shoulders, through the window. Like a, you know, silhouette. Not even clothes. That's all I could see. I swear.'

'Which window?'

'That one there, in the front?' She pointed. It was horizontal.

'You came out for a smoke and saw this person? What time?'

'Eleven, eleven thirty.'

'Did you see a car? Or when the person left?'

'No.'

Then she noticed to her alarm that Madigan had given up shooting hate rays at her, had turned and was nearly at the door of Bobby's trailer. 'Thank you, Tabatha. Go be with your children.'

'Will I have to testify?'

As Dance sprinted towards the trailer she called over her shoulder, 'We'll look after you, I promise!' Then shouting, 'Detective! Stop!'

P. K. Madigan's hand was nearly on the doorknob. His eyes slid Dance's way and she saw his face cloud with irritation. But he also seemed to understand that she had a point about not wanting him to go inside. He stepped back. So did Harutyun.

Dance hurried across the street and joined them.

'Anybody inside?' the chief detective asked sharply.

Dance steadied her breathing. 'Don't think so. But I don't know. The thing is the perp—or somebody—was here this morning. Eleven, eleven thirty. You don't want to contaminate anything.'

'In *here?*'

'I think we should assume it was the killer.'

'She know the time for sure?' Nodding at Tabatha's trailer.

'Probably. The TV was on and it would've been all morning. She'd know the time according to the show she was watching.'

'Who'd she see? Can she ID 'em?'

'No. And I believe her. She didn't see a face or vehicle.'

A deep sigh. He muttered to Harutyun, 'Get CSU over here.'

The deputy made a call. Madigan and Dance both stepped away from the trailer and stood on the crumbling walk.

'What'd Edwin, or whoever, be doing here?'

'I don't know. It could have been a friend maybe. I talked to the crew. They would've said something about being here or acting deceptive. And none of them did. I told her, Tabatha, that we'd keep an eye on her.'

'We can do that,' Madigan said.

'It's important.'

'We can do that,' he repeated, with a bit of edge. To Harutyun, 'Get a car over here. Keep an eye on the place. That trailer across the street too.'

'Thanks,' Dance told Madigan. He didn't respond.

Dance and Madigan waited in silence for the Crime Scene Unit to arrive and, when they did, Dance was impressed at their efficiency. The team dressed fast, in bodysuits, masks and boots, and two of them with weapons drawn cleared the interior of the trailer, making sure there were no threats.

CSU proceeded to process the trailer, dusting and using alternative light sources for prints, taking trace evidence samples, electrostatic footprints on the front stoop and inside, looking for tyre treads and anything else the perp might have discarded or shed.

Dance's friend, Lincoln Rhyme, was perhaps the country's leading expert in forensic evidence and crime scene work. Rhyme and his partner, Amelia Sachs, had worked miracles in identifying and convicting suspects on the basis of nearly nonexistent evidence.

She noted that Madigan's eyes grew animated as he watched the team scour the grounds and move in and out of the trailer.

An hour later they'd finished and carted out some boxes and bags, and announced that they were releasing the scene.

Dance made quickly for the trailer. Stepping inside, she froze. It was a museum, devoted to Country music, starting in the Fifties and going up to the present day. Posters, record jackets, guitars, statuettes of musicians and many vinyl records, mostly from the Sixties through to the Eighties. She spotted photos and concert souvenirs of Waylon Jennings, Hank Williams, Dolly Parton, Shania Twain and, of course, Kayleigh Towne.

Dance felt a pang that Bobby's devotion to archiving Country music in the twentieth century had died with him. She walked carefully through the place. She stepped over to a book shelf containing binders and folders of official documents like tax bills and boxes of reel-to-reel tapes, including some labelled 'Master Tapes'.

Dance was studying this portion of the trailer carefully when she happened to pass the window where Tabatha had said she'd seen the intruder that morning. Dance blinked in surprise as she found herself staring eye-to-eye at a very unhappy P. K. Madigan, a foot away on the other side of the glass.

She summoned him, calling, 'I've found something.'

He grimaced and hesitated, then reluctantly joined her.

'Actually I've found something *missing*.'

He looked around. 'Body language of the trailer tell you that?'

Madigan was being snide. But Dance said, 'You could say that. People have patterns in their gestures and speech and expressions. They also have patterns in their living spaces. Bobby's an organised person. People who are organised aren't that way accidentally. It's a psychological drive. Look at his shelves.' She pointed.

'They're messy but so? I got a teenage boy.'

'None of the others are. And your Crime Scene Unit marked where they'd taken things. Somebody else went through those boxes. It's near the window where Tabatha saw somebody.'

'Why do you say something's missing?'

'I'm making the deduction that if only those shelves were disturbed, the intruder was looking for something and he found it so he stopped.'

Madigan reluctantly walked over to the shelves and, pulling on latex gloves, poked through the tapes, the papers and the pictures. He said, 'Some of these snaps of Kayleigh, they're not souvenirs. They're personal. The sort of thing a stalker'd want for a souvenir.'

'That could be it, yes,' Dance said.

Madigan ran a finger over the shelf and examined it. The coat of dust was thick. Bobby was organised but not particularly concerned about cleaning. 'Cement plant right up the road here. Looks like dust from there.' A cool glance her way. 'You find anything else?'

'No.'

Without a word he left the trailer, Dance after him. He called to Harutyun, 'You guys find anything? Witnesses?'

'Nothing.'

Madigan pulled a phone off his thick shiny belt and placed a call. He stepped away from the others and had a brief conversation. Dance couldn't hear what was said.

As he disconnected, Madigan said to Harutyun, 'I want you to find this Edwin Sharp. Bring him in. I need to talk to him. Now.'

'Arrest him?'

'No. Make it seem like it'd be good for him to come in. In his interest, you know.'

Dance heard a harsh exhalation as Madigan regarded her expression. 'What? You don't think that's a good idea?'

She said, 'No, I don't. I'd vote for surveillance.'

Madigan squinted towards Harutyun. 'Do it.'

'Sure, Chief.' Harutyun climbed into his cruiser and left.

Madigan strode to his car. He grunted, 'Crystal, I need you to come with me in my cruiser. We'll pick yours up later.'

The woman dutifully climbed into the passenger seat of Madigan's cruiser. A moment later they were headed out onto the highway, without a word of farewell to Dance.

She fished for her keys and turned towards her SUV. She stopped, closed her eyes in frustration and gave a sharp laugh. Crystal Stanning's squad car was tight on the rear bumper of Dance's Pathfinder. In front was a carport full of junk. A V-8 engine block, weighing half a ton, she guessed, sat six inches in front of her SUV.

She wasn't going anywhere.

3

At the Fresno-Madera Sheriff's Office complex, P. K. Madigan stopped by the Crime Scene Unit, a block away, after returning from Bobby Prescott's trailer. He wanted to urge the unit to make this case a priority, which they'd do. Anything for Kayleigh Towne, the girl who'd helped put Fresno on the map. And anything for Chief Madigan, too.

He was also thinking about Kathryn Dance and her beached car. Some people you needed to hit over the head to deliver a message. He'd send Crystal back in an hour or two, spring the gal from her automotive jail.

He'd simply had it with people using Kayleigh like Dance was. If Kayleigh hadn't been involved, Kathryn Dance would never have come to Fresno, never have taken the time even to say howdy-do to a soul here. He expected better from the CBI, thought they'd be above publicity-grabbing.

Just happened to be in the area and a friend of Kayleigh's? My ass.

You don't mind if I take over your investigation, do you, P. K.?

Yeah, she'd come up with a few helpful things, but P. K. Madigan didn't believe much in that mumbo jumbo kinesics. Cases were made nowadays on forensics, not voodoo. They'd have evidence from the convention centre, they'd have forensics from Bobby's trailer—that cement dust, about as unique as trace could be, was a godsend. Armed with that, Madigan would wear down the suspect and get a confession in an hour or two.

He and Stanning walked into the CSU's lab.

'Charlie,' he called.

The pudgy, rosy-cheeked CSU director, Charlie Shean, looked up from a computer in his office—the only four-walled space in the large room. The rest of the place had workstations and up-to-date forensic *stuff* that Madigan had fought hard to get for his people.

'Hey, Chief.'

Madigan thought Shean was the best forensic tech his budget could afford and he was one of the few employees on the force the detective was deferential to, though he'd get in a few good ones about the CSU man's name from time to time, despite the spelling.

'Need you to push everything through on this Towne case.'

The round man shook his head. 'Poor thing. She's got to be shook up. And that big concert this weekend. I got tickets, the wife and me. You going?'

'I am,' Stanning said.

Madigan wasn't. He liked music but he liked music you could shut off with a switch when you wanted to. 'What've we got?'

Shean nodded towards several techs in goggles, gloves and white jackets, working with quiet intensity at several stations not far away.

'Three scenes: convention centre, Bobby's trailer and Sharp's rental. We're processing about two hundred unknown prints. We have what we *think* are Sharp's from his rental but he's not in AIFIS.'

The FBI's Automated Integrated Fingerprint Identification System was, in Madigan's opinion, one of the few things the federal government was good for.

'But we aren't sure they're his.'

'I'll be talking to Sharp. I'll get his with the water-bottle trick.'

Shean continued, 'You were right; that's the cement dust at Bobby's trailer. It's unique to that area.'

'Have you got a match from Edwin's place? Lopez said there was plenty of dust on the Kayleigh memorabilia in his house.'

'Lots of trace, but no results yet. Should know soon. And one more thing? The team found something in the orchestra pit. Some boxes had been moved—the manager said they usually kept stacks of them there to break somebody's fall in an accident. Whoever moved them, looked like he was wearing latex gloves. And similar marks on the smoke detectors; they'd had the batteries taken out.'

Bingo! Miguel Lopez, who'd searched Edwin's rental, had found a box of latex gloves.

'The same as we got from Edwin's place?'

'We don't know that yet either. Wrinkle marks and manufacturer's trace'll tell us.'

'Good, Charlie. Interrupt me if there're any breakthroughs.'

Madigan and Stanning left and walked to the sheriff's office proper. Madigan pushed through a swinging door on which was painted a fading sign, DETECTIVE DIVISION. Detective Gabriel Fuentes, a bulldog of a man, stood near the reception desk.

Edwin Sharp was here too. Madigan recognised the gangling man from the photos Kayleigh's lawyers had sent them, though he'd lost weight. He was standing over Fuentes. The stalker's eyes were sunken below thick brows, which gave him an ominous look. Those eyes were curious, Madigan thought. They weren't the least bit troubled. His smile was odd, too, a faint upward curving of the thin lips but mostly at the very ends.

Those underpass eyes now turned to him. 'Detective Madigan, hi. How you doing? I'm Edwin Sharp.'

'I'll just be a second, son. Thanks for coming in.'

'Just for the record, I'm not under arrest. You've asked me here and I've come voluntarily. I can leave at any time. Is that correct?'

'That's right. You want some ice cream?'

'Do I . . . what?'

'Ice cream?'

'No, thanks. I'll pass. What's this all about?'

'You go by Ed, Eddie?'

The smile. It was damn eerie. 'No. I like Edwin, Pike.'

Madigan paused. Why is he using my first name? And how did he know it? A lot of *deputies* here don't know what it is.

'Then, Edwin it is. Be back in a second.'

He stepped into the lunch room, opened the freezer and scooped some ice cream into a paper cup. He loved ice cream. Today he was having mint chocolate chip. He returned to the Detective Division. 'OK, Edwin. I'd like to have a conversation with you, you'd be so kind.'

They'd just started towards the interview room when the door to the Detective Division swung open and Kathryn Dance entered the lobby.

SHE'D TAKEN A CAB.

The chief detective and Crystal Stanning had been gone from Bobby's trailer for ten minutes when she gave up her futile back-and-forth attempt to free the wide-wheel-base Nissan.

She'd pulled out her mobile, found a business search app and got a cab to pick her up and take her straight to the sheriff's office.

The stalker seemed the more amused of the two men she now walked up to. 'Agent Dance, hope you're well,' Edwin said, getting her title right—name too. Madigan's expression said: so much for the improvised detention centre at the trailer.

She said firmly, 'I'd like to talk to you, Deputy,' using the less impressive of his job titles, because she was really pissed off.

Madigan replied, 'I'm pretty busy now, Kathryn. Come on, Edwin.' He said to the assistant, 'We'll be in number three.'

And they vanished down the hall.

After a frustrating five minutes, Dance noticed Detective Dennis Harutyun walking up the corridor towards her. He'd left before Madigan's little game with the cars and might not know she was persona non grata. She made a decision, taking her ID card from her bag, wedging the holder into her belt, shield on display, something she never did, even on duty. She approached Harutyun.

'Dennis.'

'Hello, Kathryn.'

She remembered how Madigan was referred to by intimates. 'The Chief's interviewing Edwin now. Where's observation for Interview Room Three? I got lost.'

The bluff worked. Assuming that she was sanctioned to be here, Harutyun guided her up the corridor and even held the door open politely. He flicked the light on in the small, close chamber.

She felt a little bad, using Harutyun like this. But Dance was determined to keep Kayleigh Towne safe, and she wasn't at all sure of Madigan's competence when it came to a suspect like Edwin.

She examined the interrogation room. It was austere. In the centre were a large table, a half-dozen chairs, and a utility table on which sat bottles of water and pads of paper. No decorations on the walls.

No pencils or pens.

Madigan sat forward, in a focused but unthreatening manner. He was confident but dropped the authoritarian, imperious attitude she'd seen earlier. He was respectful of Edwin, asking if he was comfortable.

Dance supposed the ice cream was going to be a prop of some sort. Every single word or gesture by an interrogator tells the subject something about the questioner. You should never say or do anything that doesn't further the session. Sipping coffee, scratching your head, frowning . . . But seemingly the mint chocolate chip wasn't part of the detective's plan. He finished it with relish and tossed the cup away. Edwin's eyes followed every second of the process.

Madigan made a few mistakes, though. He made a clumsy show of offering Edwin water. He simply pointed at the Clear Spring, rather than picking up a bottle and handing it to Edwin. It was probably an attempt to lift Edwin's fingerprints—and it seemed that Edwin deduced this since he chose not to touch the bottle.

But the big mistake, in Dance's opinion, came next.

'Can I ask what this is all about, Pike?'

'Robert Prescott.'

Wouldn't've done that, she thought.

'Oh, Kayleigh's road manager,' Edwin said, nodding.

'Where were you last night at the time he died?'

Oh, no.

Dance realised she must have said this aloud because Harutyun tilted his head her way.

'What? No, he's dead?' Edwin looked alarmed. 'That's terrible. He and Kayleigh were real close. What happened?'

'Got himself burned up. So, you're telling me you weren't at the convention centre last night?' He now leaned towards Edwin ominously.

Dance understood Madigan's approach. It was referred to as a blunt-force attack. With blunt force, officers would inundate suspects with information about them and about the case, suggesting knowledge they didn't have and connections that were tenuous at best. When delivered with confidence, as Madigan clearly had, the details sometimes got suspects to confess quickly.

But if it didn't work right away, you ended up with a subject who stonewalled; any chance of getting helpful information would be ruined. Accordingly, Dance never used this technique. Her belief was that information was the most valuable thing an interrogator has. To be effective it had to be fed out slowly to lure the suspect into revealing details that could later be used to trip him up. Madigan had just given away the most important facts—notably that Bobby was dead, where the crime had occurred and how it had happened. Had she been conducting the interview, she would have kept those details secret for the time being.

Edwin looked over the deputy sombrely. 'Well, I'm very sorry to hear that about Bobby. That's sad for Kayleigh.'

Madigan didn't respond. He said quickly, 'Could you tell me where you were when Prescott died? Midnight last night.'

'I'm sure you know I don't have to tell you anything. Really, Detective. You clearly think I hurt Bobby. Why on earth would I do that? I'd never hurt anybody close to Kayleigh. But the answer to your question is I was home in my rental.'

'Any witnesses?'

'Maybe somebody driving by saw me; I was in the living room, listening to music most of the night. I don't have curtains up yet.'

'I see. OK.' Then Madigan sprung the trap. 'But what do you say to the fact that we've got two witnesses that place you at the convention centre around the time he died and then at Bobby's trailer this morning?'

WHAT EDWIN SAID in reply was probably not what Madigan expected. With a frown, further blending his dense eyebrows, he asked simply, 'Did they have clear views?'

Don't answer, Dance thought to Madison.

'They sure did. The house right across the road from the convention centre stage door. And directly across from Bobby's trailer.'

Hell, Dance thought. Edwin could now figure out exactly who the witnesses were.

He said, shrugging, 'Well, they're mistaken. I was home.'

Dance said to Harutyun, 'Tabatha didn't ID anybody. She couldn't. Was there somebody else there?'

A pause. 'Not that I know of.'

'And is there really a witness by the convention centre?'

'Apparently.' Harutyun hesitated, then decided to tell her. 'Some woman who lived nearby saw somebody around midnight.'

'She positively ID'd Edwin?'

'I don't . . . I don't think so.'

The gap in his sentence meant a definitive no. 'Well, Madigan just told a possible homicide suspect about two witnesses and it wouldn't be that hard to find out their identities. They need looking after. He said he'd get some protection for Tabatha. Do you know if he did?'

'Tabatha, yes. The other one, I don't know.'

'We need to.'

'OK.'

And in the interrogation room, the one-on-one continued. Madigan said, 'We've just been through your house, Edwin. We found a lot of interesting things, including latex gloves, the same sort that were used in the murder. And trace evidence.'

Edwin said calmly, 'I see. My house, hm? Did you get a warrant?'

'We didn't need one. My deputy noticed things in plain sight.'

'Well, I don't really think you had the right to take anything,' the stalker said. 'I want it returned.'

Dance turned to Harutyun. 'Did he get a warrant?'

'No, after we saw things were missing from Bobby's, the Chief sent a deputy over there—Miguel Lopez—and he saw things through Edwin's window, in plain sight . . . What's the matter?'

Dance didn't reply.

Inside the interrogation room Edwin was saying, 'Well, I haven't been in Bobby's trailer, so—'

'Just confess,' Madigan said. 'I know you want to.'

A text-book line from blunt-force interrogation. This is the moment when the perp might start to cry and, indeed, confess.

But Edwin said, 'Can I collect my things now?'

The detective blinked. Then he said, 'Look, let's be realistic here. I'll talk to the prosecutor. I'm sure he'll cut a deal. Maybe you were arguing with Bobby. You know, that incident at the Cowboy Saloon that afternoon? It escalated. These things happen. We could be talking reduced counts. And maybe he'll cut out the stalking charge altogether.'

'Stalking?' Edwin seemed perplexed. 'I'm not a stalker. Kayleigh's a friend. I know it and she knows it.'

'Friend? That's not the story according to her lawyers.'

'Oh, she's afraid of them. They're controller by her father. They've all been telling her lies about me.'

'That's not the way it is,' Madigan said. 'You're in town to stalk her. And you killed her friend because he threw you out of the Cowboy Saloon.'

Edwin remained placid. 'No, I came to Fresno to get out of the Seattle rain for a time, to come to a public concert and to pay respect to a performer I like, a woman who's shown some interest in me. You accuse me of stalking but I'm sorry, *I'm* the victim here. You never did anything about my call.'

Madigan's face revealed confusion. 'What do you mean?'

'You don't know? I thought that was why you had asked me here. *My* complaint. Saturday night, I called nine-one-one and reported a Peeping Tom behind my house. But nobody did anything about it. You've got, what? A thousand, twelve hundred deputies? I just needed one to come out and see where this guy was standing, talk to the neighbours. But did they? No. Not for an out-of-towner.'

With a grim laugh, Madigan responded, 'We have *four* hundred deputies in Fresno and sixty in Madera. They cover over six thousand square miles of territory from the Valley all the way up to the mountains. I'm afraid a Peeping Tom, if there really was one, isn't going to be all-hands-on-deck.'

Edwin kept up the offensive. 'Your home-town girl is quote "stalked" and you think it's the end of the world. I'm a newcomer and nobody cares that somebody's casing out my house. If Bobby Prescott was murdered and witnesses place me at his trailer, then I'm being set up. Somebody had another reason to kill him and they're using me as a fall guy. You have to understand, Detective, I love her. I'd never hurt anybody close to her.'

'You don't love her, Edwin. You're obsessed with a celebrity who doesn't know you. And Kayleigh doesn't love you at all.'

Edwin shrugged. 'You say that but you know she sent me emails and letters. She practically said she loved me.'

Madigan said, 'Son, you have to get real here. She sent you the same emails she sent to a hundred thousand fans. We've been briefed by her lawyers. You got a half-dozen form emails and a couple of form letters.'

'That's what they're telling you. Doesn't mean it's true.'

Madigan hesitated. 'We got you dead to rights, son. Tell me the truth. Tell me you killed Robert Prescott and we'll work something out. Tell me and you'll feel better. Believe me.'

Edwin said, 'You know, Pike, I think I don't want to say anything more. I'd like to leave. And I'd like to pick up my things now. You know *People v. Williams*. You have to arrest me or let me go.'

In the dim observation area Dance asked Harutyun, 'The evidence? It places Edwin at the scene?'

She didn't even bother to wait for a reply. Harutyun's shift of eye away from her was all she needed. 'He doesn't have any forensics, does he?'

'We think it'll probably match. But, no, he doesn't have any yet.'

'Dennis, ask the Chief to come in here.'

'What?'

'I need to talk to him. It's very important.'

Harutyun glanced at the ID on her belt. His mouth tightened beneath the moustache. He realised that she'd deceived her way in.

'I'm sorry,' Dance said. 'I had to do it.'

He grimaced and sighed. Then snatched up a phone and dialled a number. They could hear it buzz inside. Madigan looked at it with surprise and irritation. Edwin turned to look into the reflective glass. He couldn't see the occupants of the room, but the mere transit of his eyes in Dance and Harutyun's direction was unsettling.

'Yes?' Madigan said casually into the phone.

'Detective? I'm here with Agent Dance. She'd . . . like to have a word with you? If possible.'

His incredulous eyes started to swivel towards the mirrored window too. 'Wonder how she ended up in there. I'm busy.'

Dance grabbed the phone. 'Detective, let him go. Don't arrest him.'

Madigan dropped the phone into the cradle. 'Edwin, have some water.'

'I want to leave,' he repeated, the essence of calm.

Madigan ignored him and stepped outside. The door flew open in the observation room and he was storming up to Dance.

'What the hell do you think you're doing?'

'You've got to let him go. If you don't have probable cause.'

'This's my case. Just 'cause you figured out somebody dropped that light on Prescott doesn't mean I need more of your opinions.'

So, she reflected. Dennis Harutyun had given her credit for that deduction, back at the convention centre.

'He has to be released. Edwin may very well've killed Bobby. But if he goes to trial and gets off, that's double jeopardy. He's got away with murder. Let him go and monitor him. It's the only way to make a case.'

'And what if he gives the deputy the slip and decides it's time to kill Kayleigh? You just saw his, what do you call it? Kinesics? Was he lying when he said he was being set up?'

'I couldn't tell under those circumstances. I didn't have time. But he's asked to leave and you haven't let him. That's a problem.'

Madigan looked at Edwin in the room, then he called to Harutyun, 'Book him. Cuff him and get him to detention. Breaking and entering at Bobby's only at this point. The evidence'll back us up on that.' He turned to Dance. 'Crystal'll take you to your car. You better go now. You being in here's trespass and, as you can probably tell, I'm in an arresting mood at the moment.'

AFTER FIFTEEN MINUTES of silent driving, Crystal Stanning said to Kathryn Dance, 'I didn't block you in on purpose. I just parked there.'

'I know that.'

In Stanning's personal car, a sun-faded Toyota, they were just pulling into the drive of Bobby's trailer. The young detective stopped, brakes squealing. The grass here, pale and thin, looked dustier and more spiky than before. Heat rose like sheets of flowing water above the Pathfinder.

Stanning fished another set of keys from her bag and said, 'You'll want to mind the steering wheel. People've got burns.' They climbed out.

'I'll take care.'

'You can buy windshield shades that work pretty good though I imagine you won't be staying around.'

Dance wondered if Madigan had asked his deputy to drop that into the conversation to see where it went. She said only, 'Thanks.'

'Just between us?' Stanning said.

'Sure.'

'Kayleigh Towne's a big deal here. Fresno's not the glitziest place on earth and Kayleigh's made us famous. I don't know, maybe the Chief thinks you're here to boost yourself up, you and the CBI, I mean. Take her away from us, you might say, with this investigation.'

'I see.'

Without another word the deputy drove off.

Dance walked to her vehicle.

So what do I do? Even if she wanted to take on the case, which would mean working with a wholly uncooperative local team, a stalking case wasn't the sort the Bureau would take on. Whatever Madigan felt, the CBI was the least political law-enforcement organisation she'd had contact with. Yet, Kayleigh was a good friend, other people were in danger, she was convinced, and Madigan was outgunned by Edwin Sharp.

That odd smile, the calculation, the calm demeanour, the research. They were armour and they were weapons. And what was beneath that smile? To a degree unlike any other suspect she'd known, Edwin Sharp was a mystery.

Dance got into the Pathfinder. Got out again immediately. It had to be 130 degrees inside. She leaned in, started the engine and rolled down the windows. Then turned the air conditioning on full blast.

As she waited for the interior to moderate, she walked closer to Bobby Prescott's trailer, now marked with crime scene tape. It was deserted here, aside from the squad car in which a young Asian-American deputy sat with a view of both Bobby's and Tabatha's trailers.

Despite the absorbing heat, Dance felt a chill of ill ease. She's thought of another implication of Madigan's arresting Edwin Sharp. If someone else was the killer, and he was using 'Your Shadow' as a template, then he'd have free rein to carry out the next murder without fear the police were searching for him.

Finally the Pathfinder was cool enough to drive. Dance put the vehicle in gear and drove away from the scene, debating.

I don't want to do this. It'll be a nightmare.

But ten seconds later she made the decision and was on her phone to the CBI office in Monterey, on her boss's voicemail. 'Charles. It's Kathryn. I need to take over an investigation in Fresno. Call me for the details.'

KAYLEIGH TOWNE'S Victorian squatted on a plot north of Fresno. The house wasn't large, but it was comfortable and comforting. She was a nester— tough for a performer who travels seven months out of the year—and she wanted a home that cried cosy, cried family.

When she was twelve, Bishop Towne had sold the old house she and her sister had grown up in, a ramshackle place north of Fresno, in the mountains. He'd said it was hard to get to in the winter, though the real reasons were that, one, his father had built it and Bishop would do anything he could to separate himself from his old man. And two, the rustic family manse hadn't fitted the image of the lifestyle he'd wanted to lead: that of the high-powered Country superstar. He'd built a $10 million working ranch in the Valley and had then populated it with cattle and sheep he had no interest in or knowledge about raising.

The move had been horrifying to Kayleigh, but worse was that he'd sold the beloved family house and land to a silver-mining company that owned the adjacent property. They'd bulldozed the structure, planning to expand, though the company'd gone bankrupt; the unnecessary destruction was all the more traumatic to the girl. She'd written a song about it, which became a huge hit.

> *I've lived in LA, I've lived in Maine,*
> *New York City and the Midwest Plains,*
> *But there's only one place I consider home.*

When I was a kid the house we owned.
Life was perfect and all was fine,
In that big old house . . . near the silver mine.

Now, the man responsible for this displacement walked into Kayleigh's living room and awkwardly bent down and hugged her.

Bishop's fourth wife, Sheri, also embraced Kayleigh then sat. Ash-blonde hair sprayed in place, the petite yet busty woman was a dozen years older than Kayleigh, unlike Wife Number Three, who could have attended the same high school as his daughter. Kayleigh couldn't remember much about Number Two.

Bishop Towne then manoeuvred his massive frame onto a couch, moving slowly. He was in cheap jeans and his ubiquitous black shirt, the belly rolling over his impressive belt.

'Was he still there, across the road?' Kayleigh asked, looking out, noting Darthur Morgan, vigilant as ever, in the front seat of the SUV.

'Didn't see anybody,' Bishop said. Sheri shook her head.

Edwin—the first thing she had seen this morning, looking out of the window of her first-floor bedroom. Well, his *car*, the big red car.

Kayleigh lived on the way to Yosemite and Sierra National Park. Across the two-lane road in front of her property was a public recreation area and arboretum, filled with rolling hills, jogging paths, groves of trees and gardens. The lot allowed twenty-four-hour parking, just the place for a sick stalker to perch.

'He was there a while ago. Just sitting, staring at the house.' She closed her eyes briefly.

'Well, nobody's there now,' Bishop repeated, noticing a wad of tissues on the coffee table where Kayleigh'd been sitting with her mobile, on which she'd called friends and family about Bobby's death. 'Sorry about Bobby, KT. I know you . . . I mean, I'm sorry.'

Sheri offered, 'It's terrible, honey. I feel so bad for you.'

Kayleigh stepped into the kitchen, got a milk for her father and an iced tea for Sheri. She returned to the living room.

'Thank you, honey,' the woman offered tentatively.

Her father lifted the milk as if toasting.

'Daddy.' Her eyes avoiding his, Kayleigh said quickly, 'I'm thinking of cancelling.' It was easier to stare towards where a murderous stalker had been spying on her than to make eye contact with Bishop Towne.

'The concert?' the big man grunted.

'I'm thinking of it.'

Sheri tried to deflect what might be an awkward moment. 'If there's anything I can do . . .'

'I'll think on it,' Kayleigh said. 'Thanks, Sheri.'

Kayleigh didn't hate her stepmother. Either you were a woman of steel, like Margaret, her mother, and you fought with a man like Bishop Towne, or you took the residual prestige and the undeniable charisma and you surrendered. That was Sheri.

Bishop grumbled, 'You tell Barry?'

'He was the first one I called. He's in Carmel with Neil.'

Tall, fidgeting Barry Zeigler, her producer, was full of nervous energy. He was a genius in the studio. If anybody had created a Kayleigh Towne sound it was Barry Zeigler.

Sheri said, 'Just one thing. I mean—' a glance at Bishop, sipping the milk he drank as religiously as he had once drunk bourbon,'—that luncheon tomorrow, for the fan of the month? You think we can still do that?'

It was a promotion Alicia Sessions had put together on Kayleigh's web site. Bishop had shoehorned Sheri into working on marketing projects for Kayleigh. The woman had been in retail all her life and had made some valuable contributions.

'It's all scheduled, right?' Bishop asked.

Sheri nodded. 'We've rented the room at the country club. It'd mean a lot to him. He's a big fan.'

Not as big as someone I know, thought Kayleigh.

'And there'll be some publicity too,' Sheri added.

'No reporters,' Kayleigh said. 'I don't want to talk about Bobby.'

Bishop said, 'We'll set the ground rules.'

'I can do that,' Sheri said, with an uncertain glance towards Bishop. 'I'll coordinate with Alicia.'

Kayleigh finally said, 'Sure, I guess.' She pictured the last time she'd had lunch alone with Bobby, a week ago. She wanted to cry again.

'Good,' Bishop said. 'We'll keep it short. Tell that fan it'll have to be short.'

Having conceded one issue, Kayleigh said, 'But I really want to think about the concert, Daddy.'

'Hey, baby doll, whatever you're happiest doing. We'll see how you feel in a day or so. Want you to be in good form. Happy too. That's what matters.' He said to Sheri, 'Got that meeting.'

The woman rose instantly and reached for Bishop's arm.

Kayleigh saw them to the door, amused that Darthur Morgan seemed to regard them with some suspicion. The couple piled into a dusty SUV and left, petite Sheri behind the wheel of the massive vehicle. Bishop had given up driving eight years ago.

KATHRYN DANCE was in south Fresno, trying to find a restaurant that Stanning had recommended.

Her thoughts, though, were on how to handle the explosion when Charles Overby or, more likely, the CBI director in Sacramento told Sheriff Gonzalez that Dance was going to be running the Bobby Prescott homicide.

She actually jumped when the phone buzzed. But the number on caller ID was a local one.

'Hello?'

'Kathryn? It's Pike Madigan.'

She said nothing.

'What're you up to?'

She said, 'Going for chicken *mole* at Julio's.'

'Good choice.' A pause on his part now. 'I got a call from the head of our Crime Scene Unit, Charlie Shean. Spelled S-H-E-A-N. Not like the actor. Takes some grief for that. Anyway, all the forensics were negative. None of the dust or other trace on the pictures and memorabilia in Edwin's rental matched what was in Bobby's trailer. And one of our people ran Edwin's credit card data. He bought everything we found in his house on eBay. We got his prints when we booked him. None of the ones at Bobby's or the convention centre match. No footprints, no nothin'. The treads on his car, zip. Was a washout.'

'You let him go.'

'Yeah, an hour ago. And released everything we took.'

This was, Dance supposed, the best someone like Madigan could do for contrition. But she was wrong.

'I wanted to say I'm sorry. You were right, I was wrong. I got outgunned by that fellow. It was like the only reason he came in was to find out information about the investigation.'

'If he's the perp, then, yes, I think that's a possibility.'

'This guy's pretty different from what I've been used to. You have a handle on him better than me. If you're still game would you be willing to help us out? We sure could use you.'

Without hesitation, 'I am, yes.' She'd be sure to call Overby and withdraw her prior request.

'That's much appreciated.'

Dance thought back to what Crystal Stanning had said about Madigan's concerns. 'One thing I wanted to say, Detective. This is your case. I'm a consultant only.'

In other words, the glory and the press conferences are all yours.

'Well, thank you for that. Now get yourself back here, if you would. Oh, and welcome to the FMCSO, Deputy Dance. Hey, that's got a nice ring to it, don'tcha think?'

KATHRYN DANCE stood in front of the Fresno-Madera Consolidated Sheriff's Office briefing room with P. K. Madigan and Dennis Harutyun. Detectives Crystal Stanning and Miguel Lopez were here too. They, along with Detective Gabriel Fuentes, presently in the field, would be the Prescott homicide/Kayleigh Towne stalker task force, backed up by TJ Scanlon in Monterey.

Two civilians were in the room as well. Dance had called Kayleigh Towne and asked her to join them. The woman had reluctantly agreed and Alicia Sessions had come along for moral support. Kayleigh was bleary-eyed and sallow, her hair tied back in a taut ponytail and protruding from a burgundy sports cap. She wore baggy jeans and a long-sleeved shirt, as if trying to disguise herself.

Kayleigh reported that Edwin had been spying on her again this morning, in the parking lot across the road from her house.

Alicia was dressed the opposite of her boss, almost pick-a-fight defiant. Tight jeans, light blue cowboy boots, a green tank top. Her face was grim and angry, some of that directed, it seemed, towards the deputies as if they weren't doing enough to protect her boss.

Dance said, 'Chief Madigan's been kind enough to invite the CBI to assist in the Prescott murder case, and we're going to be focusing on the possibility that it's linked to the stalker who's been troubling Kayleigh. I'm not here to step on toes. I'm helping because I've got some experience with stalkers.'

'Personally?' Lopez said.

Everyone laughed.

'First of all, my associate in Monterey's found out that there are no warrants or court orders on Edwin—nothing federal or in California, Washington or Oregon. Which is a little unusual for a stalker; normally there's a history of complaints. But, on the other hand, he could simply be very careful. And we know he's smart.

'Now, I'll tell you a little about stalking and where I think Edwin fits into the diagnosis. The first type of stalker is known as simple obsessional. These are domestic situations. The stalker and the object have had some romantic or sexual contact. Relationships, marriages or even one-night stands that go bad. Then there are erotomanic stalkers.'

'Like sex perverts?' Madigan wondered aloud.

'No, it's more about love then sex. Traditionally, erotomanic stalkers were women who fell in love with powerful men in higher economic or social classes. Like secretaries fawning over their bosses. But now as many men fall into the category as women. Usually, there's some minor, innocuous contact that the stalker misreads. They become convinced the subject of their obsession is in love with them but is too shy to reciprocate.

'The third type is called love obsessional. These go after celebrities, people they've worshipped from afar and believe they're soul mates with. I think Edwin is a mix of erotomania and love obsessional. He believes that you're the woman for him, Kayleigh. He wants a relationship with you and believes you feel the same about him.'

'That damned "XO",' Kayleigh muttered. 'It was just a form letter.'

Alicia said, 'We send out thousands of them a week.'

'Well, you have to understand all stalkers are more or less delusional,' Dance said. 'They range from serious neurosis to borderline personalities to truly psychotic, schizophrenic to severely bipolar. We have to assume that Edwin has a reality problem.'

Crystal Stanning asked, 'But what's his motive for killing Bobby Prescott—if he's the one who did?'

Dance said, 'It's the one thing that doesn't quite fit. Erotomanic and love-obsessional stalkers are the least dangerous.'

Madigan added, 'Bobby could just have been at the wrong place at the wrong time. If that song *was* an announcement, it was just about the concert hall. Maybe had nothing to do with Bobby. The perp might just've been waiting for anybody to show up.'

'Good point,' Dance said. 'But we'll look into Bobby's life a little more, see what he was up to, anything illegal, for instance.'

'He wasn't,' Kayleigh said firmly. 'He had a problem a few years ago, drugs and drinking, but he was clean recently.'

'That doesn't mean somebody wouldn't want him dead,' Dance said. 'Remember that an intruder—likely the killer—took some things from his trailer the morning after he was killed.'

'I could look into his personal life, his background,' Harutyun offered in his low, easy voice.

Dance glanced at Madigan, who nodded his agreement. 'Dennis's our librarian. Mean that in a good way. He does his homework. He knew what Google was when I thought it was a cartoon character on TV.'

Dance talked about the difficulty of kinesically analysing suspects like Edwin. 'People on the borderline of psychosis, like stalkers, might tell you facts that can lead to your uncovering their deception. But such people are often impossible to analyse kinesically. They don't feel stress when lying— because their goal of getting close to the object of their obsession trumps everything.'

Alicia grimaced in frustration. 'Isn't there a stalking law here?'

Dance paraphrased the statute: 'You're guilty of stalking if you wilfully, maliciously and repeatedly harass the victim and make a credible threat with the intent to place that person in reasonable fear for his or her safety, or the safety of the immediate family. It doesn't have a lot of teeth, though. Some jail time and a fine.'

'Well, it's something; arrest him anyway,' Kayleigh said.

'It may not be that easy. Tell me about his stalking.'

'He sent me about a hundred and fifty emails and thirty or so letters. He'd ask me out, hint about a life together. And he sent me some presents. We sent everything back.'

Alicia said, 'We threatened him with restraining orders and everything but . . . he just ignored the letters and the lawyers said he was never quite across the line of legality.'

Madigan then asked, 'In all those letters was there any threat at all? Under the statute there has to be a credible threat.'

Kayleigh reluctantly said, 'No, no threats. It's just the opposite, really. He was always telling me how he wanted to protect me. How he'd be there for me—just like in the song, "Your Shadow".'

It was then that Dance's phone sang out with an incoming message. It was from TJ Scanlon. She read quickly then looked up.

'You want to hear a bio of our stalker?'

But the question, of course, needed no answer.

Dennis Harutyun helped Dance log on to her email from a terminal in the room and she printed out TJ's document.

'There isn't much, I'm afraid,' Dance said. Edwin Stanton Sharp had been born in Yakima, a town in Washington state. His father was a travelling salesman, his mother worked in retail. 'To judge from her income, she must have had several jobs. This could mean that the boy spent a lot of time alone. Psychologists think stalking begins from attachment issues.

'His grades were very good. But he was held back a year in the seventh grade, so that suggests emotional problems in school. When he was sixteen his parents split up and he went to live with his mother outside Seattle. He went to the University of Washington for two years. Again, he did fairly well, but he dropped out after the start of his third year. No record of why. He started working at jobs stalkers sometimes gravitate towards: security guard, part-time retail sales, door-to-door selling. They're good professions for those with voyeuristic or stalking tendencies because you get to see a lot of people and are largely unsupervised. And invisible.

'His mother died in July of last year, cancer. His father hasn't filed a tax return in six years and the IRS can't find him. TJ, my associate in Monterey, has checked out Edwin's online activity. He posts to a lot of music blogs. Typically a stalker is more engaged in online activities than he is—and a lot darker ones too.' Dance continued to read. 'Ah, looks like he went through a breakup last year. TJ found a reference to someone named Sally in a blog. He was talking about your song, "You and Me".'

'That's right,' Kayleigh said. 'It's about a breakup.'

'The posting was in December.' Dance asked Kayleigh, 'Not long before the stalking started, right?'

'Yes, January.'

'Trauma often precipitates stalking.' Dance nodded towards TJ's email. 'He said the song meant a lot to him. He talked about the trouble he was having with Sally. He said it's like you knew exactly what he was going through. Then a few days later he posted about your single "Near the Silver Mine". He said he'd been feeling bad because he'd lost his house when he was about that age too.'

Kayleigh's lips tightened. 'He knew about my house?' She said that she'd loved the house she'd grown up in, north of Fresno, but her dad had sold it to a mining company when she was young. 'I probably mentioned in an interview that I wished he hadn't.'

Dance read some more. 'His spelling and grammar are very good. Which tells me he's in control. If he's the one who killed Bobby, he's going to be covering his tracks and planning out the stalking very carefully.'

'Where do you think we should go from here?' Madigan asked.

'First, we've got to keep him under surveillance.'

'Deputy Fuentes is doing that. Edwin is seeing a movie. In the Rialto.'

Harutyun explained that this was an old movie theatre in Fresno in an eclectic area of galleries, restaurants, tattoo parlours and shops.

'We need to find his former girlfriend. Sally,' Dance said.

'Lopez, you handle that. Find her. Have her call Agent Dance.'

'Sure, Chief.'

Madigan added, 'We should identify other possible victims. Keep an eye on them. Who'd be at particular risk?'

Dance said, 'Probably first is anybody he sees as a romantic rival.' To Kayleigh: 'You and Bobby dated?'

Apparently this wasn't public knowledge. Kayleigh blushed. 'Well, yes, a while ago. It wasn't a big deal. How'd you know?'

Because, Dance thought, when I saw you together yesterday I noticed a decrease in the angle of your shoulders when you were speaking, signifying relaxation. Bobby's leaning forward slightly when he spoke to you, indicating that what he was saying was meant for you alone.

What she said to Kayleigh was, 'A hunch.'

Crystal Stanning said, 'So anyone that Kayleigh ever dated or men she was real friendly with are at risk?'

'Yes, possibly, though women too. Stalkers are jealous. A stalker's likely to target anybody who's a threat to you, or has even offended you. He's taking real seriously his role as a protector; I could see that yesterday. Can you think of any enemies you might have that he'd know about?'

Kayleigh looked around. 'Not really.'

Dance continued, 'He could also consider going after critics who'd dissed you. Or fans who were critical of your work. Then, next, he could target anyone he saw as keeping you two apart.'

'Like Darthur?'

'Yes, him. But it could also be your lawyers.' She glanced at Alicia. 'Or you. You seem very protective of Kayleigh.'

The broad-shouldered woman shrugged. '*Somebody's* got to be.'

A sentence with many possible implications.

'And it could also be us. The police. Truly obsessive stalkers have a different sense of right and wrong. In extreme obsession cases, the stalker's murdering a policeman is no worse than killing a fly.'

'My family? The crew?' Kayleigh asked.

'Generally, family and nonromantic friends are at risk only if they try to protect the object from the stalker. I talked to some of the crew about what they'd seen yesterday but I think I should interview all of them. Assess if they're at risk,' Dance said.

Or potential perps, she thought but didn't say aloud.

'The crew's at the convention centre now,' Kayleigh said. But added, 'The band's in Nashville still, finishing up some studio work for our new album. They won't be here till Thursday or Friday.'

That was good news. Fewer potential victims to worry about. Fewer suspects too.

Dance said, 'Finally, there's the Hinckley scenario. Killing someone of some notoriety to impress Kayleigh.'

She reminded them that John Hinckley, Jr., was obsessed with Jodie Foster. 'He figured that by assassinating Ronald Reagan he'd be linked forever to the actress.'

'And in a sick way,' Harutyun observed, 'he accomplished his goal.'

Madigan said, 'I've talked to Edwin. You have too. He doesn't seem like a psycho. How could he possibly think killing people is going to get him closer to Kayleigh?'

'Oh, he doesn't think about it. Not on a conscious level. Even if Edwin seems functional on the surface, there's more at work. Remember, it's his reality, not ours.'

Madigan said, 'I've ordered a box on Kayleigh's phone. And we're still on those numbers of the other mobiles he bought in Burlingame. So if he powers them up again we can get a car there fast.'

Harutyun said to Kayleigh, 'Kathryn asked me to look into the second verse of the song that was played to you the other night.' He passed out copies to everyone. 'I've been trying to think of where an attack could be planned. But I can't come up with much.'

You sit by the river, wondering what you got wrong.
How many chances you've missed all along.
Like your troubles had somehow turned to stone
And the water was whispering, why don't you come home?

Dance focused on the words. 'A river.'

Madigan laughed. 'We got plenty of those around here.'

Harutyun pointed out, 'Could be anywhere.'

Madigan peered down at the lyrics. 'I'll tell patrol officers to pay special attention to riversides, ones out of view of any roads.'

Alicia gave the first smile Dance could recall seeing on the tough woman's face. 'But I guess the good news is that Kayleigh's not at risk, if he's that much in love with her.'

'That's true. But only for a time. Remember his separation from reality? He's been in the courting stage for a while.' Dance turned to Kayleigh. 'Now he's under the illusion that you care for him. At some point, though, he'll see your behaviour as if you're breaking up with him. When that happens, he'll become dangerous. He'll want revenge. Or he'll want to kill you so nobody else can have you.'

4

The convention centre had been sanitised.

Music at Kayleigh Towne's level was a very serious business so Kathryn Dance wasn't surprised that the crime scene had been cleaned as quickly as possible, all traces of the death removed, to make sure the concert could proceed as planned.

Kayleigh was here to block out stage direction for the show. Tye Slocum, the guitar technician, was temporarily chief roadie, until Alicia could fill the job with a pro; they needed someone who knew equipment and could mix sound at the console, as complicated as a plane's cockpit. The quiet, heavyset young man was distracted and not particularly confident but trying to rise to the occasion.

With Kayleigh's OK, Dance called Tye over and explained what she needed—to speak to the crew. He rounded them up, all of them from their early twenties to forties, and fit, suggesting the physical nature of their jobs.

Dance noted great camaraderie among them and Kayleigh, but no one stood out as approaching Bobby's level of closeness to Kayleigh, and therefore an obvious threat to Edwin. Nor did she sense that any of them might have had a motive to kill Prescott—another reason for her mission here.

The only one Dance didn't interview was Alicia. She'd been at the convention centre earlier when Dance arrived, standing outside beside a Ford pick-up with a trailer hitch on the back and a bumper sticker that announced:

I ♥ MY QUARTER HORSE

A cigarette had dangled from her lips and she'd looked more like a local Teamster than a personal assistant. Of anyone on the staff, Alicia was probably the most at risk; she'd defied Edwin the most at the Cowboy Saloon and would present an obstacle to the stalker's getting close to Kayleigh.

Dance, however, couldn't impart this warning in person, only via a phone message. The assistant had left the convention centre by the time Dance went to find her.

As she looked over her notes, Dance noticed Kayleigh pull her ringing mobile from her pocket. The look on the young woman's face left little doubt. It would be a call she didn't recognise.

She stared for a moment and then lifted the unit to her ear.

The woman gasped. Her head swivelled towards Dance and she said, 'It's another call, Kathryn. It's the second verse!'

IN A QUARTER OF AN HOUR, Dance was at the sheriff's office, hurrying inside. Harutyun met her at the door.

She asked, 'Did the mobile providers triangulate on his phone?'

Harutyun said evenly, 'It wasn't a mobile. The call was from a payphone, on the Fresno College campus. School's not in session yet. It's pretty deserted there. Nobody saw the caller.'

'Well, where's Edwin?'

'That's the curious thing. Still in the Rialto—the theatre. It must be somebody else.'

They stepped into Madigan's office, where both the chief detective and Stanning, next to her boss, were on their phones.

Madigan looked up. He disconnected his mobile and ignored his desk phone when it rang, after a glance at caller ID. He looked too at a half-empty ice-cream cup and pitched it out. Rocky Road.

'Where's Kayleigh?' Harutyun asked.

Dance said, 'She and the crew are at the convention centre. Darthur Morgan's with her. Alicia's the only one not accounted for. I called her on the way here and left a message. I haven't heard back.'

Madigan glanced towards his phone. 'That was Fuentes. Edwin's still watching his movie.'

Harutyun asked, 'Any way that he could've called from the theatre, either the land line or another mobile, and routed the call through the phone at the college?'

Good question. But Madigan had a good answer. 'No, we checked with the Bell folks, or whoever they are nowadays. The call was made from the phone at the school, direct to Kayleigh's.'

Dance asked, 'Any way he could've got out of the theatre?'

'No, Fuentes is in a restaurant on Olive. He's watching the front entrance. The back doors're alarmed. He checked.'

Dance supposed that Edwin was just what he seemed to be: a sad young man without a life, drawn to a woman who existed in a different universe. And yet she couldn't help but recall his icy demeanour, his calm attitude, his laserlike focus on Kayleigh, that phoney smile.

And his intelligence.

Which prompted her to ask, 'Basements?'

'What?' Madigan asked.

'In that block, are there connecting basements?'

'I don't know.' Madigan hit a button on the land line. A tone sounded, then the rapid eleven digits of a number being dialled.

'Fuentes.'

Madigan barked, 'Could he have snuck out through the basement? The hardware store next door? Do they share a basement?'

A pause. 'Let me check. I'll get right back.'

Three minutes later they got the news that Dance suspected they would. 'Yep, Chief. I went down there. There's an unlocked door.'

'Evacuate the theatre,' Dance said. 'We need to be sure.'

'Evacuate?' Fuentes asked.

Madigan was staring at her. Then he said firmly, 'You heard Agent Dance, Gabe. Get the lights on and evacuate.'

'The theatre isn't going to want to . . .' His voice faded. 'I'll get on it.'

Ten minutes later, Fuentes came back on the line. Dance knew from the first word, 'Chief', what the story was going to be.

Madigan sighed. 'You're sure he's gone?'

'There weren't that many people inside, being early. Yeah, I'm sure.' But the limp in Fuentes's voice came from another source as well. 'And I have to tell you . . . While I was keeping an eye on the theatre? I was in the restaurant and somebody broke into my cruiser. I had a Glock on the back seat. It was in a box and under my jacket.'

'Damn it!' Madigan shouted.

'I'm sorry. It should've been in the trunk.'

'It shoulda been *home*. That's your personal weapon.'

'I was going to the range tonight,' the deputy said miserably.

'You know what I gotta do, Gabe. Don't have any options.'

'I know. You want my service piece and shield?'

'Need 'em. Yeah. We'll have the inquiry as fast as we can but it'll be three or four days. You're out of commission till then.' He stabbed the speaker-phone button.

Harutyun said in his low, stress-free voice, 'It could be a gang.'

'It's not a gang,' Madigan snapped. 'It's our stalker. At least if we find him he'll go to jail for a long, long time. Hell, this's one clever son of a bitch. He got Fuentes in the doghouse and suspended and ended up with a nice big gun, to boot.'

Dance looked at the lyric sheet they had pinned up on a badly mounted cork board. 'Where's he going to strike? A river?'

'And,' Crystal Stanning added, 'who's he got in mind for the next victim?'

'MARY-GORDON, stay off that. See the sign?'

'It's not moving, Mommy,' the six-year-old pointed out.

Suellyn Sanchez reflected what perfect logic that was. The warning sign on the baggage carousel: STAY OFF THE MOVING BELT.

'It could start at any minute.'

'But when the light comes on I can get off.'

How they tested the limits.

The mother and daughter were at the Arrivals area in Fresno-Yosemite Airport; their flight from Portland had arrived twenty minutes early. Suellyn looked around for their ride. Saw no one yet and turned back to the girl.

'It's filthy. Your dress'll get stained.'

That risk apparently didn't carry much weight either. But all it took was one 'Mary-Gordon' uttered in a certain tone, that very special tone, and the cute blonde stepped back immediately.

Suellyn reminded herself to chill. Bobby Prescott's death had cast a pall over everything. And how was Kayleigh holding up? She and Bobby had had quite a history and Suellyn knew that her kid sister would be reeling from the loss.

Bishop had called that morning, after she'd learned the sad news from Kayleigh. The conversation with her father had been conducted in the clumsy way he bobbled nearly everything personal. Suellyn was thinking it was odd that he'd called to ask if she'd come to Fresno to support her sister during this tough time until Suellyn realised: Bishop would want to share the bereavement duty with someone else. Well, no, he'd want to hand off the job completely if he could.

Suellyn resembled her younger sister in a vague way. Eight years separated the two, and Suellyn was taller, of broader build and fuller face, though her light brown hair was of the same fine, flowing texture. Today she was prepared for the assault of a late Fresno summer, in a burgundy sundress, cut low at the front and back, and Brighton sandals, whose silver hearts covering the first two toes fascinated Mary-Gordon.

Even in this outfit, she was hot. Portland had clocked in at sixty-two degrees that morning.

'Where's Aunt Kayleigh?' Mary-Gordon asked.

'She's getting ready to sing a show. We're going to it on Friday.'

Maybe. Her sister hadn't actually invited her to the concert.

'Good. I like it when she sings.'

With a blare of a horn and a flashing orange light, the baggage belt started to move. Mary-Gordon spotted the first suitcase and gleefully charged towards it, her pink dress fluttering around her.

The luggage was retrieved and they both walked away from the belt and the crowds and paused in front of one of the doors.

Suellyn's mobile rang. She answered it. 'Hey, Daddy.'

'You're in,' the man growled.

And hello and nice day to you too.

'Richie's on his way to pick you up.'

Or you could've come to collect your daughter and granddaughter in person. Bishop Towne didn't drive but he had plenty in his crew to play chauffeur—if he'd wanted to come.

'I can take a cab,' Suellyn said.

'No, you won't. Richie'll be there.' And he disconnected.

I'm taking a cab, she thought. I'm not hanging around. 'Do you need to use the girls' room?' Suellyn asked Mary-Gordon.

'No.'

'Excuse me, Suellyn?'

She turned to see Bishop's minion, Richie, a young man looking every inch the member of a Country musician's entourage. 'I'm your chauffeur.' He shook her hand and smiled towards Mary-Gordon. 'Hello.'

'Hello,' she said.

'Welcome to Fresno. You're Mary-Gordon, I'll bet.'

'He said my name right.' She beamed. Hers wasn't Mary with Gordon as a middle name. It was a double-barrelled Southern name and the girl wasn't shy about correcting anyone who got it wrong.

'Let me get those for you,' the man said and took both suitcases. 'You going to your father's or Kayleigh's?' he asked Suellyn.

'Kayleigh's. We're going to surprise her.'

'That'll be fun.'

Suellyn hoped so. Bishop had been adamant that Suellyn not call Kayleigh and tell her of the visit—because Kayleigh would have told her not to come. She wouldn't want any sympathy because of Bobby's death, Bishop said. But family had to stick together.

They stepped outside. Bishop's associate whispered to Suellyn, 'It's good you're here. Kayleigh's pretty upset about Bobby.'

'I can imagine. Do they know what happened?'

'Not yet.' He lifted his voice and said to Mary-Gordon, 'Hey, before we go to your aunt's, you want to see something fun?'

'Yeah!'

'It's really neat and you'll like it.' He glanced at Suellyn. 'Little detour? There's this park practically on the way.'

'Please, Mommy!'

'All right. But we don't want to be too late, Richie.'

He blinked. 'Oh, I'm not Richie. I came to fetch you instead.' And they arrived at his car. He stashed the suitcases in the trunk of the big old Buick. It was bright red—a colour you didn't see much nowadays.

KATHRYN DANCE was in the living room of Kayleigh's house. Kayleigh was upstairs, changing clothes. Darthur Morgan was sitting near the front door.

Dance looked around the living room at the many awards and gold and platinum records hanging on the walls. In a few minutes, Kayleigh joined them, wearing blue jeans and a thick, dark grey blouse. The singer sat down on a floral upholstered couch.

Dance said, 'I just talked to the deputy at the convention centre. All of the crew are accounted for except Alicia.'

'Oh, she called ten minutes ago. I told her about the second verse and made sure she was looking out for herself.' Kayleigh smiled. 'She almost sounded like she was hoping Edwin'd try something with her. She's tough.'

Darthur Morgan sat calmly and didn't even seem to hear the conversation. Then he stiffened, got to his feet, looking out of the front window. 'Visitors. Hm, whole entourage. It looks official.'

'Entourage' described it pretty well, Kayleigh decided. Two SUVs—a white Lexus, Bishop's, and a black Lincoln Navigator.

Bishop and Sheri climbed out and turned to the other vehicle.

Four passengers, it seemed. First was security, it was easy to tell. A solid, sunglassed man, over six feet. He looked around, whispered something into the interior of the SUV. The next to climb out was a slim, thoughtful-looking man with thinning hair. The third, in a dark suit, was taller and had a politician's head of hair. Which made sense because, Kayleigh realised, that's exactly who he was: California's star congressman, William Davis, a two-term Democrat.

A woman was the last to climb out of the Navigator, dressed in a conservative navy jacket and skirt, flesh-coloured stockings.

The guard stayed with the SUV and the others followed Bishop and his wife into the house.

Inside, Bishop hugged his daughter and as if in an afterthought asked how she was holding up. He said to his daughter, 'This here's Congressman Davis. And his aides, Peter Simesky and . . .'

'Myra Babbage.' The slim, unsmiling woman with square-cut brunette hair nodded formally.

'Ms Towne, it's an honour,' the congressman said.

'Hey, call me Kayleigh. You're making me older than I want to be.'

Davis laughed. 'And I'm Bill. It's easy to remember. I've sponsored a few of them in Congress.'

Kayleigh gave a brief smile. And she introduced Dance and Morgan.

'We just flew into San Francisco a few days ago and have been making our way south. I was in touch with your father, asking about getting to your concert. Oh, I'm paying for tickets, don't you worry. I'm afraid we just need a little extra security.'

Bishop said, 'We've got it all taken care of.'

'I was hoping for a chance to meet you and to say hi in person. Your father suggested bringing me along today, before the concert.'

So, that was it. Kayleigh understood. Her father had said they'd think about cancelling the show and yet he was going to do whatever he needed to make sure it went forward. He'd be thinking that knowing the congressman would be in the audience would pressure her not to cancel.

Kayleigh fumed but smiled pleasantly, as Davis rambled like a schoolboy, talking about songs of hers he particularly loved. He really was quite a fan. He knew every word of every tune, it seemed.

Myra Babbage added, 'We can't thank you enough for letting us use "Leaving Home" on the web site. It's really become an anthem for Bill's campaign.'

Kathryn Dance said, 'I heard you on the radio, Congressman. On the drive over here—NPR was replaying that debate on immigration issues. That was some heated discussion.'

'It sure was.'

'I think you won, by the way. You drove 'em into the ground.'

'Thanks. It was a lot of fun,' Davis said with a gleam in his eye. 'I love debates. That was my quote "sport" at school. Less painful to talk than getting run into on the football field. Not necessarily safer, though.'

Kayleigh didn't follow politics much. Some of her fellow performers were active in campaigns and causes, but then again she'd known them before they'd hit it big and they hadn't seemed particularly interested in animal rights or hunger before they started drawing the public limelight. She suspected that a number had been tapped by their public relations firms or their record company publicity departments to take up a cause because it would look good in the press.

She knew, though, about US Congressman Bill Davis. He was a politico with an eclectic mix of positions, the most controversial of which was relaxing border controls to let in more foreigners, subject to requirements like an absence of criminal conviction, an English language test and guarantees of employment prospects, which is why he sought permission to use 'Leaving Home'. He was a front-runner for the next Presidential campaign.

Peter Simesky said, 'Kayleigh, I'll confirm he's a fan. On our campaign bus, you're up there with Taylor Swift, James Taylor and the Stones for our listening pleasure. Hope you're OK with that company.'

'I'll take it, you bet.'

Then the congressman grew serious. 'Your father said there's a bit of a problem at the moment, somebody who might be stalking you?' This was half directed to Dance, as well. Kayleigh's father must have mentioned that she was an agent.

'Afraid that's true,' Dance said.

'You're . . . with Fresno?' Myra Babbage asked. 'We've been working with a few people there on security.'

'No, CBI.' The fact she was here would normally mean the case was a major one. She added, 'I'm based in Monterey, but was here unofficially and heard about the incident. I volunteered to help.'

'We were just campaigning in Monterey too,' Davis said. 'Campaigning at Cannery Row.'

'That's why the traffic was so bad back at home before I left,' Dance joked.

'I wish it had been worse. It was a good turnout, not a great turnout.'

Kayleigh supposed Monterey voters would not be particularly happy about a pro-immigration candidate.

The congressman nodded towards the agent. 'I'm sure the CBI and the local authorities are doing all they can but if you need any help from me, let me know. Stalking can be a federal crime too.'

Kayleigh thanked him, Dance did too and Simesky gave the agent his card. 'You need any help,' he said, 'give me a call.'

'I'll do that,' Dance replied as her phone buzzed. 'It's a text from Detective Harutyun,' she announced to the room. She read it and sighed. 'They've found the next crime scene. It's another killing, another fire. But it was a lot worse than at the concert hall. He says there might be more than one victim. They just can't tell.'

'THE FIRE'S STILL GOING,' Harutyun told her over the phone. 'It's in a shed beside the San Joaquin river.'

'Any witnesses?' Dance asked.

'No.'

'How do you know it's related to the stalking?'

'Well, out front we found a little shrine to Kayleigh. A mound of rocks and a couple of her CDs next to them in front of the shed. And, you know what was weird? A twenty-dollar bill under a rock.'

'And no idea of the victim?'

'Or victims,' he reminded. 'The team got a look inside and saw a couple of legs. That's about all that was left. Then the roof came down. It was part of an old gas station so they're being careful, thinking there could be a buried tank nearby. Charlie Shean has his CS people running the scene outside, as close as they can. It's hot as Hades out there. No footprints or tyre treads. We've found two shell casings, nine millimetre. Same as Fuentes's gun. But that could be a coincidence.'

An altar to Kayleigh. Well, it was in keeping with stalker behaviour.

'Charlie's folks also ran the scene of the phone booth where he called Kayleigh. They got some trace, but the fingerprints don't match anything else and they're not in the AIFIS database. I've got to go. I'll call you when I know more, Kathryn.'

'Thanks.' She turned to Kayleigh, her father and the others and gave them a report.

Bishop closed his eyes, muttered what might've been a prayer.

'Who's the victim?' Kayleigh asked breathlessly.

'We don't know. It could be more than one. But because of the fire they couldn't get a good look inside.'

The singer's voice cracked. 'Where's Alicia? And Tye?'

But then Kayleigh called and got through to both of them. Alicia had been out riding her horse. All the rest of the crew was accounted for too, Kayleigh reported after speaking to Tye Slocum.

The congressman and his entourage looked uneasy. Davis seemed to be thinking that a visit now had not been a good idea. He said, 'We've got some campaigning to do. Sorry to have bothered you.'

'Not at all,' said Bishop. Davis reiterated he'd help out however he could. He'd see her at the concert.

'I'm not . . .' Kayleigh fell silent, looking at her father, who gave no reaction. 'Hey, thanks for your support.'

Peter Simesky, the aide, stepped up to Dance again. He shook her hand. 'You have my card. If there's anything else you need, just let me know.'

Kinesics is a skill that doesn't shut off when you leave the office. The instant he'd made eye contact with her earlier, she knew that Simesky wanted to get to know her better, if circumstances allowed. But in Dance's personal life, there was no inclination for expansion. She nodded politely to Simesky and made sure their handshake was brief and professional. She couldn't tell if he got the message.

Then Davis, followed by Simesky and Myra Babbage, left the house and made their way to the SUV. The security man opened the doors for them. In a minute they were speeding down the gravel driveway.

Then Kayleigh's eyes flashed in shock and she began to cry. 'Wait, he burned them?' she whispered.

'That's right,' said Dance.

'No, no! *This*'s my fault too!' Her shoulders rose, jaw tight. She angrily wiped away tears. 'My song! He's using another one of my songs.'

Dance pointed out, 'The crime scene's by the river, as in the second verse.'

'No, the fire! First, Bobby and now these other people. Edwin sent me an email, well, a bunch of them, saying how much he liked my song "Fire and Flame".'

She picked up the CD of *Your Shadow* from a shelf containing hundreds of discs and showed Dance the liner notes.

> *Love is fire, love is flame*
> *It warms your heart, it lights the way.*
> *It burns forever just like the sun.*
> *It welds two souls and makes them one.*
> *Love is fire, love is flame.*

Bishop said to his daughter, 'Hey, KT, don't go blaming yourself. You can't take inta account all the crazies out there.'

'He *burned* those people to death, Daddy!'

Bishop didn't know what to say. He looked at his watch on a big, ruddy wrist. 'Hey, you heard from your sister?'

'I talked to her this morning. I called her about Bobby. Why?'

'They shoulda been here by now. Or maybe—'

Kayleigh's mouth dropped. 'What do you mean, Daddy?'

Bishop looked down. 'I thought it'd be good for her to come. Moral support, with Bobby. Called her this morning. Suellyn and Mary-Gordon flew up, landed an hour ago.'

'Why didn't you tell me?' Kayleigh raged. 'And why on earth would you do that? With this madman around. A little girl?'

'Moral support,' he growled back, flustered. 'Like I said.'

'Oh, God.' Kayleigh sat down. Her voice rose to a high pitch. 'The fire, the attack. Oh, you don't think . . .? It's not *them?*'

'Settle there, KT. How would this Sharp fella even know they were at the airport? And what flight they were coming in on?'

Kayleigh grabbed her phone and dialled. She slammed the disconnect button. 'Voicemail. Who was going to pick them up?'

'I sent Richie. I'll give him a call.' Bishop placed a call on his mobile. 'Hey. Me. Where are they? . . . Who d'you think I mean? Suellyn and her kid . . . *What?* . . . When? . . . Oh, damn.' He disconnected, glanced at Kayleigh. 'What happened was he got a call from a friend of yours. *He* was going to give them a ride here.'

'Who?' Kayleigh cried. 'Who was it?'

'Richie doesn't remember the name. But he knew the flight number, knew their names. Said you'd rather he picked them up.'

Sheri said, 'But if it was him, Edwin, how'd he know Richie was going to pick them up?'

Bishop's eyes bored into the carpet at his feet. 'Well . . . this morning, we had breakfast at Herndon Café, Sheri and me. We were pretty much alone in the place. Except there was somebody, sitting nearby, his back to us. He coulda overheard me talking to Suellyn and calling Richie. I doubt it but coulda happened.'

'But how would he know Richie?' Kayleigh asked. 'To get his number and call him?'

'Could he be connected to you on your site?' Dance asked.

'He's listed on the last album's acknowledgments, he was one of my assistants and drivers.' Kayleigh began to cry. 'What're we going to do?'

Dance called Harutyun and told him their concern. He said he was going to check something. He came back on after an interminable five minutes. 'Video at the airport. A woman in her thirties and a little girl got into Edwin's Buick thirty minutes after the flight from Portland landed.'

Dance looked at the expectant faces. She told them what the deputy had said.

'No!' Kayleigh screamed. 'No!'

'And. Agent Dance . . . Kathryn,' Harutyun was saying on the line. 'Just heard from the fire team. There's only one body inside.' He hesitated. 'Not too big. Could be a teenager or a woman. At least, if it is the sister, the little girl's still alive. But that also means he's got her.'

Dance had just hung up the phone when Darthur Morgan called from the entryway, 'Another car coming.'

A moment later there was the clunk of car doors closing and the sound of a vehicle accelerating away on the gravel drive.

Then the front door opened and in walked a woman in her thirties and an adorable little girl of about six, in a pink dress. She held a stuffed plush toy. She ignored everyone in the room except the singer, whom she ran to and hugged hard. 'Aunt Kayleigh, we went to this museum and we brought you a stuffed redwood tree!'

KATHRYN DANCE SMILED a greeting to the woman she'd been introduced to—Suellyn Sanchez, Kayleigh's sister—and walked to the front door. She noted the big red Buick speeding away.

'It was him,' Kayleigh whispered, looking out of the window.

Suellyn embraced her father and greeted Sheri, too, more affectionately than Kayleigh had. 'What's with the police? Is this about Bobby?'

Kayleigh, however, glanced icily towards her father and turned her attention to Mary-Gordon. 'Honey, let me show you some games I got for when you visited.'

'Yay! . . . Where's Freddie?'

'He's in the stable at Grandpa's house. You and your mommy are going to be staying there. Come on.'

Her arm round the girl, the two vanished into the den.

Dance called Harutyun and told him that the sister and niece were safe. He reported they still had no ID on the victim but the fire was out and the CS unit and medical examiners were about to go inside, process the body and run the scene.

When Kayleigh returned, she steamed up to her sister and said, 'What *were* you thinking? Do you know who gave you that ride?'

'A friend of yours. Said his name was Stan.'

Dance pointed out, 'Stanton. Middle name.'

Kayleigh's voice dropped. 'It's my damn *stalker*. Did you think to call?'

'What? But you said he was fat, disgusting.'

'Well, he made himself unfat.' Kayleigh snapped, looking angrily into her sister's eyes. 'Sorry. It's not your fault. You just . . . you shouldn't be here.' A glance towards Bishop.

Dance said, 'We aren't sure who's behind it. Edwin Sharp is a possible suspect. But you should avoid any more contact with him.'

'Where did you go?' Kayleigh asked.

'He asked if we wanted to see something Mary-Gordon might like. He said it was on the way. We went to the tree museum near the Bluffs. He said you liked to spend time hiking in the forest.'

Kayleigh closed her eyes. 'He knew that too?' Her hands were shaking. 'I was so scared! Why didn't you pick up when I called?'

'The phone was in my computer bag. He put that in the trunk. I'm sorry, K, but he knew *everything* about you. He knew about everybody in the band, he knew about Sheri. I thought he was a good friend.'

Morgan said, 'So the other killing just now. By the river? That couldn't have been him?'

Dance considered the timing again. She decided that Edwin could have abducted and shot the victim, set fire to the body and made it to the airport in time to pick up Suellyn and her daughter.

'Oh God. We were in the car with somebody who'd just killed someone?' Suellyn whispered.

Bishop said, 'Well, you're safe now. That's all that matters.'

Kayleigh said she didn't want Mary-Gordon here any longer. She was afraid Edwin would come back again and might try to make approaches to the girl. They should go with Bishop and Sheri to their house, outside town. And they should leave now.

Suellyn went into the den to collect her daughter and the toys Kayleigh had bought her.

At that moment Dance's phone rang; Dennis Harutyun was calling. She asked, 'So you've identified the victim?'

'That's right.'

'Is there any connection with Kayleigh?' she asked.

'Yes and no. You better come and see.'

THE STENCH WAS BAD, but so much rubber and plastic and oil had burned that the smell of human flesh and hair was obscured.

Love is fire, love is flame.

The scene was a broad dusty field, a cracked and crumbling parking lot, a long-closed gas station collapsed in on itself and the burnt shed, of which there wasn't much left. The smoke was still rising in furious plumes. The heat you could feel from the road, thirty yards distant. Not far away was the grey-brown strip of low river that had inspired this location for the killing.

The CSU team was still at work, though the fire-fighters outnumbered the police. Harutyun explained what they'd found: the shell casings, the CDs, the money—the altar to Kayleigh. But even the twenty-dollar bill seemed to have been washed—literally laundered. And the fire had been such a serious threat that the firemen and women had charged onto the grounds with hoses to contain the flames; the scene was badly contaminated now.

Besides, Dance guessed, if Edwin was behind the killing he wouldn't have left much evidence. He was too clever for that.

Harutyun continued the explanation he'd begun over the phone. The victim had indeed known Kayleigh—and about 1,000 other performers. His name was Frederick Blanton. 'He was a crook,' Harutyun summarised.

Dance thought of the CDs, the altar . . . and what she knew of the music business. 'Into illegal file sharing?'

'That's very good, Kathryn. Yes. There were close to ten thousand computers on the network. People would download songs, music videos too. Kayleigh's were among the most popular.'

'How'd you ID him?'

'We found his wallet in a part of the shed that didn't burn so bad. We checked his address—he lived in the Tower District. A team's going through his house now. They found his door kicked and it was a mess—all his computers were wrecked. We figured the perp forced him to destroy the file-sharing servers then made him get into the trunk of his car. Drove him here, shot him and started the fire.'

Dance mused, 'How easy would it have been for Edwin to find him?'

'Google "torrent" and "Kayleigh Towne" and "download", and his site was in the top ten. Some basic research and he'd've come up with the address, I'd guess.'

'And he left the altar as a warning not to steal from Kayleigh.'

A stalker's likely to target anybody who's a threat to you, or even offended you. He's taking real seriously his role as a protector . . .

'The crime scene at his house. Any evidence?'

'Nothing. No prints, foot or finger. They *did* find he had a partner, but he's not in the area.'

'You don't need to be next-door neighbours with your co-conspirator if you're doing computer crimes. Where's he based?'

'Salinas. Monterey County.'

'You have the guy's name—and a physical or computer address?'

'CSU'd have it.' The detective made a call and asked that the information be sent to her phone. She noted that he'd memorised her number.

The unit chimed a moment later with the incoming message.

'I'll send it to some people I know there. They can follow up with him.' Dance composed an email and sent it off.

Harutyun then said, 'I'm trying to keep an open mind. I know it looks like Edwin but I'm still looking into motives anybody else would have had to kill Bobby. I've been getting a lot of information about him but so far nothing jumps out. And now I guess I better add this guy into the mix. But, well, there've gotta be a lot of people who'd like to murder a file sharer.'

Another squad car arrived, crunching over the gravel. It parked near a faded Conoco sign depicting a green dinosaur. Dance's daughter, Maggie, was presently in a Jurassic phase. Her room was littered with plastic versions of the reptiles. Dance tamped down a pang, missing her children.

P. K. Madigan climbed out, surveyed the scene with hands on hips, then he joined Dance and Harutyun. 'So, he was stealing her songs?'

'That's right.'

Madigan grumbled, 'Never thought he'd switch to land lines. Should have.'

'We all should have.'

'And where the hell is he? He's got a car as big as my boat and it's bright red, to boot. I don't see how he keeps losing my folks.' His phone rang and he regarded the scene. 'Hello? . . . You don't say . . . Naw, I'll go myself.' He disconnected. 'Well, I can't tell you where Edwin was when this fella died, but I can tell you where he is now. He's parked in the lot across the road from Kayleigh's house. And he's sitting on the hood of his car, happy as a clam, having himself a picnic. I want to have a talk with him. Well, actually, I'd like *you* to have a talk with him, Kathryn. You up for that?'

'You bet I am.'

THAT CONVERSATION DID NOT, however, occur.

Driving in tandem, they were at Kayleigh's house fast, in twenty-five minutes, but Edwin Sharp had left by then.

He has a sixth sense, Dance thought, though she did not believe in sixth senses. Was it her imagination, or did she see a cloud of dust hanging over the spot where he might have just sped off? Hard to tell. There was a lot of dust in Fresno.

Dance and Madigan both parked in the lot and climbed out. This side of the road was lush, thanks to the park. Kayleigh's garden, too, on the other side of the road, was thickly landscaped. In the distance, south and west, was a vista of low fields, recently harvested.

The detective gave a knowing glance towards her, acknowledging frustration at their missing quarry, and leaned against his car to make a call.

From the brief conversation, Dance deduced it was to the deputy at Kayleigh's house—an extra guard Madigan had provided to supplement Darthur Morgan, when the manpower allowed. He disconnected. 'Was Jose, at the house.' A nod. 'Edwin was here ten minutes ago. They didn't see which way he went.'

Dance could understand why. From here you could see only the first floor of the house, which was about 300 feet away, down the gravel driveway. She wondered if the windows visible from here—the ones Edwin had presumably been staring at while he had his picnic—were Kayleigh's bedroom.

Silence for a time. The sun was low and Dance could feel the day shedding heat in layers.

'All righty.' Madigan stood with hands on his hips again, looking over the park. 'You're in town all alone. You want to come over for dinner? My wife, she's a pretty good cook.'

'Thanks, but I'll probably just get something back at the motel. Get some sleep.'

Dance returned to Mountain View. She had not put out the privacy sign and the maids had cleaned—and left the window blinds open. But the locks on her suitcases were intact and nothing seemed to have been disturbed. Dance glanced out of the window at the park, saw no surveillance, and closed the blinds.

As soon as she did, the hotel phone rang.

'Agent Dance?' A pleasant male voice.

'That's right.'

'It's Peter Simesky, Congressman Davis's aide. I'm in the lobby . . . of your motel. Could I talk to you?'

She could find no credible excuse and said she'd be out in a minute.

In the lobby she found the man on his phone and he politely ended the call when he spotted her. They shook hands and he grinned, though the smile morphed into a frown. 'I heard they confirmed another attack. Anyone connected to Kayleigh?'

'Not directly.'

'Is there anything we can do?'

'So far, no. But appreciate that.'

'It's this stalker?'

'Pointing to him but we don't know for sure. He's persistent and smart. And obsessed. The most dangerous kind of perp.'

Simesky cocked his head in a certain way and Dance knew a related story would be forthcoming. 'The congressman's had a few problems himself. A couple of campaign workers and interns.'

Dance explained about erotomania. 'Fits the classic profile. A powerful man and somebody in a lower professional position. Any physical threats?'

'No, no, just got awkward.'

Simesky had a bottle of water and he drank it thirstily. She noticed his white shirt was sweat-stained. He followed her glance and laughed. 'The congressman's been delivering his eco-friendly speech at farms from Watsonville to Fresno. The temperature was a lot more pleasant in your neighbourhood.'

Watsonville, just north of where Dance lived, was on the coast. And, she agreed, a lot more pleasant, weather-wise, than the San Joaquin Valley.

'You got a good turnout, I'll bet.'

'At the farms, because of his immigrant position, you mean? Oh, you bet. We considered it a success—there were only forty protesters.'

Dance smiled.

Simesky looked towards the motel's bar. 'How about a glass of wine?'

She hesitated, recalling his look at Kayleigh's house, his slightly overlong handshake. She said, 'Just to set the record straight, I'm seeing someone.'

He gave a wistful, embarrassed smile. 'You caught that, hm?'

'I do this for a living.'

'I better watch my body language. Yeah, I was flirting a bit—then and just a few seconds ago. And I'm disappointed to hear about your friend. Never hurts to ask. OK, let's get that wine.'

In the tacky bar, Dance ordered a merlot and Simesky a chardonnay. They chatted pleasantly for a while then parted company.

Dance returned to her room. It was nine thirty, hardly late, but she was exhausted. It was time for yet another shower and sleep.

But that too was interrupted. Her phone rang once more and she didn't recognise the caller ID number. Let it go?

But the investigator within her decided to answer. Just as well. It turned out that the caller was Edwin Sharp's former girlfriend.

SALLY DOCKING was her name.

Deputy Miguel Lopez had tracked her down in Seattle and left a message for her to she call Dance.

The agent now thanked her for being in touch.

A hesitant, melodious voice. 'Like, sure.'

'I'd like to talk to you about Edwin Sharp.'

'Oh, Edwin? Is he OK?'

Odd question.

'Yes, he is. I wonder if you could answer a few questions for me. You were in a relationship with him, correct?'

'Yeah, for a while. We met in February a year ago. We worked in the same mall. We started going out and moved in for a few months. It didn't work out. We broke up around Christmas. What's . . . I mean, I'm curious why you're asking.'

Sometimes you can be too evasive and the subject clams up. 'He's been showing some inappropriate interest in someone in California. We're looking into whether he's guilty of stalking.'

'Edwin?' She sounded genuinely surprised.

Dance jotted this impression in her notebook.

'Have you heard from him lately?'

'No. It's been months and months.'

'Sally, tell me: did he ever threaten you?'

'Threaten? No, never.'

'Did he ever threaten or show excessive interest in other women that you know about?'

'No. I can't even picture it.'

'Did you ever see him engage in any obsessive behaviour?'

'I don't know what you mean exactly. He got pretty intense. He'd get like totally excited about a Wii game.'

'How about people, stars, musicians?'

'He liked movies. But his big thing was music. He was really into Cassie McGuire and Kayleigh Towne and Charlie Holmes.'

'After you left him, did you have a problem with him following you, calling you? Harassing you?'

'No. I mean, he'd call sometimes about something he'd left at my apartment. But, stalking, no, nothing like that. Only one thing? You said when I left him. That's not what happened. He left me.'

Dance could have kicked herself. Earlier she'd been mentally chastising P. K. Madigan for leading Edwin during the interview; here she was doing exactly the same.

'Tell me what happened.'

'He just said the relationship wasn't working. I was bummed. Edwin was sort of romantic and he was dependable. He didn't drink and he'd pretty much given up smoking when I was with him.'

'So he used to smoke,' Dance said, thinking of her own voyeur outside the motel.

'Yeah, but only when he was stressed.'

'Did he go out with anybody else after he left?'

'Not really. He dated a few girls. I don't know who.'

'One last question. Did you ever see him get violent?'

A pause. 'Yeah, I did. Once me and my girlfriend and Edwin were walking down the street and this drunk guy came up, I mean, way, way drunk. And he called us sluts. And Edwin goes up to him and shouts, "Apologise right now, you asshole." And the guy did.'

Dance waited. 'That was it? He never hit this man?'

'Oh, no. Edwin'd never do that. He'd never hurt anybody.'

Dance thanked the young woman and disconnected. She jotted a summary of the conversation in her notebook. So, what do I make of this? A relatively normal relationship with one woman didn't mean he couldn't stalk another. But stalking was habitual. For Sally to be involved for a year and to live with him for part of that time yet not see any danger signs was significant.

On the other hand, he'd exhibited *some* obsessive interest in music and performers.

After an examination of the park revealed no cigarette-smoking surveillance, Dance took a shower. She dried off, then slipped into the Mountain View bathrobe and curled up on the bed, wishing Jon Boling were here with her. She was thinking of the recent overnight trip they'd taken to Ventana, south of Carmel. The trip had been a milestone—it was the first time she'd told the children that she and Boling were going away overnight.

She'd offered nothing more about the trip and the news was greeted with no interest whatsoever by either Wes or Maggie. At their ages, though, the broader implications had possibly been lost on them. But their bored response was a huge victory for Dance, who'd stressed about their reaction to the fact that Mom was travelling with another man.

The weekend away had been wonderful and Dance had been pleased that the last hold-out of widowhood—the discomfort with intimacy—was finally vanishing.

She wanted Boling here now. And was thinking it curious that they hadn't spoken for two days. They'd traded messages but voicemail had reared its head at every instance. She was involved in a murder investigation so she had an excuse, she reflected. But Boling was a computer consultant. She wasn't sure why he was so inaccessible.

Dance called her parents, chatted with her father for a few minutes then asked to speak to the children.

It was pure joy, hearing their voices ramble on enthusiastically about their days at camp. Dance laughed when they signed off with a 'Loveyoumom' (Maggie) and 'Gottagoseeya' (Wes).

Then her mother came on the phone. Edie reported that Dance's father was finishing up some work at Kathryn's house to get it ready for the party she was throwing this weekend; house guests would be staying for a few days, after driving down from San Jose on Saturday.

And then there was a pause.

Dance tried not to practise her profession in her personal life. But now she noted that something was up.

'How's it going there?' Edie Dance offered some clumsy verbal padding.

'Good. Fresno's actually kind of interesting. Parts of it are anyway.' Get to the point, Dance thought.

'There's something I found out. I wasn't sure what to do. If it weren't for the kids . . .'

Dance said bluntly, 'What? Tell me.'

'Jon brought some computer games over for the kids. And he got a phone call . . . Honey, he was talking to a broker. I heard him say he'd got a job and wanted to take a look at a house.'

This was interesting. But why the concern in her mother's voice? 'And?'

'It's in San Diego. He's moving in a couple of weeks.'

Oh.

Weeks?

Dance now understood what Edie meant about the children. They were still vulnerable from the death of their father. For them to lose the new man in their life would be very hurtful, if not devastating.

And then there's me. What was he *thinking* of, not telling me anything?

Weeks?

So that's why he hadn't picked up the phone but had used the coward's hideout of voicemail.

But the first rule of law enforcement was not to make assumptions. 'Are you sure? You couldn't have misunderstood?'

'No, no. He was alone, in the back by the pool. He thought I couldn't hear. And when Wes stepped out, he hung up on the broker.'

Dance could say nothing for a moment.

'I'm sorry, honey.'

'Yeah. Thanks, Mom. Just need to think about this a little.'

'You get some sleep now. The kids are happy. We had a fun dinner. They love camp.' She tried to be light. 'And more importantly, can you believe it? They're looking forward to school. We're going book shopping tomorrow.'

'Thanks. 'Night.'

A moment later Dance found she was still holding the phone, disconnected, in front of her face. She lowered it, then got into bed, turned the lights out, and lay staring at the ceiling until she fell asleep.

TUESDAY

5

Kathryn Dance was in the sheriff's office with P. K. Madigan, Dennis Harutyun and Miguel Lopez. There was another law-enforcement jurisdiction present too: Monterey County.

Via Skype, Michael O'Neil's calm eyes looked back at them from 150 miles away. O'Neil was a detective with the Monterey County Office of the Sheriff. He and Dance had worked together for years and were close friends. She'd tapped him to look into the Salinas partner of Frederick Blanton, the murdered file sharer.

Madigan was briefing the Monterey deputy. 'Edwin never went home last night. Kayleigh said that at about ten thirty she heard a car in the park out front of her house. Kathryn and I want to interview him but we don't know where he is. This morning a deputy spotted his car on Forty-one, a pretty major road here. He tried to follow but Edwin must've seen him and wove around in traffic and got away.'

O'Neil said, 'Kathryn told me he'd picked up Kayleigh's sister and niece at the airport. Any charges possible there?'

'Doesn't look like it,' Madigan said. 'He behaved himself, was a gentleman. The little girl loved him and the sister thought he was—get this—the nicest of Kayleigh's *boyfriends* in recent years.'

Dance regarded the man on the screen—strong and solid but not heavy. O'Neil was wearing a light blue shirt and a dark sports coat. Most detectives in the Monterey County Sheriff's Office—like here—wore uniforms but O'Neil didn't. He thought casual clothing got you further in investigations than khaki and pointed metal stars.

Dance briefed them about the interview with Sally Docking, Edwin's former girlfriend. 'I have to tell you that his behaviour with her doesn't fall into a stalker's profile.'

'Still don't trust him,' Madigan said.

'No. It's just odd.'

O'Neil said, 'Now, I paid a visit to Josh Eberhardt.'

The file-sharing partner in Salinas.

'How polite a visit?' Dance asked.

'I talked Amy into going with me.'

Amy Grabe, the FBI's special agent in charge in San Francisco.

'They decided there'd been enough federal copyright violations to justify a raid. Joint task force.' Which meant it wasn't very polite. 'Feet apart, spread 'em' had probably been involved.

'Good job, sir,' Madigan said and enjoyed a bite of what Dance believed to be pistachio ice cream. She'd missed breakfast and was thinking of asking for a cup of her own.

The Monterey detective continued, 'They did find some file sharing going on but Eberhardt was more of a researcher. He keeps track of hundreds of above- and underground fan sites for musicians. Looks like he'd comb through them and get potential customers for illegal downloads. It really wasn't all file sharing—it was also file *stealing* and *selling*. They charged a fee for the songs. They'd ripped off albums by about a thousand artists.

'There's this dark underground of web sites out there. They have to do with cultural things mostly: books, TV shows, music. A lot of them are about stealing the artists' work, but most of them are about the celebrities themselves. Stephen King, Lindsey Lohan, George Clooney, Justin Bieber, Kayleigh Towne. And it's all off the radar. The people posting use portals and anonymous accounts. None of this shows up on Google.'

Michael O'Neil gave them the list of web sites whose addresses were only numbers or letters. Once you were inside you found pages that seemed nonsensical. But navigating through the links, he explained, you got to the true substance of the sites: the world of celebrities.

None of these troubling sites TJ Scanlon had found.

O'Neil said, 'It looks like that's where Edwin's getting a lot of information. He posted plenty about the file sharer in Fresno who got killed.'

Madigan said, 'Anything that'd implicate Edwin in the killing?'

'No, he just urged people not to use their services. It wasn't quote "respectful" to Kayleigh. He didn't even write anything to Blanton directly.'

Of course he wouldn't. Not clever Mr Edwin Sharp.

O'Neil turned away for a moment and typed. Dance received an email containing several URLs. Harutyun took her phone when she offered it to him and he set to work typing them into a computer nearby.

O'Neil asked the room, 'You're monitoring all her calls?'

'That's right, but we're trying to buy some time, make it harder for him to contact her with another verse,' Harutyun said. 'We've given her and her family new phones, all unlisted. He'll probably find the numbers eventually but by then we hope we'll nail him on the evidence or witnesses.'

'I'd dig through those sites,' O'Neil advised. 'You should be able to get some good information about him. Looks like he spends a lot of time online.'

O'Neil took a brief call and turned back to the screen. He said he had to leave, an interrogation was on the schedule. His eyes crinkled with a smile. 'You need anything, let me know.'

Madigan thanked him and the screen went dark.

They turned to a second monitor, on which Miguel Lopez had called up one of the underground sites O'Neil had found.

The site, which boasted more than 125,000 fans, was a stalker's paradise. It had pages for several hundred celebrities. Within Kayleigh's pages was one headed 'Kayleigh Spotting' and was a real-time bulletin board about where she was at the moment. 'She Can't Fool Us!' contained pictures of

Kayleigh in various outfits—disguises almost—so fans could recognise her when she was trying to remain anonymous. Other pages contained extensive bios of the crew and band members, fans' stories about concerts they'd attended, discussions of which venues were good and bad acoustically.

There was also a feed from her official site, giving updates about events, like Friday's concert and the lunch today at a local country club for a 'Fan of the Month'. Dance read the press release, written by Kayleigh's stepmother, Sheri, noting to her relief that Edwin was not the winner.

Additional links led to even more troubling pages, which offered bootleg albums, recorded illegally at concerts, and links to file-sharing services. One page gave gossip about disputes within celebrities' families, Kayleigh's included, although aside from a few public spats with Bishop and Sheri, the page was pretty sparse.

This explained Edwin's innocuous, moderate online activity that TJ Scanlon had found earlier. That was the public side of Edwin Sharp; this was the stalker's real Internet life. A number of the posts with initials ES or ESS in the username were probably his. But as with the more public sites, most of the posts that might be his didn't appear threatening; if anything, he staunchly defended Kayleigh. He came across as nothing more than a loyal, if strident, fan.

Crystal Stanning took a phone call. Dance paid no attention until she noticed the deputy's shoulders rise and her brow furrow: a posture often signalling bad, or at least perplexing, news. 'You sure?' she asked.

She disconnected, grimacing. 'That was my husband. He took Taylor, our son, to football practice. And, it was weird. I told him about the song the perp's playing, Kayleigh's song? And he said somebody got into the PA system at the high-school field and rigged the tape player so the third verse played over and over.'

'Oh, hell,' Madigan muttered. 'He's not using the phones.'

Thinking ahead of them once again.

And what were the clues in the lyrics? Dance looked over the sheet that Harutyun had printed out.

> *One night there's a call, and at first you don't know*
> *What the troopers are saying from the side of the road.*
> *Then you see in an instant that your whole life has changed.*
> *Everything gone, all the plans rearranged.*

Where did the perp have in mind for attacking next? Dance thought. Somewhere by a roadside?

Madigan said, ' "Road" could mean more than just a highway.'

Dance nodded. 'Road crew. Let's call them. We ought to let them know he's played another song. And Alicia Sessions too. At the Cowboy Saloon, I could see Edwin didn't like her any more than he did Bobby.'

Dance, Harutyun and Stanning notified everyone in the crew. Half of the crew were at the convention centre; the other half were at the country club for the luncheon. Kayleigh would be performing a few songs so they'd set up a banquet room.

Madigan was speaking into his phone, 'Come on, how hard is it? The car is a mile long! And bright red.'

Dance called Kayleigh, who'd just arrived at the luncheon, on the singer's new mobile number and told her of the possible threat.

'No! Again? Are you sure?'

'Afraid we are. Where are your sister and niece?'

'They're at home with Daddy and Sheri.'

'Darthur's with you?'

'Yes. We're expecting a hundred or so people. There's lots of security. You need a ticket to get in.'

'Kayleigh, this fan who's going to the lunch, who is it?'

'I think his name's . . . hold on. Sam Gerber. Do you think he's in danger?'

'So he's not there?'

'No, we don't get started for another forty-five minutes.'

'Do you have his number?'

'I'll find it.'

As she waited, Dance looked down and her eyes caught a series of posts on the fan site. They'd been made just that morning.

Who is this Gerber? Is he worthy of our wonderful Kayleigh? He hasn't posted much about her, hardly anything. Doesn't seem fair to some of us that he's going.

—ESKayleighfan

Come on, he won a contest, whats the big deal? I'm happy for him, he gets to have LUNCH with Kayleigh!!!!!

—Suzi09091

He doesn't deserve it. Other people do. That's my point.

—ESKayleighfan

Kayleigh came back on the line with Sam Gerber's number. Dance jotted it down. 'Thanks. We're doing everything we can.'

She called Gerber and got voicemail. She left an urgent message.

'He lives in Madera,' Madigan said. 'I'll get a car to his house. If we're lucky he may not have left yet.'

'The road,' Dance mused. 'Let's assume Edwin's going to try something on the route from Madera to here.'

She realised that, despite Sally Docking's report, she was making the assumption that Edwin was the killer. She continued to scroll through the fan site, trying to put herself into the young man's troubled mind.

WHAT SHE WANTED MOST was for Kayleigh to love her.

Sheri Towne knew that she started from a disadvantage. She was a lot younger than Bishop and in her own opinion didn't bring a lot to the table. She was insecure and knew she was worlds away from Margaret, the strong woman who was Kayleigh's and Suellyn's mother. Sheri knew about her not because anyone in the Towne family talked about Margaret in front of her, least of all Bishop, but because she'd listened to and memorised all of Kayleigh's songs; many of the early ones were about her mother.

Despite the tension, though, Sheri liked Kayleigh a lot, and she liked Suellyn and her husband, Roberto, and Mary-Gordon too.

Sheri badly wanted to fit in. She loved Bishop, loved the odd mix of his power and his neediness, loved his talent—brilliant in the past and still glimmering now. Still, her connection with her new husband wouldn't be complete if she couldn't form a real relationship with Kayleigh. And not just that superficial cordiality.

She turned the car off the long drive from their house on the route to the highway. The car bounded along; road wasn't much better than gravel.

Maybe, just maybe, things could change. There'd been crumbs of hope. Kayleigh's sending Sheri the occasional greeting card. A present on her birthday. And then a half-hour ago she'd received an email from her step-daughter saying when she came to the luncheon, could she bring a couple of dozen of her CDs from Bishop's house as giveaways to fans? Kayleigh'd forgotten them.

The woman had been hurt that Kayleigh hadn't even asked her to the event, which she had helped put together. But she'd noted the word '*when*' she came to the luncheon. So the girl hadn't snubbed her at all. Maybe she'd assumed all along Sheri would be attending.

The condition of the road improved and she pressed the accelerator of the Mercedes down further, speeding along the deserted highway, groves of trees on either side.

The flat happened so fast she couldn't respond before the car was careering along the shoulder. Sheri struggled to control the vehicle, swerving perilously close to the trees, streaking by at seventy miles an hour. But Sheri Marshal Towne had grown up in the Midwest and had started driving at fourteen. Snow and powerful engines conspired to teach her how to handle skids. She now steered into the swerve, easing off the gas but never touching the brake.

Slower, slower . . . the car fishtailed, went straight, fishtailed some more, spewing gravel and leaves and twigs from the tyres. But she managed to keep it from flying over the thirty-foot cliff to the right or slamming into the row of pines close by the opposite side. In the end, though, the ground was too slippery—gravel and pebbles on hard pack—and she couldn't quite prevent the crash as the big Merc slid off the road towards the trees, wedging itself into a ditch, and shuddered to a stop.

Her hands sweaty, her heart thudding, Sheri rested her head against the steering wheel. God had looked out for her.

She was thinking about Him when there was a loud crack and the windshield spider-webbed; fragments of glass hit her in the head.

She blinked, more startled than hurt. How would a stone—

Then again, a crack and flying glass—and this time she heard a loud bang outside.

Oh God, no! Somebody was shooting at her! These were *bullets!*

She saw motion from the shadows between a tall stand of trees. Another flash. And the car resounded with a ringing thud. He'd missed the windshield this time.

Hunters? Or was it that crazy man obsessed with Kayleigh?

Sheri popped the seat belt and slithered down to the floor as best she could. One more shot. This too wasn't aimed for the windows but, like the other, for the rear of the car. A resonating bang as it hit.

Why would somebody shoot there? Sheri wondered numbly.

And then realised: he was aiming for the gas tank!

She tried to roll down the side window of the passenger seat but the power was off. And the doors were wedged closed by the ditch.

Then the sweet smell of gasoline grew thicker. As she sobbed, kicking futilely at the windshield, a thought occurred to her: the email about the luncheon hadn't been from Kayleigh after all. It had been Edwin Sharp, who'd created an email address with Kayleigh's name in it and sent the message to Sheri, luring her here.

Kayleigh hadn't wanted her at the luncheon after all.

DANCE HAD LEFT the sheriff's office fifteen minutes earlier.

After word that 'Your Shadow' had been played at the football stadium, the task force had split into three groups: one was trying to intercept Sam Gerber. Others were at the luncheon at the country club, thinking that Edwin might try to find Gerber there. And yet others were trying to find Edwin and his car.

Dance was en route to the luncheon. She thought it was best simply to be the point person at the country club and to reassure Kayleigh with her presence. But as she piloted the SUV through traffic, a thought occurred. Edwin would be aware of the logistical difficulties of targeting a victim at the luncheon. But the event *would* provide a good distraction and draw off the police. And was Sam Gerber really a likely target? No. Edwin wouldn't go after somebody he'd commented on in a posting. It was too obvious.

The crew was safe. Alicia was among people. So who else might the target be? Dance asked herself again if Edwin was the stalker, what was his goal? Killing someone who threatened to keep Kayleigh and him apart, who could be perceived as Kayleigh's enemy or who'd offended her.

Dance had recalled the gossip pages in one of the underground web sites O'Neil had found, involving sensational stories reported by fans. A hot topic was the tension between Kayleigh and her stepmother. There was even a mobile phone video about a recent argument in Bakersfield.

This wasn't a full-blown feud; Kayleigh seemed incapable of the mean-spiritedness that would involve. And Sheri seemed like a decent woman, solid, loyal to her new husband and even helpful in Kayleigh's career. But Sheri and Kayleigh never seemed to get along. Sheri hadn't even been invited to the luncheon she'd helped organise.

Dance now called Bishop Towne and identified herself.

'Where's your wife?'

'Gone off to that luncheon thing. Kayleigh invited her, after all.'

An alarm pinged within Dance. 'When did she leave?'

''Bout twenty minutes ago,' Bishop said.

'Did Kayleigh call her?'

'No, she emailed.'

'Sheri might be in danger. Edwin might've sent that email.'

'No!'

'Maybe. Which way would she go?'

'From the house, have to be Los Banos Road to Forty-one. You've got to do something! Don't let anything happen to her.'

'Give me her number.'

Dance memorised it. Then told him, 'I'll call you when I know something. What's she driving?'

'I think she's in . . . yeah, it's the Mercedes. Silver.'

Dance first tried Sheri but the woman didn't answer. She then called Kayleigh and learned, after a brief, awkward pause, that, no, Kayleigh hadn't really wanted Sheri at the luncheon and hadn't emailed her. Dance hit *disconnect* with her thumb and the brake with her foot, skidding to a stop on the shoulder. She punched Los Banos Road into her GPS and raced back onto the highway.

Los Banos was a narrow asphalt strip snaking through the foothills toward Yosemite. It would be the only place where Edwin could attack Sheri. If she'd reached Forty-one—a wide, multi-lane road—then she would probably be OK.

In two minutes Dance was speeding on Los Banos.

It was then she saw the smoke, maybe half a mile ahead.

She jammed the accelerator down hard as she took a curve. She called Madigan and left a message, telling him where she was and to get cars there immediately, fire trucks too.

As Dance skidded round a bend she saw a horrific scene before her—the Mercedes had gone off the road and was in a ditch. The back end of the car was burning, though the front, not yet. The angle of the accident—with the car's hood in the air—meant the gasoline from the ruptured tank was flowing backwards. Still, the flames were spreading forward.

There was movement from inside the car. Dance knew it was Sheri, whose feet were kicking desperately against the windshield.

Dance brought the Pathfinder to a skidding stop on the shoulder and leaped out, opening the back door and reaching behind the seat to snag the small fire extinguisher. She pulled it out and turned towards the Merc but dropped the heavy canister. She bent to pick it up.

Which is what saved her from a bullet.

'Jesus,' she gasped, dropping to the ground, earning a scraped elbow.

The bullet had slammed, loud, into the sheet steel of the Pathfinder a foot or so from her head and shoulders. Where was the shooter?

He was somewhere in the pine forest. In shadows, of course.

Reaching for her phone, which sat on the passenger seat, to call 911, she rose. But the shooter fired again and a slug snapped over her head, then another. Dance flattened herself on the ground as another bullet punctured the side of the driver's seat.

A cry echoed from the Mercedes.

Crawling fast, cradling the extinguisher, Dance made it to a fallen tree, about forty feet from the Mercedes. She risked a look. The flames were moving faster now, washing towards the front seat.

And from the gap in the dense pine forest she saw a ragged flash of gunshot. A bullet snapped over her head before she could duck.

Dance then heard another wailing scream from the Mercedes.

'I SHOULD CHECK IN with my people,' P. K. Madigan said angrily, nodding towards his office. 'We've got a possible homicide going here. It's urgent.' The bewildered chief was feeling panic.

Two California Department of Justice officers stood in front of him. One was redheaded and one had black hair. Polite. Very polite. Madigan was so shaken he'd forgotten their names.

The redhead said, 'Yessir, I'm afraid calls'll have to wait.'

FMCSO sheriff Anita Gonzalez stood nearby, her face too a mask of dismay. 'This is nonsense, gentlemen. Utter nonsense.'

The two officers obviously didn't consider their present assignment as nonsense, utter or otherwise.

In fact, the two suspects didn't either: detectives Madigan and Miguel Lopez, who were being arrested for breaking and entering, false imprisonment, misuse of legal authority, criminal trespass.

Madigan said, 'Look, this is part of a plan by the perp we're investigating. He's trying to get some of us out of commission.'

Madigan knew the reason for the arrest was his decision to keep Edwin

Sharp in the interrogation room longer than he should have. And to have Miguel Lopez go to Edwin's house to gather evidence.

The dark-haired agent was saying, 'Here's how it'll work, Detective. We'll take you in and I'm sure the magistrate'll expedite arraignment. Probably recognisance. You'll be out in a few hours.'

'I don't care when I'll be out. The problem is I'll be suspended until it's resolved. That's procedure.'

Gonzalez said to the officers, 'We can't afford to have the chief down now—not with the perp on the streets.'

The redhead said, 'We know how you feel about this singer. But . . .' He didn't add, That's not enough to bend the law over.

Madigan wanted to hit him. The panic swelled. Hell, this could be the end of his career. Damn Edwin Sharp!

The officers were debating but it was only the cuff issue.

'Oh, please,' Madigan said desperately. 'You can't—'

'Look, gentlemen,' Sheriff Gonzalez said. 'This is a critical operation. We think a murder could be occurring at any moment.'

The redhead offered to Gonzalez, 'You understand a warrant has been issued for his arrest? I'm sorry. We don't have any choice.'

And they also decided yea on the cuffs.

DANCE HUDDLED BEHIND a fallen pine tree.

There'd been no more shots; was the assailant still there? He'd assume that Dance had called in reinforcements. He couldn't risk staying any longer. Or could he? Clutching the fire extinguisher, she debated. If I don't do something now, Sheri'll die. She'll burn to death. Dance looked up cautiously. No gunshots.

Another cry from the car, but muted. Sheri was losing the battle.

Now. It has to be now.

She leaped to her feet and began to sprint to the Mercedes, just as the flames were reaching into the passenger compartment.

Dance dived into the ditch, out of the line of fire, and crawled fast to the car. Inside, Sheri was pounding on the windshield with bloody hands. She was retching and coughing as the smoke roiled. Dance's skin prickled in the heat from a grass fire surrounding the car. The woman inside turned desperate eyes to her.

Dance gestured for her to move back and she slammed the extinguisher base into the passenger-side window. It shattered. Dance tossed the extinguisher away—it wasn't going to do any good on a fire like this—and reached inside to yank the woman out.

The agent dragged her thirty feet from the car, crouching, in case the attacker was still there with his gun. They sprawled on the ground in a depression by the roadside.

The woman dropped to her knees and then tried to stand.

'No, stay down,' Dance said and started for her SUV to see if Madigan had got her message and, if not, to call 911.

Which was when she heard a loud bang behind her and felt something slam into her lower back. She pitched forward onto the sunbaked earth.

DENNIS HARUTYUN was standing over the stretcher Kathryn Dance lay on, face down. A medic was on the opposite side from the deputy, labouring away on her back.

'No leads yet,' the detective said.

Dance could see the CSU team scouring the grounds where the attacker had nearly killed Sheri Towne . . . and Dance herself.

Finally the paramedic finished working on Dance. 'That'll do it.'

She pulled her shirt down.

'Just a scratch. Wasn't deep at all.'

Dance was sure she'd been shot in the back—her immediate thought was of her friend, the crime scene expert Lincoln Rhyme, who was a quadriplegic. How can I be a good mother if I can't walk? she'd thought, tumbling over Sheri Towne from the impact. In fact, what had happened was that the fire extinguisher she'd tossed aside had landed in the burning grass and exploded, sending either a stone or a piece of its own casing flying into her back. She'd lain stunned for a moment then had turned to see a big disk of white foam or powder from the detonated extinguisher on the ground. And she'd understood, then crawled on to the SUV and retrieved her phone and called 911. A quarter of an hour later the police, fire and medical teams arrived.

The medic wandered off to tend to Sheri, who was sitting next to her husband, breathing oxygen and staring at her bandaged hand.

'It's a real mess,' Harutyun said, explaining that Edwin had complained to the state DOJ about his detention and the illegal search. Madigan and Miguel Lopez had just been arrested, though released right away, but were no longer active-duty law enforcers.

'Oh, no,' Dance said. 'Madigan's out of commission?'

'Sure is.' Harutyun added bitterly, 'The perp took out Gabriel Fuentes, stealing his gun. Now it's the Chief and Miguel. The whole team's Crystal, me and you.'

'Any sightings of Edwin?' Dance asked.

'No sign of him or that bull's-eye red car of his. The luncheon went on as scheduled. Kayleigh didn't look too good, to hear the stories. She sang a few songs, had lunch with the fan and then left.'

Dance nodded towards the smouldering Mercedes. 'Pretty dangerous to be on Kayleigh's bad side.'

Harutyun looked at Sheri. 'She nearly burned to death but what she took hardest was Kayleigh didn't really ask her to the lunch.'

There was silence for a time.

'Hey, Charlie.' Harutyun nodded to a round, pinkish man, approaching. He wore a jumpsuit. 'You know Kathryn Dance, CBI? This's Charlie Shean, head of our Crime Scene Unit.'

He nodded to her. 'That true about P. K.? He's suspended? And Miguel?'

'Afraid so.'

'And this stalker fellow's the one orchestrated it?'

'We don't know. What'd your folks find, Charlie? Business cards? Phone bills with Edwin's name on it?' Harutyun seemed to be loosening up.

'He's good, whoever he—or she—is. No footprints, tyre treads or trace, though we did get a little cigarette ash that's recent, just past the perimeter of the burn. Analysis'll take time.'

Dance explained about seeing the person smoking across the road from her motel-room window. 'I didn't catch a description, though.' She added, 'Edwin did smoke. Still may.'

Shean said, 'The gun was a nine—like Gabe's Glock—but we don't have any casings or slugs from his so we don't know if there's a match. No immediate prints on the casings we found.'

Just then Kayleigh Towne's dark green SUV, driven by Darthur Morgan, sped up to the scene. The vehicle hadn't stopped completely before the singer was out of the Suburban and running towards Bishop and Sheri. She threw her arms round her stepmother. Dance was too far away to hear the conversation but there was no doubt about the messages in the body language: apology, regret and humour. A reconciliation was underway.

Bishop Towne stood and embraced them both.

K ayleigh packed several suitcases and lugged them downstairs to the living room of her house, where Darthur Morgan took them from her and placed them in the SUV.

Alicia Sessions was here too, helping her with the move, with her Ford F150. Kayleigh hadn't wanted her to go to the trouble but the woman insisted, schlepping guitars, amps and boxes of provisions.

'I really can manage.'

'No problem at all,' Alicia said.

'Well, stay for dinner, at least.'

'I'm seeing some friends in town.'

As efficient as she was, Alicia remained largely a mystery to Kayleigh. She was a loner, who'd lived on the periphery of the professional music scene for years, performing alternative and post-punk in New York and San Francisco, without much success. She'd get her job done for Kayleigh and then disappear in the evenings and at weekends, to go off horse riding and listening to music.

After the SUV and Alicia's pick-up were loaded, Kayleigh climbed into the driver's seat of the SUV, Morgan in the passenger seat, for a change, and headed down the long drive, Alicia's truck following. Kayleigh glanced into the rearview mirror but there were no red cars following their caravan.

When they arrived at Bishop Towne's house, Morgan helped Alicia carry the boxes, musical equipment and suitcases to the porch, then the guard went to check out the perimeter. The two women went inside.

Mary-Gordon came running up to Kayleigh and flew into her arms. 'Aunt Kayleigh! Yay! You've gotta come and look. We're doing a puzzle! I rode Freddie today. I wore my helmet, like you always say.'

Kayleigh slipped to her knees for a proper hug, then rose and embraced her sister. Suellyn asked, 'How you doing, K?'

'Hanging in there.'

Kayleigh introduced her and Mary-Gordon to Alicia.

'Wow.' The girl looked at Alicia's tattoos. 'Those are neat!'

'Uh-oh,' Suellyn said. 'I see trouble.' The women laughed.

Kayleigh greeted her father and Sheri, whose voice was still ragged from the smoke inhalation. She looked pale. She had been examined at the local hospital and then released. Kayleigh's attitude towards her stepmother had changed 180 degrees since the attack, and she regretted her pettiness towards the woman. She hugged Sheri, in whose eyes tears appeared at the display of affection.

Alicia gave Bishop and Sheri some details of the ad plans for the upcoming Canadian tour and then she glanced at her watch and headed off.

'Better you're here,' Bishop said to Kayleigh. 'I told you you should've come. Sheri's got a room made up. For that guard too. Where is he?'

Kayleigh explained that Morgan was outside checking the property.

'I did a picture for your room, Aunt Kayleigh. I'll show you.'

Mary-Gordon gripped the handle of the wheelie suitcase and sped off down the hallway to one of the two guest rooms on this floor. 'In here!'

Kayleigh had seen this guest room before and it had been functional, stark. Now the bed had new blue gingham linens, frilly pillow cases, and framed pictures of young Kayleigh and her family—photos that had been in boxes when last seen, before Sheri. It was really a very comfortable space. She'd be sure to thank her stepmother. Kayleigh admired Mary-Gordon's picture of the pony and set it on the bedside table.

'Can we go riding tomorrow?'

'We'll have to see, Mary-Gordon. It's a busy time. But we'll have breakfast together.'

'Grandma Sheri and Mommy made pancakes. They were pretty good. Not the best but pretty good.'

Kayleigh laughed and watched the little girl help unpack the suitcases and, with an expectant gaze towards Kayleigh, put away each article of clothing or toiletry where directed. She seemed to get huge pleasure from the simple tasks.

A tap in her mind, like a finger flicking a crystal glass. Kayleigh had looked forward to being a mother but those plans had been delayed by her father, who felt that a career wasn't compatible with a home life. '*KT, you're a child yourself. What's the hurry?*'

Kayleigh had gone along but the maternal urge within her grew.

She continued to unpack, pausing to look at a picture from fifteen years ago: Bishop, Margaret, Suellyn and Kayleigh on the porch of the old house in the hills an hour north of here.

The girl turned to the singer. 'Are you crying, Aunt Kayleigh?'

The singer blinked. 'Well, a little, Mary-Gordon, but you know sometimes people cry because they're happy.'

'I didn't know that. Where does this go?' She picked up a pair of jeans. And placed them in the drawer to which Kayleigh pointed.

IT WAS ABOUT EIGHT THIRTY in the evening when Kathryn Dance got to Bishop Towne's house. She greeted Kayleigh and the family, who flocked around her and thanked her for saving Sheri's life. Damp-eyed, the stepmother again hugged Dance and bled gratitude.

Dance updated them on the case, telling them that Madigan, along with two other deputies, had been suspended. When Mary-Gordon left the room with her grandfather, Dance spent time talking to Sheri and Suellyn to see if they could provide any more leads on the case. She was hoping to find something that she could use to infer threatening behaviour, which would, in turn, justify an arrest for stalking. That would give her access to Edwin— with his lawyer's approval—and she hoped to conduct a full kinesic analysis. But Sheri could provide no more information about the attacker. She'd seen flashes of gunshots and that was all. Not even an outline of the assailant. Not even a shadow.

Suellyn tried hard to recall something helpful but she confessed to Dance that she was still astonished that Edwin was the suspect. 'He was just so nice. And it sounded like he knew Kayleigh so well, they *had* to be friends.'

As they left the den, Suellyn said, 'Not much to use, right?'

'Don't think so but appreciate the help.'

Mary-Gordon ran into the hallway and hugged her mother, just as Darthur Morgan entered through the front door, his overnight bag in one hand. Suellyn and Mary-Gordon showed him to his room.

Dance said good night to Bishop and Sheri and then stepped outside, joining Kayleigh, who was on the front porch swing. Dance sat on a rattan chair next to her. The singer lifted her hands, indicating her father's house. 'Look at this,' she said, an edge to her voice, 'People're dead, lives're ruined. I'm hiding out with my dad. My life's a mess. And we don't even know for sure Edwin's behind it. He is, don't you think?'

'I honestly don't know,' Dance said. 'We always build cases slowly, but generally there's some definite evidence to tell us we're headed in the right direction. With Edwin, it's all ambiguous.'

Kayleigh lowered her voice. 'Kathryn. I'm really thinking of cancelling the show on Friday. My heart is totally not in it.'

'And your father's OK with it?' Dance asked.

'Yes,' she said, but uncertainly. 'He seems to agree but then he goes on like I never mentioned anything.' Kayleigh waved her hand, indicating where they sat. 'Remember what I told you after you recorded the group at Villalobos's? This is all the stage I'd like, my front porch. Play for the kids and family, have a bunch of Mary-Gordons and Henrys. Don't know why I picked that name. Don't know a single Henry in the world.'

'You could have a family and still be a pro.'

'I don't see how. That kind of life takes its toll.'

With that, Kayleigh dug into her pocket and pulled out a pen and small pad of lined paper and jotted words and musical notes.

'A song?'

'"Just can't stop".'

'You have to write your songs, you mean?'

Kayleigh laughed. 'Well, that's true. But what I mean is, that's a line that just occurred to me. "Just can't stop . . . spending hours . . . with you." I'll write it up tonight.'

'The whole song?'

'Hank Williams said a song that takes more than twenty minutes to write isn't going to be any good. Sometimes it takes me a day or two but for that one, it's pretty much done.' She hummed a few bars.

'You record it, I'll buy it,' Dance said. 'You . . .' Her voice faded as lights appeared through the trees. A car was approaching slowly.

Kayleigh stiffened. 'It can't be him. We weren't followed. Edwin wasn't at my place. He doesn't even know I'm not there.'

The lights stopped, then continued on as if the driver wasn't sure of the route. Or didn't want to be seen.

Dance eyed the vehicle carefully but it was impossible to see anything specific. What was the driver doing? Was it Edwin?

Dance stood up and pulled Kayleigh to her feet.

BUT THE VEHICLE turned out to be a very unthreatening—and slow-moving—powder-blue Ford Taurus.

And one did not need to be a kinesics expert to note the sea change in Kayleigh's body language when she saw the driver.

'Oh, it's Barry!' she cried, offering a smile.

A very tall man, lanky and long-faced handsome, was climbing out. Kayleigh ran down the stairs and embraced him hard.

She said, 'I didn't expect you for a couple of days.'

Glancing towards Dance, Zeigler said, 'I was in Carmel seeing Neil. I got your message about Bobby. I'm so sorry.'

'It's the worst, Barry.' Kayleigh introduced Dance.

Zeigler, Kayleigh's producer at her record label, was based in Los Angeles. In jeans, a white T-shirt and dark jacket, Zeigler seemed a bit Nineties to Dance, but it was a reasonable look for a record producer.

'And Sheri was attacked too?'

'She was hurt but she'll be all right.'

'You have any leads?' he asked Dance. 'Is it that guy Sharp?'

Kayleigh explained, 'Barry knows all about our friend. Edwin's sent plenty of letters to the label, complaining about production standards, orchestration, technical quality.'

The law-enforcement disclaimer. 'We're just gathering information at this point. But tell me, did he ever threaten you?'

Zeigler shook his head. 'He's been more insulting. I mean, BHRC's been producing Kayleigh for six years. She's had eight gold and four platinums. We must be doing something right. But just last week Sharp sent us a two-page email about the acoustic dynamics on the download of *Your Shadow*. He said the album was off in the high ranges. He wrote, "Kayleigh deserves better than this."'

Dance didn't think comments regarding tonal quality, however harsh, rose to the level of threat under the California Penal Code.

Zeigler said to Kayleigh, 'Bobby was the greatest guy in the world. I can't believe somebody'd hurt him. And to die that way. You must be . . .' He grew silent, apparently deciding he shouldn't be revisiting the horror. Then he said to Dance, 'Can't you arrest him?'

She demurred but Kayleigh said, 'He's too smart. They haven't been able to find anything he's done that breaks the law.' Her eyes welled with tears, but she tamed the emotion.

Zeigler's voice dimmed as he said to Kayleigh, 'I want to say hi to Bishop and Sheri. But could I talk to you for a minute? Alone?'

'Sure.' To Dance she said, 'Be right back.'

The producer and singer walked into the living room, the producer ducking automatically as they approached the doorway arch. He had to be six feet seven inches tall, Dance estimated.

She rose and moved to the swing Kayleigh had occupied, next to a half-opened window. From here she could hear their conversation. Whatever Zeigler was going to tell Kayleigh might have something to do with the case, even if neither of them realised it.

'This is a terrible time to bring this up,' Zeigler said. 'But I . . . I have to ask. Are you talking to JBT Global?'

'What?'

'JBT Global Entertainment.'

'I know who they are,' Kayleigh said. 'And no, I'm not talking to them. Why are you asking?'

Zeigler was explaining how a friend of a friend of a friend in the entertainment world had told him that Global wanted to sign her. 'You were in discussions, I'd heard.'

'Barry, we get calls all the time. You know I'd never leave you guys. You're the ones who made me. Hey, what's this all about?'

'I told you I was in Carmel?' Zeigler asked.

'Seeing Neil, you said.'

Neil Watson was one of the superstars of the pop music world of the past twenty years.

'Yeah, to get fired,' Zeigler said.

'No!'

'He's going with . . . get this, SAV-More, the big box discount store. They're producing him and backing his road shows.'

'Well, I'm sorry about that. But there've been zero discussions with Global. I promise.'

Dance's web site flew below the radar of the big business of music but she was aware of what Zeigler was talking about—a complete shift in how people got that most addictive of drugs: music. It used to be that early in the twentieth century, people played music in their homes on phonographs. In the 1930s the miracle substance of vinyl became the standard for records. After a few decades, cassette tapes became popular, followed by CDs.

And though the media had changed over the years, people could be counted on to spend millions and millions of dollars to bring music into their homes and cars. Artists often performed, of course, but concerts were mostly a form of promotion to sell the albums.

But then something happened.

Computers. On which you could download and listen to any song or piece of music ever recorded.

In the new world order, discs and tapes weren't needed, and the record labels, which made fortunes—for themselves and artists—by producing, pressing and distributing albums, weren't needed either.

No longer did you have to buy a whole album; if you liked only two songs on it, you could pick what you wanted, thanks to cheap download and streaming companies like Napster and other services that let you listen to millions of tunes for a few dollars a month.

And you could even have much of your heart's desires for free. Dozens of illegal file-sharing networks have made virtually any song available, free as air. Record companies used to sue file sharers—winning judgments against broke college kids and housewives, and earning a public relations black eye in the process. Now they've largely given up their police work.

Today many artists recognise the value of offering some content at no charge to the public. The theory is that free music downloads can generate new fans who'll buy future albums and attend concerts—where all the money is being made nowadays.

All of which renders traditional record stores and labels relics of the past. People like Barry Zeigler are still needed as producers but as for-fee technicians only.

Dance had heard of JBT Global Entertainment—it was a competitor of Live Nation, which owned entertainment arenas, concert halls and Ticketmaster and had contracts with many rock, pop and Country superstars. Global handled all aspects of a musician's professional life—producing the albums, pressing the few CDs that were still sold, cutting deals with download services and booking musicians into live performances.

Zeigler's world was vanishing and Dance understood his desperate concern that Kayleigh might leave him. But the conversation had nothing to do with the Edwin Sharp case. Dance gave up her eavesdropping, deciding to get back to the motel.

AN HOUR LATER Kathryn Dance was doing some stalking herself. She'd returned to the Mountain View, where she debated calling Jon Boling. Then decided not to. Partly because she was a coward, she chided herself. But she also had work to do.

Stalking . . .

She turned on the TV, so the flickers from the screen on the window shade would suggest someone was inside. She pulled on the only night camouflage she had: a navy sports coat, black jeans and a burgundy T-shirt. For shoes, pumps; she had no tactical boots. The outfit would have to do. Finally ready, Dance slipped outside into the parking lot.

Her mission was to find out who the person with the bad habits of nicotine and espionage might be. She'd just seen the glow of the cigarette again, in nearly the same place she'd seen it earlier, in the park across the road. She glanced out from behind a caravan filled with dog show paraphernalia. Dance focused again on the tiny orange glow in a recess between two thick stands of pine.

Dance waited until a car entered the lot and drove past her, parking at the entrance. Then she stepped out of the shadows and made her way to the four-lane road and hurried across.

Aware of the lightness on her hip where her pistol normally was, she circled wide and entered the park through one of the gaps in a rusty chain-link fence surrounding the ten-acre park.

She stayed close to the trees and moved forward steadily. Twenty feet farther on she smelled cigarette smoke. She slowed, crouching.

She couldn't see him yet but noted that the place where he was sitting seemed to be a picnic area; there were several tables nearby.

She moved closer yet, one careful step at a time.

The orange glow was evident but thick pine boughs completely obscured her view of the smoker, about twenty feet away.

She reached out and gripped the bough, moving it aside.

Oh, no. Dance gasped.

The lit cigarette was stuck into the fork of a sapling near a picnic table.

That meant only one thing: Edwin or whoever it might be had seen her leave the motel and had drawn her into a trap.

She spun round but saw no attacker. She dropped to her knees fast, remembering that his weapon of choice was a pistol, probably Gabe Fuentes's stolen Glock. She wasn't much of a target in the moonlight, but you can spray twelve rounds very quickly with a weapon like that and all you needed to do was point in the general direction of your victim.

Still no sign of him.

Where could he be?

Or had he lured her here to get into her room, steal her computer and notes?

No, she decided he'd be coming after her.

A snap of branch nearby confirmed this. She rose fast and turned back. But instead of returning in the same direction that she'd come from, she decided to head directly for the motel. This route was closer though it required her to vault the six-foot fence. She headed that way now, moving as fast as she could towards the road.

It was then that he sprang the trap.

Or rather, she sprang it herself, tripping over the fishing line—or maybe guitar string—he'd strung across the route he'd anticipated she would take back. She fell hard, slamming into the packed dirt. She lay gasping, breath knocked from her lungs.

She heard fast footsteps, not far away, moving in.

She tried to rise but couldn't; there was no air in her chest.

Then behind her she heard the double snap of an automatic pistol's slide, back and forward, chambering a round.

As Dance tried once more to get to cover, a man's voice from not far away called in a sharp whisper, 'Kathryn!'

She glanced about but could see no one.

Then the speaker called, 'You there. I have a weapon. I'm a county deputy. Do not move!'

Dance tried to see who this was. She couldn't spot her attacker either. Then from behind her she heard fleeing footsteps as the attacker escaped. Her rescuer was running too, in pursuit. Dance rose unsteadily, trying to breathe. Who was it? Harutyun?

She expected to hear gunshots but there were none, only the sounds of returning steps and her rescuer saying in a whisper, 'Kathryn, where are you?' The voice was familiar.

'Here.'

He approached, and she blinked in surprise.

Walking through the woods, holstering his weapon, was Michael O'Neil.

THEY SAT IN THE BAR, drinking Sonoma cabernet.

Dance asked, 'That was your car I saw pulling in fifteen minutes ago?'

'Yeah, I saw you cross the street. You looked . . . furtive. So I followed.'

'Oh, Michael, I never thought it'd be a trap. What did you see?'

'Nothing. A shadow.'

She sipped her wine. 'That's the theme of the case: shadows.'

'He's still using that song you told me about?'

'Right.' She updated him on what had happened, on how the information on the web site he'd found from the file sharer's partner in Salinas had let them save the life of Kayleigh's stepmother.

'So he's targeting family?' O'Neil, as a Major Crimes detective, had some experience with stalker cases too. 'That's rare.'

'Yes, it is. So,' Dance asked, looking him over, 'you just jumped in the car and drove three and a half hours after supper?'

O'Neil was not big on eye contact and he examined the bar refracted through his wineglass. 'With that fellow in Salinas, there was a Monterey connection. It made sense I come on over here. And I figured I should bring you a present. The sort I couldn't send FedEx. TJ said you came here unarmed. I checked out a Glock for you from CBI.' He reached into his computer bag and handed her a black gun case.

She smiled, took his arm, squeezed it. 'This was a vacation. That's all it was.'

Just then Dennis Harutyun walked into the bar and Dance introduced them. The local deputy remembered O'Neil from the Skype conference call. He said, 'Charlie's folks've been through the park. Nothing other than the cigarette and the fishing line used as a tripwire. We'll send the cigarette in for DNA but there probably isn't any. If he was smart, which he seems to be, he just lit the end, probably wore gloves. The line is nylon, the sort you'd buy in any one of a hundred sports or superstores.'

Dance glanced out of the window and noted a few cars slowing as they drove past the now brightly lit park, filled with crime scene officers and uniformed deputies, flashing lights from cruisers.

'I think I'd better get some sleep.' Dance glanced towards O'Neil. 'You must be tired too.'

'Haven't checked in yet either.'

As Dance signed the drinks to her room, her mobile dinged with an incoming text.

'What is it?' O'Neil noted that she was staring at the screen.

'It's a text.' She barked a laugh. 'From Edwin Sharp. He'd like to see me, to talk, he says.'

She texted back that she'd meet him at nine at the sheriff's office.

7

At nine on the dot Kathryn Dance met Edwin Sharp in an FMCSO office, not an interrogation room. No intimidating decor, no mirrors. The location was Dance's idea, to put Edwin at ease.

He entered ahead of her and sat, regarding her with curious eyes. He was wearing a plaid shirt and tight jeans. His boots, with pointed toes tipped in metal, were scuffed but looked expensive.

'You mind if I take notes?' she asked.

'Not at all. You can even record this.' He looked around the room as if he knew someone was doing just that. Dance wasn't obligated to tell him that they were recording the interview. They'd got a magistrate's OK, since he was a suspect in the murders.

Dance was troubled by his perception. And his calm demeanour. That false wisp of a smile added to the eeriness. 'Any time you want to take a break for some coffee or a smoke, you let me know.'

'I stay away from coffee,' he said and gave no reaction to the other offer. Dance had been fishing to find out about his current smoking habit. But whether he'd outmanoeuvred her or just hadn't thought to refer to the vice didn't matter; she'd raised the issue once and couldn't bring it up again without giving something away.

He then surprised her further by asking casually, 'How long've you been in law enforcement, Agent Dance?'

'For some time now. But please call me Kathryn. Now, what can I do for you?'

He smiled. 'You can call me Edwin. You enjoying Fresno?'

'I am.'

'Little different from Monterey, isn't it?'

Dance wasn't surprised that she herself had been the subject of Edwin's own research.

He continued, 'It's pretty there. Do you live near the water?'

'So, what can I do for you, Edwin?'

'You're busy I know. I wanted to talk to someone involved in this situation who's smart. The deputies here won't listen to me. End. Of. Story.'

'Well, I'll be happy to hear what you have to say.'

'Thanks, Kathryn. Basically, it's real simple. I didn't kill Bobby Prescott. I don't believe in file sharing but I wouldn't kill anybody because they did it. And I didn't attack Sheri Towne.'

'Edwin, I don't know you well enough to determine if you're capable or inclined to hurt anybody. Tell me a little about yourself.'

He played along. He went through facts that she largely knew—his unfortunate family history. His jobs in Seattle. His impatience with formal education. He said he often got bored in class—which might explain his chequered record at school. He didn't deny his skill at computers. He didn't mention his romantic life.

'You have a girlfriend?'

That caught him a bit off guard. 'Last year I dated somebody in Seattle. Sally was OK but she wasn't into doing anything fun. I couldn't get her to go to concerts or anything. I had to break up with her. Felt bad about it, but it wouldn't've worked out.'

Dance asked, 'When did you break up?'

'Around Christmas.'

'I'm sorry about that. It must've been tough.'

'It was. I hate hurting people. And Sally was real nice. Just . . . you know, with some people things click, some not.'

She decided it was time to start her kinesic analysis. She asked him again what she could do for him, noting his behaviour closely.

'OK, I'm not the brightest bulb on the tree. But I'm smart enough to figure out that I'm the victim here. Somebody's setting me up—probably the same people who were spying on me last weekend. They were behind the house, checking me out, my car, even the trash.'

'I see.'

'Look, I'm not the ogre everybody says I am. Deputy Madigan and Lopez? I'm sorry I had to have them arrested but they broke the Fourth and Fourteenth Amendments by detaining me and searching my house. Those souvenirs were important to me.'

'Did you get a look at who was watching you?'

'No. They stayed in the shadows.' Did his smile deepen at the word 'shadows'? Just a faint reaction? She couldn't tell.

'Why didn't you call the police?'

'Why do you assume I didn't?'

She'd known that he had; he'd told Madigan about the incident when she'd been observing in the interrogation room when Edwin was detained. She'd wanted to see his consistency. 'You did?'

His eyes narrowed. 'Nine-one-one. And they asked me if the man was trespassing and I guess technically he wasn't.'

'You're sure it was a man?'

A hesitation. 'Well, no. I just assumed.' His odd smile.

'Why would somebody make you a fall guy?'

'I don't know. All I know is I haven't hurt anybody but someone wants to make it look like I have.' His eyes scanned her face closely. 'I was by myself when Bobby was killed and the file sharer too. But when Sheri Towne was attacked, I have an alibi. I was going to the luncheon, for the fan. I didn't think they'd let me in but I thought I could watch from a distance. Anyway, I got lost. Around Cal State I stopped and asked directions. It was twelve thirty.'

Yes, just around the time of the attack. 'Who'd you talk to?'

'I don't know her name. It was a residential area near the sports stadium. This woman was working in a garden. She went inside to get a map and I stayed at the door. The noon news was finishing.'

'The street name?'

'Don't know. But I can describe her house. It had a lot of plants hanging from baskets. Bright red little flowers. What're they called?'

'Geraniums?'

'I think so. Kayleigh likes to garden. Me, not so much.'

As if he were talking about his wife.

'Anything more about the house?'

'Dark green. On the corner. And the house had a carport, not a garage. She was nice so I moved some bags of grass seed for her. She was in her seventies. White. That's all I remember. Oh, she had cats.'

'All right, Edwin. We'll look into that.' Dance noted the information. 'Will you give us permission to search the yard where you saw that intruder?'

'Of course, sure.'

She didn't look up but asked, 'And inside your house too?'

'Yes.' A second of hesitation? She couldn't tell.

Dance asked herself the big question: what did the kinesics reveal? Was Edwin Sharp telling the truth?

She frankly couldn't say. A stalker is usually psychotic with reality issues. That meant he might be reciting what he believed was the truth, even though it was completely false; therefore his kinesics when lying would be the same as his baseline.

Adding to the difficulty was Edwin's diminished affect—ability to feel and display emotion, such as stress. Body language analysis works only when the stress of lying alters the subject's behaviour.

Still, interviewing is a complex art. With most suspects, the best information is gathered by observations of, first, body language, then, second, verbal quality—pitch of voice and how fast one talks, for instance.

The third way in which humans communicate can sometimes be helpful: verbal content—*what* we say, the words themselves.

But what had he offered that could be helpful?

His smile deepened. She wished he'd lose the grin. It was more unnerving to her than the worst glare from a murderer.

'You know, with everything that's been happening, don't you think it might make sense for you to get back to Seattle, forget about the concert? You could see Kayleigh some other time.'

She said this to prime the pump, see if he'd offer facts about his life and plans—facts that she might use for content-based analysis.

She didn't expect the laugh of disbelief and what he then said: 'I can hardly do that, now, can I? You know that song of hers, "Your Shadow"?'

There wasn't a single clue in his face that this song was a calling card for murder. She said casually, 'Sure. Her big hit.'

The grin took on a patina of the genuine. 'It's about her, you know. There's a verse about that car crash—when her mother died. Kayleigh was fifteen. You know Bishop was driving, drunk.'

No, Dance had not been aware of that.

'He spent eight months in jail. Never drove a car after that. Then the verse about the river? I think something bad happened to her when she was sixteen. She disappeared for a while. I think she tried to kill herself by drowning. That's the second verse in the song.'

Was that true? Dance had never heard of this either.

Now the uncomfortable smile faded. 'How sad is that? Writing a song to comfort yourself, because nobody else is there for you? Awful . . . Kayleigh sent me a dozen emails and a few real letters, and you know what I read between the lines in every one? She needs me, Agent Dance. If I left, who else would look out for her?'

DEPUTY CRYSTAL STANNING, Michael O'Neil and Kathryn Dance were in the briefing room of the FMCSO with Acting Chief Detective Dennis Harutyun.

Dance was reporting about the interview with Edwin. 'I'll have to be honest. He's very hard to read kinesically. He's coming off as completely nondeceptive, which either means he's telling the whole truth or he's completely delusional.'

'He did it,' Stanning grumbled.

It seemed the woman had grown more self-confident and edgier as the case had progressed. Or maybe it was just Madigan's absence.

A call to the Joint County Emergency Communications headquarters revealed that Edwin had in fact called 911 to report a Peeping Tom on Saturday night at seven. He complained that somebody was watching him from the back yard. No details. The dispatcher said to call back if the perp actually trespassed or threatened him.

Charlie Shean's crime scene team had just gone out to the place and conducted a search for where the intruder might have been. He was due any moment with the results.

O'Neil asked, 'Saturday—the night before Bobby was killed. Who could've been watching him, who knew he was in town?'

Dance said, 'Anybody could've found out where he was.' She added that on the fan web sites Sharp had posted that he was going to Fresno 'for a while'.

Harutyun took a call, spoke for a few minutes and then disconnected. 'Patrol's canvassing the area around Bulldog Stadium. Cal State. Lotta people. It's slow going.'

This was to find the woman who'd given Edwin directions at the time of Sheri's attack. Dance was calling her Alibi Woman.

A moment later Charlie Shean walked into the office.

He said, 'We went through his house and collected some trace but it was clean. I wonder if he scrubbed it down, after he gave you permission to search.' A glance towards Dance.

She recalled the faint hesitation before Edwin gave his OK.

'Cigarettes?' Dance had asked them to check.

'No. No lighters or matches or ashtrays. No odour of cigarettes either. Now, the latex gloves in Edwin's kitchen probably aren't the same as at the Bobby Prescott homicide. The wrinkle patterns are different. Outside, where the alleged perp was spying on him? We found some shoe prints in the dust, cowboy boots, it looks like. Can't tell size, male, female or age. And we collected about thirty samples of trace but the preliminaries are pretty useless.

'Now, we confirmed that the cigarette from last night at your motel is a Marlboro. We have cigarette ash from the site of the Sheri Towne attack, but we don't have the equipment to analyse it properly to tell what brand it is or how long ago it was left.'

It was then that Dennis Harutyun's assistant came to the door and handed him a sheaf of papers. 'These're those emails you were waiting for, about Bobby Prescott. They finally came in.'

The deputy read them over, laughed. He said to the officers, 'One of the things I was looking into was another motive for killing Bobby Prescott, somebody other than Edwin.'

'Right,' Dance said.

'Well, I may've found one,' he said. 'You ever hear about these guys, John, Paul, George and Ringo?'

DANCE AND O'NEIL conducted the search themselves.

The scene was Bobby Prescott's trailer and what had inspired the search here was the revelation by Harutyun about the Fab Four.

Dance believed she now knew what had been stolen the morning after the roadie had been murdered—by the person Tabatha Nysmith had seen in Bobby's trailer. And the object of this theft wasn't Kayleigh Towne memorabilia. Indeed, it had nothing to do with the singer at all or with the stalker—except to the extent that, yes, Edwin Sharp probably *was* a fall guy as he'd claimed all along.

'Well,' she said breathlessly, examining a binder from the shelves where she'd noted something missing several days ago.

She and O'Neil looked over a spiral notebook in which Bobby's father had jotted details about recordings he'd helped engineer at Abbey Road Studios in London during the Sixties and Seventies.

Dance recalled that Tabatha had mentioned Bobby's father's illustrious career.

It was a breathtaking list of talent from the era: Cliff Richard, Pink Floyd and, of course, the Beatles. Much of the man's scribbling was cryptic. But they found a copy of a letter to Bobby's father.

June 13, 1969

Bob Prescott:

Hey mate, thanks for the GREAT job, you're the best engineer, we mean it. Loved working with you. So, in appreciation of all those sleepless nights, the tapes to those songs we did playing around after 'Abbey Road' are yours, all the rights, everything. The list's below. Cheers!

'Wait,' O'Neil said. 'Are those . . . ?'

Dance said, 'I think they are.' At the end of the letter were four song titles. None of them was a known Beatles song.

She explained that the composing and recording of the songs on the *Abbey Road* album began in the spring of 1969. It was the group's last studio album. 'Let It Be' was released a year later, though that song was finished by the January of 1969.

Dennis Harutyun—the 'librarian' of the FMCSO, as Madigan dubbed him—had indeed done some impressive research into the life of Bobby Prescott and his family to see if anyone else might have had a motive to kill him. The deputy had found some rumours, buried on the Internet, that his father might have had some outtakes of Beatles songs he'd helped engineer in London years ago.

But these weren't outtakes; they were complete songs, original and never heard in public.

'And the Beatles just gave them away?' O'Neil asked.

'The band was breaking up then. They were rich. Maybe they just didn't care about them.'

'The letter's not signed by any of them.'

Dance shrugged. 'They talk about "after *Abbey Road*". Who else could it be? They must've stayed around the studio afterwards and just thrown a few songs together. Doesn't matter; they're still Beatles' songs.'

'Bobby got the tapes from his father.'

'Right,' Dance said, gesturing at the shelves. 'The perp found out and has been waiting for a chance to kill him and steal them.'

'Waiting for Edwin or somebody like him to show up as the fall guy.'

'Exactly.'

O'Neil said, 'So it's somebody who knew Bobby and his archives and would have heard the rumours about the Beatles songs. We know the motive. The second question is, who's the perp?'

Dance looked around the trailer. 'I need you to do something.' She took him by the shoulders and walked him backwards five feet. She then stepped away. 'Just stand there and don't move.'

As she walked out of the door, O'Neil said, 'I can do that.'

A HALF-HOUR LATER, Dance and O'Neil, along with a contingent of FMCSO deputies, sped towards a motel off Highway 41.

The four cars moved in silently. Dance and O'Neil weren't here to claim the trophy, merely to help out. The three police cars, and Dance's Nissan, slipped up to the motel and parked. Dance and O'Neil waited while Harutyun, Stanning and four other deputies sprinted through the halls to the suspect's room.

The nervous perp had been anticipating the visit; he'd seen the cars approach and he'd literally leaped out the window of his room onto a patch of grass. He righted himself fast, wrapped his computer-bag strap round his chest and poised for a sprint, then wisely chose to stop as he glanced at the guns in the hands of Dance and O'Neil, both of the muzzles pointed steadily at his head.

Two deputies slapped the cuffs on Kayleigh's producer, Barry Zeigler. It was Kathryn Dance who took possession of the computer bag that would contain the priceless songs he'd stolen from Bobby Prescott's trailer the morning after he'd killed the roadie.

'YOUR HEIGHT,' Dance explained to him.

Zeigler sat, miserable, in the back seat of a sheriff's office cruiser, hands shackled behind him.

She elaborated, answering his question about how she knew it was he. 'The perp knew Bobby well and had probably been in his trailer before. He'd be familiar with the band. And he was tall.'

She explained about her interview with Tabatha, across the street. 'She said she'd seen somebody inside that morning. Except, she couldn't see the intruder's head, only his chest.'

This was why she'd put O'Neil in front of the window of the trailer a half-hour ago. Recalling that she'd been eye-to-eye with P. K. Madigan outside, when she'd searched the trailer, she'd positioned the detective about where Tabatha had seen the intruder. She'd then walked across the street. Looking back, she'd clearly seen O'Neil's face.

Which meant that the intruder on Monday morning had been over O'Neil's height of six feet. The only person she'd met recently with an interest in Kayleigh Towne, who knew Bobby and who fitted that stature, was Barry Zeigler.

'I'm sorry,' the man muttered.

Sorry. What it meant, ten times out of ten, was: I'm sorry I got caught.

'When I met you at Kayleigh's house, you said you'd just driven there from Carmel,' Dance said. 'But we talked to the desk clerk here. You checked in the morning after Bobby was killed.'

'I know, I know. I lied. I'm sorry.'

That again.

Dance said, 'And then there was the recording of Kayleigh singing "Your Shadow". That you played to announce the attacks? It was done on a high-quality digital recorder. The sort that pros use—pros like you, producers and engineers.'

'Recording?' he asked, frowning.

She glanced at Dennis Harutyun, who ran through the Miranda warning. He added, 'You're under arrest for murder, for—'

'Murder? What do you mean?'

'You're being arrested for the murder of Bobby Prescott, sir,' the Fresno detective said. 'And Frederick Blanton. And assault and battery on Sheri Towne and Agent Dance. Do you wish to—'

'No, I didn't kill anyone! I didn't attack anyone!' The producer's face was shocked. 'I'd never do that!'

'You'll have your day in court. Do you understand your rights?'

'You're thinking I killed Bobby? No! And I'd never hurt Sheri.'

'Do you wish to waive your right to remain silent?'

'Sure, yes. This is ridiculous. This is a huge misunderstanding.'

Harutyun asked, 'Did you drive up here on Sunday and kill Bobby Prescott that night?'

'No, no. I drove in on Monday morning, about eleven. After I heard from Kayleigh that Bobby had died. Yes, I broke into Bobby's trailer but it was just to get some personal things.'

'The Beatles' songs,' Harutyun said. 'We know all about them.'

'What are you talking about?'

Dance added, 'Bobby's father was a technician at Abbey Road in the Sixties and Seventies.'

'Right. But what does that have to do with anything?'

'The Beatles gave him four original songs they wrote after they finished *Abbey Road*. You killed him and stole the songs.'

The producer laughed. 'It's an urban legend. All those rumours about outtakes and secret recordings. There's nothing to it.'

Dance said, 'What about this?' She showed him the plastic envelope containing the letter to Bobby's father.

Zeigler looked at it. 'Those aren't Beatles' songs. It was some local group from London. After the Beatles wrapped *Abbey Road*, this group booked studio time. They laid down fifteen or sixteen tracks and used twelve for their album. I guess they liked Bobby's father so much they let him have the ones they didn't use. Nothing ever came of the group. They wrote pretty sucky songs.'

Dance looked at the language of the note again. Yes, it could just refer to studio time after the Beatles had finished recording their album. 'But you just admitted you stole something from Bobby's trailer that morning,' she said.

Zeigler looked to O'Neil and the other deputies. 'Leave us alone, Agent Dance and me. I want to talk to her alone.'

She considered this and said, 'It's all right.'

The others walked away from the squad car. Dance crossed her arms and said, 'OK, talk.'

'You can't tell a soul.'

'You know I can't agree to that.'

'All right. But take a look first, then decide. In the bag, there's a zipper liner. Some papers. *That's* what I took from Bobby's.'

Dance opened the computer bag and found the compartment. She withdrew a document and read it. 'Oh my God,' she whispered.

What Ziegler had stolen was a letter from Bobby Prescott about how he wanted his property distributed in the event of his death.

Most of it would go to one person: the child who was his and Kayleigh Towne's, Mary-Gordon.

Apparently Kayleigh had had the child at sixteen and Suellyn and her husband had adopted the little girl within weeks of her birth.

The envelope included a copy of the adoption papers and some personal messages to the girl, for her to read when she was older.

'He told me a few years ago that he'd written it,' Zeigler said. 'I couldn't let it become public.'

Dance recalled the closeness she'd sensed between Bobby and Kayleigh at the restaurant. And other things she'd noted: Mary-Gordon's golden hair. Her eyes were Kayleigh's bright blue, while Suellyn's—and presumably her Latino husband's—were brown.

She thought too about Edwin's comment in the recent interview.

I think something pretty bad happened to her when she was about sixteen.

Dance asked, 'But how come no one knew she was pregnant?'

'Oh, Kayleigh didn't start performing professionally until she was seventeen. But Bishop had big plans for her. He pulled her out of school when she was about two months' pregnant, got a home tutor. He kept it secret and spun the story pretty well to friends—Kayleigh was real upset her mother had died. She was depressed. Made sense for her to disappear for eight, nine months. He suggested to people she'd had a breakdown.'

Dance was appalled. 'And he forced her to give the baby up?'

Zeigler's long face moved up and down. 'Bobby was twenty-two, she was six years younger. OK, that's bad, no question. But he was a nice guy and if anybody would fall for a father figure, it'd be Kayleigh. Her mother had just died, her father was on the road most of the time. She was vulnerable. And they wanted to get married. They were in love. But when Bishop heard, he flew back to town and said if they didn't agree to the adoption he was going to get Bobby arrested for statutory rape.'

'He did *that?*'

'Sure did. Kayleigh agreed to the adoption—but only placing the girl with her sister so she could still see her. And she insisted that Bobby stay with the band.'

'But why couldn't she keep the baby?' Dance asked. 'She wants children.'

'Oh, that wouldn't work,' Zeigler said bitterly. 'Bishop's own career was dying at that point. All he had left was Kayleigh.'

'And he was convinced that she needed to build her career on a good-girl image to be successful.'

'He was ahead of the curve there. Parents—the ones with the credit cards—love that image. If word had got out that she was pregnant at sixteen, that could have been the end of her career.'

Dance looked at the letter. 'Mary-Gordon doesn't know?'

'No. Bishop forced Suellyn and Roberto to sign a nondisclosure agreement. If they said a word they might lose custody.'

This news about Bishop Towne disturbed but didn't surprise Dance.

Zeigler gave a bitter laugh. 'I'm not the only desperate person in this business.'

She slipped the documents into her bag. 'I'll think about it. For now, you were looking for some personal papers at Bobby's. What you found and took had no value and nothing to do with the case. But you're still a suspect in the murders.'

'I was in Carmel, at a hotel, when Bobby died.'

'Can anybody verify that?'

'I was by myself. I was really upset—I'd just been fired by my other major artist. I left a message for my wife.' He glanced up at Dance with miserable eyes. 'Is that any good—a voicemail where you're sobbing like a ten-year-old that your career is probably over?'

'It could be,' Dance told him.

'No Beatles?' Dennis Harutyun asked.

'Doesn't look that way.'

Dance, Harutyun and Crystal Stanning stood in a cluster in the parking lot of the Red Roof Inn. O'Neil was on the phone. Finally he ended the call and looked up. 'His alibi? It's good.'

The cell phone data and the voiceprint of the 'sobbing ten-year-old' confirmed that at the moment Bobby was being murdered inside the Fresno convention centre, Zeigler was over two hours away.

'Why'd he break into Bobby's trailer?' Harutyun asked.

Dance shrugged. 'Apparently he was looking for something personal. Nothing to do with the case. I believe him.'

Harutyun said, 'Hardly seems worth the trouble, collaring him for that.' He walked over to his car, got Zeigler out and uncuffed him, then gave him a stern talking-to. The producer collected his computer bag and returned to his room, rubbing his wrists.

Dance decided to give the documents to Kayleigh and let her decide how to handle the matter.

'So,' Harutyun said, returning to them. 'No leads. No suspect.'

'We have the evidence,' Crystal Stanning offered. 'From the crime scenes and what we collected in Edwin's back yard.'

'Life's not like *CSI*,' Harutyun muttered. 'Charlie's folks are good but you need more than finding. You need figuring out.'

Dance pulled out her phone and made a call.

8

Two hours later the same foursome reconvened in the sheriff's office. Dance received a text, read it and then asked the deputies, 'Can you show me your service door?'

Stanning said, 'Sure, I guess. Follow me.'

Dance and others did so, and after a brief walk stopped at a wide doorway in a delivery area at the back of the main building in the sheriff's office, opening on to a ramp that led to the parking lot.

'This'll do.' She made a call and gave directions to this entrance. Dance disconnected and explained, 'I'm having house guests this weekend. They're from New York, but they've been in San Jose at a conference. I took the liberty of asking them here.'

Just then a white van pulled up and stopped. The side door opened and a disabled passenger ramp extended to the ground. A handsome man with dark hair drove a red motorised wheelchair quickly down the ramp and through the doorway of the service area. Wearing tan slacks and a long-sleeved burgundy shirt, he was pale. Joining him was a tall, redheaded woman in jeans, black T-shirt and black jacket, and a slim, younger man.

'Lincoln!' Dance bent down, pressing her cheek against that of the man in the wheelchair. 'Amelia.' She embraced the redhead, Amelia Sachs, Lincoln Rhyme's partner. 'Hello, Thom,' she said to Rhyme's caregiver, who also hugged her warmly.

'Been way, way too long,' the aide said.

'Kathryn,' Rhyme said.

After Dance introduced him to Michael O'Neil, Rhyme made a slight movement of his neck and his right arm extended smoothly. He shook O'Neil's hand. Dance knew he'd recently had surgery to improve his condition—he was quadriplegic, mostly paralysed from the neck down; he'd been injured on the job as head of the NYPD Crime Scene Unit years ago. The operation was successful and he'd regained nearly all the use of his right arm and hand.

He similarly greeted Harutyun and Stanning, and Sachs introduced Thom Reston, Rhyme's caregiver.

'Kathryn said she'd called in an expert but I never thought it'd be some-one like you. Thanks for coming,' Harutyun said.

Dance had known and worked with Rhyme for several years. She'd been after him and Sachs to come for a visit. Rhyme was disinclined to travel, but he was in demand as a consultant in forensics and crime scene work and he had decided to accept a lecture assignment on that subject in San Jose.

The preparations for her house that her father was taking care of, in antic-ipation of their weekend visit, involved building a ramp to let Rhyme motor up to the front door and some modifications to the bathroom. Rhyme had told them not to bother; they'd stay at a motel. But retired Stuart Dance loved any excuse to use his many woodworking tools.

Harutyun continued, 'It's a pleasure to meet you, Detective Rhyme—'

A fast, '"Lincoln" is fine. I'm decommissioned.' He looked around the storage facility with a grimace as if he expected this to be the crime lab. 'You have some things you'd like me to look over?'

'We have a pretty good lab,' Harutyun offered.

'Do you now?' There was cynicism in his voice. Dance had been to Rhyme's town house in Manhattan; he'd turned the parlour into a forensics lab, where he, as a consultant, Sachs and other officers would run the crime scene side of major cases in the metro area.

Not picking up on the sardonic tone, Stanning said proudly, 'Yes, sir. Sheriff Madigan's fought pretty hard to build up our CSU. Officers as far away as Bakersfield send samples here.'

'Bakersfield,' Rhyme said, even more ironically, drawing a sharp glance from Thom, a reminder that condescension was not necessary. 'Well, we better get to it.'

They walked and wheeled through the building then out through a side door. Dance briefed them on the case, explaining that their main suspect had proved to be slippery. 'His name's Edwin Sharp. He could be the perp, he could be a fall guy, could be innocent.'

Harutyun said, 'He announces the attacks by playing a verse from one of Kayleigh's songs.'

This clearly intrigued Rhyme. 'Interesting, good,' he said. 'And he's smart, right? He started with phones, then switched to other ways to play the song, like radio call-in requests?'

'Very good, sir,' Stanning said. 'Not call-ins but most recently he played a song over a high-school-stadium PA system.'

Dance added, 'He claims somebody's been conducting surveillance on *him*, presumably to set him up for the crimes. That's part of the evidence we need you to look at. He gave us permission to search his house, though he might've scrubbed the place down before the team searched.'

Harutyun added that an earlier search, without a warrant, had resulted in getting the chief of detectives and another deputy suspended. The perp had also stolen the gun of another detective, temporarily removing him from the force.

'Crazy like a fox,' Rhyme commented and seemed oddly pleased at this news—maybe because he liked adversaries who were particularly smart and challenging. His number-one nemesis was boredom.

Soon they were entering the lab and meeting Charlie Shean. If Harutyun had been impressed that Rhyme was here, Shean was beside himself, having a crime scene legend in his 'modest abode'.

Rhyme, though, was visibly impressed at the sophistication of the operation, despite his apparent misgivings earlier.

Charlie Shean said, 'We've searched and done the analysis. But most of the results're just raw data. We don't know what to make of it. If you could offer some thoughts it'd be much appreciated.'

Rhyme said, 'Let's get to work. Entrance and exit routes from the convention centre?'

Shean explained, 'There're twenty-nine of them, including the windows and infrastructure access doorways and loading docks. There were thousands of prints and samples of trace.'

Rhyme said, 'Yes, yes, sometimes the problem is too *much* evidence, rather than not enough.'

When Rhyme learned that there were two places behind Edwin's house where an intruder might have stood to spy, he asked which trace came from which area. The tags on the half-dozen collection bags reported only: *Trace evidence from behind E. Sharp's house, Woodward Circle West.*

'Well, we didn't really differentiate them.'

From Rhyme, 'Oh.' It was the same as a loud dressing-down. 'Might want to think about that in the future.'

On the other hand, Shean had satisfied Lincoln Rhyme's number-one requirement when it came to trace: isolating 'unique' materials—those that might have been shed by the perp—at the scene. This was done by taking many samples from spots nearby: samplars, they were called. If certain materials differed from the indigenous ones they might have come from the perp. Shean's officers had collected hundreds of samplars at all the scenes for comparison.

'That was competent,' Rhyme said. One of his more enthusiastic compliments. He then said, 'And now, the cigarette ash.'

Stanning said, 'We'd like to know if the samples of ash match.'

'Yes, well, they wouldn't *match*, of course.' He turned to the young woman. '*Matching* is when two or more items are identical,' Rhyme muttered. 'Very few things actually match. Friction ridge—fingerprints *and* footprints, of course. DNA. Tool marks under rare circumstances. But as for trace? I could make the argument about some substances *matching* by analysing half-life but that's on a nuclear level.'

'You get a lot of convictions when you testify, I'd imagine,' Shean offered.

'Nearly one hundred per cent,' Rhyme said, with only a veneer of modesty. 'Of course, if the odds aren't good up-front I recommend not going to trial. Though I'm not above bluffing somebody into a confession. Now, I need to run an inductively coupled plasma test.'

Shean said, 'We can do that. But why that, if you're analysing ash?'

'For the metals,' Amelia Sachs said.

Shean tapped his forehead. 'Trace metals in cigarette ash. Brilliant. I never thought of that.'

Rhyme lectured absently, 'It's the most definitive way to determine the brand of cigarettes when all you have is ash.'

Shean prepared the sample and ran the test and a short time later they had their answer.

Looking at the computer screen, Rhyme offered, 'Zinc 351.18, iron 2785.74, chromium 5.59. Yep, that's Marlboro. It's likely that the same person was at both scenes. But Person A could have been where Sheri Towne was attacked, smoking a Marlboro. Person B could have bummed one off him and set up the trap at the Mountain View Motel. Not likely but it could be. How long for the DNA?'

'Another few days.'

A grimace. 'But it's not any better in New York. I don't think you'll find any, though. Your perp is smart. He probably lit it by blowing on the tip, not holding it in his lips. So, does this Sharp smoke?'

'He used to,' Dance said. 'Still may but we don't know.'

Rhyme couldn't draw any conclusions from the boot print—really just the toe.

Sachs studied the electrostatic print. 'It's probably a cowboy boot.'

'Let's look at the shell casings,' Rhyme said.

Shean reiterated that he believed the gun at both the Blanton shooting and the Sheri Towne attack was probably the same.

'Gun was stolen from an officer, you said?' Rhyme said.

'Possibly—Gabriel Fuentes. Sharp was near Gabe's car when the gun was stolen. But we don't know for sure.'

'No? Let me have the close-ups of the extractor marks and scratches,' Rhyme said. 'And the ones of the lands and grooves on the slugs.'

Shean placed them on a table for Rhyme to examine. 'But we don't have known samples from Gabe's Glock. I asked him and—'

'I know you don't.'

'Oh, right, otherwise we would have identified the gun.'

'Exactly.' Rhyme examined the pictures. 'Sachs?'

She studied the pictures too. 'I'd say four thousand.'

'Good,' Rhyme announced. Then, 'I need the serial number of Fuentes's gun.' A fast computer search revealed it. 'OK, the gun was made four years ago by our talented friends in Austria. Call this Fuentes and ask him when he got it and how often he fired it.'

Harutyun made this call. The answer was that he'd bought the weapon new—three years ago—and took it to the range twice a month or so. He would typically fire fifty rounds.

'Fifty rounds, every two weeks, for three years means it's been fired about thirty-nine hundred times. From pictures of the shells and the slugs, Sachs estimated they came from a gun that had been fired about four thousand times. Good eye.' Rhyme glanced at her.

Shean nodded. 'So. It *is* Gabe's weapon.'

'Most likely,' Sachs said.

'Microscope! Charlie, I need a 'scope!' Rhyme called.

'Sure.' The man had a tech wheel over two heavy compound microscopes—one a biological, which illuminated translucent samples from beneath, and one a metallurgic model, which shone light down onto opaque samples. Shean was setting it up when Rhyme shooed him away. Using his right hand he prepared several slides from the trace and examined them one by one, using both scopes.

Rhyme set the slides out and pointed. 'Fungi database on that one and I need a fast reagent test on those.'

A tech ran the reagent tests. But Charlie Shean said, 'We don't exactly have a fungus database.'

'Really?' Rhyme said. And gave the man a web site, user name and passcode. In five minutes Shean was browsing through Rhyme's own database on moulds and fungi, jotting notes.

Eyes on the screen, Rhyme said, '"Harutyun". Armenian.'

The detective nodded. 'Big community here in Fresno.'

'I know.'

And how *did* Rhyme know that? Dance wondered. But speculating about the criminalist's encyclopedic mind was useless. Some facts that even children knew he was completely ignorant of. Others, far more esoteric, were stored front and centre. The key, she knew, was whether they had helped him analyse evidence, or might help him do so in the future.

Finally the results from the new tests were compiled and Rhyme reviewed them. 'Now, outside Edwin's house. The fungus is often used in place of traditional toxic chemical pesticides. Also, at his house and at the convention centre, the triglycerides . . . With that colour temperature and melting point, I'd say it's neat's-foot oil. Used for treating baseball gloves, equestrian tack and gun slings. Snipers use it quite a bit. The limonite, goethite and calcite? It's gangue.'

'What's gangue?' O'Neil asked.

'It's by-product, produced in industrial operations, often found in ore collection and processing. The same materials were in the trace at the public phone at Fresno College, where he called Kayleigh before one of the attacks.' Rhyme wheeled back to the microscope. 'Still a few things I want to look at. Ammonium oxalate . . .'

It was then that Dance's mobile buzzed. She regarded the text with a frown. 'I'll be right back,' she told the others.

She walked outside and into the parking lot of the sheriff's office. She nearly laughed to see P. K. Madigan undercover—he was in khakis, a plaid shirt and tan sweater, a cap and aviator sunglasses.

Dance smiled. 'Hi, I—'

But Madigan interrupted and said, 'We've got a situation. I mean *you've* got a situation. I've spent the last sixteen hours online, looking up everything I could find about Edwin, Kayleigh, fans . . . everything.'

Madigan had come to see Dance a few days ago. Restless after being suspended from his job, he had asked her if there was anything he could do unofficially to help with the case. This was the assignment Dance had given him. She had told him it would be 'unpleasant', since it involved sitting at a desk, not the greatest job in the world for an active law enforcer. But Dance believed it was important to continue to monitor Edwin's online activity. With their limited manpower, she'd enlisted Madigan.

'Where's Edwin now? He under surveillance?' Madigan asked.

'He was. I'll check,' Dance replied and placed a call. She put the question to Dennis Harutyun, who was a bit mystified by Dance's disappearance. But he just said, 'Hold on.' A moment later he came back on the line. 'This is odd. Edwin went to the mall—Fashion Fair on Shaw. Parked in the lot near East Santa Ana. The deputy thought Edwin'd lose him in the stores so he stayed with the car. That was two hours ago. He hasn't been back.'

'He knew he was being tailed and he jumped. OK, I'll be back in a few minutes.'

After she disconnected she told this information to Madigan, who grimaced. 'Well, I'm pretty worried about something. A half-hour ago there were some anonymous postings on some of Kayleigh's fan sites where Edwin has posted in the past. The posts said something to the effect of "Watch the news, Kayleigh. Maybe you'll finally understand how much I love you."'

'John Hinckley.'

'Yep. I remember what you told us in the first briefing.'

That occasionally a stalker had a total break with reality and when he gave up hope that he'd be with his love, he'd kill someone to cement himself in her thoughts forever.

'Here're the URLs of those sites.' Madigan handed her a sheet of yellow-lined paper. 'Have Computer Crimes track 'em down and see where they were made from.'

'Thanks, Chief.'

'No,' he said, offering a wan smile, 'thank *you*, Deputy.'

Dance returned to the office and handed Dennis Harutyun the sheet of paper. She explained about the threatening posts, without mentioning Madigan's name. 'We need to trace them.'

Harutyun called the office's computer crimes operation and ordered them to locate the posts and try to trace them.

Crystal Stanning went online and reviewed the posts. O'Neil said, 'It may not be him. Kayleigh has to have other obsessive fans. We can't forget that.'

But a moment later Harutyun's phone hummed. He took the call, listened for a moment. 'OK. Thanks.' He disconnected. 'That was Computer Crimes. The posting was from Java Hut at Fashion Fair, where Edwin is now.' He called Dispatch to order deputies to the shopping centre to find Edwin, reminding them that he was probably armed.

Stanning asked, 'He's thinking of a mass shooting at the mall?'

Sachs said, 'That could be it but the typical stalker killing profile is more one-on-one. An assassination.'

'True,' Dance said. 'And it's usually somebody famous. So that he'll get the attention of his object.'

'But who's the victim going to be?' Harutyun wondered aloud.

O'Neil had gone online and was reading the posts. 'They don't mention anybody in particular.'

Dance joined him, arm against arm, and they scanned the posts.

'There, that one,' Dance muttered, pointing. She read it aloud, '"I've seen all your postings, about Kayleigh. You claim you like her, you claim you love her music. But you use her like everybody does, you stole Leaving Home to keep the hispanics happy. Your a damn hypocrit . . ."'

Rhyme asked, 'You have any idea who he's talking about?'

'I know exactly who he means,' Dance replied.

'IT'LL BE ALL RIGHT, Congressman,' Peter Simesky said.

Davis didn't need reassurance. He needed his family taken care of. He called Suze again and left another message for her to lock the door and stay in the house with the kids.

'Please have Jessie find my wife, Peter.'

'I'll do that, sir. But there's no indication that this Sharp wants to hurt anybody but you. Besides, I don't think there's any way he could get to Los Angeles. He was at a mall in Fresno, this morning, according to the police. And everybody's looking for him.'

'He actually thinks I'm exploiting Kayleigh?'

'Using her—well, and that song, "Leaving Home"—just to increase your Latino voter base.'

'But I've been a huge supporter of hers all along! I been posting on her site and the blogs for a couple of years. Before she even wrote the song.'

Simesky reminded him, 'Oh, he's a psycho, Bill. Agent Dance said he has no sense of reality.'

'She said he could be like Hinckley?'

'Could be.'

'Jesus. The police've got to find him. If he can't kill me maybe he'll just go on a rampage.'

The men were in the Coronado, one of the nicer hotels in Fresno, and to Davis it seemed plenty secure. But Davis's aides, Simesky and Myra Babbage, and the police thought he should move to a more secure location.

If it wasn't for his family's safety, Davis would have been amused. He was extremely unpopular in certain circles. Just mention relaxing the laws on immigration at a cocktail party and see what happens; imagine the consequences when it's a campaign position of a potential presidential candidate. And yet here he was being threatened not by any rabid right-wingers but by a crazy guy who probably didn't know what the word 'immigration' meant.

A knock on the door. The aide called, 'Yes?'

'Kathryn Dance and Deputy Harutyun are here,' the campaign staff security man, named Tim Raymond, called from outside.

Simesky opened the door and the two entered. The aide smiled at Dance.

'Congressman, Peter,' Dance said. Her green eyes quickly but calmly took in all the rooms, presumably for security threats.

Simesky asked, 'Where are we with all this? What do we know?'

Dance said, 'We're still trying to find Edwin. Until we have a better idea where he is we want to get you to that safe house as soon as possible. Are you ready to leave now?'

'Sure. Where is it?'

Harutyun said, 'A place we use about a half-hour north of here.'

'All right.' Davis thought of something. Kathryn Dance was with a statewide agency so he said to her, 'Could you get police to my house in Los Angeles? It's just . . . I'm worried about my family.'

'Of course. I'll call our office and get a CBI team there.'

'Thanks.' He gave her the address and Susan's phone number.

Dance made the call and then disconnected. Officers, she told the congressman, were en route. A few minutes later, Davis's wife called. CBI agents had arrived and she said that she was safe.

Simesky called Davis's other aide, Myra Babbage, at the local campaign headquarters, and told her to join them at the safe house.

Then, the group moved quickly through the hotel and down into the parking garage, where they climbed into a sheriff's office SUV.

Dance said to Harutyun, who was driving, 'I'd say lights, no sirens for two or three miles. But really move and use side streets. Then flashers off and normal stream of traffic to the safe house.'

'Sure thing.'

'You think he's nearby?' Simesky looked out of the windows uneasily.

'He's invisible,' Dance said cryptically. 'We just don't know.'

The big vehicle accelerated fast. Ten minutes later, when it seemed clear that Edwin was not following, they slowed and entered a highway. After a half-hour of driving, the deputy turned down a deserted road, drove for another mile or so and, passing no houses along the way, finally approached a fancy log cabin. There were, Davis could see, only a few windows and all of them were shuttered.

Dance climbed out of the SUV and watched Harutyun approach the house and punch keys on a number pad. A green light came on. He stepped inside and deactivated another security system. Dance exchanged mobile numbers with Tim Raymond, the security man, who remained outside. Then she joined the others. Harutyun turned on the lights, revealing a functional interior: brown carpet, Mediterranean-style lamps and furniture with scrolls.

Harutyun shut the door and locked it. Then the mustachioed detective walked through the house to make sure it was secure. Simesky accompanied him. A few minutes later Raymond called Dance and told her that everything seemed fine along the perimeter.

Simesky and Harutyun returned from their survey of the cabin. 'Window and doors secure and armed,' the deputy told them.

Dance's phone hummed with an incoming email. She smiled at the header: Bird Shit. The message was from Rhyme and had to do with additional analysis of the trace outside Edwin's house.

Finally managed to isolate the other trace in the ammonium oxalate. They were phosphates and residue of animal matter. It's bird shit. Exactly what kind, I can't say. But I can say the excreting birds were most likely resident in a coastal region. Fish had been the mainstay of their diet.

Dance closed her eyes and let her mind wander where it would. Then she went to the web site they'd looked at earlier, the one containing the threat to Davis. She scrolled through the posts.

PLAN YOUR ACTS and act your plan.

Peter Simesky's analytical mind continued to measure the actual milestones of his plan against the projected ones, and he found it proceeding apace. In general, the events were in harmony with what he and Myra Babbage had been working on for the past ten months.

He now stood in a den behind the living room, reviewing text messages on one of his many anonymous and untraceable accounts. He looked out into the living room where Kathryn Dance, Congressman Davis and Deputy Harutyun sat, looking at an old TV. Some game was on. Davis wasn't happy but he didn't look particularly scared.

Simesky turned and walked into the kitchen at the back of the safe house.

The goal of Simesky's plan was simple: to eliminate Congressman William Garrett Davis, who would sell the country out to people who didn't belong here, who used it for their own gain, who despised the red, white and blue but were pleased to rob this glorious nation blind. How difficult it had been for Simesky to feign admiration and devotion to Davis and get a job on the staff. He had, however, done a good job of it. He'd ingratiated himself into the man's inner circle and had gathered as much information as he needed so they could stop the traitor, who—if elected President—would ruin our great nation.

A little over a year ago, when Davis's popularity began surging, Simesky was with a think tank based in Texas, with offices in Washington, New York, Chicago and Los Angeles. It was part of an informal association of wealthy businessmen in the Midwest and South, who ran companies and even a few universities. This group of men—and, yes, they were exclusively men and, by the way, white—had no official name but informally and with wry humour, they'd adopted one, which had been bestowed by a liberal media blogger. The journalist had referred to the cabal contemptuously as the 'Keyholders', because, he reported, the senior leaders believed they held the key to curing all of the nation's woes.

The group loved it.

The Keyholders funnelled huge sums to candidates they thought would best uphold proper ideals to keep America strong: reduced federal government, limited taxation, minimal participation in world geopolitics and, most importantly, the elimination of virtually all immigration. Generally, the Keyholders' efforts involved financial support for candidates, and misinformation campaigns against traitorous politicos and reporters.

But sometimes more was needed.

And that's when Peter Simesky's obscure think tank would receive a call, asking him to handle a particularly critical matter.

However he thought best.

However extreme the solution.

The Keyholders knew that whatever the mission, Simesky would create a careful plan, so it was obvious that the death of this muckraking liberal journalist had to be an accident, or of that environmental activist had to be a suicide, or of that reformer congressman had to be an assassination spawned by a stalker's love for a famous singer.

And those clever plans often involved a fall guy.

Hello, Edwin.

Using the stalker had come to mind last winter after he and Myra Babbage—his business partner and occasional lover—had infiltrated Davis's ranks. Doing his typically exhaustive research, Simesky had learned that Davis was a huge fan of Kayleigh Towne. The congressman had used the star's pro-immigration song 'Leaving Home' at rallies and in campaign ads.

Simesky reviewed Kayleigh's web sites and learned of a fanatical fan named Edwin Sharp, who posted hundreds of comments about the singer and was described by other fans as a 'weirdo'.

Perfect.

The Keyholders had some significant resources and it took only a day to get into the Internet service providers handling Kayleigh's and Edwin's email accounts. Unfortunately, there didn't seem to be anything particularly threatening about Edwin's letters and posts, but he was clearly unhinged and troublingly persistent and that would be enough for Simesky's plan. He and Myra sent emails and letters to Edwin, posing as Kayleigh, writing that she was flattered by his attention and suggesting that she'd like to get together with him. But she had to put on a façade of indifference or her father could cause problems. The notes suggested that, whatever she said in public, she'd enjoy seeing him at the concert on Friday. If possible she'd see him later too. In private.

And Edwin had done just what they'd wanted, descended on Fresno in all his psychotic glory, far more of a nutjob than they'd hoped.

He and Myra Babbage had conducted surveillance at Edwin's rental to learn his routine and steal some evidence that could be planted at the site of

Davis's assassination to implicate the stalker. Then, today, it was time to act. Myra had called Edwin, pretending to work for Kayleigh. She explained the singer had decided she wanted to see him but they had to be careful. He should go to the Fashion Fair shopping mall and lose the police, then wait at Macy's loading dock for one of Kayleigh's friends to pick him up.

Myra had cruised past and waved. The fool had jumped into the SUV, grinning in anticipation. Myra had hit him with the stun gun, injected a sedative and taped his wrists and ankles. She'd gone into the mall, uploaded the announcement from Java Hut that someone was about to do something that would make Kayleigh remember him forever. The context made it clear that Bill Davis was to be the victim.

And now, Myra and a barely conscious Edwin Sharp were en route to the safe house.

In a few minutes the plan would be completed: Myra would arrive, smile at the security man, Tim Raymond, and then blow him away with her pistol. At the same time Simesky would step into the living room and shoot the congressman and the others. He and Myra would drag Edwin into the room, shoot him in the head with Harutyun's gun and dust the stalker's hand with gunshot residue.

Simesky would make a panicked call begging for help and an ambulance, explaining that he'd got the gun away from the stalker and had shot the man.

Kathryn Dance's appearance could help smooth over one matter he'd been worried about—that there might be some suspicion if only he and Myra were left alive. If Dance survived too, the scene would seem a bit more legitimate. Though he'd have to orchestrate it so that, of course, she couldn't see him as the shooter.

Simesky would shoot Dance in the back, paralysing but not killing her, then he'd murder Davis and Harutyun. After they were dead, Simesky would call out something like, 'Edwin, no! What are you doing?'

Ideally, Dance would be conscious and she'd hear his cry. She'd later report the story to the police, confirming that Edwin was the sole shooter.

Simesky glanced at his Rolex. Three minutes to go.

Myra would be heading towards the safe house now, moving up the drive. Simesky couldn't detect the sound of the tyres because of the thick walls, but, over the noise of the game on TV, he could hear Dance saying, 'What's that? You hear something? A car?'

'I think so. Wait, no, I'm not sure.' The voice was Davis's.

In the living room Davis's phone trilled. 'Hello . . . Hi, we're inside.' Then to the others, 'It's Myra Babbage. She just got here.'

One minute, according to Simesky's Rolex.

Remaining out of sight in the den, Simesky pulled on latex gloves, opened his bag and removed the pistol, a cold one—stolen.

He knew it was loaded and he knew how it worked. And he'd already fired it to extract some gunshot residue, now in a bag, which he'd plant on Edwin's hands. He checked the weapon again.

'Peter?' the congressman called from the living room.

Simesky replied, 'Be there in a sec.' He slipped closer to the living-room doorway, pressing his back against the adjoining wall.

'Hey, look, the game,' Davis said. 'Triple play!' The volume on the TV went up. Spectators roared.

A glance at the Rolex. Right about now Myra would shoot.

But no shots sounded.

Another minute passed, silence except for the game on TV.

What was going on? Sweat on Simesky's brow.

And then at last: gunfire from outside. A half-dozen shots.

Damn, Simesky thought. Had a local cop happened by and noticed a woman with a weapon or a tied-and-bound Edwin Sharp?

Now, all was silent.

Act your plan . . . Simesky, thinking: sometimes you *couldn't*. Sometimes you needed to improvise. But to do that, you needed facts.

Only there were no facts.

He decided to go ahead anyway. Two, two and two . . . Kill Tim Raymond when he walked inside, if he was still alive. Too bad about Myra; he assumed she was gone.

Simesky turned fast and stepped into the living room, aiming the gun at where Harutyun and Dance had been, then he froze.

The room was empty.

The light on the alarm pad by the door was green. Someone had disarmed the system so that Davis, Dance and Harutyun could leave. But he hadn't heard the door. What the hell was this? And then he saw that the side window was up. That's how they'd escaped.

Simesky noticed too in the middle of the floor a pad of yellow paper. On it was scrawled a message: PLOT AGAINST YOUR LIFE SIMESKY INVOLVED MYRA TOO MAYBE OTHERS WE LEAVE NOW SIDE WINDOW NOW

Oh, no . . . Who? he thought.

But then realised: why even ask? Kathryn Dance, of course.

She had probably texted for back-up and alerted Raymond, who'd fired on Myra when she got out of the car and presented a threat.

He heard a man's voice from behind him, Dennis Harutyun's. 'Simesky, drop the weapon and raise your hands over your head.'

The deputy would have snuck through the back door. Dance probably covered the front. Simesky assessed the situation. He reflected that Harutyun had probably never fired his weapon in the line of duty. Simesky, on the other hand, had killed eight people in his life.

He glanced back. 'I'm just trying to protect the congressman from that killer. I heard gunshots. I haven't done anything!'

'I'm not going to tell you again. Drop the weapon.'

Simesky was thinking, I have a Cayman Islands account. I have any one of the Keyholders' private jets at my disposal.

Just fight your way out. Turn and shoot. He'll panic. He's a small-town cop.

Simesky started to turn, keeping the gun low, unthreatening. 'I just—'

He heard a stunning bang, felt a burn in his chest.

'Both dead?'

'That's right,' Harutyun told Sheriff Anita Gonzalez. Ten people were in her office at the FMCSO, which made it pretty cramped.

P. K. Madigan was back—though unofficially—because his research had contributed to uncovering the plot. He was enjoying a cup of butter pecan.

Lincoln Rhyme, Thom Reston and Amelia Sachs were here too, along with Michael O'Neil and Tim Raymond, the congressman's own security man. In the interest of safety Congressman Davis was on board his private jet, heading back to Los Angeles.

Gonzalez asked, 'Any other perps working with Simesky and Babbage?'

Dance replied, 'I'm sure there are. But they were the only active participants on the scene. Our office and the FBI's agent in charge in San Francisco are tracing associates and connections.'

Michael O'Neil said, 'There seems to be some affiliation with that outfit they call the Keyholders. Some political action group.'

'Political action? Wackos,' muttered Madigan, digging into his ice cream.

'Did either say anything before they died?' Gonzalez asked.

Raymond said, 'No, Myra was walking towards me when I got the text from Agent Dance to treat her like a hostile. I lifted my weapon when she was thirty feet away. She was hiding a forty-five under her coat and she engaged. I couldn't take any chances.'

Harutyun said, 'And Simesky didn't believe me when I said, "I'm not going to tell you again."'

'And Edwin?' the sheriff asked.

'He was in the back of the SUV. The stun gun that Myra used was powerful and he's doped up. But the medics said he's fine.'

'How'd you figure it out, Kathryn?' Madigan asked.

'It wasn't just me.' She nodded towards Lincoln Rhyme.

The criminalist said offhandedly, 'Combination of things. Your man Charlie, by the way, is pretty good. Don't let him come to visit me in New York. I might steal him away.'

Dance said, 'There were questions raised about what Charlie's crime scene people found at the convention centre and behind Edwin's house, where he said somebody'd been spying on him. One was bird droppings from seagulls.'

Rhyme corrected, 'The actual phrase was shit from quote "birds most likely resident in a coastal region". The birds in question probably spent time recently on the coast, eating oceanic fish. And then we identified some fungus used in organic farming.'

Dance elaborated, 'I remembered that Davis, Simesky and Babbage had been in Monterey campaigning, which is on the coast, where they might've picked up the bird-droppings trace. And they'd been stumping at eco-friendly organic farms, from Watsonville to the Valley here.'

'But why'd you get suspicious enough to consider that maybe Edwin wasn't the killer in the first place?' Madigan asked.

Dance said, 'When I was looking again at the web-site post threatening the congressman, I realised it didn't sound like Edwin.'

She showed them the post that had raised some alarms.

I've seen all your postings, about Kayleigh. You claim you like her, you claim you love her music. But you use her like everybody does, you stole Leaving Home to keep the hispanics happy. Your a damn hypocrit . . .

'That's not Edwin's tone. I've never heard him say or write an expletive. And there're grammatical mistakes: commas that weren't necessary and the misspelling of "hypocrite" and "you're", which he never did in his emails to

Kayleigh. It struck me that the post that threatened Davis could have been written by somebody who *thought* that's what a crazy stalker would post.

'Then there were some inconsistent facts that came up during my interview with Edwin. Like the number of letters and emails Edwin received from Kayleigh. She said Edwin was sent a half-dozen replies—all form emails or snail-mail letters. But in the interview Edwin told me he'd received more than that . . . and he suggested to Pike that he'd found them encouraging. I thought at first that was a product of his problems with reality awareness. But then I realised that stalkers may misinterpret the *implications* of facts but they'll know what those facts *are*. However Edwin misconstrued Kayleigh's message in the letters, he'd know for certain exactly how many letters he received. Did that mean somebody else, posing as Kayleigh, had been sending him emails and letters?

'And then I wondered why Peter Simesky was interested in me. He wanted to see how we were progressing with the investigation and what we knew. When we met in Kayleigh's house, Myra Babbage seemed interested in who I worked for. It was as an odd question, out of place. And the two of them, and Davis, had flown into San Francisco the other day; they might've bought the prepaid mobiles in Burlingame then. It's near the airport.'

Madigan muttered, 'So they killed Bobby and the file sharer to establish the pattern of Edwin's guilt.'

'Yeah, I think that's the only reason those two died,' Dance said, She glanced at Rhyme. 'After I got your text about the bird excrement, I became suspicious about people close to Davis. I emailed my associate, TJ Scanlon, to run deep background checks on Davis's staff. Everybody was clean—but Simesky and Myra were too clean. And they'd joined the campaign on the same day. And it was impossible to find out anything about them before they joined. TJ kept digging and found some connection with a group called the Keyholders, who were on record as condemning Davis's stand on easier immigration. I decided to play it safe and we got out through the side window of the safe house just as Myra arrived and engaged Tim.' A nod towards Raymond. 'We know what happened next.'

Deputy Crystal Stanning walked into the sheriff's office. 'We just found the woman who gave Edwin directions when he got lost.'

Ah, Alibi Woman.

'Edwin was right. It was at the same time Sheri Towne was attacked. And she positively identified him.'

Madigan sighed. 'Well, we got this one wrong, boys and girls. Get Sharp in here. I for one am going to apologise.'

A moment later Edwin was escorted into the office and he looked around a little bewildered, though he was fascinated with Rhyme.

Gonzalez explained that most of the emails Edwin had received from Kayleigh were fake, not from her at all.

Dance noted his face fall. 'She didn't send them?'

Dance said, 'I'm sorry, Edwin, the ones actually from her were just form letters. Like she sent to everybody.'

Edwin slipped his hands into his pockets. 'I never would've got so . . . funny about her, if I knew.'

'I understand, Edwin,' Dance said.

Madigan said, 'I'm sorry too, son.'

Edwin said nothing for a moment. 'So, I'm not a suspect?'

'Nope,' Harutyun said.

Edwin nodded and then focused on Madigan. 'Well, then, I don't have much interest in that complaint I made against you and Deputy Lopez. I was just doing what I needed to, you understand?'

'I do, and that's good of you, Edwin.'

'I'd kind of like to leave now. Is that OK?'

'Sure is, son. We'll get a statement from you tomorrow about what hap-pened during the kidnapping. I'll have somebody get you home now. You're in no shape to drive.'

'Thanks, Detective.' Shoulders down, chest collapsed, he headed out of the door. Dance could see genuine sorrow in his posture.

Shortly afterwards Lincoln Rhyme and his New York companions said their goodbyes. They were headed back to San Jose but would all be meet-ing up again at Kathryn's party on Sunday.

Dance walked outside with O'Neil. He was leaving too. He needed to get back to Monterey. Dance watched as he got into his car.

'I'll see you on Sunday,' he said.

'Drive carefully,' she said. A phrase that had set her on edge when her parents would tell teenage Kathryn the same. As if, oh, right, I was going to drive off the road until you reminded me.

But as a woman who'd lost one husband to the highway, it was a sentence she could not stop herself from uttering occasionally.

O'Neil closed the door and put the car in gear, then pulled out of the lot.

THURSDAY

9

Kathryn Dance spent the following day not as a law-enforcement agent but as a recording engineer and producer in a garage recording a band who played the traditional style of music from northeastern Mexico. After the session ended, just after 5 p.m., she packed up her cables and microphones and wandered back to the Pathfinder. Her phone hummed and she saw Madigan's text, asking if she would come in and review the transcript of her report about the Peter Simesky–Myra Babbage case, which she'd dictated last night. Scrolling through her iPhone she also saw a missed call. Jon Boling. Her finger hit redial. A trill of numbers. Then . . . voicemail. She didn't leave a message.

A half-hour later she arrived at Madigan's office. The chief detective had been officially reinstated.

'Don't you ever do sprinkles or whipped cream or syrup on your ice cream?' she asked, sitting down on the battered couch, eyeing the cardboard cup he was enthusiastically excavating.

'Naw, it's a waste of taste. Calories too. This's yours.' He produced another cup. Chocolate chip. A metal spoon too.

'No, I—'

'You say no too quick, Deputy,' Madigan grumbled. 'You want some ice cream. I know you do.'

True. She took it and ate several mouthfuls. 'It's good.'

'Course it's good. It's ice cream. There's the statement, you want to take a look-see.' He slid the papers towards her and she read.

Crystal Stanning had transcribed it from Dance's tape—and it was pretty accurate. She was expanding on a thought or two when the detective's phone rang and he hit the speaker button. 'Yeah?'

'Hey, Chief, it's Miguel Lopez. Something kind of funny. I was listening to radio station KDHT on my way home and there's a call-in show. About five minutes ago some listener requests a song. I mean, *part* of a song. One of Kayleigh's.'

Dance froze. Madigan barked, 'And?'

'The request was in an email. It was for "Your Shadow", the last verse only. The DJ thought it was kind of funny, just one verse, and played the whole song. But I got to thinking—'

'Oh God,' Dance whispered. 'Nobody ever played the fourth verse—to announce Congressman Davis's killing!'

'Shoot.' Madigan was nodding. He asked Lopez if the radio show caller's email had said anything else.

'No. Just that.'

Madigan disconnected without saying goodbye. He called the station, got put through to the studio, told the DJ it was police business and asked that the caller's email be forwarded to him. As he and Dance waited, he muttered, 'And, hell, you know, we're still looking for the connection between Simesky and Babbage and Bobby and that file sharer—or the attack on Sheri Towne. But nobody's found anything.'

A moment later an email popped up on his computer screen. The request to the studio was from a cryptic account, of random letters and numbers. Madigan called the Computer Crimes Division and forwarded it. They soon learned that it was an anonymous free email account and had been sent from a hotel in the Tower District.

'Let's get the list of guests staying there,' Madigan said.

But Dance frowned. 'He won't be a guest. He would've just picked up the wireless signal in the lobby or from the parking lot.'

'You think that the assassination plot was just a coincidence? And there really *is* a stalker?'

'Well, we know it can't be Edwin. He has an alibi. And it doesn't need to be a stalker. It could be *anybody* trying to frame Edwin to cover up the killings—of Bobby or the file sharer—or Sheri Towne's attack.' She shook her head. 'Or maybe those were just to establish a pattern . . . and the intended victim's *next* on his list.'

'But who's the new vic? What's the fourth verse?'

Dance recited:

> '*You can't keep down smiles; happiness floats.*
> *But trouble can find us in the heart of our homes.*
> *Life never seems to go quite right,*
> *You can't watch your back from morning to night.*'

Madigan sighed. 'Kill somebody in their home. That's like the other verse, about the road—not very helpful.'

'OK, we've got to narrow it down more.' Dance thought for a moment. 'You know, there was some physical evidence that Charlie's people found that we never really looked at—because we had enough to figure out what Simesky and Myra were up to.'

Madigan called Charlie Shean, at CSU, had a conversation with him and jotted notes. After hanging up, he said, 'What wasn't accounted for was gangue, industrial by-product stuff. And Marlboros. Also the boot print, with the really sharp toe. And some neat's-foot oil—leather treatment for baseball gloves. Maybe the dearly departed Peter Simesky played in a fascist softball league.'

Dance cocked her head. 'That's not all it's used for.'

FINALLY, KAYLEIGH TOWNE was back in her own house, her sanctuary. Alicia Sessions had texted that she wanted to see her about some matters having to do with the concert but she didn't want to meet her at Bishop's house. When Alicia suggested they meet at Kayleigh's she readily agreed. Darthur Morgan had driven her back here and then he'd collected his own car and said goodbye.

After he'd driven away, Kayleigh was alone. But the relief she felt because Edwin wasn't a dangerous stalker was fading, and discomfort that struck closer to home seeped in to replace it.

'Hey, look at the good news, KT. The bad guys're dead and Edwin's out of the picture. So, no more talk about cancelling any concerts,' her father had said yesterday after Kathryn Dance had visited them and told them how Edwin had been set up.

Why hadn't she said no to her father? Just *insisted* that they cancel the concert? It wasn't that Bobby was dead, that Sheri'd nearly died . . . She just plain and simple didn't want to get up onstage.

I'm not Superwoman, Daddy. Your goals aren't my goals.

Why was he so oblivious to that? The whole industry was a huge bulldozer, pushing forward, and if somebody got crushed—Bobby's life, Kayleigh's joy—so what? It was unstoppable.

No, of course Bishop Towne didn't get that. All he got was that Kayleigh had to make money, had to feed her staff and family, had to feed the voracious fans, had to keep the record label happy.

And screw his daughter's own peace of mind.

Screw what mattered most to her: just having a simple life.

Kayleigh glanced at her watch. Alicia wasn't due for another half-hour. She walked upstairs to her bedroom. Through her mind went a verse from the now-infamous 'Your Shadow':

> *You sit by the river, wondering what you got wrong,*
> *How many chances you've missed all along.*
> *Like your troubles had somehow turned you to stone*
> *And the water was whispering, why don't you come home?*

What a time that had been, just sixteen, missing her mother, missing her baby; her father, just out of jail for the car accident, pressuring her to launch her own career. It had been too much for her. She'd driven to Yosemite by herself. And she'd looked down at the clear river and walked into it. Not really intending to hurt herself—or maybe she had been. A minute later a hiker had plucked her out and sped her to the hospital. She was in danger more of hypothermia than drowning but not even much threat of that.

Now Kayleigh sat on the bed and read once more the copy of Bobby's letter, which Kathryn had given her last night. It expressed his desire that most everything he had should go to Mary-Gordon. She didn't know if this was legal as a will but if she took it to a lawyer she supposed the news would become public about Mary-Gordon's parentage.

Bishop would explode. And the fans? Would they desert her? There was also a chance that the girl herself would find out. She'd learn at some point. But not at this age. Kayleigh didn't want to disrupt the girl's life. She slipped the envelope into a drawer in her dressing table.

It was too late for Kayleigh when it came to Bobby and Mary-Gordon. But it wasn't too late for the life she dreamed of. Find a man, get married, have other babies, play music on the front porch, maybe a few concerts now and then.

Since Bobby, there'd been no one she had felt really intense about. Oh, Bobby . . . Kayleigh cried for a few minutes. Then she went to the bathroom, filled the tub and stripped. She sank into the deep water. It felt wonderful.

THEY HAD THEIR ANSWER.

Dance, Harutyun and Madigan were in Alicia Sessions's apartment, surveying the evidence. Cowboy boots, with needle-sharp toes, like those that made the prints behind Edwin's house. And in the kitchen was neat's-foot oil for treating Alicia's equestrian tack. They found cartons of Marlboros in her apartment. The dwelling was in the Tower District, too, near the hotel from which the email request for the fourth song had been sent.

But far more incriminating were two garbage bags full of Edwin Sharp's trash, stolen from his house in Fresno, to plant at Kayleigh's, to convince the police and jury that Edwin was behind the attacks and that he had killed Kayleigh. And under Alicia's bed was Deputy Gabriel Fuentes's pistol case—without the weapon—stolen from near the theatre when the cop was tailing Edwin.

At first they hadn't come up with a motive for her setting up Sharp. But a moment ago Dance had learned the answer. To Madigan and Harutyun, she displayed two dozen sheets of paper, all pretty much the same—attempts to forge Kayleigh's handwriting on a note that read:

Just want to say a few things to the people close to me if anything happens to me on the road . . . Can't help but thinking about Patsy Cline in that airplane. Well, if anything does, I'd like Alicia to take over as front for the band. She knows the songs as good as me and can hit those high notes better. I see you in heaven, luv you all! Kayleigh

'Oh my God,' Madigan muttered, 'Kayleigh's the fourth victim. The last verse: "Trouble can find us in the heart of our homes". Alicia's going to kill her in her house.'

Dance punched the singer's number into her phone.

KAYLEIGH WAS thoroughly enjoying the bath when in the other room she heard her phone ring. She debated. *Ignore it.*

Then, hearing the mobile trill again, she thought of Mary-Gordon. Was Suellyn calling because she was sick? Concern for the little girl was what prodded Kayleigh out of the tub. She dried off and dressed fast in jeans and a blouse. Pulled on socks.

She picked up the phone. Ah, Kathryn. She hit the CALLBACK button. As it rang, she glanced out of the window. It was dark but she made out Alicia's blue pick-up truck sitting in the drive. Kayleigh hadn't heard her arrive but she could let herself in. She had a key.

Dance's phone clicked.

Kayleigh started to say, 'Hey, how're—?'

But the agent said urgently, 'Kayleigh, listen to me. Alicia is on her way there. She's going to kill you. Get out of the house. Now!'

'What?'

'Just get out!'

Downstairs, the kitchen door opened and Alicia called out, 'Hey, Kayleigh. It's me. You decent?'

THROUGH HER PHONE Kathryn Dance heard Kayleigh's voice catch. Then she whispered, 'She's here! She's downstairs. Alicia!'

Dance, Harutyun and Madigan were in the FMCSO cruiser speeding away from Alicia's apartment. Dance said into the phone, 'Get out. Can you run into the woods?'

'I . . . I'm upstairs. I don't think I can jump. And I'd have to go past her if I went downstairs. Can I talk to her? Why does she—'

'No, you have to hide, stay away. She has a gun. We'll have troopers there in twenty minutes. Are you in a room with a lock?'

'My bedroom. Yes. But it's not much.'

'Just barricade yourself in the room and stall. We'll be there soon.'

The siren spread outwards on the hot, dry air and the blue and white lights ricocheted off cars as they raced through the evening.

'KAYLEIGH?' ALICIA CALLED again from downstairs.

'Just out of the shower. I'll be down in five.' Kayleigh closed and locked the door. But the chair she tried to wedge under the knob was too low. Her dressing table was too heavy to move.

Don't be an idiot, jump!

She ran to the window. Below her was not only concrete but a wrought-iron fence. If she didn't break her back she'd be impaled.

Then her phone rang. The caller ID said that it was Edwin Sharp!

'Hello, Edwin?'

He said tentatively, 'Hey, Kayleigh, listen. I'm almost there. Alicia asked me not to call you, just to come over. But, I don't know, what's this all about? I don't want anything from you. It wasn't your fault what that guy with the congressman did.'

And with a heart-shaking jolt, Kayleigh understood. Alicia had set up Edwin. She'd asked *him* here too and was going to make it look like *he* killed her.

'Oh, Edwin, stay away! Alicia's here. She's going to kill me—'

A pause. 'You're not, like, serious?'

'She's setting you up. She's here now.'

'I'll call the police.'

She said, 'I did. They're on their way.'

'I'm five minutes away.'

'No, Edwin, don't come here! That way nobody can blame you for whatever happens.'

It was then that Kayleigh smelled smoke. Edwin was saying something. She ignored him and turned her ear towards the door. Yes, the crackle of flames was coming from downstairs. *Like Bobby, the file sharer and Sheri, she's going to burn me too.*

'Kayleigh, Kayleigh?' Edwin's voice rose from her phone.

'There's a fire, Edwin. Call the fire department too. But don't come here. Whatever you do.' She disconnected.

THE SMOKE AND FLAMES were growing. Outside the window, reflections of the flames flickered across trees and the lawn.

Kayleigh debated. Where was Alicia? She couldn't stay downstairs in the flames, of course. She'd probably left.

Kayleigh ran into the bathroom, grabbed a fire extinguisher. She unlocked the bedroom door, eased it open. The fire was in the hallway on the ground floor and on the stairs. Kayleigh caught a full breath of the foul stench and retched. She lowered her head and got a breath of clean air. The fire wasn't out of control yet. If Alicia had left she could beat down the flames enough to get to the kitchen, where there was a bigger extinguisher. And the hose in the garden. She eased out.

Just then a huge bang from downstairs resounded through the house, a flash in the smoke. A bullet ploughed into the door near her head. Two more.

Screaming, she dived back into her room and slammed the door, locked it. Kayleigh decided she had no choice but to risk a twenty-five-foot jump to the ground. Running to the window, she flung it open and looked towards the road. No flashing lights yet. Then she gazed down, trying to judge angles and distances.

She found a place she might land, just past the fence. But then she saw, at the exact spot where she'd land, Alicia's shadow moving back and forth, almost leisurely. She was at the front door and probably anticipating Kayleigh's jump and aiming at that very spot.

Kayleigh put down the fire extinguisher and sat down on the bed, grabbed a picture she had of Mary-Gordon and hugged it to her chest. So, this was it. *Mama, Bobby, I'll be with you soon.* More tears.

But just then another gunshot resounded from downstairs . . . then two or three more. Kayleigh gasped. Could the police be here after all? She ran to the window and looked out. No, no one was here. The driveway was empty, except for Alicia's pick-up.

And from downstairs, a man's voice calling her name. 'Kayleigh, come on, hurry!'

She picked up the extinguisher, opened the door cautiously and peered down. Through the smoke she could make out Edwin Sharp, beating down the flames on the stairs with his jacket. Alicia lay on her back in the hallway, eyes gazing up, unseeing. Her clothes were on fire.

Kayleigh understood. Edwin had ignored her warning and continued to the house anyway.

'Hurry!' he cried. 'Come on! I called the fire department but I don't know when they'll be here. You have to get out!'

His slapping at the flames wasn't doing much to stop the spread, though he'd beaten out a path down the stairs to the ground floor.

Kayleigh made her way along this now. He was pointing into the den. 'We can get out that way, through the window!'

But she said, 'You go! I'm going to fight it.' She turned the small extinguisher on the flames.

Edwin hesitated, coughing hard. 'I'll help you.'

She shouted, 'In the kitchen, there's another extinguisher!'

Choking, Edwin staggered through the arched doorway and returned a moment later with the extinguisher, much bigger than Kayleigh's, and started to douse the flames too.

Kayleigh ran out of the back door and came back with the garden hose. She began attacking the stubborn fire as Edwin, next to her, blew bursts of foam from the big extinguisher. They both retched and coughed and tried to blink away tears from the smoke.

Soon sirens sounded and outside the evening darkness filled with flashing lights as the first fire trucks arrived. Men and women in their thick yellow outfits hurried into the house with hoses and began battling the flames. One fireman bent over Alicia's body and felt for a pulse. He looked up and shook his head.

Another ushered Kayleigh and Edwin towards the front door and they staggered outside. Kayleigh made her way down the stairs into the garden, coughing and spitting terrible bits of soot and ash from her mouth. She looked back, realising that Edwin was lagging behind.

She saw him on his knees on the porch. His hand was at his throat. He lifted his fingers away and she could see they were dark but not stained with soot. It was blood flowing from a wound in his neck.

Alicia had shot him before he'd wrestled the gun away from her.

He blinked and looked at Kayleigh. 'I think . . . I think she . . .' His eyes closed and he collapsed back on the wooden deck.

KATHRYN DANCE was sitting next to Kayleigh Towne on the steps of her house. They were bathed in a sweep of coloured lights, blue and red, with flashes of white. The young woman was smeared with Edwin Sharp's blood, from trying to staunch the bleeding.

P. K. Madigan was directing the FMCSO's crime scene team in their search of the house.

'I don't understand any of this,' Kayleigh whispered.

Dance explained what they'd learned about Alicia and found in her apartment—the things she'd stolen from Edwin's rental. 'She was going to plant them here. There was a note too. She'd forged your handwriting. If anything happened to you, you wanted her to take over the band.'

'So she asked Edwin here tonight so it'd look like he'd killed me. He gets arrested, nobody believes him when he says he's innocent.'

'Exactly.'

Kayleigh's jaw tightened. 'Alicia wanted fame and money and power. That's what this business does to people. It seduces them. I told Edwin not to come. I knew he'd get blamed if anything happened. But he came anyway.'

As some medical techs got Edwin into an ambulance, another approached them. 'Agent Dance. Ms Towne . . . Mr Sharp's lost a lot of blood. We have to get him to the hospital for surgery.'

'Is he going to live?' Kayleigh asked.

'We don't know at this time. Was he a friend?'

Kayleigh said softly, 'In a way. He's a fan of mine.'

TWO HOURS LATER, a tired-looking surgeon walked slowly down the bleached-lit hallway of Fresno Community Hospital towards the waiting area. Dance looked at Kayleigh and together they rose.

The man said that Edwin Sharp would survive. 'The bullet missed the carotid and his spine.' Edwin would be coming round from the anaesthetic now. They could see him for a few minutes.

Dance and Kayleigh found the recovery room and stepped inside to find Edwin staring groggily at the ceiling.

'Hey,' he mumbled. 'Feels like it did when I had my tonsils out.' He spoke softly and a bit garbled. And he seemed drained.

Kayleigh said, 'You look pretty good, all things considered.'

Though the bullet hole would be fairly small, the bruise extended well beyond the thick bandage covering the wound.

'Doesn't, uhm, you know, hurt much yet.' He studied an IV drip, probably morphine. He added, 'I'm getting discharged tomorrow morning.' He had a loopy grin on his face.

'I'm glad you're feeling better,' Kayleigh said. 'I was worried.'

He frowned. Speaking slowly, 'Didn't bring me flowers, I notice. No flowers. Afraid I'd misinterpret it?' Then he laughed. 'Joking.'

Kayleigh did a double take, then smiled too.

Edwin's face grew sombre. 'Alicia . . . what was that all about? Did she go crazy? I mean, Alicia. What happened?'

Dance said, 'She was going to kill Kayleigh and plant some things she got from your house so you'd get blamed for it. She forged a note saying that Kayleigh wanted Alicia to front the band.'

'She killed Bobby Prescott too? And attacked your stepmother?'

Kayleigh nodded, her eyes damp. She whispered, 'I don't know what to say, Edwin. What a mess this's all been.'

He tried to shrug but winced from the pain.

'You didn't need to come to the house. I told you it was dangerous.'

'What happened back there at Kayleigh's?' Dance asked.

He struggled to focus. 'Well, she told me about Alicia and the fire so I called the fire department but I couldn't stop. You told me to stop, right?'

'I did.'

'But I couldn't. I kept going to the house. I parked on the shoulder at the front, so Alicia wouldn't see me. When I got to the house, the kitchen door was open and I saw Alicia by the stairs. She didn't see me. I tackled her. She was really strong. The gun went off before I got it away from her. She jumped at me and I didn't think. I just pulled the trigger. I didn't even know *I* got shot. All I remember is we were trying to put the fire out . . . and then

I woke up here.' His eyes closed slowly then opened. 'After I get out of the hospital, I'm headed back to Seattle.' A wan smile.

'Leaving?'

'Better for you, I think.' He laughed. 'Better for me too, you know. You think a famous star kind of likes you, then next thing some crazy people want to use you to assassinate a politician and some psycho's stolen your trash to frame you for murder. Never thought being a fan could be so dangerous. Think I'm . . . better off in Seattle.' His head eased towards his chest.

Kayleigh smiled but said earnestly, 'Edwin, you can't drive like this. Wait a couple of days. Please. And if you're feeling up to it, come to the concert. I'll get you a ticket front row centre.'

He was fading fast. 'No . . . Better. It's better if I . . .'

Then he was sound asleep.

FRIDAY

10

The day of the show. The band had arrived from Nashville at 9 a.m. and come straight to the convention centre, where Kayleigh and the crew were waiting. They got right to work.

The rehearsal was informal; the band had performed most of the material so often, it probably wasn't even necessary, but there was a new song order and Kayleigh had written two new songs, which she'd faxed to the band last night. One was dedicated to Bobby.

After the rehearsal, Kayleigh announced to the band, 'OK, that's it for now; reconvene at six for the final sound check.'

She picked up her phone and did something she couldn't have imagined until today. Kayleigh Towne called Edwin Sharp.

'Hello?' He still sounded a bit groggy.

'Hey, it's Kayleigh. Are you in the hospital still?'

He laughed. 'Didn't think I'd hear from you. No. I got sprung.'

'How you feeling?'

'Sore, sore, sore.'

'Well, I hope you're well enough to come to the show,' she said firmly. 'I got you a ticket.'

There was silence and she wondered if he was going to refuse. But he said, 'OK. Thanks.'

'I've got it now. Meet you for lunch?'

She could have left it at the box office but that seemed petty, considering what he'd done for her.

He said, 'Sure.'

He suggested a diner he'd been to. She agreed and they disconnected. Kayleigh headed for the stage door.

She had woken that morning at her father's house, thinking that the concert was the last thing she wanted. But once she'd arrived here and walked out onstage, her attitude changed. Now she couldn't wait for the concert. Nothing was going to stop her from giving the audience the best show they'd ever seen.

KAYLEIGH MET EDWIN in the front of the diner. The restaurant was in a quiet part of town. He greeted her at the door and let her precede him into the restaurant, which was nearly empty.

They sat at a booth and ordered iced teas and, for Kayleigh, a burger. Edwin got a milk shake; the wound in his neck made chewing painful, he explained.

They talked about Congressman Davis and Alicia for a time, then life in Fresno and Seattle. Then their order came and they ate, and sipped. He asked, 'How's your house?'

'I'll need new carpets, have to replace a lot of floor and a wall. The big problem is the smoke damage. It got into everything.'

'Sorry.'

When they were through with lunch, Kayleigh gave Edwin his ticket. 'Front and centre.'

The bill came and Edwin insisted on paying.

They walked into the parking lot. As they approached her Suburban, Kayleigh noticed Edwin's old red car, a few spaces down from hers.

'Hey, now that you know I'm not the crazy person you thought I was, how about dinner after the concert?' Edwin asked.

'I usually go out with the band.'

'Oh, that's right. Well, some time maybe . . . how 'bout Sunday? You don't leave again for two weeks. The Vancouver show.'

'Well . . . weren't you leaving?'

He pointed to his throat. 'Taking pain pills. Better if I don't do any long-distance driving. I'm back in the rental for a few days.'

'Oh, sure, you have to be careful.' They were at her SUV. 'OK, thank you again, Edwin. For everything you did.'

'"I'd Do It All Again",' he said, smiling. One of her first hits. Kayleigh laughed, and he said, 'Hey, I could drive up to Canada. Vancouver's not that far from Seattle. I know some great places—'

She smiled. 'Edwin, it's probably best if we don't get together.'

'Sure. Only . . . well, after everything, I just thought . . .'

'It's probably best,' she repeated. 'Goodbye, Edwin.'

'So . . . you're breaking up with me?' he asked.

She started to laugh, thinking he was making light of her comments—like his reference to the flowers in the hospital last night. But his eyes narrowed. And the smile morphed into the one she recognised from before. The faint twisting of his lip, fake.

'You take care,' she said quickly, unlocking the car door.

'Don't go,' he said in a breathy whisper.

Kayleigh looked around. The parking lot was deserted. 'Edwin.'

He said quickly, 'Wait. I'm sorry. Look, let's just take a drive and talk. We can just talk.'

'I think I should go.'

She turned fast but Edwin stepped forward, quickly gripping her arm. 'Please, just a little drive.' He looked at his watch. 'You don't have to be at the concert hall for six hours and thirty minutes.'

'No, Edwin. Stop it! Get out of my way. Let go of me!' She tried to push him away. It was like trying to move a sack of concrete.

He said ominously, 'I was almost killed.' He pointed to his neck. 'I was almost killed saving you! Did you forget that?'

Oh Jesus Lord. He shot himself. Alicia was innocent. He set her up. Edwin had killed Bobby, he killed Alicia! I don't know how but he did it.

'Please, Edwin!'

He released her and looked contrite. 'I'm so sorry. Here's the thing, you need a place to stay. You could stay with me until your house is fixed.'

She tried to bolt. But his hand went round her face. An arm gripped her chest and he dragged her to the back of his Buick and opened the trunk. The struggle for air became hopeless. As her vision crumbled to black, she heard a voice, singing, 'Always with you, always with you, your shadow.'

THE CASE WAS OVER. But for Kathryn Dance a greater problem loomed: Jon Boling.

She told herself: *Call Jon. Have it out.* Her intention was to ask why he was moving to San Diego without talking to her first.

Dance scrutinised her mobile and hit CALL.

Boling's phone rang once. Twice. Three times.

She disconnected fast. Not because she'd lost her nerve about talking to him; no, another thought had surfaced.

How did Edwin Sharp know that Alicia had stolen his trash? That's what he'd said in the hospital. Yet she'd never mentioned the fact. Dance had said only that Alicia had taken some things of his. That she had garbage bags in her apartment was never mentioned.

Slow down, she told herself. Think.

Could he have learned about it another way? She decided no. At Kayleigh's house last night he was unconscious for most of the time. Only the medics spoke to him. A logical deduction on his part? If Alicia had planted something of his it made sense for her to have taken his trash.

Surely possible. But another explanation was that *Edwin* had put the two bags of his trash in Alicia's apartment himself, along with the notes supposedly forged by her, but that he himself had produced. He'd then planted the evidence outside his own house, like the neat's-foot oil trace and the boot print to implicate Alicia, as the spy.

No, no, this was absurd. The shooting incident at Kayleigh's house? That surely had been Alicia.

Or had it?

Rethink the scenario, Dance told herself. Was there any possible way Edwin had orchestrated it? Think. How would *you* have set it up?

And the ideas began to form.

He goes to Alicia's, ties her up, plants his own trash, Gabriel Fuentes's gun case and the forgeries of Kayleigh's note there. Uses her phone to send texts to Kayleigh and to his own phone about meeting at Kayleigh's house, and goes to the hotel near Alicia's to send the request for the fourth verse to the radio station.

But there were two cars at Kayleigh's. His own and Alicia's. Well, maybe he pays someone to drive his car to the front of Kayleigh's house and leave it there, then vanish. Then he drives to Kayleigh's in Alicia's pick-up, with her tied up in the back. Maybe she was already dead at that point.

But Kayleigh heard Alicia calling her name in the house.

A tape recorder!

Edwin could have threatened her back at the apartment to say Kayleigh's name into a high-def digital recorder—the same one used to play 'Your Shadow' to announce the impending murder.

With your eyes closed, you couldn't tell the difference between someone really singing or the digital replay. Only a pro would have a recorder like that.

Dance recalled her reply to Kayleigh: *Or a fanatical fan.*

He'd probably planned out several scenarios for the 'rescue' of Kayleigh Towne—depending on where the singer was in the house when he got there. But when he'd arrived at the house he would have seen her in the bedroom. That gave him the chance to get inside and masquerade as Alicia—all thanks to Dance herself, of course, who'd called Kayleigh and told her to barricade herself upstairs.

And Edwin's wound? Well, if he was mobile now, the gunshot may have been dramatic but obviously it wasn't that serious.

Dance pulled a portion of her own skin away from her neck. Yes, he could easily have shot himself and missed anything vital.

It's a wild theory. But . . .

Close enough for me, Dance decided and called Kayleigh. No answer. She called Bishop Towne and told him what she suspected.

'Oh, damn,' the man growled. 'She's having lunch with Edwin right now! Sheri was at the convention centre for the rehearsal. Kayleigh left an hour ago to meet him.'

'Where?'

'The San Joaquin Diner, on Third. Do you—'

Dance hung up and dialled the sheriff's office.

'Madigan,' came the voice.

'Chief, it's Kathryn. I think Edwin's our perp after all.'

'What? But . . . Alicia?'

'Later. Listen. He and Kayleigh're at the San Joaquin Diner. On Third. We need a car there now.'

'Gotcha. I'll get back to you.'

Dance paced along the carpet until P. K. Madigan called back and, in a rattled voice blurted, 'She and Edwin left the diner a half-hour ago. But her SUV's still in the lot. And her keys were on the ground nearby.'

'She dropped them to let us know what happened. Her phone?'

'Battery's out or been crushed. No signal to trace. I sent Lopez to Edwin's house and the red Buick's there. But the place looks like he's moved out.'

'He's got new wheels.'

'Yep. But I checked. Either stolen or bought private. Nothing at DMV in his name, no rentals at any of the companies in our database. He could be driving anything. And going anywhere.'

ALIBI WOMAN HAD LIED. When Dance had spoken to her on the phone twenty minutes earlier, seventy-two-year-old Mrs Rachel Webber had once again—and very quickly—verified Edwin's story about the time he'd been at her house on Tuesday. But it took the agent only three minutes of questioning to learn what had really happened: Edwin had found her in the garden early that morning. He'd forced her inside with a gun and got the names of her children and grandchildren and said that when the police came to ask her, she was to say he was there at twelve thirty.

Now Dance was in Madigan's office. How did I miss it? She hadn't been able to read Edwin's deception but she'd known that body language analysis of someone like him would be difficult. So she'd looked at the facts he'd mentioned, tried to analyse his verbal content. Was there anything that might help them find where Edwin would go with his love?

Something was eating away at her. Something elusive. Facts again . . . verbal content. Facts were not meshing.

What is it? She sighed.

Then: Wait . . . Yes! That's it!

She grabbed the phone and placed a call to her colleague, Amy Grabe, FBI Special Agent in Charge, San Francisco.

The woman's low, sultry voice said, 'Kathryn, saw the wire—kidnapping and possible interstate flight. What can we do?'

'That's why I'm calling.' Dance asked for a couple of field agents in the Seattle area who could conduct an interview for her with a witness.

'Can't you do it over the phone?' Grabe asked.

'I tried that. It didn't work.'

WELL, THOUGHT KATHRYN DANCE, staring at the computer screen. Look at this. The woman she was gazing at, presently in Seattle and connected via Skype, could have been Kayleigh Towne's sister.

Straight blonde hair, a petite frame, a long, pretty face.

Edwin's former girlfriend, Sally Docking, stared nervously at the computer screen. Her voice broke as she said, 'These people, I don't understand. I didn't do anything wrong.' There were two FBI agents behind her in the living room of her Seattle apartment.

Dance said casually, 'I just needed them to bring one of their computers so you and I could have another chat.'

'Sure.'

Now that Sharp had been revealed to be the perp, his behaviour with Sally Docking didn't ring true. Her earlier account of life with Edwin had been credible over the phone but a kinesic expert needs to *see* her subject, not just hear, to spot deception. And so Amy Grabe had sent two agents to Sally's apartment. They had brought with them an expensive laptop, with a high-definition webcam.

Dance was in a conference room in the sheriff's office, the overhead lights off but a desk lamp not far from her face. She needed Sally to see her very clearly—and under ominous lighting.

Dance asked a number of questions about the girl, her family, her job as she drew a baseline of her behaviour. She was getting a feel for the woman, who appeared nervous and uncertain even when she was being asked simple questions and answering truthfully. After ten minutes of this, Dance said, 'Now, I'd like to talk to you about Edwin some more.'

'Everything I told you was true!' Her eyes bored into the camera.

Dance said calmly, 'We need your help, Sally. I'm worried that Edwin could hurt somebody in Fresno. Or hurt himself.'

'No!'

'That's right.' Dance had made certain that not a single soul leaked to the public the news that Edwin had snatched Kayleigh. Sally Docking wouldn't know. 'And we need to find him. We need to know where he might go, places that're important to him, other residences he might have.'

'Oh, I don't know anywhere like that. I haven't heard from him in a long time.' Her eyes whipped to the computer screen.

A baseline variation. It confirmed that she did have some ideas.

'You might know more than you think, Sally. Not necessarily someplace he wanted to move to. Just a place he mentioned when you were together.'

Sally was thinking quickly. 'He was pretty much into Seattle. He didn't travel much. He was, like, a homebody kind of guy.'

'Never mentioned anything, really?' A glance at the sheet in front of her.

Sally caught the glance. 'He talked about going on vacations some. Nashville was one place he wanted to go. To see the Grand Ole Opry. And New York so he could go to some concerts.'

Edwin Sharp probably did say that but he was not going to run off to Nashville or Manhattan with Kayleigh Towne and set up housekeeping, however skewed was his sense of reality.

But Dance said, 'That's just the sort of thing we're looking for. Can you think of any other places?'

'No.' Eyes on the web camera.

Lie. Dance grimaced. 'I don't know what I'm going to do. You were really the only person we could turn to. I mean you had a different relationship with Edwin from some people. You won't believe it but he can be very abusive and obsessive.'

'No, really?'

Dance's heart tapped faster. She was on the trail of her prey and closing in. 'That's right. When people reject him, that pushes a button. Edwin has issues about abandonment and rejection. He clings to people. Since *he* broke up with *you*, you're not a negative in his life. In fact, he told me he still feels bad about the breakup.'

'You were talking about me with Edwin? Like, recently?' Delivered fast.

'That's right. Funny, you could get the impression, from what he said, that he kind of misses you.' Dance crafted her words carefully. She never intentionally deceived her subjects but sometimes let them do it for her. 'I wouldn't be surprised if he was curious what you're up to.'

Sally asked in a higher pitch—a stress tone—'What did he want to know?'

'Just general things.' Dance saw a glistening of sweat on Sally's forehead. 'Your brother in Spokane? And your mother in Tacoma?'

'I just . . . my brother, my mother?'

'Edwin was close to them?'

The stalker had not said more than one or two sentences about Sally Docking and nothing at all about her family. Dance had looked up the details through Washington state and federal records.

'Did he say anything about *them?*' Sally asked.

'What's the matter, Sally? Would you be concerned if Edwin showed some interest in your family?'

'What did he *say?* Please tell me!' The tears began.

Dance said, 'Why are you troubled? Tell me.'

'He's going to hurt my family! He won't understand that I did what he wanted. If he mentioned them to you it means he's going to hurt them to get back at me. Please, you have to do something!'

'Wait.' Dance looked troubled. 'I hope you're not telling me that *you're* the one who wanted to break up.'

'I—'

'Oh, no. That changes everything.' She peered at Sally uneasily.

'Please! No! Where is he? Is Edwin going to Tacoma, Spokane? Don't let him hurt my mama!' She was sobbing now. 'Please! And my brother's got two babies!'

The scenario was playing out just as Dance had planned. She had needed to plant the seeds of fear within Sally to get her to open up.

Breathless with tears. 'I did what he wanted. Why is he going to hurt us?'

Dance said, 'We can help you, Sally. But we can't do anything for you or your mother or brother if you're not honest.'

Sally struggled for breath. 'I'm sorry I lied. He told me if anybody asked, I was to tell them that he was the greatest guy and never stalked me and *he* broke up with *me*, not the other way around. I'm sorry but I was scared. Send the police to my mom's and my brother. I'll give you the addresses.'

'First, tell me the truth, Sally. Then we'll see about the police. What's the real story between Edwin and you?'

'Last year Edwin was a security guard in the mall where I worked and he saw me and he got obsessed with me. One thing led to another and we started going out. Only he got weird. I wasn't allowed to do this, couldn't do that. Sometimes he just wanted to sit and look at me. It was so creepy! He'd tell me how beautiful I was. The fact is he thought I looked like this singer—Kayleigh Towne.'

Sally scoffed, 'We had to play her music all the time. He talked about her every day. Mostly it was "poor Kayleigh this, poor Kayleigh that". Nobody understood her, her father sold the family house she loved, her mother died, the fans don't treat her right, the label doesn't record her right. He went on and on. I couldn't take it. I just left one night. He stalked me, but it wasn't terrible. But then his mother died and he freaked out. I mean totally.'

The stressor event that had pushed him over the edge.

'He came over, crying, like his life was over with. I felt bad for him—and I was scared—so we got back together. But he wouldn't go out, he made me drop all my friends. All he wanted was for me to be at home with him, so we could have sex. He'd play her music when we did that. It was horrible! Finally . . .' Sally pulled her sleeve up and displayed an impressive scar on her wrist. 'It was the only way I could get free. But he found me and got me to the emergency room. I think that convinced him to back off.'

'When was this?'

'December, last year.'

The second stressor event that had initiated his stalking Kayleigh.

Dance made a decision. 'He's kidnapped her, Sally.'

'Who, Kayleigh Towne?' Sally whispered.

'We'll protect you and your family. And we'll put him in jail for the rest of his life—he's also killed some people. But we can do that only if you help us. Do you have any idea where he might go?'

'Well, he said he had this, like, religious experience, seeing Kayleigh sing for the first time. An outdoor concert, two years ago. He said if he could live anywhere, that's where it would be. In a cabin in the woods near some town in California, on the ocean. Monterey. I don't know exactly where it is.'

Dance looked at the tear-stained face of her subject. 'That's all right, Sally. I do.'

As THEY DROVE ALONG, Edwin Sharp called into the back of the van, 'We had to say goodbye to her. My red Buick. Sorry.'

Kayleigh was concentrating on not crying. Her nose was stuffed up and she was sure if she started sobbing she'd suffocate. The tape on her mouth was a tight seal. Her hands were cuffed in front of her. She was in the back of the windowless van, on the floor. He'd pulled her boots off, lovingly smelled the leather. She'd been disgusted.

They were about an hour from Fresno, probably in the foothills towards Yosemite or the Sierras because the road seemed to be at an incline. They'd stopped once, after Edwin had glanced into the rearview mirror at her and he'd frowned. He'd pulled off the road and climbed into the back; she'd shied away. A thick strand of her hair had been imprisoned by the duct tape. Edwin had carefully worked the hair free from the adhesive. He'd recited again how long it had been since she'd cut it. 'Ten years, four months.' Then to her horror he'd pulled a brush from his pocket and run it through her hair gently. 'You're so beautiful,' he'd whispered.

Afterwards the drive had resumed.

Kayleigh felt the van turn off the main road and drive along a smaller highway. Ten minutes later the tyres began to crunch over dirt and gravel. Finally the van levelled off and came to a stop.

Edwin climbed out. There was silence for a long moment.

This just isn't fair, Kayleigh thought.

'Hey there!' Edwin was opening the rear door, revealing a field surrounded by a pine forest. He helped her out and gently pulled the tape off her mouth. She inhaled hard, shivering with relief.

Edwin gestured at a small single-wide trailer, covered with camouflage netting. It sat in the middle of the clearing. 'Familiar?'

'Look, if you let me go, you can have a head start. Six hours, ten hours. And I'll arrange to get you money. A million dollars.'

'Doesn't it look familiar?' he repeated, clearly irritated that she wasn't understanding.

She gazed around. It did, yes. Oh my God. Kayleigh realised, stunned, that this was the property she'd grown up on! Where her grandfather had built the family house. Edwin had put the trailer pretty much where the house had been. She remembered that he had been aware that she'd been upset when Bishop sold the property. How had he found the land? A deed search, she supposed.

Kayleigh knew too that because the company that had bought the property here had gone bankrupt, there wasn't a soul around for twenty miles.

Edwin said with a sincere intensity, 'I knew how much this meant. This property. I wanted to give it back to you. You'll have to show me where you rode your pony and walked your dogs.'

She supposed she should have played along, pretended she was touched and then, when his back was turned, grabbed a stone and broke his skull then ran. But revulsion and anger swirled within her. 'How the hell can you say you love me and do this?'

He grinned and gently stroked her hair. 'Kayleigh . . . from the first time I heard your opening number at that concert in Monterey, I knew we were soul mates. It'll take you a little longer but you'll figure it out too. I'll make you the happiest woman in the world.'

He covered the van with a camouflaged tarp and slipped his arm round her shoulders, very firmly. He guided her towards the trailer.

'I don't love you!'

He only laughed. But as they approached the trailer, his gaze morphed from adoring to chill. 'He had sex with you, didn't he? Bobby. Don't say he didn't.' He eyed her carefully.

'Edwin!'

'I have a right to know.' They were at the trailer door. He calmed. 'Sorry. I get my hackles up, thinking about him.' His gaze morphed from adoring to chilling. 'I should carry you over the threshold. The wedding night thing, you know.'

'Don't touch me!'

He pushed the door open and swept her up into his arms as if she weighed nothing at all. He carried her inside. Kayleigh didn't resist; one of his massive hands insistently cradled her throat.

'WE'RE ON OUR WAY,' Kathryn Dance said into her phone, speaking to Michael O'Neil.

She then gasped as Dennis Harutyun nearly demirrored his cruiser as the passenger side of the car came within inches of the truck he was passing. He skidded back into the lane and sped up.

'Are you OK?' O'Neil asked. 'Are you there?'

'Yes. I'm . . .' She closed her eyes as Harutyun took on another tractor-trailer, then opened them. 'What's in place?'

O'Neil was at his desk in his own sheriff's office. 'Two helicopters around Point Lobos—that's where Edwin first saw Kayleigh at the concert two years ago. Highway Patrol's setting up roadblocks around Pacific Grove, Pebble Beach and Carmel.'

'Good.'

'What's your ETA?' O'Neil asked.

She glanced at Harutyun and posed the question.

'A half-hour,' he said.

Dance relayed this to O'Neil. 'Better go, Michael. We're doing about two hundred miles an hour here.' They disconnected.

Drawing a rare smile from the mustachioed deputy.

'You want me to slow down?' Harutyun asked.

'No, I want you to go faster,' Dance said.

'WHAT DO YOU THINK?' Edwin waved his arm around the trailer, which was perfectly neat and scrubbed. It was also stiflingly hot.

Standing in the kitchenette, still cuffed, Kayleigh didn't answer.

'Look, a high-def TV and I've got about a hundred DVDs. And plenty of your favourite foods. And your favourite soap too.'

Yes, it was, she noted. Her heart sank at this foresight on his part.

She also noticed several lengths of chain in the trailer, fixed to the walls, ending in shackles.

Then, once again, his smile faded. 'If you'd gone out with me, like I asked,' Edwin said, 'we wouldn't've had to go through all of this. Just dinner. What was the big deal?' His voice grew cold again. 'I know you're not a virgin . . . I'm sure it just sort of happened. You did have sex with Bobby, didn't you? No, I don't want to know.' He looked at her closely. But then, like a light switch clicking on, his face warmed and he was smiling. 'Hey, it's OK. You're mine now. It's going to be OK.'

He showed her the trailer more closely. The place was a shrine to her, of course. Posters and memorabilia, clothing and photos.

Kayleigh Towne everywhere. But no weapons.

No sharp knives in the kitchen—the first thing she looked for. Also, no glass or ceramic. It was all metal and plastic.

Sweat poured. 'This is hopeless, Edwin. You don't think ten thousand people are going to be looking for me?'

'Maybe not. They might think you ran off with somebody you realised loved you. They'll still be thinking Alicia killed Bobby and tried to kill you. But even if they *are* looking, they aren't going to find us. They think we're in Monterey. This girl I went out with for a while will have told them that's where we'd be. I set that up a long time ago. No, they'll never find us here.'

'You put this all together . . . to, what? Win me over?'

'To make you see reason. Who else would go to all this trouble, except somebody who loved you?'

'But . . . the congressman? I don't understand.'

He laughed. 'Oh, that was interesting. I learned a lesson there. I've stopped posting things online. That's how Simesky found out about you and me. But something good came out of that. I *did* see somebody outside my house on Saturday night. It was Simesky or Babbage but at the time I thought it was just kids. That got me thinking. I set it up so that it looked like Alicia had been spying on me. I planted evidence that'd make the police think she was the stalker.'

Then Edwin grew impatient, looking at her hair, her breasts. 'You know what it's time for.' He glanced towards the rumpled bed.

'Please, no, Edwin. Please.'

He stared at her. 'You shouldn't be so . . . standoffish. I did you a favour. Fred Blanton was a creep who stole your music. And Alicia, well, she probably *did* want your career. And Sheri? Oh, please. She's a store clerk who got lucky with Bishop. You deserve a better stepmother than her. And Bobby? All he wanted to do was have sex with you.'

She said, 'At least let me clean up? Just a shower, please?'

'I don't think so.'

She snapped, 'And you say you're Mr Today? Bullshit. I just want to take a fucking shower and you won't let me?'

He frowned. 'All right. But don't say words like that. Don't ever say words like that again. You can take a shower. But I have the only keys and there're no weapons here. And all the windows are barred.'

'I figured that. I really just want to clean up.'

He undid the cuffs, and smiled. 'Hurry back, love.' He went back into the bedroom to wait.

Shoulders slumped, she walked into the bathroom.

EDWIN CLICKED the air conditioner on a little higher—with the camouflage tarp covering the trailer it was beastly hot inside.

He listened to the running water, pictured Kayleigh inside the shower. He turned on the radio and caught the news. It seemed the police hadn't gone with the innocent interpretation of Kayleigh's disappearance. Pike Madigan's voice was explaining about the kidnapping, alerting people that it was likely that Edwin Sharp and Kayleigh Towne were heading towards the Monterey area.

'We don't know the vehicle they're in, but go to the web site we've set up and you can find Sharp's picture.'

Ah, I knew I could count on you, Sally, you liar. He wondered who'd got her to talk. Kathryn Dance came to mind. Had to be her.

Of course, the diversion about Monterey would buy them only so much time. They'd have to move but this place would be safe for a month or so.

The shower water stopped. She'd be towelling off now.

'Edwin,' Kayleigh said, a playful tone. 'I made myself ready for you.'

Smiling, he walked to the doorway and found her in front of the bathroom door, fully clothed. Edwin Sharp's eyes grew wide. Then he cried out in horror. 'NO, no, no! What'd you do?'

She'd found tiny blunt-end fingernail scissors in the vanity kit he'd bought. TSA approved for air travel and therefore safe. But they would still cut. And she'd used them to shear off all her hair.

He stared in horror at the pile of glistening blonde strands on the bathroom floor. A two- to three-inch mop of ragged fringe covered her head. She hadn't showered at all; she'd spent the ten minutes destroying her beautiful hair.

In a singsong voice, she mocked, 'What's the matter, Edwin? Don't you like me now? Don't you want to stalk me any more? . . . You love *me*, right? It doesn't matter what I look like.'

'No, no, of course not. It's just . . .' He thought he'd be sick. He was thinking, how long does it take for hair to grow?

Ten years, four months . . .

Kayleigh taunted, 'You want to have sex with me now? Now that I look like a boy?'

He walked forward slowly, staring at the pile of hair.

'Here!' she screamed and grabbed a handful, flung it at him. It flowed to the floor and Edwin dropped to his knees, desperately grabbing at the strands.

'I knew it,' she muttered contemptuously, backing into the bathroom. 'You don't know me. You don't have a clue who I am.'

And then he got angry too. 'Yes, I do. You're the bitch I'm going to have sex with in about sixty seconds.'

He started to rise. Then saw something in her hand. What—? Oh, it was just a cup. It had to be plastic. There wasn't anything inside that could be broken or made into a knife. He'd thought of that.

But one thing he hadn't thought of. What the cup held: ammonia, from under the sink. Kayleigh'd filled the cup to the brim.

She flung the chemical into his face. It spread up his nose, into his mouth. The fumes slipped up under his eyelids and burned like red-hot steel. He cried at the pain, wiping frantically at his face. Anything to get away! Choking, gasping, coughing.

Then more pain as she hit him hard in the throat, the wound where he'd fired the bullet into his own neck. He screamed again.

Doubling over, paralysed, he felt her rip the keys from his pocket. He tried to grab her arm but she was quickly out of reach.

The bitter, biting chemical flowed deeper into his mouth and nose. Edwin staggered to his feet and shoved his face under the tap in the kitchen sink to rinse the fire away.

But there was no water. Kayleigh had run the supply dry.

Edwin stumbled to the refrigerator and yanked it open, feeling for a bottle of water. He found one and flushed his face, the liquid little by little dulling the sting. His vision, though fuzzy, returned. He stumbled to the front door, opened it, then hurried outside. He spotted Kayleigh running down the road that led to the highway.

As the pain diminished, Edwin relaxed. He actually smiled.

The road was three miles long. Gravel. She was barefoot.

She wasn't going to get away.

Edwin started after her, jogging at first, then sprinting.

He saw her disappear around a curve in the road, only a hundred feet away. He was closing fast. Seventy feet, fifty . . .

And then he turned the corner.

He ran for ten more steps, five, three, slowing, slowing. And then Edwin stopped. Kayleigh stood with two people: a uniformed deputy and a woman, who had her arm around the singer.

The man was a deputy he recognised from Fresno, with the thick black moustache. And the woman, of course, was Kathryn Dance.

The deputy held a pistol, aimed squarely at Edwin's chest.

'Lie down,' he called, 'on your belly, hands to your side.'

Edwin debated. If I take one step I'll die. If I lie down I'll go to jail. In jail at least he'd have a chance to talk to Kayleigh. She'd come and visit him. They could talk. He could help her understand how bad everybody else was for her. How he was the man for her.

Edwin Sharp lay down.

As Kathryn Dance covered him with her pistol, the deputy circled around, cuffed his hands and lifted him to his feet.

'Could I get some water for my eyes, please. They're burning.'

The officer got a bottle and poured it over Edwin's face.

'Thank you.'

Other cars were arriving.

Edwin said, 'The news. I heard on the news—you thought we were in Monterey. Why did you come here?'

Dance replied, 'We have teams in Monterey, true, but mostly for the press. So you'd think you'd fooled us if you listened to the radio or went online. To me, it didn't make sense for you to go there. Why would you tell Sally Docking anything about a location unless you figured she'd tell us eventually? That *is* a pattern of yours, you know. Misinformation and scaring witnesses into lying.

'As for here? CSU found trace evidence near your house that could have come from a mining operation. I remembered Kayleigh's song "Near the Silver Mine". You knew she was unhappy that Bishop had sold the place and it made sense you wanted to bring her back here. We looked at some satellite pictures and saw the trailer. Camouflage netting doesn't work.'

Edwin looked towards Kayleigh, standing defiant, staring back coldly. Still, he had the impression that there was a spark of flirt in her eyes. As soon as her hair grew back, she'd be beautiful again.

God, did he love her.

11

At seven thirty that night Kathryn Dance was backstage at the convention centre. There'd been talk about cancelling the concert, but Kayleigh Towne was the one who'd insisted that it should go on. The crowds were rapidly filling the venue.

The singer was dressed for the concert—in her good-girl outfit, of course. The only difference was that tonight she was the good girl who'd been playing softball with friends; on her head a Cal State Fresno Bulldog's cap covered her shorn hair. She had just spoken to the band about changing a verse in one of her original songs that was meant for Bobby. Now, it included a few lines for Alicia.

A man in chinos and a starched dress shirt came up to Kayleigh and Dance. He was in his mid-thirties and had a boyish grin.

'Kayleigh, hi.' A polite nod to Dance. 'I'm Art Francesco.' Kayleigh and Dance regarded him cautiously until his all-access badge dangled forward.

'Hi,' Kayleigh said absently.

'I'm so sorry about everything's that happened. Your dad told me. Well, just wanted to say how happy I am we're going to do business together.'

'Uh-hum. And who are you again?'

'Art. Art Francesco.' When she gave no reaction the man added, 'Your father mentioned I'd be coming tonight, didn't he?'

'Afraid he didn't.'

He laughed. 'Isn't that just like Bishop.' A card appeared.

Shock went through Kayleigh's body. The agent glanced at the singer's hand. The card was for JBT Global Entertainment.

'What do you mean, doing business?'

Francesco said, 'Your father . . . He hadn't told you—'

'Told me what?' Kayleigh snapped.

'He said he was going to tell you this morning, after we signed up everything. But with that crazy man, maybe he forgot.'

'Signed up *what?*'

'Well, you. Signed up *you*. I'm sorry. I thought you knew.' Francesco looked miserable. 'He just signed you with Global. He's not renewing with Barry Zeigler and your label.'

'Can he do that?' Dance asked.

Jaw set in anger, Kayleigh muttered, 'Yeah, he can. It was set up that way when I was a minor. I never changed it. But he never did anything that I didn't agree with. Until now.'

Francesco said, 'Oh, but it's a great deal, Kayleigh. And you won't believe the money. You've got a hundred per cent creative control. We'll handle all your concert tours, your recordings, production, CDs, download platforms, marketing . . . You'll go international, big-time. We'll get you into Vegas. You'll never have to play little places like this again.'

'This little place happens to be my home town.'

He held up his hand. 'I didn't mean it that way. It's just, this'll expand your career exponentially. I'm sorry it happened this way, Kayleigh. Let's start over.' He extended his hand.

She ignored it.

Bishop Towne had seen the exchange and, with a disgusted look on his face, ambled over. He said, 'Artie.'

'I'm sorry, Bishop, I didn't know. I thought you'd told her.'

'Yeah,' he growled. 'Stuff happened today. Didn't get around to it. Give us a minute, Artie.'

'Sure. I'm sorry.'

Kayleigh turned on her father. 'How could you? I told Barry we weren't talking to Global. I told him that!'

'Barry's part of the past,' he said. 'That world is gone now.'

'He was loyal. He was always there. He made me platinum.'

'And in a few years, there won't be any platinum. It's going to be downloads and TV and concerts and deals with retailers.'

Kayleigh's eyes narrowed and Dance saw within them an anger and defiance that had never been present when speaking with her father. She laughed coldly. 'You think I don't see what's going on here? This isn't about me. It's all about you, isn't it? You screwed up your career. You let your voice go to hell and now you can't sing or write your way out of a paper bag. So you become the great impresario. What's Barry going to do?'

'Barry?' As if Bishop hadn't thought about it. 'He'll change with the times or he'll get into a new line of work.'

'So that's how you treat your friends. It's sure how you treated me, isn't it? You made me give up my . . .' She tailed off. 'You made me give up so much, so you could stay in the Industry.' She wheeled round and walked away.

He shouted, 'KT!'

She paused and turned back defiantly. Bishop approached. 'You want the truth? Yeah, I asked your sister and Congressman Davis here to keep you from cancelling. And, yeah, I cut the deal with Global. But, why I did that, it's *not* about me. And it's not about *you* either.' Bishop pointed to the filling seats. 'It's about *them*, KT. They are the only thing that matters.'

'I don't know what you're saying.'

'What you've got comes along once or twice in a generation. Your voice, your music, your stage presence, your writing. Do you know how rare that is?' His voice softened. 'Music's the truth nowadays, KT. We don't get answers from religion, we don't get them from politicians, we sure as hell don't get 'em from TV news. We get answers from *music*. The whole world needs people who can take away their sadness, make 'em understand everybody goes through lousy times too, show 'em there's hope, make 'em laugh. For you, doing that's easy as fallin' off a log. Tell me, KT, how many songs you think up in the last coupla days? Without even tryin'? A dozen, I'll bet.'

Kayleigh blinked and Dance saw that he was right.

'That's a gift, honey.' A mournful smile. 'Pushing you was never about me. It was 'cause I knew you had that gift.' He pointed out to the audience. 'They need you.'

'Then they're gonna be pretty disappointed tonight. Because this concert's going on without me.' With that, she was gone.

The two dozen people backstage were all staring at the old man. He'd screwed up not telling her about the Global deal so she'd go ahead with the concert. But Dance's heart went out to him. He looked shattered.

Just then she heard a familiar voice behind her. 'Hey there.' She turned.

Jon Boling's common greeting, just like his personality, was easy, friendly. And more than a little sexy, Dance had always felt.

Until now. She stared blankly. He gave a surprised laugh, assuming she was caught up in whatever drama was going on backstage at the moment— all the sombre faces. And he wrapped his arms round her.

She returned the pressure anaemically, feeling the weight of the blunt realisation that he'd come all the way here—three hours—to tell her he was leaving her and moving to San Diego.

'You look more surprised than I thought you would,' Boling said, stepping back from the embrace. 'Your secret lover must be here. And, dammit, I *bought* a ticket. You probably got him comped.'

Dance laughed, a reminder of the many good times they'd shared. They walked to a deserted part of the backstage area.

Boling looked around. 'What's going on? Everybody OK?'

'Hard to say.' She couldn't avoid the cryptic response.

He looked her over. 'We've had the worst phone luck. I've been doing ten-hour days. And your mom said you were working on that kidnapping case. Some vacation you had, hm? And Lincoln and Amelia were here?'

'Couldn't've done it without them. That's how we traced him.'

Boling leaned forward and kissed her quickly on the lips.

'Good turnout.' He gestured towards the filling house. 'I listened to one of Kayleigh's CDs on the way here. I can't wait for the show.'

'About that . . . there may be a rain-check situation.'

And she told him about the blowup between father and daughter.

The crew and Kayleigh's band were standing around awkwardly. Kayleigh was the least temperamental performer on earth. If she stormed out it was not diva drama, with her in the trailer waiting to be coaxed back.

Bishop Towne, alone, wiped his hands on his slacks. It was five minutes past show time. The audience weren't restless but they soon would be.

Dance found her shoulders in a terrible knot. She glanced back at Boling's handsome face. At least there wasn't—she assumed—somebody else in his life. She would make sure that Boling and the children stayed in touch. Thank God they hadn't actually moved in together.

Kathryn Dance told herself: no tears.

'Everything OK?'

She explained, 'Tough case.'

'I was worried about you when we kept missing calls.'

Quit doing that! she silently raged. Make me hate you.

Boling said, 'Hey, wanted to talk to you about something.'

Oh, that tone. How she hated that tone.

'I know this is going to seem a little odd but . . . sorry, I'm a little nervous.'

'Jon, it's OK,' she said, finding her voice. 'Go on.'

'I know we've had a, well, policy of not travelling with the kids, not overnight. Well . . . I'm thinking I'd like all of us to take a trip. For this consulting gig, they need me down in San Diego for two weeks—La Jolla. The company rented me a place near the beach. It's a month's rental. So I was thinking we could all drive down and go to Legoland and Disneyland for the kids. So, what do you think? A week in San Diego, all four of us?'

'A week?'

He grimaced. 'I know it's hard for you to get off, especially after you took time now. But if there's any way you could . . . See, it's a four-bedroom place. We'd have separate rooms, all of us. You and me too. But still, it's a good step forward, with the kids, I was thinking.'

'A week?' Dance was stammering too. Oh God—the move was temporary. Her mother hadn't got all the information.

'I . . . hey!' He stumbled back as she threw her arms around him, euphoric and utterly ashamed of her assumption, which was based on the worst thing a law enforcer can be swayed by—faulty information.

She kissed him. 'Yes, yes, yes! We'll work it out. I'd love to.'

She took Boling's hand as Bishop Towne ambled out onstage to an active microphone. There was a resounding thunderclap of applause and shouts; this was Mr Country himself greeting them.

Dance and Boling walked into the wings to see better. As the spotlight found Towne, he looked diminished and old.

He rasped, 'Good evening, y'all. I . . .' His voice caught and he started again. 'I surely do 'preciate you coming out tonight.'

More whistles and shouts and applause.

'Listen up. Uhm, I have an announcement I'd like to make.'

The crowd grew silent. Collective dismay was starting to brew.

'Again, we 'preciate your being here and appreciate all the support you've shown to Kayleigh and the band and her family during this difficult time.' As he said, 'I gotta tell you—' the applause began again and kept swelling. Within two or three seconds, the crowd was on its feet.

Bishop was confused. What was this about?

Dance too didn't have a clue, until she looked stage left and saw Kayleigh Towne walking forward, carrying a guitar.

She paused and blew the crowd a kiss.

Dance noticed that Suellyn and Mary-Gordon were now standing with Sheri Towne in the wings opposite.

Bishop hugged his daughter and she kissed him on his cheek. Kayleigh lowered a second microphone to her mouth and waited until the crowd grew silent. 'Thank you all! Thank you! . . . My daddy was going to tell you we have a big surprise for you tonight. But I decided I couldn't let him get away with hogging the spotlight, like he usually does.'

Huge laughter.

'What we want to do tonight is open the show with a father-daughter duet.' She handed Bishop the guitar. 'Y'all probably know my daddy's a better picker than me so I'm going to let him have the git-fiddle and sing and I'm going to do a bit of harmony. This's a song Daddy used to sing to me when I was a little girl. It's called "I Think You're Going to Be a Lot Like Me".'

A glance his way and he nodded, a smile curling his weathered face.

As the surge of applause settled, Bishop Towne swung the guitar strap over his broad shoulders, and strummed to test the tuning.

Then he turned his attention back to the thousands of expectant fans. He started tapping his foot, leaned forward and counted out into the microphone, 'One . . . two . . . three . . . four . . .'

jeffery **deaver**

Profile

Born:
Chicago, Illinois.

Lives:
North Carolina.

Writes:
Anywhere: hotel rooms,
planes, the kitchen.

Passions:
Fast cars, skiing, whisky,
themed dinner parties.

Books to date:
29 titles.

Degrees:
Batchelor of Journalism
from the University of
Missouri and a law degree
from Fordham University.

Previous careers:
Folksinger, journalist,
lawyer.

It may be a publishing first: Jeffery Deaver's new thriller, *XO*—the title represents a kiss and a hug in text-message form—has inspired a music album. The novel, which tells of a beautiful and successful Country singer, Kayleigh Towne, who falls prey to a stalker, has a backdrop that provides fascinating glimpses into America's Country music industry.

Deaver, it turns out, knows a great deal about music—and its creation. For a time, as a young law graduate back in the 1970s, he even made a living by performing and teaching music in clubs in the San Francisco Bay and Chicago areas. 'Growing up, I had two passions,' he remembers. 'I read everything I could get my hands on and—with the hubris of youth—wrote fiction and poetry non-stop. As for music, I listened to every genre and decided, also at a young age, to become a singer-songwriter, following in the footsteps of my idols, like Bob Dylan, Joni Mitchell, Leonard Cohen and Paul Simon (did I mention hubris?). My goal was not to be a superstar but to be a working singer-songwriter.

'Alas, it was not to be because, of course, it's not enough to be a good wordsmith; one must be a stellar performer to succeed in the business. The phrase 'singer-song-writer' carries two indispensable components. The second part—writing—I was pretty good at; the former, not so much. When I began writing novels, years ago, I was always looking for the opportunity to incorporate lyrics of mine into a thriller. I experimented with this in a short story called *The Fan*, six or seven years ago, and then went all out and wrote a number of original country-and-western/pop songs for my book *XO*, or updated some of my early songs. A few of them contain actual clues to help the reader figure out who the villain is. The album of these songs—lyrics by me, music by Clay and Ken Landers, sung by the brilliant Treva Blomquist—is now being released. (Readers can find out more at http://jefferydeaverxomusic.com.) 'There's nothing like music,' Deaver concludes enthusiastically. 'It's seductive, it's all-consuming, it's emotional, it is infinitely creative.'

He says that he enjoys keeping the reader guessing, and he refers to his carefully seeded narrative surprises as 'misdirection'—much as a magician or illusionist uses the term. 'I live to fool people, it's my goal in life. I want to make sure that a reader *could* figure out every twist in the book from what goes before. I try really hard to give clues and suggestions, double or triple meanings, and to steer (the reader) in a different direction. But the opportunity, if one *chose* to figure out what's going to happen, should be there.'

Deaver is best known for his series detective, Lincoln Rhyme, a wheelchair-bound quadriplegic with a prodigious talent for forensics. Rhyme has appeared in no less than nine of Deaver's twenty-nine thrillers, in fact. In *XO*, however, we see a different breed of investigator in Kathryn Dance, who is relatively new to the *oeuvre*. She first appeared in the 2006 Lincoln Rhyme thriller, *The Cold Moon*, and Deaver refers to that as her 'job interview'. He got such an overwhelmingly enthusiastic response from fans that he decided she should regularly have a starring role. Kathryn, who works with the California Bureau of Investigation, is an expert in kinesics—the study of non-verbal communication, and this brings a further, fascinating aspect to *XO*.

So has the research into kinesics given him more insight into the behaviour of other people? 'It's not really a one-shot deal,' he explains. 'You need to establish various baselines of behaviour through the course of several conversations. A true interrogation would require days, if not weeks, of conversation. Only then can one draw truly significant conclusions. But there's a lot of shorthand, and, I'll tell you, it's a little nerve-racking if you're out on a date checking out the girl.'

Through his first career as a lawyer, Jeffery Deaver came to appreciate the importance of logical structure—a discipline that he brings to every one of his artfully plotted thrillers during their eight-month, eight-hour-day, gestation period. 'No one goes to court or closes a business deal without knowing exactly what will happen ahead of time. A book should be the same,' he explains. Just like a song, each new novel requires a spark of inspiration, too, and usually this comes best when Deaver spends time just sitting alone in a darkened room, allowing his thoughts to wander and his mind to conceive. Luckily, he was born with a very vivid imagination. And silence really *is* golden, it seems.

the ManWho Forgot his Wife

John O'Farrell

Imagine sitting on a train, unable to remember why you're there, or a single thing about your past. That's the position Jack Vaughan finds himself in: forty years of memories completely gone.

As he starts to piece together his identity, a striking redhead triggers a memory. Her name is Madeleine and he's about to divorce her. Shocked and bewildered, Vaughan vows to learn about his life all over again—this time with eyes wide open.

CHAPTER 1

I remember when I was a child I used to watch *Mr & Mrs*. We all did; it seemed like the only option available, so everyone just put up with it. A bit like all those marriages on the programme, now I think about it. Obviously *Mr & Mrs* wasn't the cultural highlight of our week; we didn't all rush to school next morning and share our outrage that Geoff from Coventry didn't know that Julie's favourite foreign food was spaghetti. But unquestioningly we just watched the procession of unglamorous couples go through the embarrassment of revealing all the little things that they didn't know about each other. Or worse still, that there weren't any.

If ITV had wanted to increase the ratings, perhaps they should have done more research about the big stuff the partners didn't know. 'So, Geoff, do you think that Julie's favourite way to spend a Saturday night is: (a) Watching television? (b) Going to the cinema? or (c) Secretly meeting her illicit lover Gerald?'

But the subtext of *Mr & Mrs* was that all there was to marriage was knowing each other very well. The heart-covered cards of Valentine's Day should say '*Love is . . . knowing every single thing you're going to say before you even bloody say it.*' Like two lifers sharing a prison cell, you spend so much time in each other's company that there shouldn't be anything that might surprise either of you.

My marriage was not like that.

Lots of husbands forget things. They forget to pick up the dry-cleaning, or to buy their wife a birthday present until they are passing the Texaco minimart the night before. It drives their partners mad, that men can be so self-obsessed as to overlook a major event in the life of their other half.

I didn't suffer from this careless absent-mindedness. I just completely forgot who my wife was. Her name, her face, our history together was all wiped, leaving me with no knowledge that she even existed. I would not have done very well on *Mr & Mrs*. When the hostess escorted my wife out of the soundproof box, I would have been losing points already for optimistically asking which one I was married to. Apparently women hate that.

In my defence, it wasn't just my wife I forgot, it was everything else as well. When I say 'I remember watching *Mr & Mrs*', that is actually quite a momentous statement for me. The phrase 'I remember' was not always in my vocabulary. There was a period in my life when I might have been aware of the TV show but would have had no personal memory of ever having seen it. During the dark ages of my amnesia, I had no idea who *I* was either. I had no memory of friends, family, personal experience or identity; I didn't even know what my name was.

MY BIZARRE REAWAKENING occurred on a London Underground train at some point after it had emerged into the daylight. It was a drizzly afternoon in the autumn. There was no blinding flash, just a creeping confusion about where I was. The humming tube carriage started up again and then I became aware that I had no idea why I was on this journey. 'Hounslow East' said the sign outside the grimy window as the train came to a halt, but no one got on or off. Perhaps this was a momentary blackout; perhaps this blank nothingness was what everyone felt as they reached 'Hounslow East'.

Then I realised that not only did I not know where I was going, but I couldn't remember where I had come from either. Am I going to work? What is my work? I don't know. Now the panic was rising inside me. I'm not well; I need to go home and go to bed. Where is home? I don't know where I live. Think! Think—it will come back to me!

'Come on . . .' I said out loud, intending to address myself by my own name. But the end of the sentence wasn't there; it was like a missing rung on a ladder. I searched for a wallet, a diary, a mobile phone, anything that might make it all fall back into place. My pockets were empty—just a ticket and a bit of money. There was a small red stain on my jeans. I wonder how that got there? I thought. My brain had rebooted, but all the old files had been wiped.

I was pacing up the empty carriage now, bewildered. Should I get off at the next station and try to get help? It's just a temporary blip, I told myself.

I sat and pressed my hands against my temples as if I could force some sense out of my head.

I noticed on the map that the train would do a loop at Heathrow Airport. If I travelled back in the direction in which I had come, maybe some visual prompt might help me relocate myself? And people were bound to get on the train at the airport; surely then I would find someone who could help me? But at Heathrow Terminal 2 I went from travelling alone to being trapped in a jam-packed carriage, with luggage-laden travellers talking a hundred different languages, none of them mine. I was on a tube train with maps clearly stating the route, thousands of people travelling with me, and yet I felt as lost and lonely as it is possible to be.

HALF AN HOUR LATER, the only person standing still in a teeming railway terminal, I scanned the boards for some route back to my previous life. Ceaseless information scrolled across screens and distorted announcements filled my ears. I ventured into a public toilet just to stare into a mirror and was shocked by the age of the bearded stranger I saw frowning back at me. I guessed I was around forty, greying at the temples and thinning on top. I'd presumed I was somewhere in my early twenties, but now I could see that I was actually two decades older than that. I learned later that this was nothing to do with my particular neurological condition; that's just how everyone feels in middle age.

'Can you help me? I'm lost . . .' I said to a young man in a smart suit.

'Where do you want to go?'

'I can't remember.'

Other passers-by just ignored my requests for help; eye contact was avoided, wired-up ears were deaf to my pleas.

'Excuse me—I don't know who I am!' I said to a sympathetic-looking vicar pulling a suitcase on wheels.

'Ah yes . . . I don't think any of us knows who we really are, do we?'

'No, I mean I really don't know who I am. I've forgotten everything.'

His body language suggested he was keen to be on his way. 'Well, we may all sometimes feel as though we don't know if there is any meaning to it all, but in fact each of us really is very special . . . Now *I'm* forgetting that I'm already late for my train!'

Seeing the clergyman made me wonder if I had actually died and was on the way to Heaven. It seemed unlikely that God's sense of humour was so warped that he would make us travel to Heaven on the London Underground during the rush hour. In fact, this experience did feel like a kind of death. Trapped as I was in some dreamlike suspended state, I knew of no one who cared if I lived or died. I think I learned the most basic human need of all—the reassurance that you are alive and will be acknowledged by other human beings. 'I exist!' declare all those Stone Age cave paintings. That's the whole point of the Internet—it's given everyone the chance to proclaim their existence to the world. 'This is me. Look, I have photos, friends, interests. No one can say I was never born—here is the proof.' That is the central tenet of twenty-first-century Western philosophy: 'I Facebook, therefore I am.'

I was trapped in something worse than solitary confinement. Even the travellers around me, thousands of miles from their homes, would have their friends and family with them, efficiently packed away in their heads.

I was shaking and short of breath. I watched a rushing commuter aim an empty coffee cup at the trolley of a litter-collector, then continue on her way when it fell to the floor. I picked it up and added it to the other rubbish that was being collected by the elderly Asian man.

'Thank you,' he said.

'Um, excuse me, I think I've had some sort of stroke or something . . .' I said as I began to explain my predicament.

'You need the hospital. King Edward's is up the road,' he said, pointing. 'I would take you there, but . . . I'd lose my job.'

It was the first compassion anyone had shown me and suddenly I felt like crying. Of course—medical help, I thought. That's what I need.

'Thank you! Thank you!' I gushed. The location of the hospital was confirmed by a map on the side of a bus shelter. Now I was going somewhere; just this mission gave me a fragment of hope. And so I strode up the busy main road like an alien from another planet, trying to take it all in, some of it strangely familiar, some of it completely bizarre. And then the concrete block ahead turned into the hospital and I felt my pace quicken, as if the people in there might somehow immediately make everything better.

'EXCUSE ME—I really need to see a doctor,' I gabbled at the front desk of Accident and Emergency. 'I think I've had a sort of brain freeze or something. I can't remember who I am.'

'Right. Could I take your name, please?'

There was a split second when I actually went to answer this question in the casual manner in which it had been posed.

'That's what I'm saying—I can't even remember my own name! It's like, all personal information has suddenly been erased . . .'

'I see, well could I take your address then, please?'

'Um—sorry—I can't remember a single thing about myself.'

The receptionist managed to look harassed and bored at the same time.

'Right. Who's your registered doctor?'

'Well, *I don't know*, obviously. I can't remember where I live, where I work, what my name is, or even if this has ever happened to me before.'

'I'm sorry, but we're not allowed to process you without asking these questions,' she said. 'Are you currently on any prescriptions or regular medications?'

'I don't know!'

'And could you please provide the name and contact details for your spouse or next of kin?'

That's when I first noticed it. The indented ring of white flesh on my fourth finger. The ghostly scar where a wedding ring had been.

'Yes, next of kin! I have a wife maybe?' I said excitedly. Perhaps I had been robbed and concussed and maybe my dear wife was looking for me right now. The shadow of a wedding ring filled me with hope. 'Maybe my wife is ringing round all the hospitals, trying to find me,' I said.

A week later I was still in the hospital waiting for her call.

I HAD A LABEL on my wrist that said 'UNKNOWN WHITE MALE', though the hospital porters had dubbed me 'Jason' after the fictional amnesiac in *The Bourne Identity*. However, it turned out that knowing nothing about yourself was not quite as exciting as it appeared in Hollywood blockbusters. My status seemed to have evolved from emergency inpatient to layabout lodger at King Edward's Hospital in West London. Already I found myself feeling sufficiently established to refer to the place as 'Teddy's'.

I had no illness as such. I had been examined on the first day but there was no logical explanation for why on Tuesday, October 22, my brain had suddenly decided to restore factory settings. I had been seen by a regular stream of doctors, neurologists and attendant students, for whom I was paraded as something of a novelty. None of them had the faintest idea what had happened to me. One medical student asked me rather accusingly,

'If you've forgotten everything, how come you remember how to talk?'

It only compounded my depression to realise that, at the moment, my best friend in the whole world was Annoying Bernard in the next bed. In one way Bernard provided a valuable service to me during those first seven days. On the inside I was almost crippled with anxiety about what had happened to me, who I was and whether I would ever recover the rest of my life. But I never had much time to dwell on this, being in a constant state of mild irritation at the man in the next bed.

Bernard meant well; he wasn't unpleasant—in fact, he was unremittingly jolly. I just found it a bit wearing to have to spend twenty-four hours a day with someone who seemed to think that my neurological disorder could be overcome if I was just upbeat about the whole 'bloomin' business'.

'I tell you what, there's a few embarrassing things in my past that I wouldn't mind forgetting, I can tell you!' he chuckled. 'New Year's Eve 1999—I wouldn't mind forgetting that one! And a certain lady from the Swindon Salsa Dance Club . . . I wouldn't mind that episode being struck from the official record, please, Mr Chairman!'

Eventually one doctor seemed to take the lead on my case. Dr Anne Lewington was a slightly mad-looking consultant neurologist in her fifties, who was so perplexed by my condition that she made a point of seeing me every day. Under her supervision I had a brain scan, I had wires attached to my head, I had audiovisual stimuli tests; but in every case the activity in my brain was apparently 'completely normal'.

It took me a day or two to work out that Dr Lewington's excitement at my results bore no relation to understanding what had happened to me.

'Oooh, that's interesting! Both hippocampi are normal, the volumes of both entorhinal cortices and temporal lobes are normal.'

'Right—so does that explain anything?'

'Nothing at all. That's what's so interesting! It would appear that your extrapersonal memories have been consolidated in the neocortex independently of the medial temporal lobe.'

'Is that good or bad?'

'Well, there's no discernible logic or pattern to any of it,' she said, clapping her hands together in delight. 'That's what makes it so utterly compelling! And as for how memories are processed and stored—that is one of the most baffling areas of all. It's such a thrilling subject to be researching.'

'Great . . .' I nodded blankly. It was like having open-heart surgery and hearing, 'Wow—what's this big muscle in here pumping away?'

It was quite a few days before Dr Lewington sat by my bed to explain what she thought had happened. She talked so quietly that Bernard was forced to turn off his radio on the other side of the curtain.

'From cases similar to your own, it seems that you have experienced a "psychogenic fugue": literally a "flight" from your previous life, possibly triggered by extreme stress.'

'A fugue?'

'Yes, this happens to only a handful of people every year in the whole world, though no two cases seem to be identical. The loss of personal items was probably deliberate on your part as you slipped into the "fugue state", and it's usual to have no recall of consciously abandoning all traces of your former life. Clearly you have not forgotten everything, but typically with "retrograde amnesia", the patient would know, say, who Princess Diana was, but might not know that she had died.'

'Paris. 1998,' I said, showing off a little.

'1997!' came Bernard's voice from the other side of the curtain.

'Your recall of these *extrapersonal* memories suggests you stand a good chance of getting your personal memories back.'

'But when exactly?'

'Thirty-first of August,' said Bernard. 'She was pronounced dead around four a.m.'

Dr Lewington had to concede that there was no guarantee that I would definitely recover. And so I was left wondering if I would ever make contact with my previous life again.

'Maybe you're a serial killer?' came Bernard's nonchalant voice.

'Sorry, Bernard, are you talking to me?'

'Well, she said it might have been caused by a need to shut out your past; perhaps it's because you couldn't stand the torment of being an undetected murderer.'

'That's a lovely thought. Thank you.'

'Or perhaps you're a terrorist. A drug dealer. On the run from the Chinese triads!'

I resolved to say nothing in the hope that the speculation might peter out.

'A pimp . . . A compulsive arsonist . . .'

I dismissed Bernard's speculation as ridiculous, and then later that afternoon felt a flush of fear and guilt as I was informed that there were two policemen waiting for me in the ward sister's office. It turned out that they had come with a large file of 'Missing Persons', which they now went through very slowly, staring carefully at each photo before looking studiously at me.

'Well, that one's clearly not me,' I found myself interjecting, desperate to see if I was on any of the later pages.

'We have to give due consideration to every single file, sir.'

'Yes, but I'm not that fat. Or black. Or a woman.'

They reluctantly turned the page.

'Hmmm, what do you think?' said the officer, looking between my face and the photo of a wizened old pensioner.

'He's about eighty!' I objected.

'How long have you had that beard?'

'I don't know! Like the nurse said, I am suffering from retrograde amnesia, so my mind is a blank about everything prior to last Tuesday.'

They shook their heads in exasperation, then continued looking for similarities between my appearance and a teenage girl, a Sikh and a Jack Russell terrier, which they conceded had been put in the wrong file.

The fact that no one had reported me missing seemed to tell a story of its own. Had I been this lonely before my fugue? I wondered; had that been the stress that provoked my mental Etch A Sketch into shaking the screen clear to start again?

'Could we get something in the newspaper?' I kept suggesting to the ward sister. 'A sort of "Do you know this man?" feature next to my photo?' She eventually agreed that this might be a good idea, and I sat in her office while she rang the news desk at the *London Evening Standard*. I heard only her side of the conversation.

'They want to know if you are brilliant at the piano or anything like that?'

'Well—I can't remember.'

'He doesn't know.' Another pause. 'Are you, like, an incredible linguist or a maths genius or anything?'

'I don't think so. I can only do the easy puzzles in Bernard's Sudoku book . . . Should I speak to them?'

'Er, he can do easy Sudoku puzzles. Does that help at all?'

The paper said they might run the story if we sent over all the details with an up-to-date photo. The next day there was a huge double spread headed WHO'S THE MYSTERY MAN? Beneath it was a picture of a well-groomed young man standing beside Pippa Middleton at a charity polo match. There was nothing about me. It transpired that they had been intending to run my story, but the editor had ruled that they couldn't have two 'mystery man' stories in the same edition. The journalist who had taken our call was now on holiday, so the potential story had been assigned to another reporter.

'Tell me,' she asked, 'are you, like, really brilliant at the piano or anything?'

SOMETIMES I WOULD PASS a few hours in the television room. It was on one such visit that I discovered *Mr & Mrs*, which had been reinvented featuring celebrities. This programme became something of an obsession. I just loved how these couples could remember so much about one another.

'Ah, found you!' declared Bernard, just as the second half of the programme was about to begin. 'Look, I got a couple of books for you from the newsagent's in the lobby: *How to Improve Your Memory in Just Fifteen Minutes a Day!*'

'That's very kind of you, Bernard, but I'm guessing that's more for general forgetfulness than retrograde amnesia.'

'Well, it's all degrees of the same thing, isn't it?'

'Er, no. I can remember everything I've done since coming to this hospital. But I just can't remember a single thing about my life before that day.'

'Yes, I see. So you might need to do more than fifteen minutes a day,' he conceded, opening the book at random. '"*When you are introduced to a new person for the first time . . . try repeating their name out loud to lodge it in your memory.*" Well, you could try doing that for a start!'

'I don't think that's going to unlock the first forty years of my life . . .'

'Ooh, this is a good one: "*If you have problems remembering telephone numbers, try making associations. If a friend's number is 2012 1066, then remember it by thinking, London Olympics and the Battle of Hastings.*"'

'OK. If that number comes up, I'll remember it like that.'

'You see!' said Bernard, gratified that he'd been such a help. 'Ooh, *All-Star Mr & Mrs*! I'd love to go on that. You know, like, if I was famous . . . and had a wife.'

When my favourite TV show was over for another day, I announced I was heading back to my bed, but Bernard jumped up 'to keep me company', triumphantly revealing the other book he had bought. He had decided that one way to trigger a memory of my own identity might be to read out every single male name in *Name Your Baby*.

During the course of that long afternoon it became clear why *Name Your Baby* has never been a huge hit as an audiobook. Sure there are lots of characters, but none of them is ever developed. 'Aaron', for example, has a walk-on part right at the beginning but then we never hear from him again. And there are no clues as to whether that might be the sort of name my parents might have given me.

'I'm not sure you should lie down like that,' said Bernard. 'You're still really concentrating, aren't you?'

'I'm just closing my eyes so I can be sure there's nothing to distract me.'

I WOKE UP to 'Francis? Frank? Franklin?' Bernard was still declaring every name with extraordinary gusto and optimism. I had just had the same dream I'd experienced a couple of times now: a snapshot of a moment sharing laughter with a woman. I couldn't remember a face or a name, but she seemed to love me as I loved her. The sensation was pure happiness, and I was crushed when I awoke to the huge void that was my life right now.

'Garth? Garvin? Gary?'

And then something extraordinary happened. On hearing the word 'Gary', I heard myself mumble 'Zero-seven-seven-zero-zero . . .'

'What was that?' said Bernard.

'I don't know,' I said, sitting up. 'It just came out when you said "Gary".'

'Is that it? Is that you? Are you *Gary*?'

'I don't think so. Say it again.'

'Gary!'

'Zero-seven-seven-zero-zero . . .' There was more. 'Nine-zero-zero . . . nine-zero-three.' It just felt natural that those numbers followed that name.

'That's a telephone number!' said Bernard excitedly, writing it down.

We had discovered a fragment of DNA from my past life. Bernard had successfully shown the way to my hinterland. I'd been sceptical and negative and he had proved me wrong. I might have congratulated him if I hadn't noticed him reach for his mobile phone and start dialling.

'What are you doing?' I screamed.

'Ringing Gary.'

'No, don't! I'm not ready! We should talk to the doctor! You're not allowed to use that in here—'

'It's ringing!' and he threw the handset over to me.

Slowly I raised it to my ear.

'Hello?' said a male voice, on a weak, distorted signal.

'Um . . . hello? Is that . . . er, Gary, by any chance?' I stammered.

'Vaughan! Is that you? Where the hell have you been? It's like you suddenly disappeared off the face of the earth!'

In a panic I dropped the call and threw the handset back to Bernard.

'Did you recognise his voice?'

'Er, no. No, I . . . It's probably just some random bloke,' I stammered. But the stranger was ringing straight back. And soon they were having quite an animated chat about me.

'Not any more,' said Bernard.

GARY HUGGED ME MEANINGFULLY while I just stood there, enduring the physical contact like some teenage boy cuddled by his aunt at Christmas.

'Vaughan! I was so worried about you. I love you, man!'

'You love me?' I stammered. 'Are we, like, *homosexuals?*'

The meaningful embrace ended very suddenly. 'No, I don't love you like *that*. I mean I love you like a brother.'

'You're my brother?'

'No—I mean we're like brothers, you and me. Gazoody-baby!'

'What?'

'That's what we used to say, isn't it? Gazooooooody-baby! Remember?' and he gave me a little playful punch on the arm that actually hurt.

This was my visitor being reserved after he'd been given a little talk by the doctor. She had warned him on the phone that I was unlikely to know who he was, and might react nervously if he was too presumptuous or over-familiar. It was good that he had taken so much of this on board. Despite the solitude I'd felt up to this point, the sudden friendliness of this stranger felt inappropriate.

'Look, I know this is going to sound a bit rude, but I really don't know who you are. Until you called me "Vaughan" I didn't even know that was my Christian name.'

'Actually it's your surname. That's just what everybody calls you.'

'See? I didn't know that! I don't know anything. Do I have a mother, for example? I don't know.'

The man paused and placed his hand on my shoulder. 'I'm sorry, mate. Your old mum kicked the bucket about five years ago.'

'Oh, OK.' I shrugged. 'Well, I don't remember her anyway.'

And he laughed as if I was making a joke. 'Do you want to go and get a pint or two? I really fancy a pickled gherkin.'

And then I found myself emitting an unexpected laugh. It was the first time I had laughed since Day Zero, and my visitor hadn't even been trying to be funny. Just the randomness of his thought processes felt comical and refreshing. My own personality had been a mystery to me when I walked into the hospital. Bernard had lit up my irritable side; Gary had shown me what made me laugh.

'Put some clothes on, Vaughan. You can't go to the pub in your pyjamas!'

'He's not allowed to leave the hospital!' interjected Bernard, looking put out by this interloper's arrival. After a week in an institution, part of me was actually tempted to jump at this opportunity for a trip into the outside world. I might have remained in two minds, had Bernard not explicitly forbidden me to leave the ward.

WALKING OUT OF THE HOSPITAL with Gary felt both exhilarating and terrifying. I had almost forgotten what fresh air smelled like and here was someone who knew all the secrets of my past life. Gary was a tall, spindly man about my age who dressed in the clothes of someone twenty years younger. He wore a leather jacket and exuded an air of confidence and a reek of nicotine. It was refreshing to be talked to as if I was normal. It made me like him—this was my friend 'Gary' and we were off to the pub together.

'So we might as well get this out of the way . . .' he said, as we got to the street corner, 'but you do remember you owe me two grand?'

'Do I? Sorry, I don't have any money . . . I . . . if you could just hang on a bit?' and then I caught the glint in his eye.

'It's all right!' He burst out laughing. 'Can you not remember anything?'

'I have no idea what I've been doing for the past forty years.'

'Yeah, well I know how you feel.'

Forty years had been a good guess. It turned out I was thirty-nine, and according to Gary my fugue state was just 'a typical midlife crisis'. I got the impression that he didn't consider my medical condition to be a big deal—as if he'd done so many drugs down the years that this was just one of many altered states on the spectrum.

The pub was filling up with lunch-time customers so we grabbed the last booth. I chose a pint of Guinness because Gary told me that's what I usually had. Now I had free rein to ask him whatever I wanted, the infinite possibilities felt overwhelming—I might be a father of seven, an Olympic sailing champion or a bankrupt criminal.

I resolved to ask the questions in chronological order, but my attempt to pin down some basics about my early years did not start well.

'So. Have I got any brothers and sisters?'

'Nope. You're an only child. Oh, I forgot to get anything to eat—'

'OK. Where am I from?'

'Nowhere really. Your dad was in the forces, so you lived in West Germany, Cyprus, Malaysia, er . . . Yorkshire. I remember you saying that you were never in the same school for more than a year.'

'So I'm the son of a soldier?'

'Air force. He was quite high ranking, though he only did the accounts or something. Poor bloke had a heart attack soon after your mum died.'

'Oh.'

'But I remember your parents from when we were younger. A lovely couple, God bless them. Very powerful homemade wine.'

My mother and father felt like abstract concepts. Everything he told me about myself might as well have happened to another person, in some made-up story. In fact, Gary knew very little about my early years. 'How do I know what grades you got in your GCSEs?' he protested.

'Sorry, I just feel a bit nervous about getting my exam results. I feel nervous about all of it. So did I go to university?'

'This is where we met,' he recalled with more enthusiasm. 'I was doing English and American Studies. I switched from doing straight English—'

'Sorry, where was this? Oxford? Cambridge?'

'Bangor. I chose there because this gorgeous girl at my school had put it down, although she ended up in East Anglia so it didn't really work out . . .'

Over the next ten minutes I learned that Gary and I had shared a student house in North Wales, that I had been in a college football team with Gary, and that I had taken a degree in history, though I had not copied my entire dissertation off a student from Aberystwyth like Gary. Frankly, it was fascinating to find out so much about myself.

He came back from the bar with another pint and a greying pickled egg. The whole time he'd been at the bar I had found myself staring down at the white shadow where the ring had been. I was almost too nervous to broach the subject. If there was a wife out there, I wanted to know who I was when I got married.

'So you don't remember this pub at all?' said Gary sitting down.

'No. Why, have we been here before?'

'Yeah—you used to sell crack in here before all that shit with the Russian mafia kicked off—'

'Of course, the Russian mafia. They left a beetroot head in my bed, didn't they?' I felt a shiver of pride at succeeding in making Gary chuckle. 'It's weird. I don't know who I am but I know I wasn't a crack dealer.'

'No, drugs were never your scene. You fret about whether it's acceptable to give your kids a Lemsip.'

That was how I discovered I was a father. Your *kids*, Gary had said.

'Yeah, you've got two nippers,' said Gary, when I pressed him for more information. 'Boy and a girl: Jamie who's about fifteen or twelve or something, and there's Dillie, who's younger, like ten maybe. Actually, she must be eleven, cos they're both at secondary school. Though not at your school.'

'What do you mean "my school"?'

'Your school where you teach.'

'So I'm a teacher? Slow down a minute, will you? See, this is why I wanted to do everything chronologically. Tell me about my children first.'

'Well, they're just kids, you know. They're cute. I'm actually godfather to Jamie. Or is it Dillie? I can't remember. But, yeah, great kids. You can be really proud of them.'

But I couldn't be really proud of them. I wanted to be really proud of them, but they were just a cold, historical fact.

'Mind if we sit here?' interjected a woman carrying shopping bags, and she slumped into one of the two spare places at our table. 'Over here, Meg!'

I was a parent to two strangers. But these children would know me; hopefully, they would love me.

'Get a menu!' shouted the lady to her companion, her daughter maybe. This woman's face was now imprinted on my mind, yet I had no idea what my own children looked like.

'So what are my kids like?'

The woman did a poor job of pretending not to listen.

'Well, Jamie looks just like you, actually. He doesn't say a great deal, but that's probably just his age. He's getting quite tall now, trendy, into music.'

'What about my daughter—Dillie? Is that her real name or is it short for something?'

'Could be Dilys,' said the woman at our table.

'Sorry?'

'Your daughter's name? Dillie could be short for Dilys. Or "Dillwyn" is a name. Welsh, I think. You're not Welsh, are you?'

'I dunno. Am I Welsh?'

'Nah, don't think so.'

The detail of my own parenthood suddenly recast everything in an even more serious light. Now my mental breakdown was not just something that had happened to me, but to a whole family.

'Been in prison, have you?' enquired the woman nonchalantly.

'Er, something like that.' I smiled.

'Murder,' added Gary, in the hope of scaring her off. But she didn't seem thrown by this detail.

'My husband walked out on us when Meg was two. We never heard from him again. He wouldn't recognise her if he passed her in the street.'

'Right . . .'

'Er, so what other news can I tell you?' Gary said. 'The Tories are back in power. And everyone has mobile phones and home computers and Woolworth's went out of business—'

'I know all that stuff. It's just everything about *my life* that's been forgotten. I know every Christmas Number One. But I just can't remember anyone's name or anything about them.'

'Ha! That's just being a bloke, isn't it?' said the woman with a sigh.

After that we talked in hushed mumbles. Now that we seemed to have abandoned any idea of doing my life in chronological order, I jumped to the question that had been gnawing away at me.

'So, I'm father to two children. Tell me about their mother.'

There was a pause.

'Er—she's cool, yeah. God, actually this egg is disgusting. I might get something else. I wonder if they sell Peperamis—'

'No, no—hang on. What's her name?'

'Her name? Madeleine. Maddy.'

'My wife is called Madeleine!' I rolled the name about in my head, feeling how it fitted with my own. This would surely be the foundation stone on which my life would be rebuilt. 'So where did I meet her?'

'You hooked up in your first term at university, didn't you? It was like "Bye-bye Mummy, hello Wifey!" You were like so totally into one another, it was actually quite annoying for the rest of us.'

'Thanks.'

'After college you both spent a few years doing nothing. And 'cos you didn't have the faintest idea what to do, you decided to be a teacher.'

'Wow! That's a vocation! A teacher . . .' I stroked my beard as I pictured myself as Robin Williams in *Dead Poets Society*.

'Yeah—some comprehensive next to the Wandsworth one-way system,' he said. 'You said your school specialises in Business and Enterprise. So you don't produce drug addicts. Your kids learn to be the dealers—'

'A teacher. I like that. What do I teach? Tell me it's not metalwork . . .'

'You teach history—and sometimes "citizenship", whatever that is.'

'A history teacher? Ha! The historian with no history of his own.'

'I suppose that is ironic. You don't know anything about the past, but then neither do any of your pupils.'

A food order was called out from the bar and Gary looked forlornly at the plate of fish and chips being handed out.

'But hang on, we need to tell Madeleine and the kids I'm OK, don't we? I've been missing for over a week. Were they worried about me?'

'I dunno, mate. I haven't spoken to her.'

'I was missing for a week and she didn't call you?'

'Well, it wasn't really like that . . . Do you fancy sharing a plate of chips?'

'Wasn't like what? Is Madeleine away, or ill or something?'

'Maybe I'll eat a sachet of ketchup to get rid of that disgusting egg flavour. At least they're free.'

The woman gave Gary a disbelieving look.

'What do you mean, "it wasn't really like that"? What's wrong?'

'You and Maddy have been through a bit of a tough time recently.' He was tugging wildly at the ketchup sachet. 'When I spoke to that doctor on the phone she asked if you'd experienced any stress prior to your memory-wipe and I said, yeah, he's just split up with his wife, hasn't he?'

At this point the sachet ripped open, and ketchup splattered everywhere on me and on the mother and daughter sharing our booth. The two of them jumped up and made an enormous fuss, while I was still trying to digest the crippling news that the wife I had only just learned about had split up with me. It must have been the shortest marriage in history.

'Oh, sorry about that,' said Gary to the woman. 'Here—have some of these napkins. Or you could always lick it off your blouse.'

'*You* might do that—'

'I'm not licking ketchup off your blouse, love—that's crossing the line. Vaughan, mate—you got sauce on your shirt there . . .'

'Gary,' I said quietly, 'I think I want to go back to the hospital.'

I FOUND MYSELF SQUINTING at the bright sunshine as we stepped out of the dingy pub. Gary lit a cigarette and offered me one.

'No, thanks.'

'No? You normally smoke like a beagle.'

'Really?' So far Gary had told me that I was a chain-smoking teacher in a sink school whose marriage was on the rocks. Normally one would discover this about oneself over a period of decades.

'Are you all right, mate? You look kinda weird.'

'Can I just go back to the hospital, please?'

'You know, you can always shack up at my place. You stayed for a bit when things started to go a bit wrong on the marriage front.'

'When things started to go a bit wrong?'

'Yeah,' he chuckled. 'You turned up at my place with this blood-soaked bandage on your hand, saying the marriage was over.'

Then the penny dropped. 'Oh, I get it! This is another of your stupid jokes, isn't it? Maddy and I aren't separated at all, are we?'

Gary winced. 'No joke, mate. You and Maddy can't stand each other no more. Oh, and that's the other reason you can't stay in the hospital. You're divorcing her on Thursday. Oh, hang on, no, I've got that wrong—'

'What, so it *is* a joke?'

'When's the first of November? That's Friday, isn't it? You're divorcing her on Friday. Is there a snack machine at the hospital?'

CHAPTER 2

Google Images had revealed that there was more than one person in the world called 'Madeleine Vaughan'. Now I could see why the marriage hadn't worked out. She was either nine years old, a labradoodle puppy or a very tanned porn actress.

That night I had gone upstairs to spend some time on the computer terminal 'provided by the Friends of Teddy's'. The only time you could get on it was late at night, but this added to the shady sense of espionage I felt.

Researching details about myself had been no easier. Facebook wouldn't let me log in. I couldn't believe I hadn't asked Gary what my first name actually was. But it had eventually been possible to track a man down who quite possibly could have been me. I found a secondary school in the location Gary had described and on a list of staff members at 'Wandle Academy' was 'Jack Vaughan—History'. There were a couple of references to 'Jack Vaughan' at an education conference in Kettering at which I'd spoken a year earlier. On the school web site I scanned photographs and finally spotted myself on the edge of a staff group shot. I felt as if some identity thief had been walking around pretending to be me: teaching history, talking at conferences, alienating my wife.

It was nearly dawn by the time I forced myself to stop. I spent the following morning trying to catch up on my sleep, attempting to ignore Bernard.

Suddenly the curtain round my bed was pulled back and there stood Gary with a smartly dressed blonde woman who looked younger than us.

'Ta da!' exclaimed Gary. 'Vaughan—meet the missus!'

The woman beside him gave me a nervous smile and attempted a rather girlie wave.

'Hello, Vaughan. Remember me?'

'Erm . . . no, I don't, sorry. Are you Maddy?' My voice was shaking. My wife was just a complete stranger—a woman towards whom I felt no particular hostility, nor, indeed, any attraction.

'Not *your* missus, *my* missus! This is Linda!'

I felt the back of my head hit the pillow. Gary turned to her. 'See, I told you, didn't I? He's forgotten everything. So he won't remember that embarrassing affair the two of you had in Lanzarote.'

She giggled and gave him a playful slap. 'Honestly, Gary! What are you like? Don't worry, Vaughan—we didn't. Gary's explained what happened, and we're going to take you back home and look after you, aren't we, Gaz?'

Linda had rung the ward to make her offer earlier that morning. It had been a big decision. Various medics had given their professional opinions on my fragile psychological state and whether a change of location might impede my progress. Then they balanced that against how much the hospital needed my bed and said, 'How quickly can he leave?'

Dr Lewington formally presented me with a leaving present. 'There is no guarantee that your memory will not wipe itself all over again, leaving you lost as before. So I want you to wear this identity tag round your neck at all times; it has emergency contact details for this hospital.'

'Do pop over and say hello when you're back for your checkups . . .' said Bernard, a little forlornly.

'Of course, Bernard. If you're not out of here by then.'

'Have you got the same thing as Mr Memory Man here?' Gary asked.

'No. I've got a brain tumour,' Bernard said brightly. 'I don't let it get me down. I say anything that rhymes with "humour" can't be all that bad.'

'Right . . .' reflected Gary. 'Well, that makes me feel a lot better about that dose I had, that rhymes with "Snap!"'

Linda giggled and slapped him on the arm. She was not the spouse I would have cast for Gary. I would have expected some spiky-haired punk chick with piercings. Linda was not only conventional, but surprisingly young and posh, and she glowed with vigorous good health.

'Actually, we do have some rather big news since we last saw you,' she said, smiling at her husband. 'You know we've been trying for a baby?'

'No?'

'No, of course not. Well the wonderful thing is—it's happened! We're going to be a proper family.'

She said this as if it was the cue for me to scream in excitement, and when I merely gave my polite congratulations she looked a little put out. As we travelled down in the lift she began to provide anecdotes and accounts of past episodes as if to prove that I did know them very well. Apparently I had been Gary's best man at their recent wedding; I had played football with Gary every Tuesday night for years; I had even been on holiday with them.

'I'm sorry, I don't remember any of it,' I mumbled. 'It's like I was the best man at your wedding but now I don't even know what Gary and I have in common. I mean, what did we used to talk about?'

'I don't think you ever had an actual conversation,' said Linda. 'You just compared apps on your iPhones.'

Beside me in the back of Gary and Linda's car was a new baby seat with the label still attached. 'So when exactly is it due?'

'In about nine months' time,' sighed Gary.

'No, it's less than that,' corrected Linda. 'But we want to make sure everything is perfect for Baby.'

'*The* baby,' corrected Gary.

It was a sunny, windy day as we drove out of the hospital car park. I had presumed that we would be going straight back to Gary and Linda's flat, but they clearly had other plans.

'OK, groovy people, we are welcoming you aboard on Gary and Linda's famous Magicking Mystery Tour!' announced my driver, doing his best impression of a German tour guide. 'On this evening's super-hip sightsee trip, we will be point out some of most famous landmarks of Vaughan's life.' Linda was laughing at his German/Scandinavian/American accent.

Gary pointed out a pub we popped into about ten years ago, and then a sports shop where he'd bought some trainers, though he was pretty sure I hadn't been with him. He had given up on the comedy foreign accent, though the concept of the tour guide was still just clinging on. 'If you look out of the left-hand window you can see a branch of McDonald's, which is where your parents hoped you might work if you realised your full potential. Tragically, you became a history teacher instead.'

We crossed the river and Gary pointed out a couple more pubs we had frequented. Gary and Linda were surprised that I recognised some roads and not others; it seemed that a generic knowledge of London's main streets and bridges had survived. We pulled up outside a modern comprehensive.

'This is where I teach?'

'Wow, you remember it!'

'No—you just said my school was in Wandsworth and so I found Wandle Academy on the Internet.'

'Oh. Well, anyway, not exactly Hogwarts, is it?'

The concrete edifice did look a bit shabby and foreboding. The entrance was litter-strewn and a couple of silver birch saplings had been snapped off.

'So am I just a classroom teacher or a head of year or anything?'

Linda explained that during my decade at the school I had been promoted to 'Head of Humans, or something'.

'Humanities?'

'Yeah, that sounds right.'

I felt a twinge of worry that there were classes of children wondering what had happened to Mr Vaughan.

'But my own kids don't come here?'

'Don't be ridiculous! Maddy knows what the teachers are like!'

'They go to a school closer to where you live,' explained Linda. 'Dillie's only just left that primary. That's where we want Baby to go, isn't it, Gary?'

'*The* baby.'

'So—er—anyway, what do you two do for a living?'

'What is this, a Rotarians' Christmas soirée or something?'

'I don't know—it just felt a bit impolite to keep talking about me all the time. I didn't want to appear self-obsessed or whatever.'

'OK. Well, I'm—this is weird—I am in recruitment,' said Linda, 'and Gary is in computers—Internet and all that.'

'Right.' I nodded neutrally. 'Not data-recovery by any chance, is it?'

'Ha! No, though I know a few people who do specialise in that. They'll just say you should have backed your brain up on a memory stick. No, I work for myself, designing web sites, developing new ideas for the net.'

'Wow! What sort of ideas?'

'OK, well, I might as well tell you about our big project then.'

'*Our* big project?'

'Yeah, you and me have been developing a site that will revolutionise how we consume news.' I noticed a sudden degree of self-belief in Gary. 'See, currently all news is top down. Some fascist corporation decides the most important story, then serves up all the lies to the trusting public.'

Linda was nodding supportively.

'The Internet allows you to turn that model on its head. Imagine millions of readers writing up whatever they might have just witnessed around the globe, uploading their own photos, video footage and text. Hey presto! The story with the most hits becomes the main item of news on the world's most democratic and unbiased news outlet! YouNews is the future, you said so yourself. You can search by region, subject, protest movement, whatever.'

'You must check it out,' said Linda. 'I put up a lovely bit of video yesterday: this cute kitten being surprised by a cuckoo clock!'

'No, Linda, that's not news. That's not what the site is for.'

'So no reporters or editors?' I observed.

'Exactly! No hacks filing their expenses from around the world and no press barons protecting their political allies or paymasters.'

I thought about this for a moment. 'But how do you know it's true?'

'True?'

'Yes, a story that some member of the public has uploaded. How do you know they haven't just made it up?'

'Well, if they've made it up,' explained Gary, 'then you always said that other members of the public will say so in the comment thread and it will lose credibility. Or they can re-edit it themselves—it's like Wikipedia, but for current affairs. You're really into it, believe me.'

My feelings about Gary's web site echoed a deeper worry. How could I know whether anything was true? I was still fighting a tiny voice in my head that questioned whether my name was really 'Vaughan', that I was in fact a teacher and that my marriage was really over.

Eventually we reached the address where I had been living right up until my fugue. I learned that between moving out of my family home and taking up a residency in King Edward's Hospital, I had sofa-surfed between a number of temporary addresses, most recently housesitting for a rich family who were in New York for three months.

'Wow! What an amazing house. And I had it all to myself?'

'Yeah—but you didn't like it. It made you, like, really tense being responsible for all the fancy furniture and that.'

The family were apparently now back home, so this private mansion was no longer an option for me.

'And you don't recognise that either? That is really amazing! So is there anything you can remember?'

'Actually, I have this vague memory of really laughing with a girl when I was younger. And we're sheltering under a canopy or something but still getting wet, but we don't mind. But I can't remember who she was. I just remember being really, really happy.'

Gary and Linda looked at one another but said nothing. We turned into a residential street just off Clapham Common. Rows of midsize Victorian houses were interspersed with a few ugly 1950s blocks. On the corner was number 27, which looked like the best house in the street, with dormer windows at the top and a little turret that gazed out over the London skyline.

'Recognise this?'

'Don't tell me—it's where I was born? Ah, but there's no blue plaque.'

'No—have another go.'

At that moment the front door opened and a striking redhead stepped out into the autumn sunshine and dropped a bag into the wheelie bin.

'Wow! Who is that?' I whispered. 'She is gorgeous!'

The woman paused as if to check the weather.

'Was she living there when I was? Should we go and say hello?'

'Blimey, Vaughan, you've gone bright red,' said Linda. 'Gary, we probably shouldn't hang about. We don't want her to see us here.'

He was already putting the car in gear and pulling away.

'Hang on. Where are we? Who is that beautiful woman?'

'That, Vaughan, was the house you lived in for years,' said my tour guide. 'And that was Madeleine, the woman you're about to divorce.'

As YOU CAME IN the front door, the first thing you saw was a baby-gate across the foot of the stairs and a brand-new stroller folded up by the coat hooks. There were plastic safety covers over the electrical sockets and in the lounge was a big Thomas the Tank Engine rug.

'Sorry, are you expecting *another* baby, or will this one be your first?'

'No, it's just the two of us at the moment,' confirmed Gary. 'It's just that Linda likes buying all the stuff, you know.'

'I always loved your home, Vaughan,' enthused Linda, 'brimming with children's toys and everything.'

She proudly showed me into the room where I would be staying. In the corner was a brand-new cot, surrounded by musical mobiles with rotating light patterns. Teddy-bear wallpaper was softly lit by the low-wattage light from a Disney lampshade. Linda lovingly adjusted one of the soft toys, who looked settled in for a long wait. The extended sofa bed that had been made up for me rather spoiled the nursery atmosphere.

'Isn't this a lovely room?' Linda said proudly. 'Obviously you'll have to move out when Baby comes . . .'

'*The* baby,' came Gary's voice from down the hall.

In a wardrobe hung a range of men's clothes. These had either been collected for Baby when he reached middle age, or were the jeans, shirts and sweaters that belonged to me before my fugue. There were a few frayed-looking suits, presumably my teaching uniform, and some uninspiring ties.

Linda had kindly prepared everything for my stay and there was even a new toothbrush still in its packet. 'This is the bathroom, Vaughan— I thought you might fancy a bath.'

'Do you think she looked sad?'

'Who?'

'Maddy? I thought she looked a little sad . . .'

'Er, no, she looked pretty much how she usually looks to me . . . Dirty laundry goes in there, and I'll show you how to use the washing machine.'

A few minutes later I was taking off my clothes in the private space of virtual strangers. I felt like the intruder in a family bathroom. I still wanted to ask them so much more; I felt like I'd just had the barest glimpse of who I was. When did things go wrong with Maddy? Did I move out? Did she kick me out? Did one of us have an affair?

The bath was foamy and scented and I submerged my aching head under the suds, letting my senses deaden to the outside world. I slowly came up for air. This was the most relaxed I could remember feeling. My head felt completely empty. And then it happened. From nowhere, I recovered my first memory—the whole episode fell into my head all at once.

MADDY AND I are walking up a grassy hill hand in hand until we stand at the summit and feel the wind and sun on our faces before indulging in another quick kiss. We continue on to the next hill, the backpacks and camping gear doing little to slow us down as we march optimistically across the Irish countryside. This is our first holiday together—it is sunny, we have a brand-new tent—what can possibly go wrong?

'Oh, no! I don't believe it!' exclaims Maddy, sounding genuinely alarmed.

'What is it?'

'I forgot to send off that postcard to Great-Auntie Brenda. Again!'

'What, the racist one?'

'It's not racist. It's just an affectionate Irish stereotype.'

The postcard to Great-Auntie Brenda features a smiling cartoon leprechaun drinking a pint of Guinness and bears the caption 'Top o' the mornin' to yers!!' I suggest that it might be of questionable taste, but Maddy stands firmly by her selection for her elderly great-aunt.

'I thought she'd like it. She has gnomes in her garden.'

The leprechaun is not looking any less cheerful for having been stuffed into the side pocket of Madeleine's rucksack for three days. Maddy has already written a message on the back, completed the address and affixed a stamp. Just that last detail of putting the card in a postbox keeps eluding her. And when Maddy gets back to England and unpacks her bag, there is the leprechaun, still wishing her the top o' the mornin'. She gives it to me to post when I am going out that evening, and I place it carefully in my inside jacket pocket. It is several months later that I find it there.

Maddy and I have hitched and walked through west Cork and now gaze down on a huge stretch of sand known as Barleycove. Hills on either side lead down to a perfect beach with steep, grassy dunes behind. The hazy horizon is punctured by the tiny outline of the Fastnet lighthouse.

'Why don't we camp for the night?' I suggest. 'We could swim and make a fire out of driftwood and barbecue those sausages?'

'But the lady in the pub said there was going to be a storm, remember? We could go back to Crookhaven. That pub had a few rooms upstairs.'

'Come on—it's blazing sunshine. This is the perfect spot. This is what it's all about!' and I am already taking off my backpack.

Six hours later, we are awoken by the tent's top sheet coming loose in the gale. Now the rain drums even more noisily against the canvas sound box in which we're supposed to be sleeping as water trickles down the tent pole. Despite the foolhardy decision to ignore the local prophet, the night-time storm has actually made us even cosier inside.

'I told you to take no notice of that woman in the pub.'

'You were right. Everyone knows it never rains in Ireland.'

Another violent gust of wind makes the tent shudder, and then the guy ropes break free on one side and the roof collapses on top of us. I swear loudly, which prompts shrieks of laughter from Maddy, who is still enjoying the effects of a bottle of white wine. I attempt to right the tent poles from inside, but the gale pulls the tent flat again, as a stream of water flows onto our things. Maddy sticks her head out of the tent to see what she can see.

'Maybe you should go out and try to fix it from the outside?' she suggests.

'But I'm completely naked!'

'Yeah—well there's not going to be anyone out there on a night like this, is there?' she points out.

And so my pale, naked frame steps out into the night to do battle against the wind and rain. From inside the tent Maddy hears an elderly-sounding Irishman nonchalantly ask me if I am 'all right there'.

'Oh, hello, er, yes, thank you very much. Our tent blew over . . .'

'Ah well, I saw that you'd camped down here,' the old man muses from the shelter of a golfing umbrella, 'so I thought I'd better check you hadn't blown away, like.'

I can just hear Maddy giggling inside the tent—she had obviously seen him coming and had deliberately set me up.

'Not yet,' I quip and my fake laughter goes on far too long.

'There's a barn up the lane. You could move up there if you want.'

'Thank you, that's very kind.'

'But you don't want to be prancing about in this weather stark naked. You'll catch your death of cold.'

'Good advice. I'll get back inside right now. Thanks for checking on us.'

The guy ropes are never reset, and the tent stays collapsed on us all night, but it doesn't matter that we barely sleep and have to dry out our things tomorrow, because right now all we want to do is laugh and laugh. Maddy doesn't mind that I ignored her advice and was proved wrong; nothing is going to be allowed to spoil our happiness. We are young and can doze with canvas on our faces, and arms half wrapped round one another; we are immunised against discomfort by the euphoria of just being together.

'I'VE HAD A MEMORY!' I exclaimed, running out of the bathroom. 'I've just recovered a whole episode of my life!' Gary and Linda were delighted for me, though their joy was slightly tempered by the vision of an almost-naked man dripping foamy bathwater all over their kitchen floor. I wondered if being stripped and soaking wet was the association that triggered the memory, but somehow I knew that it was having seen Maddy. Linda fetched me her pink towelling dressing gown and put the hand towel I had used to protect my modesty straight into the washing machine.

We sat round their kitchen table and they assured me that this was only the beginning, that other memories would surely start to flow back. But while I wanted to find out more about my marriage, Gary felt I needed to focus on the ending of it. I was reminded that I was due in court on Friday, for the final stage of what they earnestly assured me had been a long, painful and expensive business.

The proposition that Gary was putting to me was that I was going to have to go to a court of law and pretend to a judge that nothing had happened to me in order to terminate a marriage I knew nothing about.

'But what if they ask a question I don't know the answer to?'

'Your lawyer will tell you what to say,' Gary assured me.

'And he'll know about my condition?'

'Er, probably not,' said Gary. 'We could risk telling them, but what will they do? Postpone the case and charge you another ten grand.'

'Maddy and the kids are geared up to it happening on Friday. They need closure,' said Linda.

Gary was insistent that I would deeply regret not having gone through with the divorce if my memory suddenly returned and I awoke to discover that I had lost the chance to break free from an unhappy marriage.

'Yes, you *say* it was an unhappy marriage . . .' I ventured.

'Well, you *are* getting divorced,' pointed out Gary.

On digging deeper I learned that it was not until the actual divorce process was underway that things had turned nasty. It was only after Maddy and I learned of the provocative claims being made by the other side's lawyers that personal hostilities spiralled out of control. 'You compared the divorce process to war,' recalled Gary.

However persuasive they were that we'd be better off apart, I couldn't agree there and then to take this momentous step in the dark. I announced that I'd like to go out for a walk, to have a bit of a think, and somewhere between Linda's nervous concern and Gary's total indifference, we reached a compromise that it would be fine as long as I took an *A–Z* with their address and phone number written in the back and twenty pounds in cash.

As soon as their front door was closed behind me, I began retracing my steps the mile or so to where we had seen Maddy. I was going to meet my wife. I had resolved that she had to know about my condition; the event had major consequences for her own life, our children, the court case. I owed it to her to tell her face to face what had happened. It should be done before the children were home from school and with time to postpone the court hearing; and that meant I had to do it right now.

In any case, I told myself, before I divorce my wife I'd like to get to know her a bit.

GARY HAD RELATED the course of events that had led to Maddy and me becoming the owners of a Victorian house in Clapham. After university, Maddy and I had been friends with a group of housing activists who'd identified the long-abandoned property as a potential squat. But when it actually came to it, Maddy had been the bravest of all of us. While I hovered behind, Maddy took a jemmy to the heavily fortified front windows. It transpired that the council was too chaotic ever to evict us.

A few years later we formed ourselves into a registered housing association; it was easier then for the authorities to permit us to stay there. But it was apparently *me* who did all the paperwork. Maddy and I were the only ones still living there when the law was changed permitting housing association tenants the right to buy. In two decades Maddy and I had made the journey from radical squatters to respectable owner-occupiers. The bay window where Maddy had taken a crowbar to the corrugated iron now had a poster advertising our kids' School Autumn Fayre.

And now I stood before the family home once again, a place with so many memories, but none of them currently mine. My intention had been to march right up and ring the doorbell, but I was thrown by the fact that the bell was actually an intercom system, which meant that my first words to my wife might have to be through a voice-distorting microphone. My finger was shaking as I reached for the button. I left it hovering there uncertainly. What if one of my children was off school and rushed down to say hello? I imagined the scenario of my daughter emerging with a friend and me not knowing to which girl I was father. It was not just my own mental health that was at issue here.

But it had to be done. I pressed the buzzer. To my surprise this prompted the sound of loud barking from the other side of the door. There was a dog! This was the furious bark of a guard dog in the house on his own—an angry warning that was not mollified by any owner calling him away from the door. Maddy was out. I peered through the letterbox, calling an optimistic 'Hello?' and instantly the dog's demeanour changed. Suddenly he was howling with excitement as he recognised me. He was a big golden retriever, licking the hand that held open the letterbox, then breaking off to howl his emotional hellos. I had never thought about whether I liked dogs or not, but I instinctively felt affection for this one.

'Hello, boy! Remember me? Did I used to take you walkies?'

That word made the dog even more manic, and I felt guilty for getting him so excited when I was going to have to walk away again.

I crossed the road to get a better view of the house. I was struck by what a beautiful home we'd created. It was brimming with character, with brightly painted shutters and blooming window boxes. Dormer windows peeked out from the slate-tiled roof and the middle floor had a balcony. From the side I spotted a faded sun canopy, which overlooked the back garden where a chaotic Virginia creeper was in its final blush of copper.

I tried to imagine myself sitting out on the balcony with Maddy, sharing a bottle of white wine on a summer's night, as the kids played in the garden. Was I recovering a vague memory, or was this some fantasy? Looking at it all with fresh eyes, I couldn't help thinking it was the old Vaughan that had needed the psychiatric help for letting all this go.

So lost was I in speculation that I didn't notice a car drawing up a few spaces away. I felt terror-stricken and thrilled all at once when I realised who it was and dived behind a parked van. I watched in the van's wing mirror as Maddy reversed into the tightest of spaces, rather expertly I thought. She stepped out, wearing a funky orange coat that flared out below the waist. Her hair was up and she wore small earrings.

Seeing her again, I couldn't help but feel as if some enormous administrative mistake must have occurred and the authorities were proceeding with the wrong divorce. Why would I want to stop being married to such a beautiful woman? Well, now was my chance to introduce myself to my wife.

But just as I stepped out from behind the van, the passenger door of Maddy's car opened, and now I slipped out of view again as I spied a man getting out. The two of them set about taking large frames out of the back of the car and began carrying them up to the front door. The man was younger than me, and too snappily dressed to be a delivery man. He was very matter-of-fact about the job in hand, stacking the frames and going back for more. Was Maddy a painter? An art dealer? Crouched down on the pavement out of view, I was transfixed as I scanned the situation for any further clues. There was nothing to suggest that these two were in any sort of relationship. My guess was that Maddy had bought the frames off him and now he was helping to deliver them. But that was a more personal service than you'd expect from a high-street picture framer. I wanted to see if this man followed her into the house.

Maddy unlocked the front door and patted the excited dog, who circled her, wagging his backside. The dog sniffed the air as she went inside, but instead of following her, he started down the steps. Maddy called his name, but the dog had got the scent of something and then I saw the panic in her face as he headed towards the road. The dog had clearly got something in his nostrils and looked unstoppable.

That was the moment I realised that the scent the dog had picked up was mine and he was running across the road to where I was hiding. Maddy was following and would find me lurking here, and my first encounter with her since my breakdown would be as some creepy stalker. Behind me was a passageway that led down the side of the house opposite ours. I ran down there and dived round the back of a wooden shed. Almost immediately the dog caught up with me, excitedly jumping up to lick my face.

'Woody! Woody!' Maddy was desperately calling, getting closer.

'*Woody, you bad dog!*' I scolded in hushed desperation. '*Go home now!*' and, amazingly, a rather disappointed Woody scampered back in the direction from which he'd come. I heard her say 'There you are, you naughty dog!' She had a slight northern accent, Liverpool maybe—it was hard to tell.

I was safe. She wouldn't come down here. I closed my eyes and leaned my head on the creosote-scented shed as I let out a huge sigh of relief.

'What are you doing in my garden?' said an indignant upper-class voice. I turned round to see a rotund figure in his early sixties. 'Oh, Vaughan, it's you! How are you? Haven't seen you for ages.'

'Oh, er—hello!'

'I think I know why you're here.' My mind was racing. Had he seen me spying on my own wife? 'You want your thingamajig back, don't you?'

'My thingamajig?'

'I meant to bring it back ages ago—very remiss of me. Anyway, help yourself—it's in the shed.'

I obediently opened the shed door and stared at the chaotic arrangement of garden furniture, abandoned lawn mowers, rusting barbecues and plant pots piled up before me.

'How's Madeleine?' he enquired as I pretended to scan the space in front of me.

'She's, er, fine,' I blurted.

'Well, you two must come round for dinner soon.'

'Thank you. That's very nice of you.'

'Really?'

I seemed to have given a reply that surprised him. In that moment I understood that previous offers must have always been rebuffed.

'Great, well what about this weekend? Arabella was just saying we hadn't seen much of you and we're not doing anything on Saturday.'

Without even knowing him or his wife, I could already sense that the bitterness of my marital breakup would not be ameliorated by committing Maddy and myself to a dinner party with these neighbours.

'Er, it's a bit difficult, actually. Maddy and I are having a trial separation.'

'A trial separation?'

'Yeah, you know . . . a trial divorce. Just to see how that goes for a while.'

At least this embarrassing news cut the conversation short. The neighbour came into the shed himself, where it turned out the thing I had come round to collect was right under my nose. 'Silly me!' I tutted.

Ten minutes later I was standing on a busy underground train, noticing that people were giving me more space than might usually be expected.

Perhaps it was the three-foot-long serrated blade of the electric hedge trimmer I was clutching. I affected to carry the unwieldy weapon as if I often travelled on the tube during rush hour with a yard of sharpened steel teeth in my right hand. A couple of hoodies were eyeing me warily. 'Respect!' muttered one as he got off at the next stop.

CHAPTER 3

I felt as if I had stared at my bedroom clock for an entire night. Lying there, in the half-light of the nursery, everything was quiet and still except for the manic pendulum on the wall opposite. It featured a happy clown clinging onto a rainbow, swinging back and forth, for ever. His situation still seemed to make more sense than my own. By about half past three it became clear that the clown was not going to take a rest, and so I got up and tiptoed into the kitchen for a glass of water.

When dawn came it would be the day of my court case. I sat at the pine table for a while, listening to the rhythmical dripping of the tap. Pinned on the notice board by the fridge was a telephone bill. I spotted Gary and Linda's address book and started to flick through the pages. 'Vaughan and Maddy' was filed under 'V', with the address set out underneath. A green biro had crossed my name out and scrawled a new address sideways down the margin. That had subsequently been crossed out and then another address scribbled in blue underneath that. There was my family's telephone number glaring at me, a series of digits that I must have effortlessly recited a thousand times. I could just dial that number right now. Although ringing up my ex-wife at half past three in the morning might not be the best way to reassure her of my sanity.

My personal effects had been rediscovered in a jacket pocket and now, seated at the kitchen table, I carefully dealt out the cards from my wallet: that's the Blockbuster video card, a sign that you might be the sort of person who would enjoy renting movies. Combined with a Lambeth Library Services card and a Clapham Picturehouse membership, this suggests you are quite a cultured person. In terms of wealth, there is only one basic credit card, not a series of high-status gold or platinum cards. On the plus side, your Caffè Nero loyalty card shows that you are only two stamps away from a free cappuccino . . .

I took a pen and attempted to copy the signature on my bank cards. I could produce nothing even vaguely similar. My phone was out of battery, which had been something of a relief. I had been frightened that names would flash on the screen and I would know nothing at all about them. But now, under cover of darkness, I plugged it in and watched the screen come back to life. I had forty-seven missed calls and seventeen messages.

I didn't recognise the first caller. 'Vaughan, hi, it's me, there's a curriculum problem I need you to sort out. If you could check the rota for Day Six—' And then I stopped it and just pressed 'Delete All'.

I rested my forehead on the kitchen table for a while and thought about the ordeal of the day ahead. The court case had not been postponed because I had never been assertive enough to insist that Maddy or my lawyer was informed about my condition. Gary had maintained that we were definitely doing the right thing, and that my life could begin again once this 'last little formality' was out of the way. I was to learn the hard way about the wisdom of taking legal advice from a man with an earring.

I WAS WOKEN by the sound of crockery being placed on the kitchen table beside my head.

'Sorry to wake you there, Vaughan, mate. I'm just doing breakfast. Do you want any prawn balls?'

'What?'

'With sweet-and-sour sauce. And some special fried rice, though it's a bit less special than it was a couple of days ago.'

The microwave gave out a beep and Gary bit into a reheated spring roll.

'Er—no, thanks. What time is it?'

'It's getting on a bit actually. You're supposed to be in court in an hour.'

GARY OBSERVED that I wasn't as laid-back as I used to be. He felt there was no need to run from the underground station to the court. 'Relax, they're not going to start without you, are they?'

'Vaughan! There you are!' said a posh young man with a voice even louder than his tie. 'I thought you wanted to meet a bit earlier?'

'Are you Vaughan's lawyer?' said Gary. 'We spoke on the phone.'

'Yes, hello. So, Vaughan, according to your friend here you wanted to go through the questions likely to come up in court *again*,' he said pointedly.

'Again?' I asked without checking myself.

'That's exactly what we did last time I saw you.'

'Er, Vaughan said that was incredibly useful,' interjected Gary, 'but, when I was just doing a final rehearsal with him, it turned out that he was a little confused about one or two minor aspects.'

'I see,' said the lawyer. 'Which particular areas?'

I looked forlornly at Gary, hoping that he might have the words to answer this. He didn't. 'Well, the whole thing, really. Getting divorced?'

I found it difficult to concentrate when I was looking over his shoulder to see if I could spot Maddy coming in.

'Mrs Vaughan is being incredibly unreasonable,' commented the lawyer on one of the points of contention relating to our financial settlement.

'There are two sides to everything,' I interjected. 'I mean, her lawyer probably thinks I'm being incredibly unreasonable too.'

He seemed to be pulled up short by this comment. 'Well, Mr Vaughan, I must say you seem to have mellowed somewhat.'

Gary was anxious that my attitude did not arouse suspicions. 'I think with the actual divorce so close, you're preparing for the next psychological stage, aren't you, mate? Forgiveness, reconciliation, cooperation. It's all in *Divorce for Dummies*.'

'I haven't read that one,' said the lawyer. He had never actually told us his name. 'So you're completely clear about the CETV?'

'What?' I stuttered. 'Will the judge ask me what that stands for?'

'No! The Cash Equivalent Transfer Value is the valuation technique both parties have agreed to pursue with regard to the pension.'

'I knew that—'

'The difficulty being that Maddy is demanding half.'

'Sounds reasonable,' I commented cheerfully.

His stunned silence went on for so long I was worried the extra time would be added on to my bill. 'I'm sorry, Mr Vaughan, but we have been absolutely adamant on this point up till now.'

'See mate, you paid nearly all of the contributions into the pension,' interjected Gary, 'so you didn't see why she should receive half of it.'

'But if she was looking after the kids, how could she pay any money in? She was making, like, a non-cash contribution, wasn't she?'

'That is the point that *her* lawyer will be making. But we have consistently agreed that although she could have worked, she *chose* not to.'

'Ah, well that's a difficult one, isn't it?' I mused philosophically. 'I mean, if I was working so hard at my job perhaps that closed off the possibility of her resuming any meaningful career after we had children? I just think we are pursuing a rather hard-line stance.'

The lawyer pressed his fingers to his temples as if he had suddenly developed a powerful headache. 'This is the Divorce Court, Mr Vaughan, not Disneyland. You either fight your corner or you get utterly destroyed.'

He insisted that there was no alternative but to proceed on the basis already agreed. But I was alarmed at some of the stands adopted by my former self. To solve the practical problems of my demand that I have custody of the children, my lawyer had suggested that the kids move to the school where I was a teacher. It seemed wrong to cause further disruption to the children's lives; I couldn't understand the thinking of the Vaughan who had gone along with this. Finding out about myself was like peeling an onion. And the more I peeled, the more I felt like crying.

'Shall we go in?' suggested the lawyer. I discovered that Gary would not be allowed in the courtroom, and so I alone was solemnly escorted to the chamber where marriages went to die.

THE COURTROOM ITSELF was smaller and more modern than I had anticipated. We were joined by a barrister pupil and then a solicitor and trainee, and eventually Maddy and her team bustled in and placed themselves at the parallel bench. I leaned over and attempted a smile, but Maddy had clearly decided that our divorce hearing was not the occasion for friendly little waves. Her lawyer mumbled at her for several minutes and she listened in intense concentration, glancing up only once, accidentally making eye contact with me and then quickly looking away. I was troubled by how little Maddy seemed able to smile. Of course I understood that this was not a happy occasion, but I still found myself wanting to make her feel better. As it turned out, my performance was to have the opposite effect.

There followed some procedural overtures before the hearing began in earnest. It was as if the judge and the two lawyers were performing some sort of secret coded mumbling game. I gradually understood that they were establishing the stages of the divorce process so far, during which I found my eye wandering back to the other half that I hadn't known I'd had. She was looking straight ahead, just enduring the ordeal. I so wanted to make this easier for her, to make that blank expression crack into a smile.

The previous night I had worked hard to think of every possible question that might be thrown at me. Gary had said I should go into court feeling confident. 'This is only for insurance, mate. I'm pretty certain you won't have to say anything at all.'

I was wishing that he could be in there just to see how very wrong he had been. Right at the beginning they caught me out with a trick question.

'Could you state your full name, please?'

'Ooh, erm . . . let me see . . . Well, I'm Jack Vaughan, though everyone calls me Vaughan, but my full, complete, legal name with the middle name . . . or names, well that would be . . . Sorry, I've gone blank.'

The whole room was now staring at me as if I had decided to come to court completely naked. 'Bit nervous, sorry.'

My lawyer gazed at me perplexed. 'Your full name, is er, well, it will be on the original submission. I didn't think to check you knew that . . .'

'It's Jack Joseph Neil Vaughan,' recited Maddy in a tone suggesting years of exasperation with the uselessness of the man she was divorcing.

I leaned across and mouthed 'thank you' and her look back seemed to say 'What the hell are you doing?'

'My name is Jack Joseph Neal Vaughan,' I declared with exaggerated confidence.

'Is that Neil with an "i" or with an "a"?' interjected the overweight clerk.

'It's with an "a"!' I declared confidently.

'It's with an "i",' came the voice from the other side of the court.

The judge stared at me silently for a moment; he seemed to be lamenting the long-lost power of the judiciary to impose the death penalty at will.

The next section was manageable if a little uncomfortable. I swore an oath on the Holy Bible, that everything that I would say would be the truth. I learned that I was the petitioner (amazingly, *I* was the one who had initiated divorce proceedings) and I confirmed my date of birth as the one I had seen printed on the forms. So what does that make me? I thought. What star sign is May? Mind you, it's a load of rubbish anyway . . .

'And your occupation?'

'Teacher!' I snapped back like a smug contestant in a TV quiz show.

Above us a large, angry fly was trapped inside the light casing. To my heightened senses, its manic buzzing was as loud as the monotone voices of the two lawyers talking a language I barely understood. Eventually we came to the part of the proceedings when I was to be cross-examined by my wife's lawyer.

'Mr Vaughan, I want you to cast your mind back to 1998. You and your wife first employed the service of a financial advisor in that year, did you not?'

'I have no reason to disbelieve Madeleine if she says that we did.'

'And did you not make a decision at that meeting on February 17, 1998, that, in addition to your teacher's pension, you would also make voluntary contributions in your name only, because, as the only taxpayer then, you could benefit from more tax relief than if they had been in Madeleine's name?'

I would have struggled to follow these financial details even with my brain in normal working order.

'Er, it sounds quite possible. If there is a record of the payments after that date, then obviously I did take out an additional pension in my name.'

'The existence of this pension plan is not the issue, Mr Vaughan. The point is that you verbally assured your wife that this personal pension was intended for your joint benefit, but that it was taken out in your name only to save tax. Is this not the case?'

I thought of lying and just going along with the plausible picture being presented to me, but I felt a higher duty to be as honest as possible.

'I really can't remember,' I declared. Maddy's lawyer looked stumped.

'Brilliant!' whispered my own counsel.

'How convenient for you . . .' scorned the opposing barrister.

'It was a long time ago and I just can't recall.'

The judge intervened. 'Can we move on?'

'You don't remember any subsequent assurances to your wife, do you, Mr Vaughan?' improvised her lawyer, now sounding a little desperate.

'Er, no. No, I don't.'

Maddy shook her head in contempt. 'It's not enough that you have all the money,' she spat. 'You have to come and take the hedge trimmer as well. You don't even have a garden any more.'

'I don't want the hedge trimmer. You can have it back . . .'

'Quiet, please!' insisted the judge, and as her lawyer moved on to the next matter, I tried to catch Maddy's eye. She couldn't even bear to look at me.

The memory test now moved on to the years of our marriage and how they reflected the respective investment made by both parties.

'Mr Vaughan, while you were at work, would you attempt to claim you were also doing fifty per cent of the child care?'

'Er, I doubt it. It sounds like I was always still at work when they came home from school for a start.'

'Quite,' he commented meaningfully. 'Would you even attempt to put a figure on the proportion of the child care you did?' He theatrically pretended to imagine the sort of tasks this might involve. 'Picking them up from school? Helping with homework? Cooking their tea?'

'It's hard to say *exactly*,' I said truthfully. 'Much less than Madeleine, I'm sure.' I glanced nervously at my lawyer.

'Would it be fair to say that if Madeleine had not done so much of the domestic work, then you would not have been able to work the long hours that both parties accept you put into your career?'

'I guess you're right . . .'

I noticed Maddy look up.

'So would you not agree that seventy/thirty represents an unfair reflection of the paid *and unpaid* work done by the two of you?'

'Yes, it is unfair. I think a fifty/fifty split would be fairer.' And I stared directly at my wife.

She looked astonished.

There was a moment of confused silence, punctuated only by the mad spinning of the fly trapped in the light. It was as if Maddy's lawyer was programmed only to disagree and contradict; he tried to reach for words but none would come. Now my own representative stood up.

'Your honour, the respondent's counsel is putting words into my client's mouth. Surely it is for the court to make a ruling after we have put our own case for a seventy/thirty split.' And he urgently gestured for me to shut up.

'It appears, Mr Cottington, that you and your client have come to court without agreeing in advance on the apportionment you are seeking.'

Mr *Cottington*, I thought. So that's my lawyer's name.

The judge entered into a whispered exchange with the clerk while I was left standing there. Although I felt certain I had done the right thing, I could feel my legs shaking.

Then I suddenly got my first negative memory. Maddy was angrily berating me and I was shouting back. I even felt a twinge of resentment rise up in me as I recalled how over the top she had been about a battery in a smoke alarm. The argument had arisen because I had apparently 'endangered the family' by taking the battery out of the smoke alarm to put in my bike light.

'Why the hell didn't you replace the battery?' she is shouting.
'I forgot, OK? Don't you ever forget things?'
'Not where the safety of our children is concerned.'
'Well, this was for the safety of your husband on the dark road!'
'You could have bought a replacement battery—you just forgot
about us but remembered you.'

Looking at Madeleine, I couldn't believe that she was capable of so much anger about something as trivial as one AA battery.

The court had come to consider the key point in the settlement, the decision on the Property Adjustment Order. With no agreement on the house, it would have to be sold, but negotiations had broken down over a fair split of the money. The more I listened to the arguments from both sides, the clearer it became that neither Maddy nor I would be able to afford a house in the same area that would accommodate two children and an excitable golden retriever. It would mean moving the kids far away from their school; it would mean no garden and the children having tiny bedrooms and no space for friends to come and stay.

One blindingly obvious solution to all this was not being suggested by anyone in the courtroom and I felt a duty to point it out.

'Excuse me, your honour—is it possible to . . . change my mind?'

'You want a different arrangement regarding the property assets?'

'No, no—about the whole divorce thing,' I heard myself say. 'I wonder if we ought to try and give the marriage another go?'

'Vaughan, stop it!' said Maddy. 'This is not a game.'

'Vaughan, what are you doing?' pleaded my lawyer.

'If I'm the petitioner—can't I, like, withdraw the petition?'

It seemed like a reasonable question. But the judge's patience had now been exhausted and he seemed at a loss over what to say. Deep down I had been hoping for him to declare, 'This is most irregular, but, given the circumstances, this court instructs Vaughan and Madeleine to jet off to the Caribbean for a second honeymoon and for Mrs Vaughan to fall in love with her husband all over again.'

Instead, he declared this case 'a disaster' and said he was faced with no alternative but an adjournment. Inside I felt a rush of elation that lasted for just a split second as I watched Maddy burst into tears then dash outside.

Mr Cottington looked utterly shell-shocked. He chose to say nothing at all to me; he just left, followed by his trainees. I sat there in silence, trying to take in what it was I'd just done.

'Well, I've been in this job over twenty years and I've never seen anything like that before,' said the clerk.

I attempted a brave smile. 'I just think we should be really sure,' I ventured. 'You know, before we finally cut the knot.'

'Right.' The clerk was straightening the chairs. 'As I say, people are usually pretty sure by the time they get here.'

I felt embarrassed and a little bit foolish. Part of me had wanted to rush after Maddy, but I didn't want to experience the angry side of her that I had just remembered. I sat staring straight ahead.

The clerk had finished gathering her things. 'That was the last case before lunch, but I'm afraid I can't leave you in here on your own.'

'No, of course,' I said. 'Only—would you mind if I unclipped this light fitting? There's a big fly trapped inside and he's been going mad.'

'Oh. Well, yes, all right. I think it unclips on the side there.'

And so I climbed up on a chair and released the light cover, and stood back to watch the grateful insect fly free. Instead it fell straight to the floor and spun around buzzing on its back.

'Urgh, he's enormous, isn't he?' said the clerk. And the buzzing gave way to a final crunch as her big fat foot came squelching down on it.

'There!' she said with a smile. 'Good luck sorting out your marriage—or we'll see you back here in a couple of months . . .'

MADDY AND I are on a train. We have not been out of university that long and don't view this space as a train so much as a moving pub. I find the perfect double seat in the smoking compartment and buy enough drinks for the whole journey; an hour or so later Maddy goes off to buy the food I neglected to get. But she is taking much longer than I had. There is still no sign of her when a message comes over the tannoy.

'This is a passenger announcement . . .' For a split second I think, A female train guard—you don't hear that very often.

'British Rail would like to apologise for the man serving in the buffet car. British Rail now accept that none of the female passengers on this train wishes to be asked for her phone number by a middle-aged man wearing a wedding ring and a name badge saying Jeff.' Maddy has the monotone delivery to perfection. People in the seats around me are looking at each other

with widening grins. 'They would also appreciate it if Jeff could attempt to maintain eye contact while serving the All-Day Breakfast Bap instead of staring at the breasts of the female on the other side of the counter.'

There is a spontaneous round of applause from all the women customers in our carriage. A couple of them even cheer.

I can't wait for Maddy to come back. I am so fantastically proud of her; she has made total strangers on a train start laughing and talking to one another. The hubbub is still going as she saunters through the door with a completely straight face. 'There's our rogue announcer!' I boast loudly. It is probably a mistake to tell the whole carriage, but we don't particularly mind being turfed off the train at Didcot Parkway.

THE DEFINING CHARACTERISTIC of this memory was the powerful sensations of love and pride it conjured up. And yet it was deeply frustrating to have so little else of our past lives in which to place it. My life-map was incredibly detailed on everything I remembered since October 22 and then there were just a few aerial snapshots of the uncharted continent beyond.

The train-tannoy memory had come to me as I had woken up, with no identifiable trigger. It was a few days after the court case and I desperately wanted to have the story officially verified by Gary and Linda, but the two of them had already left for their appointment at the hospital.

I resolved that I was going to talk to Maddy alone. I felt I owed it to her to tell her, one to one, what had happened to me. If she was not at home, I had the address of 'the studio' where she worked. I had learned that Madeleine was not a painter, but an artist none the less, selling huge framed photos she had taken of London landmarks, which funded her more experimental photographic works. Maddy was a photographer, and a classy one by the sound of it. It made me that little bit more proud of her.

'WHAT THE HELL are you doing here?' said Maddy, opening her front door.

'I wanted to meet—I mean, *talk* to you. Properly.'

'You've got a nerve.'

Our first moments alone together. In my fantasy reunion I had imagined her being more pleased to see me.

'I thought I owed you an explanation. Are you alone?'

The dog was barking from the back garden.

'What business is it of yours?'

'It's just—well, it's complicated, and if the kids are in, then . . .'

'No, they're at school, obviously.' I hovered there for a decade or so. 'All right, well you'd better come in,' and she headed inside. I stood in the doorway, looking at a huge black and white photo of Barleycove for far too long, until she said, 'Well? Are you coming in or not?'

The dog came bounding down the hallway and nearly knocked me over with his enthusiasm. I tried to give him some attention as I gazed around in wonder. I could feel myself shaking as we entered the kitchen. I didn't know quite where to start. A battered iPod was plugged into some speakers and I recognised the song.

'Hey, you like Coldplay. I love Coldplay,' I said.

'No, you don't. You hate Coldplay. You always made me turn it off.'

'Oh. Well, I like it now . . .'

'So what's going on, Vaughan? You ignore all my emails and texts and then you turn up to the court and pull a stunt like that.' Her brow went all creased when she looked concerned.

'Erm, well, the thing is, that a couple of weeks ago—October 22 to be precise—at some point in the late afternoon I was sort of . . . reborn.'

She looked at me with suspicion. 'What are you talking about?'

'I was in hospital for a week or so, following a psychogenic fugue.'

'A what?'

'It means that my mind completely wiped itself of personal memories. I lost all knowledge of my own name, identity, family, friends. I've been told I've known you for twenty years. But standing here right now, it's like I'm talking to you for the first time.'

She regarded me suspiciously. 'I don't know what your scam is, but you're not getting this house.'

'Yeah, Gary told me that we were getting a divorce, although I don't remember why. The doctor said the stress I experienced from the marriage breakup might be what triggered the fugue.'

'You weren't ever here to experience any stress; you were staying late at work or going round to Gary's to fart around on computers.'

'It's a lovely kitchen. Really homey.'

'Why are you being so weird, Vaughan? And why are you patting the dog like that, you know he doesn't like it—'

'No, *I don't know!* For most of last week I had a hospital label on my wrist saying "UNKNOWN WHITE MALE". Look, I've still got it. And see this metal tag round my neck? It has my name and contact numbers on it in case my brain wipes all over again and I am left wandering the streets.'

She plonked a mug of tea in front of me.

'Do you have any sugar?' I asked.

'You don't take sugar.'

'That's what Gary said. He reckoned I used to smoke as well.'

She leaned closer and smelled me. 'That's what's different about you. You don't stink of stale nicotine. I can't believe you finally gave up.'

'I didn't give up. It was wiped along with everything else.'

She pulled out her phone and I heard one end of a conversation with Linda. She was looking at me as she talked, her eyes widening and her face draining of colour. When she had finished she slumped down on a chair.

'That is so typical of you! All that crap I'm dealing with and then you just wipe the slate clean and forget all about it . . .'

'Oh. Sorry.' Part of me wanted to comfort her, but her body language did not suggest I should move in for a hug.

'How are the kids going to take this? It's bad enough that we've split up, but now their own father doesn't even know them! They'll be home from school in a few hours. You can't be here—they'll be scarred for life.'

'Whatever you say. You know what's best for them—I don't.'

'Yeah, well, no change there.' She glanced up and then softened slightly. 'I thought you were being odd in court. All that trying to catch my eye.'

'It's just that normally you get to meet your wife *before* you divorce her.'

'So . . . you literally cannot remember us? Or any of this?'

'Not really.'

'Not really?'

'All right—not at all. Although a couple of moments have come back. I remember the tent collapsing in Ireland and you using the guard's tannoy on some long rail journey?'

'Oh, yeah, we got kicked off the train for that.'

'But that's all so far. Except the other night I had a powerful dream about someone nicknamed Bambi.'

Maddy blushed slightly but said nothing.

'What? You know, don't you? Who's Bambi?'

'Bambi is what you used to call me when we were at university. You said I had the same eyes. Can't believe I fell for that.' She mimed putting her fingers down her throat.

'Well—if it's not too forward of me—you have got very nice eyes.'

Maddy sipped her tea. 'You really have forgotten everything, haven't you? I have "nice eyes"? Where the hell does that come from? You said I was a selfish cow; you said I was ruining your life.'

'Did I? I'm sorry if I said that. But I just don't remember.'

'Yeah, well, how nice for you.'

'It's not very nice really,' I said slowly, staring at the floor. 'It was incredibly distressing to start with.'

'Sorry. It's just a bit hard to get my head around it. So—like, you didn't know your own name or anything?'

'Not for the whole week I was in hospital. All I could think about was who I might have been before my amnesia. I began to worry whether my life had been a good one, whether I had been a good person, you know?'

'I suppose you would.'

'But now I discover my marriage failed and I've been sleeping on people's sofas and have spent all my money on divorce lawyers.'

She didn't know what to say to that. Instead her eyes welled up and then she began quietly crying. I so wanted to kiss her at that point; just to put my arms round my wife would have been wonderful. I finally leaned across and gently rubbed her arm.

'What are you doing?'

'Er—comforting you?'

'Well, don't!'

Then I spotted a photo on the fridge. 'Are these our children? Is this what they look like?' The girl had a big, open-hearted smile for the camera, while the boy was doing his best to look cool. Dillie looked just like her mother and Jamie looked just like me.

'Wow! They're beautiful,' I said. And she nodded and stood to share the moment with me.

'That was in France. Dillie's a bit taller than that now. Jamie hates having his photo taken.'

It was a surreal moment. The mother couldn't help but be proud of her children as she showed their father what they looked like. Maddy put her tongue out slightly as she straightened the photo and in that moment all the emptiness I had felt since October 22 was filled with an overwhelming certainty. Just that sweet movement of her mouth made me feel whole.

'Beautiful,' I said again. 'Really beautiful.'

ON THE WALK HOME the whole world seemed different. I wanted to tell passing strangers that I had just met this wonderful girl. I was still elated when I found Gary in his kitchen with the insides of a laptop spread across the table.

'Gary! Something incredible has happened! I think I've fallen in love!'

'Wow! That's great news, man! What's her name?'

'Maddy. I've just met my wife and she is something else, isn't she? Her eyes are this beautiful hazel brown—'

Gary groaned. 'Yeah, she is *something else*, Vaughan—she is your ex-wife. Listen, mate, this must be related to your condition.' He indicated the computer circuit boards scattered on the pine table. 'Your hard drive has wiped and this is like an emotional memory coming back. It'll soon fade.'

'No, it's not going to fade, Gary. This is for ever. It feels as if all my life I've been waiting for that special someone and I've finally met Miss Right.'

'OK. Except that all your adult life you've been married to her and finally decided she was Miss Wrong.'

'All right, I know we're getting divorced and that. But every relationship has to overcome a few obstacles—look at Romeo and Juliet.'

'Yeah, they both die. You don't love her, Vaughan. You're delirious.' Gary sat me down at the kitchen table. 'Look, if you are looking for someone who might be interested in making a future with you, I'd say the very last woman you should go after is the woman who has tried being married to you for fifteen years and decided she can't stand the sight of you.'

'It's not like that. You don't know Maddy like I do—'

'No—I know her *better*. It's not going to happen, Vaughan. You've got to move on. Listen, I've had a brilliant idea for how you can find out more about your past . . .'

DEAR ALL,

As you may be aware, I recently experienced a form of amnesia that has wiped all my personal memories. This means that I cannot recall anything before October 22 this year. However, with your help I am hoping I can reconstruct my personal history from the fragments that you yourselves can remember.

It would be greatly appreciated if you could look at this Wikipedia page, which I have begun, and then add any details you remember. For example, if you were there with me at the University of Bangor, you might add the names of tutors I had or clubs I joined. My hope is that

this online document will grow to become a complete account of my
life before my amnesia.
   Many thanks,
   Vaughan

With his belief in the power of user-generated content, Gary had come up with an initiative to establish a detailed account of my life to date. My appeal went out via email, Facebook and, for what it was worth, the features pages of YouNews. I was going to have my own memoir collaboratively written online. I wondered how this perspective might affect the reader's sympathies. It would be like the United States having its history rewritten from scratch by Britain, Mexico, Japan, the native Americans and Iraq.

'IT'S AN INTERESTING IDEA,' said Dr Lewington as I proudly told her how my personal memories were going to be compiled by others. It was now three weeks since I had had the fugue and this was my first appointment back at the hospital. 'Though you should continue to keep a separate record.'

'I have a little notepad by my bed. With lots of blank pages.'

'And how are you feeling in yourself? I can refer you to a psychiatrist or a counsellor if you feel that would be at all helpful.'

'No, I'm fine, really. I think I've fallen in love . . .'

'That's wonderful. Because I remember you were getting divorced.'

'Yup, that's her. She still wants to get divorced, but I was hoping she might marry me again after that . . .'

'Right. As I say, the offer of a psychiatrist is always there . . .'

At the end of our session Dr Lewington asked to see my online biography, and I found myself feeling a little nervous as she clicked on the link. But I had not anticipated the viciousness of the treatment I had received. No one had written a single word about me.

Over the next day or so I kept returning to the document but my life story just read: *This neurology-related article is a stub. Please help Wikipedia by expanding it.* I could tell from checking the article history that a few people had opened the page, but no one had taken the trouble to write anything.

Not even Maddy had responded and I worried about how she was dealing with the bombshell that her husband had forgotten their entire marriage. But then Linda took a phone call from Maddy; apparently she wanted to meet up with me 'and have a serious talk'.

'Ha, that's almost like a date, isn't it?' I suggested optimistically.

'Um, I don't think so, Vaughan.'

A few minutes later I came out of my room to ask Linda's advice.

'What do you think—is this shirt too bright? Would this one be better?'

'They're both fine. It doesn't matter what you wear. Just be yourself.'

'Fine. Just be myself. So, er, what is "myself", exactly?'

I WAS RIDICULOUSLY EARLY to the café in Covent Garden and chose a seat outside so I'd be able to see her coming. Finally, Madeleine approached and I stood up. I went to give her a peck on the cheek, but she didn't move towards me. I was forced to pretend I was leaning over to pull out her chair.

'Hi! Great to see you! You look nice . . .'

'Shall we get on with it?' she said, playing it rather cool I thought.

Today she was wearing her hair down, and I decided that she wasn't so much a redhead as a strawberry blonde. She requested a double espresso.

'Same as me!' I said with enthusiasm, wondering what it might taste like.

'No, you always have a cappuccino.'

With her already knowing me so well, there was less of the exploratory trivia that I would have liked to warm up with.

'Anyway, listen, I talked to my lawyer and I think it's actually good that the final hearing got postponed.'

'Oh great!' I said, trying not to wince at the strength of my black coffee.

'Yes—he said that if the hearing had gone ahead and it was then discovered that you were not in a fit state, then the whole divorce might have been invalidated. Better to get divorced when we know it would be cast-iron.'

'Oh.' I sighed. 'I see.'

'I told him about your amnesia and he says you have to get medical attestation that you have the mental capacity to give instruction. So you need to see a psychiatrist or neurologist or whatever as soon as possible so that we can finalise the divorce.'

She had already crushed that tiny part of me that had hoped she might be just a little bit flirty.

'So have you seen a psychiatrist yet?'

'I'm not mad. Why does everyone think I need a psychiatrist?'

'What, you and me give the marriage another go? That was pretty mad, you must admit.'

If she could only get to know me, she would surely forget all that negative stuff she'd heard about me from her divorce lawyer and would be convinced that here, finally, was the man for her.

'How are the kids?'

'I've tried to give them an inkling of what's happened to you, but Dillie was quite upset by it all. We're going to have to handle it very carefully.'

Privately I was frightened of being introduced to my own children. I was desperate to make the right first impression. 'OK, I'll follow your lead. But tell them I can't wait to meet them.'

'No, I won't say that.'

'I mean see them. *Again.*'

I ripped open the top of a sugar sachet and shared the contents between my coffee cup and the surface of the table.

'Still taking sugar then?'

'For as long as I can remember . . .'

'But you're not smoking? All those years I begged you to give up and you said it was impossible. And then you give up just like that!'

'That's all it takes, a bit of will power. And a psychogenic fugue. Are you sure I can't get you a blueberry muffin or anything?'

'When have I ever eaten blueberry muffins?'

'I don't know, do I? I do not have the *mental capacity* to choose you a muffin.'

'So just how much can you remember now? If you can remember the camping holiday and the time you got us kicked off the train . . . is it all starting to come back?'

I thought about her shouting at me about the smoke alarm. 'No, there's not much else yet.'

'Well, maybe that's a blessing.'

'I don't remember why we split up. I was serious about what I said in the courtroom. About us giving it another go.'

'Come off it, Vaughan—our marriage was over a long time ago.' And then her demeanour changed. 'God, when I think of the shit I put up with!'

'Hey, it takes two people to make a marriage fail.'

'Yeah, that's what Dr Crippen said.'

'There is something else I remember,' I said triumphantly. 'I remember you being too cross about trivial things. Going ballistic because I forgot to replace the battery in the smoke alarm—'

'Trivial?'

'I don't see why it was such a big deal.'

She looked at me as if I was stupid. 'Because there was a fire. That's why I was cross. There was a fire in our kitchen while we were all asleep, and the smoke alarm failed to go off because you had taken the battery out.'

This is why it is best to be in full command of the facts when you get into an argument. 'I . . . I don't remember that bit . . .' I mumbled.

'But you remember me being cross about it?'

'Vaguely . . . Were we outside?'

'Er, yes, because our house was on fire. The whole family was standing in the back garden in our pyjamas while the fire brigade chucked all the smouldering kitchen units out onto the patio.'

I tried to picture the scene but it was still lost to me. 'Blimey. So who raised the alarm?'

'You nudged me and asked if I could smell smoke.'

'Oh well, so that sort of cancels out removing the battery.'

'No, it does not—we could all have been killed!'

'Maybe I smelled smoke quicker than the alarm would have detected it.'

'OK—you were the hero of the hour. Wow, that is quite a rewriting of history there. Silly me—I must have remembered it all wrong.'

I couldn't help thinking that this was our first argument, but thought it best not to mention it.

'A rose for the lady?' said a flower seller in a powerful Eastern European accent. The scent of roses was slightly lost in the fug of tobacco smoke from the wet cigarette hanging from his lip.

'Er, no. No, thank you.'

The vendor wandered off, but his appearance had punctured the increasingly dangerous atmosphere.

'You can't just wipe the slate clean. You're attracted to this romantic idea of Vaughan and his happy wife, because you are understandably desperate to get your past back. But your past wasn't all drunken giggling in a tent.'

'Look, people change,' I pleaded. 'I'm really sorry about all the things that hurt you when our marriage went wrong. I can't imagine why I would have done them, but I clearly found it all so traumatic that my brain completely wiped any memory of it. And now the only thing I can remember about you is how passionately I felt when we first met.'

'Well, you wait till you get the rest of your memory back. You don't love me, Vaughan. Your mind is still playing tricks on you.'

The flower seller had started on the next café along from us.

'Excuse me!' I called across to him. 'How much are the roses?'

'Vaughan—do *not* buy me a rose.'

But nicotine-stained fingers were already pulling out one cellophane-wrapped instant love token.

'I'll give you fifty pounds for the whole lot.'

'Vaughan—you're wasting your money.'

The man gave an impassive nod and quickly exchanged the notes in my hand for a huge bunch of skinny red roses. 'He love you very much.'

'Actually, we were just finalising our divorce,' she explained.

'Your wife—funny lady!' laughed the flower seller. But neither of us joined in. My dramatic gesture had only irritated Maddy further and now she brusquely worked her way through her checklist of things she needed to sort out. Though our lives would require contact and cooperation, she did not want to be my friend. Desperately, I made one last pitch to her.

'My memory loss might be the best thing that ever happened to us.'

'For God's sake, Vaughan, one of the things that used to drive me mad about you was that you forgot everything I told you. If it was anything about *your* life then you remembered it all right, but if it was something I was doing, then it wasn't important enough to register. I don't see what the big deal is with the doctors and neurologists, because you forgot I existed years ago. This isn't a mental illness. This is just who you are. It's over, Vaughan! We are getting a divorce. End of story. End of us.'

And she got up and walked away, leaving fifty red roses on the table in front of me.

CHAPTER 4

'Vaughan. I've got some bad news, mate.' It was exactly a month since my fugue and I had come in to find Gary seated in the kitchen. 'It's your father. He's had another heart attack.'

A stunned pause followed.

'*My father?* My father is alive? Why didn't you say so?'

'You never specifically asked.' Gary raised his hands defensively.

'But you talked about my parents in the *past tense*. You said they *were* a great couple.'

'Well—the past is like, when I knew them. So, anyway, that's good news then, if you thought he was dead. He's not—he's alive. Just. Although you might not want to leave it too long, mate . . .'

Questions I wished I had asked long before were fired at Gary. 'How old is he?' 'When was his last heart attack?' and 'What do I call him?'

'I dunno. "Dad", I think.'

All Gary knew was that Madeleine had called Linda to say that she was going to the hospital with the kids to see their grandfather. He was out of intensive care and could be visited for a short period.

'Maybe I should call her. You know—to find out what time she's going to be there and how it works and everything.'

'You could do. Except she said don't call her.'

I had not felt ready to meet my own children yet. But with my father, events now forced me to arrange an immediate introduction. I had to get to know him so that I could be properly upset if he died.

THERE WAS A MOMENT as I entered the hospital when I wondered if I ought to buy my dad something from the gift shop. But of course I had no knowledge of my father's tastes or interests. 'Dad' was currently an amalgam of all the paternal role models that had survived my amnesia. Baron von Trapp and King Lear were mixed up with Homer Simpson.

On the fourth floor I was directed towards my father's room, and I was pleasantly surprised by the apparent health of the stout, dark-haired old man lying in the bed in front of me. So this was my father. I sat down and dutifully took his podgy hand.

'Hi, Dad, it's me. I got here as soon as I could.'

The old man regarded me for a second. 'Who the hell are you?' he said in a foreign accent. I saw the Arabic name on the patient's wristband and leaped up and out of the room.

Now I was standing outside a room where the occupant shared the same surname as myself. Lying in the hospital bed, surrounded by purring machines, was a skeletal old man. There was no one else there.

'Is that you, son?' he said through his oxygen mask.

'Yes. Yes, it's me.'

'You are very good. To come and see me.' His voice was very weak.

'That's OK. How are you feeling?'

'Ooh, you know. Just pleased to be here.'

'Is there anything I can get you?'

'Large whisky. No ice.'

I smiled. I realised I already liked my dad. He managed to be humorous even though he was at death's door.

'Maddy and the kids. Were here . . . Wonderful children. So charming.'

'They are. And they've coped so well with it all.'

The old man processed what I'd just said. 'Coped with what?'

Instantly it hit me that he knew nothing about our marriage breakup. Of course—my father had a heart condition, why would we have added the stress of telling him that his only child's marriage had failed? And by the same token, he clearly hadn't been told that I was suffering from amnesia.

'I mean, they've coped very well with their grandfather having a heart attack.' And in a perverse way I was grateful to this medical emergency for coming to my rescue.

On the side was a homemade card, and I could see it had been signed 'Dillie'.

'I like Dillie's card.'

'Bless her. So thoughtful.'

I tried to imagine this man holding my infant hand and leading me across the road; I visualised us kicking a leather football together in some imaginary back garden. But none of it came into focus.

'Do you remember us playing football when I was little?' I asked.

'How could I forget? You were always . . .' and he paused for a moment as his ageing mind searched for the right words '. . . so *useless*!'

I attempted to move on. 'Well, football was never really my thing. Gary was reminding me how I used to sing in a band.'

'Oh, yes. What a voice!'

'Oh . . . thanks.'

'Like a strangled cat.'

It seemed that this was another relationship based on mickey-taking. I realised it was wonderful that my father was still able to tease me like this from his hospital bed. This was clearly Dad's way of showing his affection.

'But none of that matters, because the big thing in life . . . you got right.' His voice was growing increasingly strained now.

'What—my job?'

'No. *Your wife.* You married the right girl.' I struggled to hear the whispered sentences under his mask. 'You two. Are perfect together.'

I suppose my father's physical condition added a little extra value to these words. Any sentence can seem apt and profound if it's uttered on your deathbed. But for my own father to spare the breath to tell me that Madeleine and I were perfect together—it was the first time anyone had had anything positive to say about my marriage.

Then suddenly my time was up. 'Bit tired now, son. Can't talk any more.'

'OK.' And then I forced myself to say it. 'OK, *Dad.*'

The noise of his breathing changed gear as he sank almost instantly into a deep sleep. I sat there, trying to spot myself in those weathered features. I had worried that seeing an unrecognisable parent would make me want to cry, but actually I found myself feeling uplifted. His instinct about Madeleine was the same as mine. 'Perfect together' is what he had said.

I WAS DISAPPOINTED to find Gary and Linda's flat empty when I got back. I had so wanted to tell them all about my father. Maybe I could call Maddy now and talk to her about him. What could be more natural, the two of us catching up about our respective visits to the hospital? I had already learned the number off by heart and pressed the buttons on the phone. I was shocked that it was answered almost immediately.

'Hello?' said a girl's voice. 'Hello, who is it, please?' she said after a pause. 'Mum, they're not saying anything but I think there's someone there.' Then the line was cut off. That was the first time I had heard my daughter's voice.

I had used my own mobile phone, but had withheld the caller's ID. Looking at the phone I suddenly noticed the camera icon on the menu. I excitedly scrolled across to find another icon labelled 'Photos'. Just one click and I uncovered a whole gallery of pictures of Jamie with the dog, or Maddy with the dog or myself with the dog. Then there were images of Dillie as well, giving a big smile to the photographer. I scrolled through them all slowly and then nearly ran down the battery staring at pictures of Maddy, trying to discern her feelings in every photo, imagining the actual moment that had been captured. No rational thought could counter the overwhelming gravitational pull I felt towards the woman my father had said was perfect for me.

An hour later I stood in front of the bathroom mirror and raised the blade to my throat. I took one last look and then went for it. Soon, big grey-streaked tufts of beard were falling into the basin. Bit by bit, I saw the shape of my face emerge from where it had been hiding since the late 1980s. I tried to persuade myself I looked rather square-jawed and handsome, like James Bond or Action Man—an effect only slightly spoiled by the specks of blood and deadheaded spots that needed immediate patching. The clean-shaven figure was still wearing the shabby old clothes I'd found in Gary and Linda's bedroom cupboard, but now I set about part two of my action plan.

Gary had said to me that my fugue was just some sort of midlife crisis. 'Honestly, what a fuss about approaching forty. Why can't you just get an earring and a red sports car and have done with it?' His words came back to me as I strode into the menswear section of a large department store.

The makers of the suits I liked best had spent money where no one else would see it: there were flowered linings and little extra pockets on the inside. I felt myself standing an inch taller in front of the mirror; I looked sharp and in control.

But I couldn't remember the PIN number on my credit card. A frantic text to Maddy informed me of my PIN, my mother's maiden name and my secret password. Rearmed with the knowledge required to survive modern life, I bought three designer suits, three shirts and two pairs of shoes. I kept one of the suits on; my old clothes were placed inside shopping bags, even though I could never imagine wearing them again.

One month after my fugue I was self-consciously launching Vaughan 2.0. Yes, there had been teething problems with the operating system, and the memory was limited, but this model would look cleaner and sleeker; it would have a more user-friendly interface; it would not emit smoke or cause battery problems. My hope was that it would be exactly the sort of hardware that someone like Maddy, for example, might find desirable.

'There you are, sir!' said the shop assistant, passing over the suits in big, expensive-looking bags. 'Special occasion, is it?'

'Sort of. I've just met my wife.'

'Congratulations! When are you getting married?'

'Well, let's not get too hasty,' I said. 'I've got to divorce her first . . .'

I BROWSED THE SHELVES of overpriced greetings cards, bewildered at the choice. Did Dillie like cute animals? Surely she was too old for Disney princesses? I so wanted to get it right. Here was one specifically for me.

'*Sorry I forgot your birthday . . .*' I opened it up to read the punch line: '*I was having a bad hair day*.' There were quite a few cards that said '*Sorry I forgot your birthday*' but none of them went on to say '*because I suffered an incredibly rare neurological disorder known as a psychogenic fugue*.'

I wrote in Dillie's card that I would like to take her out and buy her a birthday present. Inside, I placed a small passport photo so that the kids would not be too taken aback by the image of their beardless, suited father.

When I came back from the post office, Linda was in the kitchen stirring a saucepan. She let out a startled scream, then fought off this approaching stranger by striking me with a spoon covered in leek and potato soup.

'Linda! It's me!'

'Bloody hell, Vaughan—you look completely different.'

'You've got gunge all over my new suit!'

'Sorry, I didn't recognise you. You look so smart! Well you *did* anyway . . .'

She took my jacket and was wiping it clean as Gary wandered in.

'Well?' she said to her husband expectantly. 'What about Vaughan?'

'What?'

'He's shaved his beard off!!'

'Oh, that's what's different. I thought he'd just washed or something.'

'And the suit?'

'Of course, it's the big day on Monday, isn't it? First day back at work . . .'

I had indeed resolved to return to my former workplace.

'You didn't tell me that, Gary,' snapped Linda, sounding dangerous. 'Why didn't you tell me that? You never tell me anything.'

'Well, that's not actually possible, is it? If I *never* told you anything, you wouldn't know my name or anything about me . . .'

There are few things quite as embarrassing as being stuck with a husband and wife having a bitter, personal argument. Every marriage has its own San Andreas Fault running below the surface. It wouldn't have taken a professor of advanced psychology to work out that the tension underlying Gary and Linda's marriage was their differing levels of enthusiasm for Baby/*the* baby. There were men in history who had looked forward to a baby less than Gary. King Herod springs to mind. But although every argument was really about this, they almost never argued about it directly.

'You're so wrapped up in yourself, you don't ever tell me anything. Stop fiddling with your bloody iPhone!'

'I'm not fiddling. I'm activating the Voice Record app.'

'YOU ARE RECORDING OUR ARGUMENT?!!'

'Yes, because you always misquote me afterwards.'

'Oh, not this again! You always say that—'

'I think if you listen back through the files, you'll find I said it once.'

'You mean you recorded other fights too?'

'I told you that ages ago—'

'No, you didn't.'

'Yes, I did—hang on, I've got the recording here—you can listen yourself.'

It transpired that Gary had a definitive record of all their marital disputes, dated and filed in chronological order. At some point he was planning to cross-reference them by subject index as well.

This was the only relationship I had witnessed first hand since my memory loss, and it perplexed me that this must be a stronger marriage than my own failed one. What had been the ancient fault line that eventually ripped Maddy and me apart? I wondered.

I RESOLVED THAT as part of my mission to seize control of my life, I would move out. With Gary and Linda's new arrival now only six months away, it was time to give them a bit of space to shout at each other in peace.

It had been a few weeks since the debutante Vaughan had first been presented to society. To begin with I had felt like a gatecrasher at my old life. I had, however, quickly developed a new skill: I could measure the degree of shared personal history on a new face. Those who had known me for years seemed to plead for some sort of recognition, whereas the indifferent glance of casual acquaintances demanded nothing in return.

'Hello, Vaughan, great to have you back,' said the receptionist at my old school as I walked into the building, and I could judge exactly how well she had known me. Helpfully, Jane Marshall wore a card round her neck that told you her name.

I had made sure I knew the principal's name but now I didn't know whether to call him 'Peter' or 'Mr Scott'. He had personally undertaken the job of welcoming me back and talking to me about my 'reintegration into the school community'. The two of us were walking around the corridors, giving me a chance to meet staff and 'refamiliarise' myself with the building. Everyone was behaving so normally, they'd obviously had a serious talk about behaving normally. Each of them smiled and proffered a warm hello as I passed, and then got back to pretending to work.

I had been paid in full for all the time I had been off on leave, and today there would be a meeting at which we'd discuss what work I might realistically be able to undertake.

'I've been rereading the syllabus—I'm keen to start teaching as soon as possible,' I declared. 'I owe it to the students to get back to work a.s.a.p.'

'Goodness. You really have forgotten everything, haven't you?'

Two pupils disappearing round a corner shouted 'Oi, Boggy Vaughan! Where's your bog brush?' and then ran away laughing.

'Boggy Vaughan?'

'It's just a minority of students who call you that. You're known for many other things apart from the time you cleaned all the toilets.'

'All right, Boggy? Good to see you,' said a dinner lady walking past us.

'Why did I clean all the toilets?'

'To set an example to the students about "declining lavatory standards". I wouldn't have held up a toilet brush in assembly myself, but you got their attention, I suppose.'

'Boggy Vaughan's back!' came a voice from the atrium as we passed.

'Oh well, I'm sure it'll blow over . . .'

'Maybe. To be frank, Vaughan, I know you were having problems at home, but you stopped loving your job as well. Kids can always tell.'

Perhaps I wasn't quite ready to face the students just yet. So we agreed that I might start with a little administration in the school office. But I was starting work again! This was my place of work.

SLOWLY, I WAS GROPING my way towards some sort of purpose. I still didn't have a past, but like everything else in the modern world, you simply had to look it up on the Internet. That evening I logged on to see that my online memoir had changed completely. Now my life story was filling out. Although not everyone had entered into the exercise with the serious academic rigour that I had hoped for.

Jack Joseph Neil Vaughan, commonly known as 'Vaughan', was born on May 6, 1971. Vaughan spent his childhood in many different parts of the world. He attended Bangor University where he got a 2.2 in History, unlike his friend Gary Barnett who got a 2.1 (and a distinction in his dissertation). The two friends played football together, although Vaughan became a substitute while Gary became the top scorer for two seasons in a row. In his first year at Bangor, he met his future wife, Madeleine. Maddy is hot. She's my secret fantasy, even if she's like 35 or something.

In 2001 Mr Vaughan began teaching history at Wandle Academy. His nickname is 'Boggy Vaughan' because he loves cleaning the bog. He is the Bogmeister General, Bogimus Maximus, the Boginator; Boggy! Boggy! Boggy! Oi! Oi! Oi!

Vaughan was a speaker at the 'Lessons Worth Behaving For' Conference at Kettering and was very boring. Like, dull, dull, dull. His home is four doors down from Mr Kenneth Oakes, member of the Magic Circle and popular choice for corporate events and family parties—'a great traditional magic act' says *The Stage*. Vaughan plays 5-a-side football every Tuesday night and has all the grace and skill of an ostrich. Hello, Vaughan, long time no see, mate! Cheers! Karl.

I went to bed telling myself that the past was past and there was nothing I could do to change it. Apart from deleting the bit about how boring I was at Kettering—I could change that bit. And the references to how bad at football I was—it didn't need those.

IT IS THE EARLY 1990s, and Madeleine and I have been a couple for less than a year. Maddy has gone to Brussels with a friend. When she checks in at the hotel, the concierge says there is a letter waiting for her. She opens the envelope to find the battered postcard of the leprechaun still raising a pint of Guinness. She never mentions it to me.

Months after that, I receive a huge parcel in the post. Inside is another cardboard box. Inside that is some packing material protecting a posh presentation case. After a dozen layers, I finally get through to a small embossed envelope, and although I now realise that someone is playing an elaborate joke, it still has not occurred to me that I am about to get back the postcard I was supposed to have sent to Great-Auntie Brenda.

AND SO THE ICONIC SYMBOL was passed back and forth down the years, with neither of us ever mentioning the game to the other. I would simply smile to myself at the ingenuity of my partner and bide my time as I plotted an even more elaborate way of placing it back into Maddy's custody. Receipt of the card meant that it was now that person's responsibility to post this bloody thing to Great-Auntie Brenda, even though she had long since died and the address on the card was now occupied by a family from Bangladesh.

One day, when Maddy turned on her new computer, the screen was filled with a digital photo of the leprechaun. When she suggested I order a pizza from my usual home-delivery service, I opened the box to find that she had arranged to deliver me Great-Auntie Brenda's card instead. When Maddy had put tasteful framed black and white photographs of the children up the stairs, she came home one day to notice that every frame contained a photocopy of a grinning leprechaun saying 'Top o' the mornin' to yers!'

The memory of all this came back to me in one split second, sitting in front of a computer terminal during my first day back at work. I wanted to tell everyone seated around me, but the school admin team seemed uncomfortable enough with having one of the teachers parked in their office, without me drawing attention to my strange mental illness.

My first day in my new job felt empowering. I was making a contribution; I had a reason to get up in the morning. My task for the day was supposed to be entering data on 540 Key Stage 3 pupils. But I couldn't prevent my mind from returning to two children in particular.

I had agreed to go to the house at six o'clock that evening to take my son and daughter to the Christmas funfair on the Common. Then we would meet Maddy for a pizza and, by the end of the evening I would, I hoped, feel like a father again. They had been told about my neurological condition, though I was not confident they would understand the extent of my amnesia.

I ARRIVED AT THE HOUSE twenty minutes early. I walked up and down on the frosty pavement for a while until Madeleine opened the front door and shouted over to me. 'So are you going to ring on the buzzer or what?' She was wearing a red spotty dress that had an almost humorous edge to it, but, standing at the open door, she folded her arms against the cold as I approached. 'Kids!' she called out. 'Your dad's here!'

An avalanche of enthusiasm came thundering down the stairs, knocking me off balance as both children threw their arms round me and hugged me tightly. They smelled of washing powder and hair conditioner—my children were all fresh and new. The dog, circling this melee, barked in enthusiasm. My heart definitely remembered what my head had forgotten: I felt like I had regained a couple of limbs that I had not realised had been amputated. I would need months of practice to be able to love them properly, but it was still a miracle—Maddy and I had made these beautiful human beings.

I asked them what they'd been up to, and listened to funny stories from school, and I could sense Maddy watching me interact with them and noticed her smile a couple of times. They were confident and chatty—when Dillie was excited she talked faster than I had imagined was humanly possible, segueing wildly from one subject to the next in midsentence. 'Oh-my-god-it-was-so-funny-Miss-Kerrins-told-Nadim-in-science-not-to-bring-in-his-rat-yeah-cos-like-it-always-gets-out-oh-I-like-your-suit-is-that-new-anyway-he-put-it-in-her-handbag-on-her-desk-oh-I-got-an-A-in-Maths-by-the-way-so-she-is-like-totally-phobic-about-rats-so-she-screamed-and-ran-out-of-the-classroom-can-we-record-*Friends*-before-we-go?'

It seemed her brother had the skill to extricate the important points. 'Yeah, why are you wearing a suit, Dad? And why did you shave your beard off? Are you having a midlife crisis?'

'Oh, fresh start and all that. Is it too much?'

'No,' said Maddy. 'It looks very nice.'

'Dad, you're blushing. Why are you blushing?'

The kids were impatient to go to the funfair but, standing in the hallway by the radiator, they insisted that it wasn't cold enough to require woolly hats and gloves. I suggested I carried all their insulation until they'd been outside for a few minutes, by which time they'd be begging for extra layers.

'Are you sure you don't want to come?'

'No,' said Maddy with a half-smile. 'You've got too much catching up to do to have me in the way.'

'Well, I have a lot of catching up to do with you as well.'

Maddy raised her eyebrows as if to suggest that I was close to crossing the line. 'See you at the pizza place at half seven.' And the door was closed.

INSIDE THE HALL OF MIRRORS I saw my distorted face smiling at the kids laughing and waving at our bizarre reflections.

'Of course, this might be what we actually look like,' I ventured.

'No, because then our eyes would have to be wrong as well,' pointed out Jamie, whose intelligent point was rather undermined by his forehead being longer than his legs.

'Depends what our brain does with the info it receives. Maybe we just see everything the way we want to see it.'

'Dad?' Dillie asked. 'Did you really completely forget me and Jamie?'

'Erm—well—it's all still in there,' I said. 'At the moment I don't remember lots of facts about you, but I haven't forgotten how I feel about you. I haven't forgotten . . . how much I love you.'

'Aaaah,' she said, while in the mirror I could see Jamie miming putting his fingers down his throat.

Jamie and Dillie dashed about, jumping forwards and backwards. I stopped looking at my own distorted image and watched my new son and daughter instead. They made me feel as if my lost past wasn't important; it was right here, right now that really mattered.

'Urgh—look what's happened to my body!' shrieked Jamie.

'That's what I say to the mirror every morning.'

'Ahh no, Dad,' said Dillie. 'You're in quite good shape. You know, for someone who's, like, really old.'

I actually felt ten years younger today. The children's energy and optimism was infectious, and I felt a cocktail of pleasure, anxiety, responsibility and delight that I realised was how it must feel to be a parent.

'Dad, can we go on the waltzer now?'

'Sure, we'll all go.'

The children looked unsure, and explained that I couldn't go on rides like that because they used to make me throw up.

'Really? Nah, that was the old Dad. Now I'll probably really enjoy it.'

Five minutes later I staggered off the waltzer and puked up at the back of a generator.

'Are you all right, Dad?'

'Do you want me to get you a bottle of water?'

'No, it's OK. Sorry,' I groaned. 'I'll be all right in a minute.'

MADDY WAS ALREADY SEATED in Pizza Express when we arrived. She laughed when she saw her two kids with candy floss stuck to their hair and faces. This response was surely a signal of approval, I thought. A woman who was 100 per cent set on divorce would have interpreted this as evidence of my incompetence or irresponsibility.

The comfortable atmosphere prompted Dillie to ask if I was going to come and stay for Christmas, but Maddy took this opportunity to go to the Ladies. Not a good sign. Or maybe she was rehearsing the right words to suggest I move back home so we could give the marriage another chance?

'So, kids, let's go out again soon. Or, if your mum is busy one day, I could come round to the house and look after you.'

'Hey yeah!' said Dillie. 'Or when Mum goes away after Christmas, you could come and stay instead of Granny. Please, Dad, please!'

'Oh, that would be wonderful. I'd love that.'

It was almost too perfect. I had somehow got myself invited to come and stay in the house while Maddy was away.

'So, where's Mum going?'

'She's going to Venice with Ralph,' said Dillie, as Jamie shot her a look.

'Ralph? Who's Ralph?'

'Durr! Ralph is Mum's boyfriend.'

And Maddy returned to the table. 'Everything all right?'

CHAPTER 5

'Oh, Vaughan *is* marvellous!' said Maddy's mother, Jean, as I placed a couple of dirty plates near the dishwasher. 'Look at that, Ron. Isn't he marvellous, Madeleine?'

'It's only a couple of plates, Mum. It was *me* who bought the food, made the stuffing, set the table and carved the turkey.'

'Well, I think it's wonderful when a man helps around the kitchen. Look at that! He's scraping the plates into the bin. He *is* good.'

I couldn't resist stirring things a little more by offering to make coffee.

'Oh, you are a dear. No, you sit down; you've done enough already. I'll make the coffee. Madeleine, can you give me a hand, dear?'

Christmas dinner had been easier than I had expected. Maddy's mother had showed no hostility to her estranged son-in-law; on the contrary, I found my apparently abundant qualities constantly highlighted, usually when Jean's own husband was in earshot. 'Vaughan has brought Christmas crackers! How thoughtful. Did you see that, Ron?'

It might have been more honest for Jean to hold up large cards explaining the sledgehammer subtext every time she spoke. 'Did you hear that, Ron? Vaughan took the children to the funfair the other day. They are lucky children to have him . . .' That would have come with the subtitle: '*You never did anything with the children, Ron.*' Or 'Your father never helped around the house, Madeleine. You must be finding it harder now, without

Vaughan here to help?' telegraphed the message: '*My husband was much worse than yours, but I stuck with it.*'

Maddy's father, Ron, might have felt offended by the stream of unsubtle reminders of his apparent failings as a father and husband, but long ago he had developed the skill of tuning out his wife, reacting only to occasional trigger words that might be of interest to him.

'Vaughan offered to make the coffee, Ron. That was nice of him.'

'Coffee? Oh, yes, please.'

The whole day had gone reasonably well. I gave the children their presents, having spent a happy afternoon at the shops so that Jamie could come with me to the cashpoint and choose his money himself. Dillie had wanted a little electronic diary into which you could type your secrets and no one could read them because only you knew how to access it. A bit like my brain, I thought, except that she hadn't forgotten the password yet.

I had been unsure whether I should get Maddy anything. But I happened to stumble upon a beautiful but understated gold necklace after browsing through a number of jewellery shops. And there was a satisfactory moment of tension after lunch when Madeleine unwrapped my present and murmured, 'You shouldn't have.' I knew she really meant it. I had clearly spent a great deal of time and money choosing the perfect gift. Right now Maddy would have preferred a present from her ex-partner that confirmed how wrong for her I really was.

Jean was very effusive about what a lovely present the necklace was. 'What have you got Vaughan, Madeleine?'

'I didn't get him a present, Mum. We're getting divorced.'

'He's still your husband till then, dear.'

My gift had been more than a casual act of generosity and Maddy knew it. This was me resolutely defending the moral high ground that I felt I had seized after discovering that she was seeing another man.

So throughout Christmas Day I played the role of attentive husband with my unexpected ally, Jean, making the trip to Venice seem selfish and unnecessary. Jean was particularly worried about her daughter going on a boat after some of the stories she had seen on the news.

'Jean, Venice is in Europe,' repeated her exasperated husband. 'She is not going to be kidnapped by Somali pirates.'

'Well, it's all in the same direction, isn't it? Venice, Somalia.'

Undaunted by this obvious danger, Maddy would head off to the airport the following morning at six, and I would be left alone with my children. I had initially worried that my mother-in-law might be indignant that she was no longer required to look after her grandchildren, but it transpired that Jean thought the idea of me returning to the family home was an excellent one. 'Isn't it wonderful that Vaughan's moving back in?'

'He's not moving back in, Mum; he's staying here while I'm away.'

'Still,' said Jean, 'it'll be lovely for the children to have their father home.'

Ron initiated only two conversations: one asking after my father, who had been sleeping when I had seen him that morning; and the other enquiring about my own condition, during which he surprised me by sharing two books he had got from the library on amnesia and neuropsychology.

'He doesn't want to look at those,' said Jean. 'Christmas is supposed to be a happy time, not for reminding people they've gone mental.'

In the evening we watched a film together. Dillie had got the DVD of *Love Actually* for Christmas and I was entranced by Emma Thompson as the betrayed wife holding the family together. And I was utterly unconvinced by the little boy jumping the barriers and not being gunned down. 'I remember this bit!' I declared. 'Where he talks about how much love there is in the world by looking at the arrivals lounge in the airport.'

'Yes, but of course they love each other then!' said Maddy scornfully. 'That's because they've spent months in separate continents. Film the same couples a week later and they'd be back to screaming at one another.'

THE GRANDPARENTS went to bed and then it was just the four of us around the fire in the family home: mother, father and the two children.

'Let's play a game,' enthused Dillie.

'What about the water game?' suggested Jamie to excited agreement from his sister.

'The water game? I don't like the sound of that.'

'You think of a category—like "Premiership football teams"—and one person has the name of a club, say "Fulham", in his head. Then he goes around behind everyone, holding an egg cup full of water above their head, and the first person to say "Fulham" gets a drenching!'

'OK, why don't you go first, Jamie?'

Jamie chose '*Simpsons* characters' and although I could recall only Bart and Homer, the latter was sufficient to get the water tipped over my head, which the kids thought was hilarious.

Now it was my turn to wield the egg cup. I chose 'Fruits' and selected 'orange' as the detonator.

'Banana,' said Dillie nervously.

'Starfruit,' declared Jamie, tactically. I moved on to Maddy.

'Orange,' she said.

There was a split-second pause. 'No . . .' and I moved on. I quickly revised my chosen fruit to 'apple', but Maddy said that next time round so I changed it again. Because Dillie was so desperate to have a go I decided to pour the water over her whatever she said, which looked a bit suspicious when she said 'potato'. As she was wiping her head with the tea towel I suddenly had a memory of the four of us together, doing exactly this.

'We played this before. On holiday, by a swimming pool?'

'That's right,' said Maddy. 'In France. You've had another memory!'

'And instead of tipping the cup on my head,' remembered Jamie, 'you picked me up and threw me in the pool!'

The room fell quiet for a moment and then Dillie said, 'Can we go back there? All of us. And play the water game by the pool?'

I struggled to find anything to say to fill the heavy silence. Eventually Jamie rescued the situation. 'No, stupid. They're getting divorced.'

FINALLY CAME THE MOMENT when the children had gone to bed and there was only Maddy and me left downstairs. We flopped onto the sofa.

'Well, that all went as well as can be expected,' I suggested.

'Better than last year, that's for sure.'

'Sorry, you'll have to remind me . . .'

'Last Christmas we had a huge row after you drank yourself into a stupor, which you claimed "was the only way to make this marriage bearable".'

'Forgive me for asking, but did we ever try counselling?'

'Yeah, but we couldn't even agree on that. I wanted a woman counsellor, and you said not having a bloke would tip the scales against you.'

This did strike me as a difficult stand-off in which to find a compromise. Maddy filled up her wineglass and offered the last of the bottle to me.

'I thought my drinking was one of the reasons why you didn't want to be with me?'

'It doesn't matter any more, does it?'

I poured my wine into the potted plant she had just been given by her mother. 'OK, so I'll stop drinking. What else was it?'

'I don't want to have this discussion now.'

'No, I have to know, because it doesn't make any sense. What was so impossible for us to work out? You have to give me concrete examples.'

'I don't know.' Her head stared up at the ceiling. 'When you were young you were so incisive about what was wrong with the world and how we had to change it. But over the years that just turned into general moaning.'

'OK, that's one thing,' I noted. 'Allegedly—'

'It was so boring! All these unimportant things making you cross.' She was in full flow now. 'I mean, I didn't mind that your hair turned grey, or the lines on your face. It was the ageing of your soul that made you so much harder to love; all the goodness in you got flabby and unexercised.'

I got up and disposed of the wine bottle rather too forcefully. 'That's hardly grounds for divorce, is it? You still haven't given me a good reason.'

'We weren't happy.' She sighed. 'We were fighting all the time and it made the kids miserable. What better reason do you need?'

'But what did we fight about?'

'Lots of things. You'd always encouraged me to do more photography. But once it finally started to take off, you resented having to accommodate me not being home all the time. You talked the talk of a supportive husband, but when it came to it—getting home from school in time, or giving up stuff like fiddling around on Gary's Internet site—you were never there.'

'I must admit I don't understand why I wanted to get involved with YouNews.'

'It was just a reason not to be here, wasn't it? And then you couldn't believe that a certain gallery owner could be interested in exhibiting my photography. You said it was just because he fancied me.'

'OK—well, that does sound annoying. Clearly, I was jealous of other men. You are very attractive, and perhaps this gallery owner thought so too.'

'But it shows you couldn't see me as anything other than a bit of skirt. I mean, why couldn't he exhibit my stuff because I was an interesting photographer? Why did you presume it was only because Ralph fancied me?'

I nearly dropped the empty glass in my hand.

'So this "certain gallery owner" was Ralph? You're saying I shouldn't have suggested he fancied you and tomorrow he's taking you to Venice?'

'Yes, but back then he was just a professional acquaintance.'

'Who fancied you! I was right. Well, at least I was never unfaithful.'

'What are you talking about? Neither was I.'

'No? Isn't that your suitcase waiting by the front door?'

'That's what this is about, isn't it? You can't accept I might have met someone else.'

'No—I can't accept that you won't give our marriage another go—when I still don't see why it failed.'

EARLY THE FOLLOWING MORNING Maddy crept downstairs to find me already dressed in the kitchen.

'Wow—you're up early!'

'I wanted to get the kids' breakfast things ready. Here—I've made you a cup of tea.'

'Thanks. *"Did you see that, Ron? He made his wife a cup of tea."*' And the two of us were able to smile in a way that put the previous night's argument behind us.

'What was it like sleeping on the sofa bed?'

'It was fine. Except Woody hogged most of the duvet . . .'

Maddy got a text message. 'Oh, that's . . . er, the car's outside.'

She wheeled her bag to the doorway and the two of us hovered there for a moment. 'OK—bye.' It was clear that I was not to lean in and kiss her. 'Send my love to your wonderful dad when you see him.'

'I'm taking the kids to see him on Wednesday. Hope that's OK?'

'Yeah—that's good.'

'So, have a great time.'

'Thanks.' She unlocked the front door and forced an awkward smile.

'Just out of interest,' I mused, 'did we ever go to Venice?'

'No. You always said you'd take me but it never happened.'

'Oh. Sorry.'

'It's OK. I'm going now, aren't I? Bye.'

And the door closed and I heard a muffled man's voice and Maddy's upbeat response and the sound of a car taking her away.

IF THE NAME OF THE PLACE was supposed to fill you with excitement and wonder, it didn't work on me.

'Splash City?'

'It's like a giant swimming complex with wave machines.'

'It's a lovely idea, kids, but I don't think it'll be open on Boxing Day.'

'Yeah, it is. We checked online.'

'Ah, but, the thing is . . .' I stammered. 'I don't think I can take you swimming . . . because I don't think I can remember how to swim.'

'We'll teach you,' squealed Dillie excitedly. 'Just like you taught us.'

An hour later I found myself standing in a pair of baggy swimming shorts, plucking up courage to skip through the freezing footbath between the changing rooms and the pools. I was struck by the scale of the place. It was an enormous postmodern cathedral. Huge human-swallowing tubes spiralled through the air; children and adults alike were digested one by one, screaming as they disappeared down the fibreglass gullet.

We had agreed to start my lesson in the Little Tadpoles pool, where a sprinkling of under-fours splashed around with overkeen parents. The water came halfway up my thighs, so I decided it might be less embarrassing to squat down as the children debated the best way to proceed.

'We could both sort of hold him underneath while he practised kicking his feet,' said Jamie.

'Or there are some inflatable water wings in that basket.'

'I can't wear those!' I protested. 'They're for the under-fives!'

'No answering back in the learner pool,' declared Dillie.

'Yes, be a good boy and if you're very brave we'll buy you an ice cream.'

'And *do not* wee in the pool!' said Dillie too loudly.

They were in hysterics now. I was sure that when I had taught them to swim it wouldn't have involved me utterly humiliating them first.

'So how are we going to do this, then?' I demanded as a four-year-old swam confidently past me.

'Well, er . . . why don't you just start kicking your legs and moving your arms and see if you can do it?' suggested Jamie.

'All right! I will. Here goes . . .'

And then I just fell forward into the water. It felt unnatural and foolhardy, but I closed my eyes and found my arms were instinctively sculling and my legs flexing and pushing me onwards. I was swimming!

I could hear my two kids cheering and applauding, but I didn't want to stop, so I swam to the end of the pool in a forceful front crawl. I did a flawless tumble-turn and powered my way through the water. Then I became aware of a lifeguard blowing a whistle, and I stood up to see the parents of toddlers in armbands clutching their frightened children and staring at me.

'Oi, mate, this is the children's pool,' said the young Australian. 'Use the Olympic pool, you idiot.'

I HAD A MEMORABLE LUNCH with my children at the burger franchise within the Splash City fun park. Because families came to this complex for the whole day, the eatery boasted a convenient waterside location at which it was traditional to dine in the ultra-casual dress of soggy swimming trunks.

'So are you going to move back out when Mum comes home?' asked my daughter, finally taking a break from a huge vanilla chocolate shake.

I blushed with suppressed satisfaction at this question. Clearly the implication was that my daughter would prefer me to stay at home for ever.

'I think when couples get divorced they're generally supposed to live apart. I've been looking for a little flat as near to home as possible—they're just very expensive. But wherever I live, we'll still see lots of each other.'

'I want you to move back home,' said my daughter straight out.

'Well, that's very nice of you . . .' My smile faded as I noticed the thunderous expression on Jamie's face.

'No! No, you can't do that!' he snapped. 'Because then you and Mum will just end up shouting at each other all the time again . . .' His plastic white chair fell over as he stood up and stomped off.

'Jamie! Jamie, come back!'

I didn't know whether to run after him or just give him some time to cool off. Dillie took advantage of the opportunity to help herself to his chips.

'Dillie, don't do that. He's upset!'

'If you get down from the table it means you've finished eating. That's what you always said.'

I watched my son march round the perimeter of the big pool, his pace gradually slowing before he sat down on a plastic octopus. I watched him for a while, aware that he was casting the occasional sideways glance in our direction. Then, while Dillie was queuing for a giant slide, I walked round the pool and flopped down next to him.

'You know, the whole point of me moving out of the house was so that you and Dillie didn't have to put up with all that shit any more.'

'Yeah, but then it's just different shit, isn't it?'

'What sort of different shit?'

'Mum crying in her room at night. Us having to move house.'

'But eventually things move on and you realise that the new shit isn't as shitty as the old shit. You know, I don't think this casual use of swear words is making me seem like a cool dad.'

And then Jamie's face broke into a smile.

When we got back home, I asked him to help me see if I could still ride a bike and, to my amazement, it came back to me instinctively. Jamie clapped and cheered and proudly claimed to have taught his father to ride a bicycle, and I allowed that little bit of distorted history to stand.

THOUGH SWIMMING AND CYCLING had returned easily, it seemed that other skills would have to be relearned. I did my best around the home, but it was difficult because I had clearly forgotten how to use an iron or a Hoover.

'Dad's using the Hoover!' said Jamie. 'I've never seen that before.'

I felt empowered by discovering that physical memories had been unaffected by my amnesia.

'So if I can still do all the things I learned before,' I reasoned, 'that means I can still drive.' I waited until the children were out at friends' and then picked up the car keys.

Forty minutes later the garage truck arrived to hoist the car off the ornamental wall at the front of number 23. Previously the Parkers' front garden had been separate from the pavement, but now it was all open-plan.

'I'm terribly sorry. Obviously I'll pay for all the damage,' I said to Mrs Parker, a very nervous American woman.

'I thought it was a terrorist attack,' she stammered.

A couple of police officers arrived fairly promptly. One officer fiddled uncertainly with a laptop on which he was supposed to log the accident details, while the other was perplexed that I tested negative for alcohol and that no calls seem to have been made on my mobile phone.

'So there was no other vehicle involved,' continued the older policeman, 'and it was broad daylight on a straight road . . . I'm struggling to understand how you managed to crash into a garden wall.'

'Well, I sort of forgot how to drive.'

'You forgot how to drive?'

'Er, Dave, there's no box for that.'

'What?'

'On the new form—there's no box for "Forget how to drive".'

'Let's have a look? Hmm . . . Are you sure you didn't "swerve to avoid a pedestrian or animal", sir?'

'Sure. It was completely my fault. I'm sure I used to be able to drive.'

'And when did you forget, exactly?'

'The twenty-second of October.'

The older policeman looked at me uncertainly. 'And are you planning to attempt to drive again?'

'Not until I remember.'

The policeman on the computer chuckled at this unintended jest, but immediately dropped his smile when the senior officer shot him a glare. It was time to bring this to a close. 'Put that he swerved to avoid a cat.'

'Got it,' said the second policeman as he ticked the appropriate box, and another little bit of history was made official.

'What were you thinking?' said Maddy on the phone from Italy. 'Why did you imagine you'd suddenly be able to drive?'

'You mean I *couldn't* drive?'

'No! You never learned on principle.'

WHEN THE HONDA was finally delivered back from the garage, I gave it a good clean in the street outside, prompting the raffish neighbour who had borrowed our hedge trimmer to wander across for an extended chat.

'Hello there, Vaughan. Giving the old motor a wash and set?'

'Ha ha!' I chuckled politely. 'Yes . . . it wouldn't fit in the dishwasher.'

The neighbour thought this was hilarious and I was unsure about the etiquette of resuming washing the car before the laughter had died down. I offered just a bit too much eye contact and suddenly he pounced.

'Arabella was saying that with Maddy away at the moment, you must bring the kids over for their tea one evening.'

Behind him I spotted Jamie and Dillie, returning from the Common with the dog. The word 'No!' was mouthed over and over again.

'That's very kind,' I said, 'but I've already planned their meals for the whole week, so another time perhaps?'

I was growing more confident in the kitchen, cooking from recipe books and serving up the kids' favourite dishes by special request. They were incredibly supportive, telling me exactly how it all used to work before. Apparently I always stacked the dishwasher and they weren't expected to do any clearing up because Mum and I were insistent that they watched *Family Guy* 'while their food went down'.

I knew that they were winding me up, but I let them watch television anyway on the grounds that they'd made me laugh. That was the rule: if their pleas or excuses were witty enough, they generally got their way. 'Dad, I haven't had my pocket money—have you got six pounds fifty?'

'Six pounds fifty? Mum said you got a fiver.'

'Yeah, but there's a one pound fifty handling charge.'

I had said no to Dillie's suggestion that the twins from her class came for a sleepover. Then she insisted that the twins couldn't stay at home because their house was possessed by the Antichrist.

'It's true,' added Jamie. 'The council are sending round an exorcist.'

Minutes later I was dragging the double mattress into Dillie's room.

Dillie's own bed was a masterpiece of creative carpentry. Angled steps at the rear led up to an upper bunk, while underneath was a den that hid a pull-down desk featuring hand-built drawers. Stereo speakers were built into either side of the headboard, leading to an iPod dock, radio and CD player.

'Wow—fantastic bed!' I said. 'Where did you get that from?'

'You built it!' she said.

I learned that I had put a lot of effort into the renovations. It had been me who had done the refit of the kitchen, who'd made the built-in wardrobes. I had even constructed the wooden summerhouse at the bottom of the garden and the decking outside the kitchen door. It was strange that I was able to feel a little abstract pride at these achievements. This contrasted with all the negative stories that were nothing to do with the new Vaughan.

I was still consumed with the mystery of how this had become a 'broken home', so that night, when the children were asleep, I furtively connected an old VHS player to watch some old home movies with promising titles, such as 'Christmas 2007'. Baby Jamie had clearly been something of a super-star, playing the title role in countless thrilling-sounding movies such as 'Jamie's First Mashed Banana' or 'Jamie Sees the Sea!'. The second baby must have failed a screen test, because she barely made an appearance.

Seeing them as toddlers was thrilling and heart-wrenching at the same time. There was more footage of them as they got a bit older; once they could be put down, the camcorder could be picked back up again. An angelic little Dillie sang a song in her Brownie uniform and Jamie was filmed running towards the finishing line at his infant school sports day.

I got another couple of beers from the fridge before resuming the home-movie marathon. There was footage of my wife and kids at the seaside. Woody was a puppy, barking at the waves and then running up the beach. The children were fantastically cute, and yet I could see that they were essentially the same people as now. This whole experience was teaching me that memories are continually revised. The view from the divorce courts would have pushed Maddy's negative memories to the fore.

I sifted through the films, looking for more positive evidence for the Counsel for the Defence. And there I was—perhaps just a couple of years ago, judging by the age of the children—in the back garden, tending a barbecue.

'I could always cook the meat in the oven first? And then you could put it on the barbecue to finish it off?' suggested Maddy.

'No, it's getting there,' insisted the chef, despite all evidence to the contrary. With the light fading, Dillie did a spoof appeal into the camera lens on behalf of the starving children of South London and Maddy came into shot with a grill pan to transfer the meat to her own domain.

Then the atmosphere turned.

'Just let me do it, will you?' I snapped as I took the chicken back. 'Why do you have to be such a control freak?'

'I'm not. I'm just making sure the kids get something to eat.'

'So dinner is a bit later than usual—so what? You moan that I don't cook enough and then when I do, you march in and take over.'

'What cooking? The chicken is raw two hours after you started.'

The footage moved indoors as Jamie, who had been filming, crept away and the domestic rancour faded into the background.

I watched the tape a couple more times, noticing that I'd had a beer bottle in my hand, and that there were empties on the table nearby. Dillie's nine-year-old face had a resigned sadness to it, as if she had witnessed scenes like this before.

I lined the tape up to the end of Dillie's comic appeal and pressed 'Record' on the VHS player. The last five minutes of this story would now be wiped clear.

'Do you remember that lovely evening when we had a barbecue and the coals wouldn't light?' I imagined Maddy fondly reminiscing.

'Oh, yeah—and Dillie did that mock charity appeal to camera?'

'That was a funny evening, wasn't it . . .?'

When I returned to the kitchen, I noticed the recycling bin brimming with empty lager bottles. Then I noticed Ralph's business card in the kitchen and, even though it was the middle of the night, I dialled 141 to block my number followed by his mobile number. 'Hi, this is Ralph,' said the recording. 'I'm in Venice at the moment. Please leave a message and I'll get back to you in the New Year.' He didn't have to boast about it.

I WATCHED the re-edited videos with the children on New Year's Eve, and they were thrilled and delighted to see the way we used to be. Then Dillie fetched a box of photos and the two of them narrated me through the blurred cast of relations and family friends.

'Who's that lady?' I asked, looking at a very old picture of a woman standing alone in some tropical location.

'That's Granny Vaughan. That's . . . your mum . . .'

I held the faded colour photo in my hand. She was smiling directly at me, wearing a smart two-piece and clutching a leather handbag over her arm. I wish I could report experiencing some sort of instant bond, but I was aware only of a vacuum where sentiment and longing were supposed to be.

'Are you OK, Dad?' said Dillie.

'Yeah—I'm fine. It's just . . . she looks nice.'

'Yeah, she was,' said Jamie. 'She always gave us chocolate and pound coins and said, "Don't tell your dad!"'

We found more photos of my mum and dad and of me as a child, and they made me laugh with family stories and tales from the olden days.

'Happy New Year, Dad!'

THE NEXT DAY I took Jamie and Dillie to see their grandfather and I felt an enormous pride in them being so affectionate towards him, unembarrassed at showing that they cared. His face looked slightly yellow, but Dillie didn't hesitate to lean in and kiss him. She had brought a handmade card and Jamie lent his grandfather his iPod; he had cleared his own music collection to fill it up with audiobooks. Even though I doubted whether his grandfather would have the energy to listen to an audiobook, the vision of my teenage son taking this much trouble brought me close to tears.

'You are so kind,' said my father. The children told him all about their Christmas, and when it was time to go, they hugged him long and hard.

'What lovely grandchildren. Thank you for coming. You must have more important things to do.'

'No,' said his grandson firmly. 'Not more important than you.'

THE WEEK PASSED far too quickly. On the final day I cleaned the house, prepared a dinner and packed my bags. Maddy arrived alone at the front door and embraced the children as I hovered in the hallway. She had presents for them and an inscrutable smile and a hello for me.

'Wow, it all looks very clean. We should send photos to my mum!'

I had invited myself to stay for dinner by cooking a big casserole, and afterwards Maddy and I had the chance to talk on our own.

'So how was your holiday?'

'Oh, one minute I was travelling in great comfort in a gondola, the next I was travelling in extreme discomfort with a budget airline. They sort of cancel each other out.'

'Well, it was great being here with the kids. They are so funny and clever and interesting and everything . . .'

'Listen—I've been thinking,' Maddy announced. 'What you said in the courtroom . . . we don't actually have to get legally divorced, if you really don't want to.'

I stood up and gently pushed the kitchen door closed.

'You are so much easier to talk to since your amnesia that I wondered if we could just work something out like adults? If we didn't spend so much on lawyers, we might just be able to hang on to the house.'

'For you and the kids to live in without me?'

'Well—this is my proposal. The kids live here all the time, keep their rooms, keep walking to school with their friends. But you and I split the cost of a little flat somewhere cheap, and take turns to live in that when it's not our turn to be here. Once the children have grown up and left home we can sell the house and work out how to split the proceeds. But for the next seven or eight years, we could both have the same second home.'

Privately I had to concede that this seemed like a constructive suggestion. I'd get to have every weekend in this house with the children.

'So part of the time you'd be here,' she said with a smile, 'and the rest of the time it would be me and Ralph.'

'So this is Ralph's idea, is it?' I said, feeling my face heating up.

'Not exactly . . . I only meant if Ralph and I decide we want to live together. The kids would have to be cool with it of course.'

'So your great plan is, we don't have to legally get divorced to save money so that Vaughan lives in a shoebox in the slums, while Ralph moves into my half of the double bed here?'

'You're distorting it. Ralph said we shouldn't rush into anything—'

'Oh well, if that's what Ralph suggests, then that's definitely what we should do! I can't believe you try and dress it up as what's best for the kids, when really it's just your fancy man trying to save on his rent bill!'

Madeleine was still trying to talk to me as I marched to the door and put on my old coat, which was hanging by the door.

'Um . . . that's Ralph's coat,' mumbled Maddy.

'What? No, this is mine—I've been wearing it all week.'

'No—it's Ralph's. He left it here. It's his. But I'm sure he wouldn't mind you borrowing it . . .'

CHAPTER 6

'Right, Year Elevens, it's good to be teaching you again. Today we are going to be talking about the causes of the Second World War,' I predicted a little optimistically. 'Now Ms Coney, who I understand was taking you while I was away, has told you all about the Treaty of Versailles—'

'Sir! Mr Vaughan, sir?'

'Yes, Tanika?' I was pleased to demonstrate my apparently effortless grasp of all their names. It had involved much time staring at school photos.

'Are you a mentalist, sir?'

'I beg your pardon?'

'Dean said you'd gone mental in the nut and didn't know nothin'.'

'Well, it is no secret that my absence last term was due to me suffering a rare neurological condition, which in no way affects my abilities to teach you about the fall of the Weimar Republic.'

'Yeah, but are you a loony? Do you, like, bark at the moon?'

'No, but I might be in a minute. Since Tanika insists on referring to my memory loss, it's worth asking whether it is possible for whole countries to lose their memory as well. That's why history is so important—'

A few different hands went up.

'Yes—Dean?'

'Do you think you're the Messiah, sir? Are you going on a shooting spree in McDonald's?'

'Could we concentrate on the lesson plan, please? Now, the failure of democracy in Germany—'

'Did you find them, sir?'

'Did I find what?'

'Your marbles, sir.'

'Do you want some fruit-cake, sir? It's really nutty . . .'

'Do you foam at the mouth, sir? Are you afraid of water?'

'Look!' I finally snapped. 'This is the easy stuff! The rise of Hitler and the Nazis. This is the easiest history I can teach! So listen or we'll do module four and we'll talk about the repeal of the Corn Laws, all right?'

'Ooooh!' said Tanika, vindicated. 'Boggy Vaughan's gone mental.'

AFTER MY FIRST LESSON with Year 11, I reflected on the distressing revelation that I seemed to lack the natural authority required to teach inner-city teenagers. I was not the inspiring, life-changing teacher I had imagined when I had first learned of my occupation.

Perhaps there might be something positive on my online memoir? Perhaps by now former pupils had recalled how I had transformed their lives? When I logged on I found that a number of students had indeed discovered my Wikipedia page, although their accounts of my past did not smack of rigorous accuracy.

For example, I was sceptical about whether I had indeed been the so-called 'Fifth member of Abba', playing the tambourine on 'Gimme, Gimme, Gimme (A Man After Midnight)'. It seemed that a competition had ensued for the most outlandish back story to the mystery of Mr Vaughan's life before he taught history. I learned that I had been assistant editor of *What Caravan?* but had been sacked following a fist-fight with the editor over the merits of the new Alpine Sprite. I was pleased to learn that I had single-handedly identified the genome of the Giant African Badger, though less proud that I had threatened to kill myself unless Nestlé promised that in future Quality Street would have more of the yummy green triangle ones.

I considered taking down the Wikipedia page, but decided that it was providing a valuable outlet for student creativity on the blurred borders of fiction and nonfiction.

DR LEWINGTON had asked me to come up with some memories that I had recovered, and to think of some significant life events that were still out of reach in my memory banks. I duly arrived for another brain scan with a wide selection of episodes from my past life. I was to concentrate on these and my brain activity would be compared to the chemical and temperature changes that occurred when I tried to recall chapters that were still blank.

There was a gentle whirr as the conveyor transported me inside the pod of the new brain scanner, and it seemed to know when to stop once my skull was in place for the internal mapping to commence. Over the hum of the machine I could hear Dr Lewington giving me instructions into her microphone and so I duly summoned up a significant recollection.

IT IS THE SUMMER OF 1997, and I am feeling a little nervous in my new suit as I stand outside the nonreligious venue for our marriage service. Madeleine did not want a traditional church wedding with a white dress and bridesmaids and the church organist playing Bach.

'Madeleine's not pregnant,' explains Maddy's mother to elderly relatives. 'Doesn't she look lovely in red? She didn't want a traditional white dress.'

'Mum, it's perfectly normal to want a nonreligious service.'

'I just don't want people thinking the church wouldn't have you. Or they might take the red dress as a sign . . . that you were a fallen woman.'

'A fallen woman! It's the Nineties, Mum. It doesn't matter if a woman is pregnant when she gets married!'

'Oh, are you pregnant?' says Great-Auntie Brenda. 'Well, it's good you're getting married, dear. It's better that the baby isn't a little bastard.'

'No, she's not pregnant, Brenda,' says Maddy's mum slightly too desperately. 'She's just very political. You know—doesn't believe in things.'

'Mum, I do believe in things. That's why . . . oh, it doesn't matter.'

'Don't let it spoil your day, Madeleine,' says Auntie Brenda. 'You're still the bride, dear, even if, you know . . .' And after Brenda has done the rounds, Maddy can be overheard politely thanking other relatives for the compliment that she looks 'blooming'.

LATER MOMENTS from the wedding day melted into each other like an edited-highlights package. I thought of Maddy waltzing with my father, as he gracefully led her around the scuffed wooden floor. I could picture a rather drunk Gary remembering every move to 'The Birdie Song'. And I remembered Maddy giving me a long and meaningful hug at the end of the evening. We could have skipped the service and the party; that embrace was what made me realise that she wanted to be with me always.

One tradition had been upheld during the ceremony, when Maddy and her dad had been the last people to enter the chamber. Her entrance had been delayed outside when a young lawyer had handed her an important-looking wax-sealed envelope that he insisted she must open before she could proceed with her marriage. Was it a legal bar to the marriage? Did her intended already have a wife? Was her intended an illegal alien? A flustered Maddy tore open the envelope and pulled out the contents. It was a postcard of a leprechaun saying 'Top o' the mornin' to yers!'

The brain scanner hummed and whirred and Dr Lewington instructed me to try to think about something significant of which I currently had no remembrance. I tried to picture my mother, searching for the moment when I had learned of her death, or the funeral that I must have attended. Now I could see myself standing in a country churchyard, throwing earth onto a wooden coffin. I could have easily convinced myself that this was exactly as it happened, except that I had learned that my mother had been cremated. Even though I knew it was pure fiction, I found it vaguely comforting to have this classic funeral scene to cling to.

Now I was instructed to concentrate on any episodes I had that were partially reconstructed. I had deliberately saved the most negative moment I could recall to contrast with the bittersweet memories of my wedding. It was the day Madeleine said she didn't want to be married to me any more.

Maddy and I are getting ready for bed one night. I attempt to suggest that I have had a tough day at school, but she is not interested. What I have forgotten is that Maddy has just had the results of a test for a health scare. She had found a lump under her arm and had become convinced it was cancer.

'You can't diagnose something like that from looking it up on the Internet,' I had said when she first mentioned it.

'A couple of people said my symptoms sound serious . . .'

'What people?'

'I don't know their real names. It was on a blog about women's health.'

From the outset she has interpreted my scorn for online medical chat as lack of interest in her well-being. Now she gets into bed, as far away from me as it is physically possible to be, and starts sobbing.

'What? What is it?'

'I got the results of my cancer test today.'

Two blows strike me almost simultaneously. First, there is the sudden shame I feel at not having remembered, but that counts for nothing as

I absorb the far greater blow. Maddy's sobbing tells me that the cancer test must have been positive. Suddenly I see a future in which Maddy will have to endure chemotherapy and the kids might lose their mother.

She shakes off my tentative offer of a comforting arm as I try to ascertain what exactly the doctor has said to her and what the treatment options are.

'It was negative. I don't have cancer. The lump is benign,' she weeps.

'Oh, thank God for that!' and I go to hug her but she pushes me away.

'Maddy—it's fantastic news! You had me going there, the way you were crying and everything! God, what a relief.'

She wipes her face. 'You forgot to ask me about the results.'

'Yeah, I know—I'm really sorry, but can I just tell you what happened at school today and you might understand—'

'You didn't even remember to ask! You don't care enough to ask if I am going to live or die, to find out whether I have cancer or not.'

'That's just ridiculous. As it happens, I never thought that you did have cancer, although I could see you were worried about it.'

'But you didn't come to the hospital, did you?'

'Because you never asked me to.'

'You still should have offered.'

'For God's sake, you don't have cancer—why are we arguing again?'

'Our marriage has cancer. If you can't be there for me when I go through something like this, then I don't think I want to be married to you.'

'Look you're getting this out of proportion. I'll take a couple of days off work, and maybe we should take the kids down to your parents—'

'It's too late, Vaughan. You've never been there for me. It's always been about you, never about us . . .'

And I realise that she wouldn't have sobbed like this about the uncertainty of cancer. She is crying because she feels that something has died.

LYING IN THE SCANNER, I could almost feel my head throbbing as I trawled over that terrible night again, honing in on the tiny details that made it feel so real. The moment when we finished talking and she went to sleep in the spare room, never to return again for all the time that we stayed under the same roof. The broken light bulb in the bedside lamp. The ache on the back of my skull that kept me company until dawn.

Then, lying inside that machine, I realised I had just had an actual new memory. I had had a blow on the head! The whole time this marriage-ending argument was going on, I could feel a large swelling on the back of my head. I had been concussed. That was what I had been trying to tell her: I had been confronted outside the school by an angry father. He had shoved me over and I had hit the back of my head on the kerb. I had refused to go to hospital, but I knew it had been a pretty bad blow.

Now I realised that my amnesia might be a delayed reaction to this injury. That was why I had forgotten Maddy's medical results! It was the first symptom of an amnesia that was later to swallow me completely.

Back in her office, Dr Lewington showed me the results of the different scans. One image showed lots of blues and reds in the middle part of my brain. And in all the others there were lots of blues and reds in the same part of my brain. 'Absolutely no difference whatsoever!' she enthused. 'The brain really is such a fascinating enigma.' Even the moment when I recovered the brand-new memory revealed no brain activity that was different.

'Of course we have to be aware that the memories you are recovering may not be all that accurate,' she commented cautiously. 'You might be regaining memories that were already distorted, and they might have been twisted further in the recovery—they might even be completely false.'

'False?' I exclaimed, vaguely offended.

'Certainly. I've had patients with vivid recollections of things that happened when they weren't there. They can become quite angry when their versions of their own past are challenged. Such is the power of memory to affect our emotions!' She made an appointment to see me in a couple of months and I realised that that would be after I was officially divorced.

'Just as a matter of interest,' I said as I stood up. 'Is there any scientific basis for what they say, that "there's a fine line between love and hate"?'

'Yes, actually. Both emotions occur in the same neural circuits. Neurologists at UCL recently logged levels of emotion from the amount of activity in that part of the subcortex.'

'So you can scientifically measure how much you love someone?'

'Well, it might be love. It might be hate. Their scans measured only the strength of feeling.'

THE MEMORY OF MY CONCUSSION increased the sense of injustice I was already feeling inside. I had to confront Maddy with this new development; she had played the neglected martyr about her health, but at the end of that fateful day she did not have a serious medical condition and I did. I went directly to the house to share my revelation with her. I knew the children would be at school and I think I was actually looking forward to a really good argument with her. In the fantasy scenario spinning around in my head, she was actually pleading with me to take her back. 'No, it's too late now,' I told her. 'You had your chance but you threw it away.'

Forty minutes later I had worked myself up into a state of indignation as I pressed the entry-phone buzzer. 'It's Vaughan! I need to talk to you.'

There was a long pause and then the door lock clicked and I pushed my way in. The dog greeted me enthusiastically, but Maddy did not appear as quickly as my state of excitement demanded. Through the ceiling I could hear her walking about. Eventually a toilet flushed and I heard her footsteps. I stiffened in anticipation of the coming difficult conversation. But it would be more awkward than I expected. Coming down the stairs was not Maddy, but her boyfriend, Ralph.

I RECOGNISED HIM before he introduced himself. I had already guessed that the man I had seen helping Maddy with the picture frames must have been Ralph. In any case, the confident way he jumped down two steps at a time wearing a towelling dressing gown suggested that he was probably not a burglar. He was maybe a decade younger than me, and indeed Maddy.

'Hi, Vaughan—I'm Ralph! Great to meet you.' I felt I had no alternative to accepting the outstretched hand. 'Maddy's out at the moment. Sorry about my state of undress—just showered after my run!'

'Ah, right. Hence the dressing gown. "Hilton Hotels"!' I hadn't intended this to come across like an accusation of theft, but that was how it sounded.

'Yes, it's Egyptian cotton. They were selling them in the Venice Hilton so I thought, why not?'

I was disorientated by the detail that he had taken Maddy to a luxury hotel. 'Yes, Venice, of course. How was that?'

'Amazing! What a city! You ever been?'

'Er, no. Maddy always wanted to go—but, you know . . . Wasn't there some problem with Venice sinking or something?'

'I dunno if they sorted that out or not. But I suppose even if they did stop it sinking, now sea levels are rising it's going to be back to square one.'

'Honestly, if it's not one thing it's another,' I tutted. 'I mean, I used to order the Veneziana in Pizza Express because they added twenty-five pence onto your bill for the Venice in Peril fund.'

'Well, that's great! And do you still have the Veneziana now?'

'No—I got fed up with the sultanas.'

'Urgh, sultanas on a pizza? No!'

The dog yawned and I knew that it was time to say something about Ralph's relationship with Maddy.

'So . . .' I said ominously, and I saw him prepare himself. 'I wonder . . . if they've thought about building, like, a huge tidal barrier across the strait of Gibraltar? So it could stop the rising Atlantic flowing into the Med and flooding all the low-lying coastal areas?'

'Nah—it's about twenty miles between Spain and Morocco,' he said. 'I mean, the engineering logistics alone would be insurmountable.'

The arrogance with which he dismissed my idea rubbed me up the wrong way. 'Well, something's got to be done!' I said, hearing my voice rising.

'There's no point. It's all too late anyway.'

'Oh right, so we can put a man on the moon, but don't bother trying to safeguard the homes and livelihoods of a billion people?'

'All the other coasts are going to disappear anyway—just deal with it!'

'No—I'm going to try to do something about it. I'm going to start having the Veneziana again. Even if I have to pick off all the sultanas.'

Admittedly my idea had been a bold one, and Ralph might have tried to clinch the argument by pointing out the geopolitical strategic power that control of this barrier would bestow upon Spain or Morocco, but instead he opted for a personal blow below the belt.

'So, I understand you've been having some mental-health issues?'

It was at this point that I felt that my argument for this massive engineering project would become unanswerable if I punched Ralph in the face. I felt my fist clench and my face redden as an alarmed Ralph suddenly took a step back. Only in the last nanoseconds of this thought process did something inside me put the brakes on. I had just remembered how stupid and upsetting the incident with the psycho-dad at school had been. That's why I had come here—to tell Maddy about my concussion.

'Where's Maddy?' I demanded.

When he told me, I knew I wanted to be there too.

Failing to bother with the niceties of saying goodbye, I slammed the door on my way out, feeling my hands shaking as I unlocked my bike. It was not a short cycle ride, but it was made considerably quicker by just how fired up I was.

'Hello, Maddy,' I said quietly as I pushed the door open.

'Oh, hi. I didn't know you were coming.'

'No, well . . . Hi, Dad, how you feeling? You're looking a little better.'

My father's gaunt face peeked out of the top of the NHS blanket.

'That's for seeing. Your lovely wife!' he suggested breathlessly. 'You don't. Normally. Come together.'

Maddy and I glanced at one another. 'Well, we thought you'd prefer more frequent visits, so we take it in turns,' improvised Maddy.

'Yes, that!' I blurted. 'But—it's nice to be here together, isn't it, Maddy?'

I was still angry with her and Ralph and realised that there would be nothing she could do if I put my arm round her waist. I felt her stiffen, but I held it there as we stood before the old man's approving gaze. There was a perfect hand-shaped ledge above her hip that felt like the most natural place in the world for a man to place his hand.

'Look at you,' wheezed my dad. 'You still make such a lovely couple.'

I gave Maddy an extra squeeze and was contemplating planting a kiss on her cheek, but she quickly sat down and told my father what the children had been up to. I sat beside her, chipping in with inferior contributions.

'Maddy's the daughter. I never had.' His breath seemed weaker now; the effort of this visit could not be sustained much longer.

'You have a sleep, Keith,' Maddy said. I was startled to see that her eyes had welled up. 'I'm just popping to the loo!' she blurted as she dashed out.

Soon the old man was asleep and I went out and found our family car and waited to catch her there.

'Hi. You OK?'

'Your father is such a wonderful man,' she mused, her eyes still red.

'Yeah, I wish I could remember more of what he was like before . . . Look, I need to talk to you, Maddy. Any chance of a lift back?' Madeleine was too grown up to refuse me.

'You didn't have to do the whole lovey-dovey thing in front of him. Do that again and I'll stamp on your foot.'

'Yeah, well, I'll take whatever attention I can get.'

Maddy had put her seat belt on and was just checking her texts when she suddenly looked up. 'So you met Ralph?'

'Oh—yes. We had a brief conversation.'

'What did you say to him? What did he say back?'

'You wouldn't be interested.'

'What, my ex-husband and father of my children meets my boyfriend and you think I wouldn't be interested?'

She had put her ticket in the machine and the barrier juddered upwards.

'OK, well he said you could never build a tidal barrier across the strait of Gibraltar.'

She took her eyes off the road to look at me in confusion. 'Sorry?'

'Rising sea levels? Venice in Peril? He was actually quite dismissive of my idea of a massive Thames Barrier-type sea wall.'

'So you didn't talk about anything important?'

'Rising sea levels are important. But, no, we never really talked about the elephant in the room.'

'What was the elephant in the room?'

'Well, *you*, obviously . . .'

Her phone beeped again, and she read the next message at the traffic lights. 'He says he thought you were going to hit him!'

'What? Over a discussion on sea levels? As if I'd hit a man in a dressing gown! From which I am deducing that he's already moved in.'

'No! The kids were on sleepovers, so he stayed the night. They don't know he ever stays either, so don't say anything.'

'Anyway, I went round there because I wanted to talk to you about something. I had another brain scan today—'

'OK—back to *you* then.'

'It's important. I remembered something. The day you had the results of your cancer test. The thing is I had concussion that day—I had been shoved to the ground by an aggressive parent and I banged my head on the kerb. I think it might be related to my amnesia since October.'

'Did you tell the doctor?' She was being deliberately obtuse.

'That's not the point. There was a *medical* reason why I forgot to ask you about your test. Remember it was the final straw for you that I forgot to ask you about it?'

'The point of that phrase is that it takes a lot of other straws as well.'

'But the more I remember, the more I see that we didn't need to break up. I knew that from the moment I fell in love with you back in the autumn.'

'You didn't fall in love with me. You just loved the idea of being married.' She was cross now. 'And now I have to put up with everyone saying "Poor Vaughan—he can't even remember his own wife!" But you always forgot your own wife—you just took your world view to its logical conclusion.'

The light had changed to green and a car behind was tooting impatiently.

I was knocked back by the depth of her resentment, but had one more line I had prepared and polished and was ready to detonate.

'Have you any idea what it is like to lose your identity? And then to find out who you were, only to have that taken away from you too?'

'Do I know what it's like to lose my identity?' she spat in disbelief. 'Are you serious? Before I married you I was "Madeleine". Not "Vaughan's wife" or "Jamie's mum", or "Dillie's mum"; I existed in my own right. I was Maddy the photographer, who earned her own money doing something she loved. Then suddenly it was all "What does your husband do?" And "How old are your children?" So I do know what it is like to lose my identity. Yes, I do.'

'Maddy, you are doing nearly seventy in a thirty-miles-an-hour zone—'

'And now I am doing what I want for the first time I can remember. I'm going to Venice, I'm working towards an exhibition, and I don't have to compromise my entire existence.'

'I think that speed camera just flashed twice—'

'Yeah, well, I'll appeal, explaining that my ex-husband was being really annoying. You think because you got a bang on the head I am going to go, "Oh, that changes everything! It was all *my* fault"?' She pulled the car over to the kerb. 'Why don't you get out here, before you make me run someone over? Or, even better, get out here and then maybe I can run *you* over.'

'Oh. But—couldn't you at least drop me where my bike is locked up?'

'Where's that?'

'At the hospital.'

It seemed that everything I said was somehow really annoying. I watched Maddy speed off without glancing in her mirror. I stood there in the winter drizzle and eventually crossed the road to catch the bus back in the opposite direction. When nothing came for ten minutes, I began to walk. Eventually I reached Chelsea Bridge.

Around my neck I could feel the dog tag that I had always worn in case my amnesia recurred. But so what if I lost my memory all over again? I might handle it all better second time around. This ID tag weighed a few grams but felt like a couple of kilos; it rubbed against my neck, a constant reminder of my broken brain. I undid the little clasp and then cast it down into the swirling, murky Thames. I heard no sound and saw no splash. And then I walked on to face the rest of my life without Madeleine.

CHAPTER 7

'I am never, ever, getting a mobile phone.'

'Yeah, you say that now . . .' laughs my fiancée.

'No—' I confirm. 'Come back to me in the year 2000 and even if I'm the last man in Britain without one, I guarantee you will never catch me shouting into a handset.'

'It's different for a woman,' asserts Maddy. 'I might be stuck somewhere at night and be worried about being mugged or something.'

'Oh, right, so you make sure that you advertise you have something worth nicking ringing away in your handbag!'

THIS CONVERSATION came back to me twenty years later as I sat in the pub with Gary taking turns to show off the stupid apps on our iPhones. 'This one finds your location and tells you how many crack houses have been closed down in the area.'

'Hey—that's useful.'

I had now officially moved out of Gary and Linda's flat, having felt increasingly less comfortable there as the weeks passed. When I had popped back to leave a gift and return their keys, I found myself hovering on the step, unsure whether I should intrude on a screaming match. I let myself in and tiptoed into the kitchen to find that there was no argument. Gary was alone, listening to an old fight on the iPod speakers while he was peeling some potatoes.

'Hi, Gary. Listening to your Greatest Hits tape?'

'Yeah. Fifteenth of August last year—it's an interesting one.'

From the speakers, a tearful Linda shouted, 'You never talk to me about anything! You always go all quiet if I want to discuss things . . .'

'Because *this* is the alternative to quiet!' Gary's voice shouted back. 'You don't really want me to "talk", as in "put alternative point of view"; you just want me to be like your friends who think it's supportive to go along with every nutty thing you say.'

'Good comeback line, eh?' commented Gary. 'It's like the presidential debates—you've got to have your counter-arguments rehearsed.'

'Isn't the point to try to avoid the arguments?'

'No, you've got to have fights in a marriage. What is it you see tattooed on people's fingers? "L.O.V.E." on one hand, "H.A.T.E." on the other. They're two sides of the same coin.'

'I don't hate Maddy.'

'You did before your brain wiped it all. You hated her because you loved her—that's how it works.'

IT WAS A SHORT WALK to the pub, or it would have been, if we hadn't taken the route suggested by Gary's new 'Barfinder App'. In my defence, when I said I would never get a mobile phone, it was before you could do so many useful things with them.

Many weeks had passed since Maddy and I had fought in the car and I had decided to make the most of my freedom and live in one of the world's great tourist locations at the perfect time of year. Which one was it to be: Paris in the spring, New England in the fall, or Streatham in March?

'So what's the Hi Klass Hotel in Streatham like?' said Gary.

'Well, it's very cheap for me, because I'm the only guest who wants a room for more than half an hour. They have a sort of chambermaid pit-stop team changing the sheets after every punter all through the night.'

'Maybe you should make the most of the convenience. When was the last time you had sex?'

'I can't remember ever having sex. The experience has been completely wiped from my brain.'

Gary almost fell off his bar stool with laughter. 'Oh, you know what that means, don't you? For all intents and purposes, that makes you a virgin!'

'Don't be ridiculous. I've got two kids.'

'Makes no odds. You're a *born-again virgin*. You do not know what it is like to make love to a woman. We, my friend, are going to make a night of this.'

Before we left, Gary popped to the toilets and came out with a small foil square, which he thrust into my hand.

'It's a condom. Take it. You'll thank me later. This is a once-in-a-lifetime opportunity! Most men would love to be in your position.'

UNSURPRISINGLY, MY CONDOM stayed in its packet that night, despite Gary doing his best to re-create the cliché he'd seen in films, where two men spot two unattached women in a bar and offer to buy them a drink. In six different pubs and wine bars, we found just one pair of women who were not with boyfriends or husbands and it turned out they were waiting for the rest of their book group to turn up.

'How old are you anyway?' one of them had said to Gary, who came back with, 'Old enough.' This failed to make them want to abandon discussing their magic realist novel and sleep with two middle-aged strangers instead.

But away from the vicarious prowling of Gary, I did soon find myself in a situation where some women were interested in me. The night after school had broken up for Easter I accepted the invitation of the younger teachers to go to the pub. My work colleagues had always been cautious not to appear nosy about my medical condition, but, after a few bottles of wine, a group of female teachers broached the subject of how much I could remember.

'Can you remember your childhood and stuff like that?'

'Bits of it are coming back. I don't really remember my parents, or growing up or going to university or anything.'

'It must be weird to have no past,' said Sally, the English teacher. 'It means you don't quite know who you are in the present.'

'Exactly. Though it's made me think none of us really knows who we actually are—we just invent a persona, put it out there and hope everyone else goes along with it.'

The others reflected on this profound thought for a moment.

'And my friend Gary says I'm a virgin because I don't remember having sex!' I joked, but this information sent an electric ripple through the group.

'What, you haven't had sex since your amnesia?'

'Well, no—my wife and I are separated.'

'And you don't remember having sex beforehand?'

'No—it's a complete blank.'

This bewitching detail instantly seemed to elevate me to the status of the most desirable man in all Europe. Suddenly my jokes were hilarious, my anecdotes deeply fascinating, and I was subjected to an hour of intensive flirting from a collection of vivacious women.

I told them about having no memory of my friends and family and then discovering my marriage had failed and that my father was dying.

'Ah, come here—you need a big hug,' said Jennifer, who helped late developers with special needs.

'Yes, you are badly in need of a cuddle,' agreed Caroline, who taught media studies and drama but seemed keen to expand to adult education.

I realised I was thoroughly enjoying the undivided attention of these women, even though it felt slightly scary.

The topography of the pub, coupled with the perseverance of one particular woman, meant that eventually I was no longer talking to a group of ladies but just to one. Suzanne was a tall, thin Australian brunette in her early thirties who worked in the PE department. She had previously been a dancer, and it showed in her impeccable posture and penchant for woolly leggings.

She had seemed fairly attractive at the beginning of the evening, but following several pints of beer and a bottle of red wine, I was even better able to appreciate her seductive allure. She taunted me with her provocative story of how she had introduced a B.Tech in dance for those not able to do the GCSE; her account of how she was unfairly passed over for the vacancy of Assistant Principal (Curriculum) seemed positively erotic.

'You know you said you were going to Greenwich Market on Sunday?' I said. 'I have an *A–Z* back in my desk that you could borrow. A ring-binder one so you could keep the map open on the Greenwich page . . .'

'Oh, that would be really useful, actually, yeah . . .'

There was a moment's silence while we both wondered how to get round the second problem.

'It might take me a while to find it.' I was concentrating hard now. 'So, if you like, you could finish your drink, with the rest of your department over there, and I could meet you in school in about ten minutes?'

Kofi and John the security guards were well used to teachers coming in at all hours and thought there was nothing unusual in seeing me walk past the reception desk around midnight.

'Hello, Mr Vaughan, sir. You working too hard, sir.'

'Aha ha, yes, work, work, work! Just picking something up, actually.'

I swiped my smart card to pass through the main doors and then headed up the stairs. It felt illicit to be in school so late. Looking at myself in the cracked mirror in the staff toilets, I was excited and nervous that this could be the night when it was finally going to happen.

In my form room, I grabbed the *A–Z* from my drawer. Now it could lead me to my first sexual experience: you just followed the route from talking to touching, kept going till you reached kissing and eventually that lead you straight to . . . And then I realised that I had no idea how you actually went from one to the next. Perhaps I should make an excuse and forget the whole idea? At that moment the beep of my phone made me jump. The text message read: 'Hve bought wine. Am in gym store. S.x'

Now I felt myself physically shaking. I was going to lose my virginity in the gym, like some jock in an American teen movie.

SUZANNE WAS SITTING cross-legged on a pile of exercise mats with a bottle of red wine and two plastic cups in front of her. I perched myself on the edge of a low bench and drank my wine far too quickly.

'I'm sure there are rules about members of staff drinking alcohol in the gymnasium after midnight,' I joked.

'Who's going to know? Kofi and John never leave the reception desk, and anyway, I can always lock the door.' She got up and did so with a suggestively raised eyebrow and I worried that I may have given a slight whimper.

But still the Rubicon had to be crossed.

'It's incredible to think that you have no memory of having sex,' she chuckled as she sat beside me, looking directly into my eyes.

'Yeah, but you know, I got in the swimming pool and immediately remembered how to swim. And I got on a bike and I remembered that . . .'

'Oh, right, so you can still cycle and drive and everything?'

'Well, I tried driving. And I demolished my neighbour's wall—'

Her insane laughter made me realise that she was drunker than I was.

'Maybe I should give you a few driving lessons?'

'No, I think it's important to have a proper instructor—' The sentence was cut off at source as she kissed me full on the lips.

OK, we're doing this now, I thought. I wondered how many women I had kissed like this in my previous life. Finally I broke off the kiss, ostensibly to have another glug of wine. I had tried but failed to keep Maddy out of my mind. This woman's body was completely different from that of the mother of my children. And I knew which I preferred. Madeleine had curving hips and breasts and tumbling red hair that wasn't cropped short for sport. And then I did something I did not feel proud of. As Suzanne launched her face at mine once more, I imagined it was Madeleine. I closed my eyes and eagerly pulled her close. I kissed her with passion, pretending she was the woman I had told myself that I was over. My mission this evening was to lose my virginity. I had to remain focused on my goal.

I was surprised by how forward she was, effortlessly undoing my buttons to rub her hands over my chest. At each stage she was ahead of me. She wriggled out of her top and her bra in one deft movement and then moved to pull my shirt and vest over my head. Even though we hardly knew each other, she seemed to have no qualms about baring the upper half of her body to me. She wriggled out of her tights and I thought I ought to follow suit by taking off my trousers.

'Have you got a condom?' she suddenly enquired.

That was definitely it, then. That surely was confirmation it was going to happen. 'Yes. I've got one in my wallet.' I reached across to my discarded trousers to find the sachet that Gary had bought me a few days earlier. I tugged at the foil, and was unable to open the packet. In my desperation I attacked it with my teeth, recoiling as the seal broke and I got a tiny taste of the sterile lubricant inside. Finally Suzanne lay below me and I was ready to make love to her. Actually 'love' was far too strong a word. I barely knew her, I quite liked her; I would be 'making quite like' to her.

And so with a shift of my body, and a clumsy grope to find my way, I became a man again. That Rudyard Kipling poem really should have included something about this bit, I thought, as I focused on the achievement, the milestone that *this was it*.

'Whoa! Whoa! Slow down a bit, Vaughan—it's not a race to the finish!'

'Sorry . . . Is that better?'

'Nice and gentle—that's right.'

I did my best to be considerate and attentive. I had got into a rhythm now, and felt pretty much in control. Unfortunately, my foot seemed to have got tangled in the netting of a folded-up five-a-side goal that was propped against the wall. That foot was not shaking free, however much I tried to wiggle it about. While still ostensibly focusing on Suzanne, I gave one final tug and suddenly the whole metal goal frame came crashing to the floor.

'Jesus, what was that?' She had leaped up in fear.

'Sorry! Sorry! The goal net was tangled in my foot.'

'Do you think the guys will have heard that from the reception desk?'

'I doubt it. It didn't make that much noise,' I claimed, despite the ringing in my head. 'Shall we just go back to where we left off?'

But the moment had gone. Before her drunkenness had made her adventurous; now she was paranoid and I was appalled to see her getting dressed.

It was over before it was finished. I had learned to put on a condom, but it hadn't really been required. Did this count? I wondered. Yes, it definitely counted, I concluded. I had lost my second virginity.

The two of us got dressed and there was no pretence that we ought to spend the rest of the night together. She suggested I should leave first and she would tidy up and leave ten minutes later, so that the blokes on the door didn't suspect anything. I gave her a peck on the cheek and headed out into the main part of the gym, still feeling like a superhero. There in the middle of the wooden floor was an abandoned football. I saw the goal at the far end of the room, and I took a short run-up and kicked the ball with all my might, watching it curl into the corner of the net. And I raised both arms in the air in triumph. 'He shoots! Goooooaaaallll!'

I was still feeling mightily proud when I said good night to Kofi and John, who seemed a little red around the eyes as if they had been crying. Or laughing, perhaps. I looked up to the security monitor above the desk, to see a black and white image of Suzanne putting her coat on in the gym, and then I heard them burst out laughing as I slunk out of the main door.

WHEN MADDY WAS FED UP with the city, she would buy a property-porn magazine called *Coastal Living*. It featured sun-bleached seaside cottages where the only item on the kitchen table was an artistically positioned shell.

I wondered if there should be a special lifestyle magazine for where I found myself now: '*Vaughan divides his time between his cosy bedroom in Streatham's Hi Klass Hotel and the en suite bathroom, where he is cultivating a range of black and green moulds. "I love living in a cheap South London hostel used mainly by prostitutes," says Vaughan, thirty-nine. "From my grubby fourth-floor window I have a perfect view of the huge extractor ducts of the kebab shop opposite."*'

In my imagination, the Easter holidays had loomed as a vast tract of unlimited free time during which I would get on top of all my marking, lesson plans and personal admin, while also grabbing some quality time with my children and visiting my still-hospitalised father. It was not until I emerged from under the sheets to glance at my bedside clock on Wednesday afternoon that I accepted I might be letting the opportunity slip by.

I occupied just one side of the double bed, as I always did. I'd only just realised that I instinctively preferred to take the left half of the mattress, subconsciously leaving the other side free. But now I was staring at a piece of paper that would do away with the need for such considerations.

I had verbally agreed to all the terms in this document some time ago; now all I had to do was sign where indicated, in front of a witness, return it in the stamped addressed envelope, and my marriage would be history. It was a five-second task, yet during four whole days of doing nothing I had still not found the time to do it. It wasn't just the final act of formally ending the marriage that crippled me, but that extra little humiliation of having to ask a witness to watch me sign the form.

I had wondered if I could ask the fat man from the former Soviet republic of Something-astan who ran the Hi Klass Hotel. Except that I sensed he rather resented the way that I paid for my room and then proceeded to sleep in it for the entire night. Every time I saw him, I felt guilty that I wasn't sheepishly vacating my room fifteen minutes after arrival. I could always ask one of the ladies who regularly entertained clients here, I thought: '*Witness Occupation: Prostitute*'. That would look impressive.

Occasionally I looked back on that moment in the gym store, but more significant than the physical experience of the night with Suzanne was the recovery of my memories of sex with Madeleine. I remembered that Maddy talked during sex. Not in the way that women are scripted in male fantasies— she didn't groan an ecstatic 'Oh yes, yes!' That wasn't Madeleine's style. No, on the night of passion that came to mind, she had suddenly said, 'I must remember to give in the form for Dillie's school trip . . .'

I recalled that she had often done this. When I'd imagined that she was consumed in the intimacy of the moment, she would volunteer the information that she had booked the car in for a service, or would wonder out loud whether she could move an appointment from Monday to Wednesday.

I suppose Maddy had been saying that she was comfortable with me. Like the two trees in our garden that had grown side by side, their trunks intertwined over the decades to accommodate and support one another.

And then I recovered another memory. It was an argument that had begun with Maddy wanting to throw out a plastic shower curtain and me insisting that it just needed cleaning.

'*Just needs cleaning by me, is what you mean,*' *she says.* '*Because it would never occur to you to clean a shower curtain.*'
    '*A shower curtain doesn't need cleaning; it has a shower every day.*'
    '*Yeah, you take a shower every day and I have a bath, and you said you would clean the shower. Why didn't you clean the curtain as well?*'

But the argument is actually about sex. We have not so much as touched one another for weeks, and I feel angry and frustrated.

*'You notice a bit of grime on the curtain, but you don't even notice
your own husband,' I say, escalating the conflict.*

'Why are you being so horrible?'

*'Oh look, the top is off the toothpaste because Vaughan forgot to
put it back on!' and I run to the toothpaste and make a big show of
replacing the top. 'Ooh look, the toilet seat is up because Vaughan
forgot to put it down.' And I slam down the toilet lid. 'Well, it's better
than forgetting you're supposed to be married to someone!'*

I was able to place this incident to about a year before we had separated.
I felt ashamed that my frustration had translated into anger. But with hind-
sight, I understood that sex is so important in keeping a marriage together
that it really shouldn't be left to husband and wife alone. We have health
checks and visits to the dentist, and an engineer who makes sure the gas
boiler is safe. There ought to be someone from the council who pops round
to make sure that married couples are having sex every weekend. 'Hmm . . .
I see there's a two-week gap at the beginning of the month. You will receive
an official letter warning of the dangers of neglecting physical intimacy.'

The document from my ex-wife's solicitors had to be signed. I owed it to
Maddy. I pulled on my shoes and threw on a jacket before I presented
myself to the outside world. My reintegration into civilisation seemed to go
unnoticed by the rest of society; evening shoppers and busy commuters
passed me by. It reminded me of the time before I found my identity, the
sense of separateness from the rest of the world, as if everyone else knew
the part they were playing but I'd never been given a script. Inside my jacket
pocket, however, was the death certificate for my marriage. In my head
I was scrolling through all the people who could witness my signature, but
somehow I didn't want to admit my final failure to any of my friends.

I found myself at the door of the only person I felt I could ask. Suzanne,
the dance teacher, seemed surprised and a little alarmed to see me.

'Vaughan! What the hell are you doing here?'

'I came to ask a favour.'

'Er—it's not very convenient . . .' she glanced back down the hallway.

'Who is it?' said a gruff man from inside the flat.

'Just someone from school.'

Despite Suzanne's embarrassment, I persuaded her that this wouldn't
take a minute and I produced the divorce agreement for her to witness.

'Vaughan,' she whispered, 'I don't want you to divorce your wife just because of what happened the other night . . .'

'No, I was going to divorce her anyway.'

'Brian and I are very happy. I can't leave him for you, Vaughan, just because of one naughty little fling.'

'Really. I just need someone to witness my signature.'

'You won't tell anyone what happened, will you?' She glanced nervously in the direction of the lounge. 'I mean, it didn't mean anything, did it?'

Her name was hastily scribbled. The deed was done.

I STOOD BEFORE the pillar box, nervously checking that the envelope was properly sealed and that the stamps would not fall off. Then, in a short ceremony, The Future formally surrendered to The Past and I put the letter in the box. Rather than return to my dismal hotel room, I picked up a free newspaper and went into a high-street 'tavern'. The pub had got a signwriter to advertise its many attractions in old-fashioned Shakespearean script. This worked quite well for 'Ye Real Ales' and 'Ye Fine Foods' but looked less convincing for 'Sky Sports in High Definition'. Even with the sound turned down, the large TV screen was impossible to ignore, as the silent presenters on Sky News searched for the least appropriate footage to match the song playing on the pub jukebox. The info-bar scrolled the changes in the stock markets as I finished a third packet of pork scratchings and tied the foil packets into tiny knots. A couple came into the pub hand in hand, and I was disgusted by such an ostentatious public display of passion.

In the toilets I paused to stare at the craggy face of the man whose life I had inherited. 'You stupid idiot!' I shouted at my reflection. 'You only get one life and you completely screwed your one up, didn't you, eh? You don't know your own kids! Your wife hates you. You can't even remember people's names, you senile bastard—'

Then a slurred voice spoke up from behind a locked cubicle door. 'Who is this? How do you know so much about me?'

I set off to walk the length of Streatham High Road, the night lit briefly by the blue strobe of a passing police car. Alcohol used to make me excited and up for a laugh, but these days it just made me really drowsy. Walking down the wide, uneven pavement, I found myself overcompensating for the sudden appearance of a litter bin and, in trying to give it a wide berth, nearly staggered into some bike racks. Finally I skipped up the steps to the hotel's front door, displaying a certain casual aplomb, I felt. But aiming the front-door key at the uncooperative lock was a more demanding challenge and I missed the keyhole several times.

I leaned against the unlocked door and discovered it just needed pushing open, then I was surprised to see someone sitting in the chair in the corridor. Occasionally this seat was occupied by punters waiting for a lady, or a lady waiting for a room, and in my drunken confusion I could not work out why my ex-wife Madeleine was now working as a prostitute at the Hi Klass Hotel in Streatham.

'Maddy? What are you doing here?'

'Hello, Vaughan,' she said calmly.

Her unexpected appearance at this time of night alarmed me. 'Look, I'm sorry,' I blustered. 'I posted it today.'

'It's not that. We've been trying to ring you . . .'

'What is it?'

'Your father. It happened in his sleep. I'm so sorry.'

I could almost feel my body sobering up as I stood there trying to comprehend the news that my father had died.

'But—that's not fair,' I heard myself blurting out. 'That's just not fair.'

'I'm really sorry, Vaughan,' repeated Maddy, but I felt too numb to respond. My grief was for something I hadn't had. He'd died before I had got to know him properly or before memories of him had returned.

Maddy and I just stood there for a moment looking at one another. Then she put her arms out to embrace me and I accepted the invitation. Now my emotions were really confused. My only living parent had been taken from me. But the woman I had given up on was hugging me, and it felt right. I raised my hands round her and hugged her back.

MADELEINE SUGGESTED that I should come and stay in the spare room at home, so that I didn't wake up on my own and could be with the children in the morning. We stayed up for an hour or two, sharing a bottle of wine and talking about my dad. There was no friction in the air; in fact, looking at her sitting opposite me on the sofa, I couldn't understand how I had ever not been in love with her. Eventually I took a moment to visit the toilet and, looking at the family pictures on the wall, I recovered another memory. I was regaining them every day now, and this one was of a trip to central London with the kids.

WE ARE IN MADAME TUSSAUDS. There must have been an era when a visit here was a great family treat, but as far as our own kids are concerned, looking at waxy replicas of has-been celebrities has not been their idea of a thrilling day out. The display of the British Royal Family has singularly failed to compare with the excitement of the Nemesis ride at Alton Towers; in fact, I think it is actually a bonus for our kids that a couple of the figures have been removed for refurbishment. After an increasingly fractious hour or so, we are close to abandoning the whole trip, when a little light goes on in my wife's eye. Just as a group of tourists is about to join us in the room, Maddy steps over the velvet rope and strikes up a pose on the empty pedestal, where she stares into the middle distance.

Dillie and Jamie are already thrilled at her mischievousness, when some foreign tourists join me as I stare hard at the apparent wax model.

'Dad—who is this model of?' says Dillie pointedly.

'That's Princess Rita. Of Lakeside Thurrock . . .'

Maddy's expression does not alter one iota.

'What relation would she be to the Queen?' asks an American lady.

'Princess Rita is not actually related to the Queen. Rita is the bastard off-spring of the Duke of Edinburgh and, um, Eleanor Rigby,' I explain.

'Eleanor Rigby? Like the Beatles song?'

'Yeah, that's why she was so lonely—the Duke wouldn't leave the Queen for her. He couldn't afford the alimony.'

'Oh, I never knew—that's really interesting! Thank you.'

And then as they walk away their teenage daughter lets out a scream. 'Dad! Dad! Princess Rita just winked at me!'

WHEN I REJOINED HER in the kitchen, Maddy was putting the wineglasses in the dishwasher and turning off the downstairs lights.

'When did you stop doing stupid stuff?' I asked her. 'You were always making us laugh with daft stunts like pretending to be a statue at Madame Tussaud's.'

She shrugged. 'I think life probably knocks the fun out of us all in the end.'

Ten minutes later I was lying in the dark in the spare room, reflecting on what she had said and thinking of my father, a shadow of the man I had seen in photos. Is that how people die? I wondered. Incrementally? Maddy's spirit had diminished since our marriage had crashed; a part of us both must have died with every disappointment.

This little room where I now lay had once been Dillie and Jamie's nursery. Luminous stars still glowed on the ceiling from where they had been stuck by a younger, optimistic father. I stared at the random constellations, thinking of the centuries that seemed to have passed in between me putting up the stickers for my newborn baby and this lonely moment.

I recalled how delighted Maddy was when she saw what I'd done. I remembered a few years later, how thrilled Dillie was when I'd shown her the stars and we both just lay on our backs in the dark, pointing at the magic of the tiny lights on the ceiling.

Now I was surprised to feel an emotional geyser building up inside me. So much had been lost, so many moments gone for ever. I pictured the old man I had got to know on the hospital bed. And I thought of Dillie and Jamie visiting him, and the last time they hugged him, understanding that he would soon be dead. Now I wept out loud at the simple sadness of it all—at the hollow sense of loss: disappearing childhoods, irrecoverable decades, a family I had taken for granted but one that I now understood could not be there for ever. And when at last I was quiet, I could hear Maddy crying on the other side of the bedroom wall.

In the morning I hugged my daughter long and hard as she wept for the loss of her grandfather. Dillie wore her emotions on her sleeve. Her brother, on the other hand, attempted to play the stoic young male, but he too crumbled when I asked him for a hug. Maddy herself could not help but break down as she watched them. Then the group hug was joined by the excited dog, who jumped up and wrapped his front paws round my jeans.

The kids switched from grieving for their grandfather to eating their cornflakes in front of the television, and Maddy and I tidied up. Maddy's mobile phone got a text with a comical ringtone.

'Ralph?'

'Yes. He was saying he was sorry to hear about your father. He said he lost his own dad a few years back so he knows what you're going through.'

'I doubt that.' I wiped down the surfaces, perhaps a little too vigorously.

'You know, it's OK. I don't expect you to like him.'

'No, he was fine.' I pouted. 'I just thought he wasn't very "can do", that's all. He came across as one of those people who sees the problems first.'

Maddy laughed out loud. 'Because he foresaw difficulties in building some massive dam?'

Without realising it, we were unloading the dishwasher in tandem, Maddy doing the glasses, me doing the cutlery as I had always done. Madeleine could have been angered by my criticism of Ralph, but she actually found it quite amusing. Still, the subject of her new partner hung in the air and I felt the need to show a little humility.

'So, is Ralph going to move in here?' I asked. 'I mean, have you got a timetable in your head for it or anything?'

Maddy let out a long sigh. 'Oh, I don't know. Sometimes I think it would have been so much easier to be a lesbian.'

'What does that mean?'

'It doesn't matter . . .'

'It's OK, you can tell me. I was married to you for fifteen years.'

'All right. We had a big fight. He's filled his gallery with awful abstracts by this new painter. I think it's just because he fancies her.'

'Oh dear,' I lied.

'Maybe I was never meant to be with anyone. I'll be one of those old ladies with seventeen cats and a council injunction about the smell.'

Inside I was surprised to feel as if I wanted to punch the air in triumph, but I remained determined to carry on as normal. I announced that I should be on my way and thanked her for letting me stay the night, and added that it had been good to have someone to talk to. Maddy avoided eye contact, embarrassed that she had revealed more than she had intended. She wanted to leave me with a clear signal that we both had to move on.

'You know what you need, Vaughan? You need a girlfriend.'

Even though I had my coat on, I began stacking the dirty plates into the dishwasher. 'Hmm. I don't think I could handle the emotional involvement.'

'It doesn't have to be Miss Right straightaway. Just someone to make you realise that there are plenty of other women out there.'

'What, you'd like me to have a fling?'

'Well, it's nothing to do with me. I just think it might help you move on.'

'Actually, there was this woman from school—'

'What woman?'

'Suzanne. She's a dance teacher, Australian.'

'And you fancy her?'

'In the cold light of day, I can't say I do really.'

She had stopped the housework and just stood there looking at me.

'But I had a one-night stand with her. Like you said—just to try to help myself move on.'

274 | JOHN O'FARRELL

'Oh.' Suddenly it seemed her eyes didn't know where to look. 'A dance teacher? Skinny, is she?'

The dirty mugs were being placed in the dishwasher with more force than was strictly necessary.

'Yeah, not really my type. I mean, I wasn't seeking it or anything. Suzy just happened to come along.'

'Oh, she's called "Suzy"? It's all right—*I'm* stacking the dishwasher. It doesn't take two of us.' And we both pretended not to notice that she had just chipped Kate Middleton's face on the Royal Wedding mug.

WESTERN SOCIETY has decided that what the bereaved family really need is a huge in-tray of complicated admin. Suddenly I was responsible for all sorts of legal duties and tasks that took me the entire week. I learned that I was the executor of the will, that it fell to me to register the death, choose the hymns, book the cremation, and decide on the appropriate number of sliced carrots for the hummous dip.

Who was I supposed to invite to the funeral anyway? I settled on a tactic of writing to all the names that had not been crossed out of my father's address book. And so, a couple of weeks after his death, I stood at the top of the drive of a suburban crematorium, ready to fulfil my duty as the chief mourner and only son of Air Commodore Keith Vaughan.

The first guests to turn up were a couple of elderly ladies from the rest home where my dad had spent his last years. They were followed by a reasonably young man in an RAF uniform, who marched straight past without making eye contact. Then my heart lifted as I saw Maddy and the children.

'Are you OK, Dad?' asked Dillie, giving me a hug.

Maddy told me that I didn't have to stand outside waiting for everyone and, once her parents had arrived, we all went inside to take our seats.

Our host for the afternoon led the traditional mumbling of the hymns and did an impressive piece of reading from the Bible, in which he managed not to change the emphasis of his voice by one iota for the entire passage. I had requested in an email that we would require 'the standard traditional service'. I should have checked exactly what this involved. I ought to have guessed that this would include a speech from a close relative.

My mind drifted off during another incomprehensible prayer, then I heard the vicar say, 'And now Keith's only child will say a few words about his father.' Surely I imagined that? But there was the vicar, gesturing to me to come up and share a lifetime of recollections of my dad, unaware that I had none. I saw the elderly mourners looking at me in anticipation. I made eye contact with Maddy, who looked slightly panic-stricken on my behalf.

'So,' he repeated with a firm smile, 'Vaughan, if you would—'

'Oh, no, I er . . . I can't. I mean . . .' I mumbled.

'Obviously it can be very difficult,' said the vicar.

You have no idea, I thought as I slowly walked to the pulpit. I took a deep breath. My legs felt unreliable behind the lectern as I gripped on tight.

'What can I say about my Dad?'

I gave a long, significant pause. One retired RAF colleague nodded meaningfully at this rhetorical question.

'Dad! My old dad . . .'

There was a wheezy cough from the back row.

'Well, there's so much to say it almost seems wrong to attempt to sum it all up in a few minutes . . . but obviously I'm going to have to. He had a distinguished career in the Royal Air Force, rising to the very senior rank of Air Commodore and serving his country with distinction. Er, he was posted all over the world, but always wanted his family with him.' Time just to start making stuff up. 'Because he was always a great father and a wonderful husband to my late mother . . .' This prompted a few nods. I saw Dillie looking up at me admiringly.

'But he was a wonderful grandfather too. I remember on family holidays in Cornwall'—I chuckled to myself at the memory of it—'he was always so patient with his grandchildren.' There was another cough. 'He and my mother made very powerful homemade wine.' A few smiles at that. 'And he had a long and distinguished career in the Royal Air Force . . .' I realised I'd already said that. I was out of things I could say. I let out an extended sigh. 'To be honest, there isn't much else.' I could feel a bead of sweat run down my back. In my panic, I could think of no other course but the lowest one available. I clutched my thumb and forefinger to the bridge of my nose and just said, 'And I'm going to really miss him.'

In fact, having resorted to this posture, I realised that I did really miss him. He had always been so delighted to see me, and made the world seem such a positive place, lifting my spirits when I was supposed to be lifting his. As I glanced up I saw the ladies who had been the first to arrive clutching their tissues to their noses. And right in front of me sat Maddy with tears streaming down her cheeks.

Witnessing Maddy so upset suddenly flicked a switch inside me. 'My dad really thought the world of Maddy,' I said, looking directly at her and starting to speak with a fluency that had been absent till now. 'When he was in the hospital at the end, her regular visits were the highlight of his day. He pointed out her kindness and intelligence to me, as if to warn me against the risk of ever losing his beloved daughter-in-law. He was not to know that he was too late. With him being so ill, we took the decision that he should be protected from the bleak truth that his son was unable to hold a marriage together in the way that he had done.

'Maddy brought his grandchildren to see him one last time, and I think we all knew then that he would never see them again. He refused to let his imminent death get him down. "What a lucky man I am,"' I said, impersonating him, '"to have such a wonderful family!"'

I had stumbled on my thesis now and was conveying it with a missionary zeal. 'And maybe the best way we could all remember my father is for each of us to take that world view away from this crematorium, and try to remember Keith whenever we are feeling sorry for ourselves. My wife and children don't live with me any more. But what a lucky man I am to be able to recall so many wonderful times together, and to have so much to look forward to as they grow up.

'Believe me when I say that I wish I'd had a bit more time with him. It's made me determined to spend every possible moment with my own family, to grab every memory that I can—even though I can't be there as much as I would like and Maddy now has someone else.'

'No,' interjected Dillie. 'She dumped him.'

The heckle had not been a loud one. The children were in the second row. It was more a mumbled point of order than a public declaration. But I had heard her clear enough, and then caught her whisper, 'But they have!' when Jamie chastised her for speaking out.

So Maddy and Ralph had broken up. Madeleine avoided eye contact, but I looked at her mother and the undisguised satisfaction on her face confirmed that this was indeed the case.

'What a lucky man I am!' I said, but I didn't qualify this any further. 'That's what I think.' And I sat down, trying to hold back a beatific smile.

Now I understood the therapeutic value of a funeral, because the world seemed like a better place as the coffin set off on its short journey to the sound of the Carpenters. They had been Dad's favourite band, although in retrospect I realised that 'We've Only Just Begun' was probably not the best choice of song to mark an old man's demise.

'Don't sing along, Vaughan,' whispered Maddy behind me.

'SIR, MR VAUGHAN, sir, why weren't you in on Friday? Were you in the loony bin, sir?'

'That's enough, Tanika.'

'Have you been sectioned though? Do you have a padded cell?'

'Tanika, you are on a first warning. Any more disrespect and failure to focus on today's lesson outcomes and you will be one step away from removal from this classroom, detention and a telephone call home.'

I had relearned the official script and was hoping that my most difficult pupils would recognise the magic words and change their behaviour.

'Are you a serial killer, sir? Do you eat your victims?'

'Second warning, Tanika!'

'Sir, do you bury your victims under the patio? Is that where you was on Friday? Burying a victim?'

'If you must know, I *was* burying someone.'

The moment I said it, I felt it was probably a mistake, but the room fell into a stunned silence that demanded some further explanation.

'Well, it was a cremation, actually. I was at my father's funeral, OK? He died during the holidays, so that's why you had a supply teacher on Friday, for which I apologise.'

The teacher-baiting stopped after that. They cooperated with the lesson, answered the questions and wrote down their homework assignments at the end. In fact, I was wondering if I could get away with announcing a family bereavement at the start of every class.

After the students had all filed out, I noticed Tanika hanging back.

'I'm sorry about your dad, sir. I didn't mean to disrespect him.'

'That's OK, Tanika. Only . . . let's drop it with the "mentalist" thing, eh? I didn't have all my memories of my father back before he died, so I do have some sort of mental condition that can be quite difficult at times.'

'Sir? My dad died . . .'

I had never seen Tanika drop her cocksure guard before, but could sense that this was anything but a wind-up.

'I'm very sorry to hear that, Tanika. Was that recently?'

'No, it was when I was three. He was shot.'

'Shot!' I exclaimed, unprofessionally revealing my alarm.

'It was on the London news and that. They said it was a drugs-related murder, but it wasn't. Would you like to see a picture of him?'

She had already got a photograph from the little plastic wallet that held her travel pass and her dinner card. Through the misty plastic was a toddler version of Tanika standing next to a tall man smiling for the camera.

'He looks like a very nice man.'

'It wasn't drugs-related though. They just said that to make everyone feel better. If people see a picture of a murdered black man and then the newspaper says it was like "drugs-related", all the posh white people think, "Oh, that's all right then, it won't happen to me."'

This was a level of analysis that I had not witnessed in Tanika before.

'Losing your father at three is much, much harder than losing your dad at my age. I can't imagine what you must have gone through.'

She was no longer staring at the floor but making direct eye contact with me. There wasn't any sadness or emotion there; instead I understood the hard shell that had grown over her to make her top dog in the classroom.

'Tanika? You know you have to do an independent history module for your coursework? Why don't you set the history straight on your dad?'

'What?'

'Why don't you gather all the records of your dad's murder—in the newspapers, online or whatever—and then set about correcting them with the true story of what really happened?'

'Are we allowed to do that?'

'What you said about how things get distorted to make people feel more comfortable has to be part of it. That's how history gets rewritten.'

I was already worrying that I should have reflected upon this perilous idea before suggesting it, but Tanika's education was going to end soon unless I could find a way of getting her engaged. 'Anyway, have a think about it,' I said, and she nodded blankly, put the photo away and headed out.

AFTER SCHOOL I sat at the computer screen in my form room. Gary's user-generated news site had a front-page story explaining how the BP oil spill in the Gulf of Mexico had been deliberately staged as part of a white supremacist conspiracy between Buckingham Palace and the American Military-Industrial Complex to destabilise Barack Obama. Surprisingly, none of the major news outlets had picked up on the YouNews exclusive.

It made me feel marginally less guilty for having told Gary I didn't want to resume my involvement in YouNews. He couldn't believe that I didn't want to topple those evil, all-powerful, super-rich media moguls and become an all-powerful, super-rich media mogul.

I had not looked at my online Wiki-biography for a week, following a session when I had methodically reversed all the facetious edits. In the time since I had last corrected the document no further changes had been made. Clearly, the young writers had got bored reinventing Mr Vaughan's life and had now moved on to other things. I couldn't help but feel a little hurt.

But then I noticed a new paragraph under 'Career'. It said:

Mr Vaughan was the best teacher I ever had. When I left the sixth form to work in JD Sports he kept coming into the shop to persuade me to come back. I would never have got my A levels or gone to university if it wasn't for Mr Vaughan.

This one comment from a former pupil utterly changed my mood. There *had* been a time when I had transformed lives. 'Now I am manager of JD Sports,' boasted my former pupil.

Despite the accumulating evidence and recovering memory, I still found myself regarding the negative side of Vaughan Mk 1 with a dispassionate objectivity. The marital breakup was an event that had happened to another man. And the Maddy before the fugue was a fictional character from some half-remembered domestic drama; the other was a living, breathing woman who seemed to understand me better than I did myself. But what was so irrational about this Maddy was that she kept getting the two genres mixed up. She resented real-life Vaughan for things that fictional Vaughan had done. I was different now, she acknowledged as much; but I was not to be allowed to forget things I couldn't remember.

I had found myself pondering how much my brainwipe had altered my actual character. I suggested to Gary that this question raised all sorts of issues about the philosophical relationship between memory and experience. We were sitting in a busy pub, beside a noisy quiz machine. Probably not the best setting for a debate.

'What I'm trying to say is: is it possible that all the character-defining experiences of my life were wiped along with the memories of them? Do I still have the mental scars of a failed marriage and all the other disappointments and unrealised ambitions, whatever they may have been?'

'Well, you were shit at football before and you are now.'

'I'm about average at football, actually—'

'You run like a girl and the last goal you scored bounced in off your arse. You can't drive a car . . . can't hold your drink . . . appalling dress sense—'

'All right, you don't have to list them. I'm just saying, surely we don't have to remember something to be affected by it? None of us can recall everything that's happened to us, yet all of it helps shape our personalities.'

'Nah,' Gary said, taking a sip of his beer. 'You were always into all that philosophical bollocks. Can I eat your crisps?'

But even Gary's rhinoceros sensitivity was gradually being affected by the outside world. The photo on his iPhone was from the scan of his unborn child. He even had an idea about a possible girlfriend for me.

'Do you know who I thought you ought to ask out on a date? Maddy!' he declared, as if this was the brainwave of a genius. 'You've got loads in common—and I've a hunch you've still got a bit of a soft spot for her.'

'Wow! Thanks, Gary. I'll bear that in mind.'

Deep down, I feared that as more memories of my marriage came back, I might reacquire some of the bitterness and cynicism of my pre-fugue incarnation. I could now recall various stages of our marriage. The power struggle at home seemed to have escalated like a small regional war. I had been insistent that the shelves above the television were the historic homeland of my vinyl LP collection, and Madeleine upped the tension with the infamous July 10 massacre of all the history programmes stored on the TV planner.

We ended up fighting about all sorts of stupid things. And the tension following any fight would continue for days, with a coded war of attrition fought on a dozen different fronts. Maddy's critical appraisal of detective thrillers on the television became unreasonably sympathetic towards the deranged wife who murdered her husband. Traditional little kindnesses disappeared: favourite treats were no longer placed in the supermarket trolley; just a single cup of tea was made at any one time. Years earlier the news of other couples splitting up would have been recounted in the same tones as a car crash. Now such events sounded more like an innocent person being let out of prison.

None of this, of course, featured in this Wiki-memoir that I had pulled together, where I had taken care to be as neutral and objective as I could be. In any case, I was uneasy about trusting my own memories of the marriage; in the narrative I had reconstructed, the unhappy ending still didn't seem to work. I could remember the Maddy who had been my companion, my best friend, my soul mate. Was a bitter divorce always going to be our final chapter? Over the past months, I had spent many hours wanting to understand why this relationship had fallen apart. Then in a flash I saw what was wrong. *I was thinking only about me.* Could it be that the problem with my marriage had been that I had approached it as an individual, not as one half of a pair?

Feeling inspired by this flash of insight, I created a new document and wrote at the top: 'The life story of Madeleine R. Vaughan'. Then I deleted that and put in her maiden name. In no particular order, I began to recall everything I knew about her story. Her family background, her interests and, with all the objectivity I could muster, details of boyfriends before me. I took care to write as much as I could about the struggle of being a professional photographer. I recalled the excitement she had felt when buyers began to be interested, and the indignant fury she had sometimes expressed when she suspected me of regarding her job as less important than my own.

I attempted to chronicle our own entire relationship from her point of view. Memories I was unaware I had recovered poured out of me. I wrote about her pregnancy and the birth of Jamie. I wrote about the time she was called up at home by a telephone salesman and she pretended to be really stupid. 'Yer wha?' she grunted to every question.

My fingers were still pecking away at the keyboard two hours later. Even if I did not agree with what I understood to be her analysis of my own faults and mistakes, I recorded them. I was determined to see our two lives from her point of view. My first draft of Maddy's biography ended with her splitting up with Ralph and then grieving for her father-in-law.

In just a couple of hours of trying to see the world through her eyes, I felt as if I had discovered an extra hemisphere in my brain. I didn't pretend that now I completely understood Maddy's psyche, but I had found a way in.

We used to have stupid arguments about nothing. 'What's wrong with you?' I would finally ask. 'If there's something wrong, tell me what it is.'

'I shouldn't have to tell you. You should just know.'

Now I think I understood what she had meant.

She had seemed so quiet after the funeral, pensive and distracted. Obviously she was upset about my dad, and splitting up with Ralph must have been distressing, but there was something else going on. At one point I had caught her alone in the kitchen and had asked if she was all right.

'I just don't know what I think any more,' had been her enigmatic reply.

'Don't know what you think about what?'

'About anything,' and I thought for a moment she might be about to put her head on my shoulder.

'I don't know what I think about anchovies,' boomed Gary, striding into the kitchen. 'Sometimes I love them; sometimes I hate them.'

'Maybe you should have married an anchovy, Gary?' said Maddy, and I laughed, but she was already wandering back out to the reception. I didn't get another chance to talk to her after that; there were just a few words about practical arrangements. I had wanted to be her counsellor and confidant, but instead I was watching her car drive away as I listened to an old man in a beret explain that he had been stationed with my dad at Northolt.

Sitting in the empty classroom on my own, I felt a deepening worry on Maddy's behalf. I glanced at the time and realised it was now too late to go round there. I should have rung her over the weekend, I thought; I should have gone round to see her. I could go past in the street and just see if any lights were on? Then I shut down my computer and hurried out of the door.

Even before I was close, I could see that lights were on all over our house, which struck me as quite unlike Maddy. Even the outside porch light was still glowing like a beacon. I climbed up the steps and hesitantly reached for the button. I was relieved to see movement from the other side of the glass, though it wasn't Maddy but her mother, looking anxious.

'It's not her!' Jean called back into the house. 'It's Vaughan!' She urgently beckoned me in. 'I was going to ring you if we didn't hear from her this evening. It's been two days—we've been worried sick . . .'

'What? What is it? Where's my wife?'

'She's disappeared, Vaughan. She's completely vanished.'

CHAPTER 8

My first thought was that Madeleine had experienced the same sort of neurological breakdown that had befallen me. This was not such a fantastical notion; one of the early theories put to me by Dr Lewington was that I had contracted viral encephalitis—perhaps Maddy could have literally caught this amnesia virus off her ex-husband?

I hoped that nothing so severe had befallen Maddy. She might be in a hospital somewhere labelled 'UNKNOWN WHITE FEMALE'. Then I wondered: If she had been struck with retrograde amnesia, would this manifest itself in the same way? Would she now fall in love with me all over again? Isn't that every middle-aged couple's fantasy—to feel that white-hot passion burning as fiercely as when they first fused together?

But the more I heard about Madeleine's disappearance, the less likely it felt. If Maddy's brain had suddenly wiped all memories, it was a convenient moment at which to do so. On the Saturday morning both children had left for the school's skiing trip. It occurred to me that this would have been the first time in twenty years that she'd had her home to herself. At least it would have been, had her mother not insisted that they stay for the week. Maddy's disappearance had occurred at the end of a period of enormous stress: she'd had her ex-husband disappear and then resurface wanting to turn back the clock; she'd got involved with another man and then broken it off; she'd taken her children to their grandfather's funeral.

Enduring all that and then having her mother in her house, focusing on her twenty-four hours a day, might be more than any sane person could be expected to endure.

'I can't comprehend why Madeleine would just disappear like that. I can't comprehend it. Can you comprehend it, Ron? You see, Ron can't comprehend it either; it's completely incomprehendible—'

'Incomprehensible . . .'

'It is! Ron, will you phone the police? It's nine, nine, nine.'

'Let's not phone the police just yet,' I counselled.

'It's all right, I'd forgotten the number anyway,' said Ron with a twinkling smile towards me. He had clearly come to the same conclusion as me: that his daughter's disappearance might not be so mysterious after all.

'The thing is, Jean,' I said, 'perhaps Maddy just needed a bit of space?'

'She's got lots of space. You had the loft converted, didn't you?'

'No, I mean headspace—from all the pressures she's been under recently. You know, some time on her own.'

I assured Jean that Madeleine would call soon, but privately I remained worried. To leave her parents alone in the house without so much as an explanation was unlike the ultra-considerate Maddy I thought I remembered.

I knew where she kept the family passports. If she had really wanted to flee abroad for a few days, that would be an obvious clue. I slipped upstairs to the large Victorian bureau beneath the bedroom window. I slid open the little drawer for essential documents. My hunch had been correct. Maddy had stolen herself away; the person who had always put herself second had emerged from her cocoon of commitments and responsibilities and flown.

I imagined her hastily packing a bag while her parents were out walking the dog. I wished I could have seen it as a spontaneous declaration of independence. But she had left no note, no text message; it smacked of a moment of crisis, a woman at the end of her tether. Then I sat on the edge of the bed and tried to imagine where she might possibly be.

Putting myself back into Maddy's mindset, this is the sequence of events that I finally projected onto her.

IT WAS UNSEASONABLY HOT for April and I pictured her skipping over some rocks to where the water was deep enough to dive in. She would have stopped and just inhaled the sense of space that was her favourite beach in the world. In the distance a few sheep populated the grey-green hills that surrounded the bay, but no cars came along the coast road.

I saw Maddy positioning her bag and towel, and then an unhesitant leap and a splash. The grace of her dive would probably have been undermined by her surfacing and swearing loudly about the iciness of the Atlantic Ocean in springtime. But Maddy was a strong swimmer and I saw her doing a powerful front crawl across the bay. She would have checked the tides and stayed close to the shore, and maybe she had spotted a local, collecting wood at the far end of the beach, who might be keeping one eye on the mad swimmer.

I could see her hauling herself back onto the rocks. She knew she could climb out here—she had never forgotten that swim on this beach all those years ago, the shared bottle of wine and the snugness of the tent before the storm pulled it from its moorings. Now the light spring breeze felt like an icy wind and her towel seemed inadequate as it wrapped round her shoulders. The figure at the far end of the beach had lit a fire, which sent a plume of white smoke up over the dunes. She wanted to go and warm herself by its flames but she could hardly wander up to a strange man in her wet swimming costume. Then again, this was Ireland; to wander over and chat would be a perfectly normal thing to do here.

She walked barefoot along the length of the dunes. It was hard to see in all the smoke whether the man was still there or not, and she was quite close before she attempted a friendly good afternoon.

'Good afternoon,' replied an English accent she recognised. And then the smoke changed direction and right before her stood her ex-husband, smiling warmly, holding out a canvas bag.

'I brought your cashmere hoodie,' I said.

Once I became certain that this would be where Maddy had gone, it had been easy to follow her. I had already done the difficult journey: getting to the point where I understood her. Now Maddy looked at me as if too many thoughts were racing through her head for her to articulate any one of them.

'And I just made a fire to warm you up. But I know you probably came here to get a bit of space, so I'll be on my way. If you fancy meeting up for a drink later, it's up to you,' and with that I turned to head back up the beach.

She took quite a few bewildered seconds to call after me and I started to worry that she was actually going to let me just walk away.

'Wait! How did you . . . How come . . . Are Mum and Dad all right?'

Now I stopped and turned. 'They're fine.' I laughed. 'See, you can't help it. You can't help thinking about other people.'

'How did you guess I'd come here? How did you find me?'

'Well, I remembered that whenever you couldn't hear yourself think, you'd always say "I wish I was at Barleycove."'

'You remembered that?'

'I saw your passport had gone but then I saw that you hadn't taken your cashmere, and I thought, oh, she's going to want that.'

She had already pulled it on and her sea-scrubbed cheeks were glowing in the warmth of the fire.

'And I've got some sausages by the way, if you fancy a sandwich?'

To Madeleine's post-swim appetite, these bonfire-roasted Irish sausages were the best meal she'd ever eaten, and when I brought out a small bottle of wine and a plastic cup, I think she had to stop herself from hugging me. We sat on the dunes looking out at the blurred horizon, chatting and laughing as the tide went out and our shadows lengthened.

Madeleine explained that she had decided to disappear abroad without saying anything to her mother, as the only other option would have been to bludgeon her to death with a saucepan.

'Mum thought she might cheer me up by listing all the things that her lucky daughter had that *she* hadn't had when she was bringing up children. So I thought I would slip away.'

Maddy had spotted a cheap flight to Cork and realised that she could make that flight and ring her parents later. 'But then my phone was out of battery and the telephone was broken.'

'Don't worry—we'll say that you rang me and asked me to tell them. But then my dodgy memory wiped any trace of it.'

'Good idea. On second thoughts, that's exactly what *did* happen!'

We watched a distant tanker disappear round the headland and threw our crusts to a slightly scary seagull. When she offered to fill up my glass she noticed I wasn't drinking.

'Well, actually, I've got a little rented car up the hill . . .'

'You learned to drive?'

'Yes. I did this intensive course and haven't demolished a single garden wall yet. I can chauffeur you back to Crookhaven later if you like, in my luxury Nissan Micra.'

She didn't say anything; she just looked at me long and hard.

When the fire had faded, we headed back to the village and Maddy tried not to grip onto the passenger seat too obviously as we weaved around the coast road. We had a drink at the pub where she had booked a room and we both got an excited skiing update text from the children. Maddy rang her parents and apologised.

I asked Maddy about her work, then she asked me about mine and I went on for far too long about the breakthrough I had had with my most difficult pupil, finding myself getting carried away: '. . . and then Tanika stood up in front of the class and talked about how her father's death had been misrepresented in the media and you should have seen it, Maddy—I was so proud of her. She did this really impassioned speech and it was all the stuff we'd talked about in history—how getting the past wrong will send you off into the wrong future. And she's written to the *South London Press* to ask them to print an article setting the record straight on her dad's death, and the class was cheering her, and she shouted that she was going to *kill the lie*: "Me and Mr Vaughan are going to kill the lie," she repeated over the cheers, "and I know my dad is looking down from heaven, saying thank you."'

'So you've remembered why you loved teaching,' Maddy said with a smile. 'You used to talk with that sort of passion often in the old days. I always loved that about you . . .'

Eventually Maddy went up to her room, and since the pub had a couple of other rooms free, I took the cheapest of those. An hour later I was still wide awake.

Something momentous had occurred. The two of us had forgiven one another. Eventually I felt the adventure of the day catching up with me: the flight, the anxious drive, and most of all the worry that she would be utterly appalled that I had followed her. But it had gone far better than I had dared hope. Then my door opened and Maddy whispered, 'Budge up!' and climbed into bed beside me.

I wanted to hug her, but something told me she'd prefer it if I just shifted across the bed and made sure there was enough quilt for my ex-wife. Or my wife, maybe? I couldn't be sure.

'How did you know which room I was in?'

'I didn't—I tiptoed into the room opposite first. Anyway, I don't think finding the right door is quite as impressive as the feat of mind-reading you pulled off today.'

She put her head on my shoulder. 'You knew I'd come here!' she said in amazement. 'You just knew!'

And we didn't talk any more, but just lay beside one another, my arm round her. I had remembered things I never would have remembered before my amnesia. I had remembered her favourite place, I had remembered that she loved to swim but never took warm-enough clothes, I had remembered that she'd said that sausage sandwich we'd shared on that perfect beach had been the best meal she'd ever had.

And I had also remembered her Gmail log-in so I could check where she had booked her flight and accommodation—but it didn't seem the moment to mention that right now.

IF A HISTORIAN had to put a date on the absolute low point in our marriage it would most likely be 11.15 p.m. on February 13, eight months before the sudden onset of my amnesia. On that night I had come home late to discover that Maddy had actually carried out her threat to change the locks on our front door. In my anger I struck my hand against the front panel, smashed the glass and ended up taking myself to Accident and Emergency, where I had a few stitches, the precise number varying with the level of injustice I felt at the time of recounting the episode. I refused to speak to Maddy for weeks after that, until I had got divorce proceedings underway.

The undignified exit from my marriage was not a new memory to me; but this morning the memory came back to me again, lying in bed with Madeleine in West Cork. I had heard the sound of broken glass being swept up outside and the episode leaped into my consciousness. I glanced down at Maddy and was glad the noise hadn't jolted her awake.

After I woke that morning I had been unable to remember where I was for a few seconds. Then there had been a surge of elation as I remembered how Maddy had tiptoed to my bed the night before and cuddled up next to me. And there she still was, her dozing head on the Madeleine-shaped dip below my shoulder as in a previous life.

We had not had sex. I was stroking her hair as she dozed, but now I could not get the memory of February 13 out of my head. I recalled feeling utterly humiliated as I stood on my own front doorstep, screaming through the letter-box to be let in. It had felt like she was stealing my whole life from me.

I stopped stroking Maddy's hair and shifted my body so her head fell onto the pillow. She had actually changed the locks on the house where I lived with my children! I hadn't been violent or unfaithful. How was that not a monstrous thing to have done? I felt my indignation rising as I thought about the injustice that had been done to me. I climbed out of bed, thinking I might go and have breakfast alone, but she opened her eyes and smiled dreamily at me.

'I seem to be in your bedroom . . .' she said playfully.

'Yes,' I mumbled coldly, avoiding eye contact and focusing on the kettle on the side table instead.

'Why don't you come back to bed?'

'No, I'm, er, just going to see if I can make some tea.'

And I took the kettle to the basin, but it banged quite hard against the tap. 'Are you OK?'

'Fine,' I said. 'The bloody kettle doesn't fit in the basin—'

'Fill it up using the cup. Or use the cold tap in the bath.' Now she was sitting up in bed. She was wearing my T-shirt, which I understood was quite significant in the complex code of marital diplomacy.

Maddy said how lovely it was to be brought a cup of tea in bed and I countered that I hated those little cartons of UHT milk. The moment had come to vocalise my fury about what she had done. I knew it might ruin everything, but I couldn't hold down my anger. She looked at me with a coy smile and pulled the T-shirt over her head so that she was now completely naked in the middle of a soft white bed. 'So, why don't we have sex and then go downstairs for a big cooked breakfast?'

'Oh God . . .' I groaned a few minutes later. 'You are so beautiful . . .'

'Shut up!' she tutted. 'Blimey, I must look a right state.'

Now that sexual intercourse had occurred, the case of the lock-changing was re-examined and found to be inconsequential. Actually, now I thought about it again, the fact that in my drunken state I had smashed a window rather vindicated Maddy's decision to keep me locked out. I recalled that 'make-up sex' had always had an extra passionate edge to it, so it was unsurprising that 'make-up after getting divorced' sex proved to be even more potent. I couldn't remember sex like that with Maddy. At no point had she mentioned that the car was making a funny rattling noise or wondered out loud if her mother still had her school reports in the attic.

After breakfast we walked by the port. Only the post office/general store was open at this time of year: the village felt ghostly and suspended.

'Do you want to go back to Barleycove for one last swim?'

'No, thanks, I'm not risking pneumonia a second time. Anyway, it's nice here—we could walk up to the headland maybe?'

'You're right, it's a lovely spot. We should have stayed at that pub when we were students instead of camping.'

'Well . . . Some things take you twenty years to learn.'

Now that the words were out it seemed to demand some sort of clarification about where the two of us stood. We stared out at the bobbing yachts.

'I came out to West Cork to decide something,' Maddy said finally. 'And yesterday, at Barleycove, I came to a conclusion.'

I felt my heart accelerate. 'What did you decide?'

She took both my hands in hers as she looked me in the eye. 'That next time I go swimming in the Atlantic in April, I'm buying a wetsuit.'

'Seems reasonable . . . I might not always be there with your cashmere.'

'That was the other thing.' She looked back out across the water. 'It would be quite nice if you were.' A couple of seagulls seemed to laugh together in the distance. After about twenty seconds Maddy said, 'Can you stop hugging me now as I'm having trouble breathing?'

We walked out of the village and towards the cliffs. Finally we were looking down on the bay, sitting on a weathered bench that a bereaved husband had erected in memory of his late wife.

'Look at those dates,' I said. 'Fifty-five years they were married. Do you think we could stay together fifty-five years?'

'Depends. You might go off and have an affair tomorrow, and then I would have to kill you . . .'

'Really? Is that the very worst thing?'

'No, actually. If you immediately confessed I might just forgive you. But if you didn't tell me and then I found out, well I would kill you slowly and post the video on YouTube.'

'So, tell me, are we legally divorced yet?'

'No, there's one last court thing, but we're not expected to go to it.'

'Well, maybe we should go?' I half joked.

'Yeah! I could wear my wedding dress again—and we could have confetti outside and a big reception afterwards?'

'Oh, fantastic!'

'Fantastic?'

'Yeah—you're up for doing stupid stuff again!'

Suddenly I decided I really ought to do this properly and I took her hand and got down on one knee. 'Madeleine Vaughan, would you do me the immense privilege of becoming my ex-wife? Will you divorce me?'

'I would be honoured!'

WE BOTH ACCEPTED it would be far too complex and expensive to try to reverse the whole process now, so we resolved we would have a different kind of *decree nisi* with a big party to celebrate that we were going to live happily ever after now that we were finally divorced.

'I'm sorry I couldn't just take you back after your fugue. But I had to be really sure that you wouldn't walk out on us again.'

I was shocked by how distorted her version of our split was.

'Erm . . . it seems a shame to drag this up now, but . . . it was you who changed the locks, if you remember?'

'Changed the locks? What are you talking about?'

'You changed the lock on the front door, like you threatened. That was the moment I realised I had to start divorce proceedings.'

'I didn't change the locks, you stupid idiot!'

'Yes, you did. And you pretended to be out—even after I cut my hand on the glass in the door.'

'What? That was you? We thought someone had tried to break in! I'd taken the kids to stay at my parents to give them a break from all the fighting—I left you a note and everything. When I came back the window was smashed and you weren't there and wouldn't return my calls . . .'

'Yeah, because you'd gone and changed the locks!'

Maddy turned to look directly at me. 'Had you been drinking? When the key didn't work in the front-door lock? Had you been drinking?'

There was a long pause.

'Look, er, if you like, I can move my vinyl LPs out of the lounge . . .'

IT WAS SPRING, when a middle-aged man's fancy turns to divorce. Maddy and I entered the court arm in arm and walked ceremoniously down the central aisle. Madeleine was unmistakably a bride, in a crimson-silk, three-quarter-length dress, clutching a bunch of roses that matched the single rose in her coquettish hat. I complimented her that after two children and fifteen years she could still get into it.

Despite giving up alcohol, I failed to fit into the suit I'd worn on my wedding day, which was just as well considering the size of the shoulder pads. But I hired a smart grey morning suit and wore a rose in my button-hole, and we stood side by side in the Principal Registry of the Family Division, ready for the judge to pronounce us man and ex-wife.

The judge himself initially checked that we weren't in the wrong building. Both our long-suffering lawyers were present, finding some sort of common cause in the obstinate refusal of this impossible couple to follow the traditional script of bitter acrimony. Only a few minutes were normally allotted for such cases, all disputes having been sorted before this final formality. It seemed the judge's day had been brightened up by this unconventional couple. 'Sounds more like a marriage than a divorce!' he observed.

'You could say that, m'lud,' said an embarrassed lawyer.

'Are you certain, Mr Vaughan, that you wish to divorce this woman?'

'Oh, yes, your honour.' I looked lovingly at Maddy, who smiled back. 'I've never been so sure of anything in my whole life.'

The judge then declared that the *decree nisi* was granted and my lawyer mumbled sarcastically, 'You may now kiss the divorcee.' So I did.

As Maddy and I emerged hand in hand, a small gathering of friends and family showered us in tiny coloured bits of tissue paper. Our children were particularly generous with the confetti, tipping boxes of the stuff onto their parents' heads, before asking if they could ride in the white Rolls-Royce that had been booked to drive their parents to the reception. And so the whole family climbed inside and pulled away to the applause of the crowd.

For Jamie and Dillie's benefit, the Rolls-Royce took a scenic route home and by the time we pulled up at our home, most of the guests were already sipping champagne in the marquee that took up most of the garden.

Our friends had happily dressed up in their best wedding outfits to mark the occasion. Only Madeleine's mother struggled to process the irony of the thing and was explaining that we would probably get married again like Richard Burton and Elizabeth Taylor.

Most of our social circle had been delighted to learn that one of their favourite couples were back together. There was a sense of real euphoria among the friends gathered here on this special day. 'This is so romantic!' said the heavily pregnant Linda. 'Why can't we get divorced?'

Today Gary was taking the role of best man, or 'worst man' as he enjoyed telling everyone. In his waistcoat pocket he checked he still had the wedding rings we had not worn for months but would later place on one another's finger in front of everyone we knew and loved.

Dillie was officially the world's most delightful twelve-year-old girl, and Jamie would have blushed when he was asked if he had a girlfriend, had he not already been asked the same question eleven times already that day. 'No, I'm saving myself for Miss Right' got an appreciative chuckle from elderly relatives. Ron danced an old-fashioned dance with his beautiful daughter and Jean looked on with pride. With the champagne flowing through her veins, she suddenly erupted into tears of joy. 'He always was a splendid dancer,' she slurred. 'He's always been such a wonderful husband.'

Eventually it was time for the mock ceremony, and Gary guided people towards the raised decking in preparation for the service. For this special 'second time around' ceremony we had resolved that we should still publicly commit to one another, but with revised, more realistic vows. 'I promise sometimes to pretend to listen to you going on about stuff, when really I am thinking about something completely different.' 'I promise to love you in an everyday, familiar, best-friend sort of way, but not expect gushing declarations of devotion every five minutes.' And 'I promise to tolerate your imperfections and varying moods as you tolerate mine, and not to use these as private justification for entering my old girlfriends' names on Google.'

Gary, now dressed for some reason as a bishop, reminded the guests once again what a special occasion this was. 'Earlier today, Vaughan and Maddy finally took the big step that so many of us have often thought about but never quite had the courage to do, and finally got themselves divorced.' A big drunken cheer went up from the crowd.

'Now, Maddy and Vaughan appreciate that some of you came to their original wedding fifteen years ago, and brought them some lovely gifts, which they now feel morally obliged to return to you . . .'

One lone voice heckled, 'They've bought them back off eBay?'

'Mark and Erena,' he continued, 'with a heavy heart they are returning the twenty-two-piece dining set you gave them, which after one particularly fierce argument is now a ninety-two-piece dining set.

'Pete and Kate—to you they are returning the set of six crystal wineglasses, which is now a set of eleven crystal wineglasses, as Maddy and Vaughan buy their petrol from the same garage as you.'

Gary was milking this chance to perform to a generous crowd but after a while, though I could hear his voice, I ceased to hear the actual words. My mind was taking in a hundred other things at once: I saw friends I had got to know all over again, other teachers from my department at school, and the next-door neighbour with the cravat whose name I feared I might never find out. And I saw Madeleine nodding in agreement at Gary's jokes or feigning outrage at some of his humorous suggestions. And then I closed my eyes and felt the warmth of the sun on my face, the swirling sunspots floating me somewhere else. When suddenly it happened—an entire sequence of memories arrived in my head uninvited.

I had had an affair. Her name was Yolande, a twenty-something French language assistant at school, who had eventually returned to France. But for a month or so I had seen her secretly after work, and eventually I had been bold enough to gatecrash a school trip to Paris, creeping into Yolande's hotel bedroom after the other staff and students were asleep.

I felt appalled. I remembered that the affair had come at a point in our marriage when normal communication had broken down, months after Maddy and I had ceased to have sex. But if I'd felt that there had been any moral justification, why had I kept this secret locked up so tightly that it was one of the very last memories to re-emerge?

Details of my affair were churning in my brain. I could recall the potent illegality of that first time. There were so many good reasons why I should not proceed to have sex with this French language assistant, I remembered thinking. However, ranged against all the valid and persuasive arguments was the incontrovertible fact that she was lying naked in front of me . . .

I remembered the first time I had come home after having had sex with another woman, wondering if Maddy would be able to tell. But there was too much hostility in the air for Maddy's antennae to detect any suppressed contrition. Nor could I possibly tell her. She was already furious with me on so many counts and I was angry in return. If she knew, it would only make everything worse.

But that was then. Standing here now, surely she had to know the truth before the two of us began our new life together? If not now, then when? When is the best time to tell your wife you've had an affair—before or after you make a set of vows in front of friends and family? 'If you immediately confessed I might just forgive you . . .' That was what she had said.

Gary had finished his speech, but before the climax of the afternoon's entertainment Maddy just wanted to say a few words. She wanted to thank all the people who had helped make today's party possible: she thanked her mother and father, Dillie and Jamie, thanked Gary for being so entertaining; in fact, she was thanking so many people there was a chance the marriage would run its natural course before I had the chance to come clean.

'Gary!' I whispered, gesturing him to step back inside the kitchen. 'Listen—I just remembered something.' I lowered my voice to almost inaudible, 'I had an affair.'

Gary grinned at me. 'Yeah, right! And it was you who smashed up the Blue Peter garden . . . You won't get me on a wind-up, mate.'

'No, I swear I did. Really—a couple of years ago.'

'Bloody hell, Vaughan. Why are you telling me this now?'

'I only just remembered it. I have to tell Madeleine before the vows!'

The two of us looked at Maddy out on the makeshift stage.

'Are you insane? Don't tell her now. Don't tell her ever, but especially not now. Don't throw it all away, you idiot.'

'But it has to be before we commit. Withholding it is deception.'

'Deception is fine. Deception is normal. You should never, ever be completely honest with your wife. That's the worst thing you can possibly do.'

'But later is too late. She said she'd forgive me if I told her *immediately*.'

'Don't ruin her big day. Cos this whole thing is actually like a wedding,' observed Gary, as if this was a perceptive insight.

Now the moment had come for the spoof ceremony and the symbolic (and unironic) exchange of rings. I stepped back outside with Gary, who seemed less assured than he had before and stammered and mumbled his explanation of the next section of the proceedings.

I caught Maddy's eye and she raised her eyebrows at me with a slightly coy grin. This might possibly be the last smile I ever got from her, I thought. Which was better: a happy marriage based on a lie, or the risk of no marriage because I'd told the truth?

'Maddy!' I whispered behind Gary's back. 'There's something I have to tell you. It's about before we split up. I've only just remembered it, but you have to know now.'

'Vaughan, you're freaking me out. Shut up!'

With just a gesture of my head, I indicated that we move back from the exposed stage and, looking perplexed, Maddy stepped inside.

'So what's the big deal?' she whispered.

'You know when I went to Paris with the school? It wasn't just with the school. I went because there was another woman.'

No amount of blusher or lipstick could hide the colour draining from Maddy's face. 'What do you mean? How . . . who is she?'

'She was a French language assistant at school. It was over in a month. I'm really, really sorry, but I had to be honest with you. It'll never happen again, I promise. Maddy, say something.'

But Maddy had nothing to say, though her mascara was being diluted and a dark line ran down her cheek.

'So Vaughan and Madeleine, step forward, please!' demanded Gary, the unconvincing clergyman. We hovered on the other side of the open doors for a second. 'Come on, come on, don't be shy!' said Gary, ushering us back out into the open air. 'So, if any person or golden retriever knows of any just impediment why this man and this woman should not be disunited in unholy divorce, let them speak now or forever hold their peace.'

I glanced at Maddy, who seemed stunned.

'Jack Joseph Neil Vaughan, do you take Madeleine Rose Vaughan of this parish to be your legally separated ex-wife, to live with in sin from this day forth? Will you notice when she's been to the hairdresser's and accept her choice of driving routes as a reasonable alternative?'

'I, um . . . I will.' I glanced at her; at least the crying seemed to be at a minimum.

'And Madeleine Rose Vaughan, do you take Jack Joseph Neil Vaughan to be your legally separated ex-husband, to live with in sin from this day forth? Will you tolerate him and humour him? Will you laugh at jokes you've heard a hundred times before?'

A silence followed.

'She's forgotten her lines, ladies and gentlemen—it's a very big day . . .' Gary had been aware of us whispering inside and feared the worst. 'Just say "I will",' he whispered to her. She looked down and saw her friends staring expectantly at her—almost mouthing the two words on her behalf.

'She's changed her mind!' shouted a drunken heckler, whose wife then slapped him on the arm because she realised that maybe Maddy had.

'Take your time, Maddy—it's a big decision . . .' The humour had gone from Gary's voice, as if he was speaking to her sincerely now.

Finally Maddy seemed ready to speak . 'You . . . you . . .' She was staring directly at me. 'You BASTARD!'

A couple of people attempted to laugh, as if this was all part of the day's ironic script, but their hearts weren't really in it. And now she really did burst into tears as she threw her bouquet at my face. 'I never want to see you again for as long as I live.' And then she ran off the stage into the house, until the stunned crowd heard the front door slamming behind her.

CHAPTER 9

Apparently, the party went downhill a bit after Madeleine left. Gary still tried to do one or two of his prepared jokes, but even he soon realised that perhaps the moment had gone. I eventually ran out after Maddy, but she'd grabbed the car keys and sped off as aggressively as is possible in a Honda Jazz automatic.

The party guests drifted off, mumbling embarrassed 'thankyous' to me, and saying that most of the party had been very enjoyable. Later that evening Jean came round to collect a few things of Maddy's, explaining to the children that their mummy was going to stay with her mummy for a night or two and that she would ring them later.

'Could you tell her that I need to talk to her?' I pleaded.

'She just needs a bit of *headspace* at the moment, Vaughan. Every relationship goes through this . . .'

I was pretty sure that every relationship did not go through this. Husband and wife split up, he has a mental breakdown resulting in total amnesia, eventually sees his estranged wife as if for the first time, changes his mind about getting a divorce, eventually wins his wife back, then at the party to celebrate their new beginning remembers that he was unfaithful, tells her and she breaks up with him all over again.

In fact, Maddy stayed away for more than a couple of nights, and now I was the stressed single parent, getting the kids off to school, dashing on to work, then rushing back and cooking their tea and failing to be of any assistance with their maths homework.

Maddy rang Jamie's mobile every night and he grunted his few words before passing the handset to Dillie, who used up the talk-plan minutes within the first couple of days. I had texted and emailed Maddy but she couldn't bring herself to speak to me just yet.

I offered to move out if Maddy wanted to be back at the house with Dillie and Jamie, but she interpreted this as me not wanting to be responsible for the children so that I would be free to chase female members of staff.

Gary and Linda had me round for supper and I learned that they had talked to Maddy about me, pointing out, in my defence, that I had at least told her the truth.

'OK, it was wrong, he admits that,' Linda had said. 'But not every bloke would have owned up—'

'I wouldn't have,' Gary had chipped in brightly. But now Gary had reasons of his own to be depressed. He reported to me that he had finally decided to close down YouNews.

'User-generated news doesn't work. People were just making stuff up.'

'What, unlike tabloid journalists?'

It felt like everything went wrong in the end.

I HAD A FINAL APPOINTMENT with Dr Lewington, who said she had been meaning to call me back in to monitor the progress on my amnesia. 'But here's the funny thing—I forgot!' she chuckled. When she asked me if I had regained any more significant memories I said, 'No. None at all.' The curious thing that I should have shared with her was that this was the first memory I had regained and then subsequently lost again. I clearly recalled the moment it all came back to me, but the details of Yolande and Paris were now a vague blur.

Finally she announced, 'Well, I don't think there is anything else we can do for you. You can walk out of here and get on with the rest of your life.'

I had decided that, since I was back in the hospital, I would try to locate

Bernard. I had kept meaning to visit him but had never got round to it.

'Bernard?' said Dr Lewington, when I asked where I could find him.

'You remember Bernard? Talkative bloke in the bed next to me. Had a brain tumour, but wasn't going to let it get him down.'

'Oh, yes, him. You won't be able to visit him, I'm afraid.'

'Is he not here any more?'

'No. He died.'

ON THE FOURTH DAY of limbo, I was surprised to receive a call from Maddy's father. Ron wanted to meet me and suggested the café at the British Library at Euston. I was reassured by his choice of venue. If he wanted to punch me in the face for betraying his daughter, the British Library did not seem the most obvious place to do it.

Ron was already waiting for me when I arrived; he was seated at a booth and got up to shake my hand. He showed no hostility towards me for the trauma I had caused his daughter, though I felt too embarrassed to look him in the eye. 'How's Maddy?' I asked.

'She's been staying in her old room most of the time. Her mother puts plates of food beside her bed, then takes them away again later . . .'

'Right. So . . . this is a long way from home.'

'Yes, I've been commuting to London to do a bit of research on your medical condition. I hope you don't mind?'

Inside I felt a pang of disappointment that this was what he had come to talk about. I had hoped he might have a message from Maddy.

'I think I may have unearthed some interesting case studies,' he said. I gave a neutral nod. I was going to have to indulge him. I'd already read everything there was to read on retrograde amnesia and dissociative fugues.

At the next table a young student couple were staring at one another, their two straws intimately sharing the same iced mocha.

'Now I'm not saying that this applies in your case; but it's something I think you should be aware of.' He indicated the pages he had photocopied from various reference books and old journals. 'In 1957, this businessman in New York had exactly the same thing as you. He had been under great stress as a chief executive, with millions of dollars riding on his decisions, when one day he disappeared and was found a week later with no knowledge of who he was. Like you, this gentleman gradually regained all his memories, and the board voted to reinstate him.'

The student took his straw out of the cup and presented the foam on the end for his girlfriend to lick off.

'But at the moment when he returned to his old life, he suddenly remembered that he had defrauded the company. He was racked with guilt, confessed and resigned.'

'Sorry, Ron—but I don't quite see how that helps me now? I remembered all the worst stuff last as well.'

'I think this might have some bearing on your indiscretion in Paris.'

I blushed. 'The funny thing is, I don't even remember that any more. It came back to me as clear as anything on the day of our party. But it's the first memory I have regained and then lost again.'

'But that's one of the symptoms!!' said Ron excitedly. 'Look, this is the interesting bit. His company investigated his confession, and *it wasn't true*. There had been no fraud; it was a false memory!'

I had never seen Ron so animated.

'A false memory? How does that work?'

'Deep down he was frightened of returning to the challenges of his old life and subconsciously needed an excuse not to make that final leap.'

'Where did you get all this from?'

'From books. These examples are from years back, long before online medical journals and suchlike. It is amazing what you can find in libraries.'

'You mean there are others?' Only now did I look properly at the photo-copied pages on the table.

'Yes—look. This was in a 1930s book about psychiatry. A local alderman in Lincoln confessed to killing a woman who, it transpired, was still alive.'

'I don't get it.'

'The sufferers aren't pretending to have these memories; they really do believe they did these bad things.'

I hurriedly scanned the dense print of the photocopied book. The psychi-atrist's theory was that this handful of individuals had experienced false memories for the same reason that they had suffered their original amnesia. Unable to cope, their brains had created an extreme solution: wipe all memories of the stressful life or create new memories that would make a return to that stressful life impossible.

'When I told a language teacher at school the reason Maddy and I had split up again, he said that Yolande never went on the Paris trip. He said she'd already left at that point. I thought he must have got it wrong.'

'Well, it seems like your brain has been playing tricks on you again.'

'Oh, Ron, this is fantastic! I feel like I've been let out of prison. I *didn't* have an affair! Does Maddy know about this?'

'Yes. She suggested I came to tell you.'

'Right. Was she happy?'

'She said, "So Vaughan may not be an adulterer, he's just a total nutter."'

'Oh.'

Nearby there was the sudden scrape of a chair as the teenage girl stormed off, her confused boyfriend calling after her.

'Will you tell her that Yolande didn't even go to Paris? That proves my innocence, doesn't it? Will you tell her and get her to call me?'

'You're not really mad at all, are you? You're just mad about Maddy,' he said with a smile. 'But then, who wouldn't be?'

A FEW HOURS LATER I was seated in the hall at my children's school, saving the empty seat beside me. Jamie and Dillie were appearing in the school production of *South Pacific*. I had texted Maddy to say that I would leave her ticket at the desk. The nerves of all the children on the stage were nothing compared to those of one of the adults watching them.

The band struck up the overture, and Jamie looked as though he wished his guitar was big enough to hide him. All the parents were looking directly ahead except one, who kept looking round. I knew that Dillie's entrance was coming up, so I endeavoured to concentrate. It was at that moment that a body slipped quietly in beside me and I heard Maddy whisper, 'Hi.'

I felt a surge of elation. What better time for my wonderful wife to make an appearance than during the chorus of 'There Is Nothing Like a Dame'. I turned to her and exclaimed, 'Maddy!' so loudly that several parents glared at me for interrupting. 'You haven't missed Dillie yet,' I whispered.

She said nothing else to me for most of the first act, which made me anxious and distracted throughout 'Some Enchanted Evening' and 'A Cockeyed Optimist'. Finally, during 'Younger Than Springtime', I whispered, 'I spoke to your dad.'

'Yeah, he called me immediately afterwards.'

'Isn't it fantastic?'

'What's fantastic about it?'

'Shhh!' said a couple of teachers in front of us.

I tried to establish how her father's discovery could be anything other than positive, but every time I whispered loud enough for her to hear, heads would turn.

'Can you please stop talking!' came the harsh whisper from behind us.

There was a round of applause for the end of the song, so Maddy gestured to me to come outside. At that moment Dillie made her big entrance. Just in time to see both her parents getting up and scurrying to the exit.

The two of us stood and talked in the school corridor. I tried to fathom why Maddy was still so cool with me.

'Look, I remember Yolande being at the school, but it's like I hardly knew her. I don't understand why you aren't pleased. I *didn't* sleep with the French language assistant!' The group of teenage girls in grass skirts rushing down the corridor gave me a strange look. I gestured to hug Maddy, but she did not accept the invitation.

'So why,' she asked accusingly, 'did you imagine you had an affair with this Yolande woman?'

'You're not going to hold it against me that I *imagined* I had sex with another woman, are you? That's every male in the known universe . . .'

'I don't care who you imagine you have sex with.'

'Hello, Mrs Vaughan,' said one of Jamie's friends.

'Hello, Danny. The first question is, did you imagine you had sex with Yolande because you fancied her?'

'Hello, Mrs Vaughan.'

'Hello, Ade. Well, did you?'

'This isn't fair. You're giving me a hard time because of something I didn't actually do.'

'But did you fancy Yolande the French language assistant?'

'Of course I fancied Yolande. Everyone did—she was gorgeous.'

'Thank you.'

'What's more pathetic is that my subconscious believed that a stunning young thing like Yolande would ever have an affair with an old fart like me! It's ridiculous.'

At that moment, the double doors of the hall burst open and the audience swept towards the dining room, where the catering students would be selling interval drinks. Maddy and I went through with the rest of the crowd, feeling mortified when someone congratulated us on Dillie's performance.

'Maddy—come home with me, Jamie and Dillie tonight. They've really missed you. I miss you. You were all set to give our relationship another go until I tried to be honest about something that had happened in the past. Well, now you've got the best of both worlds: I *wasn't* unfaithful, but you know I'd tell you if I had been.'

'It's not as simple as that.'

'It *is* as simple as that.'

'Didn't Dillie look fantastic up there?' said a teacher I didn't recognise. 'And Jamie in the band as well! What a great night for the Vaughan family!'

'Well, let's see how it turns out . . .' I said.

'It such a great musical, isn't it?' said Maddy, grateful that the teacher was still there. 'Great songs.'

'Oh, yes, wonderful songs.'

'Yeah, tell me, Maddy, which number do you prefer?' I asked. '"I'm Gonna Wash That Man Right Out Of My Hair" or "I'm In Love With A Wonderful Guy"?'

The teacher hovered to see the outcome of this interesting question.

'I'd say the best is yet to come. "You've Got To Be Carefully Taught".'

'Good answer!' said the teacher.

Other families we knew joined us and I didn't get another chance to talk with Maddy before we returned to our seats. Finally, during the applause for 'Happy Talk', I grabbed my opportunity.

'You said the "*first* question" is did I fancy Yolande. What was the second question?'

I had to wait until the end of the next song to get a response.

'Why did your mind need to create a false memory?' she said.

'I dunno.'

'Because at some deep level, you don't want to commit. Your brain invented a reason not to be with me because it doesn't want to be with me.'

'But—'

She put her fingers to her lips as the room fell quiet. All the way through 'This Nearly Was Mine' I wanted to scream at the unfairness of it. My memory was like some involuntary muscle: acting independently, wiping files, making up stuff, while I was held to account for the way it was trashing my past and future.

'But I *do* want to be with you. In sickness and in mental health. Remember our wedding vows.'

'Yeah. Except we got divorced.'

Now Dillie was on stage again and we clapped loudly, making sure she could see us in the audience. Only at the end did we have another opportunity to talk. During the repeated curtain calls, while we waved enthusiastically to our children on stage, we tried to work out whether their mum and dad were going to stay together.

'You have a psychological condition,' sighed Maddy. 'And your psyche doesn't want you to be with me. That will manifest itself sooner or later, and I'm not going through all that again.'

'This is so unfair. I want you back home, OK? The kids want you back home, I didn't sleep with anyone else, and now you know you can trust me to tell you if I ever had. What else do I have to do?'

'Dillie's waving—wave back!'

I waved at my daughter, then gave two thumbs ups to Jamie.

'Oh God, I don't know,' sighed Maddy. 'I spoke to the lawyers before this false-memory stuff came up. Under the terms of the divorce, you have to vacate the house and I have to allow you access to the children every weekend. They're waiting for me to direct them to instruct you.'

'No, Maddy, think about it. Give us another chance.'

'Look, we can't put the kids through another breakup. I'll go back to Mum and Dad's and I'll be in touch, OK?'

THAT NIGHT I tucked Dillie up like I used to when she was little. 'Why did you and Mum walk out just as I came on stage?'

'Oh dear, you saw that, did you? I'm very sorry we weren't there for your big debut moment. It was because we were trying to sort out whether we are both going to be there all the rest of the time.'

'What did you decide?' said Jamie, standing at his sister's doorway.

'Oh, hi, Jamie. Well, we aren't sure yet. We're both going to be in your lives a lot. It's just whether we do it together or apart.'

'Can we have some crisps?'

'Look, just because you know I'm feeling guilty about missing Dillie's debut and Mum not being here and everything, you think I am going to be a soft touch for junk food after you've both brushed your teeth? Well . . . there's a big cheese-and-onion grab bag in the cupboard.'

FOR TWO DAYS I waited for any message from Maddy. I had sent her a long email listing all the reasons why I felt that we should be together, but heard nothing back. I didn't dare leave the house in case she came round.

On the third day, a solitary letter landed face up on the doormat and in that moment I feared the worst. A formal letter, addressed to me, from her lawyer; that could only be an official instruction to vacate the house and adhere to the terms of the divorce.

I was not sure where I wanted to be when I opened this emotional letter bomb. I took it into the kitchen, but decided I didn't want to read it there. I wandered into the lounge and then back to the hallway. I held the letter up to the light, but the envelope was too expensive to see through. And finally I ripped it open to have my fate confirmed to me.

Inside there was no letter from the lawyers. Just a tatty green postcard featuring a cartoon leprechaun saying 'Top o' the mornin' to yers!!'

'SHE'S BEAUTIFUL; she's absolutely perfect!' I said, looking at the newborn baby in Maddy's arms, or possibly at Maddy, I never actually specified.

'Would you like to hold her, Vaughan?' suggested Linda from the hospital bed, and Madeleine passed the baby over.

Linda's birth plan had specified a traditional birthing experience, which Gary had taken as his cue to play it like a 1950s husband and remain in the pub the entire evening. He only just made it in time.

But now, incredibly, here the new baby was. And here was Maddy with our own children, marvelling at the miracle of a whole new life.

I looked into the unfocused eyes of the tiny baby, feeling some sort of vague affinity with this new arrival. And Maddy smiled as she looked at the baby staring up in the direction of her newborn man.

'Does it take you back to when you first held our two?' said Maddy.

'God, yeah, I'll never forget that—'

'*Again* . . .' heckled Jamie.

Linda took the baby back to breastfeed her, and I fixed Gary directly in my gaze and asked him if he was planning to do any late-night bottle feeds.

'It depends whether Linda is able to express enough. We don't want to use formula milk when obviously breast is best for Baby.'

He said 'best for Baby', I thought. No definite article. They've got him too. 'Oh, we brought you a present,' I remembered.

Gary ripped open the paper to reveal a specially commissioned family tree, surrounded by various photos of the baby's parents and grandparents and with an empty space for her own image right at the bottom.

'Wow—look at that! That's really kind of you.'

'It's a present for the whole family really,' I said. 'Your history is important. It sort of defines who you are.'

We left Gary and Linda to make the disappointing discovery that none of Baby's ancestors had gone down with the *Titanic* or been hanged for horse-stealing, and headed home.

Family life had quickly reverted to normality after Maddy had returned. The children found it irritating that their parents were trying really hard to be nice to one another, and shouted, 'Get a room!' every time we so much as cuddled. But they obviously appreciated having both their father and their mother around to tell them to do their homework, tidy their rooms and clear the dinner table. It was just at such a profound level that the children wouldn't have realised quite how much they appreciated it.

But Madeleine and I hadn't got back together for the sake of our kids. Maddy told me she realised that I was, in fact, 'the light of her life'. I was amazed to hear her being this romantic, until she added, 'OK, so the light flickers a bit and the bulbs don't last five minutes, but frankly I can't be bothered to get another bloody light now.'

Despite our kids' outwardly confident and contented manner, I worried about how much they might have been affected by our original breakup. I'd been particularly worried about how Jamie might react to the reunion. I was still haunted by his outburst at the swimming pool.

I contrived an opportunity to walk Woody on the Common with Jamie to give me a chance to have a grown-up talk.

'I won't let it ever get like it was before,' I said.

'You can't promise that,' he said, like the admonishing parent.

'Well, I can promise that I've changed.'

'We'll see,' said Jamie, which is what adults always say when they don't want to agree to something. We walked on in awkward silence for a while. Then from nowhere he piped up, 'Still, at least it means we won't have to see Ralph any more.'

In the distance a tractor chugged and rattled, and the delicious aroma of fresh-cut grass mingled with the smoke of the first summer barbecues as impromptu picnics spread out across the giant green tablecloth of the Common. Then Maddy and Dillie were spotted, approaching on their bicycles, my daughter puffed and pink-cheeked from racing to catch up with us.

'We thought we could all go to the bandstand and get an ice cream.'

'Great idea. Get me a coffee,' I said as they cycled ahead.

It was just a perfectly ordinary scene, a family sitting outside a café in a London park, spooning the chocolate froth off their parents' coffee or sharing a taste of each other's cones. But as I chatted and laughed along, I felt myself detach, like some lab scientist gazing down in wonder at the whole incredibly unlikely scenario. How fragile a thing was human happiness. This might turn out to be the best moment ever, right here, right now.

Maddy was so beautiful, her face showing the creases of forty years of smiling at everyone. Jamie was quiet and dignified, always so judicious when he did choose to speak. Dillie glowed with enthusiasm and unshakeable trust in the goodness of people. And there was I in the middle of them all, consciously recording this precious memory. I felt like a born-again father.

Maddy had told me something remarkable about our quiet, contemplative son. During that terrifying purgatory when Madeleine had been staying with her parents in Berkshire, she had answered the front door to see Jamie standing there in his school uniform, clutching the present of a chocolate orange. And while he was supposed to be in double maths, mother and son sat on a bench in a pretty back garden in the country, sharing his gift.

'Me and Dillie were talking,' he had said. 'We just thought you should know that whatever you do, it should be what you want, not what you think we want. Because what we want is what you want.'

'Well, that's no good,' she told him, 'because all I want is what you two want, so now we're completely stuck!' And she kissed the top of his head so he couldn't see that she was crying. I later noticed that Maddy kept the packaging of that chocolate orange in her bedside drawer.

As for the leprechaun postcard, that was officially decommissioned and put on display in the public gallery that was the downstairs toilet. It had become a bit battered and faded down the years, but the little leprechaun's upbeat message still made me smile every time I looked at it.

THE DAY AFTER Gary finally became a father I offered to take my old friend out for a celebratory lager, or, in my case, sparkling mineral water. Gary took the last empty table, dangerously close to the dartboard.

'Well, here's to your new arrival!'

'I'll drink to that . . . Gazoody-baby!'

'A girl! Now that's two people in your home you won't understand.'

'Talking of which—how are things with Maddy?' ventured Gary.

'Great! Really great. It's early days, but I think we're both really happy.'

'That's good.' He took a large sip of beer. 'So she's still hasn't twigged that her father-in-law forged all that false-memory bollocks?'

'*What?*' My mouth hung open.

'Don't give me that!' said Gary, looking slightly disgusted. 'I clearly remember you boasting about the French girl to me at the time. He did a good job, old Ron, with his phony photocopies and made-up psychiatrists.'

'You mean . . . ? So I did commit . . .' A wave of sickness washed over me. Could I have been unfaithful to Maddy after all? Would I have to tell her, or was living a lie actually the only possible option? Gary burst out laughing at my intense mortification.

'I tell you one thing that has never changed. You were gullible when I first met you, and you're just as gullible now!'

'Bull's-eye!' came the cry from behind us.

'Ah, you should see your face!' laughed Gary. And I affected a good-natured smile, using muscles normally intended for screaming.

THE NEXT MORNING in school, I found myself wandering off the curriculum during my last lesson with Year 11. 'So all this history we have done over the past year—is it all true, do you think?'

'Yeah, 'cos if it's not true, it's not history.'

'But who's to say what's true? Is "true" what everyone thinks happened? Tanika's letter to the *South London Press* about how her dad really died has changed the official history, hasn't it, Tanika?'

'Yeah, and we're planting a tree and we're going to put a notice underneath. Will you come, sir?'

'I'd be honoured.'

Six months ago, an exchange like this would have prompted jeers to the effect that Tanika loved Boggy Vaughan, but all that had been left behind.

'You see, it's all a question of perception. Sometimes we think we remember something, but have actually reinvented it, because the fictional memory suits us better. And the same is true in history—'

'Nah,' interjected Dean, ''cos in history I never remember anything.'

'We all put our own angle on everything that happens to us, consciously and subconsciously. Governments, countries and individuals—'

'So what you have been teaching us all year might be a load of old bull?'

'I wouldn't put it quite like that. I'm just saying that history is not what definitely happened. History is . . . well, history is just old spin.'

THAT EVENING, Maddy and I sat out on the wooden decking as the light gently fell away.

'Linda and Gary took the baby home today.'

'Blimey! I wonder how their marriage will cope.'

'Oh, I'm sure they'll get through it,' said Maddy. 'Gary's probably got a special app for it on his iPhone.'

'Ha! I could have used one of those. GPS technology to tell me where I'd gone wrong in my life . . .'

'I think the secret is just to find what it is that really makes you happy. And then drink a few glasses of it every evening.'

She took a sip.

'I must tell that to my Year Eleven class. We had a really interesting discussion today. About the nature of history. They so want to be certain about what definitely happened.'

'Yeah, well, you might not be the best judge of all that . . .'

'Fair point. But having completely lost my past, it makes you realise how all that stuff can actually get in the way. Countries go to war over distorted versions of history; couples get divorced from accumulating bitterness about stuff that never quite happened the way they remember it.'

'So everyone should get chronic amnesia?'

'No, I'm just saying that you've got *your* version of the past, and now I've got mine back, and we should each respect the differences.'

She went to pour some wine into my empty water glass, but I covered the top of it with my hand.

'Not drinking any more—remember?'

'Oh, yeah—old habits die hard.' But the end of the bottle somehow knocked my fingers and the glass fell and broke in two.

'Sorry! I thought I had it.'

'No, that was me—I knocked your hand.'

We burst out laughing at ourselves and I picked up the broken glass.

'Give it a few months and I'll remember that was definitely your fault.'

'In ten years' time, I'll say you smashed the glass. After you threw it at me.'

'Ten years' time! Do you think we'll still be together in ten years' time?'

'Maybe. Maybe not.' She put her bare feet up onto my lap. 'Who knows what the past will hold?'

And then I recovered perhaps my final unreclaimed memory.

A STRIKING REDHEAD walks into the Students' Union bar. I have never seen anyone so beautiful and once she sits down I place myself in an empty seat nearby and hope she might notice the fellow first-year directly in her eye-line. I pull my brand-new textbook from the bookshop bag, but decide it will look more impressive if I open it somewhere near the final chapter. I can't help glancing up every few minutes to catch her eye.

'That's a very scholarly sounding book,' she says eventually.

'This? I'm just reading this for pleasure; it's not part of my course.'

'Hmm . . . Do you mind me asking, why are you starting at the back?'

'That's just how I prefer history.' I feel myself blushing at having been caught out. 'I can never wait to find out what happens at the end . . .' I glance down at the final page and exclaim, 'Oh no! The Romans win!'

'Oh . . . Now there's no point in me reading it.'

'Sorry about that. I'm Vaughan, by the way.'

'I'm Madeleine . . . Sociology.'

'Unusual surname.'

'Yeah—Russian or something . . . Are you here for the Experimental Poetry Performance?'

'What? Er, yeah. I love that stuff. Oh, you just made that up, didn't you?'

And she grins and that is the moment I decide this is the woman I want to marry. Then a couple of Maddy's friends arrive. 'This is Vaughan, everyone. He's studying history,' she explains. 'Backwards.'

john o'farrell

Profile

Born:
March, 1962.

Education:
Read English and Drama
at Exeter University.

Comedy scriptwriter on:
*Spitting Image, Murder
Most Horrid, Chicken Run.*

Fiction:
*The Best a Man Can Get,
This is Your Life, May*

Contain Nuts.

Nonfiction:
*Things Can Only Get
Better, Global Village Idiot,
I Blame the Scapegoats, I
Have a Bream, An Utterly
Impartial History of Britain,
An Utterly Exasperated
History of Modern Britain.*

Supports:
Fulham FC.

Why, when, or how do you think you developed such an eye for human foibles?
My father had aspirations to be a writer. He had poems published and even completed
a novel, so maybe I inherited something from him. I think we all notice human foibles,
don't we? The trick is to find a way to write them down.

Where did you grow up, and what are your most vivid childhood memories?
I grew up in Maidenhead, besides the Thames. I remember rowing down the backwater
near our house, the magic secrecy of the place. I remember everything from then
down to the finest detail. That's why there is no room left in my hard drive for whatever
I was told this morning.

What was the initial spark of inspiration behind *The Man Who Forgot His Wife*?
I had seen contemporaries get divorced and be just as miserable afterwards, and I
spent ages trying to think of a way in which a protagonist might look at his life with
fresh eyes.

**Your earlier novel, *The Best A Man Can Get*, brought a sharp, witty eye to family
life and, in particular, to fatherhood. How many children do you have and what,
for you, has been the best part of the journey?**
I have two kids, now virtually grown up at seventeen and nineteen. It's just been fantastic having such interesting and funny people living with us, and now sharing the things
that interest them.

You've also written a best-selling history book, *An Utterly Impartial History of*

Britain: Or 2000 Years of Upper Class Idiots in Charge. **What makes you angriest about British society these days?**

I suppose it is the enormous and growing gap between rich and poor in our society, and the problems that are created when the people making the decisions have absolutely no experience or comprehension of what it must be like for people at the other end of the social scale. Sadly, the subtitle of my history book is as true as ever.

Television viewers will have seen you on *Have I Got News For You*, *Grumpy Old Men* and other shows. Are the TV appearances fun or hard work?

I usually enjoy going on television, although the writing comes first. TV helps remind people about the books. Believe it or not, there are plenty of shows that I turn down because they would send the wrong message about what I write. The hardest work is a show like *Question Time*, because you have to have read up on all the possible news stories and you might need to know what you think about a difficult moral issue.

Do you usually find it easy to come up with something to be grumpy about?

I first did *Grumpy Old Men* when I was thirty-nine, and just as I didn't think that I was particularly old back then, I don't consider myself very grumpy. But, since you have asked, I dislike people being rude, especially if they are in a position of power (eg over a waiter). I get irritated by the modern syndrome of customers being expected to do all the work for themselves—from self-check-outs in supermarkets to having to print out your own boarding pass. Oh, and the little packets of UHT milk when you order a cup of tea. Actually, I am quite grumpy aren't I?

When were you at your happiest, or do you feel you're not there yet?

I've always been pretty happy, but it could be that when both kids have left home I will look back at the years when we were all together as the happiest time of my life. But then, there are always other things to look forward to. Like shouting at passing strangers from my electric trolley.

What is the best advice you could give to your children?

To try to make the world a better place for them having been in it. Don't wait for anyone else to discover your talents—go right out there and have a go at achieving your highest ambition, because otherwise you will never know what could have been.

And, finally, what makes you laugh?

As a teenager, I loved the classic TV sitcoms such as *Fawlty Towers*, *Porridge*, *Yes, Minister*, and *The Likely Lads*. Now, I enjoy re-watching cleverly crafted films like *Groundhog Day* and *The Odd Couple* over and over again. My kids have introduced me to a whole new range of TV comedies from *Modern Family* to *The Simpsons* and *Curb Your Enthusiasm*. Plus, I always try to laugh along when my kids see something hilarious—even if it's usually my fashion sense.

Inspector Singh has been sent from Singapore to Kuala Lumpur to help solve a high-profile case—Chelsea Liew, a former Singaporean model, is on trial for shooting her ex-husband, who was using Islamic law to take her children away from her.

And then someone else confesses to the crime!

As Inspector Singh employs all his cunning to find the true murderer, he asks himself: What hope of justice, when politics, love and religion trump rational behaviour?

ONE

The accused, Chelsea Liew, was in court. She sat on a wooden bench in a wooden box, handcuffed to a policewoman.

The prosecutor watched the court official read out the charge in a slow, ponderous voice: '. . . that you, Chelsea Liew, on or about the eighteenth day of July, committed murder by causing the death of Alan Lee.'

The judge said, 'How does the accused plead? Guilty or *not* guilty?' He managed to inject a wealth of disbelief into the possibility of a not guilty plea.

Chelsea's lawyer, a tall, thin Indian man, struggled for words that would not involve criticising any party for whom the judge had sympathy—basically, everyone except his client. 'My lord, the evidence is circumstantial. The police and prosecution have rushed to judgment because this is a high-profile case. The charges should be dismissed outright.'

The judge simply said again, 'Guilty or not guilty?'

The lawyer stole a quick, nervous glance at the woman in the dock. At last she muttered, 'Not guilty.' Her lawyer sighed with relief.

The judge rapped his gavel. 'Accused to be remanded in custody until trial dates fixed.'

Her defence lawyer made one last attempt to assist his client. 'My lord, this is an unusual case involving a mother of three. Although bail is not usually granted where the charge is murder . . .'

He was interrupted. 'Application for bail denied!' Gown billowing, the judge walked out.

The prosecution team looked pleased. The accused did not react. Her anger and emotion had been spent long before her marriage had culminated in the murder of her husband. A policewoman led her out.

INSPECTOR SINGH WAS wedged into a small plastic seat at Changi Airport. Hunched up, his belly compressed his lungs. His fleshy, sweaty knees were pressed together to avoid inadvertent brushes with the people on either side. Inspector Singh had a strong dislike of physical contact with strangers. Unfortunately, his girth made it difficult for him not to encroach onto their seats. Patches of damp were visible under his armpits and just above his belly. Only his white sneakers looked as fresh as when he had put them on before setting out for the office—blissfully unaware that he was about to be assigned to the case that he had, that morning, been reading about in the newspapers. He remembered feeling sorry for the policeman who had the dismal task of finding the murderer of Alan Lee. He felt much sorrier now that he knew it was himself.

Inspector Singh was waiting for a flight to Kuala Lumpur. He sighed, a breathy, wheezy sound. A heavy smoker, he needed a cigarette, but smoking was prohibited indoors, and pretty much everywhere else in Singapore.

Singh knew he would not be on the case if he had not been the unofficial 'most likely to be forced into early retirement' entry in the Singapore police yearbook. He sighed again, causing his neighbour, a middle-aged white woman, to glance at him surreptitiously. Singh knew what she was thinking. A dark man in a turban who seemed worried and preoccupied? She was hoping not to be on the same flight as him. Singh did not feel like explaining to her that the six metres of cloth that he had wound round his head expertly that morning reflected his heritage as a Sikh. It did not indicate terrorist proclivities, and neither, for that matter, did anyone else's turban.

FORTY-FIVE MINUTES LATER, he was on the plane, looking out of the window. He could see the coastline of Peninsular Malaysia. Singapore, a small island separated from the Malaysian mainland by a thin strip of water, the Straits of Johor, and connected by two bridges, had disappeared from view.

He forced his mind back to the matter at hand—the reason for this unexpected trip to Malaysia. He had the file in his briefcase and knew the skimpy facts by heart. It was the depth of passion running beneath the surface that had occupied the newspapers in Malaysia and Singapore for the last couple of weeks, and promised to make the case a nightmare.

Inspector Singh also knew that if he managed to find a way through the thicket of politics overwhelming the case, his superiors would claim the credit. If he failed, they would hang him out to dry. His was not an organisation that appreciated instinct over method, results over means, footwork over paperwork. He was the elephant in the room that no one talked about but everyone hoped would do the decent thing and take early retirement. As he had not done it so far, he was on a small plane, enduring a bumpy flight, to a town up in arms.

Inspector Singh was quite convinced there was no possibility of a successful resolution to the case. There never was when religion trumped rational behaviour and politics influenced police work. Malaysia and Singapore were former British colonies, once part of the same country but now suspicious and independent neighbours. Every act of state was potentially a threat or an insult to the other. There was none of the polite distance and formal dispute resolution of strangers—every difference of opinion was a family feud. And there were all too many opinions being vented in newspapers and on-line about his new case.

The plane came in to land over undulating hills covered in neat grids of oil palm. Singh caught a train linking the Kuala Lumpur International Airport terminal building and the arrival hall. Moments later, he stepped out into the sweltering tropical heat. He strolled to the massed ranks of Mercedes Benz taxis and climbed into the back of the first one.

The Malay driver's car was immaculate, with a verse of the Quran plastered on the rear window. Inspector Singh did not read Arabic but he knew the expression was, 'There is no God but Allah and Muhammad is his only Prophet'. Across the glove compartment there was another sticker, with the words 'Liverpool Football Club' emblazoned next to a logo.

Inspector Singh smiled, then pulled out the newspaper to read the latest on the matter that had brought him to Kuala Lumpur.

TWO

'There is nothing for you to do here! I don't know why you came. The Malaysian police can handle everything. You should go back now.'

The speaker's moustache, a neat black brush with flecks of grey, bristled angrily as he shouted at the man across the desk from him. His eyes, under thick brows, glared at the inspector from a nut-brown face.

Inspector Singh remained expressionless. He said, 'You have no choice and I have no choice. So we can do this the easy way or the hard way.'

The Malaysian Superintendent of Police did not respond. He sat at his desk, drumming his fingers on the table. His desktop was devoid of anything that looked work-related. Singh knew from his own experience in Singapore that the further up the ladder one got, the more the job was about politics and statistics than actually dealing with crime.

He wondered if he was expected to head back to Singapore with his tail between his legs—surely it was obvious that his superiors in Singapore had more leverage over him than the officer glowering at him across the desk? Still, if there was a waiting game to be played, Singh was a past master. He sat nonchalantly in the chair, eyeing a display of plastic flowers in a vase.

The Malaysian was the first to blink. He stood up, walked over to a filing cabinet, slid open a drawer and took out a large folder. 'I do not like it but certain quarters have demanded that I cooperate,' he said. 'This is what we have done so far. We have the wife in custody. You can see her if you like. You can interview any person in Malaysia but only if they agree. We cannot make anyone talk to you. I will send you my ADC. He will assist you.'

And watch my every move and report back to you, thought Singh, but he did not say anything. This was a higher level of cooperation, however reluctant, than he had expected. He nodded his thanks to the scowling man, got up and picked up the folder.

A few strides later he was out of the door. A muffled sound of footsteps caused him to turn round and he saw a young policeman hurrying after him. Singh stopped and waited.

'Sir!' A smart salute accompanied the greeting. 'I am Sergeant Shukor, aide-de-camp to Superintendent Khalid Ibrahim. He asked me to help you.'

'Good. You can start by finding me a place to sit down and read this report,' ordered Singh. 'And then I'll need some tea.'

Inspector Singh lumbered after the young policeman assigned to be his minder and was shown into a small room with a desk and filing cabinet. He sat down heavily in the lone chair in the room. It creaked a noisy protest. Having spread out some papers from the folder, Singh lit a cigarette and wedged his large posterior more firmly into his chair.

He glanced at Sergeant Shukor, who was standing smartly to attention. The young man had a tanned strong jaw, a broad flat nose and eyes that were slightly too widely spaced. His dark blue uniform was pressed to perfection and tight enough to grip muscular thighs and forearms. His regulation service revolver—shiny, black and dangerous—was neatly holstered.

Singh asked, 'Who is in charge of the Lee murder investigation?'

'Inspector Mohammad, sir.'

'Shouldn't I be talking to him before getting to work?'

The sergeant looked uncomfortable. He was remarkably transparent for a police officer.

Singh asked, 'What is it?'

'He was supposed to be here to meet you, sir. But he hasn't turned up.'

Singh grimaced. 'Not another Malaysian policeman with a bad attitude?'

'He's not exactly like that, sir.'

Singh was just about to probe deeper when there was a quiet knock on the door. Shukor opened it.

A very tall man with thick, short, iron-grey hair and a thin face walked in. He was dressed in a smart dark suit, wore a pale blue shirt and a darker blue tie and had cufflinks with a college crest on them.

He said, 'Inspector Singh? I'm Inspector Mohammad. Thank you for coming to help us poor Malaysians stumbling around in the dark on this case.'

His voice matched his looks—smooth and effortlessly classy. And his hostility was going to be subtle and difficult to overcome. Singh, suddenly conscious of his damp shirt, took the cigarette out of his mouth and said, 'It's my pleasure, Inspector Mohammad.'

'Please call me Mohammad.'

Inspector Singh nodded. 'I understand you're in charge of this case?'

'The murder of Alan Lee? Yes, I'm afraid so. Still, it seems a fairly open-and-shut case, doesn't it?'

Singh gestured to the pile of papers in front of him. 'I was just making myself familiar with the facts.'

Inspector Mohammad's lip curled. 'It's not pretty, I'm afraid. Well, I'd better leave you to it. Shukor here will get you anything you need, and I'm in my office when you're done.' He walked out, closing the door quietly behind him.

Inspector Singh whistled softly. 'Now where did that come from?'

Sergeant Shukor did not pretend to misunderstand the question. 'He's from a very wealthy family, sir. Perak royalty, actually.'

Singh nodded his head. Nine of the thirteen states in Malaysia were former sultanates and had hereditary royalty.

Shukor continued, 'He went to boarding school in England and has a doctorate from Cambridge in Criminal Psychology.'

'Then what's he doing here?'

'They say he loves the job and doesn't want to be promoted to where it's all management and no police work.'

Inspector Singh could understand the reluctance to turn into a bureaucrat. He had the same instincts.

Singh set aside his curiosity about the Malaysian policeman, and said brusquely, 'Can you get me in to see the suspect?'

The young man nodded. 'Yes, sir. Inspector Mohammad said you would want to see her first so I have already arranged it.'

'I would like to see her in two hours' time. I will familiarise myself with the investigation first.'

The young man saluted. 'In that case, I will get you a cup of tea, sir.'

As the sergeant left the room, Inspector Singh sorted through the papers on the desk and started to read.

The file heading was 'Chelsea Liew' and in brackets were the words 'Singapore IC'. In that short reference was the whole reason for his being in Malaysia: Chelsea Liew was a Singapore citizen. She held a Singapore identity card. She had married a Malaysian and had lived in the Kuala Lumpur suburb of Bangsar for the last twenty years. She had three children who held Malaysian passports. But she was Singaporean. And she was accused of murdering her ex-husband.

As a rule, the arrest of a Singaporean by any foreign country would not have involved the Singapore police. This case was different, though. The religious overtones, custody battles, public outcry in both countries and political sensitivities between Malaysia and Singapore had resulted in a request by the Singapore government—keen to be seen to be doing something—to the Malaysian government—keen to be seen to be above the fray—that a Singaporean policeman be seconded to the investigation. So here he was, sitting in a grubby room in the Malaysian Police Bukit Aman headquarters, with a file three inches thick, feeling very sorry for himself.

Singh looked at the folder. He thought he recognised the efficiency of Sergeant Shukor in the neatly labelled piles of newspaper clippings, court transcripts and police interview notes. He was familiar with the essentials of the matter. But now he sat back in his protesting chair and let the full story unfold before him.

THREE

From the day of their white wedding twenty years before, Chelsea Liew and her Malaysian husband, Alan Lee, had featured regularly in the gossip columns. Even Inspector Singh was aware of the beautiful Singaporean model swept off her feet in a whirlwind romance by the dashing Malaysian, heir to a timber fortune. The fairy tale of a poor but beautiful girl who had gone on to marry one of the most eligible bachelors in Malaysia had captured the public imagination.

Chelsea had given up her modelling career upon marriage. It was rumoured that she had wanted to continue working but her husband had put his foot down. Singh vaguely remembered that his own wife—she of the firm opinions and grim forebodings—had warned that no good ever came of a woman giving up her independence for a man. The inspector had been vaguely irritated by this. She, Mrs Singh, had abandoned her job as a teacher on marrying him and never hinted at a desire to go back, not even when it became apparent that no children would be forthcoming from the marriage. Her bleak outlook for the couple had caused Singh to secretly wish the rich man and his trophy bride well.

But his wife was proved right. The gossip and innuendo had started almost immediately the honeymoon was over. Chelsea Liew's husband was seen out on the town. She had an unexplained black eye. Magazines started to carry pictures of her turning away hurriedly or holding up her handbag to obscure her face. She had three difficult pregnancies, and bore her husband three fine sons.

Alan Lee had been reported as being ecstatic over the birth of his sons and heirs. His business dealings were also generating publicity. He had taken over the family business upon his father's death, bypassing the elder brother, Jasper, who had rejected the timber business and become a wildlife activist. Alan Lee was an important man and his patronage was sought by politicians.

As Chelsea disappeared completely from the public eye, Alan Lee was often photographed with other women, described coyly as his friends or colleagues. Finally, twenty years into the marriage, Chelsea had sued for divorce and sole custody of the children, alleging abuse and adultery.

THE ACCUSATIONS and counter-accusations involved in the case were a large part of the file. The transcripts of the divorce proceedings, with both parties fighting tooth and nail for custody of the children, made vicious and ugly reading. Her medical records showed evidence of traumatic injuries consistent with beatings. Alan had insisted they were self-inflicted and the symptoms of a deranged woman who should not have the care of her children. She had, through her lawyers, asserted persistent adultery. Lee had looked sorry and insisted that he had just needed some comfort after his wife had turned on him. It did not affect his ability to be a good father.

The renegade brother, Jasper Lee, had testified—appearing on behalf of Chelsea. He claimed that Alan Lee, far from being a model parent, was an absent father whose business dealings were so tainted with criminality that he would be an unfit father for his children. Alan Lee's lawyers had done their best to discredit his brother on the grounds he was the frustrated black sheep of the family who, not content with breaking his father's heart by walking out on the family business, was now seeking revenge against the brother who had taken over.

The youngest son of the family, Kian Min, had then stepped in to contradict Jasper, by testifying to Alan Lee's strong character and kind heart. This had caused some surprise. It was no secret that the youngest son had tried to persuade the father, when Jasper had walked out of the business, to give him control of Lee Timber. It had not been an unreasonable request. Alan was a playboy pursuing beautiful women, and had not completed the engineering degree for which he had been sent to the United States. The father had been tempted to bypass his middle son in favour of the youngest.

But Alan, perhaps suspecting that he had pushed his luck far enough, had returned home in the nick of time, settled down with Chelsea, shown a tepid interest in the business; and the rules of primogeniture had triumphed. It was implied in the newspapers that Kian Min, who still worked at the company but was barely on speaking terms with Alan, must have received quite a sweetener to perjure himself on behalf of his despised brother.

Public opinion was favouring the wife when court was adjourned suddenly for two weeks. There was much speculation in the interim as to the reason for the sudden delay. Did Alan believe he was going to lose? Did he have a plan to kidnap the children? Did she? And there was the inevitable suggestion that the judge had an interest in reaching a particular outcome. After all, Alan Lee had money. And money had been known to subvert justice.

In the end, it had been none of these things.

When court reconvened, Alan Lee had dropped his bombshell. Sergeant Shukor had a flair for the dramatic because he had included the court transcript of proceedings and artist sketches of the main characters. Inspector Singh was soon absorbed in the courtroom drama.

THE POLICEMAN HAD INTONED, '*Bangun*' or 'All rise' in a solemn voice. The judge, a huge Indian man with a beak for a nose, walked through the hidden door behind the dais on which he sat. The courtroom had been packed. This was the first day back after the unexpected two-week adjournment. The press, including members of the Singapore press, had queued since early morning to ensure a seat. The lawyers made a show of rustling papers.

The judge had glared at the packed courtroom and waited until there was silence. He asked, 'Are all parties present in the matter of Liew versus Lee?'

He spoke in English, not Malay, holding that Chelsea Liew, a Singaporean, would not be able to follow proceedings.

At the judge's question, Chelsea Liew's counsel said, 'Yes, my lord.'

Alan Lee's lawyer, Mr Loh, was a feisty Chinese man who had a reputation for using every trick in the book to ensure success for his clients. He said now, brightly, 'Yes, my lord!'

'I assume counsel for both parties are ready to proceed with the custody hearings?'

Mr Loh had said unexpectedly, 'We are making an oral application to dismiss these custody proceedings, my lord.'

Chelsea Liew's lawyer had leapt to his feet. 'On what grounds? My lord, the respondent is wasting the court's time!'

The judge said, 'Mr Chandra has a point. On what grounds could I possibly dismiss proceedings? We have almost reached the conclusion of the custody hearings.'

Mr Loh said firmly, 'We are invoking Article 121(1A) of the Constitution of the Federation of Malaysia, my lord.'

There was a muttering in the court as journalists had asked each other what the provision was, and members of the public echoed the question. Alan Lee was smiling. Chelsea Liew had sat up straight on the wooden bench, her anxiety peaking as she had looked from the judge to her lawyer.

Her lawyer did his best. He said, 'Article 121(1A)? But what has that got to do with anything, my lord?' He looked at the judge almost pleadingly.

The judge said, 'You *are* trying my patience, Mr Loh.'

Mr Loh said firmly, 'We are applying to dismiss proceedings on the grounds that this court has no jurisdiction to hear this matter. The proper forum for a custody dispute between the parties is the Syariah court.'

There had been uproar as the massed audience got wind of where the argument was going. The judge rapped his gavel loudly and glared around the court. The volume of noise subsided, although there were still low murmurs.

He turned back to Mr Loh and asked in a long-suffering voice, 'Why should the Moslem religious court—the Syariah court—have jurisdiction?'

Mr Loh had replied, 'My client, Alan Lee, has recently become a Moslem, my lord. All family law matters concerning Moslems are within the jurisdiction of the Syariah court under Article 121(1A) of the Constitution.'

Mr Chandra had said indignantly, 'But Chelsea Liew is not a Moslem. Neither are her children!'

Mr Loh had known he had the upper hand: 'I am not an expert, of course, but I understand the religion of minors under Islamic law is that of the father . . . or he can declare them to be Moslem, which he has done.'

The transcript that Inspector Singh was reading ended rather prosaically with, '*Court adjourned. Applicant, Mdm. Chelsea Liew, caused a disturbance and had to be removed.*'

The newspapers were less reticent about the 'disturbance in court' caused by Chelsea Liew. Inspector Singh found an article from the *Malay Mail*. It had taken the intervention of three policewomen to restrain Chelsea Liew, who was taken into custody and later released without charge.

Her last words to her husband as she was dragged from the courts were, 'I will kill you for this!'

FOUR

In an interview with the press afterwards, Alan Lee had said, 'It is an insult to me and my religion to suggest that I converted to Islam to get custody of my children. Since the break-up of my marriage, I have been looking for spiritual guidance. I found it in Islam. I am proud to be Moslem and look forward to raising my children in the one true faith.'

Turning the page, Inspector Singh saw that the next document was the autopsy report on Alan Lee, killed exactly one week after the tumultuous court hearing. The autopsy had established that Alan Lee had died of injuries sustained from a bullet wound to the chest. He had been shot on a deserted street, 200 yards from his front gate. The gun had not been traced. His wallet, Rolex watch and gold chain were left undisturbed. He was pronounced dead on arrival at the Kuala Lumpur General Hospital.

His ex-wife, Chelsea Liew, had been arrested within hours and charged with his murder.

Inspector Singh tapped his foot, in his trademark white sneakers, against the ground. It was hard, he thought, to believe that Alan Lee's sudden discovery of religion was anything except cynical.

The judge had agreed to adjourn the custody hearing until the various issues of jurisdiction were determined. He had not hidden his contempt for what he saw as a cheap legal trick that brought the administration of justice into disrepute, but the conversion to Islam, suspect as a matter of faith, was a powerful weapon as a matter of law.

Inspector Singh extricated himself from his chair with difficulty, stretched and went in search of Sergeant Shukor. He found him waiting outside the door. He stood to attention and saluted smartly as the inspector came out.

'Have you been here all this while?' asked the inspector.

'Yes, sir. I have been told to stay close to you.'

Inspector Singh shrugged. 'Well then, take me to the widow.'

'I'M HERE TO HELP YOU,' said the inspector, almost pleadingly.

There was no response from the woman sitting opposite him at the table. She was in the small interview room when they arrived, brought up from her cell. But she had not yet uttered a word nor even looked at them. She sat, as she had from the moment they entered the room, knees together, shoulders rounded, head bowed.

The inspector tried again. 'You are a Singapore citizen. The Singapore government sent me to make sure that you are treated fairly.'

This was not an exact truth. The government was largely indifferent to the fate of this woman. It did, however, want to look authoritative and caring in an election year. And public opinion in Singapore was incensed by what it saw as the victimisation of someone they felt they knew personally, so intense and detailed had been the media coverage of the divorce and custody battles.

The policeman could see just enough of Chelsea Liew's face to understand her success as a supermodel, although her recent experiences had left their mark. Her cheekbones were high, almost protruding through translucent skin. She had large almond eyes but they were red-rimmed, with deep blue shadows underneath. Her hair was scraped back firmly and tied in a ponytail. Her lips, so luscious in those cosmetic adverts of the late eighties, were bloodless, dry and chapped. Her neck, thin and long, protruded from an oversized T-shirt. The inspector could see that she was at least six inches taller than him. Even seated and slumped, it was evident that the long legs in baggy prison pyjamas, feet slipped into flip-flops, were of a length to have stridden down catwalks—before marriage and murder had reduced her to silence.

He said, 'If you do not help me, I cannot help you.'

She looked up for the first time, her brown eyes filled with pain. She spoke, the words wrenched out of her. 'Nobody can help me now.'

'Why do you say that?' he asked, more gently than was his wont. The case-hardened policeman felt an unusual sympathy for the accused.

She gestured at the prison walls around her. 'I will only leave this place to walk to my death.'

'Did you kill your husband?'

'You would use that word for twenty years of brutality?'

'What about the children?'

'What can I do for them now?'

'Not much while you're in here.'

Quiet descended on the room again.

The inspector said, 'At least let me talk to people. Find out what happened. Please! It will cost you nothing if I fail. But if I succeed, we might get you out of here and back with your kids.'

She nodded once, a terse gesture, as if she was conferring a favour on him rather than dependent on him to find her an escape route.

Chelsea Liew rose to her feet. Inspector Singh got up too, and watched her shuffle to the door. Sergeant Shukor—Singh had almost forgotten the sergeant was there—opened it for her and she walked out. The waiting policewoman handcuffed her briskly and led her away.

The two men left in the room were a study in physical contrasts. One fit, clean-shaven, well groomed. The other dishevelled, overweight and bearded.

Inspector Singh asked, 'What do you think? Did she do it?'

Shukor shrugged. 'She had the best motive.'

The senior policeman nodded. 'She certainly did. What does Inspector Mohammad think?'

'That she's one hundred per cent guilty, sir.'

The policeman was not surprised. Police work was rarely complicated: locked-door mysteries and multiple suspects were the stuff of fiction. Usually, the person last heard threatening to kill someone who was later found dead was the murderer. He could not even blame Inspector Mohammad; he was not leaping to conclusions, just following the facts.

'What now, sir?' asked Shukor, interrupting his reverie.

'I go to my sister's house for the evening and then back to my hotel.'

'I will get the car, sir—and wait for you in the front.'

ALAN LEE'S BROTHER, Jasper, sat in a small office on the second floor of an old shop house near Chinatown. From his shuttered windows, he could see the red, pagoda-roofed entrance to Petaling Street, bustling and crowded as always.

Jasper was indifferent to the sounds of horns blaring and engines revving under his window: he had learnt to tune out the sounds. He ignored the stink of overflowing, garbage-filled drains mingled with the pungent, eye-watering odour of dried anchovies piled high on the pavements. In the early days, when the freedom of having walked away from the family business and his father's expectations had filled him with a sense of profound relief, he had been delighted by the sights and sounds that were in such contrast to his own privileged upbringing. It was so colourful and raw compared to his stultifying existence under the watchful eye of a stern father.

Those heady, early days of autonomy were behind him, however. His past had caught up with him. He remembered his father's last words, shouted after him in angry Cantonese, as he had stormed out of the family home: 'One day you will understand that your family is what is most important.'

He had disagreed with the old man, insisting instead that shared values were more important than shared blood. He was not so sure any more. His younger brother had been gunned down on a Bangsar street. His sister-in-law was in prison. His mother was in a state of collapse. His three nephews were in the care of Chelsea's mother. God only knew what his youngest brother was doing. Perhaps it did come down to family in the end.

Jasper looked around him at the photos of orangutans stuck to the walls, all taken in the depths of the Borneo rainforest on his excursions into the wilderness. There were wizened patriarchs looking calmly at the camera; young bucks captured on film screeching their aggression at any intruder; family groups of females and their babies. The whole sense was of a gentle, separate community—so different from the ugly reality of his own existence.

He got to his feet slowly, like an old man. There was one more thing he needed to do before making up his mind.

A HEAVY THUNDERSTORM had reduced the traffic they were in to a standstill. The sky was dark although it was still early in the evening. The rain fell like large teardrops, straight down. It was a few years since Inspector Singh had been to Kuala Lumpur and he had forgotten the flash floods and gridlock that rain caused.

The inspector, who had started the day in a bad mood, was now extremely irritable. He contemplated the impossibility of the case that had been dumped on his lap as they inched forwards towards their destination. How was he to investigate the murder of Alan Lee? He had no jurisdiction. The Malaysian police did not intend to be helpful. Inspector Mohammad was going to be a handful. He was being spied on by the young man driving the car, and Chelsea Liew was not cooperating. He had assumed that she would be full of suggestions as to alternative suspects—desperate to save her own neck. Instead, she seemed indifferent to his promised efforts and had given him no information to work with. All he had got was a grudging agreement that he should try to find the truth. And that, he admitted to himself, was the rub. *Was* he looking for the truth? Or was the most obvious answer, quickly seized upon by the Malaysian police, the correct one?

Finally, they drew up outside the house of Inspector Singh's sister. The sergeant indicated that he would be round the corner having dinner at one of the stalls that lined the streets in the evening. The inspector nodded and then, mentally girding himself for the encounter with family, rang the doorbell.

His sister, a large, big-boned woman with a nose Caesar would have been proud to possess, was dressed in a cotton caftan. She nodded to her brother and held the door open to indicate that he was welcome. They did not hug or kiss, despite not having seen each other for over a year: it would have been completely out of character for either of them to have expressed emotion physically. Asians of their generation were not tactile. Affection was expressed, if at all, through food. To make an effort over dinner, to have a few extra dishes, to remember what someone liked best and serve it piping hot—that was the way to show family feeling.

Baljit had been a widow for thirty years. Her husband had died when all three of her children were still under five. He had left her well provided for with a large insurance policy as well as a house, the value of which had increased exponentially over the years as Bangsar changed from a small, rural development to the hub of the Malaysian middle class. Inspector Singh rather suspected that after the initial grief at the death of her husband, she had found the whole arrangement completely satisfactory.

She asked now, seated in the living room: 'How is Dev?'

He answered the enquiry about his wife brusquely, 'Fine; same as usual.'

'Still too thin? Not you. You should eat less. You know what happened to my poor husband!'

She poured him a mug of hot strong tea, thickened and sweetened with condensed milk, as she said this, and pushed a plate heaped with Indian sweetmeats at him.

'What is the use of telling me to diet and then serving me this sort of thing?' asked the inspector tetchily.

She changed the subject. 'Why are you here?'

'I am helping in a Malaysian murder investigation. The chief suspect is Singaporean.'

She said with relish, 'I saw it in the newspapers. I am not surprised she killed him—converting to Islam to keep the children!'

'It is not certain that she did kill him,' pointed out the inspector.

'Don't be silly. Who else?'

'That is what I am here to find out.'

'You are wasting your time, *lah*!'

Later that evening, in his hotel room, Inspector Singh wondered if his sister was right. She was insufferable but she did have a knack, with her direct, tactless observations, of hitting a core truth from time to time. The popular sentiment was that Chelsea Liew had killed her husband and for very good reason, too. Even Moslems were muted in their support for the dead man. The official line, as adopted by the religious authorities, was that any conversion to Islam had to be assumed to come from the heart. However, public sentiment was highly doubtful that a Chinese businessman of dubious repute, locked in a bitter custody battle with his abused wife, would suddenly find God, except as a matter of convenience.

THE SMALL TWO-SEATER Cessna aeroplane was buffeted by wind; it was a wild bouncy ride with the updraughts from the rolling hills. The single propeller on the nose of the aircraft spun vigorously and noisily, as if it was conscious of its responsibility as the only thing between the plane and a long downward spiral into the thick jungle below.

The few human habitations were small and far apart. The larger towns in Borneo all hugged the coast, keeping the jungle on one side and an escape route by sea on the other. The villages in the jungle were indigenous. Treks to the nearest big town could take weeks; even a river ride in a canoe with an outboard motor took days. Only the narrow, short airstrips carved out of the jungle offered a quick way out in an emergency.

Jasper Lee, at the controls of the small plane, envied the villages their seclusion. It was his idea of heaven to be a week in any direction from cities, with their brothels, cinemas and drains. He looked down at the rolling expanse of green. If he went ahead with his plan, he would never again know the rich beauty of Borneo—never hear the chattering of the orangutans nor catch a glimpse of a clouded leopard. He had forced himself to visit Borneo one last time, taking to the air in a hired plane. He had to test his resolve. Jasper wanted to remind himself of what was at stake.

ALAN LEE'S YOUNGER brother sat behind the desk of his dead brother and smiled. He was a slight man, impeccably dressed with expensive elegance. It was an extra-large desk—a little too big for the brother who had inherited it—bare except for a telephone, an Apple MacBook Pro and a notepad with a Mont Blanc pen next to it.

Lee Kian Min had waited a long time to get his feet under the desk of his father and, later, his undeserving brother. He had worked hard, learning the business while his older brothers had pursued orangutans and women respectively. He despised them for their weaknesses and envied them their seniority. But he had always known his time would come.

When Jasper Lee had walked out on the family and almost killed the old man doing so, Kian Min had been sure his moment had arrived. But in the end his father had insisted, despite misgivings, that Alan take over. Kian Min had been devastated. But rather than emulating Jasper and leaving, he stayed, worked hard behind the scenes and kept the company together. When his father died, he continued to do the same. He allowed Alan to play the timber mogul while he quietly controlled the business. He learnt to be patient, to bide his time, to hide his ire when Alan would make one of his sporadic visits to the company offices. And now he had his reward. The company was his and he was going to savour every moment.

INSPECTOR SINGH met Sergeant Shukor at the entrance to the Ritz Carlton. Replete with the hotel buffet breakfast, his belly straining against his shirt, he felt energised and ready to confront the case head on.

'Take me to the morgue,' he ordered. 'I want to meet Alan Lee.'

'I have the autopsy report if you would rather look at that.'

'I've read that. I want to meet Alan Lee!'

They weaved their way towards the hospital, parking some distance away. The morgue was difficult to find: a design feature of hospitals worldwide. An attempt, wondered the inspector, to hide the ultimate destination from those who were nearest to it? It was not conducive to the right frame of mind for recovery to have the morgue signposted for patients.

Inspector Singh was dragged to the present by a wiry hospital orderly dressed in baggy green hospital garb. He was struggling to pull out a steel drawer that contained Alan Lee. With the suddenness of a champagne cork, the drawer popped open. The orderly grinned at them in sweaty triumph.

The policeman turned his attention to the body. It was a bloodless corpse, yellow and dry skinned with closed eyes. Between a few sparse, dark chest hairs, the black hole of the bullet's entry wound was clearly visible, as were the gunpowder burns around the edges.

'He must have been shot at almost point-blank range by someone standing directly in front of him,' remarked the inspector.

'How do you know that, sir?' asked the young sergeant.

'There wouldn't have been powder burns if the bullet had travelled any distance. Also, the burns around the wound are even. That means the bullet went in straight. Otherwise, the burns would be lopsided, more towards one side or the other.'

'What else can you tell, Inspector?' asked the sergeant, trying to distract himself from a growing feeling of queasiness. Alan Lee did not look good.

'I would say that the person who killed him knew him. The killer must have stood in front of him, spoken to him and then shot him. They were face to face when it happened. Also, I think it was an amateur . . . rather than a professional hit.'

This surprised Shukor.

'Only an amateur would have chosen to shoot him in the chest—he might have survived. No, a professional always goes for the head shot. Unless, of course, it was a professional pretending to be an amateur.' His belly laugh reverberated through the cold room. 'That's what makes this job so challenging.'

Shukor grinned and said, 'Where to now, sir?'

'Back to the beautiful widow.'

'THERE IS A possibility that the Syariah court will place the boys in a home,' the inspector said brutally.

For a moment it seemed that he had still not penetrated her isolation. Then Chelsea Liew looked up, sunken eyes staring at him unblinkingly.

'What are you saying?'

'The Syariah court might take them into care.'

'But my mother has them.'

'She is not Moslem.'

'Neither are they.'

The inspector shrugged. 'They are the under-age offspring of a Moslem man who declared them Moslem before he died.'

She snapped, 'I won't let them have my children!'

It was the first real emotion she had shown the inspector. He was delighted, but he hid his pleasure. He said bluntly, 'You won't be able to stop them if you're dead.'

She was silent, so he continued. 'And you will be dead if you are not prepared to defend yourself. You know they will hang you. The judge has no choice if you are found guilty of murder.'

She nodded, more to herself than in acknowledgment of his remarks.

The inspector seemed to be getting through to her, chipping away at the protective wall to provoke an emotional response. It was a cruel thing to do—to use her children as a tool to break through her defences. Inspector Singh acknowledged the fact to himself as he looked into her wide, frightened eyes. He did not hesitate, however, to press home his advantage.

He said, 'Don't imagine there will be any mitigation. He might have beaten you but the killing was a cold-blooded execution.'

Chelsea was silent, and her eyes flickered like those of a trapped beast.

Inspector Singh continued, this time sympathetic, 'You need to be there for your children—and I can help you.'

Chelsea whispered, 'I'm so tired. I didn't want to fight any more. After all, who would believe that it wasn't me who killed him? After what he did to me, after he tried to take my children away . . .' She paused for a moment and added bitterly, 'Besides, I thought if I kept quiet, they would leave the children alone. Forget about this whole Moslem thing . . . I can't believe they're still trying to take the kids. Alan is dead, for God's sake!'

Singh seized the moment. He asked, 'Did you kill him?'

She looked at him as if seeing him with new eyes. She said firmly, 'I didn't kill him—although he deserved to die a thousand times.'

'Why didn't you kill him, if that's how you feel?'

'I considered it,' she said.

'Why didn't you?'

She smiled wryly. 'Someone else got there first? No, I did not kill him because I did not want to end up here, like this—separated from my children.'

Singh nodded. 'Well, whoever did kill your husband hasn't done you any favours. You need to help me find out who did it if you want to get out of here.'

It was her turn to nod.

Inspector Singh was beginning to see the glimmerings of the woman who had fought her powerful husband tooth and nail for custody of her children. Had this strength also led her, when other avenues were proving to be dead ends, to kill her husband?

He asked now, 'Why did you stay with him?'

She sighed, 'At first I loved him, believe it or not. I was very young when we married. Twenty-one. He swept me off my feet. The newspapers and magazines at the time, they did not have to exaggerate—it *was* a fairy tale. Rich man meets poor girl, showers her with gifts and flowers, takes her on exotic holidays, treats her like a queen. I was so naive.'

'And then?' the inspector asked quietly.

'He started to hit me—even when I was pregnant.'

'Why didn't you walk out then?'

'I'm not sure. Why don't women walk out? I used to read all the women's magazines—full of good advice to women trapped in abusive relationships. I didn't even *really* believe I was one of them. Of course, in reality, I was a textbook case. In denial, for my own sake, for my self-respect. For the sake of the children. I don't really know. Alan would always have some excuse— he was stressed with work and just snapped; I had spent too much time talk- ing to some man at a party . . . I doubted myself. Perhaps it *was* somehow my fault. Perhaps I was a lousy wife, a lousy person to have changed him into something so awful. Maybe I was a slut—talking to men at parties.' She tossed her head, a glint of pride. 'It's hard to believe now, but there was a time when men would seek my company.'

He looked at her. Hair drawn back. Pale. Hollow cheeked. Defiant. Meeting his eyes—challenging him to disbelieve that the wreck she was had once been a model.

'I imagine men would seek your company if you walked out of this prison today,' he remarked.

She was embarrassed. Pink flushed through the translucent skin. She said, 'Oh! Those would just be the reporters.'

A knock on the door put an end to the conversation. It was time for her to go back to her cell.

THEY BOTH STOOD outside the prison, young policeman and old. The inspector squinted against the sun. Sergeant Shukor pulled a pair of sunglasses out of his pocket and slipped them on. His wrap-around black shades added to his air of danger and competence. The inspector tried to recall if he had ever looked the part of a professional policeman in the way that the younger man did. He doubted it. He looked down at his sneakers, having to crane to see past his ample stomach. They were extremely grubby after a few days in the dust of Kuala Lumpur.

The inspector sighed and said, 'OK, let's start at the top. If Chelsea did not murder her husband, who did?'

'You believe her, sir?'

'Yes, I do,' said Inspector Singh firmly.

Shukor sighed. He could smell trouble. He liked the policeman from Singapore—he was honest, direct and seemed to care about the people involved in the case. But his being sure of Chelsea's innocence was unhelpful. After all, they only had her denial to go on. How was it that that was enough to convince the senior policeman? He came with a big reputation for success and a bad one for being his own man. He hadn't got either by being gullible.

Singh interrupted his train of thought. 'Well? Who else do we have?'

Shukor said, 'I have no idea, sir.'

'All right. There's work to be done, then. Let's go and find out who killed Alan Lee.'

FIVE

Jasper Lee, back from his fleeting visit to Borneo, was at a Chinese coffee shop. Since leaving the family business, he had managed on a shoestring budget, eschewing by choice his prior lifestyle.

He sat on a stool at a brown, Formica-topped table. The smell of *koay teow* frying, the flames leaping around the wok, triggered an explosion of gastric juices in his stomach. Jasper knew he would enjoy the meal far more than the expensive dishes of exotic, endangered species that an expensive Chinese restaurant would offer him.

He tucked in heartily. In the old days, he would have been unable to eat under pressure as great as he was suffering now. But years on his own had taught him that a failure to eat regularly only exacerbated the nature of the problem he faced.

A cat slipped out from a nearby drain. Heavily pregnant with a mangy coat through which ribs were visible, the cat was no different from the hundreds of other strays that lived in the vicinity of hawker centres. Jasper felt sorry for the beast. Leaving money wedged under his empty glass, he quickly tipped the remaining food on his plate onto the floor. The cat barely waited for him to step away before attacking the food with the ferocity of a mother driven by a biological imperative to look after her unborn young.

Crudely, it put him in mind of his brother's wife, Chelsea. It was no hardship for anyone to believe that she had gunned down his brother to protect her children. He did not feel any anger towards this woman accused of killing Alan. Instead, he wondered what she had eaten for lunch. He had no idea what prison food in Malaysia involved. He shuddered and then steeled himself. He had made up his mind what to do. There would be no turning back now.

'LET'S START AT the beginning and do things the old-fashioned way,' said Inspector Singh.

Shukor hazarded a guess. He had begun to understand the other policeman's elliptical references. 'Who gains from the death of Alan Lee?'

'Yes.'

'No will has turned up.'

'So the kids get everything? How old are they?'

'The oldest boy is seventeen, the other two are twelve and seven.'

'Three boys, huh? I suppose that the oldest might have fancied some spare cash if his father kept him short?' The inspector did not sound convinced by his own accusation.

Shukor said, 'It's more complicated than that, sir.'

'What do you mean?'

'If it is finally agreed that Alan Lee died a Moslem, the Islamic laws on intestacy are not the same as for non-Moslems.'

Singh rolled his eyes. 'Give it to me straight. Who gets the incredible wealth of Alan Lee under Islamic law?'

'To be frank, sir, I don't know. But I think there will be shares for the family—the brothers as well as the sons; maybe even Chelsea.'

'Let's not bring Chelsea back into it. She has motives to spare. But the brothers might get something?'

'I'll check with a lawyer, sir—but probably, yes.'

The inspector looked thoughtful.

Shukor said diffidently, 'There's one more thing, sir. The family holding in Lee Timber . . . It was placed in a trust by the father. Kian Min inherits after Alan.'

'What?'

'Kian Min gets Lee Timber, sir. It is only the rest of the wealth, cash, property and so on, that is divided up amongst the rest of the family.'

'You know something, Shukor? It sounds to me like Lee Kian Min had a damn good motive to do away with his brother.'

JASPER LEE WALKED to his appointment concentrating on the here and now. He walked along the kerb in dusty shoes looking at his feet as he put one ahead of the other. He noticed that he walked with quick, small strides and consciously slowed down. There was no particular hurry.

He understood now why people talked about their lives flashing before their eyes. In his case, it was not so much his whole life but a highlights reel. Peculiarly, he was neither seeing his past nor re-living it. It was the sensations associated with significant moments that flowed over him: he heard the door slam behind him as he left home for the last time; smelt the scent of the woman he loved the first time he met her; felt the wind rush through his hair as he piloted his little plane high above the rainforests. It was a mosaic of emotion and experience, a reward for doing the right thing.

Jasper Lee walked into the Bukit Aman police station and cleared his throat to catch the attention of the duty sergeant, who was immersed in the sports pages of the afternoon tabloid, his half-eaten packet of rice and curry, wrapped in banana leaf and newspaper and tied up with a rubber band, on the desk in front of him. The policeman dragged himself away from his newspaper long enough to look up and ask grumpily, '*Ya*?'

Jasper Lee said firmly, without hesitation, 'I have come to confess to the murder of my brother, Alan Lee.'

THE YOUNG MAN of mixed parentage looked at himself in the full-length mirror. Ravi liked what he saw. He wore a black T-shirt firmly tucked into low-cut, hip-hugging denim jeans and a broad belt with a square, masculine buckle. His hair was cut close to a well-shaped head. He looked fit, he thought. He took care of himself. But he made sure to keep his look natural. Only he knew the effort that went into his careless good looks.

Looking at his reflection with admiration, he could not understand why Chelsea had refused to see him. After all, he had taken a big risk asking for her at the prison. Nobody knew about him. About them. He had been willing to take a chance on being found out but she had rebuffed his attempt without even the courtesy of seeing him first.

Mind you, she had rebuffed his early efforts to get to know her, too. But he had played his cards well. He, Ravi, was experienced in the ways of rich, lonely women. He had treated Chelsea with studious, old-fashioned courtesy, listening to her stories with a sympathetic ear. Finally, she had started to open up, unburden herself. Really talk to him. As he had guessed from the start—it was the same with the other abused women he had targeted—she was only too willing to sleep with him the moment she started talking to him. For women like Chelsea Liew, the commitment was communication. Sex was a reward to men who had earned her trust.

They had managed their relationship very well; the husband had never suspected. Alan Lee had been a little bit too confident that he had beaten his wife into submission. It was easy to arrange assignations. Interludes between shopping trips while the kids were in school. He had Chelsea precisely where he wanted her—dependent on him for emotional solace and physical pleasure. The small gifts she gave him had turned into cash handouts.

But to his intense annoyance, she had broken off all contact the minute the custody battle for the children had begun. He had protested that they were discreet, nobody need find out about their liaison, but she was firm. She was not going to give her husband any ammunition in the battle for the children. She, who was alleging adultery as grounds for divorce and custody, did not intend to be caught, literally, with her pants round her ankles.

Ravi had hoped to go back to the well a few more times. But if it was not possible, he could live with that. He knew when to cut his losses and walk away. There were plenty of other rich, lonely women in Kuala Lumpur.

But then Alan Lee had been killed. What a euphoric moment! He had sent her a letter immediately, professing undying love, predicting a future together, talking about his willingness to be a father to her children. She had not responded but he had not been worried. With the husband out of the way, he would soon insinuate himself back into her good graces, her bed and hopefully marriage—his ticket to the good life.

He could not believe it when Chelsea was arrested for murder: his golden goose was about to be hanged from the neck. And to add insult to injury, she would not even see him. He kicked his bed in frustration and scuffed one of his ankle boots. Taking a piece of cloth, he sat down and started polishing the spot with neat circular movements.

SERGEANT SHUKOR'S mobile phone rang. He extricated the phone with his left hand: his right hand was still soiled from tucking into his lunch of *roti telur* and dhal curry.

He was sitting across from Inspector Singh, who ignored the contortions of his Malaysian colleague as he tried to answer the phone with one hand. He wiped his plate clean with his last piece of *thosai*—an Indian bread made with rice and lentil flour.

The sergeant was nodding his head, listening to the man at the other end of the phone. He waved his hand in the air, signalling for the bill. Inspector Singh glared at him, indicating with a curt shake of the head that the sergeant was being premature: the older policeman fancied some dessert.

But his subordinate tapped the phone—whatever the message was, it could not wait. As the bill arrived, Inspector Singh took a handful of grubby ringgit from his pocket and tossed them on the table. He followed Shukor out into the blazing sunshine and blinked as his eyes watered in the unexpected light.

'What's the matter? What's happened?' asked the inspector.

'There's been a confession.'

'A confession? Chelsea has confessed?' Singh's heart sank.

'No. Not her. The brother! Jasper Lee has just confessed.'

'Confessed to what?'

'His brother's murder!'

'But why? Why did he kill Alan Lee?'

'No idea, *lah*!' exclaimed the young policeman. 'Let's go and find out.'

THE MALAYSIAN POLICE now had two people in jail for the murder of Alan Lee, and Inspector Singh was incensed.

'Why can't you just release her?' he asked angrily.

'You should understand, Inspector. We cannot release her until the prosecutor drops the charges or the judge dismisses the case. The prosecutor won't dismiss the case yet because he doesn't know the details of this new confession—maybe Jasper Lee and the widow were working together?'

'Don't be ridiculous!' snapped the inspector.

Inspector Mohammad shrugged.

'OK, why doesn't the judge order her release?'

'Holiday, I'm afraid,' he said laconically.

'What?'

'The judge is on holiday.'

Inspector Singh kicked the table. It was the height of rudeness but he could not bottle up his frustration. Chelsea Liew was innocent but they would not let her go.

'What about another bail application?'

'Her lawyer is working on it, I believe. I wouldn't worry, Singh. She'll be out soon enough.'

The fight went out of him. He, of all people, knew the bureaucracy of a police force. The Malaysian police were not going to come out of this smelling of roses: having incarcerated the beautiful mother of three children while a murderer roamed free, they were not going to compound any errors by acting hastily at this late stage.

Inspector Mohammad was looking at his Singaporean colleague with interest. 'You were convinced she was innocent, weren't you? I mean, even before this confession from the brother.'

Inspector Singh nodded.

'Why? On what grounds?'

Singh thought hard, understanding that the policeman was asking him a serious question. Finally, he said, 'I'm not sure I *was* convinced, to be honest. But she had so much strength and what looked like . . . integrity, I thought I'd take her word for it and look around for another possibility. And there seemed to be a few about—although I never suspected Jasper.'

Mohammad nodded ruefully. 'Well, I owe you an apology, I suppose. I was sure she'd done it. Didn't look under many rocks after that . . .'

It was handsomely said and Singh felt respect for the man. He shook the Malaysian's hand and realised there was nothing to prevent him going back to Singapore. He had been sent to see that Chelsea got a fair deal. The outcome was even better than that. She would walk free.

His superiors in Singapore would have to find some other way of forcing him into early retirement.

Singh debated asking Shukor to take him to the airport and then thought better of it. He had a curiosity to see how things turned out. He would hang around for a few days.

Inspector Mohammad must have guessed his reluctance to leave as he said, 'Would you like to sit in on the interview with Jasper Lee?'

It was an olive branch, and Inspector Singh seized it at once. The men set off for the labyrinth of detention cells.

IT WAS AN interview with Jasper Lee but he was not saying much. The Malaysian policemen were persistent, demanding answers—pointing out that he was putting his head in a noose. The self-confessed murderer was indifferent. If anything, he seemed slightly amused by their efforts.

He said again, 'I've told you I killed him, shot him in the chest. What more do you want?'

'What weapon did you use?'

'What do you think?' asked Jasper, cuttingly. 'A gun, of course.'

'What sort of gun?'

'How do I know? The kind you point and shoot.'

'Where did you get it?'

Jasper shrugged. 'You can always buy these things if you really want to.'

His insouciance was starting to visibly irritate the policeman asking the questions. Inspector Singh suspected that if he had not been there, they might have considered roughing him up by now. And he could see why they might be tempted. This man, voluntarily confessing to murder and somehow finding it amusing, *was* extremely tiresome. But perhaps he, Singh, was doing the Malaysian police a disservice. He could not picture the placid Sergeant Shukor beating up a prisoner. As for Inspector Mohammad, he was the most correct gentleman Singh had ever come across.

Inspector Singh looked at Jasper curiously. He was a small, plump man. Conservatively, but casually, dressed. Not handsome like his brother, Alan, had been. In fact, fate had rather cruelly made him a caricature of his good-looking younger brother. He was shorter and rounder, with receding hair and big ears. Despite his bravado, there were bags under his dark eyes behind their black, plastic frames, and he looked tired. He was cheerful now but he had been losing sleep in the recent past, perhaps weighing up his decision to come in and confess. It took courage to face a mandatory death penalty.

Inspector Singh asked, 'Why did you kill him?'

Inspector Mohammad's lips thinned with displeasure that the inspector from Singapore was inserting himself into the interview process.

Singh asked again, 'Why did you do it? There must be some explanation! He was your brother.'

Jasper Lee shrugged. 'Any number of reasons, actually. Alan Lee was cruel and corrupt. I despised him for what he was doing to the environment. He deserved to die for that alone.'

'What?' said Inspector Singh. 'You killed your brother to stop him cutting down a few trees?'

'Yes. But it's not just a few trees, is it? He and his cronies are cutting swathes through the jungles of Borneo. Bribing, or if that fails, intimidating everyone who gets in their way. Men like him are destroying the rainforests. Sometimes, if you want to protect something you care about, you have to take extreme steps.'

Sergeant Shukor had the last surprised word in the face of the unexpected motive. He said, '*You dah gila, ke?*' Have you gone quite mad?

'HE'S LYING,' SAID Chelsea flatly.

The inspector stared at her in surprise. 'What do you mean?'

She said again, 'Jasper's lying. He did not kill Alan.'

'He confessed!'

She shook her head angrily. 'I don't care. Jasper is not capable of killing anyone. He's far too gentle.'

'Why would he confess, then?'

'How do I know? Maybe one of your chums beat him up.'

Inspector Singh took a deep breath, trying to keep a lid on his temper. He said patiently, 'For your information, I've just been with Jasper Lee while the Malaysian police interviewed him. No one laid a finger on him. They didn't have to. I've never seen anyone confess to premeditated murder with such enthusiasm.'

Chelsea Liew snorted. A derisive, disbelieving sound.

The inspector continued, 'You do realise what you are saying, don't you? His confession gets you off the hook. Your lawyers are applying for bail again. The prosecutor is bound to drop the charges. Or the judge will dismiss them. You will soon be a free woman!'

Chelsea Liew looked at the inspector in disgust. 'You think I'm better off because some *other* innocent goes to the gallows?'

'Actually, yes—I do think it's better that they hang the man who confesses to a murder rather than a battered wife and mother of three who has protested her innocence all along!'

Singh was alone in the cell with Chelsea. The Malaysian police had left it to him to break the news of Jasper's confession to her—washing their hands of the Singaporean whom they had wrongly held for one long month.

Singh had been more than willing to be the bearer of such good news. He had pictured her surprise as colour flooded back into her pale face. Instead, he had this unexpected, persistent denial. He did not understand it. He tried again.

'Nobody who is innocent confesses to a murder where the penalty is certain death.'

'In your experience?' she asked, her voice tinged with sarcasm.

He was stung by this and snapped angrily, 'In my many, many years of experience, yes!'

She was sitting on her chair, sunk slightly into it, knees higher than her lap with two arms round them. Now she uncoiled and stood, looking down at him from her greater height.

She said, enunciating each word carefully, as if talking to a child or an idiot, 'Jasper Lee did not kill anyone.'

He grabbed her arm. 'There is only one way you could know that for sure!'

She wrenched free angrily. 'Now you are accusing me of murder again? No! I am not confessing . . . Unlike the combined talent of the Singapore and Malaysian police force, I just know an innocent person when I see one.'

He changed tactics. 'Fine! What does it matter to you whether he did it or not? You get out and go home to your kids!'

She sat down on the seat again. Defensive, tired but not quite defeated. She said, 'I will. I will do that. I owe it to my children not to walk away from an open door. But then I will work to clear Jasper's name!'

Singh said tiredly, 'That could land you right back in here.'

'So be it.'

'JASPER HAS CONFESSED!'

The man at the other end of the phone could hear the excitement in Kian Min's voice. He asked, 'That means we can go ahead?'

There was a silence punctuated by static crackling on the line.

Again the question was asked. 'Mr Lee, are you there? Can we go ahead?'

After a few more moments of hesitation: 'Yes, OK. You can go ahead.'

Wai Ming, who preferred to be known as Bruce—after his boyhood idol, Bruce Lee—punched the air once. Then he walked out of his trailer and shouted in dialect, 'The time for waiting is over!'

A muted cheer could be heard from the men. One or two stubbed out cigarettes; a couple of others went back to the job of oiling and cleaning their guns with extra care.

The dew hung like individual teardrops at the tip of each leaf. A fine mist reduced visibility slightly. It was still cool. It would take a while for the sun to penetrate the canopy and warm the jungle at ground level.

They moved out and started walking in single file along the river bank. On their left, the muddy brown Rajang moved sluggishly through Borneo towards the South China Sea. A sudden excited chattering broke the stillness of the jungle. The men, acting of one mind, stopped in their tracks. Overhead, a group of macaque monkeys gesticulated excitedly. They soon got tired of this sport and made off as a unit, deeper into the jungle. The men started again, keeping their eyes peeled, scanning the horizon for tell-tale signs of human activity. They kept a close eye on the river, too, wary of crocodiles masquerading as logs, on the lookout for an easy breakfast.

CHELSEA LIEW'S EYES flashed. There were spots of high colour on her cheeks. She was wearing a headscarf, worn by pious Moslem women to indicate modesty and religiosity. It was a common enough sight in Malaysia where growing numbers of Moslem women had adopted the headdress worn round the head, all hair tucked away and invisible, with a full cloak reaching almost to waist level, draping the upper body. Pressure from menfolk, peer pressure, genuine choice—it was difficult to know why so many women had adopted the stricter Islamic code of dress, although the full burqa was still fairly uncommon. Those dressed in the black, shapeless gowns, with gloves and an opaque veil, tended to be part of the huge contingent of oil-rich, Arab tourists who came to Malaysia to shop for designer clothes to wear under their black coveralls.

Chelsea Liew wore a transparent gossamer headscarf lined with beads. Her hair peeped out enticingly. It could hardly have been the intention of the Syariah court, in insisting on a mandatory head covering for women appearing before the court, whether Moslem or not, to enhance the appeal of the wearer. But that was what they had achieved in the case of Chelsea Liew.

Chelsea's relief at her release from prison had immediately turned sour. She had gone home to her children. They had asked her no questions, too thankful to have their mother back to question the manner of her return. Chelsea knew that at least Marcus, the eldest boy, knew that she was out of jail because their uncle had confessed—it was in all the newspapers. But she acquiesced to his withdrawn silence, thankful for the respite from the immediate past.

And then she had received an official document from the Syariah court requiring her presence at a custody hearing regarding her children. Apparently, the Islamic Council felt it necessary to seek custody of her children, the offspring of a Moslem man, rather than have them brought up by a non-Moslem mother. It was their view that the children would be better off fostered in a Moslem home, and they had applied to the Syariah court for the children to be placed with Moslem caregivers.

Chelsea had frantically consulted her lawyers, only to discover that they did not have *locus standi*, the right to appear, before the Syariah court. Their practice was wholly before the parallel civil jurisdiction that held sway in Malaysia over most matters, except that of Moslem family law. Her lawyers could advise but they could not appear. Finally, she had found a Moslem lawyer to represent her and they had arrived for the hearing, only to be barred at the door. Her clothing, knee-length skirt and jacket over long-sleeved blouse, was not modest enough for the presiding judge. Her lawyer had hastily arranged a twenty-four-hour adjournment. Chelsea was now dressed in the customary Malay dress, the *baju kurung*, a shapeless long-sleeved, knee-length blouse with a closed neck, a long maxi-skirt and the required scarf.

In the end, in the manner of all courts, religious or secular, the hearing was postponed. The judge, dressed in long black robes and sporting the fist-length beard believed by some Moslems to be required of their religion, was anxious to usher them all out of his courtroom. The law and his personal sympathies were pulling in opposite directions. He would give everyone a few weeks to mull things over.

OUTSIDE, THE RAIN BEAT DOWN. The sky was an impenetrable dark grey. Crashes of thunder followed hard on the heels of bolts of lightning that lit up the heavens and caused the air around them to tingle with electricity. At least the rain had thinned the ranks of waiting reporters. A few stood huddled together, under voluminous raincoats, next to the main entrance of the courthouse building. Chelsea deliberately unwound her head covering, shook out her hair and stuffed the scarf into her handbag.

The inspector had found out about the hearing from the newspapers and had decided to attend. He had a curiosity about this woman, as well as a concern. Looking at the teeming downpour now, Singh did not have much hope of summoning one of the beat-up red and white taxis that plied the streets: there was hardly any traffic on the roads, an unusual occurrence in Kuala Lumpur. The inspector glanced at Chelsea and caught her eye. She shouted to be heard above the rain and beckoned imperiously, her summons emphasised by a clap of thunder. 'Come with me. I want to talk to you!'

Docilely, he walked over and her chauffeur held a large golf umbrella over his head, ushering him into the Mercedes Benz.

This was a different woman from the creature whom he had first met behind bars. That Chelsea had been tired, defeated. But now, free, rested and in a battle to maintain custody of her children, the indomitable woman he had sensed even in her darkest hours was back. And, free from prison and no longer a suspect in her ex-husband's murder, she had been allowed to resume the trappings of his wealth—the car, the clothes, the chauffeur. He did not begrudge her a cent of it. She had paid for the accoutrements of the rich in blood and tears.

Inspector Singh sat next to her on the cream leather seats in the back of the car but did not say a word. He was happy to let her break the silence when she was ready. His superiors in Singapore had got wind that Chelsea was a free woman and were insisting that he get back to Singapore—he was booked on an evening flight that day. He was glad that he would have a chance to speak to Chelsea Liew before he left. He needed to get a sense, for his own peace of mind, that she had the tools and courage to fight.

The electric gates of the Lee residence drew open and the Mercedes purred into the driveway. The gates immediately closed behind them. He could see the closed-circuit television cameras on every promontory, covering every angle. In the distance he could hear the deep sound of big dogs barking: there was a guard dog contingent on the premises.

Chelsea must have guessed the direction his thoughts were taking because she said, 'Didn't do him much good, did it?' She nodded her head in the general direction of the barking dogs to indicate what she meant.

'Where exactly was he killed?' asked the inspector. 'I know it was in the vicinity of the house.'

She nodded coolly. 'Yes, he was shot about two hundred yards down the road. If the car was needed to go and pick up one of the children from school, the driver sometimes dropped him off at the bottom of the hill. Whoever killed him knew that.'

They were out of the car now and walking in at the main door. Two children ran down the stairs and then pulled up short when they saw their mother had a guest. The inspector tried to smile at them in a friendly manner, but it was more of a nervous grimace. It was a long time since he had interacted with children. They glared at him, indifferent to his overtures.

Chelsea said, 'Boys, I have a guest I need to talk to. Will you both go upstairs and play for a while?'

The younger boy asked, 'Is he going to take you away?'

She said calmly, 'Of course not.'

Beside her, the inspector shook his head to emphasise her denial.

The boys turned and went back up the stairs, dragging their heels to indicate a general reluctance. Chelsea watched them go, an indecipherable expression on her face. Then she turned to the inspector and said in a sprightly tone, 'Tea?'

She was interrupted by the appearance of a surly youth. Chelsea said, 'Inspector Singh, this is my eldest son, Marcus.'

Singh held out his hand. Marcus looked at him in disdain and walked out of the room.

Singh watched him go. He turned to the widow. 'Kids, eh?'

SIX

Inspector Singh sipped his tea from a delicate bone-china teacup. The fragile thing looked out of place in his large hand.

Across from him, Chelsea also sipped her tea. He could smell it—it was a fragrant green tea. He hated the stuff—give him a strong black tea any day—but the smell was like a slice of heaven. Singh noticed that Chelsea's fingernails were trimmed and glossy, but colourless: she had found time for a manicure. Her hair, too, was trimmed and shining, still coiled in a bun on her head. As he stared at her, she pulled off the jewelled clips and her hair cascaded down her shoulders. He was sure that he had seen a TV shampoo advertisement once where she had done the same thing.

Chelsea shook out her hair and said, 'You have no idea how wonderful it is to be clean! I've been scrubbing for days to get prison off my skin.'

He did not respond. Inspector Singh was not the sort to indulge in small talk. Not when murder was the subtext of the conversation.

Chelsea changed tactics smoothly. She said, 'You must be wondering why I asked you back here. Now that you've done your job and I'm free.'

He shrugged to indicate a willingness to hear her out, but also to deny anything as crude as curiosity.

'I need your help.'

'What can I do?' he asked, puzzled.

'I want you to clear Jasper. You know, find out who actually killed Alan.'

'I am a policeman from Singapore, not a private investigator for hire,' he said crossly. 'My flight back is booked for tonight.'

'You have to stay.'

'I can't! And, anyway, even if I did, I would be of no use to you. I was sent here to look after your interests. You're out of jail. My job is done.' He added as an honest afterthought, 'Not that your getting out had anything to do with me, in the end.'

She did not say anything. The rigidity of her shoulders was the only sign of her tension.

The inspector asked, 'Why me?'

She looked at him, eyes pleading. 'I don't know anyone else with the skills to find a murderer. And I trust you to look out for my interests.'

'What makes you think you can trust me?'

She did not answer. He knew she was right, though. She could trust him. Somehow or other, she had got under his skin.

He said heavily, 'I could lose my job!'

A TWIG SNAPPED underfoot and the leader turned to glare at his companions. He was distracted from censuring the culprit by the sight that he was looking for—a thin, curling wisp of smoke in the distance. He pointed at it with his thumb. The men made their way towards it until they could smell the cooking fire. With a wave of one hand, the leader indicated that the men were to spread out. They did, splitting into two columns and surrounding the small native encampment. The Penan, a nomadic tribe who wander about the Borneo rainforest in small communal groups, were gathered around a small river turtle being turned on a spit. Except for one or two young men who were wearing T-shirts, the men wore loincloths and the women were bare breasted. All were barefoot. It was a cheerful breakfast get-together: a wizened old man was telling a story in a high, quavering voice to a group of young men who were largely ignoring him, while a young woman deftly lifted the spit and sliced the turtle onto a large green banana leaf.

The men waited for the signal. It came in the form of a sudden yell from their leader. They rushed into the encampment, scattering the gathered crowd. Women fled into the jungle clutching their children. A few men tried to protest. They were thrown to the ground and clubbed with thick wooden staffs. The old Penan man sat cowering, never moving from his spot.

One of the men unstrapped the jerry can he carried from his back and began to pour petrol over the area. He set the whole place on fire, stopping for a moment to admire his handiwork.

The leader grabbed the old man by the arm and yanked him to his feet. He shouted at him in Malay, 'You understand me?'

The old man nodded, his terror showing through cataract-filled eyes.

A young, pregnant woman with long black hair and a gentle face rushed over to his aid. She stood in front of the old man and glared at the intruders.

The leader grabbed her by the arm and yanked her towards him. He said, 'Go! Take your filthy kind and leave this place. If we see a Penan in this jungle, we will kill him. Do you understand?'

The woman managed a nod.

She was flung to the ground. She landed awkwardly and yelped with pain. The old man bent over her. The leader kicked him once in the knee for good measure. He fell. The man aimed another kick at him. He rolled over to escape; the pregnant woman took the whole weight of the boot. She curled up silently, trying to protect her stomach and the unborn child within.

The leader gave a whistle and his men fell in behind him. He led them back into the jungle, well satisfied. That had been quick and easy. But there were other communities to track down.

INSPECTOR SINGH TOOK a leave of absence. He had accumulated a lot of leave, hardly ever having taken time off in the course of his career. His superiors did not ask him what he intended to do. If they had, and if he had been honest, they would have ordered him back to Singapore at once. Instead, he implied that there was some sort of family crisis involving his sister. And since he was on the spot, he felt he should take a few days off and try and fix the problem.

Having been sent to try and avert a scandal, Inspector Singh was now well placed to become one himself. For, against his better judgment, he had agreed to Chelsea's request to stay on and try to help Jasper Lee. It was an absurd assignment, even more ridiculous than his original remit to keep an eye on Chelsea and make sure she got a modicum of due process. At least she had always protested her innocence. Second time around, he was being asked to look out for a man who had blithely confessed to being a murderer.

But Chelsea Liew appealed to his dormant masculinity. It was a long time, the inspector thought, since any woman had made him feel needed. Chelsea had explained her concerns in hushed, heartfelt tones. The Malaysian police were not going to look any further for a killer. They were embarrassed at having charged the wrong person once. She could not turn to any private investigator: she could not be certain that they were on her side. They would be in it for her money and the kudos of such a high-profile job. Probably they would sell any dirt they dug up to the tabloids. She needed a professional. And he was it. After all, she had pointed out, he had been sent to help her in the first place.

Finally, Singh had agreed—corpulent knight to the rescue. Afterwards, he could not quite remember the point that the conversation had ceased to be about whether he would help but about how he would help.

She had put a slender hand on his arm and said, 'Thank you. You have no idea how much this means to me.'

And he could see both that she meant it and that he was trapped.

Singh had no idea how he was going to proceed. He had no *locus* to ask questions. He had Chelsea's support, which might open a few doors but not many. And he would certainly need the cooperation of the Malaysian police if he was going to try snooping around.

He did not even know if Jasper would be willing to see him.

'MUM, IS UNCLE Jasper in jail?'

Chelsea looked at her eldest son. Marcus was a thin and wiry seventeen-year-old with a teenager's quick passions. But, of late, the feisty, combative youth had become quiet, his eyes always on the ground in front of him. She told herself that it was inevitable that recent events had taken their toll.

She had not answered his question and Marcus asked again, 'Is Uncle Jasper in prison?'

She nodded and tried to put her arms round him but he resisted and pulled away.

'For killing Daddy?'

'Yes,' she said.

'Do you believe he did it?'

She shook her head emphatically.

Marcus punched a door, hard.

Chelsea looked at him, her face creased with intense concern. Of her three sons, it was Marcus she was most worried about. The other two, with the resilience of children, were recovering from their ordeal. They were insecure, clinging and demanding—punishing her for having left them. But she did not doubt that time would restore their equilibrium. Marcus was another matter. He was the one who had understood a little of what she had gone through being married to Alan Lee.

It had started to affect his behaviour well before the divorce. Seventeen years old, with a driving licence and the Mercedes sports car his father had bought him as a birthday present over Chelsea's angry protests, he was always out or locked in his room. She knew he went clubbing. She could smell the stale cigarettes and old beer on his clothes and his breath in the morning. She knew he had girlfriends, impressing them with his fast car, moneyed background and devil-may-care attitude. She could see the hatred he felt for his father, as well as a burning anger at her, Chelsea, because she was his mother and she had let herself be hurt, and there was nothing that he could do.

As the divorce had approached, Marcus had calmed down—relieved perhaps that his mother was taking steps to leave his father. He was still out of the house at all hours but seemed happier. Chelsea had wondered if he had found a serious girlfriend. But during the custody hearings, he had reverted to his old ways: she had found bottles of alcohol in his room; he never washed or changed his clothes. She had asked him whether he was worried that his father might get custody; assured him that she was going to win.

He had laughed bitterly and said, 'I'm seventeen, Mum. Neither of you has any control over me—it doesn't matter a damn which of you has "custody".'

She had not been able to work out what was upsetting him. She could not find a way through the wall her son had erected round himself.

INSPECTOR SINGH STILL had the file on the murder. It was time to look at it again—this time with a view to exonerating Jasper. He sat down at the desk in his hotel room.

Three hours later he stood up, felt his knees creak with the effort, and left the hotel in a taxi. Any plans to think about the contents of the file he had just read were soon lost in the important business of hanging on to his seat as the driver weaved his way through traffic, missing each motorbike by inches and every car by less.

The taxi stopped some way from the scene of the murder. Singh told himself this was in order to understand the general environment of the crime better, but it was actually because he was starting to feel carsick. He got out, gave the driver a few ringgit and looked around him.

In every direction, rows of terraced houses stretched. Inspector Singh got his bearings in consultation with a road map and set off towards the murder scene. It was a quiet part of the morning. There was not much traffic on the road; the school and work rush was over and the lunch rush had not started. He would have to come back in the evening and gauge the traffic. Was it likely that nobody had seen anything, or were witnesses reluctant to come forward and be associated with this notorious case?

It took him five minutes to reach the spot where Alan had been shot. Here it was easier to imagine that the murderer had gone unnoticed. It was a quiet cul de sac. The crowded terraced houses had given way to individual bungalows hidden behind high walls and security cameras. The blue from swimming pools could be seen through front gates. Balinese-style villas complete with stone gargoyles and frangipani trees stood next door to mansions that had evidently used the White House as their design inspiration.

Inspector Singh dragged himself away from an awed perusal of the houses to contemplate the crime that had taken the life of one of its residents.

According to his chauffeur's testimony, Alan Lee had alighted from his car, waved his driver away and turned to walk up the hill along the broad, quiet road leading to his unhappy home. He had not gone further than fifty yards when he met the person who had shot him. The murder weapon had not been recovered although the police had scoured the drains and the rubbish tips over a 500-yard radius. Alan Lee's valuables were left untouched. The murderer had wanted the only thing that a man of Lee's wealth could not replace—his life.

The inspector stood silently, looking around him. Trying to understand, trying to visualise the murder. He was convinced, based on the forensics, that Alan Lee had known his killer. It was possible that the perpetrator had been frightened off before he had completed the robbery, but it struck the inspector as improbable. It seemed far-fetched that robbery was a motive or, if it was, that the killer would have abandoned his crime before completing it.

Singh walked all the way up to the gates of Alan Lee's residence. He did not know if Chelsea was home and he did not seek to find out. He had nothing to report. She wanted him to exonerate her brother-in-law, Jasper Lee. But the inspector did not conduct murder investigations based on who he most wanted to exculpate. He conducted investigations to find a murderer.

In his heart he knew he would be pleased if he could find proof, contrary to the widow's wishes, that implicated Jasper Lee. If he could prove to Chelsea that Jasper had done it, his confession was in earnest, she would abandon this effort to prove him innocent and get on with her life. Inspector Singh was not of a mind to contemplate the alternatives: if Jasper had not done it, the prime suspect would, once again, be the ex-wife of the victim.

Singh decided he needed access to Jasper Lee. He dug out his mobile phone and called Sergeant Shukor. He said without preamble, 'Singh here. I need to see Jasper Lee.'

'Why?'

'Chelsea has asked me to look into the murder. Find some mitigating circumstances if I can.'

He decided the complete truth—that he was seeking to absolve the eldest brother—would be too much for the young sergeant to stomach.

There was hesitation. At last, the policeman said, 'I can get you in. But if Inspector Mohammad finds out, I'll be in big trouble.'

'I won't tell him if you don't.'

THE MEN SITTING around the polished wood table were pleased. Things were going well. China's need for wood products was inexhaustible. Ever since the severe flooding around the Yangtze River a few years back, the Chinese government had cracked down hard on excessive or illegal logging on the mainland. But this had not in any way dampened the demand for wood for the massive ongoing construction site that was modern China. And the authorities, so belatedly mindful of the degradation to their own environment, turned a blind eye to wood sourced from overseas. As a result, primary forests across Asia, from Papua New Guinea to Borneo, were being denuded at a rate that would soon see the end of the great jungles of Asia.

None of these things was a concern to the men in the room. They were at the profitable end of the destruction. The four of them were fellow directors of Alan Lee's timber company. The boss was dead but the men were still doing their best to make money for the company under the guidance of their new boss, Lee Kian Min. Besides, Kian Min had been running the show for years. It would have been much harder to carry on if he had been the one killed.

Kian Min walked into the room, took the seat at the head of the table, received their respectful greetings and said, 'We are increasing our production out of Borneo.'

There were nods of approval all around.

'How come? I thought we had logged all the non-reserve land?' asked one of the men with nonchalant curiosity.

'Don't worry about it,' said Kian Min. 'We have found new areas.'

The others understood the implications of this. New areas, after generations of intense logging, meant wildlife reserves and protected forests.

'You need to be careful—there is a lot of concern. Those Penan are in the news every day,' said one of the men.

'I said no need to worry about it. I have everything under control.'

'What about the bio-fuels project?'

'That is also under control.'

'CHELSEA DOES NOT accept that you killed your brother.'

'And you believe her rather than me?' Jasper's question to the inspector seemed reasonable.

'Actually, no,' said the inspector.

'Then why are you here?'

'I'm not sure,' the inspector confessed with a sigh. 'I am going to lose my job when my bosses get wind of this . . . I guess I could never resist the request of a pretty woman.'

'Tell me about it,' said Jasper. 'Chelsea can be very persuasive.'

The inspector was quick to latch on to this. 'Are you saying that she persuaded you to confess?'

Jasper looked pained. 'Don't be ridiculous! She would never do that. She didn't try. And, anyway, why would I agree?'

The inspector changed tactics. 'Look, I accept you murdered your brother. At least tell me why. Then I can convince Chelsea you did it and go home. She does not seem to be prepared to accept your word for it.' He added a sweetener. 'Maybe I can find some mitigation—save you from hanging at least.'

'Like what?'

'Anything—self-defence, provocation, accident. Anything!'

Jasper looked at the inspector long and hard.

The policeman could see that prison was taking its toll on the man. He was pale. He had lost much of the colour of the outdoorsman in a few short days. His skin sagged, the weight loss too sudden for the elasticity of his skin. In prison clothes, his tragicomic face emphasised the tragic.

At last, he seemed to come to a decision. He took a deep breath, squared his shoulders and said, 'There is something.'

'Well, that's nice,' said the inspector, dryly.

The prisoner ignored the sarcasm. He sat in the plastic chair, elbows on the table, deep in thought.

The inspector waited for Jasper to speak. The act of speaking, the release from silence, invariably meant that the prisoner would say too much, give something away; let slip an honest truth in the midst of the self-justification. Inspector Singh, like a fine piano-tuner, could listen to these verbal outpourings and pick up those hints of expression or emotion that were off-key and those that rang true. And so he waited for Jasper Lee to open his mouth, and a door to the truth, at the same time.

'THERE IS SOMEONE to see you, ma'am. He says it's urgent.' The maid managed, in the great tradition of household workers, to convey far more than she said in words. Looking up at her, Chelsea could tell, from the slight emphasis on the word 'someone', that she did not approve of the guest who was waiting to see her employer.

Chelsea got out of the easy chair she had been lying in to read court papers. She went to the window and parted the curtains slightly. A short, overweight Chinese man stood at the entrance holding a file.

She said, 'Let him in.'

The man was sweaty. His eyes had disappeared so far into the rolls of fat on his face that only two small black pinpricks remained. Despite all this, he managed to convey, through a puffed chest and a big smile, that he was pleased with himself.

Chelsea said, 'Good morning, Mr Chan. What can I do for you?'

'Nothing, nothing! But I can do something for you, yes, yes.'

Chelsea waited politely.

'You remember you ask me to investigate your husband Alan Lee? Find out what he was up to . . . about other women and things?'

Chelsea said, 'Yes, of course I remember—but you might not have heard that my husband is dead. So, if this is about your fees, please send me your bill for the hours you worked.'

Mr Chan said, 'I know Mr Alan is dead. I found out some things—I was going to pass them to you—but you went to jail. When you come out of jail, I thought better to pass you the file. You can read it. Always good for the wife to know everything. I know Mr Alan dead . . .' The man wiped his brow with a short shirt sleeve and got to the point. 'My bill is on top.'

Chelsea nodded, keen to get rid of this gross little man. 'All right, I will look at the file. If the information is useful, I will send you a cheque.'

'Cash, please. Otherwise, my wife take the money.'

Chelsea nodded abruptly. Mr Chan understood that he was being dismissed and walked out of the door, smiling broadly. He did not doubt he would get his money.

IT WAS NOT APPARENT that the man was Caucasian. He was burnt nut-brown by the sun. This was not a superficial tan but deeply embedded into his skin. His hair was unkempt, streaked with grey, greasy and tied back with a length of twine. His clothes were worn through, with makeshift patches over the knees. It was only when he looked up—as he did now at the policeman behind the desk—that his piercing blue eyes gave his race away.

The accent was pure Queen's as well—England not Brooklyn. 'These people are being terrorised and I want to know what you are doing about it.'

The policeman said, 'I will report to the senior officer when he comes in—for now you fill in the incident report. That is our procedure.'

'I tell you that the weakest members of your society are being hounded off their land and this is your response?'

'You are foreigner—why you come here and shout at me? You do not understand the Malaysian way. These Penan are troublemakers. You should not believe everything they tell you.'

'I've seen the destruction with my own eyes! A pregnant woman died!'

'I will report it, sir.'

'You do that.'

The policeman watched the Englishman walk out of the door, slamming it behind him. As if the exit was his cue, the senior officer appeared at the door to his office. He had been listening to proceedings quietly in his room. The two men looked at each other.

'What should we do?' asked the junior man. 'If he calls the newspapers . . .' He trailed off into silence. There was no need to spell it out.

'He must not go to the newspapers. You know what to do.' The senior policeman went back into his office and closed the door.

The younger man unbuttoned his holster and slipped his revolver out. He had never used it except on the firing range. He checked that it was loaded, slipped it back into its case and walked out of the door onto the dusty street.

Rupert Winfield was staying at a Chinese lodging house in Kuching. It was a favourite haunt of backpackers. It was cheap and had in residence a loud-mouthed Chinese woman. She kept the place spotless, wore nylon floral dresses and fake pearls, and cooked up tasty meals in the café she ran on the ground floor for any guests who needed an inexpensive meal to go with their cheap room. She was known as Mrs Wong, although there had never been any sign of Mr Wong.

A policeman walked into the café. He looked around, searching for someone, and then walked out again. Mrs Wong, watching the street, could see him on the road, a dark silhouette against the bright sun. At last he came back in and walked over to the small desk that served as a reception for the hotel. He looked at her and asked brusquely, 'Mr Winfield—he stay here?'

She nodded.

'Which room?'

'Why you ask me that?'

'None of your business!' The young man's hand caressed the butt of his gun for a second, and she could see beads of sweat on his upper lip.

He asked again, 'Which room? I know he stay here.'

She said, 'Room one one five.'

He made for the stairs.

'Where are you going?'

'Stay out of police business, old woman!'

Mrs Wong said mildly, 'He is not in his room.' She nodded to the little pigeonholes behind her.

His strained eyes found the slot marked '115'. A key was bundled into it.

'Do you know when he will come back?'

'Not sure.' She shrugged.

The policeman said firmly, 'Don't tell him that the police are looking for him. I will come back later.'

He did not go far. She could see him standing under the limited shade of a casuarina tree across the road, watching the entrance to the hotel. Occasionally, he would glance up and down the street.

Mrs Wong went to a cupboard, took out a mop and bucket, shouted in Cantonese to the staff that she would see to the bathrooms upstairs and started up the stairs. She could feel the eyes of the policeman on her back. As she reached the semi-cool darkness at the top of the stairs, out of sight of the road, she hastily put down the bucket and hurried to room 117, tapping gently on the door. Rupert Winfield opened it, looking haggard and dishevelled. She looked past him into the room, lit with a single, bright fluorescent tube. His clothes were scattered on the bed. An empty suitcase on the floor suggested that he was starting to pack.

She said, 'You better hurry, *lah*. The police are looking for you.'

CHELSEA OPENED THE file the private investigator had given her. There was a note on the top with the name and address of a woman, 'Sharifah Abdul Rahman, #04-04, Rose Condominium, Ampang'. It was stapled to the investigator's bill for 2,000 ringgit. Her eyebrows went up. Mr Chan must be convinced of the value of the information he had provided and expected her to be willing to pay handsomely for it.

The only other thing in the file was a CD. Chelsea held it in her hand. Did she really want to see what was on this recording? Presumably, it was yet more evidence of Alan's adultery. She had always known and never needed proof. The courts had required evidence, so she had found it for them. None of it mattered any more now that Alan was dead. Reluctantly, Chelsea decided that she could not ignore it. It might contain something as simple as Alan tucking into a plate of *char siew*—roast pork—after his so-called conversion to Islam. It might eventually be good evidence that religion was purely a matter of convenience for Alan Lee.

She ran up the carpeted stairs lightly and soundlessly. She went into the spare bedroom and locked the door. There was a television and DVD player, rarely used, in there. Steeling herself, she slipped the CD in, grabbed the remote controls and perched on the edge of the bed.

The images had been shot on a recording device with fairly low resolution—a mobile phone, Chelsea decided. She had no difficulty recognising her husband as he sat on a bar stool watching the dancers at a club. Flashing lights in many colours punctuated the scene and she could almost smell the perspiring dancers. The sound was largely muffled but Chelsea could make out the persistent beat of loud music.

A young woman walked up to Alan. She was exquisite. Tall and thin, with beautifully made-up features, she strode into the shot like a model. With a start, Chelsea realised that the woman bore a strong resemblance, in height and style, to herself. Alan had not seen her as she walked up to him: he was concentrating on the dancers. She slipped a thin arm round his neck and he swivelled on his stool. She leaned down and kissed him full on the mouth. It was a smooth, sensuous action. Alan responded by standing up and folding the woman in his arms. Chelsea felt her stomach muscles clench. Knowing your husband was adulterous and watching him were two different things. Public displays of affection—*or lust*, thought Chelsea dismissively—were not common in Malaysia. A few people had turned to look at the couple kissing so uninhibitedly. This was Sharifah, she supposed. The screen went blank. She wondered why Mr Chan thought she would be willing to pay 2,000 ringgit for what he had provided.

The camera came back on. Perhaps Mr Chan had been trying to conserve the battery. A young man had marched up to the couple. He was slim, dressed in black with short dark hair. He grabbed the woman by the arm and yanked her away from Alan. She turned in surprise and then, seeing who it was, took a step backwards and said something—it was impossible to hear over the music. It was obvious that she knew the young man. He grabbed her by the shoulders and shook her—not roughly, almost pleadingly. It was clear to Chelsea what had happened. Alan had stolen this girl from the young man and he was desperate to win her back. Seeing the woman's face for the first time, Chelsea realised that despite her dress and make-up, she was very young. No doubt she had been swept off her feet by an older man with money who knew how to be charming. Chelsea could almost feel sorry for the girl.

Alan had grown tired of the young man's impassioned pleading because he grabbed him by the arm and pulled him away from the girl. The girl put out a hand, a gesture of sympathy, an apology—it might even have been a sign that she knew deep down that her affections lay with him. Alan must have recognised the possibility because he put both hands on the stranger and shoved. The boy stumbled backwards, found his balance and would have charged forwards to attack Alan if the girl had not stepped between them. She shook her head at the young man. He said something and she shook her head again, more firmly this time. The boy raised an angry finger—pointing at Alan over the girl's shoulder. Chelsea could just make out the words, 'I won't let you get away with this!' And then he had turned and almost ran away from the couple. But not before he had looked directly in the direction of Mr Chan's camera.

Chelsea collapsed backwards onto the bed.

SEVEN

'I killed him.'

The inspector said testily, 'Yes, yes! I've heard this part before. I am asking you why!'

'His job . . . his business.'

'You wanted his business?' There was no disguising the puzzlement in the inspector's voice. 'But I thought you walked away from all that. Chelsea told me that you had no interest in money matters.'

Jasper said impatiently, 'Not to get his business—to stop Alan running it!'

'Why?'

'Everything he has ever done is illegal and destructive.'

'I'm not sure what you mean.'

'The family business is logging—my father was the original timber magnate. He built an empire cutting down trees.'

The inspector nodded to indicate that he knew the potted history of the Lee family.

'Alan was expanding operations to Borneo. That is where the best logging is—most of the old-growth hardwood on the peninsula is long gone. What is left is on nature reserves, and fairly well-policed.'

'I still don't know what you're driving at.'

'He was logging illegally. Destroying the rainforest. Driving species to extinction. Hounding the indigenous tribes and chasing them off the land they have used for thousands of years.' Jasper Lee's voice was rising with anger—his genuine disgust at his brother's actions apparent in the reddening face.

The inspector's voice dripped with sarcasm. 'Are you trying to tell me that you're some sort of eco-terrorist?'

Jasper was stung into a reaction. 'I don't care what you believe! You asked me for an explanation and I've given you one.'

The inspector snorted.

'What do you want from me?' asked Jasper tiredly.

'The truth would be a good place to start.'

Jasper stared past the policeman at the grimy walls of his cell. 'You ask me for the truth,' he said, 'but you don't believe me when I tell you. I know it sounds far-fetched when you live your life in air-conditioned cities, that I could have killed my brother to save the rainforests, but if you were in Borneo, you would understand.'

Inspector Singh raised one of his expressive eyebrows.

Jasper hung his head, refusing to meet the policeman's eyes.

Finally, the inspector said, 'All right. Let's say I take your word for it and that I believe you when you say you killed your brother because of . . . jungle people. Why now?'

Jasper looked at him, brow wrinkled with perplexity.

'Presumably Alan has been up to no good for years. Why did you kill him now? Besides, I understood it was your other brother, Lee Kian Min, who was the brains behind Lee Timber, anyway. Haven't you just made things worse? You killed the wrong brother.'

KIAN MIN WAS FRANKLY MYSTIFIED. He had no idea why his brother Jasper had confessed to the murder of Alan. Even if he had committed the murder—which Kian Min thought highly unlikely; Jasper wouldn't have had the balls—surely there was no reason to implicate himself by confessing so dramatically.

Kian Min had taken Alan's messy divorce and lengthy custody battle in his stride. When Alan had asked him to testify as to his good character, he had laughed out loud and then agreed to help—for a price.

He remembered the occasion well. Alan had summoned him on the office intercom: even when he wanted a favour, he still demanded that his brother come up to the big office to see him. Kian Min had trotted up dutifully and agreed to help—if his brother would cease objecting to his big idea to expand the business.

He had never understood Alan's reluctance to adopt his most recent business development plan. Alan rarely got involved in planning and never had a view on prudent policy. Every now and then though, to Kian Min's intense irritation, he would step in and veto some plan. Kian Min was certain that Alan did it just to yank his chain—stop him getting ideas above himself about where he belonged in the company's hierarchy, and remind him who was the boss of Lee Timber.

Alan's most recent effort had been to veto Kian Min's plans to turn the land they logged in East Malaysia into oil palm plantations. Kian Min firmly believed that the future of the business was in bio-fuels. And the company had a huge advantage muscling into the market because of the land concessions they had, and which they could easily buy from corrupt government officials.

But Alan had refused. He had asserted that Lee Timber was a timber company and he was not going to compromise the legacy his father had left him. He had implied that he, Alan, had inherited the trade because his father had trusted him with the family business. In vain had Kian Min pointed out the advantages of diversifying and the dangers of staying hooked on a logging industry that was fast running out of trees. Alan was obdurate. Until, that is, he had needed his brother to testify at the custody hearings. Kian Min had spelled out the cost of his cooperation—the setting up of a bio-fuels unit. Alan had agreed immediately.

'What happened to all your big talk about protecting Father's legacy?' Kian Min had asked snidely.

'I couldn't care less. I just love that look on your face when I screw up one of your pretty little business plans.'

Kian Min, standing before his brother's desk like a schoolboy summoned to see the headmaster, had grown pale with anger, but had not said anything.

INSPECTOR SINGH LOOKED mournfully at his shoes. His snowy white sneakers were streaked with mud and covered in a fine film of grey dirt. In Singapore, where one could eat lunch off the pavements, he never had any difficulty keeping his footwear pristine. He wondered whether the time had come to abandon this affectation and buy a pair of black leather shoes.

He picked up his newspaper and settled back into his chair, waiting for his coffee and his guest.

Moving quietly as he always did, Singh did not notice the young sergeant until he was right in front of him. The older man gestured at a chair, inviting Shukor to sit down. He did not. He stood looking down at the inspector, a troubled expression on his face.

'What is it?' asked Singh.

'There's another man.'

'What do you mean?'

'Chelsea had . . . has maybe, a boyfriend.'

'How do you know?'

Sergeant Shukor slipped a letter across the table. It was handwritten with looping juvenile strokes and much underlining for emphasis. The inspector picked it up gingerly and read the enthusiastic plans of a young man, composed on the demise of his lover's husband.

'Where did you get this?'

'We were putting together the stuff we took from searches of the Lee residence after Chelsea was arrested. I came across this while I was tidying.'

'Alan Lee didn't know about this young man!'

'Why do you say that?'

'Well, I suspect it would have come up in the custody battle. It might even have stopped him from converting to Islam. Adultery is never viewed with enthusiasm by the courts. She might have lost custody without any of these religious episodes.' Singh continued thoughtfully, 'In fact, if she was still in the dock for murder, this letter would have been the final nail in the coffin.'

'Are you going to ask her about it?'

Singh grimaced. 'I would very much prefer to know as little as possible about the repulsive creature who wrote this piece of epistolary art.' He looked at the signature. 'One Ravi, apparently. But you're right. We do have to make sure this has no bearing on the case. Chelsea may not be a suspect any more, but she seems very sure that Jasper did not do it. Maybe she knows something we don't about this boyfriend of hers. If his literary effusions are to be taken seriously, he is a creature of strong emotions.'

CHELSEA GOT UP off the bed, walked to the bathroom and splashed cold water over her face. She took the soft bath towel and scrubbed herself dry. She looked at herself in the mirror. Her eyes were those of a cornered wild beast. She sucked in a few deep breaths. Everything she had ever done, she had done for the children. They needed her more than ever now. She did not know where she was to find the strength. She felt physically sick, cowed by what she had just discovered on the disk from the private investigator.

A pounding on the door distracted her.

Her youngest son was yelling for her to come out. He wanted to show her something. It was important. She unlocked the door and he came tumbling in, all excited about the grasshopper he had caught in the garden.

She said distractedly, 'That's very nice. Remember to be gentle with it. Mummy can't come to look at it now. She has to go out for a while.'

The boy looked rebellious and Chelsea put her arms round him and hugged him tight. She said, a little catch in her throat, 'I'll be back soon, honey. I promise.'

The chauffeur was outside but she waved him away and grabbed the car keys. She did not want anyone to know where she was going. She nosed the car out of the garage and into the street. The note with the address jotted down on it lay on the passenger seat. She knew where she was going. She was not sure what she was going to do when she got there.

Rose Condominiums turned out to be an elegant, low-rise development some distance away from any main road. Chelsea took the elevator up to the fourth floor and hurried down a wide, well-lit corridor until she was outside apartment 04-04. She hesitated. She noticed the number four, considered unlucky by the Chinese as signifying death, and made up her mind. She put a finger on the doorbell and pressed firmly. She could hear a faint ring through the heavy door.

A few moments later the door was opened a crack and a young face peeped out. Her mouth rounded into a literal 'o' of surprise when she realised who it was: the older woman's recent notoriety meant she was instantly recognisable wherever she went. Chelsea took a step forward, signalling her intention to enter. The woman shrugged and stepped aside. Chelsea walked into the apartment. It was a pleasant, airy place with watercolours on the walls and Persian carpets on the floor. A very large, smoky cat twined itself round her legs, mewing softly.

Chelsea remarked calmly, 'Nice place. Did my husband pay for it?'

The girl—she was no more than a girl really—did not say anything, but her guilty face spoke volumes. Sharifah picked up the cat and hugged it to her cheek. She asked quietly, 'What do you want?'

Chelsea wandered over to the dining table. It was piled high with books and papers. The girl was studying—they were mostly science texts.

She asked, genuinely curious, 'Why in the world did you get involved with him?'

'I don't know really. He was so kind. He bought me so many things. He seemed so worldly.'

Chelsea could have screamed at the other woman for being so naive. The only thing that held her back was the knowledge that she had fallen into the same trap herself so many years ago.

Sharifah said defiantly, 'He said he would marry me. I believed him. He said he was divorcing you. It was all in the newspapers so I knew it was true.'

Chelsea shrugged. 'He might have done, I suppose.'

'He even agreed to convert to Islam because I'm a Moslem!' insisted Sharifah, stung by the disbelief in Chelsea's voice.

Chelsea looked up sharply at this. 'He did convert,' she said abruptly. Could it be that he had done it to marry this woman? If he had really intended to marry her, he would have had no choice. It was the law. Marriage to a Moslem in Malaysia required the non-Moslem to convert to Islam. That would destroy her case—that the conversion was a cynical ploy to get the children, that Alan had not been a genuine Moslem and therefore the kids weren't either. The Syariah court would almost certainly take the kids away from her. She looked at Sharifah, trying to decide if Alan had really fallen in love with her. It was not impossible. She really was beautiful—young, fresh, with a gentle voice.

Sharifah said, 'I really believed he wanted to marry me. But then someone killed him. I heard at first it was you . . . but then they arrested the brother.'

'Jasper confessed.'

'I see.' But it was clear that she didn't.

'Were you upset when he died?' asked Chelsea.

'Of course,' asserted the young woman, but she looked down, sleek hair falling over her face.

Chelsea looked at her pityingly. Her regret did not ring true. Perhaps she had begun to suspect that a relationship with an older man, however rich, was not all it was cracked up to be. Probably Alan had started to hit her. Possibly she had woken up in his arms one morning and realised that things were not going to be so rosy when she was still a young woman but her husband had become an old man. Or perhaps she really cared about that young man who had begged her so passionately to come away with him.

Sharifah screwed up the courage to ask again, 'What do you want?'

'It's not about my husband, actually. It's about my son.'

Sharifah looked frightened. 'What do you mean?'

'I am not interested in your sordid affair with my ex-husband. I want to know about your . . . relationship with my son.'

'How do *you* know about it?'

Chelsea waved the question aside with a well-manicured hand. 'Tell me the truth.'

Sharifah's voice, when she spoke, was the merest whisper. She said, 'Marcus and I were at school together. We started going out. He didn't want to tell anyone because I'm a Moslem and he was afraid we would get into trouble. For a while, we were very happy.' She looked up defensively. 'I don't mean that we were making long-term plans or anything—just that we hung out and had a good time, that's all.'

'Then what happened?'

'Once, when the driver came to pick him up from school, I got in, too. We were planning to go to the movies. Marcus never wanted to go home so he was always making plans.'

Her words hurt but Chelsea gave no outward sign of it.

Sharifah continued, 'His dad was in the car. It was just a coincidence. He had a meeting nearby or something. He chatted to me a little bit. Not much. Marcus was always telling me how much he hated his dad but he seemed all right to me.'

Chelsea knew just how good Alan Lee had been at dissembling. Few people would suspect him capable of the cruelty he had shown her.

'I guess he must have found out who I was . . . he pursued me.'

'And you swapped the son for the father?'

'Marcus was a boy. Alan seemed so grown up. I didn't know what to do.' Chelsea was silent.

'When Alan was killed, I was so worried that Marcus had done it. But then they arrested you . . . and now you say his brother has confessed?'

IT WAS A PROSAIC escape. Mrs Wong led him downstairs—he stayed behind her, hidden from view by her wide girth and floral skirts. On the ground floor he fell to his knees, scurrying after her on all fours. She did not say a word but marched down the corridor to the kitchen. There she opened the shutters. Rupert Winfield climbed out of the window, only standing up when he was outside and on the opposite side of the building to the watchful policeman.

He said through the open window, 'Thank you.'

She was more practical. 'Money, passport?'

He patted his breast pocket to reassure her and himself. 'Yes, I'm OK. I have everything.'

'Don't go to airport, *lah*!'

It was good advice. He nodded. She put up her hand in a tentative gesture of goodbye. He clasped the raised hand in both of his, bringing them close to his chest. She understood that his thanks were heartfelt.

He had to get to Kuala Lumpur. There he knew people who knew people. He would get in touch with that wildlife activist, Jasper Lee. He was a good guy and he was related to the Lee family. He was pretty sure it was them who were behind the shocking events he had witnessed. Jasper might have some idea who was ultimately responsible for the attack on the Penan. But first he had to get there. And it was not going to be easy with a crooked policeman on his tail.

He had no illusions: he was a threat to a multi-million dollar industry. They feared he would approach the newspapers with his story or seek out policemen and government servants who had not been bought. The policeman who had tried to ambush him at the hostel was not pursuing him for a chat. If he disappeared here in Borneo, it would just be one more tale of a white man who had mistakenly believed he could tame the jungles.

The Englishman put on a pair of shades. With his blue eyes obscured, his race was indistinguishable to the casual observer. It was his best chance of escape.

SERGEANT SHUKOR KNEW that it would be best for his career to maintain a distance from the maverick Sikh. Instead, he was getting involved in the details of the case against Jasper Lee. His official remit was to shadow the troublesome policeman from across the border. His unofficial mandate was to encourage him to leave as soon as possible by any means, including by being obstructive. But he found himself actively helping out. He had already got the inspector in to see Jasper Lee on a number of occasions.

He had listened in on the interviews—admiring the way the inspector had mastered the use of silence as a weapon. He just sat there quietly in the cell, patiently waiting for Jasper Lee to start filling the empty spaces with words. There were no threats, no brutality expressed or implied. Just a gradual getting under the skin of an imprisoned man until he talked to pass the time or distract himself from the loneliness of certain death. And from this idle conversation had come nuggets of information, the most peculiar of which was this assertion that Jasper had killed his brother to stop his destruction of the environment. It was a lesson in interview technique that Shukor looked forward to testing the next time he was asked to interrogate a suspect or a witness. And the more the young man learned, the more he felt compelled to return the favour by arranging access for the Singaporean policeman. He knew that when his superiors got wind of it, he would be in a difficult position, but he hoped by then something concrete would have resulted from their efforts.

He and the inspector sat now in what was their favourite restaurant, sipping hot sweet tea and watching the street vendors flog their wares that ranged from prayer mats to holy beads. All the products were geared towards the Friday prayer crowd who would soon be overflowing from the mosque, forming lines on the pavement facing Mecca and chanting praise of God.

Shukor was deep in thought. At last he said, 'It is possible.'

'What?'

'It is possible that he killed his brother because of what he was doing in East Malaysia, especially Sarawak.'

'What makes you say that?'

'I've been looking at his history,' replied Shukor.

He seemed to hesitate for a moment but then slipped a folder across the table to the inspector. Another breach of protocol, handing over confidential police files. It was the haul from Jasper's office in Chinatown.

The police had been thorough. They did not want the prosecution of

Jasper for his brother's murder to end in failure. They had a confession; they wanted background information as well. After all, he would not be the first accused to retract a confession at the eleventh hour and insist it was provided under duress—whether true or not.

The inspector looked through the file with interest. The majority of papers were innocuous enough. They indicated an interest in conservation issues in Malaysia. There were World Wide Fund for Nature reports printed off the internet, flyers pleading for logging to be stopped in Sarawak, newspaper cuttings on the plight of every animal—from the orangutan to the pygmy elephant—as a result of deforestation. A draft research paper on a nomadic tribe in Borneo—the Penan—was written by one Rupert Winfield. There was also correspondence between Jasper and Rupert Winfield on the problems faced by the indigenous peoples as their symbiotic relationship with nature was thrown out of kilter by the logging industry.

'I guess it shows he genuinely cared about these issues, but that is a long way from murder,' remarked the inspector.

'That's because I haven't shown you the best part,' was Shukor's response.

'What do you mean?'

Another folder was slipped across the table. The inspector picked it up and started leafing through the pages.

At last he looked up at the young man across the table. Shukor was looking a trifle smug. It was not often in their relationship that he was one up on the fat policeman.

'Where did you get this?'

'At his office as well.'

'Well, it is not quite a smoking gun, but it does lend some credibility to his claims about his brother.'

Sergeant Shukor nodded.

They looked down at the papers in front of them. It was a collection of company annual reports, government survey maps, handwritten notes and print-outs. It was difficult to see at first what Jasper had been driving at with his highlighting of maps and scribbled margin notes, but a careful look made it clear that by putting together the company returns and estimating the volume of wood that had been sold over the years, more wood was sold by Lee Timber than appeared in their books. They had inflated the prices they received for the timber and the processed wood they exported to justify the large income flowing in. This, combined with survey maps showing logging areas, conservation areas and marked with the results of Jasper's own aerial reconnaissance, showed that logging had encroached deep into protected areas.

There were also letters written by Jasper to various authorities in Sarawak pointing out these findings, but the appended responses were always polite denials that illegal logging was going on under their noses. Their officers had checked out the allegations and found no truth in them.

In the margin of one of these replies, Jasper had scribbled angrily, '*How much did you get for this?*'

'It was certainly a subject he cared about,' remarked Inspector Singh.

Shukor nodded. 'I can almost believe that he killed his brother for this.'

'A man on a mission?'

'Yes, if he had proof that his own family company was involved in the activities.'

'Surely he would have confronted his brother, not killed him!'

'Maybe he did.'

It was a pertinent point and well made, thought the inspector. It was quite possible that Jasper had confronted his brother and been given short shrift. What was the next step? Murder? Surely, trial by publicity first.

'Wouldn't he have gone to the newspapers?'

'He might not have had much luck.'

'What do you mean?'

'Plenty of cronies around. The newspapers might have refused to publish.' The inspector pulled at his beard, now flecked with grey. It was possible that Jasper had tried all these options first, failed and then decided to kill Alan. But something did not ring true. He was still not confident that Jasper Lee had killed his brother over such an abstract issue. He thought of the murderers he had caught over the years. Crimes of passion and crimes of greed. He had never come across an altruistic murderer before. He still thought the boyfriend a more likely suspect. But Ravi had not confessed: Jasper had.

COULD SHE RISK LOSING? The first hearing had been postponed. They were due back in court the following week. Chelsea sat in the waiting room of the Syariah lawyer's office, impatiently waiting to hear his advice. She knew the lawyer was both senior and successful.

Finally, she was shown in. The lawyer's desk was piled high with books. Gold-trimmed black court robes, fraying around the edges from years of use, hung from a coat stand in the corner. The lawyer was small, almost gnomic, largely hidden by the piles of paper on his huge desk. He had large, pointy ears poking out on either side of the white cloth cap worn by Moslems who had performed the Hajj in Mecca. He stood up as she came in and she held out her hand, expecting the usual handshake.

He shook his head slightly. 'As you know, Mrs Lee, my religion forbids me from having contact with a woman who is not my wife.'

Chelsea's hand fell to her side, embarrassed.

As if to accentuate the cultural gap between them, her lawyer walked round the desk, avoiding brushing against her as he did so, and opened the door that she had closed behind her. He pushed a doorstop into place: he was not allowed to be alone with a woman who was not his wife either; not behind closed doors, anyway.

The preliminaries dealt with to his satisfaction, he smiled and said, 'May I offer you a cup of tea?'

She shook her head mutely. She needed to get down to business. This man was the most senior practising member of the Syariah bar. He came highly recommended and was expensive. She was not interested in tea.

He understood because he said, 'I know the background to your case, of course.' Left unsaid was that he would have had to have been a hermit to avoid the details of Chelsea's recent exploits.

Chelsea nodded. 'Can they take my children from me?'

She was not in a mood to beat around the bush and her lawyer looked a little pained at being put on the spot so quickly.

'This is an unusual confluence of circumstances.'

Chelsea glared at him. Apparently it did not matter whether it was within the Syariah or civil jurisdiction: all lawyers charged by the hour and would not answer a direct question.

'So what does "unusual confluence of circumstances" mean for me and my children?'

Her lawyer sighed and looked up. She saw a sincerity in him that reassured her for a moment. His answer, however, did not. 'I don't know. I don't know what the outcome will be.'

There was a tense silence between them as they both digested his admission of ignorance.

The lawyer spoke first. 'It is always unfortunate to be precedent-setting in a case that is in the public eye. All the parties involved feel that they have to adopt the harshest line because they don't want to be seen to be weak.'

She nodded. She had always lived her life on the front pages of the tabloid press. But now she had gravitated to the broadsheets, and the reputations of powerful men were at stake.

He continued, 'My contacts at the Islamic Council inform me that they are split on whether to pursue this custody matter in the first place. Not everyone is convinced that your husband's conversion was genuine.'

'Of course it wasn't!' snapped Chelsea.

'Unfortunately, the Council does not want to set a precedent of doubting the authenticity of a religious conversion. You can see why that would be. Whenever any non-Moslem converts, objecting family members will turn to the courts. A matter of faith will become a matter of evidence.'

Chelsea slumped back into her chair. 'What are you getting at?'

'The court might not let us introduce evidence that Alan was not really a Moslem. He followed the legal procedures to become a Moslem. They might take it at face value. If they do that—well, then, strictly as a matter of Islamic family law, the children should be brought up as Moslems . . . and by Moslems. The court could take the children away from you.'

'What can we do?'

'There is one sure way to avoid losing your children,' the lawyer replied.

She looked up hopefully. 'What is it?'

'You could convert to Islam, too.'

Chelsea said quietly, 'I've thought about that, of course.'

'Then why don't you do it?'

'Do you think that two conversions of convenience are the solution?'

The lawyer steepled his fingers and looked at her ruefully. 'It's best if you don't reveal to me that any conversion to Islam by you would not be genuine. It is important that your adoption of the religion appears credible.'

Chelsea snorted. 'Like Alan's?'

The lawyer could not meet her eyes. He shuffled the papers on his table and sighed.

Chelsea spoke quietly again. 'If I convert, it means Alan has won. He has reached out from beyond the grave to control what I do and how I live my life. I don't want to give him that victory . . .'

'It might be the only way of keeping your children.'

She nodded. 'I realise that. But for now I am still hoping for some justice from the courts.'

SINGH WAS NOT looking forward to his appointment with Chelsea. To ask this woman about her Achilles heel would not be pleasant. He was forced to concede that he was shocked to discover that she had a boyfriend on the side. He would not have thought it would be in her character. He supposed he was just not in a position to understand a vulnerable woman.

He had no doubt in his mind about Ravi—he was a slippery character on the lookout for women he could exploit. Singh had come across many of his ilk over the years. He would have assumed they were too cowardly to commit murder for gain, but Chelsea's potential wealth and anticipated gratitude, if her husband was removed from the picture, might have tempted Ravi to overreach. Then there was another possibility. Perhaps Chelsea had provided the backbone Ravi lacked to kill her husband.

Singh wiped his face with a big, white handkerchief. He really did not want to contemplate Chelsea's involvement in the killing, whether she pulled the trigger or not.

He sat, wedged into a spindly, cushioned chair, waiting for Chelsea. He had turned down offers of refreshments, tea, freshly squeezed watermelon juice or coffee from the demure, uniformed Indonesian maid.

The door opened and Chelsea came in. Dressed in a pair of white linen trousers, with an equally cool sky-blue shirt worn open over a white camisole, she looked fresh and well—a far cry from the traumatised woman of a couple of weeks ago.

She said now, as if theirs was a relationship of casual, gossipy friendship rather than a bond forged in the most unusual of circumstances, 'How are things going?'

He shrugged, as if he was trying to avoid speech.

She looked at him quizzically. 'Go on, you can tell me! I've had my fair share of difficult news in the past few months. Have you found some evidence against Jasper? I won't believe you if you tell me you have.' She smiled to rob her words of offence.

The inspector said heavily, 'Not as such, no. He says he killed his brother because he was cutting down the rainforests.'

'Really?' She shook her head. 'I know Jasper takes these things seriously but surely that's a bit far-fetched?'

Singh nodded. 'It strikes me as a bit odd, too.'

There was an awkward pause between them. Singh tried to look competent and menacing at the same time.

She said, holding his glance, 'That's not what you came to discuss, is it?'

He was the first to look away. He stared past her, looked at the ceiling briefly, tied a shoelace and then sat back up in his chair.

Chelsea said, half-amused and half-worried, 'For God's sake, how bad can it be?'

Singh said brusquely, 'We know about your boyfriend.'

It was her turn to sit back in her chair and avoid meeting his eye.

She said quietly, looking down at her hands, 'Ravi was the mistake of a woman with nowhere to turn . . . and no one to turn to. He is not relevant.'

'On the contrary, aside from Jasper, he's the best suspect we have.'

Chelsea looked at him. 'I've told you—Ravi meant nothing then and means nothing now.'

'Have it your way. But that leaves Jasper in the frame—by himself.'

'You've forgotten someone,' Chelsea said.

'Who?'

'Kian Min, Alan's younger brother. He's taken over the company. It's been his life's ambition to do that. Who is to say that he didn't kill Alan to inherit Lee Timber?'

'It's interesting,' remarked the inspector, 'that you are so anxious to help one brother, Jasper; but have no qualms about pointing a finger at the other.'

'It's not interesting at all,' snapped Chelsea. 'Jasper is a kind, decent man. Lee Kian Min would make Alan look like the good guy.'

Singh put up a hand. 'Fine, I'll look into it.'

THEY HAULED RAVI in for questioning. Sergeant Shukor was only too pleased to help, not even mentioning the possible reaction of his superiors. Like the inspector, he was curious to see the man who had cuckolded Alan Lee.

Ravi was extremely good looking, Singh acknowledged to himself a little ruefully. He was in perfect physical condition—strong without being excessively muscular. With his mixed Indian-Chinese parentage, he had even features, warm eyes and flawless skin.

Nevertheless, it did not take them long, either of them, to get the measure of the man.

Ravi started out blustering. 'How can you arrest me? For what? I haven't done anything!'

'You were having an affair with a wealthy woman whose husband has turned up dead,' pointed out Singh.

Ravi turned pale. His eyes shifted from one policeman to the other. He stammered, 'I . . . I didn't do it. You can't go around accusing people of murder just like that. I want a lawyer. I won't say anything more until I have a lawyer! You're violating my rights.'

Singh suspected that Ravi's knowledge of police methods was derived entirely from American television drama.

Shukor said patiently, 'You've not been arrested. This is just a chat. You can walk out if you like.'

Ravi considered his options. The policemen watched him silently. Ravi decided belatedly on cooperation.

'She pursued me,' he offered, as his opening remark.

Inspector Singh took a deep breath. He said, 'In what way?'

'We met at a party. I could see she was attracted to me.'

'How could you tell?' asked Shukor.

The inspector wondered whether the policeman was wasting valuable interview time trying to pick up tips about women from someone who fancied himself an expert.

Ravi said, 'Well, she couldn't take her eyes off me. I noticed that right away. And when we were introduced and shook hands, she held my hand for just that bit longer than necessary.' He continued smugly, 'You can always tell, can't you?'

'Moving on,' said Singh, brusquely. 'What happened next?'

'I gave her my phone number.'

'And she called you?'

'Not exactly, no. But we . . . er . . . bumped into each other a couple of days later at the Marriott and had coffee together.'

Singh had seen it so many times before. A man, little better than a gigolo, setting his sights on a rich, lonely, unhappy woman and engineering coincidences until he had wormed his way into her affections and her bed. He was just surprised that Chelsea had fallen prey to such a predator. He supposed that he had no idea what she had been through. And she was evidently an appalling judge of the male character. She had married Alan Lee, after all.

'Go on,' said Shukor.

'It was the usual story,' Ravi continued, smirking slightly. 'She pursued me. We ended up having a relationship. I was reluctant because she was married, but in the end I could not say no.' Ravi stopped to admire the picture he painted of a moral man tempted too far by a determined woman.

'How much did you take her for?' asked the inspector abruptly.

Ravi looked pained. 'I have no idea what you are talking about.'

'How did you feel when she called off the relationship?'

'Who said she called it off?'

'She did!'

Ravi looked unsure whether to contradict this version of events, but decided against it. 'She was worried about the custody battle.'

'So how did you feel when your meal ticket was threatened?'

'She was not a meal ticket. I loved her. I would have married her and been a father to her children.'

Singh could not resist sarcasm. 'You mean you would have been willing to marry an extremely wealthy and beautiful woman? You amaze me!'

Ravi started to say something and then thought better of it. He slumped in the chair.

Singh asked, 'So, did you kill Alan Lee?'

'Of course not!'

'You had every reason.'

'I did not kill him. Anyway, I thought the brother confessed.'

Later, when the policemen were alone, Shukor asked, 'Could Ravi have done it?'

Inspector Singh shrugged. 'He strikes me as a coward, but he had an excellent motive. Without Alan in the picture he must have felt sure enough of Chelsea to think that he had found the pot of gold at the end of the rainbow.'

Shukor said tentatively, 'But we've still got Jasper's confession, *lah*.'

Singh sighed. 'Yes. There is still that damned confession.'

THE OFFICE WAS CLOSED. Rupert leaned his forehead on the dusty wall and closed his eyes. Jasper Lee was his best hope. He needed someone with access and information. A conduit who knew the issues would have been perfect. Someone who he had worked with and trusted. But the door was locked and the place musty and damp. No one had been in for a while.

Outside again, and feeling the safety of anonymity in a crowd, he walked into a coffee shop at the base of the building and asked an old crone chopping vegetables where Jasper had gone. She cackled at him, showing gold teeth sporadically protruding from red gums, but did not answer. A harassed woman, cooking vegetables in a big pot of boiling water and then deftly flicking them onto a row of plates, said, 'She no speak Engris one!'

He turned to her gratefully. 'Maybe you can help me? I am looking for Jasper Lee—the man with the office upstairs? He might have eaten here.'

She looked at him curiously, pushing a strand of hair, damp with sweat, behind her ear.

'Why you want him?'

'He's an old friend of mine.'

'He not here any more.'

Rupert nodded encouragingly, willing her to continue.

Answering the silent question, she said, 'He go to jail!'

Rupert's first thought was that somehow the police had guessed where he would be going and had deprived him of his one ally in the battle against the logging companies. Then he realised that was far-fetched. 'Jail? Why is he in jail? What did he do?'

'He kill his brother. He go to jail. They sure hang him!'

She seemed to relish this unseemly end to her neighbour's career and went back to her task of scooping vegetables out of the boiling water.

Rupert walked down the street. He did not notice the noise or the crowds. He was too shocked at what he had just heard. He could not believe that the gentle man he had known, with his overwhelming compassion for every living thing, could have taken a life. What could have led him to kill his brother? Possibly it was some sort of trumped-up charge by the police to get Jasper Lee out of the way. That would not have surprised the Englishman, who had spent the last twenty-four hours escaping from corrupt policemen. He knew that Jasper's research was getting closer and closer to proving the extent of the illegal logging going on in Borneo. Someone might have seen fit to frame him for a murder he had not committed.

How was he to find out more? Rupert set out for the library newspaper archives. Sitting there half an hour later, scrolling down the history of Jasper's internment, he was not a happy man. It seemed that Jasper had confessed to killing his brother. Alan Lee, the man Rupert held responsible for the events in Borneo, was dead. He would never have the opportunity now to confront him with the consequences of his actions. But he still found it hard to believe that Jasper had killed him.

He stretched and sneezed. Even when the old newspapers were on screen they seemed to exude mustiness. It reminded him of his time researching dusty books when he was studying the indigenous tribes of Borneo. He had never anticipated that his academic interest would be so bound up in his own fate. But his life among the simplest of folk, first as a researcher, then as a defender, had completely changed his career path. Not for him the ivory towers of academe. He had traded it for a cause. And it had left him with a strong sense of fulfilment over the years.

He sat lost in the past, forgetting his troubles in memories of the jungle.

IT WOULD NOT have been Inspector Singh's choice to move in to his sister's house. But now that he was no longer in Kuala Lumpur in his official capacity, his budget did not stretch to a hotel. He had called his sister and told her he would be coming to stay for a few days. She seemed indifferent rather than enthusiastic. But there had never been any danger of refusal. The right of family to come and stay indefinitely, whatever the inconvenience and expense, was hardwired into her brain. It was the Asian way. Hospitality was paramount—especially to relatives.

He was at her door now with his small suitcase. She let him in and he sat silently in the gloomy living room waiting for her to make him a drink. It did not take her long to return with a cup of tea.

She asked, 'How come you are not staying at the hotel?'

He debated telling her that he was freelancing and decided against it. It would give her too much ammunition with which to nag at him for the duration of his stay. She would go on and on about the importance of staying on the good side of one's employers. He said instead, 'If I stay here, they will still pay me the hotel allowance.'

She nodded approvingly, sipping her tea. 'That is good!'

Singh did not know if she was referring to his cunning in getting some spare cash or the generosity of the government of Singapore in letting him get away with such an old-fashioned expense fiddle.

'What would you like for dinner?' she asked.

He shrugged indifferently. He was a fat man with a fat man's lack of fussiness over his diet.

She continued, 'I am making *chapattis*.'

'Why did you ask me what I wanted then?'

She did not answer but wandered back into the kitchen and presently he could hear the clanging of pots and pans. The rich smell of toasting ghee and baked bread soon filled the air, and Inspector Singh realised that he fancied *chapattis* for dinner after all.

'DID YOU DO IT?' asked Rupert, without preamble.

Jasper looked amused. 'I confessed,' he pointed out.

'I know. I read the newspapers. I just can't believe you would kill anyone.'

'Not even Alan?'

Rupert smiled suddenly at his friend. It was true that they had shared many a cup of *arak*—fermented coconut wine—over a campfire while Jasper had complained bitterly about his brother.

Jasper said now, 'What are you doing here anyway? Last I heard you had vanished into the jungle with a beautiful Penan girl!'

Rupert's face became serious. 'I barely got out. Thugs attacked the camp. Just after daybreak.'

'Thugs?'

'A group of armed men. I was some distance away. I heard the commotion. I dashed back. Armed men were attacking the Penan. They were just leaving as I got there.'

'Did they kill anyone?'

Rupert's voice cracked. 'A young woman. She went into early labour and mother and baby died.'

'What did you do?'

'I hid. There was no point in letting them see me. I was afraid they would kill everyone if there was a non-Penan witness. You know they don't really fear that the authorities will take the Penan seriously if they complain, but they might not be so sanguine about a foreigner. I didn't know what had happened to the girl at that point—or I would have confronted them, whatever the consequences.'

Jasper nodded thoughtfully. 'What was it about?' he asked, but he knew the answer. He wanted to see if Rupert had come to the same conclusion.

'I would guess—in fact, I know—it's the timber companies. They want to log the area. It's off-limits, in a nature reserve. Difficult to log illegally with a nomadic tribe in your midst.'

Jasper was struck by something that Rupert had said earlier. 'I agree with you—that must be the reason for the attack. But why do you say you know, rather than guess?'

'You're not going to like this, but I recognised one of the toughs.'

'Who was it?'

'That big chap with the tattoos—the one who used to work as foreman of the Borneo operations of Lee Timber.'

Jasper nodded slowly. 'You're sure it was him?'

'Positive! I remember him from that time we went to the site to protest about something or other—do you remember?—and he had us thrown out. Is he employed by Lee Timber still?'

'I think so,' replied Jasper.

Rupert sighed. 'I cannot be upset that Alan Lee is dead—but I would have liked to have forced him to acknowledge what he did.'

'I know what you mean,' said Jasper. 'The fact is, though, Kian Min—my other brother—has been running the show at Lee Timber for a long time.'

'Really?' asked Rupert, staring at Jasper fixedly.

'Oh, yes. So if you want to confront someone, the right person is still alive and well.'

EIGHT

Subhas Chandra placed another pencil in the sharpener on his desk and turned the handle furiously. He tested the tip, honed to a fine point, on his finger. The slight sting convinced him it was sharp enough. He picked another one out of its case. Sharpening pencils was what he did when things were not going well. And things were not going well.

He remembered that he had been pleased to be asked to represent Chelsea Liew during her divorce and custody battle. He would have preferred Alan Lee as a client—it was always better to represent the half of the couple that had the majority of assets. Still, he had been confident of winning, which meant that Chelsea would have got a substantial part of the family wealth in a settlement. Either way, his name and picture were in every newspaper in the country for weeks. Publicity like that was hard to come by. He had played his cards well; public opinion was on Chelsea's side—battered, long-suffering wife against violent timber tycoon. And then the rug was pulled from under his feet.

Alan Lee's conversion to Islam was a master tactical stroke and he had been taken completely by surprise. It rankled. And now there was more bad news. He reached for the phone and rang Chelsea Liew's mobile. She picked up immediately.

He paused and could sense her growing impatience on the phone. He screwed up his courage, put on his most lawyerly voice—deep, slow tones usually reserved for when he was in court—and said, 'I have some bad news. I'm afraid the court has released the body of your husband for burial in accordance with Moslem funeral rites.'

'So?'

'They've released the body to the Islamic Council to bury.'

She said, 'I could not possibly care less.'

This was not easy. 'I realise that you are not particularly concerned about what happens to the body and I understand that. But the court's decision does have legal consequences.'

'What do you mean?' Her voice was hard and suspicious.

Her lawyer swallowed a sigh. 'If you will recall, we asked the judge in the civil custody hearing to examine the conversion to Islam of your ex-husband. The idea was that if his new religion was not genuine, then his children were not Moslem—and therefore you should keep them.'

'Yes, I understand that.'

'Well, the judge, when releasing the body, ruled that he had no authority under the Constitution to look behind a conversion to Islam to determine whether it was genuine.'

'So?'

'It will affect the decision about the children.'

'What do you mean?'

'The civil courts have set a precedent saying they will not question the genuineness of a conversion to decide whether Alan Lee should be buried with Moslem rites. In other words, if he claims to be Moslem, that's enough for them. They could use the same logic about your custody claim.'

'I see,' said Chelsea, slowly. 'What do you suggest I do?'

'Appeal!'

'Can I win?'

'It is difficult to say. These are uncharted constitutional waters . . .'

Chelsea rolled her eyes. She would dearly love a lawyer who gave her a straight answer, but suspected that this restraint was endemic in the profession. She said, 'What's your best bet?'

'There is a certain safety in numbers. The Court of Appeal might be more willing to make a controversial decision than a judge sitting alone. It is not impossible that we will get a favourable result.'

Chelsea said, 'All right, go ahead and appeal,' and terminated the call.

Her lawyer carefully put another pencil into the sharpener, turned the handle mechanically and watched the shavings fall into the clear receptacle.

SERGEANT SHUKOR WAS the point man. He had to be. These tycoons were far too well advised to subject themselves to questioning by a Singapore policeman freelancing in Malaysia. They had agreed between them that Singh would come along and remain in the background.

They had made an appointment and were shown in to see Lee Kian Min. His appointment as managing director of Lee Timber had not been formalised. The company thought it would be better to wait until Alan Lee had at least been buried before the official handover.

Kian Min did not know why the police wanted to see him but he had nevertheless choreographed the encounter to ensure that his questioners were made to feel at a disadvantage. He sat behind the huge desk. On the other side there were two much smaller chairs.

He stood up as they came in and ushered them into the small chairs. His nasal voice suggested roots that were not quite as polished as his dress and surroundings implied. While Alan had ironed the Chinese *towkay* out of his voice during the course of an expensive education, Kian Min had stayed close to home and sounded it. He said, 'So why the police want to see me?'

'We just have a few questions,' said Sergeant Shukor. Singh sensed he was intimidated by the tone of wealth. He wished he could take part in the interview. He would soon have the little bastard by the balls. He ground his teeth in frustration and the two other men turned to look at him in surprise. In the quiet room, it had been audible. Singh patted his stomach apologetically.

Kian Min, his confidence increased by the embarrassment of the two policemen, said, 'What questions you want to ask me? Is it about my brother? If so, I can tell you straight that I have no idea why Jasper killed Alan.'

Shukor said, 'We have evidence that Lee Timber is logging illegally.'

Kian Min stared at him. 'What evidence? Cannot be!'

'We have maps and aerial photos showing that you have been logging on areas gazetted as national park land in East Malaysia, in Borneo.'

'Let me see it then, if you say you got evidence.'

Shukor shook his head firmly. 'We will look into it further first.'

'You cannot simply come here and make accusations! The Sarawak police have investigated and found nothing.'

'So you deny that Lee Timber is involved in anything illegal?'

'Of course I deny it.'

'Well, this is the thing,' said Inspector Singh, unable to obey his own rules about keeping out of trouble. 'Jasper claims he killed your brother to stop his illegal activity in Borneo. If what you say is true—that there is no illegal activity—then Jasper Lee has no motive . . . unlike another brother of Alan who did rather well out of his untimely demise.' As he said this, Singh looked around at Kian Min's office trappings contemptuously and then turned back to look at the man he had just implicitly accused of murder.

To his surprise, Kian Min looked unperturbed: amused even. He ignored the allegation and concentrated on Jasper's story. 'So Jasper say he kill Alan to stop him cutting down trees?' He laughed, a derisory sound. 'You know, he's so screwed up he maybe believes it. But that's not the real reason.'

Shukor jumped in. 'Why then? Why did he kill Alan?'

Kian Min eyed them. At last he said, 'Well, it's obvious, right?'

This time both policemen kept silent.

'He did it for Chelsea.'

IT WAS THE first time she had gone to see him. She had stayed away for as long as possible but then guilt had driven her to prison. She could not abandon her brother-in-law without at least a visit. He was, after all, the reason she was free.

Remembering her own experience, she was pleasantly surprised when she saw him. He looked thinner and tired but there was a bounce in his step when he came into the room. Jasper had an inner resilience which she had not suspected. They sat in silence for a while. He looked at her with a mildly amused expression on his face, guessing her conflicting emotions—relief not to be incarcerated herself, guilt that he was there.

Chelsea looked around, not saying a word, struggling to believe that a few short weeks ago she had been sitting in this room as the accused, not a visitor. She screwed up the courage to ask, 'How are you managing?'

He shrugged. 'It's not the Mandarin Oriental, but I'm fine.'

She said, 'Why did you confess?'

He looked at her, meeting her eyes fearlessly. 'Because I killed Alan.'

'I don't believe you.'

'I know. You even have that fat policeman trying to persuade me that I'm not guilty. But, really, I killed Alan and I don't regret it.' This last was said with a stubborn look, defying her to contradict him.

She shook her head gently. 'I won't pretend that I have any sorrow at Alan's death. The man I thought I married died for me a long time ago.'

In the silence, they were both remembering a wedding day from many years ago—where the radiance of a young bride had transcended the kitschy white wedding and turned it into something truly beautiful. Jasper had not been asked by his brother to be the best man; the relationship between them had soured by then. Instead, he had sat in the front pew of the big church and watched his brother marry the most beautiful woman he had ever seen.

He looked at the woman across from him, seeking in her features something of that young woman—girl almost—he had watched that day. He was lost in the past and did not hear Chelsea speak.

She said again, 'Jasper!'

She looked worried and he smiled reassuringly. 'I'm fine.'

This made her angry. 'How can you say that?' she snapped. 'I was sitting in that chair not long ago—looking forward to a dawn walk to a hangman's noose. There is nothing fine about this situation!'

He did not know what to say. Her anger was palpable. He understood that it was concern for him. But he did not know how to deal with this fiery-eyed, assertive woman. All the years he had known her, she had been retreating further into a shell until he had become accustomed to the quiet, polite, but basically secretive woman. Her release from prison into a world where there was no dominating husband had removed emotional shackles, too.

He changed the subject. 'What's happening with the custody thing?'

She said, 'It doesn't look good. The civil courts released Alan's body to the Islamic Council for burial in accordance with Moslem rites.'

Jasper said thoughtfully, 'I see—and that might be a precedent for the custody issues?'

Chelsea nodded. 'Which leaves me entirely at the mercy of the Syariah court. They must surely be even less inclined to examine whether Alan was actually a Moslem or just faking it.'

Jasper said, 'It's possible, I suppose, that they will be more willing to preserve the sanctity of the religion—by not allowing a conversion of convenience to carry any weight.'

'That's my last hope!' said Chelsea, an edge of desperation in her voice.

'The worst part is that, if Alan was alive, I might have stood a better chance. The judges would have seen with their own eyes that he could not possibly be a genuine convert. We both know Alan. It's not an act he could have sustained for very long. Can you imagine him going to the mosque every Friday? But now, with Alan dead, it has become a matter of principle—not of people . . .'

Jasper asked, 'Are you sorry he's dead, then?'

Chelsea did not answer for an interminable moment. Then she said quietly, 'No, I'm not.'

Jasper reached out and took one of her hands in his. He said, 'You need not worry about me. Really, I'm OK. If they hang me, so be it. I did what I did knowing the consequences. I just wish there was something more I could do to help you.'

'You need to concentrate on helping yourself!' said Chelsea, squeezing his hand to rob her words of the harshness. She rose to her feet, put out a hand and touched his cheek fleetingly—a small, sad farewell gesture—and knocked on the door to be let out.

He did not protest her departure. This was no place for her. It was imagining her in a cell like this one that had given him the strength to confess to the murder in the first place. He did not want to see her here, even as a visitor.

SINGH HELD a handkerchief to his nose and stared in disbelief. The sun, struggling to penetrate the gloom, was a pale moonlike orb. The streets were almost empty—a few dispatch boys on motorbikes scurried along, hankies tied firmly around their noses and mouths. The smell of burning was pervasive and Singh could almost feel the soot clogging his nostrils.

'They will have to close the schools again,' said Shukor.

'Airports, too, I suspect,' was Singh's response. 'The haze is bad this year, isn't it?'

'Forest fires in Indonesia. When the wind changes, it blows here directly from Sumatra, Borneo, Java and gets trapped in the Klang Valley,' said Shukor. The Malaysian suddenly turned on his heel and headed back into the building they had just exited. Singh hurried after him.

'Where are we going?' he asked, surprised.

The young policeman, face grim, did not answer. He headed straight for the elevator, impatiently jabbing the buttons. The lift 'pinged' and Shukor hurried towards it.

The doors slid open and Kian Min walked out. He was surprised to see the policemen still in the building—but his expression of discomfiture was quickly smoothed into the enquiring mask he had presented to them upstairs. It did not last.

Shukor grabbed him by the arm and dragged him towards the exit.

'What are you doing? Let me go!' shouted Kian Min angrily.

People in the lobby stared at the sight of a leading business figure being frog-marched out of their building. Singh, breathless at the pace, was trying to catch Shukor's eye. He had no idea what had got into the sergeant.

They stopped just outside the main entrance. Shukor let go of the slight Chinese man's arm.

He said, 'Look around you!'

Kian Min complied, rubbing his sore arm.

'What do you see?'

Kian Min shook his head. 'I don't know. I cannot see much. Very hazy!'

Shukor grabbed him by the lapels and held him on tiptoes, Kian Min's face inches away from his own.

'Yes, you can't see anything—because of this haze. Because you and your cronies are clearing land all over—burning the rainforests . . . And here in Kuala Lumpur we cannot see to the end of the street! You wear your expensive suits and hide in your expensive offices while your gangsters chase people off their own land so that you can log it and burn it to plant oil palm.'

Kian Min was over his initial shock. He hissed, 'I will have you kicked out of the police force.'

Shukor said, 'Well, you'd better be quick—because I am going to prove that it is you and your company that has caused this.' He let go of Kian Min's lapels so suddenly that the smaller man stumbled backwards and almost fell before righting himself.

Shukor gave him a last meaningful glare and then walked off at a great pace, the inspector struggling in his wake.

'What was that about?' he asked, when Shukor slowed down enough for him to catch up.

'I just got angry, *lah*.'

Kian Min dusted off his jacket and straightened his tie, wincing at the soreness in his arm. He smoothed his hair and then reached into his pocket and slipped out his mobile. He rang a number.

A man picked up the phone and said 'Hello' in an impatient voice.

'We have a problem,' said Kian Min.

BOTH POLICEMEN WERE standing, both of them looked sheepish. Inspector Mohammad was seated behind his desk, looking livid. His face was contorted with rage and it was only with the greatest difficulty that he was able to squeeze words out from behind his clenched teeth.

He said, 'Let me get this straight—although we have a man in custody who has confessed to killing Alan Lee, you two, a rookie and a foreigner, decided to keep investigating?'

Sergeant Shukor said smartly, 'Yessir!'

'And then you went to see Lee Kian Min, one of the most powerful men in the country, and accused him of murder?'

'Yessir!'

'And finally, you attacked him in a public street.'

Shukor did not feel able to speak, he simply nodded.

Mohammad looked at them in disbelief—genuinely at a loss for words at the magnitude of their insubordination. Finally, he said, pointing a finger at Shukor, 'You're suspended for two weeks. As for you'—he turned his attention to the fat man—'I want you on a plane to Singapore this evening.'

The steady whirring of the stand fan was the only sound to be heard in the room. Singh looked Inspector Mohammad in the eye and said, 'No.'

'What do you mean, "no"?' yelled Inspector Mohammad.

'I mean no—I'm not leaving. If you want to get me off the case, you'll have to arrest me.'

'Fine—have it your way. Shukor, arrest him.'

Shukor took a step forward, stopped, looked at the inspector from Singapore—a short, fat man with a determined expression and dirty white shoes—turned to his boss and said firmly, 'I can't, sir. I've been suspended.'

Singh understood what the word 'apoplectic' meant for the first time. Mohammad's face was mottled red, right up to the roots of his peppery hair. In contrast, his lips were pale and bloodless he had them pursed so tight.

Singh stepped in. He could not let the younger policeman ruin his career over his, Singh's, stubbornness. He said, 'Look, Mohammad. You're quite right. We were out of line. I was just sniffing around and things snowballed.'

Mohammad's jaw muscles unclenched slightly. Shukor heaved a tiny, inaudible sigh of relief.

Singh continued, 'If you'll just hear us out, I'll get on a plane if you insist. But I don't think Jasper Lee killed his brother. And I know you don't want to hang an innocent man.'

Inspector Mohammad exclaimed, 'What's the matter with you chaps? Chelsea Liew didn't do it. Jasper Lee didn't do it. Alan Lee has a bullet in his chest. Someone did it!'

Singh relaxed. Inspector Mohammad was listening now.

He said, 'I think I can get Jasper Lee to retract his confession. Will you let me try?'

Mohammad laughed. 'Well, that's an unusual approach. Here we usually work to *extract* confessions from suspects, not persuade them to retract. We leave that to the damned lawyers.'

Singh laughed, too. Shukor didn't dare.

Mohammad said suddenly, slapping the table with both hands and standing up, 'All right, it's a deal. If Jasper Lee recants, I'll reopen the investigation *and* let you stay.'

THE PRIVATE INVESTIGATOR was angry. The disk he had given Chelsea Liew was worth its weight in gold. He had expected her to pay up, and pay up quickly. But days had passed and no messenger had arrived bearing a sealed envelope stuffed full of cash. Mr Chan had pride. When he performed the task to which he was assigned he expected more than a pat on the head or a quiet dismissal.

He could not let this pass. If word got out that he could be cheated of his rightful fee, others would not be slow to follow suit. He thought hard. The idea came to him—the perfect punishment for rich bitches who didn't understand hard work. And the best part was that he could pretend that he had done it for all the right reasons. Mr Chan picked up his phone and rang one of his contacts.

JASPER LEE WAS in the interview cell. He looked even thinner—but still cheerful. He looked at the trio, Inspectors Singh and Mohammad and Sergeant Shukor.

'And what can I do for you, gentlemen?' he asked. 'Crime must be a bit slow at the moment if the police can waste three of their top cops on a confessed murderer.'

None of the men said anything and Jasper's face grew worried. 'Has anything happened?' he asked. 'Is Chelsea all right?'

Singh responded. 'Oh, yes! She's fine. Relieved to be out of here. The kids are OK, too.'

Jasper relaxed. He said, 'That's great. I'm glad she's recovering.'

Singh said, as one musing aloud, 'I would go as far as to say she's happy.'

'Oh? Why do you say that?'

'It's a great relief for her to be able to shack up with the boyfriend, I think. You know her better than I do—but she does not seem to be the sort who would want to hide a relationship.'

'What are you talking about?'

'Ravi, of course,' said the inspector, feigning surprise at Jasper's ignorance.

Shukor, watching the performance, felt almost sorry for Jasper Lee. He was no match for the Sikh policeman's low cunning.

Jasper looked annoyed, like someone who suspected that the joke might be on him but could not quite put his finger on the punch line. He said, as coolly as he could, 'Who is Ravi?'

'Don't you know? I thought you were bound to be in on the secret—seeing how close you and Chelsea are.'

Jasper asked with a valiant effort at a nonchalant tone: 'She's met someone, has she?'

'More than that!' exclaimed Singh. 'She's had a bit on the side all this while.' His tone was gossipy. 'What's sauce for the goose is sauce for the gander, eh?' And to Shukor's amazement, he winked at Jasper Lee.

Jasper's shock was palpable. 'What are you saying?'

'You need me to spell it out? All the while she's been playing little Miss Innocent, she's had a bit on the side.' Singh appeared to think about his statement for a moment. 'Well, I may be being just a bit unfair. It does seem she really loves this guy. They've been inseparable since she got out.'

Jasper had turned gallows pale. He said, more to himself than anyone, 'I don't believe it.'

'Well, look at this then . . .' Singh slid Ravi's love letter across the table.

It had turned the inspector's stomach to read the lies that the boyfriend was willing to tell to get his hands on some of Chelsea's money. It had a different effect on Jasper.

He let the letter slide through numb fingers and said in a voice that was so thick and choked, it sounded like his tongue had inflated suddenly, 'So what are you doing here?'

'We just wanted to ask you again why you killed Alan Lee.'

Jasper didn't answer. Instead, he stood up and said, 'Can we do this another time, please?'

THEY LEFT JASPER to his thoughts and walked out.

'Why didn't you ask him if he was sticking to his story?' asked Shukor.

'Too soon,' said Singh, and Mohammad nodded his agreement. 'In my experience, a mistake like he's made—it will take a while for him to move from disbelief to denial and then, of course, to anger. I give it about twenty-four hours—and then he'll be asking to see us.'

A young uniformed policeman came up to them and muttered something to Inspector Mohammad. The policeman handed a package over to him and, saluting smartly, retreated.

Singh asked, 'What is it?'

'A tape from an informer with an address. It might have a bearing on the Lee investigation apparently.'

'Convenient!' remarked Inspector Singh. 'Any idea what it's about?'

'Not a clue. But we can find out.'

The men walked towards a room with audio-visual equipment. Mohammad led the way, walking with long-limbed elegance. Shukor padded silently in his wake. Singh lumbered after them.

Mohammad opened the package and handed the disk to Shukor, who organised the equipment efficiently. The three men sat down and the whole episode at the night club unfolded before them. The wealthy Alan Lee, his plaything and the irate young man shunted aside.

'Maybe that woman had some reason to be jealous?' suggested Shukor.

'Yes, although more likely that young man had a surge of testosterone,' was the Malaysian inspector's response. 'We need to find out who he is.'

Singh said unexpectedly, 'Oh, no, we don't.'

'What do you mean?' asked Inspector Mohammad testily. 'You're convinced he's innocent? Leave me some suspects, for God's sake.'

Singh grinned. 'No, I don't know that he didn't do it. But I do know who that young man is. I met him only last week.'

The other two turned to him, the inspector in surprise, the sergeant, who was beginning to see the Singapore policeman as omniscient, in expectation.

'That,' said Inspector Singh laconically, 'is Marcus Lee—the murdered man's son.'

TWENTY-FOUR HOURS later, Jasper Lee asked to see Inspector Mohammad. Mohammad summoned Singh and they set off for the cells. There was no talk now about Singh returning to Singapore. Although there was no official reason for him to stay—not unless Chelsea was rearrested—he was too involved. Mohammad had changed his tune. He treated the inspector from Singapore as an ally in a hunt for the truth, not an adversary in a battle for kudos. Singh admired him for it but did not expect it to last past their next dispute over culpability.

Jasper Lee was a pale imitation of the man he had been a mere twenty-four hours earlier. His eyes were bloodshot and his hair lank. Up until he had heard about Ravi, Jasper had been waiting for certain death with dignity—now he looked as if it had caught up with him.

Singh flicked on the tape recorder and said, 'You asked to see us? Decided why you killed Alan yet?'

Jasper sat sullenly. He had called them in, but his heart still shrank from what he intended to do. The policemen saw the doubt and anxiety flit across his face. And also the disappointment: Jasper Lee had screwed up the courage to be a hero—and had only managed to land the part of the fool.

Singh sensed it was partly a reluctance to admit that his great sacrifice was a mistake. This was a man who had been branded a failure by his father and his brothers. He was vilified as being weak, lacking the hard head needed to make intelligent business judgments. Jasper must have felt secretly proud—proud of his capacity for self-sacrifice, proud of his courage in the face of death. And it had all been for nothing—merely vindicating the family view that he was a gullible idiot.

Singh said almost gently to the tortured man, 'It's not too late, you know.'

Jasper looked up at him and there were tears in his eyes. Mohammad shifted uncomfortably. He was of the old school—grown men didn't cry and boys shouldn't. Singh was from the same generation. But to him, tears were an honest reflection of emotion.

'Not too late?' asked Jasper. 'I'm afraid you're quite wrong. It was too late twenty years ago.'

'Too late to have her—not too late to save your life,' urged Mohammad.

'Save it for what?'

'For the things you care about,' said Singh.

'I was going to sacrifice it for the thing I care about.'

'We know,' said Mohammad gently.

Jasper looked at them and saw from their sympathetic expressions that they did know. It made it easier for him to put his errors into words. He said carefully, looking down at the floor, 'I did not kill my brother, Alan Lee.'

'Why did you confess?'

'I wanted to protect Chelsea. I was afraid she would be convicted of the murder.'

'Can you tell us why you wanted to protect her?'

'I love her. I've loved her since the day I met her, twenty years ago, at my brother's wedding.'

'So what changed your mind?'

Jasper struggled to articulate his reasoning. He said, 'I'm not sure. I tried to protect her because I loved her. I knew I couldn't have her, not if I was going to end up in here. But to find out she had a boyfriend all along . . . I thought she was alone, you see. That she needed me. Had no one else.'

'Why were you so sure that she killed Alan?'

The question penetrated the daze. 'I am *not* sure! But you seemed ready to hang her.'

'Do you know anything that made you suspect that she'd done it?'

'Where the smoking gun is, you mean? Look, I've decided I don't want to swing for Chelsea. Her boyfriend can do that if he wants. But that does not mean I plan to help you hang her!'

This flash of spirit quickly died down and Jasper slumped back into his chair. He said, 'What now?'

'I guess we let you go,' said Inspector Mohammad. 'But don't go too far.'

Singh tapped the Malay policeman on the shoulder and nodded in the direction of the door. 'I need a quick word,' he said.

The two men walked out and Mohammad said impatiently, 'What is it? Do you want me to thank you?'

'No, no. Don't let him go yet.'

'What?'

'Don't let him go yet!'

'Why not? Weren't you the one who couldn't bear Chelsea Liew spending one hour more than she had to in prison?'

Inspector Singh brushed aside his previous position with a quick gesture. 'Look, you don't think Chelsea did it, do you?'

'I wouldn't say that,' said Mohammad cautiously.

'At least you agree that there are a few suspects floating around?' He ticked them off on his fingers—'Kian Min, Marcus Lee, Ravi, the woman on the disk who might have been scorned.'

'And Chelsea Liew.'

'All right, and Chelsea.'

Mohammad said, 'I am willing to accept that we have a few suspects, yes. So what?'

'Let's keep Jasper here. The murderer, whichever one he is, will think he's home and dry. He might make a mistake.'

If Mohammad noticed the masculine pronoun for the murderer, he didn't show it. Instead, he nodded. 'That's actually not a bad idea. We'll try it.'

The policemen walked back in to inform Jasper Lee that he would have to wait a little bit longer to get out. He didn't seem to care.

SHARIFAH LOOKED OUT of the window. The day was so hot a shimmering haze was visible, as if the heat had warped the air. She was devastated by Chelsea's visit. It was a terrible thing to have a conversation with the woman whose husband she had slept with. She thought of her parents, who had worked hard to bring her up to know right from wrong. She thought of Marcus, who had loved her and been completely destroyed by her betrayal of him—not just with anyone, but with the father he hated. She felt very, very ashamed. She wondered if she dared call Marcus. She looked at her mobile phone on the dining table. No, she could not call him. Not after what she had done. Thank God the uncle had killed Alan. If she had provoked Marcus to murder, she could not have lived with herself.

Sharifah made up her mind. She would make amends as best as she could. And she would sell the flat bought in her name, as well as all the jewellery, and return the money to the Lee family—anonymously. She was not looking for public forgiveness, just personal redemption.

The doorbell rang and she went to answer it nervously. She hoped it was not Chelsea again.

A Sikh man said, 'We are the police. We want to ask you some questions about Alan Lee.'

She let them in reluctantly, the fat man and his handsome sidekick. They all sat down in the airy living room.

Singh did not beat around the bush. He had decided early to be aggressive, convinced that only tough questioning would have an impact on a woman so bold as to have an affair with Alan Lee. When Sharifah opened the door and peered out fearfully, he realised at once she was not the scheming woman of his imagination but a pretty young thing—a victim of Alan Lee.

Despite this, he felt a sudden anger at the woman who had added to the misery facing Chelsea Liew as she tried to escape her abusive marriage.

He said abruptly, 'We have good reason to suspect you killed Alan Lee.'

'We were going to get married! Why would I kill him?'

Inspector Singh asked rudely, 'Why in the world would a man like Alan Lee marry *you*? Here's what really happened—he showered you with attention, got you into bed and then dumped you as he had done all the women before you. You got upset, got a gun, found a quiet moment and killed him.'

Sharifah's eyes were wide with shock. She was young and had never been confronted so aggressively before. Even Chelsea, who had better reason than most to hate her, had not raised her voice. She felt tears fill her eyes. 'But he converted to Islam—he did that for me!'

'You might have given him the idea, but he converted to get custody of the kids and spite his ex-wife.'

'I don't believe you!'

Singh said in genuine disgust, 'It's naive, stupid young women like you who make it possible for men like Alan to exploit and ruin them.'

Sharifah said quietly, 'I know I made a mistake, I see that now. But I didn't kill him. At the time when he died, I still thought I loved him.'

'"I still thought I loved him,"' imitated Singh, in an irritated tone. 'If you were my daughter, I'd lock you in a room and not let you out until you developed some common sense.'

'I've told you I didn't kill him. Is there anything else I can help you with?' asked Sharifah.

Singh noted with approval that the young woman had some gumption. He wondered at Alan Lee. He had been attracted to strong, beautiful women, if Chelsea and Sharifah were anything to go by, but then was not content until he had beaten the spirit out of them.

'Did Alan beat you?' he asked abruptly.

She flinched at the sudden change of tack but she said firmly, 'No, of course not. Why would he do that? I told you—he loved me. He loved me very much. We were going to get married.'

Singh knew she was lying. She was protesting too much.

'How often did he hit you?'

'I've just told you, he didn't!'

'Just once, twice? Was it all flowers and apologies after that? What did he tell you—he was under pressure at work? He loved you so much he got jealous because you were talking to the postman? I bet you thought it was a compliment that he gave you a black eye!'

Sharifah said in a subdued tone, 'It was only the once. He slapped me. But he was really sorry about it.'

'And you believed him?' asked Shukor, speaking for the first time during the interview.

She looked at him defiantly. 'Yes.'

'So let me get this straight,' said the inspector. 'He was much, much older than you, was going through a divorce where he was accused of adultery and brutality, and was locked in a bitter custody battle for his kids. He had started to hit you—and yet you thought you were going to marry him and live happily ever after?'

She nodded and said, 'I guess it sounds unlikely.'

Singh said, 'All right then, let's suppose I believe you . . . maybe you didn't kill him.'

Sharifah looked up at him quickly, hope dawning in her eyes.

'Why don't you tell us how you drove Marcus Lee to kill his own father?'

NINE

M r Chan, the private investigator, had given a copy of the disk to the police. Chelsea Liew, he thought, would think twice about not paying up for work done in the future. And he was quite sure he had found a way to recoup the losses that he had made on the Lee investigation: he had approached the newspapers with an exclusive. The tape in exchange for 2,000 ringgit. When he explained, in lascivious detail, what was on the tape, he started a bidding war. In the end, he had walked away with 5,000 ringgit. *Not bad*, he thought smugly. His cunning had resulted in a much better outcome than he could have predicted when that woman had not paid him.

The newspaper that won the tape watched it, cut stills from it, consulted their lawyers and prepared the morning edition with an enthusiasm that had not been seen on the newsroom floor for many years. They had the Malaysian scoop of the year.

CHELSEA HAD PERSUADED Marcus to sit down with her for a coffee. It had not been easy. He had insisted he was busy, he had schoolwork—they could do it later. But she had insisted. They sat at the dining table, sipping hot coffee. The two younger boys had gone to the park with their nanny. They would not be interrupted—not for a while, anyway.

Chelsea broke the silence that was becoming oppressive. 'I'm worried about you.'

'Why?' asked Marcus. 'I'm fine.'

'I don't think you're fine. You're hardly at home. You don't speak to me or the boys any more. Your clothes stink of alcohol and cigarettes. I checked with the school—you've not been turning up there.'

'I don't like you spying on me!'

'I'm not spying on you. I'm your mother—I'm worried about you.'

'Yeah, you're a great mother . . .'

'What's that supposed to mean?'

'Nothing!'

'Marcus, I did my best for you. I'm doing my best for all you kids. Things haven't been easy—you know that.'

Marcus fidgeted in his chair. 'Can I go now?'

Chelsea said quietly, 'I know about Sharifah.'

His skinny body grew stock still. He looked up at his mother and saw the sympathy and pity on her face. Images of Sharifah flitted through his mind like a series of photos on a screen saver. And then the last time he had seen her—at that club. Standing there, all dressed up like he had never seen her, looking so much older than she had ever done before. Wearing clothes his father had bought her, wearing jewellery his father had bought her, selling herself to a rich man. He had begged her to come away with him. Promised her that he loved her. Tried to explain the sort of man his father was. He had thought, for a moment, that he was getting through to her. Her face had softened, she had looked younger. More like the girl he had known at school. And then he had realised that she was looking at him with sympathy, with pity. That same expression he now saw on his mother's face.

Marcus put his head down on his folded arms. His mother reached out and put an arm round him. He did not shake it off. For a long time they stayed in the same position, until at last Marcus sat up.

He looked at his mother with red-rimmed eyes and said, 'How do you know about Sharifah?'

'That's not important.'

'You know about Dad, too? What he did?'

She nodded, not trusting herself to speak. Her anger at her dead husband burned so hot she felt she could set fire to things simply by touching them.

'I hated him. I'm so glad he's dead,' said the boy bitterly.

'Marcus, I need to ask you an important question. And whatever you tell me, I will protect you. But I need to know the truth.'

Marcus looked at her, his face twisted with sadness.

She asked softly, 'Did you kill your father?'

'MARCUS DID NOT kill his father.' Sharifah spoke emphatically, complete conviction in her voice.

'How would you know that for a fact?' asked Singh.

'I know Marcus. He would never do a thing like that!'

'I can just see the court taking your word for it,' said Singh, snidely. 'You'd make a wonderful character witness—your behaviour in this matter has been so upstanding.'

Sharifah winced at the sarcasm but would not budge from her position. 'Marcus Lee is a very gentle boy.'

'A gentle boy, not like that big strong man, his father, eh? If that's how you spoke to him—and not just about him—no wonder he was provoked to kill his father.'

'He did not kill his father!'

'Somebody did.'

'I thought it was the uncle.'

'I bet that made you feel better,' remarked Inspector Singh, with his usual intuitive insight. 'You must have been very worried, when you heard Alan Lee was dead, that you had driven Marcus to do it.'

'I was not worried at all,' she said firmly.

'Look, the only way you could know for sure Marcus Lee did not murder his father is if you killed Alan yourself.'

'No, I know Marcus didn't do it . . . because I was with him at the time of the murder.'

Singh looked at her disbelievingly. 'That's your story?'

She nodded, pale but determined.

'So what was this? The grand reunion?'

She thought about her answer.

Trying to remember exactly what she had said earlier so that she would not contradict herself, guessed the inspector. It would be almost amusing if it wasn't an effort to mislead them in a murder investigation.

Sharifah said, 'No . . . I hadn't broken up with Alan. We were still getting married. But I wanted to apologise to Marcus—make him understand.'

'So when was this grand reconciliation and forgiveness fest?'

'I told you—the day Alan was murdered.'

'And which day was that?'

'I don't remember.'

'You don't remember the day your fiancé was killed?'

'Of course I remember. I mean I don't remember the exact date!'

'Do you remember what time this reunion with Marcus was?'

'Not exactly. But we were together quite a while.'

'Morning or afternoon?'

She was confused. 'I don't understand.'

'Were you with him in the morning or the afternoon?'

'I don't know, I don't remember. Both!'

Singh laughed out loud. He said, 'I feel sorry for you spouting these lies in front of the prosecution at Marcus Lee's trial for murder.'

'What are you going to do?'

The inspector didn't answer her question. Instead, he turned to Shukor and said, 'Come on—let's go. We've got work to do.'

Shukor nodded to Sharifah almost apologetically and trailed after his superior officer. He had no idea why Singh had been so aggressive with Sharifah and he certainly wasn't going to ask; he didn't relish feeling the rough edge of the inspector's tongue. It was bad enough to be a witness to it. Still, it had produced results. The young woman had tied herself in knots with her hastily concocted version of events, desperate to provide her ex-boyfriend with an alibi. Shukor could not decide whether her attempts had been provoked by guilt or a residual affection for Marcus.

The two men took the lift to the ground floor and got into the car. They drove quietly for a couple of minutes. At last Shukor asked, 'Are we on the way to arrest Marcus?'

'No. In fact, just pull over here.'

Shukor stopped by the side of the road. 'What now, sir?'

'I want you to go back.'

'Back?'

'Yes, to the apartment building. Find a convenient bush, hide behind it. Wait for Sharifah to come out and stay on her tail. *Don't* let her see you.'

'Yes, sir. But what are you hoping she'll do?'

'Run to Marcus and warn him.'

'Won't she just call him?'

'I suspect she'll want to see him face to face. Try and get this alibi straight. Besides'—Singh fished in his pocket—'I nicked her mobile.'

Shukor looked shocked but did not protest. He said, 'You don't believe she was with him?'

'No!'

'Me, neither,' said Shukor ruefully, climbing out of the car.

Inspector Singh got out too, and walked round to the other side, sliding into the driver's seat with difficulty and moving the seat back so his stomach had more space.

Shukor bent down to speak to him. 'Do you think she did it, sir? Or him?'

'Don't know. But both scenarios are quite possible. They might even have done it together.'

INSPECTOR MOHAMMAD WAS not at the station. He was at the Lee Building talking to Lee Kian Min. Kian Min was not amused to be at the receiving end of two visits from the police in as many days. He calmed down a little when Mohammad told him that he was just there to apologise for Sergeant Shukor's behaviour and to assure him that the policeman had been disciplined.

'He should be sacked,' asserted Kian Min, daring the inspector to contradict him.

Mohammad chose discretion. 'It was not my decision,' he said, hinting that if he was in charge, Shukor would have come out of it much the worse. 'The higher-ups thought that he should have a second chance since he had an unblemished record until the regrettable incident with you.'

'It better not happen again.'

'It won't, Mr Lee.'

Kian Min looked at the inspector expectantly. 'You want something else?'

'There is something you could help me with, sir. Did you kill Alan Lee?'

'What?'

'I asked you if you killed your brother, Alan Lee?'

'What for I would do that?'

'For this!' said Mohammad, waving a careless hand around.

'I no need to kill him to get this. I was boss of the company already.'

'That's not what I hear. My sources tell me that Alan Lee was the brains behind the success of the company.'

'Alan? The brains?' Kian Min barked with loud, angry laughter. 'Who told you that?' He jabbed his finger at the inspector to emphasise his point. 'They know nothing about Lee Timber. I have been the boss of this company since my father died. Alan was figurehead only.'

'But what about that decision to switch to growing palm oil for bio-fuels? I read in the papers that it was Alan's last decision in charge before he was killed. The analysts think it's a stroke of genius.'

'Of course it is genius—my genius!' Kian Min was almost shouting now. 'Alan did not even understand the business!'

Mohammad shook his head, like a man struggling to understand what he was being told.

Kian Min said, 'I thought Jasper killed Alan, anyway.'

'We have reason to doubt his story,' said Mohammad stolidly.

'That's a pity. But, for your information, I have nothing to do with it.'

'You think Jasper Lee did it?'

'I don't know and I don't care who killed Alan. He was useless, a piece of nothing his whole life.' There was a small speck of saliva at the corner of Kian Min's mouth.

'But you testified at the custody trial that he was a fine man, a good father and a brilliant businessman.'

'Maybe I did, I suppose . . . family must stick together.'

'You've been sitting there telling me you don't care who killed your brother but it was most likely your other brother, and then you expect me to believe that you felt a *family* obligation?'

Kian Min maintained a sullen reticence for a few seconds and then said, 'Well, murder not the same, right?'

'Perhaps, but perjury—giving false testimony under oath in court—is an offence.'

'I not committed perjury.'

'You lied about your brother's character. I could arrest you right now and drag you down to the police station in shackles.'

Kian Min turned pale. He said, 'How can I change your mind?'

'What are you offering?' asked Inspector Mohammad carefully.

'Some contribution to your retirement fund?'

Mohammad looked at the man across the table with an unreadable expression. 'How much?' he asked bluntly.

'A hundred thousand.'

Mohammad shook his head.

'Five hundred thousand? That should be enough. You can retire in style!'

'That's a lot of money,' said Mohammad, thoughtfully.

SHARIFAH LEFT HER apartment hurriedly, jumped into a small Toyota sports car—no doubt another gift from Alan—and set off at top speed. Shukor, waiting in a taxi, had no difficulty following her.

When she reached the neighbourhood where Alan Lee had his mansion, she drove past the house slowly, turned round, parked the car at the bottom of the street and waited. Shukor disembarked from the taxi some way up the street, paid off the driver and sat at a bus stop.

Some time later, the gates to the Lee residence opened. A Mercedes Benz purred out. Shukor, watching Sharifah, saw her duck down so the car she was in looked driverless. He wondered at this until he glimpsed the passenger in the back seat. It was Chelsea, her face partially obscured by a very large pair of sunglasses. Shukor realised that Sharifah must have been waiting for her to go out—unable to face the wife.

Sharifah waited a few minutes and then got out of the car. She walked slowly up the hill, each step laboured and reluctant. Shukor stayed a safe distance away but there was no danger of Sharifah turning round. All her attention was on the shiny gold gates of Marcus's home. She reached the entrance and gave the bell a good, long ring. She spoke a few words into the mike and the gates swung open mysteriously. Sharifah took a few tentative steps forward. The gates shut behind her.

SHARIFAH WAS TERRIFIED. Her chest was constricted, her movements slow and uncoordinated, her skin tingling with nerves. She was ushered inside by the housemaid, led to a sitting room, invited to sit down on a comfortable sofa and offered a drink, which she declined. Sharifah explained that she was a schoolfriend of Marcus.

The maid said, 'I will fetch Master Marcus. Your name, please.'

She said, 'I'm Sharifah. But please don't tell him. Just say it's someone from school. I want to surprise him.'

The maid nodded. She was pleased to be part of a conspiracy to cheer up the young master. He had been so miserable for so long now. She smiled at the young, beautiful visitor. She noticed that the girl looked pale. Perhaps there was something more here than met the eye. This could be a girlfriend. She could not fail to cheer Marcus up.

Marcus was slumped in bed playing with a portable Gameboy. He wore the same clothes he had gone to bed in. He smelt, not just of alcohol and cigarettes, but also rancid and unwashed. The maid hoped the girlfriend was the tolerant sort. Marcus, however, had no inclination to drag himself out of bed and go down to his guest.

'Who is it?' he asked irritably.

'I did not ask,' said the maid.

'You know you're always supposed to ask.'

'Yes, Master Marcus. I just forgot.'

'Well, just find out who it is and send him away.'

'Why don't you just come down and say "hello"? Maybe it will make you in a good mood?'

Marcus snorted, but then remembered that one of his schoolmates owed him some money. That must be who it was. He got to his feet.

'All right, I'll see him.'

The maid did not think this was a good time to mention that the visitor was female.

'WHAT ARE YOU DOING HERE?' Marcus didn't shout, but anger ran through the words like a major artery. 'Get out of my house!'

Sharifah cowered, as if his words were physical blows. Her shoulders shook and she wrapped her arms round herself—part defensive gesture, part an attempt to stop the trembling.

She tried to speak. 'Marcus . . .'

He screamed this time: 'No, I don't want to know. Get out!'

'I wouldn't be here if it wasn't important.'

She rushed the words out, but he did not appear to have heard them. He was still staring at her as if she was some sort of apparition. One small part of his brain noticed her pallor. She had lost weight and was not wearing make-up as she had done in those last days with his father.

She said again, 'You have to listen to me, Marcus. This is important or I wouldn't be here.'

Somehow that got through. 'You have something important to tell me?

That's a change, isn't it? The last time you had something *important* that you should have told me, you didn't bother, did you? But maybe—just maybe—I would have been just a little bit interested to know that my girl-friend was sleeping with my father.'

The words dripped with sarcasm, but the voice was undiluted anger.

Sharifah thought she had known, had guessed, how much she must have hurt him. But now she looked at the thin, young boy in front of her and realised that she had no idea what he must have gone through. She said, 'God, Marcus. I am so sorry. I could not have done worse and I will never forgive myself, as I know you will never forgive me.'

He shook his head, as if her words were like a mosquito buzzing in his ear.

'But I must talk to you. You must listen to me.'

Marcus stared at her fixedly, unblinkingly.

Sharifah was beginning to worry for his sanity. She said in a determined voice, 'The police have been to see me. They know about us. And about me . . . and Alan.'

He did not respond or appear to have heard her.

'Marcus, the police think you killed your father!'

'WELL, WAS IT THE GIRLFRIEND? Or the son?' The Malaysian inspector's tone was flippant but Singh ignored it. He did not know why Mohammad was in such a good mood but he did not plan to match it.

Singh said, 'Hard to say. The girl claims that she and Alan were still an item when he was killed and so she was not a woman scorned. And also that he converted to Islam to marry her.'

'Really? Did you believe that?'

'No. I think she gave him the idea and he realised it would be a powerful weapon in the custody hearings. But I doubt he would have married her.'

'What was she like, this girl?'

'Pretty, dangerously naive.'

'A killer?'

Singh said reluctantly, 'I don't see it. But I've been wrong before.'

'Wrong? Not our infallible inspector from Singapore!'

Singh scowled at his counterpart. 'Why are you in such a good mood?'

Mohammad ignored the question and said instead, 'It must be the son, then . . . Marcus Lee.'

'The girlfriend claims to have been with him at the time of the murder.'

'She's sleeping with the father but hanging out with the son? One big happy family?'

'It was a fairly shaky alibi. She had no idea when Alan was killed so was trying for a fairly broad-brush approach.'

Mohammad laughed. 'What prompted it?'

'Guilt, probably. She knows the only reason we suspect Marcus is because, thanks to her, he has a powerful motive.'

'You should have followed her. Presumably she'll rush off and warn the young man now.'

'I sent Shukor.'

'Good thinking,' said Mohammad approvingly.

'So, what's been happening around here?' asked Singh.

'Chelsea Liew came to see Jasper but was turned away.'

'By us?'

'No, by him. He's not ready to tell her that she's back on the list of suspects, I guess.'

'Which brings us to the question—why do you look like the cat that's swallowed the cream?'

Mohammad said, as nonchalantly as he could, 'I dropped in to see Lee Kian Min.'

'He agreed to see you? I would have thought he'd be reluctant to expose his person to a policeman for a while.'

'He was. I said I was the official delegation to apologise to a leading member of the business community.'

'I bet he lapped that up.'

Mohammad nodded. 'He was fine until I asked him if he had killed his brother—then he got a little bit agitated.'

'What did he say?' asked Singh.

'Well, he denied everything, of course—said that it was probably Jasper.' Mohammad shook his head at the willingness of the Lee brothers to point the finger at each other.

'No love lost between the brothers, eh?' remarked Inspector Singh.

'No. It made it very difficult for him to explain why he had testified at the custody hearings that Alan was such a fine fellow.'

'Good point. We can threaten him with—'

Mohammad interrupted him, determined that no one was going to steal his lines. 'Perjury! Yes, I pointed out to him that we could make his life miserable.'

'What did he say?'

'He tried to bribe me,' said the Malaysian policeman.

Singh refrained from saying that Kian Min must have felt on pretty safe ground if the reputation of the Malaysian police force was accurate. He asked instead, 'How much?'

'Five hundred thousand without bargaining . . .'

'Not bad. He must really want to stay out of trouble.'

'Well, I told him money would not do the trick. I needed another credible suspect.'

'Did he have one?'

'Yup,' said Mohammad, grinning.

'So who did Kian Min serve up to save his skin?' asked Inspector Singh.

'A businessman from Hong Kong,' replied Mohammad, evenly.

'What was his reason?'

'Quite complicated. This Chinaman from Hong Kong—Douglas Wee—fronts for some Chinese conglomerate looking for bio-fuels.'

'So?'

'Lee Timber has been considering diversifying into bio-fuels, partly because this syndicate, or Douglas Wee anyway, promised to buy whatever they can produce.'

'I read in the papers that they had decided to go ahead with it.'

'Yes, that's right—now that Alan Lee is dead. Apparently, he was standing in the way of the project while Kian Min was in favour of it. Alan's dying made it happen.'

'So why should this Donald or Douglas, or whatever his name is, have killed Alan?'

'According to Lee Kian Min, he needed to land the deal for his Chinese masters or wear knee-cap protectors.'

'It's possible, I suppose,' said Singh doubtfully, scratching his nose.

Mohammad laughed. 'There's no need to be polite. I know it's far-fetched. But we can get this guy in. He's in Malaysia apparently, tidying up loose ends.'

'And if it does turn out to be a load of bollocks, we'll have more to harass Lee with.'

Mohammad raised a warning finger. 'Let me make it quite clear—under no circumstances are you or Shukor to go anywhere near Lee Kian Min. He's a petty, vindictive bastard. If you annoy him again, I will not have the influence to protect you—and nobody else will give a damn.'

Singh held up a pudgy, stubby-fingered hand. 'I hear you,' he said.

'Good,' said Mohammad.

CHELSEA HEARD HER. Back early from the jail when Jasper had refused to see her, she had walked into the house and followed the sound of voices. Marcus was talking to someone. She wondered who it could be. He never invited friends home.

To her utter amazement it was Sharifah. Chelsea was speechless with shock. Was no place sacrosanct? How dare that woman set foot in her house? And then she heard the sentence that drove all other thoughts from her mind: 'Marcus, the police think you killed your father!'

She was at the door now, unseen by the two of them. Instead of throwing Sharifah off the premises with all the raw rage she could summon, she found herself asking quietly, 'How do you know? How do you know they suspect Marcus? What about Jasper?'

She might as well have yelled. Her words fell on the tableau like over-sized hailstones. The pair whirled to look at her.

Marcus spoke automatically. 'This has nothing to do with you, Mum.'

Sharifah said, 'I'm so sorry. I wouldn't have come here. But I had to warn Marcus.'

Chelsea ignored the dismissal and apology with equal indifference. She said again, 'How do you know they suspect Marcus?'

Sharifah turned to Marcus for guidance but he was looking at his mother. His expression revealed how he was torn between a desperate desire to lean on her strength and a reluctance to expose her to more pain.

Sharifah said quietly, 'The police came to see me.'

'What did they say?'

'That they were no longer certain of Jasper's guilt—they didn't say why—and their next best bet was me or Marcus.'

'Why you?'

'They thought I might have quarrelled with Alan. That perhaps he dumped me and I was angry or jealous.'

'And were you?'

Chelsea's questions were staccato and to the point. She wanted to understand fully what they were up against. She forced the fear that welled up in volcanic waves back down through a sheer effort of will. There would be time for that later. Right now, she had to question this woman until she fully understood the danger that Marcus was in.

Sharifah said, 'No. I still believed we were going to get married.'

'Still believed? What does that mean?'

The younger woman hung her head, unable to look either of them in the eye as she was forced to discuss her relationship with the husband of one and the father of the other. 'I'm beginning to realise now that Alan never had any intention of marrying me. That was not the sort of man he was.'

Chelsea dismissed this as irrelevant. She asked, 'How did the police know about your relationship with Marcus?'

Sharifah shrugged. 'I'm not sure. From the way they talked, they seemed to have some sort of tape.'

Chelsea sat down suddenly. 'My God,' she whispered to herself, completely forgetting the presence of the others. 'I forgot to send the money.'

'What are you talking about, Mum?' asked Marcus.

Chelsea's hands were shaking. She put them on the arms of the chair, trying to steady herself. Had she brought this catastrophe down on them? 'A private investigator—I hired him during the divorce and custody hearings to dig up some proof of adultery to help my case against your father. He turned up the other day with a tape. It had all three of you on it—at some club.'

From their worried faces she could tell that they knew immediately which occasion it must have been—and they both knew it would not have looked good.

'But how would the police have got a copy?' asked Sharifah, confused.

'I forgot to send the money. The investigator asked for two thousand ringgit. I came to see you.' She looked at Sharifah. 'And I just clean forgot to pay him. He must have decided to teach me a lesson.'

Marcus guessed how much his mother was suffering from the thought that she had led the police directly to him. He sat down on the arm of her chair and gave her a hug. 'They would have found out about Sharifah and me somehow. It's not your fault, Mum.'

Chelsea shook her head. 'I don't know, son.'

Sharifah interrupted them. 'I didn't finish. I said I was with you, Marcus—when your . . . when Alan was shot. But I didn't really know when that was so I wasn't very convincing. I'm not sure they believed me.'

'You alibied me? Why?'

There was a pause while she considered her answer. Her young, fresh face was thoughtful, like a student pondering an exam question; not an adulteress considering an alibi. At last, she said, 'They think you did it because of me. I guess that makes it my fault that you're in trouble. I just wanted to try and make things better.' She trailed off.

Chelsea guessed that she was longing to make things better, not just in the context of the suspicion the police had about Marcus, but with everything else she had done in the last few months. This was a young, smart woman who had somehow come adrift and made some truly appalling decisions. Chelsea might have found it in her heart to feel just a tiny bit sorry for her if it was not for the fact that the consequences of her actions were about to engulf her son.

'Do you think I did it?' The question was blurted out more stridently than Marcus intended. He was looking at her, but Chelsea suspected the tension in his body was for fear of Sharifah's answer.

Chelsea said immediately and as reassuringly as she could, 'Of course not, darling. I *know* you had nothing to do with it. You've told me so and I believe you.'

Sharifah did not say anything and Marcus said almost roughly, 'What about you?'

'No,' she said quietly, 'I don't think you did it.'

Marcus sat down suddenly. He said, 'That means a lot.'

Sharifah said briskly, 'I guess it's not what we think that's important. It's what the police believe that counts. So let's get this alibi straight.'

Marcus said, 'I don't want you to have to lie to protect me.'

Chelsea said sharply, 'Don't be ridiculous, Marcus. Sharifah is trying to help—and you're in no position to refuse.'

'But she could really get into trouble . . .'

'You could hang,' said Chelsea.

There was a silence after Chelsea had so brutally pointed out Marcus's fate if he was found guilty of murder. In their imaginations, all three could picture Marcus at dawn, a hood over his head, with only a couple of policemen and a doctor for company, waiting to drop through the trap door with the thick, rough rope round his neck.

Sharifah said, 'Your mother is right, Marcus.'

He was white-faced but resolute. 'I still don't like it.'

Chelsea brushed a greasy strand of hair away from his forehead and said gently, 'We understand that, Marcus. I don't think we're looking at Sharifah testifying in court or anything like that. But if you have an alibi, the police will keep looking for the murderer and not stop with you. Once they've found someone else, we won't have to pretend any more.'

'I wonder why they don't think Uncle Jasper killed Dad. Why haven't they released him if he didn't do it?'

Chelsea shook her head ruefully. 'That may be my fault as well. I persuaded the policeman from Singapore to keep looking into things. I just didn't believe Jasper murdered Alan. I had no idea there was evidence out there that would implicate you.'

'It was a Sikh policeman who came to see me,' said Sharifah. 'He was pretty unpleasant—really aggressive and accusing.'

'It could be that they still think Jasper did it. But thanks to my kicking up a fuss, they're looking around a bit as well.' Chelsea turned to her son and said with something approaching bleakness, 'I'm so sorry, Marcus. Everything I've done seems to have got you into more trouble—it was the last thing I intended.'

Marcus shrugged. 'Let's not concentrate on what we could have done differently, Mum. It's water under the bridge.'

Sharifah said practically, 'Someone needs to tell me when Alan was killed. And we need a good story about where we were at the time and what we were doing.'

The three sat down, wife, son and girlfriend of a murdered man, and tried to concoct an alibi.

TEN

The newspapers the next morning caught them all completely by surprise. Singh saw them first. He was up early, unable to sleep, which was very unusual for him. He normally slept like a tired six-year-old, completely and utterly knocked out by a day's exertions. He had drunk too much coffee the previous night; his sister had annoyed him with a tedious nag about some wedding that he should have attended but had not; the mattress in the room was filled with lumpy cotton; and the small bedroom was either unbearably stuffy or, if he turned on the air-conditioning, an icebox.

He got out of bed just as dawn was breaking, wandered around the house looking for a source of coffee and heard the thump of the newspaper landing on the front porch.

It was a thick wad of newsprint tied up in a rubber band that snapped against his hand the minute he picked it up. Singh grimaced. It was going to be one of those days.

To his relief, his sister appeared at the door, bleary-eyed but instinctively hospitable. 'Coffee?'

He nodded curtly and sat down at the small table outside. A few potted plants provided the only hint of green to the tiled garden. In the distance he could hear birdsong, as well as the cooing of pigeons. Singh took the coffee his sister proffered with a muttered thanks and unfolded the paper.

It was the lead story on the front page. Three large, slightly grainy but recognisable faces were side by side looking out at the reader. Sharifah looked beautiful and worried, Marcus looked distraught and Alan was smug. Singh recognised the photos as being lifted from the disk. He wondered how the papers had got hold of them. The same place the police had got them, he supposed. Not content with earning brownie points with the police, the source of the disk had cashed in as well.

It really didn't matter now. The cat was out of the bag and far away.

There were so many font sizes on the cover—headlines, by-lines, sub-headings—it was difficult to take in at first. 'Alan Lee's Girlfriend', 'Night Club Rumpus', 'Father, Son and the Woman Who Came Between Them'. There was more inside. 'See pages 3–12 for more details.' Singh read the articles slowly. The newspaper had extrapolated wildly from the facts at its disposal.

Only Marcus emerged without blame—but he was made to look like a pathetic young thing, superseded by his own father in the affections of his girlfriend. The newspaper stopped just short of suggesting that motives for murder abounded in the love triangle they had discovered. Jasper's confession was a bulwark against that particular storyline—but they would have a field day when Jasper was eventually released.

Singh shook his head. An ugly case was getting uglier. His thoughts turned to Chelsea. She was going to be a very unhappy woman when she saw the papers that morning.

MOHAMMAD ORDERED Jasper's release. When Singh heard, he was furious.

'Why, in God's name, did you do that?'

'He's innocent,' replied Mohammad, patiently.

'You know and I know that has nothing to do with it. I'm not asking you why you released him; I'm asking you why you released him *now*!'

'It seemed like good timing. The other suspects more or less know that we don't think Jasper did it any more.'

'Good timing?' Singh almost exploded with rage. 'How can this be good timing? About the only thing the newspapers didn't do this morning was accuse Marcus Lee of murder. By tomorrow, even that will change.'

'That's why I did it,' confessed Mohammad, unexpectedly.

'What do you mean?' Singh snapped at his Malaysian counterpart like a bad-tempered dog.

'Unlike you, I'm trying to find a murderer!' The phlegmatic Inspector Mohammad was getting annoyed.

'What's that supposed to mean?'

'*I* am trying to catch a murderer.' Mohammad enunciated each word carefully as if he was talking to someone of subnormal intelligence. '*You* are trying to protect Chelsea Liew from the "slings and arrows of outrageous fortune".'

Singh did not know it but it was a sign of how angry Mohammad was when he started quoting Shakespeare. Shukor tried to catch the Singaporean's eye but to no avail. The Sikh was six inches shorter but toe to toe with Mohammad, and neither was backing down.

'That's nonsense,' said Singh through gritted teeth. 'She's not even a real suspect any more.'

'That's precisely what I mean. Your remit was to protect her from being hanged for a murder she didn't commit, not shield her from the harsh winds of fate. If Marcus Lee killed his father, he's going to swing for it. If we let the newspapers have a go at him, he might do something silly and give himself away. You might not have noticed, but we are down to a small band of suspects with no way of narrowing the list further.'

Singh looked at the other man thoughtfully. Was he right? Had he, a policeman who prided himself on his objectivity, so lost his sense of perspective that he was no longer looking for a murderer but just trying to protect a woman who had caught his fancy?

Mohammad sensed that he had caused at least a pinprick of doubt and was satisfied. He said, 'I'm off to bring Douglas Wee in for questioning.' Met with blank stares from the others, he said impatiently, 'You know, Lee Kian Min's sacrificial lamb.' And then perhaps regretting his harsh words a little bit, he said, 'I'll call you when I've got him—you might want to sit in.'

Singh nodded absently and the other man beckoned to Shukor and left. Inspector Singh sat down on a stool and bent over to tie a shoelace. He pondered Mohammad's words.

It was possible, he decided, that he was not behaving as professionally as was his norm. It might be about Chelsea, but he thought it was also partly because he was not in Singapore. There, constrained by superiors who distrusted him, colleagues who were suspicious of his methods, subordinates who feared him and the endless red tape that engulfed any investigation, he did not have the freedom to follow his own instincts so single-mindedly. But here he was functioning partly as a private investigator and partly as some consultant flown in for his two cents' worth of advice. It had led to a feeling of freedom from the normal constraints of police work.

After all, back in Singapore, he would hardly have agreed to work freelance for an ex-murder suspect to prove someone innocent. He would never have gone to visit a suspect and then let a junior policeman rough the suspect up, not even one as deserving of a good kicking as Lee Kian Min. It was this free and easy Kuala Lumpur society with its hard edge of aggression that had sucked him insidiously into its culture. Singh shook his head. What did they put in the water in these parts? The stuff they pumped over to Singapore was a less potent blend.

MARCUS WOKE UP that morning in a good mood. Considering that he was suspected of murder, he had slept well. He got out of bed, showered quickly, and dressed. Marcus did not lack self-awareness, so he was perfectly aware that his good cheer was the result of Sharifah's apparent concern for his welfare. It was absurd that the goodwill of a woman who had pretty much ruined his life should have the power to raise his spirits this way. But there was no doubt—he felt great. And with the careful alibi they had worked out the previous evening, he felt safe, too.

Then he saw the newspapers. Marcus was only seventeen. When he saw how public his humiliation was to be, how impossible it would be to forget the past and reconnect with Sharifah, he sat down and sobbed—big, heavy, dehydrating tears—like a child who had lost something precious.

CHELSEA OVERSLEPT. AS a result, she did not wake up to the newspapers like the other protagonists. She missed three frantic calls from her civil lawyer and two from her Syariah lawyer.

When she woke up, she looked at the time in surprise—it was close to eleven in the morning. She did not feel like she had slept for twelve hours. Her eyes were dry and her head was full of what felt like clogging strands of cobwebs. Her mouth tasted like it had done after three weeks of prison food. She dragged herself out of bed and walked slowly to the bathroom.

Could it be that her worry about Marcus was misplaced? It was impossible to know. She liked the fat policeman from Singapore. She had appreciated his support when she was isolated in the physical confines of the Malaysian jail and the mental prison that Alan had created for her. But she was under no illusions—Singh was not going to ignore the truth for her. If Marcus had killed Alan, and he found some evidence, there would be no dereliction of duty on his part.

Chelsea stood under the hot shower and turned it on. She turned her face to the water and tried to wash away the worries. One of the true advantages of wealth, she decided, was a high-powered shower. She remembered the bathroom in the small house where she grew up. There was no hot water, of course. The whole household bathed using a plastic bucket to pour cold water from a large, tiled receptacle in one corner of the bathroom. Floors were cement, slippery and always wet. Soap was very pink and harsh on the skin. And the towels . . . Chelsea smiled when she remembered the threadbare towels, with hardly any water-absorbing qualities.

She dried herself quickly on a carpet-sized, fluffy towel and debated what her first step of the day should be. Perhaps she should contact Inspector Singh and somehow convince him that her son was innocent. She paused in the middle of the thought. Could she be convincing? She admitted to herself that she was not sure that Marcus had not killed Alan. At any time when he was growing up she would have sworn that her gentle son was incapable of harming anyone. But the perfect storm of events that he had encountered would have left him completely off-balance.

Chelsea heard the doorbell and grimaced. The last thing she wanted was a visitor right now. She peeked out from behind the curtain and saw to her surprise that it was Jasper. Her brief pleasure was immediately swamped by the confirmation of her fears. If the police had released Jasper, they must be on the trail of her son.

JASPER WAS DRESSED in clothes that were too big for him. His blue jeans and white shirt were clean but not pressed. He was not wearing socks. His hair was a little too long and he had a furtive air that would have seemed appropriate in prison but was at odds with his luxurious surroundings in Alan Lee's home. Chelsea had run down the stairs, opened the front door and hugged him tightly. He stood stiffly in her embrace and then let her usher him into the house. She made him sit down, fussed over him, asked him what he wanted to eat or drink. He sat on the edge of his chair with his hands on his knees, quite still, except for a finger and thumb that picked nervously at a loose thread on his jeans.

She realised that there was something wrong, sat down in a chair opposite him and said in a gentle tone, 'What is it, Jasper?'

He did not answer and she did not press him. She understood the first feeling of freedom. There was relief, of course, but also a sense of spaces that were too big and contained too much nothingness.

She asked, 'Did you get out yesterday?'

He shook his head. 'No, this morning.'

'And you came straight to see me? That's very kind of you, Jasper.'

He looked up at her when she said this but then turned his glance to the floor again, blinking slightly as if she was too bright a light that he had looked at directly.

Chelsea opted for a conversational tone. 'As you see, I'm bearing up.'

He spoke in a half-whisper, 'I'm glad of that, of course.'

Jasper did not sound glad; he sounded worried and tired.

'Why did they let you go?' she asked. 'Did you change your mind about the confession?'

Jasper nodded once.

She said, unconsciously echoing his words, 'Well, *I'm* glad of that!' She continued, 'Although I'll never understand why you confessed in the first place . . .'

This provoked a response. He spoke quietly. 'I did it for you.'

MARCUS MADE UP HIS MIND. He got into the small Mercedes SLK that his father had bought him. His mother had been furious but he, Marcus, had been so smug. He knew he was just a spoilt, rich kid—but damn, it had its moments. Marcus did not see himself as exceptionally wasteful or lazy. He was not dishonest. Having too much money hadn't ruined him. It was having a father who had engineered a public humiliation from the grave that had destroyed him. Marcus thought to himself that although he felt like the wronged party, he had not done Sharifah any favours by introducing her to his father. She had been a joyful, engaged teenager looking forward to a bright future as a scientist. He had never understood that ambition—he hated chemistry and physics and all the other impossible subjects. He would probably have gone to a third-rate university and then joined the family business. His mother would not have been happy about that but what choice did he have? He wasn't brimming with any particular talent.

Marcus realised that he was thinking about his future plans in the past tense. So be it—his subconscious had raced ahead of him.

The traffic lights turned green just as he got to them, and he accelerated away, leaving the other cars far behind. He rarely put the car through its paces and had never felt a strong desire to treat the highways as his own personal racetrack. But today was different. His personal misery had become a public ordeal. The newspapers had not even latched on to the possibility that he might have killed his father—that would be tomorrow's news. He thought about school. How would he ever be able to go back? And wherever he went, restaurants, bookshops, the guy under the umbrella at the bottom of the road who sold newspapers . . . all of them would know him as the poor sap who had not been able to keep his girlfriend away from a man thirty years older than him, and his own father to boot.

As he drove down the street, weaving in and out of traffic, he saw a beautiful Chinese woman with a long, easy stride and was reminded of his mother. Marcus realised that he was being cowardly compared to her. After all, she knew the sheer, bloody awfulness of being gossiped about by strangers and shunned by friends. But she had never taken the easy way out. She was still fighting for her children. Marcus wondered whether he would have had more courage if he had kids. Or was he a fatally flawed character like his own father?

He reached the spot he wanted. A wide, high curve of highway, elevated over one of the rivers that ran through Kuala Lumpur. He accelerated until the car was almost flying. When he reached the apex of the bridge he wrenched the wheel. In a shard of time, he ploughed through the barriers and was airborne. The car was propelled through the air until the laws of physics dictated that it slow down. Under the influence of gravity's insistent pull, Marcus was dragged back to earth.

DOUGLAS WEE WAS a rat. That was Singh's opinion. It was the large front teeth that stuck out and the reddened nostrils—perhaps he was recovering from a cold. His hair was short and somehow furry. The eyes were close-set in a pointy face and scanned his surroundings furtively.

'Of course I no kill Alan Lee. What for I want to do that?'

'You tell me,' said Inspector Mohammad, looking at him with disgust.

'Why you say I kill Alan Lee? He big business for my company. Better for me when he alive.'

'So you say, but we have credible evidence that your business interests were best served by his demise,' said Mohammad.

The other man's dialect was bringing out the policeman's most idiosyncratic turn of speech. It was hopelessly lost on Douglas Wee.

Singh stepped in. 'He said better for you if Alan Lee is dead.'

'That not true,' whined the rat.

'Lee Kian Min says you killed Alan,' said Inspector Singh, throwing caution to the winds.

Douglas Wee spat on the floor, angrily. 'Why he say that?'

'We don't know; you tell us!'

Wee looked as if he was gearing up to spit again. A flinty glare from Inspector Mohammad caused him to swallow instead. 'He not like me,' said Wee at last, by way of explanation.

'I don't like you either, but I'm not accusing you of murder,' pointed out Singh.

Wee reached into his breast pocket, took out a red silk handkerchief, patted his brow, wiped the beads of sweat off his upper lip, blew his nose hard and said, 'It's business.'

'You're going to have to explain that,' said Mohammad.

'Is very complicated,' said Wee.

'Try us,' said Mohammad, ironically.

'Lee Timber wants to go into bio-fuels business . . . Got two companies want to buy the oil—sign contract for future oil production. My boss in China very keen. But also another Hong Kong businessman.'

'And Alan didn't want to grow palm oil, so you killed him,' stated Singh.

'No! At first, Alan no want to grow palm oil but he change his mind.'

'That's not what Kian Min said,' pointed out Inspector Mohammad.

Wee looked cross. 'You want to hear my story or you just want to say I wrong about everything?'

Singh waved him on apologetically and Douglas looked mollified.

'At first, Alan not agree to bio-fuels. But then he make deal with his brother—he want him say that he was a good man in the court. Alan was fighting with his wife.'

'Are you saying that Alan and Kian Min made a deal—favourable character testimony in exchange for agreeing to the new business strategy?' asked Inspector Mohammad.

Wee looked doubtful. 'I think that's what I'm also saying. But Alan like my company to sign contract; Kian Min prefer other Hong Kong one. But Alan sign contract with me. Kian Min not know about it.' He was triumphant. Even in a police station, his having landed a deal against fierce competition was a source of pride.

'So what happened after that?'

'Alan got killed,' said Wee in a depressed voice. 'And Kian Min want to get out of contract. But I say "no". He very angry with me. He say contract not legal. I say if he tries to get out I . . . I sue him.'

'And now he's trying to get you out of the way by telling us you had something to do with Alan Lee's death?'

Wee understood this. He said clearly, 'I think so, yes.'

Singh asked Mohammad, 'But why would Kian Min have led us to this guy when he's just landed him in more trouble?'

Mohammad looked thoughtful. 'I would assume that he didn't know this fellow was on sufficiently good terms with Alan to know so much about their private arrangements.'

'You could be right,' said Singh.

CHELSEA DID NOT respond except to look at Jasper, eyes wide with disbelief and, he sensed, an instinctive rejection of what he was asserting.

He said again, 'I did it for you.'

She asked, in a quiet voice, her tone suggesting that she dreaded his answer, 'What do you mean?'

His nerves were taut and his answer whipped back. 'What do you think I mean?'

She said, probably untruthfully, 'I have no idea what you're getting at.'

Jasper went to stand by a window. He looked out over the well-tended grounds and could see the glint of the swimming pool under the shade of a rain tree. Without looking at Chelsea, he said, 'I love you.'

She did not respond and he dared not turn round to see her face. He could not bear to see rejection or dismay, or even amusement. The silence in the room grew until it was bigger than both of them, a thick fog of un-uttered words.

It was Jasper who spoke again; the quiet oppressed him more than her. He said, 'I guess you've never known that.'

The impulse to speak did not come with the discipline to stop. He was explaining now, begging for understanding, for sympathy, for forgiveness. But he did not beg for his love to be reciprocated because he knew about Ravi, thanks to the policeman from Singapore. Jasper said, 'Since your wedding day. Can you believe it? It was the first time I saw you. I couldn't believe that you were marrying my brother. I knew what he was like—self-ish, unfaithful, violent. Do you know, I almost spoke up—when they asked if anyone had objections . . . Can you imagine the scandal if I'd done it?'

She said, 'I wish you had.'

He turned to look at her for the first time and the pain in his heart was intensely physical. He relished it. It made him feel human. This capacity for suffering, for *feeling*, was what distinguished him from his brothers. He could not have this woman, but she had given him the most intense emotions he had ever experienced.

Jasper chuckled. 'You might not have thought so at the time.'

'I am really so sorry, Jasper. I had no idea.'

'It's all right. I was probably a bit subtle. I had nothing to offer you, you see. Not compared to this.' His glance took in their opulent surroundings.

Chelsea said, 'I still don't understand why you confessed.'

Jasper could see that there was real confusion on her face. She suspected him of having a youthful crush, the remnants of which had lasted for a bit longer than usual. No doubt she believed that his coming over and telling her he loved her was some by-product of his being in prison.

'I confessed,' he said slowly, 'because I wanted to save you from prison, from dying. I couldn't bear you to suffer.'

'But . . . but . . .' Chelsea didn't finish the sentence.

He made a clean breast of it. 'I knew I could never be with you, never have you . . . It seemed the best thing I could do was to save you. I imagined you having a life with your children . . . without Alan. It was what you deserved—the very least you deserved after what Alan put you through.' He stopped. He had reached the point where he had to explain why he stood on her thick carpet, free. He said, 'But then I found out about . . . Ravi.'

'What?' It was a single word, like the explosion of a firecracker.

Jasper said patiently, 'I found out about your boyfriend.'

Chelsea gripped the arms of her chair until her knuckles showed white. She said, 'Who told you about . . . him?'

'That fat policeman from Singapore. He said you were happy and that you'd had him on the side for a long time. He suggested I was a bit of a fool.'

Chelsea was silent for so long that Jasper walked over to her chair, willing her to say something, to explain how it was that while he was standing by, ready to offer her all the protection he was capable of, she had turned to someone else.

At last she said, 'I suppose I'm glad. I never wanted an innocent man— I never wanted *you*—to die trying to protect me. But the inspector was not entirely truthful, I'm afraid.'

She saw hope dawn on his face and knew that she had misled him. She said hurriedly, 'I did have an affair—it was brief, physical and meaningless. I ended it the minute divorce proceedings began. I've not seen Ravi since, and I have no intention or desire to do so.'

Jasper sat down so suddenly she thought he might have fallen. He was ashen, defeated.

Chelsea said, 'I'm sorry, Jasper.'

He found a vein of strength and humour he had never suspected he possessed: 'I don't suppose they'll believe me if I confess again?'

JASPER LEFT AND Chelsea sat in her chair lost in thought for a few minutes. Jasper's revelations were extraordinary. She knew at the back of her mind that his release put her back in the frame for the murder. But she tried not to think about it. Marcus was also in trouble. That would have to be her first priority. Chelsea tracked down her mobile phone and looked at the missed calls from her lawyers in disgust. What did the vultures want? More fees? She debated whether to ring the Syariah lawyer or the civil lawyer first.

The choice, such as it was, was taken out of her hands. The phone vibrated and then its old-fashioned peal filled the room. The number was that of Subhas Chandra, her civil lawyer.

She picked up, feeling a tiny frisson of dread. 'Hello?'

'Mrs Lee, is that you?'

'Yes—I'm sorry I missed your calls. Have there been any developments?'

His voice exploded like a cannon. 'Developments? What do you think? Of course the revelations will have an impact on your case!'

Chelsea was confused and her tone reflected it: 'What revelations?' she asked. There was complete silence at the other end. She continued, 'Hello, are you there?'

Subhas Chandra said tentatively, 'Today's newspapers? Have you not seen them?'

Chelsea said, 'Not yet. I've been busy this morning.'

'You should take a look.' His voice was still quiet. 'But I'm afraid it's not good news.'

Chelsea told him to hang on and she walked to the dining table where the newspapers were usually placed so she could read them with breakfast.

She had never understood the expression 'blood running cold' prior to that moment. It had seemed theatrical, impossible. Now, as she stood there and shivered, she knew precisely what it meant.

Subhas Chandra asked, 'Are you there?'

'Yes,' she whispered.

'Have you got the papers?'

'Yes.'

'It's not good news, I'm afraid.'

'What do you mean exactly?' Her voice was constricted by the bands of fear around her throat. She doubted the lawyer had heard her.

He must have guessed what she was saying though because he said, 'Custody!'

'What do you mean?'

'Alan had a Moslem girlfriend . . .'

'So?'

'His conversion may have been genuine.'

'Don't be ridiculous! He didn't convert to marry some teenager.'

'All right—you and I know what Alan was like. But the fact is that this will have an impact on the case: civil and Syariah.'

'Spell it out,' Chelsea said curtly.

'We've been arguing that the civil courts should determine whether the conversion was genuine. The reason we had a shot at persuading them to look at Alan's sudden religious awakening was because of the *prima facie* injustice of the case. It was difficult to leave you with no remedy. But now that there is a small chance Alan was genuine, they are not going to feel the same pressure to help you.'

'OK.'

'That's not all. Even if by some chance they still agree to look at the matter, there's now evidence that the conversion to Islam might have been for real—so we could lose.'

'I understand.' Her voice grew harsh. 'You're saying that just because the last of Alan's numerous infidelities happened to be with a Moslem woman, I could lose the kids?'

Subhas Chandra said, 'Yes.'

'I assume that my Syariah lawyer, who has also been trying to call me this morning, will have the same view of the matter—that the Syariah courts might use his relationship with Sharifah as evidence that the conversion to Islam was genuine.'

'I would think so. This gives the courts a loophole. It means they don't have to rule on the issue as a matter of principle. To be frank, I think they'd jump at the chance.'

Chelsea looked at her phone—a poisonous piece of plastic and circuitry that could bring her news like this.

The lawyer said, trying to be reassuring, 'At least with Jasper Lee in jail for Alan's murder, there's no danger to your son. Otherwise, this evidence—the newspaper story—would raise eyebrows with the police.'

She said automatically, 'Jasper's been released.'

'I beg your pardon?'

Chelsea repeated, 'Jasper's been released. He didn't kill Alan.' She rang off, leaving the lawyer at the other end more shocked than he had ever been in his illustrious career.

She thought about calling her Syariah lawyer and decided against it. She would have to speak to him soon, but there was no doubt he would say the same thing as Chandra. Chelsea hurried up the stairs. She had better find Marcus and prepare him for the morning papers. Unless he had seen them, in which case she would just have to try and reassure him. Marcus would not be easily convinced.

But he was not in his room. The bed was made, he had showered and changed, but he was not there. She looked out of the window. His car was gone. She guessed that Marcus had gone to see Sharifah.

The doorbell clanged, its electronic sound reverberating around the house. Chelsea hoped it was not Jasper back again. She could not cope with any further emotional outpourings.

She went down and saw the maid let two policemen into the house—Inspectors Singh and Mohammad. She could not believe it. Surely they were not there to rearrest her or arrest Marcus? Both men looked solemn.

Chelsea mentally girded herself. They watched her with deliberately impassive faces. Despite that, she sensed sympathy from them—and it annoyed her. No doubt they had seen the morning papers, too. She didn't need their commiserations. She needed them to find the murderer.

She asked brusquely, 'What do you want?'

Singh said, 'We have bad news. There's been an accident.'

ELEVEN

Rupert Winfield checked into the Mandarin Oriental. It was not his usual sort of hotel. He much preferred backpacker hangouts. On the other hand, this was not his usual sort of visit to the city. His plan required that he reinvent himself, albeit briefly, as the sort of man who stayed at luxury hotels and wore expensive, tailored suits.

Rupert had become accustomed to the Penan way. For them, nature was all-powerful. Their ability to survive depended on a symbiotic relationship with the jungle around them—not a parasitic one. Rupert wondered why the parasites who lived in cities did not understand the most fundamental tenet of nature—that a parasite eventually kills its host. How much better was the Penan way that posed no threat to its surroundings? Their practice of *molong*—never taking more than they needed—was in such contrast to the people he could see far below, scurrying about their acquisitive businesses, never content with what they had, always wanting more.

He wandered into the luxurious bathroom for a long bath and a close shave. Afterwards, he looked at himself in the mirror. His body was thin and wiry, without a spare ounce of flesh. He cupped his smooth chin in one hand. It looked peculiar. His jaw was several shades lighter than the rest of his weather-beaten face. It was the best he could do. Rupert shrugged. He had learnt from the Penan not to sweat the things he could not change.

The doorbell rang and he slipped on a dressing gown and went to answer it. It was the hairdresser he had asked to be sent up. A second ring was the delivery of the suit he had ordered. He had been fitted for it the previous day and it was ready, as had been promised, within twenty-four hours. *Amazing what efficiencies the pursuit of material wealth can engender*, thought Rupert.

SINGH DESPISED HIMSELF for his choice of words. 'We have bad news. There's been an accident.'

He had used them before; stood at other doorsteps with information that would crush the recipient and been unable to forewarn or to prepare the ground for what he needed to disclose, except with such triteness.

Watching Chelsea's face drain of blood was like watching the tide go out in fast forward. She could not speak. She opened her mouth but no words came out. Singh knew he had to break the news to her—but he could not bring himself to do it.

It was Mohammad who stepped in. He said, reaching out to her and then letting his hand fall to his side, 'It's about Marcus. He's been in an accident . . . a car accident.'

'Is . . . is he . . . dead?'

Singh took hold of Chelsea by her upper arm. She did not seem to notice. Her eyes were fixed on Mohammad's face, trying to read his answer.

He said, 'No, he's still alive. But it doesn't look good.'

Mohammad had said enough to spur Chelsea into action. She had only taken in the first part. Marcus was still alive. If he was alive, he needed his mother and she needed to get to him. She said frantically, 'Where is he?'

Singh said, 'Come, we'll take you.'

Shukor was waiting with the car. Mohammad climbed in the front and Chelsea and Singh slid in the back. Shukor set off, slipping the siren onto the roof and weaving through the traffic.

Chelsea asked, unnaturally calmly, 'What happened?'

Singh said, 'The details are sketchy. He went off a bridge and ended up in a river. He was rescued by people on the banks, just before the car was submerged entirely, and taken to hospital.'

He did not say that eye-witnesses had insisted that the car had accelerated and swerved towards the barriers intentionally. But Chelsea Liew was no fool.

She asked, 'Did he do it on purpose?'

Mohammad interjected from the front, 'Why would you think that?' He was still the policeman on the trail of a murderer.

She was not in the mood for mind games with the police. 'You must have seen the newspapers,' she said, tiredly.

Singh answered her original question quietly. 'There's some evidence that it wasn't an accident.'

Chelsea shielded her eyes with a hand and leaned her head against the car window.

CHELSEA WAS ALONE. The policemen had left. She called home and explained to the other two boys that she would be late getting back. She sounded normal, cheerful. It was only after she hung up that she allowed herself the luxury of tears. But she quickly dried them. While Marcus was alive she would continue to be strong.

A shadow fell across her and she looked up. It was Sharifah. Her eyes were bloodshot and her hair was tied up under a scarf. She saw the apprehension in the girl's eyes and felt a wave of compassion wash over her. It had a cleansing effect. It soaked away the last of the ill feeling Chelsea had for this foolish girl.

Sharifah asked, 'I heard on the radio. Is there any news?'

Chelsea shook her head. 'He's still in surgery. I haven't spoken to a doctor yet.'

As if on cue, a doctor in green scrubs and a face mask walked out of the operating theatre.

He looked at the two women and enquired politely, 'Are you Marcus Lee's family?'

Chelsea said, 'I'm his mother. How is he? Tell me, please!'

The doctor sighed. 'Well, he survived the surgery. It was touch and go.'

Chelsea sifted through the words and latched on to those she wanted to hear. 'He survived? He's going to be all right?'

The surgeon said, 'It's too early to tell. He has a lot of impact injuries: a ruptured spleen, collapsed lung, dislocated shoulder and broken bones, including all the fingers in his right hand.' The doctor continued, 'The only reason he survived the accident is that all the airbags in the car deployed on contact with the water. It just cushioned him enough—or the impact would have killed him on the spot.'

Chelsea looked at the blood on the green overalls of the surgeon and felt sick to the stomach. That was Marcus's blood, all over this man. She said, 'There's more, isn't there?'

The doctor could not meet her eyes. He said, 'There was also a blood clot in the front of his brain. We've removed it successfully. But, I'm afraid, even if Marcus makes it through post-op, there might be . . . brain damage. It's not unusual in this sort of case.'

'When will you know?'

'Not until he wakes up—which won't be for several days, I'm afraid. We need to keep him heavily sedated or the shock will be too much for his body to handle.'

Sharifah bit her bottom lip to keep from screaming with the black, spinning horror of it all.

THE THREE MEN were in the car on the way back to the police station. Each was lost in his own thoughts. There was complete quiet in the car except for the crackling of the police radio.

It was Singh who gave some expression to the conflict within. He said, 'I really, really hope we can pin the murder on Kian Min . . . or Ravi.'

There were nods of agreement from the rest. They could relate to that.

It was Mohammad who acted the spoiler this time round. 'It could be the kid.'

'Because he tried to kill himself?' Shukor was the one who asked the question.

Singh said in a depressed tone, low and gravelly and barely audible, 'It is suggestive. We let Jasper go. Marcus drives his car off a bridge.'

Shukor was the unexpected source of adamant disagreement with his superiors. 'That need not be the reason, sir. He could have been driven to it by today's papers.'

'Really?' asked Inspector Mohammad, sceptically. 'He gets a bit embarrassed and he tries to kill himself? Would you do that?'

Shukor was defensive but firm. 'I might if I were seventeen, sir.'

He could see the other two men consciously try to remember what it was like to be seventeen. It was not such a long journey for Shukor. He could easily recall the sensitivity and the insecurity of a seventeen-year-old. For sure, he thought, he might have tried to kill himself—been at least tempted—

if he had found himself in such a public mess as Marcus had done.

Mohammad said doubtfully, 'You might have a point. But I think there is every chance that he guessed we'd come looking for him once we released Jasper—and tried to find a way out.'

WHEN HE SAW on the news that Jasper had been released, Rupert called him. They agreed to meet at the hotel lobby. They almost didn't recognise each other, although it was no more than a week since Rupert had visited Jasper in prison. Jasper, who had been cheerful and relaxed, was crushed and tired, still wearing the same clothes he had gone to see Chelsea in the previous day. Rupert Winfield, who had spent a good part of the last five years living the life of a nomad in the jungle, was conspicuously smart.

The men shook hands and sat down. They ordered coffees, black for Jasper and a cappuccino for Rupert.

The latter came straight to the point. 'I was just wondering about the office set-up at Lee Timber,' he said.

'Oh? Why?'

'You remember you mentioned that Alan had never been the brains behind the company—it was your dad and, when he died, your other brother, Kian Min?'

'Yes, Alan was just a figurehead—he was too busy playing around and beating his wife to have time for business.' He paused, then Jasper asked, 'Are you still disappointed that Alan is dead?'

'It sounds like he deserved a bullet,' said Rupert, and glanced quickly at Jasper to see if he found such strong sentiment misplaced. 'Well, you know why I was so upset. I wanted to make sure he paid for what he did—evicting the Penan, causing the death of that woman. I had big plans to confront him, force him to acknowledge what he had done.'

'I suppose he did pay for what he did,' said Jasper.

Rupert nodded a half-hearted acknowledgment of the correctness of what Jasper had said. Jasper grinned at the other man, affectionate but mocking. 'I know, I know—it's not the same unless you get to shoot him yourself!'

He was surprised to see how badly Rupert took his attempt at humour.

'That's not right, Jasper. Why would you say such a thing?'

'Damn it! Give me a break, Rupert. I've been in jail for ages. I was just trying to be funny. God knows, I don't feel like being funny. My brother is dead, his wife thinks I'm a fool, my nephew is in hospital, Kian Min is making sure that the Lee legacy is safe, Lee Timber continues to destroy everything I've sought to preserve . . .'

He buried his face in his hands and Rupert patted him awkwardly on the shoulder. 'I'm sorry, mate. I'm just a bit touchy myself.'

There was no response from Jasper, so he continued hesitantly, 'I'm going to see Kian Min. I've an appointment next week.'

Jasper looked at his companion. 'What are you hoping to achieve?'

Rupert shook his head. 'I have no idea. I just want to explain what's going on in Borneo.'

'You think he doesn't know? He'd have ordered the attacks himself.'

Rupert looked at Jasper, his eyes glowing with a curious intensity. 'You really believe that?'

'Of course! But how are you going to get in, anyway? Kian Min is not stupid enough to let a Penan sympathiser into his office to harangue him.'

Rupert fingered his suit. 'What do you think this is? I'm not *laki Penan* any more, I'm Jonathan Hayward, representing the European Commission. I want to buy bio-fuels to meet European Union emissions targets.'

'It's a good plan,' acknowledged Jasper reluctantly, after a pause. 'Kian Min's greatest weakness is his greed. I like it. You give him hell!'

'I plan to,' said Rupert. 'I certainly plan to.' He drained the last of his coffee. 'There's one more thing . . .' He reached into his pocket and took out a sealed envelope. 'Can you hang on to this? Open it if . . . you'll know when to open it if it becomes necessary.'

Jasper looked at him quizzically. 'What is this? Your last will and testament? Kian Min is not going to shoot you in the middle of his office!'

Rupert leaned back in his chair. 'Better safe than sorry.'

CHELSEA LIEW DEVELOPED a routine. Get the boys ready for school and send them on their way with cheery smiles and reassurances about the condition of their older brother. Have a quick breakfast, or perhaps a sandwich in the car, and head for the intensive care unit. Sit down in the chair next to her son, talk to him, read to him or be lost in her own scattered thoughts. Head back in time to meet the younger boys when they got home from school. Spend the afternoon with them while Jasper or Sharifah took over at the hospital. It tore her apart to be away from Marcus but she felt that she had to provide the younger kids with a semblance of normality. If she disappeared from their lives again, it might be too much for them so soon after the death of their father, her incarceration in jail and the hospitalisation of Marcus. So she played Lego and did puzzles and listened to their tales of school and helped them with their homework—and all the while she hung on to her mobile with a sweaty palm and worried about Marcus.

When the boys sat down to dinner she would go back to the hospital and spend a fitful night in a hard chair—mostly awake but occasionally chased across a dreamscape by her worst nightmares. In the morning, she would make sure she was home again before the boys realised she had spent the night away.

That was the routine. It was punctuated with hushed telephone confrontations with lawyers, as her legal team warned her she was not getting anywhere in the courts. She had urgent, difficult conversations with all the specialists that she brought in for second and third and fourth opinions of Marcus's case. None of them could reassure her that Marcus would be all right.

Through it all, Sharifah was her companion and Jasper was her support. If she had had time to think thoughts that were not related to the welfare of her children, she might have appreciated the irony.

Jasper had never previously been able to be of service to the woman he loved. His big attempt had backfired: he had, in the clutches of jealousy, recanted his confession. But now, finally, he was of real use to her. Once, he came into Marcus's hospital room and found Chelsea sobbing quietly, but with such intensity that her shoulders were shaking. He put a hand on her shoulder and looked at Marcus, numb with fear. But the boy was still alive, his condition unchanged. He knelt down by the chair and wrapped his arms round her and she whispered through her heartbreak that it was Marcus's eighteenth birthday; he had come of age in a medically induced coma. But then she had wiped her eyes on the corner of her pashmina and squared her shoulders and she smiled at him, her eyes distant, lost in other thoughts.

It was the closest he got to providing her with emotional support instead of practical help—but Jasper was happy.

THE POLICE WERE at a loose end. They all had a different preference for the murderer: Mohammad was convinced it was Marcus; Singh was sure it was Kian Min; and Shukor thought that Ravi had tried to ensure his meal ticket by murdering the wealthy husband of his lover. But, despite his best efforts,

Shukor had not been able to find any evidence linking Ravi to the crime. And a motive, however persuasive, was not enough for an arrest, especially when the two senior policemen were both convinced that Ravi was too protective of his own skin to risk committing a murder.

Nobody was pointing a finger at Chelsea. Singh because, he acknowledged to himself, he was prejudiced in her favour; Shukor because he took his lead from the inspector from Singapore; and Mohammad because he could not face arresting the same woman twice. But they all acknowledged that having favourites was utterly irrelevant because they did not have any compelling evidence against any of them. Motives abounded, but evidence was thin on the ground.

Mohammad even wondered out loud if the murderer could have been the proverbial stranger—perhaps scared off before he had robbed the body. Singh was dismissive of the possibility. For a man with as many enemies as Alan Lee to be finally bumped off by a stranger would require a divine providence with a sense of irony, and that was not a possibility that Singh was prepared to give credence to—not even if it got Chelsea off the hook for good.

The police were not being idle. They had launched an appeal for witnesses again. The foot soldiers were sent to comb a wider area for the murder weapon. The Lee family home was searched once more, as well as Marcus's lockers at school and the library. Sharifah's flat was ransacked—although no one really thought she had anything to do with it. Their friends and acquaintances were questioned. Mohammad especially was convinced that Marcus might be able to buy himself a gun but would lack the experience to cover his tracks adequately and they might be able to track down his supplier. But so far he had not been able to find even a whiff of evidence. Even Kian Min's offices and bachelor flat in Ampang were searched. Shukor had reported back that the apartment was modern, stylish and soulless, a perfect habitat for the man. But there was no physical evidence tying him to the murder.

'The thing is, the only really useful evidence would be the gun,' said Mohammad, impatiently. 'And with a bit of time and a cool head, it could be almost anywhere.'

Singh rubbed his eyes with his knuckles like a child. 'And hardly anyone with a television would throw the gun away within the vicinity of the crime scene—let alone with something useful on it like fingerprints.'

'Not even Marcus . . .'

'No, he probably watches all the CSIs,' said Singh with disgust.

'None of the possibilities—Chelsea, Marcus, Kian Min—would be stupid enough to be caught with the weapon. It was an audacious murder but, having got away with it, I don't think they're going to screw up now.'

Mohammad sounded thoroughly fed up. It was the highest profile case of his career and he was clean out of clues. He brightened up. 'Have they got the car up?'

'Just, sir—and they're going through it—but so far there's been nothing in it. No gun, no farewell note, no confession—nothing.'

JASPER ASKED CHELSEA hesitantly, 'Would it be so awful to convert to Islam and keep the children?'

'Jasper, I don't believe in God. My husband became a Moslem in name only to spite me. Can the solution really be for me to fake a religious awakening in order to mislead a court of law into giving me custody over the children I have brought up, loved and who are mine by any sensible measure of parenthood?'

'When you put it like that . . .' said Jasper humorously and Chelsea smiled—a thin, tired but genuinely amused curve of her pale lips.

'Besides, if I convert to Islam it means that Alan is still dictating the way I live my life. But don't worry, I'm not going to allow anyone to separate me from my kids—and that's final.'

'You need to have an escape plan.'

She looked at him and decided after a careful scrutiny of his honest, open, ugly face that she could trust him, really trust him. 'I have made plans,' she said cryptically. She looked around the hospital ward. 'If it wasn't for this . . .' She didn't finish the sentence and Jasper did not enquire further. He was not sure he wanted to hear what she was going to do.

Chelsea stood up. 'I've got to get back to the boys.'

Jasper stood to walk her out and they both turned to look at Marcus. Chelsea always told Marcus when she was leaving and explained that she would be back as soon as she could. The doctors had told her bluntly that he would not be able to hear her but she was determined not to risk his waking up and wondering where she was.

Chelsea walked round the bed, leaned over, whispered her farewell to Marcus and saw his eyelids flutter. It was not the first time there had been some movement; the doctors had warned her that they were very, very gradually reducing the anaesthetic. But this time, his eyes flickered open, closed again and then opened once more.

Chelsea gasped and said, 'Marcus?'

Sharifah woke up and looked around bleary-eyed, remembered where she was with difficulty and then saw Chelsea leaning over Marcus and leapt to her feet. Jasper stayed at the foot of the bed, ready to go to Chelsea's assistance.

Marcus's eyes were unfocused, his pupils dilated, his corneas intricately patterned in red lines. One of his hands was in splints and bandaged, his right, where he had shattered all his fingers against the steering wheel on impact with the water. But his other hand, swollen, with the intravenous needle attached, jerked convulsively and then closed into a fist. His lids closed once more. When they opened again, his eyes were wide. His pupils narrowed to a black pinpoint in the bright, cold room. He looked at his mother and she willed him, with the entire physical and mental energy that she had at her disposal, to be all right.

Marcus said, 'Mum?'

Chelsea did not cry or fall down on her knees. Bubbles of hysteria floated around and popped against her insides—but she smiled at her son reassuringly and said, 'I'm here, son. Everything's going to be all right.'

Marcus turned his head slightly and saw Sharifah standing diffidently by his bed, nervous of her reception, and a tiny, pained, stiff smile creased his dry lips.

Sharifah said quietly, taking her cue from Chelsea, 'Your mum's right, everything is going to be fine.'

His smile widened slightly and he nodded, the tiniest of movements, almost imperceptible—but enough.

HIS APPOINTMENT WAS at two and he arrived ten minutes late. As a representative of powerful government interests, he did not want to appear needy or anxious. He wanted Kian Min on the defensive. Rupert walked in unhurriedly and shook hands with his host. He was dressed well with that hint of extra style that comes with wearing good clothes with confidence. His shades, for the bright Malaysian sun, were resting on his hair and his briefcase was leather, new and discreetly embossed with an expensive designer logo.

After Kian Min's secretary had left the room after offering coffee, Rupert said in his plummiest tones, 'Thank you for seeing me at such short notice.'

Kian Min was not to be outdone. 'It is my pleasure. We at Lee Timber are always happy to welcome people to our business.'

Rupert said solemnly, 'But I understand that I should offer you my condolences . . .'

Kian Min looked puzzled.

'Didn't your brother, the previous head of the company, die recently?'

'Oh, yes, yes. Thank you. We are all very shocked and miss Alan very much,' said Kian Min, recovering quickly.

Rupert allowed himself to look mildly sceptical but said, 'I am sure we are all glad that Lee Timber is in good hands. But perhaps we could get down to business?'

'Can also! What do you want from Lee Timber?'

'Bio-fuel,' said Rupert bluntly. 'Lots of bio-fuel.'

'Well, you come to the right place. We are shifting from logging to palm oil to enter bio-fuels business.'

'The European Union would be interested in your crops as soon as they become available. Have you contracted with anyone else?'

'No,' said Kian Min solidly, ignoring the claims of Douglas Wee as well as the expectations of his Hong Kong clients.

'That is good news,' said Rupert. 'But there is a problem'.

'What is that?'

'The European Union has strict rules about bio-fuels. We cannot have any sourced from protected virgin rainforest or at the expense of indigenous cultures.'

'We only clear secondary forest and farmland,' said Kian Min with an air of great frankness.

'That is not your reputation,' said Rupert, his tone lightly accusing.

'We cannot help that there are all these tree-huggers who always accuse us of doing the wrong thing. But the police never find anything wrong with Lee Timber.'

'Isn't that because you bribe them?'

Kian Min looked irritated. Only his desire to land a really big long-term contract kept him from evicting his visitor. He said stiffly, 'We no do that.'

Rupert patted his briefcase suggestively. 'I have testimony here from the Penan group that you are clearing them off their land. It was passed to me by wildlife activists . . .'

'They are all liars, the Penan,' interrupted Kian Min angrily. 'You should not believe what they tell you. Lee Timber never does anything illegal.'

'It is not a pretty story. A woman was killed. She was pregnant. You can see why my bosses might be worried.'

'Why the Penan not go to the police?'

'They are a nomadic tribe scattered around Borneo. They may not trust the police!'

The two men looked at each other.

Rupert changed tactics. He leaned forwards in his chair, put both hands on the table, and said, 'Look, Kian Min, we both know you can't make an omelette without breaking some eggs. I need bio-fuels. I have targets to meet, quotas to fill. There isn't any source in the world that would meet our policy guidelines. That's what you get when the rules are written by bureaucrats sitting in small offices in Brussels. I just need to know—can you keep this stuff under wraps?'

'What do you mean?' asked Kian Min cautiously.

'I know you have the officials and police in your pocket. What about the Penan? Can you stop stories like this getting out?'

'Of course,' said Kian Min. 'A few Penan in loincloths cannot stop Lee Timber!'

'What about this story about the pregnant woman. Is it true?'

Kian Min nodded. 'It was an accident. But a good thing. They will know we mean business. It will be easier next time to chase them out.'

'There will be a next time?'

'Yes—until your bio-fuels are safe.'

'Good, then we only have one more thing to discuss. Is it possible to send your secretary away? This is private.'

Kian Min recognised the drill. This was the bit where the upstanding representative of a major governmental organisation asked for a kickback.

He leaned over, pressed the buzzer on his desk and said, 'Mrs Lim, you can go home now.'

'Yes, Mr Lee.'

Rupert waited for a few moments and then went to the main door and peeked out. She was gone.

He came back in and Kian Min said jovially, 'So, how much?'

'Oh, I don't want money,' said Rupert. 'I just wanted to tell you that my real name is Rupert Winfield and the pregnant Penan woman who died was my wife. Her unborn child was my son.'

TWELVE

Chelsea was at the hospital when she got the news.

'The civil courts have decided, as a matter of law, that they have no choice but to follow the latest precedents on apostasy—the right of an individual to renounce his or her religion. Questions of whether an individual is or is not a Moslem are a matter for the Syariah courts under the Federal Constitution.' Subhas Chandra delivered the news in a sober tone.

She said, 'But they didn't ask to see me!'

'It wasn't necessary. They are not deciding as a matter of fact, but of law. They only wanted submissions on law. And the recent precedents, although dealing with apostasy, were found to have great importance.'

'All right, I guess I was not expecting much else. So now we wait for the Syariah court?'

'Yes, but apparently they are convening already . . .'

'And they don't want to see me, either?'

'They will only hear testimony if they decide that they are going to examine the authenticity of the conversion to Islam. If they decide as a matter of law that they will not . . .' He was unable to continue. How was he to explain to this woman that all the courts in the land could achieve such a result in an individual case without even hearing from the mother of the children?

As Chelsea sat by Marcus's bed, listening to him and Sharifah chat about trivial things, finding pleasure in conversation and the sound of each other's voices, her Syariah lawyer called. The Syariah court had decided: Alan Lee, having gone through the official form of conversion to Islam, had died a Moslem and the children were Moslem, too. 'In the circumstances,' he warned, 'they might send court officers to take the children into care.'

'Is there anything else I can do?'

'Appeal—but they might take the kids while you do that.'

'All right,' she said calmly. 'Thank you for trying.'

CHELSEA MOVED QUICKLY. She told Marcus and Sharifah what she was going to do. They nodded and agreed. Marcus was in hospital, over age and recovering. She would leave him. She did not like it but she had no choice and he understood. Jasper and Sharifah would look after him. She was sure of that.

She picked up the younger boys from school. They were surprised but treated the whole thing like an unexpected holiday and were excited and cheerful. Chelsea swung by the house and picked up the pre-packed suitcases, passports, cash and travellers' cheques. She had been preparing for this moment for a while.

They got to the airport without mishap. It was at the check-in for the flight to Australia that there was the first sign of trouble. They were early for the next flight to Sydney and queued up in the carpeted First Class aisle. The clerk was well dressed, well made-up, polite—and then suddenly worried. Chelsea saw the furrows on her brow appear as she stared at the screen in front of her. Chelsea gripped the hand of her youngest son so tight he protested. She loosened her hold and waited, polite, patient and, inside, a wreck. Was she too late?

The check-in girl got up suddenly, said, 'Excuse me,' and scurried away in her high heels, until she got to a counter a few rows down and had a whispered conversation with a Chinese man in a suit.

The man came over, accompanied by the clerk, looked at her screen and glanced surreptitiously at the woman and children in front of him. Perhaps he recognised them, or their names, although he showed no sign of it. In any event, he spent a bit of time fiddling with the computer while the boys fidgeted and Chelsea asked in an irritated tone, 'Is there a problem?'

He looked up at this and said heavily, 'Yes, ma'am. For some reason, and I'm sure it must be some mistake, your details, and that of your children, appear on a police list. You are not allowed to leave the country.'

'It's a mistake!' said Chelsea firmly.

'Yes, ma'am, but my hands are tied. I cannot check you in until and unless your name is removed from this list.'

Chelsea thought hard. She leaned forward and said in a low tone, 'I'm sure you recognise me and know my story. They're trying to take my children away from me. Can you please help me?'

He dropped the pretence and said, 'I think the situation is very unfair but if I don't stop you here, Immigration will stop you in there.' He nodded towards the departure gates. 'And you might be arrested.'

Chelsea bit her bottom lip to keep it from trembling. What was she going to do?

The man said softly, 'Your best bet is Johor.'

She didn't understand him. The sound of her heart thumping was muffling his words.

'The border with Singapore—there is so much traffic there, quite often they don't check everything as carefully. That might be your best chance of getting out.'

She looked at him and made up her mind. 'I'll try that,' she said.

JASPER WAS ON THE WAY to the hospital when his phone rang. He picked it up but did not recognise the voice: it was high-pitched and breathless, speaking quickly, not making sense.

Jasper interrupted the caller, 'Who is this? Can you tell me who this is, please?'

There was a surprised silence and then Rupert said clearly and slowly, 'It's me, Rupert Winfield. I just wanted to tell you . . . I've killed your brother, Kian Min.'

'What?' Jasper asked. 'Rupert, are you all right? What are you saying?'

'I'm in his office. He's dead. I stabbed him with a Penan blowpipe needle. I dipped the end in one of their poisons.'

'My God, Rupert! Why? What have you done?'

Rupert's voice broke. He had his ending and his revenge. He said, 'I told you they killed a pregnant woman?'

'Yes.' Jasper's mind was racing, trying to come to terms with what Rupert had said.

'That woman—she was my wife.'

INSPECTOR MOHAMMAD decided, without telling the others, that he was going to arrest Lee Kian Min for perjury. He doubted he would be charged—not one of the leading businessmen in the country—but he had enough evidence for an arrest. After all, he had heard it from Kian Min himself, as well as Douglas Wee, that Kian Min had lied in court about his brother's good character in exchange for agreement on the bio-fuels expansion.

Inspector Mohammad firmly believed that he needed a breakthrough in the case. He needed to shake some trees and see what fell out. He had been to see Marcus and Sharifah, trying to break their alibi for the Alan Lee murder, which he knew full well to be false. But they had improved their stories in consultation and he had not pressed as hard as he could have.

Marcus was still recovering slowly. He would wait a while before applying more pressure. But later, he would turn the screws. Perhaps threaten to charge the boy with attempted suicide. It was still a crime on the statute books, albeit not very often prosecuted.

That left Kian Min and Chelsea. As he was not about to let the other two policemen on the case near Kian Min, he decided to go on his own. It was unlikely that he would resist arrest, but Mohammad left a couple of uniformed men downstairs just in case. Probably Kian Min would behave in the customary way of the business elite when confronted with a policeman. He would go quietly, and call his expensive lawyers and influential friends en route.

SHUKOR AND SINGH were instructed to question Chelsea again. Mohammad had told them to and they were willing, not because either of them thought there was any chance she was guilty, but because they were tired of sitting around achieving nothing. Singh knew he would not object to seeing Chelsea one last time. Perhaps give her a heads-up that the police had nothing and, if she kept her cool, she would ride the murder investigation out. That would not be professional, but professionalism had not been the hallmark of his conduct in the case to date. Perhaps he was getting old.

The two policemen were disappointed to see her limousine pull out of the house with Chelsea and the boys in the back just as they got there.

Chelsea had stopped at the house to repack. If she was going to try Johor, she needed to travel light.

Singh said idly to Shukor, 'Follow them. They must be going to the hospital. We can talk to her there.'

They drove in silence for a few minutes and then Shukor said, 'She's not going to the hospital, sir. We're actually heading out of town. This is the road to Seremban.'

'Hmmm, well, do you have anything on this afternoon?'

'No, sir.'

'Well, let's see where she's going, then. Maybe she has a rendezvous with that Ravi.'

They drove on, each lost in his own thoughts. Shukor had no difficulty maintaining a discreet distance from their quarry, a silver S-Class Mercedes with a woman and her two children in the back.

'We're passing Seremban, sir. She's going further south.'

Singh was genuinely taken aback. 'I wouldn't have thought she'd leave Marcus to go for a drive in the country,' he said thoughtfully. He continued abruptly, 'Call in. Find out if there's something we don't know.'

RUPERT'S REVELATIONS HAD almost destroyed Jasper's ability to think coherently. But he knew he had to if he was to save his friend.

He said to Rupert authoritatively, 'Stay there, and don't move. I'm on my way over.'

Rupert had protested incoherently, 'No, no . . . stay away. I just called, I'm not sure why. I wanted someone to understand why . . .'

Jasper just said, 'Don't worry, Rupert. I know what to do. For God's sake, just wait there. Where's the secretary?'

'Gone home. Kian Min sent her home.'

'All right, sit tight. And lock the door if you can. I'll be there in twenty minutes.'

Jasper drove fast but not recklessly. He didn't want to be stopped by the police. He made one stop on his way and recovered a carefully wrapped package tied up in string from a locker at the railway station.

He parked his car in the Lee building. There was a security desk where visitors had to sign in but Jasper walked past like someone who belonged and no one stopped him. He was heading for his father's office, where he had played in the corner as a small boy—to Alan's office, where he had exchanged so many harsh words over the years. And now it was Kian Min's office except, if Rupert was to be believed, Kian Min was dead.

The layout worked for him. On other floors the worker bees of Lee Timber went about their cubicle business. But Kian Min had a big office on a separate floor, with an empty boardroom on one side and his secretary, long gone, protecting the entrance.

Jasper walked in and tried the door. It was unlocked. Rupert had not done as he had suggested. That did not surprise him—he had sounded beyond reason. He put a hand on the doorknob and hesitated, afraid of what he might find. Taking a deep breath, he turned the knob and pushed. The heavy door opened quietly on its hinges.

IT WAS A VERY peaceful scene. Kian Min was slumped over his desk. He might have been catching forty winks. Rupert was sitting on the sofa in the reception area tucked away in one corner of the office. His hair was tousled, his tie loosened and his suit jacket flung across a chair. But he smiled at Jasper as if he was perfectly comfortable welcoming people to the scene of his crime.

Jasper walked in, went across to his brother and felt for a pulse. Kian Min was quite dead. It was not some sort of elaborate, highly unfunny joke. He came over and sat across from Rupert in an armchair. He looked at his friend.

'She was your wife?' he asked gently.

A single teardrop followed the laughter lines on Rupert's face down to the corner of his mouth. He said in a tired voice, 'I came to Kuala Lumpur to confront Alan, but he was dead. I would have gone back to my jungle and my people, maybe died trying to blockade a logging company—I didn't really care what happened to me.' He looked up accusingly at Jasper. 'But then you told me that he'—he nodded in the direction of the slumped figure—'was the boss. He would have ordered the clearing of the land—and the killing.'

Jasper nodded but said, 'I had no idea what you had in mind.'

His friend shrugged off the regret. 'How could you?'

Jasper asked, 'How did he die?'

Rupert leaned down over the arm of his chair and picked up a slim, wooden blowpipe. 'I wanted to kill him with a weapon of the Penan. They would never consider taking a life but it seemed fitting somehow. I stabbed him with the poisoned needle.' He smiled suddenly. 'I didn't quite trust myself to use the blowpipe, I'm not that good a shot.'

'What did you use?'

'Tajem latex.'

Jasper nodded. He was familiar with the poison the Penan put on the end of their blowpipe needles to hunt wild boar and mouse deer in the forest. It affected the heart and would kill a small animal instantly and a large animal in minutes. He looked doubtfully at Rupert. 'It was strong enough to kill a grown man?'

'I distilled it a few times. He died almost immediately.'

Jasper nodded. An ancient knowledge with a modern touch.

Rupert continued conversationally, 'He admitted it, you know. He thought it would be what a buyer of his new bio-fuels might want to hear.'

'I'm not surprised,' said Jasper.

He unwrapped the bundle he had brought with him.

Rupert looked at the revealed contents in astonishment. He said, 'Why did you bring a gun?' And then, a trace of resignation in his voice, he said, 'Are you going to kill me?'

'IT'S NOT GOOD NEWS,' said Shukor. 'I spoke to HQ. The Syariah court has issued a custody order in favour of a Moslem children's home.'

'What? They are taking the kids away from Chelsea and putting them in a *home*?'

'It's the law, sir. There are no family members entitled to custody. None of them is Moslem.'

'But what about Marcus? I can't believe she left him.'

'He's eighteen. The court order did not include him.'

Singh nodded in understanding. 'She's trying to get to Singapore. I'd bet my pension on it.'

'But she's bound to be stopped at the border,' protested Shukor.

'Yes, but she probably thinks she has a better chance there than at the airport. I'm sure she's just passing through on the way to Australia or somewhere like that.'

Shukor said, 'Well, she's not going to get through Immigration.'

'Let's go and watch,' was Singh's only response.

'IF YOU'RE NOT planning to kill me and he is dead, why have you got a gun?'

In the midst of their truly bizarre encounter in an empty office with a dead man nearby, Rupert was showing resilience. It convinced Jasper that he was doing the right thing.

He said, 'Kian Min is dead. I don't want you to hang for it. There is important work still to be done amongst the Penan. You should honour your wife's memory by trying to preserve her way of life.'

'It's a nice idea,' said Rupert. 'But I just killed a man.'

'That's why I'm here,' said Jasper, picking up the gun carefully with his handkerchief.

'Where did you get that gun, anyway?'

'I bought it from a bent copper in Sarawak once. Not sure what I had in mind—defending myself if the cops or the loggers turned nasty, I suppose. It has been very useful.'

'What do you mean?'

'I used it to kill my brother Alan.'

ON REACHING the Lee building, Inspector Mohammad nosed around looking for parking. He could have just abandoned the car by the side of the road and left his police ID in the window for any passing traffic warden but he didn't like to do that. He was a conscientious man who preferred to save police privileges for when they were needed, not for when they were convenient. He finally found a spot and reversed in carefully. He uncurled his long legs, swung them out of the car and walked towards the building with a spring in his long stride. He was pleased to be doing something. Making Kian Min's life miserable was an added attraction. He was such a slimy bastard. It would be fun to make him squirm in that big office of his. He had tried to be too cunning, sending them after Douglas Wee, another desperately unattractive character—but hardly a murderer. Perjury was a crime Mohammad took seriously. As a man who did not even tell half-truths, let alone lies, he knew the importance of honest dealings in everyday life. How much more so in the administration of justice?

Inspector Mohammad stopped at the security desk and showed the overweight Indian guard his police ID. It merited a quick glance but that was all. He was waved on without any further curiosity or enquiry.

THERE WERE TWO crossing points into Singapore. The Causeway in Johor Bahru was crowded, old and narrow. Tourist buses lined up in fleets, dropping off passengers and picking them up on the other side. Goods vehicles were stopped and searched and hundreds of cars; shoppers, visitors, business people and relatives—all crossing international borders in their everyday business—clogged the Causeway up further. It was a mess. The Second Link, the other way of getting across, was new, ultra-modern, efficient and attractive. But the tolls to cross over to the other side were also too expensive for most of the flood of travellers to and from the two countries.

Singh saw that Chelsea intended to make for the Causeway. She was thinking—betting her chances were higher with tired officials and a crowded crossing.

As they got closer to the border, Chelsea surprised him, however. The limousine pulled over. She got out with the kids, tied up her hair and slipped on a pair of sunglasses. The chauffeur opened the boot. She took out a wheelie bag and passed the boys a rucksack each. She shook hands with the driver, slipped him something in an envelope and set off at a brisk, determined pace, the boys trailing in her wake.

Singh watched from the car in admiration. He said, 'She's going in on foot. It's the most crowded bit.'

He gestured for Shukor to pull over. The two men got out of the car and followed the escaping Lee family.

'YOU KILLED ALAN? Why?'

'For Chelsea . . . his wife. I've always loved her. I thought I was just going to waylay him, talk to him, threaten him to let her keep the kids—that's why I took the gun. But maybe I always knew I wanted him dead.'

'But you changed your mind about the confession . . .'

'Yes, I found out Chelsea had a boyfriend on the side. I was just destroyed by that. I decided that, even though I had killed for her, I didn't need to die for her as well.'

Rupert was stunned by the revelations. For a short while, he had almost forgotten his own despair. He was sitting up, looking intently at Jasper, his sapphire eyes flashing.

'But why did you keep the gun? It might have been found!'

'In case I ever had to prove I did it . . . I never planned to let anyone else hang for my crime.'

'Does Chelsea know?'

'Of course not!'

Rupert asked gently, 'Are you hoping for a happy ending?'

Jasper looked at him and, for the first time, there was stark, exposed emotion in his voice and eyes. 'I don't know. She depends on me now. That might have to be enough.'

Rupert's next question dragged him back to the present: 'So what do you plan to do now?'

'Where did you stab him?'

'In the neck . . .'

'Well, then, that's precisely where I plan to put a bullet. With luck the police will assume that Kian Min killed Alan and then himself in a fit of uncharacteristic remorse.'

'Do you really think we can get away with it?' asked Rupert sceptically.

Jasper sighed. He said at last, 'I don't know. But I do know I don't want you to hang. He'—he nodded in the direction of Kian Min's body—'deserved what he got. I don't have any better ideas. But you need to get back to Borneo and your people.'

Rupert asked, 'And what about you?'

'Me? I would like, more than anything, to have a second chance—to be there for Chelsea if she needs me. This is my best hope, too.'

INSPECTOR SINGH WAS growing steadily more irritable. The stench of petrol fumes from the cars, buses and lorries, all with their engines running as they waited to cross over into Singapore, was making him lightheaded. He slipped on a black patch of oil and would have fallen if Shukor had not grabbed his arm. There was not a dry patch on his shirt he was perspiring so heavily in the heat. He glared at Shukor, who was still managing to look fresh and neat.

The queue they were in wound back and forth, along the temporary aisles created by bollards. Chelsea and the children were about ten people ahead of them. He was dreading her turning round and spotting them. But he need not have worried. All her attention was focused on the distant booth, with its tired female officer sitting in a small air-conditioned box behind tinted sliding windows, stamping passports with only a cursory glance at their owners.

MOHAMMAD HEARD THE gunshot in the lift, muffled but distinct. The elevator doors opened and he stepped out into the corridor and looked up and down. Had it been a shot? How could it be? He drew his own gun from the holster tucked into the back of his trousers. He was not taking any chances.

He walked along slowly, keeping low. There was no sign of anyone. He reached Kian Min's office and straightened up. There was no one at his secretary's desk. The tycoon was probably inside dictating his unpleasant business plans to her, he thought. Nevertheless, he approached cautiously. When he got to the door, he readied his gun, turned the knob slowly, pushed it in and whirled in low.

CHELSEA SLIPPED the three passports through the slot in the Perspex window. The immigration official, a woman with bad skin from sitting in traffic fumes and grime all day, a dark blue head scarf pinned neatly under her chin with an official Immigration Department pin, and the most tired, blank eyes Chelsea had ever seen, picked up the passports, typed in the numbers quickly, picked up her big stamp, opened Chelsea's passport to a blank page, raised her hand to stamp it—and had her attention caught by her screen. Chelsea's heart sank. The official retyped the numbers to check that there was no mistake.

She turned to Chelsea, looking at her for the first time. 'You are not allowed to pass.'

JASPER LEE STOOD there, gun in hand. Inspector Mohammad's finger tightened a fraction on the trigger of his weapon. Jasper dropped the gun he was holding at his feet and put his hands in the air.

He said conversationally, 'Just in time, Inspector Mohammad.'

There was a man slumped over his desk. Inspector Mohammad went closer. He raised a limp wrist; not even the briefest flutter of life. There was a gaping artery-severing wound on his neck but not a lot of blood. Much less than Mohammad would have expected. The body seemed cold for someone who had presumably died within the last few minutes, when Mohammad had heard the gunshot. On the other hand, the policeman thought, the room was cold, too: it felt like the air-conditioning was turned up high. He raised the dead man slightly: he needed to confirm his identity. He saw that Jasper Lee was now an only child—both his brothers were dead.

Inspector Mohammad called for back-up.

'THEY'VE STOPPED HER,' said Singh urgently. He hurried forward, ignoring the angry commuters who thought he was trying to cut the queue.

They got to the counter just as Chelsea was turning away. She looked at them in surprise and then said ruefully, 'You had to hound me to the border? Don't worry. Your minions here are up to the job of separating me from my children.'

She had forgotten the boys in that bitter comment. The younger one looked at her, panic flooding his eyes, tears springing forth. 'Mum, what do you mean? Are you going to leave us again?'

The older child grabbed her arm with both his hands and hung on. Chelsea looked at the two policemen; her disgust was palpable. She asked, and each word was flung at them like a knife, 'How can this be right?'

Singh made up his mind. He had been sent to protect this woman and he would. He leaned towards the immigration official and said, 'Let them go.'

She said, 'I cannot.'

'I'm with the police. She's wanted in Singapore. This is a joint operation. Let them through!'

'ID?'

Singh pulled out his wallet and slid his police ID through. She looked at it and said, 'Singapore police. No authority here. I cannot let them pass.'

Singh was desperate. The crowd behind them was getting impatient, muttering with annoyance at being held up. They formed a phalanx at the counter, preventing people going about their business. They were beginning to attract attention. A moustachioed officer, standing some distance away, was looking at the rumpus, trying to decide whether he should intervene. Singh knew that once someone senior arrived, the game was up.

Shukor stepped in. He held up his ID to the window. He said authoritatively, 'I'm Malaysian police. This is a joint operation. Let them go.'

She visibly wavered and Shukor smiled at her charmingly. 'Don't worry, *lah*. If there is a problem, you can blame me.'

She made up her mind; the young policeman's shoulders were broad enough for her to hide behind if there was trouble. She picked up her stamp and quickly did all three passports. She passed them to Chelsea, who picked them up with numb, cold fingers. She did not say anything to the policemen. She did not dare—in case it made the immigration official suspicious again. Chelsea looked at them with gratitude in her eyes and hoped they understood. Then she grabbed the boys' hands and hurried towards Singapore.

IT TOOK THEM four hours to drive back to the police headquarters in Kuala Lumpur. Neither man said much. They were not sure what they had done or why they had done it—but it felt right.

Mohammad was waiting for them impatiently. He snapped when they came in looking tired and dishevelled: 'Where have you been?'

'Following Chelsea Liew and the two younger kids,' said Singh wearily. 'But she got away, across the Johor border into Singapore.'

Mohammad looked at them suspiciously. 'You couldn't stop her?'

'No, we just missed her . . .'

Mohammad said, 'Well, she's probably on her way to Australia by now. Still, it might be for the best.'

Shukor asked, 'You don't suspect her of the murder any more?'

Mohammad said with elaborate casualness, 'Oh, it's case closed on the Alan Lee murder.'

'What? How?' It was Singh who exclaimed.

'Jasper Lee killed his brother.'

'Jasper? How do you know? Did he confess again?'

'Yes, but that's not all,' said Mohammad, and proceeded to tell them about his day. About hearing a shot and finding Jasper Lee standing over the body of Kian Min with a gun in his hand.

'You're sure it was the gun that killed Alan?' asked Singh, trying to take the whole thing in.

'Yes, the ballistics report is back. There's no doubt.'

'And it was that same gun he used on Kian Min?'

'Something a bit odd about that,' confessed Inspector Mohammad. 'Kian Min had a load of poison in his system as well. And the forensics team almost suggests that he was dead *before* the bullet, although it's close. There just wasn't enough blood. In any event, there was a hole in Kian Min's neck that matched the gun in his brother's hand.'

Singh said hesitantly, 'But why did Jasper kill his brothers?'

'We're back to saving the rainforests, I'm afraid.'

Singh scratched his beard thoughtfully. 'I would never have put Jasper down as the type to commit multiple murders . . .'

Mohammad stood up and stuck a hand out. 'Thank you for your assistance in this matter, Inspector Singh. We look forward to greater cooperation between the Malaysian and Singapore police in the future as well. I won't fail to mention your contribution at my press conference.'

Singh's eyes twinkled as he remembered their numerous run-ins. 'Just don't get into the details,' he chortled. He shook the other man's hand and said, 'I have a plane to catch.'

RUPERT WINFIELD COULD barely understand what had happened.

Jasper had carefully shot Kian Min at close range in the neck, aiming for the point of entry of the blowpipe needle. They had been heading for the lift to get away from the scene when they saw the elevator doors slide open. Only Jasper's quick thinking had saved them. Jasper had grabbed his arm, turned the corner sharply and dragged him down the corridor, their footsteps muffled in the thick, pile carpet. They were cornered and desperate until Jasper had seen the fire escape door. He had hurried them towards it. Flung it open. Shoved Rupert through. Jasper had taken a step forward to follow him but then hesitated. He had looked back down the corridor and at Rupert. He said, 'Go back to Borneo. Honour her memory. I will handle things here.'

Rupert had started to protest but Jasper had put a hand up to stop him, put a finger to his lips to demand silence and closed the door firmly on his dumbstruck friend.

And now he was on his way back to Borneo and the Penan people. He would work to save them—do everything in his power to preserve a disappearing people. In memory of his wife, his unborn child and the friend who had given him a second chance.

EPILOGUE

Inspector Mohammad was in a cell with Jasper, recording his confession to the murder of his two brothers. At last they were finished and the two men sat looking at each other.

Mohammad said, 'That's your story, and you're sticking to it?'

Jasper smiled. 'This time I am, yes.'

The policeman nodded thoughtfully, then he asked, 'How do you explain this, then?' He slid an envelope, its seal broken and a letter sticking out of it, towards Jasper.

Jasper stared at it, puzzled. He had a horrid feeling of *déjà vu*. He was not going to be fooled into retracting his confession this time, though. Besides, he had produced the murder weapon.

He picked up the letter and read it slowly. At last, he put it back on the table, looked up, and said in an even voice, 'Where did you get this?'

'Your apartment.'

Jasper nodded in acknowledgment. 'Rupert gave it to me when we met at his hotel the other day. I'd completely forgotten about it or I would have destroyed it, of course.'

'Why?'

'Kian Min deserved to die.'

'But you didn't kill him.'

Jasper shrugged. 'I killed Alan.'

'Why would you take the blame for what this Rupert Winfield did?'

Jasper picked up the letter again between two fingers. He said, 'You've read it. He gave it to me just before he went to see Kian Min. I didn't know what he was planning . . . but he obviously wanted someone to understand why he was going to do . . . what he was going to do.'

'They killed his wife?'

Jasper nodded. 'Yes. She was pregnant. Kian Min was boasting about it just before he died.'

Both men fell silent. Rupert's letter to Jasper lay on the table between them. The plea of a broken-hearted man for some understanding.

'It explains why the body was cold even though I heard the gunshot just a few minutes before. And why Kian Min was full of poison,' remarked Mohammad. 'In fact, if you shot him after he was dead—that explains the lack of blood as well.'

Jasper asked, 'What are you going to do?'

Mohammad looked at him. 'You're sure you know what you're doing?'

'They can only hang me once.'

Mohammad fished in a pocket and brought out a clear plastic cigarette lighter. He had found it under his desk—a remnant from the visit of the inspector from Singapore. He ran his thumb over it and a blue and yellow flame flared. Inspector Mohammad picked up Rupert Winfield's letter and held the flame to a corner. He dropped the burning sheet of paper onto the concrete floor and the two men watched it burn, curling and dissolving into ashes.

Jasper said, 'Thank you.'

Mohammad nodded and put the lighter back in his pocket. He suspected that Inspector Singh would have been proud of the use to which it had just been put.

shamini **flint**

Profile

Home:
Singapore.
Family:
Husband and two children.
Career:
Practised law in Malaysia, and also worked at an international law firm in Singapore.
Other novels in the

Inspector Singh series:
Inspector Singh Investigates: A Bali Conspiracy Most Foul; *Inspector Singh Investigates: The Singapore School of Villainy; Inspector Singh Investigates: A Deadly Cambodian Crime Spree.*

What is your background?

I am an ex-lawyer and stay-at-home mum who is determined to change the world through the written word! I began writing adult and children's books four years ago. My life is now a whirlwind of playdates, soccer lessons and writing, writing and more writing. I began with the 'Sasha Books', a series of picture travel books about a little girl named Sasha visiting places in Asia. Round about the same time I caught the environmental bug. I belatedly realised that our lifestyles are unsustainable and our children are going to inherit the mess. In a panic, I began to write books (printed on recycled paper) about endangered species and did a lot of school visits to talk about environmental issues. As I am a closet workaholic, I also began a series of crime fiction stories for adults based on the ubiquitous Inspector Singh.

Apart from Inspector Singh himself, did you have a favourite character who you enjoyed writing about in this book?

Inspector Singh spends some time in Kuala Lumpur with his sister. It's actually a cameo appearance by an eccentric elderly aunt of mine who lives in KL. Fortunately for me, she didn't recognise the character, although she claims to have read and enjoyed the book!

Do you find a difference in attitude towards conservation in Singapore and Malaysia, especially over the protection of forests?

Asian society is a decade behind the West in terms of green awareness. Governments spend an awful lot of time insisting that the economic consequences of adopting higher environmental standards will be too great. I am always taken aback by an argument that suggests lining one's pockets now is more important than preserving a healthy planet for future generations. My hope is that *A Most Peculiar Malaysian Murder* will remind a few readers of the challenges of rainforest conservation in SE Asia.

Have you had letters from real-life policemen giving their opinion of Singh?

Rather to my surprise, I've had letters from a number of policemen including Malaysian, Australian and Indian ex-coppers, usually retired. So far, the feedback has been very positive, although they may have just been polite! I have to say that I think having a real-life colleague like Inspector Singh would be very tiresome. Some of these mavericks are best kept between the pages and off the streets . . .

The character of Chelsea Liew in this story is persecuted both by her husband and by the law, but she has courage. Is she based on someone you've known?

I'm a bit of a feminist in that I think women have an enormous ability to show strength and courage in difficult situations. Their courage tends to lie in a certain stoicism and quiet determination. I've known quite a few strong women, in the family, in the law, in journalism, and I think of Chelsea as a composite of all of them. I try to write about such women, hoping that I'll learn some courage from them.

Without giving the plot away, we can say that at least one person who commits murder in this novel is allowed to go unpunished. Did that cause you any dilemmas when you were writing it?

Sadly, the law and justice do not always serve the same ends, especially in the Third World, where the legal system can be a tool of oppression by authority. Many of my books deal with this schism, so I didn't feel bad about a certain character going unpunished by the law, for in many ways that person had suffered enough already.

Inspector Singh seems very much of a problem-solver, as opposed to a simple law-enforcer. Which problems is he especially qualified to solve? Would you trust him with your life, for instance?

I'd trust him with my life but not immediately before lunch! Yes, I think he is definitely more about solving the puzzle than enforcing the law, especially when he operates outside Singapore, where his role tends to be more private investigator than cop. I think of him most of all as a man with a conscience and some detecting skills.

Can you tell us where the next Inspector Singh story is set?

India! The next book in the series is *Inspector Singh Investigates: A Curious Indian Cadaver*. It allowed me to take Singh back, as an outsider, to the country of his ethnic roots. Mrs Singh and her extended family are involved as well—and I do enjoy hanging out the family dirty linen!

now you see her

JOY FIELDING

Marcy Taggart is ready to admit that the death of a child can make it hard for a marriage to survive. She's even made the trip to Ireland on a long-planned second honeymoon—without her husband, since he's left her for someone else.

But while she's touring in the historic city of Cork, Marcy suddenly throws away acceptance and fastens on to a wild hope.

What if her daughter isn't dead?

What if she's hiding in this very city?

ONE

'If you'll all just gather around me for a few seconds, I'll give you a wee bit of information about this glorious building you can see in front of you.'

The guide smiled encouragingly at the group of tired and somewhat bedraggled-looking tourists milling around at the front of St Anne's Shandon Church.

'That's it, darlin',' he cajoled in his exaggerated Irish lilt, the emerald-green scarf in his hand waving impatient circles around his portly frame. 'Move in a little closer, young lady. I won't bite you.' His smile widened, revealing a bottom row of spectacularly stained and crooked teeth.

Good thing her husband hadn't made the trip to Ireland after all, Marcy Taggart thought, taking several reluctant steps forwards. He'd have interpreted the poor man's lack of a perfect smile as a personal affront. *People spend all this money on face-lifts and designer clothes, and they forget about the most important thing of all—their teeth*, he often fumed. Peter was an orthodontist and therefore prone to such pronouncements. Hadn't he once told her that the first thing that had attracted him to her wasn't her slim figure or her large, dark brown eyes but rather her flawlessly white teeth? To think she had once found such statements romantic; Marcy marvelled at it now.

'Can I have your full attention, please?' the tour guide asked, without a hint of reproach in his voice. He was clearly used to the casual rudeness of those in his charge and had ceased to take offence. Even though the group of twenty-four men and women had paid a lot of money for the day's excursion to Cork, Ireland's second-largest city, only a handful had been paying attention to anything the man had been saying since leaving Dublin.

Marcy had tried—she really had. She had repeatedly instructed herself to focus as the guide educated them on the history of Cork during the bus ride. She had learned that the name Cork was derived from the Irish word '*corcach*', meaning 'marshy place', because of its situation on the river Lee; and that it had been founded in the sixth century A.D. Today it was known as the heart of industry in the south of Ireland, the chief industry being pharmaceuticals, its most famous product none other than Viagra.

At least that's what Marcy thought their guide had said. She couldn't be sure. Her imagination had an unfortunate tendency to get the better of her these days and, at fifty, her once prodigious memory was no longer what it used to be.

'As you can see, because of its hilltop position, the tower of St Anne's Shandon Church dominates the north side of the city,' the guide was saying now, his voice rising to be heard over the other tour groups that had suddenly materialised. He took a breath. 'You have thirty minutes to visit the inside of the church; then we'll head over to Patrick's Hill so you can get a feel for its steepness.'

'What if we're not up to the climb?' an elderly woman asked.

'I think I'm all churched out,' the man beside Marcy muttered. 'I could use a pint of Guinness.'

'For those of you who would prefer to enjoy a bit of rest before heading back to the bus, there's no shortage of pubs in the area.'

'Sounds good to me,' someone said.

'We'll meet back at Parnell Place Bus Station in one hour,' the guide announced. 'Please be prompt or we might not have enough time to visit Blarney Castle on our way back to Dublin. And you don't want to miss out on kissing the Blarney Stone, do you?'

No, we wouldn't want to miss out on that, Marcy thought, recalling Peter's revulsion at the idea of being held by his feet and suspended backwards and upside down in order to kiss 'some bacteria-soaked rock coated with other people's saliva', as he had so memorably phrased it when she had shown him the brochures. 'Who in their right mind would do such a thing?' he had asked.

Marcy had smiled and said nothing. Peter had ceased believing she was in her right mind some time ago.

Wasn't that why she had agreed to go on this trip in the first place? Hadn't everyone been telling her that it was important that she and Peter spend more time together, time in which they could come to terms with what had happened, *as a unit*? Wasn't that the term her psychiatrist had used?

So when her sister had floated the idea of a second honeymoon in honour of their twenty-fifth anniversary, Marcy had thrown herself into its planning. It had been Peter's suggestion to go to Ireland, his mother having been born in Limerick. He had been talking for years of making a pilgrimage to the land of his ancestors. Marcy had initially argued in favour of somewhere more exotic, like Tahiti. But what difference did it make where they went as long as they went there *as a unit*? So Peter's choice it was.

And ultimately, Peter had chosen someone else.

He couldn't take any more drama he had said, when he told her he was leaving. *It's better this way. We'll both be better off. You'll see, you'll be much happier. Hopefully, eventually, we can be friends.* The cowardly clichés of the deserter.

'We still have a son together,' he had told her, as if she needed reminding. No mention of their daughter.

Marcy shivered, gathering her trench coat together, and decided to join the ranks of those opting for a pint of beer. They'd been on a three-hour walking tour of the city. It was time to sit down.

Ten minutes later she found herself alone at a tiny table for two inside a traditional Irish pub overlooking the river Lee. It was dark inside, which suited the mood that was rapidly overtaking her. She was crazy to have come to Ireland, she was thinking. Only a crazy woman goes on her second honeymoon by herself, even if the trip had been paid for in advance. It wasn't as if she couldn't afford the loss of a few thousand dollars: Peter had been generous in his settlement offer. Clearly, he had wanted to get away from her quickly. Marcy found herself chuckling. Why should he put any more effort into their divorce than he had put into their marriage?

'You find something amusing, do you?' a voice asked from somewhere above her head.

Marcy looked up to see a roguishly handsome young man with straight black hair falling into luminous dark green eyes.

'What can I get you, darlin'?' he said, notepad and pencil poised to take her order.

'Would it be too ridiculous to order a cup of tea?' Marcy asked.

'Not ridiculous at all,' the waiter said.

'Tea sounds wonderful,' she heard someone say. 'Could you make that two?' Beside her a chair scraped the floor. 'Mind if I join you?' A man sat down before Marcy had a chance to respond.

Marcy recognised him as a member of her tour group, although she couldn't remember his name.

'Vic Sorvino,' he said now, extending his hand.

'Marcy Taggart,' Marcy said, without taking it. Instead, she gave a little wave she hoped would satisfy him. Why was he here?

'Taggart? So you're Irish?'

'My husband is.'

Vic looked towards the long bar that ran the entire length of the room. 'I'm sorry, I didn't realise you were with anyone,' he said.

'He's not here.'

'Doesn't like bus tours?'

'Doesn't like being married,' Marcy said. 'At least to me.'

Vic looked stunned. 'You're not big on small talk, are you?'

Marcy laughed in spite of her desire not to and pushed at the mop of curls falling into her narrow face.

So much hair, she thought in her mother's voice, *for such a tiny face.*

'I'm sorry,' she said now. 'I guess that falls under the category of too much information.'

'Nonsense. I believe information is always useful.'

'Stick around,' Marcy said, immediately regretting her choice of words. The last thing she wanted to do was encourage him.

The waiter approached with their teas.

'He probably thinks we're crazy, ordering tea in a pub,' Marcy said, following the handsome young man with her eyes as he returned to the bar. She estimated his age as early thirties and wondered if her daughter would have found him attractive.

'Actually, Americans have the wrong idea about Irish pubs,' Vic was saying, his easy baritone pulling her back into the conversation. 'They're as much about socialising as drinking. People come here to see their neighbours, and lots of them choose tea over alcohol. I've been reading the guidebooks,' he admitted sheepishly; then, when Marcy remained silent, 'Where are you from?'

'Toronto,' she answered obligingly.

'Toronto's a lovely city,' he said. 'I was there a few times on business.' He paused. 'I was in the manufacturing business. Widgets,' he said.

'You manufacture midgets?' Marcy asked, realising she had been listening with only half an ear.

Vic laughed and corrected her. 'Widgets. Small mechanical devices whose names you usually can't remember. Gadgets.'

Marcy sipped her tea and said nothing. *I'm an idiot*, she thought.

'I sold the business and retired last year,' he continued. Then, when no further questions were forthcoming: 'I'm from Chicago.'

Marcy managed a tepid smile. She had always liked Chicago. She should have gone there, she was thinking as her cell phone began ringing in her handbag. Chicago had wonderful architecture, and it didn't rain almost every day.

'Is that your phone?' Vic asked.

'Hmm? Oh. *Oh*,' she said, locating it at the bottom of her handbag and lifting it to her ear. 'Hello?'

'Where the hell are you?' her sister demanded angrily.

'Judith?'

'Where have you been? I haven't heard from you in a week.'

'Is everything all right? Has something happened to Darren?'

'Your son's fine, Marcy,' her sister said. 'It's you I'm worried about. Why haven't you returned any of my calls?'

Because I didn't want to speak to you, Marcy thought. Marcy pictured her sister, older by two years, pacing the marbled floor of her new luxury condominium. She was undoubtedly dressed in her standard uniform of black yoga pants and matching tank top, because she had either just finished working out or was about to start. She spent at least half the day exercising. Judith was on husband number five. She'd had her tubes tied when she was eighteen, having decided never to have any children of her own.

'Something's not right,' she said now. 'I'm coming by.'

'You can't. I'm not home.'

'Where are you?'

A long pause. 'Ireland.'

'What? Please tell me you're joking.'

'I'm not joking. I'm fine, Judith.' Marcy saw a shadow fall across the window. The shadow stopped and waved at the bartender. He acknowledged the shadow's wave with a sly smile.

'You aren't fine. I demand you come home instantly.'

'I can't do that.' The shadow stepped into a cone of light, then turned and disappeared. 'Oh, my God.' Marcy gasped.

'What is it?' Vic and Judith asked simultaneously.

'My God, it's Devon!' Marcy said, slamming her hip into a nearby table as she raced for the door.

'What?'

'I just saw her. She's here.'

'Marcy, calm down. You're talking crazy.'

'I'm not crazy.' Marcy pushed open the pub's door, tears stinging her eyes as her head swivelled up and down the tourist-clogged street. A light drizzle had started to fall. 'Devon!' she called out, running east along the river Lee. 'Where are you? Come back.'

'Marcy, please,' Judith urged in Marcy's ear. 'It's not Devon. You know it's not her.'

'I know what I saw.' Marcy stopped at St Patrick's Bridge. 'I'm telling you. She's here. I saw her.'

'No, you didn't,' Judith said gently. 'Devon is dead, Marcy.'

'You're wrong. She's here.'

'Your daughter is dead,' Judith repeated, tears clinging to each word.

'Go to hell,' Marcy cried. Then she tossed the phone into the river and crossed over the bridge.

WITHIN MINUTES, Marcy was lost in the labyrinth of lanes that twisted around the river Lee.

'Devon!' she cried, her eyes pushing through the crowds, straining to see over the tops of black umbrellas that were sprouting up everywhere as it began to rain. 'Devon!' Her eyes filled with tears as she circled back to the main road, wet curls clinging to her forehead. Seconds later, she found herself at the busy junction of St Patrick's Street and Merchant's Quay.

In front of her stood the hulking Merchant's Quay Shopping Centre, an enclosed shopping complex that served as the city's main mall. Marcy stood staring at it. Had Devon taken refuge from the rain in there? *What do I do now?* Marcy wondered, deciding against going inside.

Instead, she ran down St Patrick's Street, trying to fit her daughter's delicate features on the face of each young woman who hurried by. St Patrick's Street curved gently into Grand Parade, a spacious thoroughfare. Marcy continued south, scanning the street's benches. She proceeded to the South Mall, a wide tree-lined street that was Cork's financial centre, its Georgian-style architecture housing banks, law offices and insurance companies. No chance Devon would be there, Marcy decided. Her daughter had never been very good with formal institutions. She had been even less good with money.

Marcy shuddered, remembering the time she had berated Devon for taking forty dollars from her bag. Such a paltry sum, and she had made such a fuss.

'I was just borrowing it,' Devon had insisted stubbornly. 'I was going to pay it back.'

Marcy had protested in turn. 'It's not that. It's a matter of trust.'

'You're saying you don't trust me?'

'I'm saying I don't like it when you take things without asking.'

'I just borrowed it. I didn't think it was such a big deal.'

'Well, it *is* a big deal.'

'I apologised, didn't I? God, what's your problem?'

What *was* her problem? Marcy wondered now. Why had she made such a nothing incident into such a huge issue? Didn't all teenage girls occasionally steal money from their mother's purse? So what if Devon had been almost twenty-one at the time? She was still a child, still living at home, still under her mother's protection.

Her mother's protection. Marcy scoffed silently. Had Devon ever felt protected in her mother's house?

Had Marcy in hers?

Everything that happened is my fault, Marcy told herself silently, losing her footing on a patch of slippery pavement and collapsing like a discarded piece of crumpled paper. She made no move to get up. *Serves me right*, she was thinking, recalling that awful afternoon when the police had shown up at her door to tell her Devon was dead.

Except she wasn't dead. She was here.

Right here, Marcy realised with a start, her head shooting towards a young woman exiting a two-storey grey brick building directly across the street. Not only was Devon still alive, she was here in Cork. She was standing right in front of her.

Marcy pushed herself to her feet. She darted across the street and almost collided with a speeding scooter. The driver swore at her, drawing the attention of everyone in the vicinity, including Devon, whose head snapped towards the angry expletive.

Except it wasn't Devon.

Marcy saw immediately that this wasn't the same young woman she had been chasing after. This girl was three inches taller than Devon, who'd always complained that, at five feet four, she was too short. 'Why'd I have to get your legs and not Judith's?' she had asked Marcy accusingly, as if such things were in Marcy's control.

'Marcy!' she heard a voice calling. 'Marcy Taggart!' Someone was suddenly beside her. 'Marcy, are you all right?'

A man's face snapped into focus. He was tanned, and his dark hair was greying. *A nice face*, Marcy thought, *saved from blandness by unsettlingly blue eyes*. Why hadn't she noticed them before?

'It's Vic Sorvino,' the man said, his hand lingering on her arm.

'I know who you are,' Marcy said impatiently. 'I'm not crazy.'

'I'm sorry. I didn't mean to . . . I was just worried about you.'

'Why?'

'Well, the way you took off . . .' He glanced up and down the street, as if looking for someone. 'I take it you didn't find the girl you went chasing after. Devon, I think you called her.'

'Did you see her?' Marcy demanded. 'Did she come back?'

'No, I didn't see anyone,' Vic said. 'All I know is that one minute you were sitting beside me talking on the phone, and the next you were running down the street, shouting, "Devon".'

'So you followed me?'

'I tried, but I lost you in the crowd after you crossed the bridge. You looked as if you'd seen a ghost.'

Marcy stared at him. Was that what had happened? Had the girl she had seen been nothing but a figment of her desperate imagination? That's what Judith obviously thought. Was she right? It wouldn't have been the first time she had chased after ghosts.

How many times in the last twenty months had she stopped strangers on the street, certain each girl with a resemblance to Devon was the daughter she had lost? Each time, she had been wrong.

Was she wrong this time as well? Did it make any sense—any sense at all—that her daughter could be here?

It wasn't that far-fetched a possibility, Marcy quickly assured herself. How often had Devon heard her father extolling the imagined glories of Ireland? The most beautiful country in the world, he had proclaimed.

Devon had worshipped her father, so it wasn't that surprising she would choose Ireland as her place of refuge. Was that really why Marcy had come here?

'I guess I did see a ghost,' she said, when she realised Vic was waiting for some kind of response.

'It happens.'

Marcy nodded, wondering what he knew of ghosts. 'We should get back to our bus.'

He took her elbow, and gently led her back towards Parnell Place. By the time they saw the pinched face of their guide as he paced impatiently outside their waiting bus, the rain had slowed to a weak drizzle. 'I'm so sorry we're late,' Marcy said as the guide hurried them onto the coach.

Marcy felt the unabashed animosity of her fellow tourists pushing her towards her seat as the coach pulled out of the station. She lost her balance and lurched forwards.

'Careful,' Vic said, grabbing the back of her coat to steady her.

What is he still doing here? Marcy wondered, shaking free of his sturdy grip. She no longer believed in knights in shining armour.

Marcy crawled into her seat and Vic sat down beside her as the guide began to speak. 'In about twenty minutes we'll be passing through Blarney, which boasts one of the most impressive castles in all of Ireland,' he announced. 'Blarney Castle also boasts a beautiful garden and a lovely dell beside Blarney Lake. Unfortunately, we won't be able see any of those things today.' A groan swept through the bus. The guide continued. 'I'm sorry, but I did warn you about being late.' He glared at Marcy. Several angry heads swivelled in her direction.

'I'm very sorry,' she whispered, then turned to stare out of the window, seeing only her own reflection staring back. *I used to be considered beautiful*, she thought, wondering when she had become so tired-looking and old. People were always telling her she looked at least a decade younger than she was, and maybe she had at one time. Before her life had changed for ever. Before that awful October afternoon when she had watched a police car pull to a stop outside her bungalow in Hogg's Hollow, her eyes following the two officers slowly up her front walkway, her breath catching painfully.

'Aren't you going to answer that, Marcy?' Peter had called as the doorbell rang. He was in the den, watching some sporting event on TV.

'It's the police,' Marcy had managed to croak out, although her feet had turned to lead and she lacked the strength to move them. She was suddenly fifteen years old again, standing beside her sister in the principal's office.

'The police?' Peter had marched into the foyer and pulled open the front door. 'Officers?' he asked, the word suspended ominously in the air as he ushered the two men inside.

'Are you Dr Peter Taggart?'

'I am.'

'We understand you have a cottage on Georgian Bay,' one of the officers said as Marcy felt her body go numb. 'Yes, that's right,' Peter had answered. 'Our daughter is up there for the weekend with some friends. Why? Has something happened?'

'Your daughter is Devon Taggart?'

'Yes, that's right. Is she in some sort of trouble?'

'I'm afraid there's been an accident,' the policeman said. 'Perhaps you'd like to sit down.'

'Perhaps you'd like to tell me what's happened.'

Out of the corner of her eye, Marcy had seen the police officer nod, then look towards the floor. 'Neighbours saw your daughter climb into a canoe at around ten o'clock this morning. The water was pretty rough, and she wasn't wearing a life jacket. When they saw she still hadn't returned three hours later, they called the police. I'm afraid they found her overturned canoe in the middle of the bay.'

'And Devon?' Peter asked quietly.

'They're still searching.'

'So you haven't found her,' Marcy interrupted forcefully.

'Not yet.'

'Well, that's good. It means she probably swam to shore.'

'I'm afraid there's little chance of that,' the officer told her. 'The canoe was miles from anywhere.'

'Devon's a very strong swimmer.'

'The water is extremely cold,' the second officer stated. 'It's doubtful—'

'You said she went to the cottage with friends?' the first officer interrupted to ask Peter.

'Yes,' Peter had replied. 'Carrie and Michelle. I can't remember their last names,' he had added helplessly, looking to Marcy.

'Stafford and Harvey,' Marcy had informed the officers. 'I'm sure they'll be able to tell you where Devon is.'

'According to your neighbours, your daughter was at the cottage alone.'

'That's not possible. She told us she was going up there with Carrie and Michelle. Why would she lie?' *Why did she usually lie?* Marcy had thought, brushing aside a tear.

'Do you know if your daughter has been depressed lately?' she heard one of the policemen ask.

'You're saying you don't think this was an accident?' Peter said.

Marcy had had to grab her hands to keep from slapping him. How dare he even entertain such a suggestion, let alone say it out loud?

'I have to ask: do you think it's possible she took her own life?'

'No, it's not possible,' Marcy said adamantly, fleeing the room and racing down the hall before Peter could contradict her. She had flung open the door to Devon's bedroom, swallowing the room in a single glance.

The note had been propped up against Devon's pillow.

'DESPITE OUR NOT BEING ABLE to visit Blarney Castle,' the guide was saying now, 'I hope you have enjoyed our tour.' Marcy opened her eyes to see that they had arrived in Dublin. 'As you no doubt observed from our brief visit, you need more than one day to fully appreciate Cork. The library is well worth a visit, as is Cork's famous Butter Museum. And don't forget the university, whose campus is home to seventeen thousand students from all over the world.'

All those students, Marcy thought silently, thinking how easy it would be for Devon to blend in. To disappear.

'Have you ever just wanted to disappear?' Devon had asked Marcy one day not long before her overturned canoe was found. 'Just go somewhere and start all over again as someone else?'

'Please don't talk that way, sweetheart,' Marcy had said. 'You have everything.'

What a stupid thing to say, she thought now. She, of all people, should have known that having everything guaranteed nothing.

They'd never recovered Devon's body.

'That *was* you I saw,' Marcy whispered under her breath.

'Sorry. Did you say something?' Vic asked.

Marcy shook her head. 'No,' she said out loud. But inside, a voice was screaming, *You aren't dead, are you, Devon? You're here. I know you are. And whatever it takes—however long it takes—I'm going to find you.*

TWO

The message light on her phone was flashing ominously when Marcy returned to her hotel.

It must be a mistake, she thought, letting her coat fall to the thick carpet and kicking off her shoes. She balanced on the side of her bed, wondering who could have called. Nobody knew she was here. *Probably the tour company*, she decided. *Holding me responsible for the missed excursion to Blarney Castle, expecting me to cover any costs they incurred as a result*. She decided not to listen to the message until later. She leaned back against the stack of pillows at the head of the king-size bed and closed her eyes. Almost immediately the phone started ringing.

Marcy's eyes popped open. Could it be Devon? Was it possible that she had spied Marcy through the pub's window? Had she watched her mother's frantic search from a safe distance? Had she followed her, watched her board the bus back to Dublin, then started calling every first-class hotel in the city in a desperate effort to track her mother down? Was it possible?

Slowly Marcy lifted the receiver to her ear.

'Marcy? Marcy, are you there?' Peter's voice filled the large, elegant room. 'Marcy? I can hear you breathing. Answer me.'

Tears of disappointment filled Marcy's eyes. 'Hello, Peter,' she said. It was all she could think of to say to the man with whom she had shared the last twenty-five years of her life. 'How are you?'

'How am *I*?' he asked incredulously. '*I'm* fine. It's *you* I'm worried about. I've called half a dozen times, left messages . . .'

'How did you know where to find me?'

'Your sister called,' he told her. 'She's frantic. Says you've gone off to Ireland by yourself, that you think you've seen—' He broke off, took a second to regroup. 'I remembered the name of the hotel in Dublin where we—'

'Were supposed to stay together?' Marcy finished for him.

A second's silence, then slowly, cautiously, almost lovingly, 'You have to come home, Marcy. You have to come home now.'

'I saw her, Peter. I saw Devon.'

Peter sighed. 'You only *think* you saw Devon,' he told her gently. 'Marcy, please. I thought we'd got past this.'

'No, *you* got past it.'

'Because I had to. Because there was no other choice. Our daughter is dead, Marcy.'

'They never found her body.'

Another silence. Another sigh. 'So you're saying . . . what? That she faked her own death?'

'Maybe. Or maybe it was an accident and she saw an opportunity . . .'

'An opportunity for what? Why would she do something like this? Why would she let us think she was dead?'

'You know why!' Marcy shouted, silencing him.

'How did she get there?' he asked quietly. 'She didn't have a passport. She didn't have any money . . .'

'She could have had money put away.'

'Think about what you're saying, Marcy.'

'I don't have to think about it,' she insisted, refusing to be swayed. 'Our daughter is alive, Peter. She's here in Ireland.'

'And you just happened to run into her.'

'She walked right by the pub where I was sitting. I know, it's quite a coincidence,' Marcy said, before Peter had the chance.

A moment's silence, then, 'Did you talk to her?'

'No. I tried following her, but I lost her in the crowd.'

He sighed. 'Come home, Marcy.'

'Goodbye, Peter. Please tell Judith not to worry.'

She hung up the phone before he could say anything else.

The phone rang again immediately. Marcy let it go directly to voicemail. If it wasn't Peter, it was Judith, and she didn't have the strength to have the same conversation a second time. If they wanted to think she was crazy, so be it. They were probably right.

But that didn't mean she was wrong about Devon.

She would return to Cork first thing the next morning, she decided. She retrieved her suitcase from the closet. Within minutes it was packed, shoes and nightgowns at the bottom, shirts and dresses followed by T-shirts and jeans, along with a nice pair of black trousers.

She walked to the large window that overlooked College Green, across from Trinity College. It was almost eight o'clock. She hadn't had anything to eat since lunch. She thought she should call room service. Or maybe she should go out, and let the night breeze blow Peter's doubts out of her head.

Except that Peter didn't have any doubts. He never had. Wasn't that one of the things that had drawn her to him in the first place? That he had always been so sure of himself?

Marcy crossed back to the closet and opened the safety deposit box, her hand brushing against a pair of gold hoop earrings Judith had given her for her fiftieth birthday, as she reached for the envelope at the very back of the velvet-lined box.

Returning to the bed, Marcy opened the envelope and removed the half-dozen photographs, careful to avoid the smaller envelope inside it, the word 'MOMMY' scrawled across its front. She laid the pictures across the white comforter, studied each one: Devon as a baby in her mother's arms, both with the same huge brown eyes, the same cupid's-bow mouth; Devon as a child of five, wearing a pink tutu; Devon on her twelfth birthday, her mouth wide open to show off her new braces; Devon at eighteen, hovering on the edge of beauty, dark curls falling past her shoulders, her smile unsure. Marcy noted the sadness already creeping into her eyes. And, finally, Devon, only weeks before her canoe was found, her once expressive dark eyes blank, her cupid's-bow lips now a thin line.

Marcy sat staring at the pictures, wondering at Devon's transformation from giddy toddler to morose young woman. *My fault*, she thought. *Everything, my fault.*

There was another photograph inside the envelope, and Marcy pulled it out. It was a black-and-white picture of her mother, taken around the time she had turned twenty-one. She was standing in front of a large mirror, her regal profile reflected in the glass at her back. Her eyes were downcast, and her long brown hair was pulled away from her face. She was wearing a dress of pale organza. Her left hand held a gardenia that she held coyly to her chin.

Only the slightest hint of madness in her eyes.

The person who'd taken that picture had been desperately in love with her, as her mother had been fond of recounting. Theirs had been an exciting, wild affair, a whirlwind of constantly shifting emotions. And yet, in the end, her mother had opted for security. She had married George Fraser, a man whose name said it all. He was uncomplicated, straightforward, and too sane for his own good.

A man much like Peter in so many ways, Marcy acknowledged reluctantly. Both men never knew what hit them.

Marcy stuffed the pictures back inside their envelope, quickly returning it to the safety deposit box. Then she grabbed her coat and handbag and headed out of the door.

In the elegant lobby, Marcy made her way to the reception desk. 'Where do I go to rent a car?' she asked a middle-aged woman behind the counter.

'Oh, I wouldn't advise renting a car in Dublin,' the woman, whose name tag identified her as Lynette, said cheerily in her thick brogue. 'It's much easier getting around the city without one.'

'I'm thinking of driving to the countryside. I'm sure I'll be fine.'

Lynette smiled indulgently as she handed Marcy a map of the city, drawing a red circle where the major car-rental offices were located. 'Of course, they're all closed at this hour,' she said.

'Of course.' Now she would have to waste a valuable chunk of tomorrow morning just getting organised. Her stomach growled, as if underlining her displeasure. 'Do you happen to know a nice restaurant in the area? Nothing too fancy . . .'

'There's Flannery's over on O'Connell Street. The food's good.' Lynette took back the map from Marcy's hand and circled the spot.

Marcy was walking through the lobby when she heard a now-familiar voice call out her name. *What is he doing here?* she wondered, pretending she hadn't heard him.

'Marcy?' he called again.

She spun around. 'Vic.' Marcy acknowledged him, noting that he smelled of soap and shampoo and that he had changed his clothes since she had seen him less than an hour ago. He was wearing a black turtleneck sweater that emphasised the intense blueness of his eyes. 'I didn't realise you were staying at this hotel.'

'I'm not. I'm at the Morgan, just down the block.'

'How did you know where to find me?'

'The bus let you off at your hotel,' Vic said, with a shrug. 'I thought I'd take a chance you might be free for dinner.'

'You're asking me out?'

'I'm sorry if I'm not very good at it. I haven't had a lot of practice lately.'

'I can't,' Marcy said.

'You have other plans?'

'No.'

'Oh. I'm sorry. I didn't mean to bother you.'

Marcy continued unprompted. 'It's just that I'm a mess. I mean, look at me. I haven't showered or changed. My hair's a disaster.'

'You look gorgeous.'

Marcy released a long, deep breath. When was the last time a man had been so nice to her? 'I can't,' she said again. 'I just don't think I'd be very good company.'

'No need to explain.' He began backing away.

'Vic,' she said, stopping him, wondering what she was doing.

He stared at her expectantly.

'I hear there's a very nice restaurant over on O'Connell Street. Good food. Not fancy, but good.'

'Are you asking me out?' he said with a smile.

'I'm sorry if I'm not very good at it,' she parroted.

'On the contrary. You're doing just fine. It sounds wonderful.'

'Would you give me a few minutes to shower and change?'

'I'll wait right here.'

'I THINK I'll try the shepherd's pie.' Marcy handed her big, unwieldy menu back to the waiter.

'Sounds good,' Vic said. 'I'll have the same. And a glass of Irish whiskey to start.' He smiled at Marcy expectantly.

'What the hell? Why not?' Marcy said, although she had never been much of a drinker. But why not celebrate? She had seen Devon. Tomorrow morning she would rent a car and drive to Cork. Once she was settled, it shouldn't take long to find her daughter.

'The Irish call their whiskey the water of life,' Vic said.

'The Irish have a nice way of looking at things.'

'And speaking of nice ways of looking,' Vic said, 'have I told you how lovely you look?'

'Thank you.' Marcy fingered the collar of her cotton shirt self-consciously. She had had to unpack her suitcase to get at her white blouse and black trousers, but the change had made her feel better.

The waiter approached with their drinks.

'To a holiday that gets better every day,' Vic said, lifting his glass and clinking it against hers.

'I'll drink to that.' Marcy took a sip. 'Wow. That's strong stuff.'

'Good, though.'

'Getting better every sip.' She looked around the noisy, brightly lit restaurant. A large bar in the centre of the room was its dominant feature. Around the bar were small tables, all of them occupied.

'So what did you think of "the Stiletto in the Ghetto"?' Vic was asking.

Had she heard him correctly? 'The what?'

'The Millennium Spire,' he said; then, when that didn't seem to register, 'The monument we passed on the way over? The tall, stainless-steel needle in the middle of the road?' he said, clarifying further. 'It's pretty hard to miss. You missed it,' he said.

'I guess I was pretty focused on finding this place.'

'You seem to have a habit of doing that. Focusing on finding things,' he said. Marcy understood he was referring to the events earlier in the day.

'Have you been to St Stephen's Green yet?' Vic asked.

Marcy shook her head.

'I'd be happy to show it to you. If you're free tomorrow—'

'I'm not.'

A flash of disappointment registered in his eyes, although his quick smile disguised it. 'You've booked another tour?'

'No. It's just that I've already made other plans for tomorrow.'

'Well, if you should find yourself with some extra time on your hands, feel free to give me a call.' Vic reached into his pocket, pulled out a business card and handed it across the small table. 'Sold the business; kept the cell phone number.'

Marcy slipped the card into her handbag without looking at it. 'Actually, I'm leaving Dublin tomorrow.'

'Oh. I'm sorry to hear that. Where are you off to?'

'I'm meeting my sister in Paris for a few days,' she lied.

'Paris is a beautiful city. I started my trip there a few weeks ago. Paris, then London,' he said. 'Then Scotland. Now here. Next stop, Italy.'

'That's quite the trip.'

'Well, I want to see the village where my great-grandfather was born, and I figured if I wait too long, I might not make it.' He paused, as if waiting for her to ask the logical follow-up, then continued when she didn't. 'My father died of a heart attack when he was fifty-nine. My mother died of cancer at sixty-two, my first wife at fifty-three, also cancer. I've just turned fifty-seven. I figure I might not have a whole lot of time left.'

Marcy nodded, then held up her empty glass. 'In that case, do you think we could have another one of these?'

'I think that could be arranged.' He signalled the waiter for another round. 'And thank you.'

'For what?'

'Most people tell me I'm being foolish when I tell them my philosophy of life. Or death, as the case may be.'

'Sounds quite logical to me.'

'Sounds as if you also lost a loved one at too young an age.'

'Actually, my father was almost eighty when he died.'

'And your mother?'

Marcy extended her hand towards the approaching waiter, smiled when she felt the weight of the glass in her hand. 'Forty-six.' She took a swallow. 'You said *first* wife. How many have there been?'

Vic smiled. 'Just two.'

'What happened to the second?'

'We divorced a year ago. It was a disaster from the word go.'

Marcy took another sip and waited for him to continue.

'I was married to my first wife for almost thirty-three years,' he said, obliging her. 'She was my high-school sweetheart. We were the quintessential all-American couple, with three sons, a house in Lake Forest, and everything you could ask for. One day Kathy said she was feeling kind of funny, and we went to the doctor, and he said she had pancreatic cancer. Three months later she was dead.'

Marcy lowered her glass, stared at the table.

'And I was just reeling. Kathy was it for me. I'd never even been with another woman. Suddenly I was alone. I had my sons, of course, but they had their own lives to deal with. David and Mark were married with small children, and Tony was finishing up his master's degree in music. And I was acting like a lunatic. One minute I was holed up in the house, refusing to go anywhere, and the next minute I was out on the town, bedding anything that moved. Anyway, one day I decided it was time to sell the house.'

'Don't the experts usually advise not making any big moves for at least a year after the death of a spouse?'

'If they don't, they should. But real-estate agents aren't exactly big on periods of reflection.'

'So you sold your house?'

'No. I married my realtor. Reliable Vic Sorvino marries a woman twenty-five years his junior—a woman he's known for three months—barely six months after his beloved first wife passes away, without even a prenup, and the marriage is a fiasco. Six months later we agree to a divorce and, among other things, she gets the house, which, incidentally, she now has up for sale.' He sighed. 'I guess grief makes us do funny things.'

'I'm sorry. Are you all right?'

'Let's say I'm recovering. I don't think we ever fully get over the death of someone we love. We just learn to live with their absence.'

'Do we?'

'Do we have a choice?'

Marcy turned her head, grateful to see the waiter with their food.

'Looks good,' Vic said, inhaling the steam rising from his plate.

Marcy tore into her shepherd's pie. 'It's delicious,' she said.

'Tell me more about you,' said Vic.

'Not much to tell. My husband left me for one of the golf pros at our country club. Sarah's handicap was lower than mine,' she added, feeling the smile she tried to muster wobble on her mouth.

'How long were you married?' Vic asked.

'Going on twenty-five years. This trip was supposed to be a second honeymoon to celebrate our anniversary.'

'So you came by yourself. That's very brave. Do you have any children?' he asked.

'Yes. Two.'

'Boys? Girls?'

'One of each. Darren's nineteen, thinking of going into dentistry, like his dad. He's working as a camp counsellor for the summer.'

'Sounds like fun. And your daughter? What's she up to?'

'Devon is twenty-one, or no, actually, she'd be almost twenty-three now,' Marcy said, correcting herself immediately.

Vic cocked his head to one side, smiling to mask his obvious confusion. 'Devon is the girl you thought you saw this afternoon?'

'I *did* see her.'

'Your daughter is here in Ireland?' This time there was no attempt to hide his confusion.

'She's travelling through Europe for the summer,' Marcy said. 'I didn't realise we'd both be here at the same time—not until I saw her this after-noon. That's a lie,' she added in the next breath.

'I kind of figured.'

'I'm sorry.'

'That's all right. You don't owe me any explanations.'

'My daughter supposedly drowned in a canoeing accident about two years ago,' Marcy said, watching Vic's brow furrow. 'Except they never found her body. And I know, *I know,* she's still alive; that for whatever reason, she faked her death.'

'Why would she do that?' Vic asked.

'To get away. To start a new life. Start over.'

'Why would she want to start over?'

'Because she was so unhappy. Because she was in trouble . . . I'm sorry. Can we not talk about this any more?'

'We can not talk about whatever you'd like.'

Marcy continued, however, unable to stop herself. 'Everybody else is so positive she's dead. But I know what I saw. I saw my daughter. You think I'm crazy, don't you?'

'I think a mother knows her own child.'

Relief washed across Marcy's face. 'You're a nice man,' she said.

'And you've had a very eventful day. Come on. Finish up. I'll take you back to your hotel.'

Marcy reached across the table, took Vic's hand in hers. 'I have a better idea,' she said.

THREE

Her sister was right about one thing, Marcy thought, sitting up in bed and gazing through the darkness at the man snoring softly beside her: sex was like riding a bicycle. Once you knew how to do it, you never really forget the mechanics.

And her sister would know. As Judith herself admitted, she had ridden a lot of bicycles.

It was quiet although, surprisingly, even at two in the morning, there were still people out walking. The trendy area of Temple Bar never really shut down, according to Vic.

They'd gone to his room at her suggestion.

'Are you sure?' he had asked, when they first entered the elegantly under-furnished lobby of his hotel.

'I'm sure.'

They'd made love easily and effortlessly. *And repeatedly*, she thought now. When was the last time she and Peter had made love more than once in a single night? Not in at least a decade.

She sighed, reaching her hand out to touch Vic's cheek, then withdrawing it before she made contact. What had possessed her to sleep with a man she barely knew, a man who was still grieving the death of his first wife even after divorcing his second? *Grief makes us do funny things,* he had said. Was it grief that had brought her to his bed? Or was it gratitude?

I think a mother knows her own child, he had said, and she had actually had to hold herself back from leaping across the table and smothering his face with kisses. *Yes, thank you. You believe me!*

Was that all it took?

Or maybe it was hope that had brought her here. Hope that had let a virtual stranger undress and caress her; hope that had allowed her to respond so eagerly to his touch; hope that because Devon was alive, so, too, was she; that two people hadn't drowned on that horrible, cold October day, and that she could finally spit out the water that had been trapped in her lungs for far too long, and inhale and exhale without feeling a knife plunging into her chest.

Devon was alive, which meant Marcy had been given a second chance, a chance for both of them to be happy again.

Had they ever truly been happy?

'What's the matter, sweetheart?' she remembered asking one July night five years ago. The night everything had changed. The night she had had to stop pretending that everything would be OK.

It was after midnight. Devon had been out partying with friends. Marcy was lying in bed, Peter asleep beside her. She had never been able to sleep until she knew Devon was home safe. Marcy had heard Devon moving around in the kitchen, restlessly opening and closing the cupboard doors. Open, close, open, close.

Then a crash. The sound of glass breaking.

Marcy had jumped out of bed, grabbed a bathrobe, and run from the bedroom, telling herself that there was no need to be alarmed.

Except that when Marcy had entered the kitchen, she had discovered Devon standing beside the granite counter, her mouth open, her jaw slack, her eyes blank and filled with tears.

'What's the matter, sweetheart?' Marcy had asked, drawing closer.

'Don't,' Devon warned.

Marcy had noted the pieces of glass that were scattered around Devon's feet and the tulips that were lying half out of what remained of their crystal vase. Water was splashed across the top of Devon's open-toed sandals, the red polish of her toenails wet and shiny in the moonlight. Her hands were curled into tight fists at her sides, white granules squeezing out from between her clenched fingers and falling towards the floor like snow.

'What is that, sweetheart?' Marcy had asked, seeing a cardboard box of salt on the counter. 'What are you doing with the salt?'

In response, Devon had begun shovelling the salt into her mouth.

Marcy was instantly at her side, tearing Devon's hands away from her face. 'Devon, stop that. You'll make yourself sick.'

Devon's eyes had suddenly snapped into focus, as if she were seeing her mother for the first time. 'Mom?' she had said, opening her palms and letting the remaining salt spill free.

'Are you all right?' Marcy had begun frantically trying to wipe away the salt still stubbornly clinging to Devon's lips and chin.

Devon had looked from her mother to the floor. 'I'm so sorry.'

'What is it, sweetheart? What happened?'

'I don't know. I was reaching for a bag of potato chips, and I stopped to admire the flowers. You know how they say you have to stop and smell the roses? Even though these are tulips. Only I knocked over the vase and I couldn't find the potato chips. Do you remember Vicki Enquist? She's really tall, almost six feet, her nose is a little crooked? She was like my best friend in the seventh grade. Do you remember her?' she said, all in the same breath.

Marcy was about to answer that no, she had no memory of Vicki Enquist and could Devon please slow down, that she wasn't making any sense, but her daughter had already moved on.

'Her mother was this famous gardener. She had, like, her own TV show in Vancouver. Anyway, she was there tonight. At the party at Ashleigh's.

She looked so pretty,' Devon said, suddenly bursting into tears. 'Her nose didn't look crooked at all. I felt bad about all the times we teased her. I was really mean to her, Mom.'

'Sweetheart, please. Why don't we sit down?'

'I don't want to sit down. I want to go dancing.' Devon pushed herself onto her toes and did a clumsy pirouette. 'But everybody else just wants to sit around and get high,' she said.

'Are you high, Devon? Have you been doing drugs?'

'I'm so thirsty,' Devon said, ignoring the question.

'I'll get you a glass of water.'

'There's water on the floor,' Devon said. She sank to her knees and began moving the water and salt around the ceramic tile floor with the palms of her hands, as if she were a child finger-painting.

'Devon, please, sweetheart, be careful of the glass. No, don't put that in your mouth. Let me help you up.'

'I don't want to get up.'

'You need to let me help you.' Marcy had succeeded in dragging her daughter to her feet and sitting her down in one of the four kitchen chairs clustered around the oval-shaped pine table. 'I'll get you some water. Please, baby. Tell me what you've taken.'

'I'm just so thirsty,' Devon said again. 'Why am I so thirsty?'

Marcy's hands had been shaking as she went to the sink and poured a glass of water for Devon, letting the sound of the water gushing from the tap temporarily drown out Devon's insane chatter.

'Devon,' she said, turning off the tap and swivelling towards her. Except that Devon had been no longer sitting on the chair. She was curled up on the floor, her face half-submerged in a mound of soggy salt. 'Devon?' Marcy had said again, her voice a whisper.

She had collapsed to her knees beside her daughter. Devon had fallen asleep. Sound asleep, Marcy had realised when she'd tried to rouse her.

She had thought of waking Peter but decided against it. It took her almost fifteen minutes to get Devon out of the kitchen, down the hall, and into her bedroom; another twenty to get her undressed, cleaned up, and into bed; and then another fifteen to clean up the mess in the kitchen. By the time Marcy had returned to her room, she had been bathed in sweat. She had taken a shower and climbed back into bed.

'Can't you stay still?' Peter had muttered, flipping over onto his side.

'WHAT ARE YOU DOING?' Vic asked now, his eyes finding hers in the dark hotel room. 'Are you crying?'

Marcy swiped at the tears in her eyes. 'No. Well, maybe a little.'

'You were thinking about Devon,' he said.

'Yes.'

'Have you decided what you're going to do?'

'No.'

'Would you like me to go with you?' he asked with a smile. 'I'd be happy to go back with you to Cork.'

It's certainly tempting, Marcy thought. *It would be nice to have company.* 'No,' she said after a moment. It would only complicate things. 'I think this is something I need to do alone.'

He nodded. 'Promise you'll keep me posted. And if at any point you need some help, or if you just want someone to hold your hand or scratch your back . . .'

She smiled as his fingers moved up her arm to the base of her neck, disappearing into her mop of wayward curls. 'I must look awful. My hair—'

'Is fabulous. Is it possible that you don't know how beautiful you are?' he asked.

'My mother always said I had too much hair,' Marcy told him.

'My mother said I'd be six feet tall if only I'd stand up straight.'

'There's nothing wrong with your posture.'

'There's nothing wrong with your hair.'

Marcy laughed. 'Mothers,' she said.

'You said yours died when she was forty-six? That must have been very hard for you.'

'Actually,' Marcy admitted, 'in some ways it was a relief.'

'Had she been sick for long?'

'As long as I can remember.'

Vic tilted his head to one side, his eyes asking her to continue.

'She threw herself off the roof of a ten-storey building when I was fifteen years old,' Marcy said.

'My God, I'm so sorry.'

'Can you do me a favour?' Marcy asked, drawing the covers up to her chin. 'Can you just hold me?'

She felt his arms immediately surround her, his breath warm on the back of her neck as she pressed into the curve of his stomach. They lay that way until eventually his breathing drifted into the slower rhythms of sleep. She lay in the dark, absorbing the reassurance of his gentle snores. Then she extricated herself from his arms, slipped out of bed, got dressed and tiptoed from the room.

FIRST THING the next morning, Marcy checked out of her hotel.

'I notice you have a number of messages you haven't retrieved,' the clerk told her as she was settling her account.

'You can erase them, thanks. And can you get me a taxi?' Some time after she had returned to her room, Marcy had decided against renting a car.

'You'll be able to find one right outside the main entrance. Do you need help with your suitcase?'

'I can manage. Thank you.'

A line of taxis waited outside the front door. Marcy approached several before she found one willing to drive all the way to Cork.

Luckily the driver was possibly the only man in Ireland who showed absolutely no interest in carrying on a conversation. Marcy leaned back in her seat and closed her eyes.

'Where do you want me to drop you?' the driver asked in what seemed like the next moment.

'What?' Marcy snapped to attention, checking her watch to discover hours had passed and she must have fallen asleep. She looked out of the raindrop-splattered window to find the city of Cork.

'What hotel are you stayin' in?' the cabbie asked.

It suddenly occurred to Marcy that she had forgotten to make hotel reservations. 'I don't have a room. Do you happen to know somewhere nice you could recommend?'

'Well, there's Tynan's on Western,' the driver said. 'It's a bed and breakfast, and I hear it's OK, although pretty basic.'

'Basic is good.'

It was also fully booked. As were the next few B&Bs on Western Road. Finally, Marcy dragged her suitcase up the front steps of the Doyle Cork Inn, one of the few B&Bs she had yet to try.

'Can I give you a hand with that?' a young man asked, appearing at her side to grab her suitcase. He was in his late teens. A stray lock of reddish-blond hair curled onto his forehead, and his mouth was filled with large, cramped teeth.

A pair of braces would have fixed that, she heard Peter say.

'Thank you, yes.' Marcy followed the young man inside to the tiny lobby. 'Do you have a room?'

'I believe we do, yes.'

'Thank God. I was beginning to give up hope.'

'Oh, you must never do that.'

Marcy smiled. 'I won't. Thank you. That's good advice.'

'The name's Colin Doyle. My mum'll be right with you. Are you over from America?'

'Canada,' Marcy told him, as she pulled a picture of Devon out of her handbag and showed it to Colin. 'Do you know this girl?' she asked.

He studied it for several seconds. 'Can't say that I do,' he said.

'You're sure? It's possible she's a student at the university. I understand it's very close to here.'

'Just up the road a bit,' he concurred. Then, 'No. Don't know her.' He handed back the photograph. 'She looks very sad, doesn't she?'

'Sorry to have kept you,' a high-pitched voice trilled as a heavyset woman with grey-flecked reddish-blonde hair entered the small foyer. Her eyes were the same shade of hazel as her son's. 'Name's Sadie Doyle, owner of this proud establishment.' Large hands fluttered in front of her, sweeping together the foyer, the living room to her left, and the narrow staircase to her right. 'Mind if I have a look at that?' she asked, indicating the picture of Devon. 'Pretty girl. Your daughter?'

'Yes. Do you know her, by any chance?'

'I'm afraid I don't. She's here in Cork, is she?'

'Yes, she is. I'm trying to find her. We've kind of lost touch.'

Sadie Doyle smiled wistfully. 'Wish I could be of help.' She walked behind the counter in the corner and opened the guest register. 'It's one hundred and five euros a night for a single room.'

'That's fine.'

'Just how long will you be staying with us, Mrs—'

'Taggart. Marcy Taggart. I'll be staying a few days.'

'If you could just fill this out.' Sadie pushed a sheet of paper across the reception desk. 'And I'll need your passport, of course. What credit card will you be using?'

Marcy handed over her American Express card.

'You'll be in room seven.' Sadie Doyle handed Marcy a large brass key.

'Good luck with finding your daughter.'

'Thank you,' Marcy said, as she followed Colin up the stairs.

After he had gone, she looked around. The room was small and crowded with inexpensive furniture: a double bed with an old brass headboard, a shabby-looking armoire and dresser. The wallpaper was purple, and the carpet was a tired-looking mix of mauve and brown. *No more tired-looking than I am*, Marcy thought despondently, plopping down on the bed and staring at her reflection in the mirror on the opposite wall.

You're beautiful, she heard Vic whisper in her ear.

Marcy unpacked her suitcase, hanging as many clothes as she could in the tiny armoire and stuffing the rest into the chest of drawers. Then she changed into jeans and a fresh blouse, grabbed her handbag, took a deep breath and left the room.

SHE WENT DIRECTLY back to the pub where she had first spotted Devon.

Marcy approached the front door cautiously. A man was exiting the pub as she was going in, and he held the door open for her, the welcoming chatter from inside the room instantly enveloping her.

'Well, well!' a voice exclaimed above the din. 'Welcome back to Grogan's House. Come to finish your tea, have you?'

Marcy walked directly to the bar. 'You remember me?' she asked the handsome man behind it.

'I never forget a pretty face.'

Marcy felt strangely flattered. 'I was hoping you'd be here.'

The young man's green eyes sparkled as his full lips parted in an easy grin. 'Is there something I can do for you, then?'

'There was a girl,' Marcy said, reaching inside her handbag for Devon's photograph. 'Yesterday. I think it was this girl.' She pushed the picture of Devon across the bar. 'Do you know her?'

He looked at the photograph, slowly shaking his head.

'She walked by outside and waved to you,' Marcy pressed.

He smiled. 'I get lots of girls waving at me, I'm afraid.'

'Our Liam's quite the ladies' man,' a waitress said as she was walking past with a tray of empty beer mugs. 'Shall I have a look?'

'Please.' Marcy handed Devon's photo to the young woman.

'Hmm,' the waitress said encouragingly. 'She looks a bit like Audrey, don't she?' she said to the bartender.

'Audrey?' Marcy and Liam asked together.

'You know, the girl we see hanging around with that other one—the quiet one who works for the O'Connors. Shannon, I think.'

'Oh, yeah. Now I know who you mean.' Liam took another look at the photograph. 'Nah, no way that's Audrey.'

'Well, she's younger than Audrey and not so tough lookin' . . .'

'This picture was taken a few years ago,' Marcy explained.

'Well, there you go,' the waitress said.

'So you think this could be Audrey?' Marcy asked, trying to fit her tongue around the new name. Devon had always loved Audrey Hepburn, she reminded herself.

'Well, I can't be sure, of course. But it could be.'

Marcy stuffed the picture back inside her handbag, her heart threatening to leap from her chest. 'Do you know where I can find her?'

'Sorry. I've no idea,' Liam said, turning his attention to a man at the far end of the bar.

'You might try the O'Connors,' the waitress said. 'Shannon's their nanny. She could probably tell you where to find Audrey.'

'Hey, Kelly,' a customer called from his table against the wall. 'How are you coming with those refills?'

'Be right there.'

'Where do I find the O'Connors?' Marcy called after her.

'They live over on Adelaide Road. Don't know the exact address. But it's the biggest house on the street. You can't miss it.'

Marcy walked quickly to the door. 'Thank you,' she called back as she stepped outside, but both Kelly and Liam were busy with customers and neither was listening.

ADELAIDE ROAD was a wide, winding street built up the side of a steep hill. Kelly had said to look for the biggest house on the street but, so far, all the homes had looked roughly the same size.

Then she saw it. Bigger than all the other houses, it was further distinguished by its yellow-brick exterior and winding flower-lined path. An enormous driveway led to a three-car garage.

So what now? she wondered, continuing up the street, then turning around and walking back. Should she simply ring the doorbell and ask to speak to Shannon? 'The quiet one' was how Kelly had described her.

Marcy pictured a skinny girl with fair skin and strawberry-blonde hair.

Coming to a decision, Marcy walked briskly up the path and rang the bell, listening for the sound of footsteps approaching. When none was forthcoming, she rang the bell again. Silence. No one was home. Marcy looked around for a place to sit down, but there was nothing.

She began walking back down the hill, her arms swinging purposefully at her sides. She checked her watch. Four o'clock. Maybe she should grab a bite to eat, come back later. Except it was too late for lunch and too early for dinner, and she had no appetite.

'You have to eat something,' Judith had told her in the aftermath of Devon's accident. And then again after Peter had walked out. 'You have to keep up your strength,' she had insisted.

Marcy closed her eyes, trying to block out the myriad unpleasant memories that were flooding her brain. 'Enough,' she said out loud, her voice disappearing under the wheels of a passing car. *A Rolls or a Bentley*, she thought, opening her eyes to see the big black sedan disappear around the bend, knowing instinctively it belonged to the O'Connors. She raced back up the road and watched the car pull to a stop in the driveway of the yellow-brick house.

From a distance of maybe fifty yards, she saw a woman exit the passenger side of the car with shopping bags in each hand. As she reached the front door, the woman called to the driver as he was about to proceed into the garage: 'Don't forget the groceries in the boot.'

The woman was young, early thirties, and pretty, with shoulder-length auburn hair. Marcy guessed this must be Mrs O'Connor.

Now's your chance, she thought as the woman fished inside her designer bag for her keys. Marcy commanded herself to move, forcing one foot in front of the other, stopping abruptly when the man emerged from the garage, his arms loaded with groceries. He was older than the woman by a decade, and he managed to look distinguished even as he struggled to keep groceries from spilling.

'Can you manage?' the woman asked from the doorway.

'Out of my way, woman,' her husband responded, with a laugh. Seconds later, still laughing, they disappeared inside the house.

'Mr and Mrs O'Connor, I presume,' Marcy said, marvelling at their easy camaraderie and trying to remember the last time she and Peter had laughed that way together. *Maybe in the beginning*, she thought. *Before Devon.*

Marcy decided to give the O'Connors a few minutes to put their groceries away before ambushing them. 'You can do this,' she told herself, removing Devon's picture from her handbag and wondering what she was so afraid of. That the O'Connors wouldn't recognise the girl in the photograph? Or that they would?

Moments later, a baby's loud wail filled the air as a young woman pushing a pram rounded the curve at the top of the street.

Marcy found herself holding her breath as the girl came into sharper focus. *She's exactly as I imagined her*, Marcy thought. She stared at the skinny girl, taking in her fair complexion and long strawberry-blonde hair. She was dressed in blue jeans and a light jacket.

The girl turned in to the O'Connors' driveway. If she had noticed Marcy standing by the side of the road, she gave no sign.

'Now,' Marcy said, tripping over her own feet as she vaulted forwards. 'Excuse me, but could I talk to you for a minute?' She rehearsed it, her voice a whisper. 'Excuse me,' she said again, louder this time.

But the front door was opening, Mr O'Connor filling its frame. 'Well, hello there, my little angel,' he said, lifting the crying baby into his arms. 'Daddy's missed his little princess. Yes, he has.' He turned to Shannon. 'How was she this afternoon? Still colicky, I see.'

Marcy couldn't hear Shannon's response. Mr O'Connor carried the crying baby inside, shutting the door after him as Shannon wheeled the pram around to the side of the house.

You ring the bell, you ask to speak to Shannon, you show her Devon's picture, Marcy instructed herself silently. Shannon would either confirm the picture was her friend Audrey or she wouldn't.

Or what if she recognised the picture but refused to divulge Audrey's whereabouts? Suppose Devon had already told her all about her mother: how she had failed her in every way possible and how she had actually faked her own death in order to get as far away from her as she could? What then? Would Devon take off without a word to anyone, fly off to Spain or South America? Somewhere her mother would never find her?

Marcy felt her shoulders slump. Her daughter would do exactly that, she understood. Which was why she had been hesitating, why she couldn't confront Shannon and risk losing her daughter all over again. She had to be patient. She had to wait. Wait and watch.

You're sure you want to do this? Judith had asked when Marcy had first informed her she was expecting. *You'll never have another peaceful moment, you know. You'll always be waiting, watching . . .*

Rain was starting to fall. She had to find a taxi, get back to the city before she was soaked to the skin. She would return here tomorrow. And the next day. Eventually, Marcy told herself as she hurried down the hill, Shannon would lead her to Devon.

'WELL, WELL. Can't keep away, can you?' Liam said as Marcy walked through the door of Grogan's House. 'Sit down, luv. I'll get you some tea.' He waved towards an empty table in the corner.

Barely five o'clock, and already the place was almost full, Marcy observed. Didn't anyone ever go home?

'So did you find Audrey?' Kelly asked, appearing at her side.

'No, but I found Shannon.'

'Was she able to help you?'

'I didn't speak to her.'

'Why not?'

'It's complicated,' Marcy said, after a pause.

'What's complicated?' Liam asked, lowering a steaming pot of tea to the table along with two mugs, then plopping into the chair across from her. 'You don't mind if I join you, do you? I'm on my break, and you look in need of company. You're soaking wet.'

Marcy began patting at her hair. 'I couldn't find a taxi.'

'Leave your hair alone,' he said. 'It's quite sexy like that.'

Marcy laughed, flattered in spite of herself.

'That's better. So what's complicated?'

'What isn't?'

Liam's turn to laugh. 'Hunger isn't complicated,' he said. 'I bet you could use something to eat.'

'Anything you recommend?'

'I'd try the special. Kelly, can you get the lady a special? My treat,' he added. 'My way of apologising for my rudeness earlier.'

'You weren't rude.'

'I was a bit abrupt. You know, about Audrey.'

'Are you saying you *did* recognise her picture?'

He poured them each a mugful of tea. 'Well, I might have been a little hasty in my assessment. I suppose it could be Audrey.'

Marcy tried to swallow her growing excitement with another sip of tea. 'Do you know her last name?'

Liam shook his head. 'I've only talked to her a couple of times. She moved here about a year ago. From some small town west of London, I think she said.'

'She has an English accent?' Devon had always had a good ear for accents, Marcy recalled, remembering her performances in various high-school plays.

'I suppose. Definitely not Irish, but I wasn't paying that strict attention. She's not really my type. I like 'em a little older myself.' A playful smile teased his lips.

Is he flirting with me? Marcy wondered, dismissing the thought as she sank back in her chair. 'Can you do me a favour? Can you call me the next time you see her?'

'Can you at least tell me your name?'

'Marcy,' she said. 'Marcy Taggart. I believe the girl you know as Audrey is really my daughter, Devon.'

Liam's eyes revealed a long list of questions, none of which he voiced. Instead, he removed a pen from his shirt pocket and slid it across the table. 'Write your cell phone number on that napkin.'

Marcy started to print her number along the surface of the small paper napkin, then stopped. 'Oh, I can't. I threw it in the river.'

'Why on earth would you do that?'

'It's . . .'

'Complicated,' Liam said, finishing for her. 'Figured as much. So just how do you propose I get in touch with you?'

'I'm staying at the Doyle Cork Inn over on Western Road.'

Liam nodded, retrieving his pen and scribbling his own number across the top of the napkin. 'Suppose you check in with me periodically. That might be easier.'

'That's really very kind of you.'

'Sometimes we have to rely on the kindness of strangers,' he said with a twinkle in his deep green eyes.

Marcy recognised the familiar quote from Tennessee Williams's *A Streetcar Named Desire*. She lifted her mug into the air, clicked it against his. 'To the kindness of strangers.'

Liam's smile was unexpectedly shy. 'To finding your daughter.'

FOUR

It always started the same way.

With soft words and a seemingly simple request.

'Darling, come and sit beside me for a minute,' her mother might say, welcoming Marcy to her bed, although it was almost noon. 'I know you're just a little girl, but you're so wise and thoughtful. Do you think you could help me out with a little problem I'm having?' Or, 'Sweetheart, you know how much I value your opinion. Come sit on the bed and tell me which dress you think I should wear tonight—the red one or the blue?'

Marcy turned over in her bed in her room at the Doyle Cork Inn, wrapping the lumpy pillow around her ears to keep from hearing the dialogue that inevitably followed. But it was too late. Her mother was already beside her, whispering in her ear, asking for opinions she quickly discounted and advice she never took.

'You should wear the red one,' Marcy might have answered.

'You really think the red is better, darling? Why is that? Does the blue dress wash me out? Does it make me look fat?'

'You could never look fat.'

The sudden threat of tears. 'Do you think I've put on weight? My clothes have been feeling a little tight lately, although you know, I think it's the manufacturers' fault with their inconsistent labelling. I mean, you buy the same size you always buy, and suddenly it doesn't fit, and I'm wondering if it's some sort of conspiracy to confuse women. The manufacturers are playing games with our heads, making us feel fat when we're the same size we've always been. We're not fat at all. Do you think I look fat?'

'I think you look beaut—'

'I worry about Judith. She looks as if she's put on a few pounds. She has great legs, but she has a tendency to put on weight.'

'No, she—'

'I'm sure she's put on a few pounds. Designers don't make clothes for fat people, I told her. And it's not easy, because the manufacturers are conspiring to confuse women, and it's not fair.' The threat of tears would become a reality, her mother pacing back and forth in front of Marcy.

'Mom, what is it? What's wrong? Why are you crying?'

'The world is such a cruel place. Sometimes I feel such despair.'

'I'm going to get Daddy. You're scaring me.'

'Oh, sweetheart, there's nothing to be scared about. Everything's going to be just fine. If only we could do something about your hair. So much hair for such a tiny face.'

Marcy pushed the hair away from her forehead, sitting up in her bed at the Doyle Cork Inn, staring at the clock radio on the tiny bedside table next to her. Almost 4 a.m. She flopped back down, hearing echoes of her mother's closet door as it opened and closed.

'I've made a mess of things,' her mother was saying, sobbing uncontrollably now. 'What have I accomplished? I have nothing.'

'You have Daddy. You have me and Judith.'

Her mother stared at her. 'I had to have a Caesarian section with Judith,' she said. 'It was horrible. They gave me this big needle—they insert it right into your spine—and it's supposed to freeze you from the waist down, except they gave me too much and it froze me right up to my chest, and it felt as if I couldn't breathe. I thought I was dying. And I was so scared.'

Then she had dropped to the floor, curled into a ball, and fallen asleep. She slept for the rest of the day. The next morning she was gone.

'Where's Mom?' Marcy remembered asking when she came downstairs for breakfast.

Judith had shrugged, cutting her omelette into tiny pieces. 'Away.'

'Where'd she go?'

'Where she usually goes,' Judith replied.

Which meant nobody knew. Periodically, their mother simply disappeared. Usually for several weeks. Nobody ever knew where she went. Their father had stopped trying to find her after the first few times, stopped reporting her disappearances to the police, stopped hiring detectives to find her, stopped searching through homeless shelters and checking the dirty and raggedly dressed bodies asleep on downtown sewer grates.

Her father had tried to explain, using the accepted parlance of the day. 'Your mother is manic-depressive. She just gets very excited, and then she gets very depressed. But as long as she takes her medication, she'll be able to function just fine.'

Except she hated her medication. It made her feel as if she were, in her words, 'trying to do the butterfly stroke in a vat of molasses.' And so she would stop taking it. And then the cycle would begin again: the wild mood swings, the crying jags, the disappearing act.

It didn't take Marcy long to learn the signs. She got very good at predicting when her mother was about to take off. 'It's happening again,' she would say to Judith. Invariably she was right.

Except once.

'OK, enough of that,' Marcy said, pushing herself out of bed. She should have brought a book with her, she thought. Something to keep her mind occupied. She would buy one as soon as the shops opened. Along with a new cell phone, she decided, walking to the window and staring through the dusty lace curtains. She was still standing there when the night sky began to brighten and the bells of St Anne's Shandon Church announced the start of a new day.

As soon as the shops had opened, Marcy purchased a new cell phone and called Liam.

'Did I wake you?' she asked, hearing the sleep still clinging to his voice. What was the matter with her? Why had she called him, for God's sake? He didn't really care about her or her daughter. He just felt sorry for her. 'I'm so sorry to bother you,' she said.

'Has something happened? Have you found Audrey?'

'No. I . . . I . . . bought a cell phone,' she blurted out, quickly rattling off her number. 'I'm so sorry for disturbing you. I just thought this way you could call me—'

'The instant I see her,' Liam said, finishing the sentence for her. 'Promise,' he added. 'So what are the plans for the day?'

Marcy told him she intended to check out the university.

'Good luck,' he said, hanging up before she could apologise again.

I'll need it, Marcy thought, setting out for the university campus.

According to the brochure the visitors centre provided, University College Cork was established in 1845 and was one of Ireland's leading research institutes. More than seventeen thousand students attended the four main colleges: one college for arts, one for business and law, one for medicine, and one for engineering.

Knowing it was highly unlikely that Devon would have enrolled in anything to do with medicine, business, engineering or law, Marcy decided to concentrate on the arts. Her daughter had always been drawn to drama.

Marcy marched along the brick-and-concrete pedestrian road that ran through the campus. 'Excuse me,' she said, showing her photograph to a group of young women who were walking by. 'Do any of you happen to recognise this girl?'

The three girls took turns looking at the picture. 'No,' the first one said, her two friends nodding in quick agreement.

'Thank you. Excuse me.' Marcy continued in the next breath, quickly approaching a young man balancing an armload of books. 'Have you seen this girl? Her name is Devon . . .'

'No, sorry.'

It was the same with everyone she asked.

By four o'clock, Marcy had tried virtually every department on campus. She had popped her head into every office and classroom, visited every gallery, walked down every hall, investigated every nook and cranny of every building.

Marcy was just exiting the campus when she saw her.

The girl was standing on the footbridge separating Bachelor's Quay from North Mall, staring down at the water below, seemingly lost in thought. A breeze was blowing her long hair into her face.

'Devon!' Marcy cried out. She began running towards the bridge, each step bringing her closer to the daughter she feared she had lost for ever. *Please let her be happy to see me*, she prayed as she ran. Which was when she heard shouting and turned to see the bicycle coming out of nowhere, a look of horror on the cyclist's face as he tried to avoid her.

In the next second, Marcy was sprawled across the pavement like a rag doll, a small crowd gathering around her. 'Are you all right?' someone was asking. 'Is anything broken? Can you stand up?'

Marcy felt hands underneath her arms returning her to an upright position. 'I'm fine,' she said.

'You're sure? Do you need to go to hospital?' a young man asked, pushing his way to the front of the crowd.

'I don't need a hospital.' Marcy was recovering her equilibrium and deduced from the boy's ashen complexion that he was the one who'd run her down. She looked towards the footbridge. 'Please, I have to go.'

'No,' the young man insisted. 'You shouldn't move for a few minutes. You could have a concussion.'

'I didn't hit my head. Please, if you could all get out of my way.'

People immediately began dispersing until only Marcy and the young man remained. 'I'm so sorry,' he said. He looked to be in his twenties, curly brown hair framing a face that was more rugged than handsome.

'It's OK,' Marcy said, her voice flat. 'It was an accident.'

'I was just goin' along, mindin' me own business, not payin' enough attention, I guess, and suddenly there you were,' the boy elaborated in a strong Irish brogue. 'I tried turnin' the wheel—'

'It wasn't your fault,' Marcy assured him, her brain absorbing what her eyes already knew: that Devon was no longer standing on the bridge. Her daughter was gone.

THEY GREW UP always checking each other, looking for signs: a laugh that was too loud or lingered too long, a sigh that split the air with melancholy, a mood that shifted too abruptly, cascading from high to low and then back again with unnerving speed, like the roller-coaster rides they used to enjoy when they were kids.

'What's the matter?' Marcy would ask whenever she caught Judith looking even vaguely out of sorts.

'What are you still chuckling about?' Judith would demand of her sister after she had told a moderately funny joke that had Marcy still giggling moments later. 'It wasn't that funny.'

'MARCY! FOR GOD'S SAKE, where are you?' Judith was shouting.

Marcy held her new cell phone away from her ear, already regretting her decision to phone her sister. 'I'm fine.'

'I didn't ask *how* you were,' Judith shot back. 'I already know you're nuttier than a jar of cashews. I asked *where* are you?'

Marcy swallowed the giggles tickling her throat; Judith had always had a way with words. 'I've always admired your ability to express yourself,' she now said.

'What? Where are you?' Judith repeated.

Marcy looked around her tiny bathroom in the Doyle Cork Inn. She was sitting, naked, on the edge of the bath, steam rising from the hot water that filled it. 'What difference does it make?'

'What do you mean, what difference does it make? How am I supposed to come and get you if I don't know where you are?'

'I don't want you to come and get me.'

'Marcy, you're in the middle of some kind of breakdown. Which is perfectly understandable under the circumstances,' she elaborated unnecessarily. 'Your daughter died; your husband left you for another woman. Not to mention our family history . . .'

'I'm not crazy, Judith.'

'You went on a second honeymoon alone. Is that normal?'

'It might be a little unusual, but—'

'Just like it's a "little unusual" to see your dead child wandering the streets of Dublin?'

Cork, Marcy almost corrected her. 'I didn't see her,' she said instead. 'I was wrong. I realise now that the girl I thought was Devon was just a girl who maybe looked a bit like her but wasn't her.'

'You didn't see her?'

'It wasn't Devon. Devon is dead,' Marcy said.

Judith pressed her. 'You're not just saying that because you think it's what I want to hear?'

That was exactly why she was saying it, Marcy acknowledged silently. 'Devon is dead,' she repeated.

She felt her sister nodding her head. 'OK,' Judith said. 'So where are you, and when are you coming home?'

Marcy lied, the same lie she had told Vic Sorvino. 'I'm in Paris.'

'I don't believe you.'

Marcy sighed. 'I'll be home by the end of next week.'

'Wait. If you're really in Paris, why don't I book the next flight and meet you there? We can go shopping and see the sights.'

'Let me think about it. I'll call you,' Marcy said, disconnecting the phone. She hated lying to her sister. But what other choice did she have?

The truth was that she was more convinced than ever that Devon was alive. Tomorrow she would go back to the O'Connor house, wait for their nanny to emerge, spend the day following her around. She was confident Shannon would lead her to Devon eventually.

Marcy lowered herself gingerly into the bath, gasping as the hot water surrounded her. She heard her sister admonish her: *It's not good to take such a hot bath.*

'Go away, Judith,' Marcy told her impatiently, sinking down lower in the water. She closed her eyes as it reached her forehead, feeling her hair floating around her head like seaweed, only then coming up for air.

In the aftermath of the discovery of Devon's overturned canoe, Marcy had tried to imagine what it felt like to drown. Every day for weeks, she had climbed into the bath and let the water surround her. Then she would slip beneath the surface and open her mouth.

Had Devon felt panic? She had often wondered. Had she struggled to survive even as the icy water filled her lungs? Had she cried out for her mother one last time before she died?

Except she hadn't died, Marcy knew now.

'My baby's alive,' she whispered. 'She isn't dead. She isn't dead,' she repeated, the sound of her words vibrating gently.

Except it wasn't her words that were ringing, she realised. It was her cell phone. The only person it could be was Liam.

Marcy vaulted from the bath and opened her phone. 'Hello?'

'Hello?' Liam said in reply. 'Marcy, is that you?'

'Liam? Have you seen Devon?'

'No,' he said. 'Have you?'

Marcy's response was to burst into tears.

'Marcy, what's the matter?'

'Nothing. It's OK. I just thought . . .'

'You thought that my calling meant I'd seen her,' he said. 'I'm so sorry. Of course you'd think that.'

'Don't apologise. I shouldn't jump to conclusions.' Marcy told him about having seen Devon earlier.

'Wait a minute,' he said, when she was through telling her story. 'You're saying you got hit by a bicycle? Are you hurt?'

'I'm fine. A few bruises is all.'

'Except that by the time you got back on your feet . . .'

'She was gone,' Marcy said.

'Well, I wish I was calling with some news.'

'Why *are* you calling?'

She felt him smile. 'There was someone here just now askin' about you. The man you were with the other day.'

'Do you mean Vic? Vic Sorvino?' Marcy asked incredulously.

'Yep, that's him. I'm starin' at his business card right now.'

What was Vic doing there? 'Did he say what he wanted?'

'Just that he was lookin' for you. I wasn't sure what you'd want me to tell him, so I said I hadn't seen you.' Marcy couldn't tell if she was disappointed or relieved. What was Vic doing back in Cork? 'Did I do the right thing?' Liam was asking.

'You did. Thank you.'

'So what do you want me to tell him,' Liam asked, 'assuming he checks in with me again?'

'Tell him you haven't seen me.'

'You're sure?'

Marcy felt Vic's lips brushing gently against hers, felt his fingers tracing delicate lines along her flesh, heard his soft words, *You're beautiful,* as they floated tenderly across her skin. She didn't deserve to feel so good. Not yet. Not until she had found Devon. Not until she had had a chance to make things right. 'I'm sure.'

'Good. There was somethin' about the man that made me a bit uncomfortable,' Liam said.

'Uncomfortable?'

'Something just seemed a little off. You know what I mean?'

Marcy shook her head. In truth, she had no idea what Liam was talking about. Vic hadn't struck her as 'off' in any way. But she had never been a very good judge of character when it came to men.

'Marcy?' Liam asked. 'Are you still there?'

'Oh, yes. Sorry.'

'You hungry?' Liam was asking. Marcy immediately felt her stomach cramp emptily.

'I am a bit, yes.'

'Pick you up in half an hour,' he said.

'WELL, LET'S SEE. Husband number one was a musician,' Marcy was saying, a little voice in the back of her head telling her she shouldn't be discussing her sister in this way.

'You don't have to tell me,' Liam said, as if sensing her reservations. 'It's none of my business, really. I was just trying to take your mind off things.'

By 'things', he meant the fact that despite taking her to one of the most popular gathering spots for young people in all of Cork, they'd yet to spot Devon and hadn't found a single person who recognised her picture.

'Oh, well. It's early,' he had said as they settled into a booth in the crowded downscale restaurant on Grattan Street. 'Maybe she'll turn up in a bit,' he had said as they'd placed their dinner orders with the pink-haired waiter. 'We'll find her. You'll see.'

Marcy had smiled. It felt good to be a 'we'. *A unit*, she had thought, feeling Peter's instant disapproval.

'You grimaced,' Liam had said immediately. 'Are you sorry you let me ambush you into coming out tonight?'

'No. I'm glad I came. Why *did* you ask me out?' she had asked in the next breath. 'I'm sure there are dozens of young women out there you could have called.'

'Maybe I don't find young women all that interesting.'

Marcy had blushed and turned away.

Which was when he had asked about her family.

'I have an older sister,' she had told him, relieved to shift the focus off herself. 'Judith. She's been married five times.'

He had laughed. 'Obviously an optimist.'

'That's a nice way of putting it.'

'And how would you put it?'

'I think she's just afraid of being alone.'

'So . . . about those five husbands,' Liam had said, sipping his coffee.

Marcy began. 'Well, husband number one was a drummer.'

'Oh, no. The worst.'

'He really *was* awful. But she was all of nineteen. To absolutely no one's surprise, the marriage lasted less than a year.'

'Ah-ha, I see. And husband number two?'

'A photographer. It lasted two weeks. Turned out he was gay.'

Liam nodded. 'Dare I ask about husband number three?'

'An advertising executive. It lasted four years.'

'Well, now, that's an improvement. Number four?'

'A stockbroker she met at the gym. Nice enough guy until he started taking steroids. It lasted eight years,' said Marcy.

'Perfectly respectable. Which brings us to number five.'

'A lawyer. They've been married almost fifteen years now.'

'So he's a keeper, is he? Any children?'

'No. Judith never wanted kids.'

'Unlike you,' Liam stated more than asked.

'Unlike me.'

'So how many times have you been married?'

Marcy took a deep breath, exhaled slowly. 'Only once. My divorce should be final in another month or so.'

'Do you want to talk about it?'

'No,' she said. Then, 'Actually, yes, I think I do.'

Liam looked at her expectantly.

'My husband, Peter, left me for another woman, one of the golf pros at our country club. They haven't had a scandal like this in years. And all my friends . . .' She laughed, a sharp bark that scratched at the air. 'My friends. What friends? We didn't really have that many friends to begin with, and then after what happened with Devon . . .' She broke off. 'I can't really blame them. It's hard for people after a tragedy. They don't know what to say. They don't know what to do. So instead of saying or doing the wrong thing, they don't say or do anything. And then pretty soon they stop calling and coming around. And then it's just the two of you, and it makes it hard, it makes it really hard, for a marriage to survive.'

'Tell me about your daughter,' Liam said softly.

Marcy hesitated, trying to decide what facts to leave in and which ones to leave out.

'My daughter is bipolar,' Marcy began. 'She just has a chemical imbalance. It used to be known as manic depression.'

'One minute you're happy; the next you're bawlin' your eyes out.'

'I guess that about sums it up, yes.'

Liam apologised. 'Sorry. I didn't mean to sound glib.'

Marcy dismissed his apology with a brief shake of her head. 'It tends to run in families. My mother had it as well. She committed suicide when I was fifteen.'

If Liam was shocked, he didn't let on. 'Is that the reason your sister opted not to have any children of her own?'

'She tried to talk me out of having any. She said I'd always be waiting, watching for signs. She was right.'

'When did you first know?'

'Soon after Devon turned seventeen.' Marcy thought back to that awful night when she had found Devon in the kitchen, a broken flower vase at her feet, handfuls of salt at her mouth. 'I'd suspected it for a while,' she admitted. 'Her moods were getting blacker. Her behaviour was becoming increasingly erratic. But after this one incident, I couldn't deny it any longer.'

'What did you do?'

'Not enough. Oh, I took her to the doctor, got her started on medication and therapy, tried to comfort her as best I could . . .'

'Nothing helped?'

'She didn't like the way the drugs made her feel.' *Like trying to do the butterfly stroke in a vat of molasses.* 'She hated her therapist,' Marcy said. 'She hated me even more.'

'I think you're being very hard on yourself.'

'I lied to her, day in and day out. I told her if she'd just take her medication, then everything would work out; that she just had to be patient, give the haloperidol a chance . . .'

'Which is what anyone in your situation would have told her.'

'No, you don't understand.' Tears began falling down Marcy's cheeks. 'I had no patience for it—the crying jags and the craziness, the guys she'd bring home or the trouble she'd get into. You'd have thought that after everything I went through with my mother, it would have made me more understanding. But the opposite was true. I hated her for making me have to go through it all again.'

'What kind of trouble?' Liam asked.

'There were a few incidents.' Marcy sighed. 'One day she got into a fight with a neighbour who'd complained she was playing her radio too loud in the backyard. Then she stole an expensive bracelet from one of her friends' mother. Another time, she got involved with this guy I tried to tell her was trouble . . .'

'But she wouldn't listen.'

'And Peter was no help. He didn't know what to do or how to cope. Devon had always been a daddy's girl, and now here she was, his little angel, this child who'd worshipped him her entire life, and he couldn't help her. It made him feel so impotent. Which I guess explains Sarah. The other woman,' Marcy clarified. 'Anyway, he blamed me. He said he didn't, but I know he did. And he was right. It was my fault.'

'How do you figure that?'

Marcy shrugged. 'They were my genes.' *There's no mental illness on my side of the family,* she remembered Peter saying, although he had apologised later.

Marcy told Liam the story of Devon's 'accident'; about how she had faked her own death and disappeared.

'And you thought she was dead until—'

'I never believed she was dead. Not really,' Marcy insisted. 'And then I saw her walk by your pub.'

Liam shook his head. 'And I thought you were a cop.'

'What?'

'When you came back to Grogan's, when you showed me her picture and asked if I recognised her, I assumed you were some sort of copper. I just assumed Audrey's past had caught up with her.'

'Her past?'

'I've heard rumours that she'd been in some sort of trouble in London and that she'd come to Ireland to get away. So when you showed up askin' about her, I assumed you were with Interpol.'

'And now?'

'Now I know you're tellin' me the truth.' He smiled, reached across the table for her hand. 'Nobody makes up a story like that.'

Marcy smiled. 'My husband thinks I do. He thinks I'm crazy.'

'And I think *he's* crazy, letting a woman like you get away.'

Marcy slipped her hand away from his. 'You should be careful, saying things like that. It could be taken the wrong way.'

'And what way would that be?'

'Some women might think you were coming on to them.'

'And what do you think?'

'*Are* you coming on to me?' Marcy asked, amazed she was actually asking the question out loud.

'Don't know. Haven't quite made up my mind.'

Marcy smiled and shook her head. 'How old are you, Liam?'

'Thirty-four on my next birthday.'

'I'm fifty.'

'Fifty's not old. It's just a number.'

'You could have any woman you want. You just feel sorry for me.'

'Why would I feel sorry for you?' he asked. 'You're a beautiful woman with gorgeous curls who's found the daughter she thought was dead. I'd say that's cause for celebration, not pity.'

'I haven't found her yet.'

'But you will.'

'Maybe that's when I'll feel like celebrating.'

'Well, then,' Liam said, green eyes dancing. 'Looks like I'll just have to stick around and help you find her.'

FIVE

The next morning, Marcy returned to the big house on Adelaide Road. She was there by eight o'clock. Checking her watch now, it was already ten thirty, and nothing had happened since Mr O'Connor had left for work two hours earlier. At least she had managed to find a fairly secluded spot at the side of a neighbour's house across the street where she could stand and keep watch.

'Excuse me, do you mind telling me what you're doing here?' The voice was equal parts curiosity and indignation.

Marcy spun around to see a middle-aged woman in a flowered house-dress standing on the front steps of the house next door. Marcy took a few halting steps in the woman's direction.

'I'm lost,' Marcy answered. 'I went for a walk—'

'You American?' the woman interrupted. 'This isn't exactly a popular spot for tourists.'

Marcy improvised. 'Exactly. I try to avoid the usual tourist traps. I like to really explore the cities I visit, to see the way people actually live.'

'Well, it looked to me as though you were skulking. I should report you to the police.'

'Please, don't do that,' Marcy said quickly. 'I'm leaving right now.' She started to back away. In the next instant, she was running down the hill.

Marcy doubled over when she reached the bottom of the steep hill, her breath coming in sharp, painful stabs. She remembered seeing a park a few streets away. Surely there would be a bench on which she could sit down and regroup, rethink her strategy.

Minutes later, she was sitting on a wooden bench surrounded by pink hydrangea bushes. She took a deep breath and closed her eyes. Then she heard a baby's distant cries mingling with the drone of traffic.

Marcy opened her eyes to see a skinny young woman with fair skin and strawberry-blonde hair pushing a pram in her direction. *Shannon*, Marcy realised immediately.

'Do you mind if I have a seat?' the young woman asked shyly, waiting until Marcy nodded her consent before sitting down.

Marcy tried hard not to stare. Was this really Shannon?

Inside the carriage, the baby continued to cry. 'Sorry for the racket.' The young woman began pushing the pram back and forth, back and forth.

'I don't mind.' Marcy glanced inside the pram. 'A little girl?'

'A very colicky little girl, I'm afraid. I'm her nanny.'

Marcy tried to still her growing excitement. 'What's her name?'

'Caitlin. Caitlin Danielle O'Connor.'

'Pretty name. How old is she?'

'Almost five months.'

'She's beautiful.' Marcy extended her hand. 'I'm Marilyn,' she said, not confident she could trust Shannon with the truth.

'Shannon,' the girl said, shaking Marcy's hand.

'I could hold her, if you wouldn't mind,' Marcy said.

'I wouldn't mind at all,' Shannon said, as Marcy carefully lifted the screaming baby out of her pram. 'Poor Mrs O'Connor was up half the night walking her around. I tried feeding her, changing her, rocking her. Nothing did any good, so I thought I might as well take her out for a walk to give Mrs O'Connor a chance to sleep.'

'I'm sure she appreciates that.' Marcy held the baby tightly, rocking her gently. Within seconds, the crying shuddered to a halt.

'Would you look at that!' Shannon exclaimed. 'You've got the magic touch, Marilyn. How on earth did you manage that?'

'Practice,' Marcy answered, feeling a surge of pride.

'How many children do you have?' Shannon asked.

'Three,' she lied. 'Two boys and a girl.'

'I have five brothers and two sisters.'

'Are you from around here?'

'Oh, no. I'm from Glengarriff. On the coast. I couldn't wait to get out,' Shannon confessed. 'Soon as I turned eighteen, I was gone.'

'You don't look much older than that now.'

'I'll be nineteen next month,' Shannon said.

'So you've been here almost a year?'

'Well, I started out in Dublin, but I found it a little intimidating.' She blushed. 'Then I came here. It's much better.'

'Cork's a nice size,' Marcy agreed. 'Much easier to make friends here, I would think.'

Shannon nodded. 'I've always had a rather hard time making friends. I'm kind of shy.' She blushed again. 'Audrey says I'm lucky. She says boys only bring you grief.'

Marcy's breath caught in her throat at the mention of Audrey's name.

'Audrey?' she repeated. Had she heard Shannon correctly?

'My friend. Well, sort of. I've known her just a few months.'

'What does Audrey do?'

'As little as she can get away with.' Shannon's blush turned a bright tomato red, as if she'd just said the most terrible thing imaginable. 'Works as a temp. That sort of thing. My goodness, would you look at the time? I really should get going.'

Marcy returned Caitlin to her pram, laying the now-sleeping baby gently on her back. There were so many more questions she wanted to ask Shannon: where does Audrey live? Has she said anything about her past, about her mother? Where can I find her?

'It's been nice talking,' Shannon was saying. 'Hope to see you again.'

Marcy watched Shannon push the pram out of the small park and out of sight. 'Count on it,' she said.

FOR THE NEXT THREE DAYS, Marcy kept watch on Shannon's comings and goings. She would sit in the small park until she saw Shannon appear, pushing the baby in her pram, usually at around eleven in the morning and then again at two in the afternoon. In the mornings, she would follow Shannon up and down the winding roads, careful always to keep a safe distance between them. The afternoon walk was always the longer of the two outings. She never spoke to anyone.

'I'm getting very discouraged,' Marcy had confided in Liam on the phone the previous night.

'Don't be. She's bound to lead you to Audrey sooner or later.'

'I need it to be sooner.'

'What can I do to help? I could come over now . . .'

'No,' Marcy said. Much as she was attracted to him, she couldn't let herself be distracted. 'I'll call you tomorrow,' she said.

'I'll be here.'

Now Marcy watched as Shannon pushed Caitlin's pram up Mary Street towards the busy main thoroughfare that was St Patrick's Street. Although it was overcast, it was actually warm. She glanced towards the weather vane on the top of St Anne's.

It was at that moment she realised that Shannon had disappeared. Marcy looked around. Shannon was nowhere. Where could she have gone?

Marcy sighed and glanced down at her watch. She decided to call it a day. In the morning, she would return to Adelaide Road. If Shannon didn't lead her to Audrey by the end of the week, she would bite the bullet and confront her directly. Tell her that the girl she knew as Audrey was actually her daughter, Devon. Ask for her help in locating her.

Marcy was turning around when she saw a pram emerge from inside a shop near the corner. Seconds later, Shannon popped into view again, one hand pushing the pram, the other holding a bottle of cola. She manoeuvred the pram into the street, sipping her drink as she continued in the direction of Merchant's Quay.

Marcy was within half a block of Shannon when she saw a young man ride up on a bicycle. Shannon smiled as he approached. The boy stopped and dismounted, touching her arm. It wasn't until she was almost on top of them that Marcy realised she was staring at the same young man whose bicycle had sent her flying.

Was it a simple coincidence or something sinister? What was his connection to Shannon? And was he connected to Devon as well? *OK, calm down. Don't go jumping to conclusions.* Except how could she help it? She had been searching for Devon, had just spotted her on the footbridge over Bachelor's Quay, when his bicycle had appeared from out of nowhere, sending her sprawling. By the time she had extricated herself from his clumsy concern, Devon was gone. Maybe the boy had purposely knocked her down, alerting Devon to her presence and giving her time to get away? Or *was* she reading too much into things?

'Marilyn?' she heard someone calling. 'Marilyn? Yoo-hoo.'

Marcy looked up to see Shannon crossing the street, waving furiously and heading in her direction.

'It's me, Shannon,' she announced over Caitlin's loud cries.

Marcy fought hard to control her emotions. 'Shannon, of course. It's nice to see you again.'

'What an amazing coincidence! Do you fancy a spot of tea?'

'Tea sounds wonderful.'

'Why don't we head over to Grogan's?'

'Grogan's?' Marcy felt the name stick to the roof of her mouth.

'It's just up the way a bit, across St Patrick's Bridge.'

Marcy smiled, trying to collect all her conflicting thoughts. She gave up when that proved impossible. Instead, she smiled again and said, 'Lead the way.'

IF LIAM WAS SURPRISED to see her, he didn't show it. Nor did he let on that he recognised either of them.

'And how are you today, ladies?' he asked, approaching their table on the small outside patio. There were perhaps a dozen people crowded into the makeshift space.

Marcy said, 'We're good, thank you.'

Inside her pram, Caitlin started howling.

'Unfortunately, some things never change,' whispered Shannon, glancing apologetically towards the other patrons.

'And what do we have here?' Liam peered inside the pram. 'Think she'd fancy a bottle of Beamish?'

The blush that accompanied Shannon's laugh almost matched the surrounding pink rhododendrons. 'I know *I* would.'

'Two Beamishes?' He looked towards Marcy for confirmation.

'I think I'd better stick with tea,' she told him.

'Make that two,' Shannon concurred quickly. 'Mrs O'Connor would have a right fit if I came home with beer on my breath.'

An amused grin played at the corners of Liam's lips. 'So you work for the O'Connor clan over on Adelaide, do you?'

'Yes. Do you know them?' A look of apprehension suddenly clouded Shannon's small green eyes.

'I know *of* them. Who doesn't? One of the richest families in Cork,' he explained to Marcy. 'So two teas and some warm milk?'

'I have a bottle of apple juice with me, thanks,' Shannon said before Liam hurried off. 'Not that she'll take it. Unless you'd like to try?' she asked Marcy hopefully.

Marcy held out her arms, and Shannon quickly scooped up the crying baby and handed her to Marcy, along with her bottle.

'Hello, sweetheart,' Marcy cooed, kissing Caitlin's wet cheeks. 'Who's my sweet girl?' In the next instant, the baby was lying still against Marcy's breast, suckling contentedly on her bottle.

'Amazing,' Shannon marvelled. 'I don't know how you do it.'

Marcy shrugged, wondering when her power to comfort her own children had deserted her. Not that her son had ever required much comforting. A spectacularly easy baby who'd matured into an independent, easy-going young adult, Darren was his sister's opposite.

'You should come over to our house,' Shannon was saying, 'and give Mrs O'Connor a lesson. She tries really hard with Caitlin. I think she just thought it would be easier.'

Marcy nodded. *We all do*, she thought, watching Liam approach with their teas.

'I see somebody has the gift,' he remarked, putting their teapot in the middle of the table, followed by white cups and saucers.

'Isn't she amazing?' Shannon asked.

'And beautiful to boot,' Liam said with a smile. 'Can I get you anything else? Some biscuits perhaps?'

'I'd love something sweet,' Marcy said.

Liam winked. 'Sweets for the sweet.'

Shannon leaned forwards conspiratorially. 'I think he likes you,' she said, as he left the table.

Marcy felt her cheeks grow pink.

'You're blushing!' Shannon exclaimed with a laugh. 'Glad to see I'm not the only one. I blush all the time. I hate it.'

'It's very charming on you. I'm sure that the young man you were talking to earlier would agree with me.'

What the hell—it was as good an opening as she was likely to get.

A look of confusion caused Shannon's blush to spread towards her ears. 'Oh. Oh, yes, of course,' she said. 'You mean Jax.'

Marcy lifted her cup to her lips. 'So, tell me, is this Jax someone special?' she asked.

Shannon almost choked on her tea. 'Oh, no. I barely know him.'

'More like a friend of a friend, is he?' Marcy pressed.

Shannon looked a little confused, her green eyes narrowing, then suddenly widening again. 'Oh, look. Here come your biscuits.'

'Brought you a few extra,' Liam said, laying a plate carefully on the table. 'My treat.'

'I told you he likes you,' Shannon whispered as he made his retreat. 'Oh, shortbread. My favourite.'

'Have one.'

Shannon quickly grabbed one and bit off its end.

'So are Jax and Audrey friends?' Marcy asked, throwing caution to the wind.

'How did you know that? Are you psychic?'

Marcy shrugged, as if to say, *Lucky guess*. 'Isn't she the one who said boys only bring you grief?'

Shannon giggled. 'She *does* say that, yes.'

'Sounds like she's speaking from experience.'

'They used to be an item. They're over and done. She said I could have him if I wanted.'

'And do you?'

Shannon waved away the suggestion. 'I don't think Mrs O'Connor would approve of Jax. He's a bit on the wild side. Not exactly the kind of young man you bring home to mother.'

Marcy shuddered, recalling the man Devon had been involved with prior to her supposed drowning.

'Not that he fancies me or anything,' Shannon was saying.

'Why wouldn't he?'

A nervous giggle. 'Well, you don't see the boys exactly lining up, now, do you?'

'I think any boy would be lucky to have you,' Marcy offered, her frazzled brain working a mile a minute. If Audrey and Jax knew each other, she was thinking, if they'd once been lovers, surely that meant there was no way his running into her with his bicycle could have been coincidental. Which meant what?

'You really think so?' Shannon asked hopefully.

'I absolutely do.' Marcy smiled at the baby in her arms. 'She's falling asleep,' she commented, and in the same breath: 'So how long have you known Audrey?'

'I met her just after I started working for the O'Connors.'

'Is she from around here?'

'I think she's from London originally. Why are you so interested in her?'

Marcy shrugged. 'Just making small talk. These cookies are the best. Here, have another one.'

'No. I really should be getting home.' Shannon started to stand.

'Do you think it's a good idea to disturb the baby?' Marcy asked quickly.

Shannon acknowledged the sleeping baby in Marcy's arms with a deep sigh. 'You *do* have a way with her.'

'I'm sorry if I ask too many questions,' Marcy apologised. 'It just gets a little lonely,' she added, 'travelling by myself.'

'I know how you feel,' Shannon said, softening immediately. 'When I first moved to Cork, it was hard. I had no one to talk to.' She smiled. 'You fancy some more tea?'

'Sounds good.' More tea meant more time for questions.

The tavern's front door opened. Footsteps approached their table.

'Could we have another pot of tea, please?' Shannon asked.

Marcy looked up and smiled, expecting to see Liam standing there. Instead, she saw Kelly.

'Well, hello, there,' the waitress said, recognising Marcy immediately. 'I see you found Shannon all right.'

The blush instantly drained from Shannon's face. 'What?'

'I'll be right back with your tea,' Kelly said, spinning around on her heel and returning to the inside of the pub.

Shannon was already half out of her chair, the red in her cheeks having returned with a vengeance. 'What did she mean, "I see you found Shannon all right?" Have you been asking about me?'

'Of course not. She must be confusing me with someone else.'

'Do you think I'm stupid? Asking all these questions about me and my friends! Did Mrs O'Connor put you up to this?' Shannon demanded, tears filling her eyes.

'What?'

'She sent you, didn't she? To check up on me. Find out who my friends are, who I see and what I do. You're going to report back to her all the things I said . . .'

'I have no intention of saying anything to Mrs O'Connor.'

'What do you want, then? Who are you?'

Marcy kept her voice purposefully low, hoping to encourage Shannon to do the same. 'My name is Marcy—'

'It's not Marilyn?' Shannon demanded. 'Give me the baby,' she ordered, a note of hysteria creeping into her voice.

A portly man got up from a nearby table. 'Is there a problem?'

'She won't give me back my baby.'

As if on cue, Caitlin opened her eyes and started to howl.

'Give the girl back her baby,' the man instructed, as others on the patio rose from their seats.

'Of course I'll give her back the baby,' Marcy protested. 'I'm not trying to steal her, for heaven's sake.'

Caitlin's screams filled the air as Shannon lunged towards Marcy and the crowd closed in. A brawl broke out between two would-be Sir Galahads. Punches were thrown. An errant fist connected with Marcy's cheek. In the next instant, all was chaos.

SIX

'Do you want to tell us what happened?' the police officer asked.
'I've already told you.'
'Tell us again.'

Marcy lowered her head, the left side of her face still throbbing as she stared at the grey concrete floor. Could she really go through the whole sad story again? What more could she say? That she was sorry? That they were wasting precious time? 'I wasn't trying to steal the baby,' she said instead, sure that Devon was packing her bags at that very minute and preparing to leave the city.

'We know that,' the older of the two men admitted, after a pause. His name was Christopher Murphy, and he was about forty, with close-cropped blond hair. He sat on the edge of the wide desk that occupied most of the room.

'You know that?' Marcy repeated.

'The girl, Shannon Farrell, gave us a statement. Said she'd just as soon forget the whole incident.'

'Then what am I doing here?' Marcy was already beginning to rise from her chair.

'Please sit down, Mrs Taggart.'

Marcy glanced around the windowless room, surprised by how familiar it seemed. Not that she had seen the insides of many police stations. *Just one*, Marcy thought with a shudder, stifling the memory. 'I don't understand. If you already have Shannon's statement . . .' Marcy told the officer, or 'garda', as policemen in Ireland were called. She shifted her gaze towards the female garda standing against the wall. Her name was Colleen Donnelly. She had pale skin and freckles, and was maybe twenty-five. The remaining garda had given his name as John Sweeny, although Marcy noted that his colleagues always referred to him as Johnny. He was about thirty, she estimated.

'How do you know Shannon Farrell?' Colleen Donnelly asked.

'I met her in the park a few days ago,' said Marcy. 'We happened to bump into each other again today on St Patrick's Street. She asked me if I'd like to go somewhere for a cup of tea.'

'What are you doing in Ireland?' asked John Sweeny.

'How is that relevant?'

'Indulge me.'

Marcy sighed her resignation. 'I'm here on holiday.'

'Your husband didn't come with you?' the older garda asked.

'No. We're getting a divorce,' Marcy offered. Now she was not only a troublemaking foreigner, she was pathetic as well. She felt the sudden threat of tears.

'Cheek still sore? Would you like more ice?'

'No, thank you. I'm fine.' It *did* hurt, and she *wasn't* fine, but what the hell. She would tend to her black eye later. She had wasted enough time. All she wanted was to get out of there.

'Who's Audrey?' Murphy asked.

'What?'

'Miss Farrell said you seemed awfully interested in a friend of hers named Audrey.'

'Shannon mentioned her. I was just making conversation.'

'She said you asked a lot of questions about Audrey and a young man named Jax.'

'Like I said, I was just making conversation.'

'Tell us what's really going on, Mrs Taggart,' Colleen Donnelly said. 'Maybe we can help you.'

Marcy looked from one garda's face to the next. Could they help her? she wondered.

'Audrey is my daughter,' she said, after a lengthy pause.

'Your daughter,' all three repeated, their voices overlapping.

'She disappeared two years ago. We thought she was dead—'

'Why would you think that?' John Sweeny interjected.

Marcy swallowed her growing frustration. 'Because that's what she wanted us to think. Because she was confused and depressed.' She told them about Devon going up to their cottage and the discovery of her over-turned canoe in the middle of the bay. She told them of her husband's desertion. She told them of coming to Ireland and seeing Devon walk by Grogan's House, of Liam and Kelly identifying her daughter's picture as the girl they knew as Audrey, and their revelation that Audrey was friendly with Shannon, who worked as a nanny for the O'Connors.

'So let me get this straight,' Christopher Murphy said, when she had finished. 'You're saying you spied on the O'Connor house, that you fol-lowed Shannon to the park—'

'I was hoping she'd lead me to my daughter.'

'Why didn't you just ask Shannon where to find her?'

How many times had she asked herself the same thing? 'Because I was afraid that if Devon knew I was here, if she knew I'd seen her, then she'd disappear again. And I couldn't take that chance.'

'Who's Devon?' Johnny asked.

'My daughter. Audrey is the name she's using.'

'Why would she be using an alias?'

'Obviously because she doesn't want to be found,' Marcy replied testily.

'You don't think she'd be happy to see you?' Colleen asked.

'No. Devon blamed me for a lot of her problems—'

'Such as?'

'I'd really rather not get into that.'

Christopher Murphy reasserted his position as leader. 'I assume you have pictures of your daughter. Can I see them, please?'

Marcy pulled the photographs of Devon out of her handbag.

'Can't say she looks familiar,' Colleen said.

'No. Don't know her,' Murphy agreed. 'Tell me, why didn't you come to us when you first saw her?'

Marcy stared at him blankly. She had no satisfactory response.

'I understand your not wanting to confront Shannon,' he said gently, 'but we might have been able to help you find Audrey.'

'How could you have helped me?'

'Well, we could have circulated her picture, talked to Shannon in an official capacity, asked around, found out about Audrey, made sure she really *is* your daughter.'

'What are you saying? That you don't believe me? I know what I saw.'

'I don't doubt it's what you *think* you saw.'

'Look. I've had enough of this. I appreciate your wanting to help, but it's not necessary. So if you'll just give me back my passport . . .' She nodded towards the stack of papers on his desk. Her passport was lying on the top.

'This isn't the first time you've thought you've seen your daughter, is it, Mrs Taggart?' Murphy asked. 'It's happened before, hasn't it?'

Marcy closed her eyes and shook her head. 'Yes, it's happened before.' She reopened her eyes in time to catch the knowing look that passed among all three officers.

'So it's possible you could be mistaken this time as well?'

'No, it's not poss—yes, it's possible,' she said in the next breath, deciding she might as well tell them what they wanted to hear. 'Is that all?'

'Yes,' Christopher Murphy said, with a sigh. 'I believe it is.'

'Good. Then I can go?'

'You can go.' He retrieved Marcy's passport and handed it to her, along with the pictures of Devon.

Marcy tucked them into her handbag as she rose. 'Thank you.'

'Would you like us to call someone for you, Mrs Taggart?' Colleen asked, gently.

Marcy shook her head. 'No. There's no one.'

'Actually, I believe there's someone waiting for you in the hall,' Murphy said, reaching for the phone on his desk. 'Jenny, is that gentleman still waiting for Mrs Taggart?' he asked. 'Good. Tell him she'll be out straight away.'

Marcy stepped into the narrow hallway, looking for Liam. She saw the blue eyes first, the rest of him coming into focus as he pushed himself off one of the chairs lining the wall.

'Marcy,' Vic Sorvino said, rushing to her side. 'My God, look at you. What happened?' he asked, his eyes darting to her black eye. 'Are you all right? Does it hurt?'

'Vic! What are you doing here?'

A sheepish grin crept onto his sweet mouth. 'I was worried about you. The way you just took off . . .' He paused, took a deep breath. 'I couldn't stop thinking about you.'

'How did you know where to find me?' Marcy asked.

'I stopped by Grogan's House. The waitress told me what happ—' He looked around. Officers Sweeny and Donnelly were listening to their exchange from the open doorway. 'Look, why don't we go somewhere more private?'

Marcy allowed him to lead her by the elbow out of the station and onto the busy South Mall.

'Did they hurt you?' Vic was asking.

'No. The police were really very kind. What are you doing here?' she asked again. 'Aren't you supposed to be in Italy?'

'I decided Italy could wait a few more days.'

'But why?'

A flush of embarrassment stained Vic's cheeks. 'I would have thought that was pretty obvious.' He took a quick glance over both shoulders. 'Look, why don't we go grab a beer or get something to eat? It's almost six o'clock.'

On cue, the bells of St Anne's Shandon Church began ringing.

'I'm awfully tired,' Marcy said. 'It's been one hell of a day.'

'Where are you staying?'

Should I tell him? Marcy tried not to recall the tenderness of his touch, the way his hands had caressed her body. 'At a bed and breakfast on Western Road,' she told him.

'Lead the way.'

SHE HAD BEEN FIFTEEN the day she had walked into her parents' bedroom and found the now-familiar scene of her mother standing naked in the middle of the room, the contents of her closets strewn across her bed. Every necklace she owned had appeared to be hanging from the wrists of her outstretched hands. Her eyes had been red from crying.

'What are you doing?' Marcy had asked, although she knew the answer well enough to mouth the response along with her mother.

'I have nothing to wear.'

Marcy had shrugged and turned away. *So it was starting again*, she thought. Why had she come up here? She could have simply eaten her breakfast and left for school with nothing more than a casual shout of good-bye up the stairs, as Judith had done.

It had been almost a year since the last occurrence, a year in which her mother had dutifully followed her doctor's orders and stayed on her medication; a year of relative calm. A year in which Marcy had allowed herself to be lulled into a false sense of security.

'Maybe you could help me, darling,' her mother was saying, necklaces falling to the floor as she beckoned Marcy forwards.

Marcy had taken a step back. 'I'll be late for school. I have to go.'

'No. Please, don't leave me.'

'I'll call Dad.'

'No. He's in court all day today. We can't disturb him.'

'Then I'll call your doctor.'

'He's on holiday.' A note of triumph crept into her mother's voice, as if she had been planning this for some time.

Marcy had crossed the room towards the bathroom, opened the medicine cabinet, and began riffling through the various creams and lotions for her mother's medication. 'Where are your pills, Mom?'

'Gone. I flushed them down the toilet. I stopped taking them weeks ago. I don't need them any more.'

'I have to go.' Marcy headed for the door. 'I'm going to be late.'

Her mother's hand on her arm had stopped her. Another necklace rolled off her wrist and dropped to the floor. 'Why don't you wear any make-up, sweetheart? A little blush or mascara would do wonders for you; take some of the emphasis away from your hair.'

In response, Marcy had grabbed a pair of sweatpants from the bed and thrust them against her mother's chest. 'Get dressed, Mom.'

'Please, won't you stay with me a little longer?'

'I can't. I'll see you later.'

'There's so much cruelty in the world,' her mother had said, starting to cry again. 'All those poor abused children and animals, all those people dying in poverty.' She sank to the floor. 'Sometimes I feel such despair.'

'I have to go. I have a French test first period.'

'Then you should run along,' her mother said abruptly.

Marcy had turned and fled the room.

'Good luck on your test,' her mother had called after her.

'You just left her like that?' Judith demanded when they passed each other in the school corridor later that morning.

'What was I supposed to do? I didn't see you sticking around.'

'Whatever. Did you call Dad?'

'He was in court. I left him a message.'

'She'll be all right,' Judith said. 'She always is.'

'Yeah,' Marcy had agreed, thinking that maybe at lunch she would go home to make sure.

Except that when it came time for lunch, she had chosen to go out with a bunch of friends instead. If the experience of the past fifteen years had taught her anything, she had reasoned, it was that nothing she could do would make any difference. Her mother would spend the next few weeks in a downward spiral of crying and incoherent babbling, and then she would likely disappear for a few days, maybe even weeks, living on the streets and sifting through garbage bins until somebody recognised her and brought her home. And then the cycle would start all over again.

Except it didn't.

At two o'clock that afternoon, she and Judith had been summoned into the principal's office, where two uniformed officers were waiting to inform them that their mother had committed suicide by jumping off the roof of a ten-storey office building.

'Don't feel guilty,' Judith had told her as they waited for their father to pick them up from school and take them home.

Marcy had nodded. She didn't feel guilty about her mother's death. She felt relieved.

And for that, she had felt guilty ever since.

'MARCY?' VIC CALLED from the bed. 'What are you doing?'

Good question, Marcy thought. 'What time is it?' she asked, wrapping her pink cotton bathrobe tighter around her. What was Vic Sorvino doing in her bed? *Again.* Had she no self-control whatsoever?

Vic reached for his watch on the tiny bedside table. 'A little after nine,' he said. 'You hungry?'

Marcy shook her head. 'You?'

'No.' Vic patted the space beside him. 'Come back to bed.'

'I don't think that's such a good idea.'

'Why not?'

'I don't know.' Marcy shrugged. 'I don't know what I'm doing any more.' *How did this happen?* she wanted to shout. Except she already knew the answer. This was all her doing. They'd barely made it up the stairs before her lips were reaching for his. She was tearing at his shirt before she had even closed the door to her room. 'I don't know what's the matter with me.'

'There's absolutely nothing the matter with you,' Vic said.

'I practically attacked you. I normally don't act that way.' She laughed. 'Except, of course, for the last time we were together.'

'And you asked me what I'm doing here?' he said, sardonically.

'What *are* you doing here, Vic?'

The air turned serious. 'I told you. I was worried about you. It seems I've grown quite attached.'

'Why?'

'*Why?*' he repeated, shaking his head. 'I'm not sure I can answer that. I don't know. Maybe I sense a kindred soul.'

'Or maybe you just feel sorry for me.'

'I feel many things for you. Sorry isn't one of them.'

Marcy smiled in spite of her attempt not to.

'Come back to bed,' he said again.

What the hell? Marcy thought. *Why not?* She was exhausted. She lay down on the bed, Vic's arms immediately encircling her.

'We can go out again if you'd like. Make the rounds of all the pubs,' he said. 'Maybe we'll see her.'

Marcy shook her head. 'We won't see her. She knows I'm here. She doesn't want me to find her.'

'Tell me what kind of trouble she was in,' Vic said.

'She'd gotten mixed up with some guy who was into cocaine. They went to a party one night. It got kind of loud. A neighbour called the police. They found drugs. Devon was charged, along with everyone else. Our lawyer scheduled a meeting with the Crown attorney. He thought that, because of Devon's condition, we might be able to persuade him to drop the charges if she'd agree to get help.'

'And?'

'The weekend before the meeting, Devon went up to our cottage.' Marcy's voice caught in her throat. 'She never came back.'

'You'll find her, Marcy. You'll bring her home.'

There was a long silence. 'What if it's not her?' Marcy asked. 'What if I'm as crazy as everyone thinks I am?'

'I don't think you're crazy.'

'You married your realtor,' Marcy reminded him.

Vic laughed. 'I guess sometimes we just want so badly to stop hurting, we do crazy things.'

'Is that what I'm doing?'

'I don't know. But I'd like to be here when you find out.'

Marcy reached for him again. 'You really are the nicest man.'

SHE AWOKE to the sound of bells ringing.

Except they weren't bells, she realised. It was her cell phone.

Careful not to disturb Vic, sleeping beside her, Marcy grabbed her handbag and took it into the bathroom. 'Hello?' she whispered.

'I think I might have found her,' Liam said without preamble.

'What?' Was she dreaming? 'How?'

'Well, I've been asking around, as you know, and it looks like it's finally paid off. I just got a call from an acquaintance of mine. He says that a girl matching your daughter's description recently rented a small house just down the way from his ex-wife. He saw her yesterday when he went to visit his kids.'

'There are a lot of girls matching my daughter's description.'

'This one's named Audrey.'

Marcy gasped. 'Where is she?'

'A tiny village very close to here, called Youghal.'

'Yawl?' Marcy repeated, pronouncing it as he had.

'I'll pick you up in twenty minutes,' he said.

SEVEN

Marcy was halfway down the main staircase of the Doyle Cork Inn when Vic's voice stopped her. She froze, looking back to see him standing at the top of the stairs, her pink cotton bathrobe tied haphazardly around his waist, his legs and feet bare. He had been sleeping so soundly, she hadn't wanted to disturb him.

'Marcy, what's happening?'

'I have to go.' Why hadn't she told him where she was going?

'Where? It's not even seven thirty.'

'We might have found Devon,' she said.

'Who's "we"?'

Was that the reason she hadn't told Vic where she was going? Because she didn't want him to see her with Liam?

Sadie Doyle suddenly appeared in the foyer. 'Good morning, Mrs Taggart. Will you be joining us for breakfast?' Her glance drifted towards the stairs, her face registering both surprise and amusement at the sight of a half-naked Vic Sorvino. 'Oh, hello.'

'Give me a minute to get dressed,' Vic urged Marcy, ignoring Sadie Doyle's salacious gaze. 'I'll come with you.'

'No. Please. I don't know if there's room.' Marcy opened the door and rushed out onto the street.

'Marcy . . .' she heard Vic call after her.

The street was already congested with heavy morning traffic. She didn't even know what kind of car Liam drove, Marcy realised. She checked her watch. Twenty minutes had passed since Liam's phone call. In that time, she had washed, brushed her teeth, pulled on a pair of jeans and a grey sweater, and tucked her hair into a clip.

'Come on, Liam,' she muttered now. Every minute counted.

She heard a door open and turned to see Vic, now dressed, step outside. 'Marcy,' he said, and she felt herself swaying towards him.

A series of loud honks filled the air as a small black car pulled to a stop beside her, its passenger door opening. A handsome face with sleepy green eyes suddenly filled her frame of vision. 'Get in,' Liam said, taking off before she had had time to close the door.

Marcy turned back for a final glance in Vic's direction. But she had other, more important things to think about now than Vic's hurt feelings. There would be plenty of time for explanations and amends after she was reunited with her daughter.

'Sorry I'm late,' Liam said. 'The traffic's been fierce.'

Marcy pulled the seat belt around her and snapped it into place, then stole another quick glance behind her. Vic was no longer standing on the doorstep of the Doyle Cork Inn.

'I brought coffee,' Liam said, handing Marcy a large paper cup. 'Double cream, double sugar. Is that all right?'

'Sounds great,' she said, and raised the hot coffee to her lips.

'We should be in Youghal in about half an hour. So take a deep breath, try to relax, and drink up.'

Marcy did as instructed, inhaling deeply before taking a long swallow. The sugar immediately glommed onto her tongue.

'Too sweet?'

'It's fine,' Marcy said, grimacing.

Liam laughed. 'You're not a very good liar, are you?'

'OK. This is the worst cup of coffee I've ever had in my life.'

'See? That was much better, wasn't it?'

Marcy laughed, the tension of the morning starting to dissipate. She tried not to stare at the pronounced curl of his eyelashes.

'I see he found you,' Liam said.

'What? Who?'

'That guy who's been asking about you. Vic something-or-other. He stopped by Grogan's again yesterday asking more questions. Kelly told him about the altercation before I could stop her.'

'Yes, he found me.'

'Stayed the night, did he? Not that it's my business,' he added.

'It's not what you think,' she said. Then she sighed. 'OK, it's *exactly* what you think.'

He laughed. 'Well, good for you. He's a nice-looking man, rich, obviously madly in love with you.'

'What? No. That's ridiculous. We barely know each other.'

'You're very beautiful, you know,' Liam said suddenly. 'Although . . .' One hand left the wheel to reach behind her head and undo the clasp in her hair. 'There. That's much better. Shake your head.'

'You're crazy,' Marcy protested, but she did as she was told.

'Doesn't that feel much better?'

Marcy had to admit that it did. 'How do you know Vic is rich?' she asked.

Liam shrugged. 'Well, when he came by the pub looking for you, he said he was staying at the Hayfield Manor Hotel, and you pretty much have to sell the farm to stay at that place. Did you tell him where you were goin' this morning?'

'No.'

'I don't think you fully trust him.'

'What?' *Was he right?*

'You know what else?' Liam asked. 'I think I'm jealous.' He laughed, and Marcy laughed with him. 'I'm serious,' he said, the laughter coming to an abrupt halt.

'Why would you be jealous?'

'Because it should have been me last night,' he said simply.

Marcy said nothing, although her heart was beating fast. She turned away from him to observe the scenery in a concerted effort to calm down. Would they never get out of this damn city?

'We should be on the coast road in a few more minutes,' Liam said. 'Why don't you catch a bit of sleep before we get there?'

'I *am* kind of tired,' Marcy admitted, her head suddenly spinning.

'Lean back, close your eyes, think pleasant thoughts,' he instructed her, and Marcy did as she was told.

Almost immediately, she saw Devon walking towards her, her arms extended. In the next instant, she was caught in her daughter's embrace. 'Mommy,' her daughter whispered lovingly in her ear.

My baby.

'Marcy.'

'Hmm?'

'Marcy,' Liam said again. 'Marcy, wake up.'

Marcy opened her eyes to see Liam's smiling face looming above hers. It took her a second to realise the car had stopped.

'We're here,' Liam said.

'In Youghal? I can't believe I fell asleep. What time is it?'

'Eight forty-five. The traffic was absolutely brutal.'

Marcy looked at the vast expanse of majestic beach stretched out in front of her, trying to get her bearings. 'Where are we, exactly?'

'Just outside the town walls. That's the Blackwater River straight ahead.' Liam pointed towards a breathtaking expanse of water. A wide lane of grass and a pedestrian walkway separated them from the river. 'This here's Green Park Beach, which is just minutes from the centre of Youghal.'

It was an undeniably beautiful spot, unspoiled and serene. In the distance a yacht was cruising slowly by. *Lots for Devon to do*, she thought. Except that Devon was a city girl at heart. Could she really have found the happiness she craved in a tiny fishing port on the edge of nowhere?

'Where does my daughter live?' she asked Liam.

'Marcy . . . you have to be prepared in case we're wrong,' he said. 'There's a chance it might not be her.'

'We're not wrong. Where is she, Liam?'

'Within walking distance.'

'Then what are we waiting for? Let's go.' Marcy pushed open the car's passenger door and stepped onto the pavement, a strong wind almost flattening her against the side of the car. Liam took her by the elbow, guiding her across the street towards the town.

He led her past a series of shops and sandwich bars painted a host of garish colours. They veered off the main street, finding themselves on a street so narrow they could barely walk side by side. Tiny row houses lined the cobblestone street, each a different vibrant hue. Most were two-storey homes containing a single upstairs bedroom.

'Which way?' Marcy asked, when they stopped at a busy crossroads.

'Down this street.' Liam pointed to his right. 'OK, here we are,' he was saying in the next breath, stopping in front of a pink house with green trim and a purple front door.

'That's where she lives?' Pink was Devon's least-favourite colour.

'Goat Street, number fifteen,' Liam said.

Marcy took a deep breath, feeling her legs grow weak.

'Are you all right?'

'I just can't imagine Devon living in a pink house.'

'Well, there's only one way to find out.' He took her hand and led her to the front door. 'Do you want to knock or shall I?'

'I'll do it.' Marcy banged the brass knocker against the door.

No response.

'Try again,' Liam said. 'I thought I heard something.'

'What if she looked out the window and saw me?' Marcy asked. 'What if she saw it was me and now she won't answer the door?'

In response, Liam took the knocker and banged it adamantly.

'Just a minute,' a woman's voice suddenly called from inside.

'Oh God,' Marcy said, holding her breath as the door opened.

A young woman with short blonde hair and wide questioning eyes stood on the other side. 'Can I help you?' she asked.

Marcy opened her mouth to speak, but no words came out.

'We're looking for Audrey,' Liam said, in her stead.

'Who are you?' the girl asked.

'My name's Liam. This is Marcy Taggart, Audrey's mother.'

The young woman's eyes shot to Marcy. 'Audrey's mother?'

'Yes,' Marcy said, more a sigh than a word.

'Well, fancy that. Audrey,' she called towards the dark centre of the house. 'You'd better get over here. There's someone to see you.'

'Who is it? I'm a little busy trying to rescue your muffins.'

'Been cooking,' the girl explained, sheepishly. 'The muffins can wait,' she called back. 'You've got a visitor.'

'Who is it?' Cautious footsteps approached.

'See for yourself.'

A young woman stepped out of the dark hall into a warm spotlight of sun. Marcy took one look at the girl's long brown hair and sad dark eyes. Then she fainted in Liam's arms.

'WE NEED TO TALK,' Marcy had said to her daughter.

She was standing in the doorway to Devon's bedroom. Outside, rain was coming down in sheets and a strong October wind was blowing the remaining leaves off the maple tree on the front lawn.

'I don't want to talk,' Devon had said, plopping down on her bed.

'Then you don't have to,' Marcy replied, stepping into the room and navigating her way around the discarded clothes covering the carpet. Marcy had recognised some of the items as purchases from a shopping trip she had taken Devon on, hoping to cheer her up. The clothes now lay crumpled on the floor, their price tags still in place. 'I'll talk. You listen.'

Devon had shrugged. She was wearing a pair of yellow flannel pyjamas that Marcy had bought her the previous Christmas.

'You're in a lot of trouble, Devon.'

'I'm not in trouble. Our lawyer's going to get me off.'

'We don't know that for sure.'

'It wasn't my fault. I didn't know about the drugs.'

'It's irrelevant. The fact is, you were there with a man the police have identified as a known drug dealer—'

'His name is Alex, and he's not a drug dealer.'

'I don't care what he is. You're not to see him again.'

'I'm over twenty-one. You can't tell me what to do.'

'As long as you live in this house, I can and I will.'

Devon had jumped off the bed, arms flailing. 'Then I guess I'll just have to move out.'

Marcy didn't flinch. 'I remind you that one of the conditions of your bail is that you continue to live at home.'

'So now you're my jailer?'

'I'm your mother.'

'Yeah. Great job of that you're doing. This is your fault, you know. It's your rotten genes I inherited.'

'And I'm sorry for that. But at some point you have to play the cards you were given and take responsibility for your own life.'

'Which is exactly what I'm trying to do.'

'How? By getting arrested, by doing drugs?'

'I thought you wanted me to take drugs.'

'Taking your medication is hardly the same thing.'

'You're right. Your drugs make me feel bad. My drugs make me feel good.'

'Devon, this is ridiculous. You're acting like a twelve year old.'

'I *am* twelve years old! Like it or not, Mommy, that's all I am.'

'Well, I don't like it!' Marcy shot back, her patience spent. 'I'm tired of being the mother of a twelve-year-old child. I want to be the mother of a twenty-one-year-old woman. Do you understand? I'm tired of parenting.' She had burst into a flood of angry, bitter tears. 'I've been a parent since I was a child, and I'm sick of it. I can't do it any more. I don't *want* to do it any more. Do you hear me?'

She had braced herself for Devon's fiery response. Instead, Devon had wrapped her arms around her mother and held her close. 'I hear you, Mommy,' she said softly.

'CAN YOU HEAR ME? Marcy, can you hear me?'

Marcy opened her eyes to find two worried faces staring down at her. She pushed herself up onto her elbows and looked around. She was lying on a brown velvet sofa in the middle of a tiny room.

'What happened?' she asked warily.

'You fainted,' Liam told her.

Marcy swung her feet onto the worn wool carpet. 'Where's Audrey?' she asked the young blonde woman standing beside Liam.

Audrey suddenly appeared in the doorway, the tray in her hands holding a steaming pot of tea, four mugs and a plate of freshly baked muffins. 'I'm right here,' she said.

'SO HOW LONG have you been living in Youghal?' Liam asked as they sipped their tea. He was sitting on the sofa beside Marcy. The blonde girl, who was about thirty and whose name was Claire, had pulled an armchair close to the coffee table and was curled up inside it. Audrey sat on the floor at her feet.

'Just a few months,' Claire answered. 'There's still a lot we want to do with the place. How are the muffins? They any good?'

'Delicious,' Liam said. 'You like to cook, do you?'

'Well, *I* do,' Claire answered, giving Audrey an affectionate cuff on the side of her head. 'Can't say the same for this one here.'

'Hey,' Audrey said, grabbing Claire's hand and holding it.

Marcy felt her eyes widen, and she tried to look away. But it was too late. Audrey had already taken note of her response.

'Something wrong?' she asked.

Marcy shrugged, as if to say, *No, of course not. Anything you choose to do is fine with me.*

'A few of the neighbours got their noses out of joint when we first moved in,' Audrey said with a laugh.

'Yeah, but they've more or less all come around.'

'What made you settle here?' Liam asked.

'We came here on holiday about a year ago, decided we liked the look of the place, and thought we'd give it a go,' said Claire.

'Thought we might be able to save some money, and open up a bakery of our own one day.' Audrey smiled at Claire.

'Well, your muffins really are delicious.' Liam motioned towards the tray on the coffee table. 'Do you mind if I have another?'

'Please, help yourself.'

What's he doing? Marcy wondered. *Why are we prolonging this agony? Can't we just get out of here?*

'So what made you think Audrey might be your daughter?' Claire asked, as if sensing Marcy's restlessness.

Tears immediately filled Marcy's eyes.

'I'm afraid that was my fault,' Liam said.

'It's nobody's fault,' Marcy told him. 'You were told a young woman matching Devon's description lived here and that her name was Audrey.' Marcy turned her attention back to the two young women. 'My daughter disappeared about two years ago,' she explained. 'Liam has been kind enough to help me look for her. We thought we might have found her.'

'That's why you fainted when you saw me?' Audrey asked.

'Liam warned me not to get my hopes up,' Marcy said. 'But . . .'

'You couldn't help it,' Claire said, with obvious sympathy.

'Do I look like her at all?' Audrey asked.

'Superficially, yes. Same age, same height, same long hair.'

'What happened to her?' Audrey asked. 'Your daughter, I mean. She just wandered off one day?'

'Audrey'—Claire chastised her—'it's really none of our business.'

'Sorry. It's just that it's a bit like what happened with my mum and me, isn't it?'

'You didn't just wander off,' Claire said.

'No, but I haven't spoken to her in six months.'

'Audrey's parents weren't my biggest fans,' Claire explained.

'I come from a very traditional Catholic family,' Audrey clarified. 'They told me I was going straight to hell.'

'Instead, we came to Youghal,' Claire said happily.

'Does your mother know where you are?' Marcy asked.

Audrey's face clouded over. 'I told her we were leaving town, that I'd call her when we settled in.'

'And have you?'

Audrey shook her head. 'Don't really see much point in it.'

'I think you should call her,' Marcy said.

'She doesn't care.'

'She's your mother,' Marcy said forcefully. 'She cares.' There was silence.

'We really should go,' Liam said.

Marcy pushed herself to her feet. 'Thank you for your kindness.'

'Sorry it didn't work out the way you hoped,' Audrey said.

'Call your mother,' Marcy said, and followed Liam out of the door.

'When Devon was about two,' Marcy was telling Liam as they neared the outskirts of Cork, 'she took her colouring pens and drew all over the living-room walls. I'd just had them painted. I mean, the workers had literally just finished up the day before. Anyway, the point is that I was on the phone and not paying enough attention to Devon, who'd been quietly drawing at the kitchen table, and at some point she got up and went into the living room without my noticing. And then suddenly she was back, grinning from ear to ear. And she said, "Mommy, come see what I did." She always called me "Mommy", even when she was all grown-up. I always loved that.' Tears filled her eyes. 'Anyway, she grabbed my hand and led me into my freshly painted living room and showed me, very proudly—oh, she was so proud—what she'd done.' Marcy took a deep breath, not sure whether or not she could continue. She had never told this story to anyone: she had been too ashamed. 'I saw all these black and red and green swirls all over my new walls. And I'm looking from this happy little face to these graffiti-covered walls, and I'm thinking of all the money I've just spent, and I feel this anger rising inside me like lava from a volcano. And I could see how thrilled Devon was and that she was waiting for me to tell her how beautiful her drawings were, and I *knew* that's what I should do, that I could wait until later to explain that we don't draw on walls, that sort of thing, what all the advice books tell you to do. But I heard this awful voice, *my* voice, screaming, "What have you done?" And Devon was crying, begging me to stop yelling. But I couldn't. Suddenly, she let out this awful wail—I'll never forget it—like a wounded animal. It was horrible.'

'Marcy,' Liam said gently, 'Devon didn't run away because you yelled at her when she was two for scribbling on the walls.'

'There were other times.'

'What, that you yelled at her? That you were less than perfect? I'm sure there were plenty of times you made it up to her.'

Marcy refused to allow herself to be comforted by his words. 'When Devon was about eight, I decided it would be a good idea for her to take piano lessons. We hired this guy to come over and give her lessons. She was a natural. Except I noticed that when her teacher wasn't there, she was hopeless. I'd tell her to practise, and she'd sit there and bang at the keyboard. I'd get so frustrated—'

Liam interrupted. 'Marcy, why are you doing this?'

'That's what I'd say to Devon. "Why are you doing this? You know the right notes. Just read the music." Well, of course, it turned out she *didn't* know the right notes. She'd just watch what he played and copy his fingers. The next day, she couldn't remember.'

'When I was five, my mother spanked me for putting salt in the sugar bowl and ruinin' her morning coffee. I tell you, I'm scarred for life.'

'You're minimising what I did,' Marcy said.

'And you're blowin' it out of proportion. How do you get out of bed in the mornin' with the weight of that guilt on your shoulders?'

It's not easy, Marcy thought. 'I expected too much from her.'

'So what? Big deal. You expected too much. What about your son? Do you expect too much from him, too?'

The mention of her son caught Marcy off-guard, as it always did. Devon had a way of taking up every inch of space in her brain, crowding her brother out. 'Darren is different.' Marcy pictured her son's handsome face.

'He never gave me any trouble.' *I neglected him terribly*, she realised. 'Devon took all my energy.'

'What's done is done. So what's the point of beatin' yourself up about something you can't change? Unless you like wallowin' in all that guilt because it allows you to stay stuck in the past. Maybe that's what you want.'

Marcy felt a twinge of outrage. 'You think I want to be miserable?'

'Don't know,' he said, his voice provocative. 'Do you?'

'I just want things to be normal,' Marcy said. 'Maybe if I'd—'

'No,' Liam said, suddenly pulling to the side of the road and shutting off the car's engine. 'No more maybes.' He kissed her before she could say another word.

The kiss was passionate and grew even more urgent as it progressed. Marcy felt strong hands at her waist, on her cheeks, in her hair. So different from the way Vic had kissed her just last night.

What's happening? she wondered, pulling away from Liam.

Liam apologised immediately.

'Why did you do that?'

'I've been wanting to kiss you since I first laid eyes on you.'

Marcy's head was spinning. She stared at the empty field by the side of the road in order to steady it. 'Where are we?' she asked.

'Just outside the city limits. I'm really sorry,' he said again.

'No, it's my fault.'

Liam smiled. 'Not everything is your fault, Marcy.' Then, tenderly, 'Things will work out in the end. You'll see.'

Marcy reached out to touch his hand, then thought better of it. As thrilling as his embrace had been, she realised they weren't the arms she wanted around her. She pictured Vic standing outside the Doyle Cork Inn, his wounded eyes following Liam's car down the busy street. Would he be waiting for her when she got back?

Liam restarted the car's engine, pulling back onto the main road. Within minutes they were mired in traffic, the sound of nearby road drills pounding against the sides of their heads.

'My father used to work in construction,' Liam said, obviously straining for conversation. 'He was killed twelve years ago when a building he was working on collapsed. Never knew what hit him.'

'I'm so sorry.'

'Oh, well. What's done is done, right? Think I remember a very wise man once saying that there's no point beatin' yourself up over things you can't change.'

'He *is* a very wise man,' Marcy said.

'Just not the man you want.' Liam pulled to a stop in front of the Doyle Cork Inn.

'Liam . . .'

'It's all right. It'll all work out in the end,' he said, green eyes twinkling.

EIGHT

Sadie Doyle was waiting for her in the inn's small reception area, hands on her wide hips. 'That'll be an extra fifty euros for your guest,' she announced, before Marcy was through the door.

'Is he still here?' Marcy asked hopefully.

Sadie shook her head. 'Nah. He left hours ago.'

What did I expect? Marcy wondered. 'Did he leave a message?'

Another vigorous shake of Sadie's head. 'I'll just tack that extra charge on to your bill, shall I?'

'Yes.' Marcy walked up the stairs, deciding to call Vic when she got to her room. Liam had said he was staying at the posh Hayfield Manor Hotel, which was relatively close. She would ring his room, apologise for running out on him, and tell him about Youghal. He would understand. *I'll make it up to him*, she was thinking as she strode towards her room, key in hand, reaching for the door.

It took several twists of the key until she succeeded in unlocking the door, and then it suddenly swung open. Marcy froze. 'Oh, my God,' she gasped. Then, 'No. No!'

The room looked as if a storm had swept through it. The sheets had been ripped from the bed, the mattress slashed. Every drawer in the place had been upended. The closet had been emptied, her clothes left in a heap. Even her toiletries hadn't been spared—bottles smashed, her toothbrush snapped in half. 'What the—' Her words froze in her throat as she approached the bed, her shaking hand reaching for a pair of panties that had been slashed repeatedly. 'Oh God!' she exclaimed in horror, realising that every item of her clothing had been slashed, shredded, gutted. 'No!' she shouted. 'No, no, no, no!'

She heard heavy footsteps on the stairs, followed by a shrill scream. Then more footsteps, faster, nimbler than the ones before. A sharp intake of breath. 'My God. What have you done?'

Marcy spun around to see Sadie and Colin Doyle in the doorway.

'What have *I* done?' Marcy sputtered. 'You think *I* did this?'

Sadie held firm. 'You're responsible nonetheless.'

'*I'm* responsible? How do you figure that?'

'Looks like your friend didn't appreciate your runnin' off.'

Tears filled Marcy's eyes. 'He didn't do this,' she said.

'Who, then?'

'Who else had access to this room?' Marcy asked.

'Aside from your gentleman friend? The one you ran out on this mornin', the one who sat here half the day waitin' for you to come back, the one who snuck out when he thought no one was lookin'?'

'That can't be,' Marcy muttered. 'Where do you keep your keys?' she asked suddenly. 'You obviously have a master set . . .'

'They're in a safe place.'

'Where? Behind the reception desk?' The look that passed through Sadie's eyes told Marcy her guess was correct.

'And you're not always at that desk, are you, Mrs Doyle? Sometimes you're busy with other things. It's possible someone could have come in, taken those keys, and—'

'Ransacked your room? Why would anybody want to do that?'

'I don't know.' Marcy felt her knees grow weak.

'Yeah? Well, this is what *I* know. My room's been trashed, and some-body's got to pay for the damage. Frankly that guy who spent the night looked a little shifty to me. Any jewellery missin'?'

Marcy looked through her tears towards the empty drawer where she had put her earrings. 'My gold earrings are gone,' she said dully.

'Call the gardai,' Sadie instructed her son.

'WELL, MRS TAGGART,' Christopher Murphy said in greeting. He closed the door behind him, and walked towards her chair. 'It's nice to see you again.'

'Do you think we could dispense with the sarcasm?' Marcy asked, con-centrating her attention on the messy stack of papers on the garda's desk.

It seemed to have grown substantially since she was there yesterday.

'Suppose you tell me what happened this time,' Murphy said as Colleen Donnelly entered the room, followed by John Sweeny.

Marcy sighed. 'I came back to the inn—'

'You'd been out all day?' Murphy said, interrupting.

'Yes. I went to Youghal. I was looking for my daughter.'

The three officers exchanged glances. 'Did you find her?' Sweeny asked.

'No.'

'Go on, then. You returned to the inn . . .'

'I went up to my room and discovered that someone had torn it apart.'

'Mrs Doyle said you had company last night,' Murphy said.

'He never would have done this,' Marcy insisted.

'And you ran off early this morning like a bat out of hell. Meeting someone, were you?'

'Yes.'

'Mind telling us who that was, Mrs Taggart?'

'His name is Liam. I . . . I don't know his last name,' she admitted, her face flushing. 'He works at Grogan's House.'

Marcy saw Colleen Donnelly scribble down this piece of information.

'So you ran out on one man to go and meet another,' Murphy said. 'What's this other guy's name? The one who spent the night,' he added unnecessarily.

This is ridiculous, Marcy thought. 'His name is Vic Sorvino,' she said. 'He's staying at the Hayfield Manor Hotel.'

Christopher Murphy nodded towards Colleen Donnelly, who then left the room. 'Did Vic Sorvino know you were meeting Liam?'

'No.'

'I understand that after you ran out on him, he followed you onto the street and returned to your room again after you left.'

'According to Mrs Doyle.'

'Who claims he was in your room waiting for you when she went in to make up the bed,' Murphy stated. 'You don't believe her?'

'I don't know what to believe. For all I know, it could have been Mrs Doyle who trashed my things. And what about her son?'

'It appears Colin was out for most of the morning.'

'Which left the front desk largely unattended,' Marcy said, pouncing. 'Which means anybody could have wandered in off the street and taken the master key and gone up to my room.'

'You said yesterday there'd been issues with your daughter, that perhaps she might not want to be found. . . .'

'You think it was Devon who did this?'

'I'm simply suggesting it's a possibility. Maybe that was her way of telling you to go home, to leave her alone.'

'Or maybe it was someone else,' Marcy said.

Murphy shrugged as Colleen Donnelly re-entered the room. 'We checked with Hayfield Manor. Mr Sorvino checked out at noon.'

Disappointment stabbed at Marcy's chest. 'Can I go now?'

'Where is it you plan to go, Mrs Taggart?' Murphy asked.

Marcy couldn't very well go back to the Doyle Cork Inn. 'It looks as if Hayfield Manor has a vacancy,' she said.

'I'M SORRY. How much did you say?' Marcy asked the bright-eyed, dark-haired receptionist, who didn't look a day over twelve.

'Six hundred and fifty euros,' the girl repeated, with a smile that exposed her entire upper gum.

I could do something about that, Peter said from the dark recesses of Marcy's brain.

Six hundred and fifty euros translated into around a thousand dollars, Marcy calculated, thinking that Peter would have a fit when he saw this month's credit card bills, whose charges he had agreed to cover for two years—'within reason,' he had stressed—when she had agreed not to contest their divorce. *Silly man,* she thought now. Had he really expected a crazy woman to act reasonably?

'Is that all right?' the receptionist asked. 'It's a deluxe room. I'm afraid there's nothing else available at the moment.'

'It's fine.' Marcy pushed her credit card across the counter.

'Do you need help with your luggage?'

'Don't have any.' Marcy surveyed the soft peach-coloured foyer, with its marble columns and magnificent mahogany staircase. 'Is there somewhere I can buy a toothbrush and toothpaste?'

'Housekeeping can provide that, and we have a wonderful spa that sells all sorts of beauty products,' the receptionist told her. She handed Marcy a key card. 'You're in room two twelve. The lift is straight ahead.'

Marcy's room was on the second floor, only steps from the lift. She opened the door to find a wall of leaded windows overlooking a private garden, and a beautiful marble bathroom. The bed was king-size, the sheets crisp, the walls a pale apricot. A fluffy white bathrobe hung in the closet. 'I think I'll stay here for ever,' she said, lying on the bed.

Seconds later, she was asleep.

MARCY WOKE UP with a start. There was another knock on the door. 'Housekeeping,' a woman's voice announced.

Marcy threw open the door to find a grey-haired woman of around sixty holding a toothbrush and a small tube of toothpaste. 'I understand you're in need of these,' she said, brightly.

'Thank you,' Marcy said, and then, 'Could you hold on a moment?' She reached for her handbag, quickly extricating the envelope containing her daughter's pictures and holding out the most recent one. 'Do you recognise this girl, by any chance?'

'Oh, who's this now?' the woman from Housekeeping asked.

'Do you know her?' Marcy asked in return.

The woman studied the picture. 'I thought for a minute it might be Katie, my neighbour's daughter. But it's not her. Now that I have a good look, I can see they're quite different around the eyes.'

'You're sure?' Marcy asked. 'Have you known Katie long?'

'Only all her life,' the woman said, and laughed. 'She's a handful, that one. Always has been. Who's this, then?' she asked again.

'My daughter,' Marcy told her. 'Also a handful.'

The woman smiled. 'Yes, well. I guess they all are at that age.'

'Do you know the sort of places Katie likes to go?' Marcy said. 'A favourite pub? My daughter will be joining me soon,' she added, when she saw the woman's puzzled expression. 'I thought it would be nice to take her to places where there are young people.'

'Oh, there's no shortage of those.' The woman laughed. 'There's Dingles, over on Oliver Plunkett Street. And there's Mulcahy's on Cornmarket. It's a bit rough, but the kids all love it.'

'Thank you.' Cornmarket Street was in the centre of the city. No doubt she had walked past Mulcahy's without noticing it. *It might be worth a look*, she thought, deciding to shower first.

She heard her cell phone ringing as she was getting out of the shower.

'Marcy, are you all right?' Liam asked, as soon as she said hello. 'The gardai were just at Grogan's askin' questions. What the hell happened?'

Marcy struggled into her bathrobe. 'The police were there?'

'They just left. They said your room had been ransacked . . .'

Marcy quickly explained everything that had happened since Liam had dropped her off in front of the Doyle Cork Inn.

'The gardai think it was that guy you were with. Is it true he destroyed all your things?'

'Somebody did,' Marcy said. 'What did the police say?'

'Just asked how long I'd known you, your background and stuff like that—if I thought you were unstable,' he added, after a pause.

Marcy held her breath. 'And do you?' she asked.

A second's silence, then, 'What I think is you're not safe.'

'Why wouldn't I be safe?'

'Some lunatic just trashed your room,' Liam said. 'He could come back. I think you should think about goin' back to Toronto.'

'I'm not going anywhere until I find Devon.'

A pause. 'All right. I have to go. Grogan's givin' me the evil eye. Will you do me a favour and just stay put for the rest of the night?'

'I don't know. I was thinking of going over to Mulcahy's.'

'Have you taken leave of your senses? It's a dive. No way you're goin' there alone. You're to order room service and get into bed.'

'OK,' she said, agreeing reluctantly. She disconnected the line and tossed the phone onto the bed.

Liam is right, she decided, drying her hair. Her head was spinning; her eye had resumed throbbing. She was in no condition to go out again. She should just order room service and get to bed early.

At least my photographs of Devon escaped unharmed, she thought gratefully, seeing the envelope on the desk. 'My baby,' she whispered, gently laying the photographs along the desk's smooth surface, watching as Devon grew up before her bewildered eyes. 'My beautiful baby.'

My beautiful mommy, Devon whispered back.

Marcy removed the picture of her own mother from the envelope. 'My beautiful mommy,' she repeated, laying her picture down beside Devon's, breathing in their uncanny resemblance. Slowly, reluctantly, her fingers trembling, she reached back inside the envelope and removed the second, smaller envelope, the one marked 'MOMMY', carefully withdrawing the sheet of paper that was folded neatly inside, turning it over several times before unfolding it.

My beautiful Mommy, she read, Devon's awkward scrawl playing hide-and-seek with her tears. *I don't expect you to understand what I'm about to do.* Marcy trembled. When had she ever understood anything her daughter had tried to tell her? *Please don't be mad, and understand that this is not a decision I've made lightly. I know how much pain I've caused you. Believe me when I say I have no desire to cause you any more.* Marcy lowered her head, unable to continue. When she looked up again, her tears blinded her to everything except the letter's next-to-last line. '"*Please know how much I love you,*"' she read out loud.

Her hands shaking, Marcy returned the paper and photographs to her handbag. Minutes later, she crawled back into the jeans and grey sweater she had been wearing all day and headed out.

MARCY HAD TO WALK up and down Cornmarket Street twice before she spotted the sign for Mulcahy's, a ragged piece of scrap metal with *MULCAHY'S* hand-painted in black across it, with a wobbly arrow pointing towards a narrow flight of stairs at the side of a dry-cleaning shop.

This is crazy, she thought as she descended the concrete steps, stopping at the closed basement door. She tried the handle. It didn't budge. She knocked. Nobody answered. 'Hello?' she called out.

'Excuse me,' she heard someone say from above her head.

Marcy looked up towards the street. She saw an enormous pair of legs stretching for the sky. The legs were attached to a man whose head seemed disproportionately small for the rest of him, probably due to the angle from which she was viewing him.

'Can I help you with somethin'?' he asked.

'I'm looking for Mulcahy's,' Marcy said.

'It would appear you've found it. Don't think it opens until ten.'

'Ten?' Marcy repeated, glancing at her watch: seven o'clock. 'Are you sure?' she asked the man, but he had already left.

She returned to street level and turned north toward Kyrl's Quay, a smattering of raindrops falling on her head and shoulders.

The water in the North Channel of the river Lee was dark and moving swiftly. Marcy hurried along beside it until she found a pleasant-looking pub, the sound of traditional Irish music beckoning her inside. She opened the door and found herself in a crowded room. There was a podium at the front where three young men were finishing up a song. 'We'll just take a wee break and be back with you in a quarter hour,' the leader of the band said.

Marcy's eyes searched the room for an empty table.

'Lookin' for me?' a man asked, pushing a chair towards her.

Marcy smiled at the man, who was probably in his early forties, and balding. 'Thank you, but I wouldn't want to put you out.'

The man motioned for her to sit down. 'What are you drinkin'?'

What the hell, Marcy decided, sitting down. 'A beer, maybe?'

'Two Beamishes,' the man shouted at the waitress. 'Name's Kieran.' He extended his hand across the table.

'Marcy.' She shook his hand.

'Where you from, Marcy?' he asked.

'I'm from Toronto. You're from Cork, I take it.'

'Lived here all my life. Best city in the world.'

'It's lovely.'

'All the lovelier since you got here.' Brown eyes twinkled.

Marcy laughed. 'Someone's been kissing the Blarney Stone.'

'Every chance I get. You hungry?' he asked, when the waitress appeared with their beers.

'I'd love a sandwich.'

'Two ham and cheese sandwiches,' Kieran told the waitress.

'Thank you,' Marcy said. 'That's really very kind of you.' She absent-mindedly patted her rain-damp hair.

'A euro for your thoughts,' Kieran said playfully.

Marcy smiled. 'Do you know a place called Mulcahy's?' she asked.

'Over on Cornmarket? It's not your kind of place, that's for sure. It's a wee bit raunchy. Loud music, drugs, loose women. Or so I'm told.' He laughed. 'What makes you ask about Mulcahy's?'

'Someone suggested it was a place young people liked to gather,' she explained. Then, 'I'm looking for my daughter.' She quickly reached inside her handbag and withdrew her daughter's photograph. 'Do you know her, by any chance?'

Kieran studied the photo. He looked back at Marcy, his eyes burrowing deep into hers. 'I might,' he said.

Marcy felt her heartbeat quicken.

'Mind my askin' why you're lookin' for her?'

'It's a long story. Please . . . you know her?'

'I love long stories,' he said stubbornly.

Marcy chugged back a mouthful of beer, feeling her eyes sting. 'My daughter and I haven't spoken in several years,' she told him. 'I heard she was in Cork. Please, if you know anything . . . I need to see her.'

'What'd you say her name was?'

'I didn't. Devon,' she added quickly, not wanting to antagonise him. 'But she might be calling herself Audrey.'

'Audrey, yes.' He tapped the photograph with the index finger of his right hand. 'That's her, all right. Lovely girl, she is. Quiet, respectful, always a smile and a kind word.'

'You've talked to her?'

'Just "Nice day". That sort of thing.'

Marcy's eyes welled up with tears. 'How do you know her?'

'She works for the old lady who lives across the street from me mum. I've seen her a few times when I go to visit.'

Was it possible that after all her frantic efforts, a chance run-in with a stranger in a pub was going to lead her to her daughter? 'What sort of work does she do?'

'She's like a companion. Does Mrs Crocker's grocery shoppin', her laundry. In exchange, she gets a place to stay, rent-free.'

'Where does Mrs Crocker live?'

'Over in Montenotte, up in the Cork hills,' Kieran said.

Marcy reached into her handbag for her cell phone. 'If you'd give me Mrs Crocker's exact address, I'll call a cab . . .'

Kieran downed the last of his beer. 'No need,' he said, pushing himself away from the table. 'Come on. I'll take you there.'

NINE

'I don't know this part of the city,' Marcy said, staring out of the car window through the light rain that fell. It felt as if they'd been driving for hours, although less than twenty minutes had passed since they'd left the pub.

'Almost there,' Kieran said, as he continued into the Cork hills.

Marcy tried to control her excitement. She glanced at Kieran, marvelling at his willingness to put himself out for her. She brushed aside a twinge of doubt. Was it the kindness of strangers or something else entirely? *I should have taken a cab*, Marcy thought, admonishing herself.

Minutes later, they pulled into the driveway of a small, semidetached house. 'That's Mrs Crocker's place over there.' Kieran pointed to a similar house directly across the street, as they got out of the car.

'It looks awfully dark.'

'Probably at the movies. Audrey takes her at least twice a week. Let's have a look, shall we?' He took her elbow and guided her across the street towards Mrs Crocker's.

Please let her be home, Marcy prayed.

Kieran knocked on the door. After several seconds, it became obvious that her prayers would go unanswered.

'Should be back soon,' Kieran said, with assurance. 'Come on. You're gettin' soaked. We can wait over at me mum's.'

'She won't mind?' Marcy asked as they recrossed the street.

Kieran removed a key from his pocket and opened the front door. 'Not at all,' he said, flipping on the light. 'Mum?' he called as he led Marcy into the living room. No answer. 'Probably gone to the movies with Mrs Crocker and Audrey. You fancy another beer?'

Marcy looked around the room, which was comfortably furnished with an overstuffed sofa and matching chair. A large-screen TV took up most of the opposite wall. 'I don't think so, no.'

'Oh, come on,' he said, walking into the tiny kitchen and returning with a beer in each hand. 'It'll take the chill off.'

Before she could refuse, he popped the caps off the bottles and handed her one. Then he plopped down on the sofa, patting the cushion beside him. 'Sit down, luv. Take a load off.'

'I'm too anxious,' she told him honestly, recognising that her unease had little to do with seeing Devon again and everything to do with her growing apprehension at the fact that she was in the middle of nowhere, in a strange house with a man she barely knew. She walked to the window. How stupid could she be? 'This isn't your mother's house, is it?' she said, carefully.

He laughed. 'Guess you got me there.'

'Whose house is it?'

'It's mine,' he admitted sheepishly, as if he were a small boy who'd been caught with his hand in the cookie jar.

It was then that Marcy noticed a silver-framed photograph. It was of an attractive, middle-aged woman with a square jaw and short brown hair, her arms wrapped around two young boys, both wearing Kieran's vaguely guilty grin. 'I take it this is your wife and sons.'

'Charles and Walter,' he said easily.

'You have a very handsome family. Where are they?'

'In Kilkenny for the week, havin' a bit of a holiday.'

'Is there really a Mrs Crocker who lives across the street?'

Kieran rose to his feet, crossing towards her in two steps. 'Of course there's a Mrs Crocker. She's in Kilkenny with me wife.'

'And Audrey?' Marcy asked, already knowing the answer.

'Can't say I've had the pleasure.'

'So this whole thing was a ruse to get me up here.'

His response was to lean forward, kiss the side of Marcy's neck.

'You didn't recognise my daughter's picture.'

His lips moved to the side of her mouth. 'Ah, come on, darlin'. You looked like you could use a little fun.' One hand crawled underneath her sweater; the other slid toward her buttocks.

Marcy brought her bottle of beer crashing down against his skull.

Kieran staggered back, blood dripping from the gash at the side of his head. 'What the . . .'

'If you touch me again, I'll kill you,' Marcy heard herself say.

'Are you crazy? What—you think I'm gonna force you? Need I remind you that you came here of your own accord?'

'I want to go home.'

'There's the door, you crazy bitch.'

'How am I supposed to get back to the city?'

'Try flyin' there on your broomstick, why don't you? Hell, my wife's gonna have a right fit when she sees this mess.'

Marcy bolted towards the front door, opening it and quickly fleeing into the night, outraged cries of 'Crazy bitch' pursuing her down the twisting curves of the rain-soaked streets.

More than an hour later, the sharp slope of St Patrick's Hill mercifully popping into view, she heard a car pull up beside her. A door opened, blocking her path, forcing her to a stop. A man got out, his firm hand on her arm preventing her from continuing.

'Excuse me, ma'am,' the garda said. 'I think you need to come with me.'

IT WAS ALMOST ELEVEN O'CLOCK by the time Marcy made it back to the city. She was exhausted; her head ached. 'When did I get this stupid?' she asked out loud.

You were always naive, she heard Judith say.

The young garda had seemed genuinely concerned with her welfare. Was there a problem? he had asked. Was she hurt? Had she been accosted? What was she doing wandering the streets of Cork alone? He had made her sit in the front seat of his car, asking politely whether he could see her passport, examining it closely. Then a call had come in about a suspected break-in in the area.

'You go,' she had told him. 'I'll be fine.'

Still, he had hesitated. 'You'll go straight back to your hotel?'

'I swear,' she said.

She approached the steep incline of St Patrick's Hill thinking she had never been so happy to see a bridge in her life. Grogan's House was only blocks away, and Marcy fought the almost unbearable urge to head toward it, continuing down St Patrick's Street towards Cornmarket instead.

What am I doing now? she wondered. *I really am crazy.*

Crazy bitch, she heard Kieran shout from somewhere behind her.

This is *crazy,* Judith said after him. *You have to accept reality. The reality is that Devon is dead.*

Judith had always been so sure Devon had killed herself. Was that why Marcy had never shown her Devon's letter?

'Studies have shown that suicide frequently runs in families, that one suicide validates another,' Peter had pronounced.

'You think that just because my mother killed herself, that means our daughter did, too?'

'She paddled her canoe into the bay in the middle of October. She wasn't wearing a life jacket. She was depressed . . .'

Why hadn't she shown Peter the letter?

She had told herself that it had been addressed to her and her alone. 'MOMMY,' Devon had written across its clean surface. But she had always known such rationalisations were a lie. Peter was her husband. He had deserved to see what Devon had written. Not sharing Devon's letter with him had been the final nail in the coffin their marriage had become.

'Excuse me,' a voice said.

'What?' Marcy turned to see a couple of teenagers dressed in black, tattoos covering the boy's neck, assorted piercings disturbing his girl-friend's complexion.

'You're blockin' the stairway,' the boy said.

'Oh, sorry.' Marcy stepped aside. It was only then she noticed the metal hand-painted sign that said MULCAHY'S.

The basement door opened to admit the couple, and loud music shot towards the street. Cigarette smoke blasted from the room, the smell of marijuana teasing Marcy's nostrils. How many nights had Devon come home, that same smell clinging to her clothes?

Is she here? Marcy wondered. Was her daughter somewhere in that dark, smoky basement right now? It was just the sort of place Devon would be drawn to. Marcy started down the steps and pushed open the heavy steel door.

It took a few seconds for her eyes to adjust to the almost total blackness. There had to be at least a hundred people crowded into a space that comfortably held maybe forty. In the corner, a DJ was spinning records. Everywhere people were dancing to the beat of the music.

Then she saw them. They were standing against the back wall. The boy was whispering something in the girl's ear, and she was giggling, her eyes lifting towards his, then returning to the floor.

Marcy felt her heartbeat quicken as she skirted the wall, her head down, trying not to draw any attention to herself. She was almost beside them when she heard the boy shout towards his companion, 'I said, what do you think of all this?'

Marcy was suddenly grateful for the noisy crowd because it meant the boy had to yell to be heard.

'Never seen anything like it,' the girl shouted back.

'So, Shannon, are you glad you came?'

'You know I am.'

'I know *I'm* glad,' Jax said.

Shannon lowered her head, her long hair falling across her thin nose. Jax's hand moved to tuck the hair behind her ear. Marcy's gold earring glinted at her through the darkness.

Marcy gasped. So it had been Jax who'd broken into her hotel room. Why? Stealing her earrings could only have been an afterthought, an opportunity he chose not to waste. What else had he been hoping to find? The photos? Devon's letter? Or had the trashing of her room been a warning, a way of telling her to back off, leave town, leave her daughter alone?

'I thought Audrey was joinin' us,' she heard Shannon say.

'Guess she changed her mind.'

Marcy felt her eyes sting with tears. Audrey was supposed to be there, but she had changed her mind. Once again she had come so close.

'Do you think she's got a fella?' Shannon asked.

'Audrey's always got a fella,' was Jax's terse reply.

'Do you know who he is?'

'Nah. I think he's older. She keeps talkin' about how mature he is. Anyway, you're here. That's all I care about.'

Even in the dark, Marcy could see Shannon blush.

'It was a lucky thing you called when you did,' Shannon said. 'Tomorrow you'd 'a' missed me.'

'Are you goin' somewhere then?'

'Over to Kinsale for a few days. Mrs O'Connor's got an aunt who's not well.'

'So when will you be back?'

'Sunday night.'

'Oh, not so long, then. Only three days. Still, I'll miss you.'

'You will not. You're just sayin' that.'

'It's the truth. I like you a lot. You think I'd have given you those earrings if I didn't?'

An involuntary cry escaped Marcy's lips. Jax's head twisted in her direction. Was it possible he had heard her, despite all the noise? Marcy brought her hand up to hide her face.

'Hold on a minute,' Jax said.

'What is it?'

Oh, no, thought Marcy. Had he seen her? What was he going to do? She had to get out of there. Except she couldn't move. She was trapped between dozens of sweating, undulating bodies. She felt a scream rise in her throat and it took her a few seconds to realise that he wasn't moving towards her; that he was, in fact, taking off in the opposite direction.

'Jax, wait. Where you goin'?' Shannon called after him.

'Be right back,' he yelled, fighting his way towards the door.

Marcy began worming her way through the wall of revellers until she reached the door and escaped into the cold night air.

Where did he go? she wondered, running up the steps and stopping suddenly, realising how exposed she was.

She heard him before she saw him, his voice coming from around the side of the building. 'I'm tellin' you,' he was saying, 'that's what she just said, OK?'

Marcy tiptoed closer.

'Fine, I'll go over the whole thing from the beginnin',' he said, and Marcy realised he was talking on his cell phone. 'We're at Mulcahy's . . . Yes, I gave her the earrings . . . Yes, she loved 'em. Just like you said she would. So I've got the stupid girl eatin' out of the palm of me hand. Everything's movin' accordin' to plan. I'm startin' to feel like James Bond. Hey, we should call this Operation Babycakes.' He laughed. 'Anyway, that's when she lowers the boom. Says they're goin' away for a few days. Tomorrow until bloody Sunday. The whole bleedin' family. Apparently Mrs O'Connor's got a sick aunt.'

He paused to catch his breath, allowing Marcy a few seconds to try to make sense of what she had just heard. *I'm startin' to feel like James Bond. Hey, we should call this Operation Babycakes.* What were they planning? What had her daughter got herself into now?

'Yeah, I know it's only three days, but I can already taste that money . . .' Marcy's cell phone suddenly began ringing in her handbag. She frantically tried to muzzle the sound. Had Jax heard it? She ducked inside the doorway of a nearby shop. Her phone continued to ring, the sound fainter now. Would Jax find her?

A sudden burst of noise: the angry sound of Mick Jagger directing someone to get off his cloud, a girl's voice rising above everything else: 'Jax, are you out here?'

'Comin', luv,' he answered, immediately.

Marcy heard heavy footsteps descending the steps.

'I was worried about you. Is everything all right?' Shannon asked, as the door closed behind them.

Marcy extricated her cell phone from her handbag. It had stopped ringing. She decided it must have been Liam calling to check on her. Should she call him back? And tell him what? That her amateur sleuthing had almost gotten her raped? That she had stumbled upon Jax with Shannon. That she may have uncovered some possibly nefarious plot that may involve her daughter?

Shielding her head from a fresh onslaught of raindrops, she began the long walk back to her hotel.

SHE DREAMED OF CAKE. Vanilla cake with rich vanilla icing. The kind of cake that Devon always requested for her birthday. 'She has such a sweet tooth,' Marcy explained to the guests around the table.

'Sweets for the sweet,' Shannon said, blushing.

'Sugar and spice and everything nice,' Judith added.

'That's what little girls are made of,' Jax said, entering the room, a crying baby in his arms.

'Oh, let me see,' Devon gushed, running towards them.

'Take her.' Jax transferred the baby to Devon's eager arms.

And suddenly Marcy and Liam were strolling down the cobbled roads of Youghal. 'Where are we going?' she asked him.

'Haven't you heard? Claire and Audrey have opened a bakery. They make the best cakes in all of Ireland,' he said.

Somewhere in the distance, a baby started crying. Marcy entered a clearing, seeing Georgian Bay stretched out before her, an empty canoe drifting in its rough waters. Devon was sitting on a blanket at the water's edge, Shannon beside her, a baby crying in her arms.

Devon stood up, took the shrieking infant from Shannon, and walked towards Marcy. 'Here's the girl you've always wanted,' she said. Then she opened her arms and let the baby fall.

Marcy bolted upright in her bed. 'No!' she cried, frantically grabbing for the child before she hit the cold earth. Pushing her hair away from her face, she glanced at her bedside clock, amazed to see it was 8 a.m. She was so exhausted from the events of last night, she probably would have slept until noon had her nightmare not jolted her awake. 'Stupid dream,' she muttered. *Cakes and babies*, she thought, shaking her head at the ridiculousness of it all.

Babycakes.

'Operation Babycakes,' she remembered Jax saying. The O'Connor baby, Marcy realised, finding it difficult to breathe. 'Caitlin,' she whispered, her whole body growing ice cold.

What was she thinking? Was it possible?

'No,' she answered immediately. 'You're being silly and melodramatic.' Was she? What was she thinking?

I gave her the earrings. Yes, she loved 'em. Just like you said she would.

Like who said?

Audrey? Marcy thought.

Had Jax been talking to her daughter? Were he and Devon involved in some crazy scheme regarding the O'Connor baby? And did that crazy scheme include winning over Shannon, the baby's naive nanny?

Stupid girl, Jax had called her. Hardly the words of an infatuated suitor. *I can already taste that money.* Was it possible that there was a plan to kidnap Caitlin O'Connor and hold her for ransom?

Marcy jumped out of bed and pulled on the same clothes she had been wearing the day before. No time for a shower. No time to go shopping. No time to eat breakfast. No time for anything except finding her daughter and stopping this insanity once and for all. She might not know where to find Devon, but Marcy knew where the O'Connors lived. She would go there and warn them that their baby was in danger. Hopefully they hadn't left for Kinsale yet.

What would Shannon say? Would she support Marcy's story, risk incurring Mrs O'Connor's wrath by admitting the truth of where she had been and with whom? Or would she deny it, afraid of losing her job? Would she laugh derisively and dismiss Marcy's ravings as those of a seriously deranged individual who'd been pestering her for days, an obviously deluded and unbalanced woman who was well-known to the local gardai?

Which was exactly why she couldn't call officers Murphy, Donnelly and Sweeny, Marcy understood. What could she tell them, after all?

It didn't even matter if the O'Connors believed her, she decided. By warning them, they would be more vigilant regarding their daughter, and Marcy would put an end to this harebrained scheme that was sure to bring disaster down on the heads of all those involved. She would finally succeed where she had failed so often: in protecting her daughter from herself.

Assuming Devon was involved.

Was she?

MARCY DECIDED to take a taxi—a mistake, she decided, once she was in the cab's backseat, as the traffic was especially awful. Finally, the cabbie stopped the car. 'Here we are, one seventeen Adelaide Road.'

Marcy gave him a generous tip along with the fare. Then she ran up the O'Connors' front walk, rang the bell and pounded on the black double doors. 'Please be home,' she prayed.

But no one was there.

'Damn it!' Marcy exclaimed, walking round to the side of the house, knowing there was little point in knocking on the side door but doing it anyway. Now what was she supposed to do?

She returned to the front of the house. She saw curtains move in the window of the house across the road as her cell phone started ringing. She retrieved it from her handbag and flipped it open.

'Where are you?' Liam asked, before she had time to say hello.

Marcy told him.

'What?' he barked. 'What are you doing over there?'

Marcy told him about her trip to Mulcahy's, about seeing Jax with Shannon, about overhearing his phone conversation and her subsequent suspicions.

'Wait a minute,' he interrupted. 'You're saying you think there's a plot to kidnap the O'Connors' baby?'

'You think I'm crazy,' Marcy said.

He surprised her by saying, 'I think you should call the gardai.'

'Devon might be involved. I don't want to get her in trouble.'

'What if something happens to the O'Connor baby? You'll never forgive yourself.'

'I know,' Marcy said. 'I just don't know if I can.'

She heard the sound of sirens in the distance getting louder, drawing nearer. A garda car tore up the street and pulled to a stop in front of the O'Connors' driveway. She watched as the nosy neighbour emerged from her house and conferred with one of the gardai, while another garda walked purposefully towards Marcy.

'Call the gardai,' Liam said.

'That won't be necessary,' she answered.

TEN

'Really, Mrs Taggart,' Christopher Murphy said, leaning back in the chair behind his desk. 'We have to stop meeting this way.'

Marcy smiled, appreciating the senior garda's attempt at levity. 'I'm truly sorry for all the trouble I've caused,' Marcy told him. 'But as far as I know, I haven't broken any laws.'

'I think a good case might be made for being a public nuisance. This is your third visit to this station in as many days,' he said. 'Not to mention the little stunt you pulled last night.'

'The stunt?' Had that creep Kieran filed a formal complaint?

'I understand you spent some quality time with one of our boys in the front seat of his patrol car,' Murphy said.

Marcy felt her shoulders slump. 'You know about that.'

'Marcy Taggart, Canadian citizen, found wandering the Cork hills at around ten p.m.,' he recited, 'likely inebriated . . .'

'I was not drunk! I just needed some air.'

'At ten at night? In the rain? Far from your hotel?' Murphy shook his head. 'Is that what you were doing this morning? Getting some air?' Another shake of his head. 'Mrs Leary said it wasn't the first time she caught you snoopin' around the O'Connors' house.'

'I wasn't "snoopin"',' Marcy replied. 'If anybody's a snoop, it's that damn Mrs Leary.'

'She saw you peeking in at her neighbour's windows.'

'I was just trying to see if the O'Connors were still home.'

Murphy nodded. 'The fact that nobody answered when you knocked or rang their bell wasn't enough of a clue?'

'I already told the other officers—'

'You were trying to warn them,' the garda stated as the door to his office opened and Officer Sweeny stepped inside. He whispered something in Murphy's ear. Murphy nodded, and Sweeny left the room with a smile in Colleen Donnelly's direction. The female garda was standing quietly in a far corner of the room.

'That there's a plot afoot to kidnap their baby.'

'That's right,' Marcy said.

'And you think this because . . .'

Marcy sighed, understanding the drill. She wasn't going to get out of there until she went over every last detail of her story again.

'I overheard a phone conversation outside Mulcahy's.'

'At Mulcahy's, you just happened to see the lad you say ran you down with his bicycle some days ago. He was with Shannon, the girl you argued with at Grogan's House the other day. And you overheard them plotting to kidnap—'

'No,' Marcy interrupted, understanding that this was no careless mistake on his part. 'I overheard Jax on his cell phone.'

'When you followed him outside,' Murphy stated.

'Yes.'

'And he was talking about kidnapping the O'Connor baby?'

'Not exactly. He said that everything had been moving according to plan. He made a joke about "Operation Babycakes"—'

'*Operation Babycakes?*' the garda repeated incredulously. 'And you naturally assumed he was referring to the O'Connor baby.'

Marcy decided to ignore his sarcasm. 'Not right away. I had no idea what he was talking about at the time.'

'When did you figure it out?'

Marcy hesitated. This was the part she had been dreading. 'I had a dream.' She admitted it reluctantly, already picturing the bemused looks of condescension on the faces of the two gardai.

'So this epiphany came to you in a dream?'

'The dream just helped me put the pieces together.'

'Perhaps you'd be good enough to explain how.'

'Jax said that everything had been moving according to plan,' Marcy repeated, her voice rising. 'But that now everything was going to have to be delayed because the O'Connors were going away for a few days, and he was upset because he could already taste the money.'

'The money they were going to collect as ransom?'

'Yes.'

'Did he actually ever use the word "ransom"?'

Marcy shook her head. 'No.'

'If you thought there was a plot to kidnap the O'Connor baby,' Murphy asked logically, 'why didn't you call us?'

Marcy took a deep breath. 'Because I was afraid that Devon might be involved. I didn't want to get her in trouble.'

'So you rushed to the O'Connor's house to warn them?' Murphy asked, his tone indicating that he already knew the answer.

'Not right away, no. I needed time to figure things out. Believe me, I know how crazy this must sound,' Marcy said.

'It does sound a trifle far-fetched,' Colleen Donnelly said.

Christopher Murphy came around the front of his desk. 'Mrs Taggart, I don't doubt that you believe everything you've told us. I also believe your intentions are honourable and pure.'

'It's just that you don't think what I'm saying has any merit,' Marcy said.

'Can you look at it from our perspective?' Murphy took a deep breath before continuing. 'You've suffered two terrible losses in as many years: your daughter was presumed drowned, and your husband left you. You're alone in a strange country; your imagination is working overtime. You've been picked up for wandering the streets; you've been sleeping with virtual strangers—'

'Excuse me?'

'I'm sorry. I don't mean to sound judgmental. Of course, you're free to sleep with whomever you like.'

'I've slept with exactly two men in the last quarter of a century,' Marcy said. 'My husband and—'

'A man you met on a bus,' Murphy finished. 'We spoke to Vic Sorvino. We intercepted him at the airport yesterday afternoon as he was about to board a plane for Rome. He denied trashing your hotel room; said that when he left, everything was in order.'

'Poor Vic.' Of course he had had nothing to do with the trashing of her hotel room. It had been Jax.

'And Liam Flaherty?' Colleen Donnelly asked.

'What *is* your relationship with Mr Flaherty?' Murphy asked.

'He's a friend who's been helping me look for Devon.'

'He's waiting in the next room.'

'What?'

'He showed up about half an hour ago, concerned about you.'

'He begged me to call you,' Marcy told them.

'Should have listened to him.'

About a lot of things, she thought.

'If you'll excuse me a minute,' Murphy said, leaving the room.

Marcy sat back in her chair and closed her eyes. She didn't open them again until she heard the door open and Christopher Murphy announce she was free to go.

'WHAT TIME IS IT?' Marcy asked Liam, shielding her eyes from an unexpected burst of sunlight as they exited the garda station.

'A little before noon.'

'What? How is that possible?'

'You've been at the station all morning.'

Marcy shook her head. Half a day gone already. Her daughter no closer to being found. 'They think I'm crazy,' she said morosely.

'Yeah,' Liam said with a smile. 'I think they might.' He raised his hand to flag down a passing cab. 'Hayfield Manor Hotel,' he told the driver as they climbed into the back seat.

'Thanks for coming down.'

'No thanks necessary.'

She shook her head and sighed. 'I've lost all credibility as far as the police are concerned.'

Liam nodded. 'I think that last bit about the plan to kidnap the O'Connor baby might have tipped the scales.'

'I guess it sounded pretty weird. So what do I do now?'

'*You* do nothin'. Unless you want them to lock you up.'

'But what if I'm right? What if something happens . . .'

'Then it happens. They certainly can't say they weren't warned.'

'Do you think they'll at least talk to the O'Connors?'

Liam shrugged. 'Don't think it's high on their list of priorities.'

'Would *you* talk to them?' Marcy asked, after a moment's pause.

'Me?'

'*Somebody* has to warn them.' Marcy saw the look of resignation that flitted across Liam's wondrous green eyes, the look that told her she might have lost her credibility with him, too. 'Unless, of course, you don't believe me . . .'

'I believe you saw your daughter. But to go from that to thinking she might be involved in some kind of plot . . .'

'Kind of tipped the scales for you, too, did it?' Marcy asked.

Liam sighed. 'These are the facts. You overheard a one-sided conversation outside a noisy club, and then you had a dream . . .'

'Which explained everything,' she said vehemently, then stopped. He was right. Just as Christopher Murphy was right. And Judith. And Peter. Hell, everyone was right. She really *was* crazy.

'OK, look,' Liam was saying. 'If it'll make you feel better, I'll talk to the O'Connors. As soon as they get back.'

'I'll go with you,' Marcy said eagerly.

'No. You'll stay put. Do you understand? You've done quite enough. You won't budge from your hotel room. Are we agreed?'

'Agreed,' Marcy said reluctantly, then she looked down at her sweater. 'I've been wearing the same clothes for two days now. I really should stop and pick up some new things,' she said, realising they'd just passed the

Merchant's Quay Shopping Centre. 'Can you stop here?' she asked, tapping the driver on his shoulder.

'Marcy, for God's sake, what are you doing?' Liam asked as she opened the door and jumped out of the cab. 'Marcy, wait!'

'I'm fine, Liam. Really,' she called back at him. 'I just need some new clothes,' she added, watching as he scrambled to pay the driver. 'You don't have to babysit me,' she told him when he finally caught up with her inside the entrance to Marks and Spencer.

'Actually, I promised the gardai I'd keep an eye on you,' Liam said sheepishly. 'It was the only way they'd agree to your release.'

'Oh.'

'Is it so awful,' he asked, 'havin' me around?'

Marcy studied his beautifully chiselled face, losing herself momentarily in the unabashed intensity of his gaze. 'Why are you so nice to me?'

'I think you already know the answer to that,' he said, tilting his head, his lips moving slowly towards hers.

Marcy realised he was going to kiss her again: in the middle of the day, a beautiful young man fifteen years her junior was going to kiss her. And this time she was going to kiss him back.

'Hold on a minute,' Liam said, his soft, warm breath teasing her newly closed eyes.

She opened her eyes to see him moving towards the tall glass doors of the entrance to the shop. *What was he doing?* 'What is it?'

'I thought I saw that man you were with at your hotel . . .'

'Vic Sorvino?' Marcy pushed open the heavy door, her eyes pummelling their way through the crowded flock of afternoon shoppers. 'You saw Vic?'

Liam backtracked. 'I don't know for sure it was him.'

Was it possible Vic was still in Ireland? And if he *was,* in fact, in the Merchant's Quay Shopping Centre, then *why*?

'I don't see him,' Liam said, as Marcy's eyes swept the mall.

Marcy agreed seconds later. 'No.' She took a series of deep breaths in an effort to control the too-rapid thumping of her heart.

'Are you all right?' Liam asked. 'You look a little pale.'

'I really need to find some new clothes,' Marcy heard herself say, her voice coming from somewhere outside her body.

Twenty minutes later she approached the sales counter, her arms loaded with two pairs of trousers—one black, one khaki; two T-shirts—one white and one beige; a blue-and-white-striped cotton blouse; a navy pea jacket; some socks and underwear; and a pair of flannel pyjamas.

Marcy handed over her credit card to be swiped.

'There seems to be a problem with your card,' the shop assistant said seconds later. 'It's not going through.'

'That's impossible. Try again,' said Marcy.

The girl ran the card through again. 'It's not acceptin' it. Sorry.'

'I don't understand,' Marcy mumbled.

'Is it possible you forgot to pay your bill?' Liam asked.

'No. Peter takes care of that,' she said, her knees growing weak.

'Here.' Liam handed his card to the sales assistant. 'Use this.'

'No,' Marcy protested. 'I can't ask you to do that.'

'You'll pay me back as soon as you get this straightened out.'

Get what straightened out? Marcy wondered. *My credit? My daughter? My life?* 'I don't understand,' she muttered. Except she did understand. Peter, alarmed by her recent actions, had cut off her access to her credit cards. The room began spinning. In the next instant, her knees gave out.

The last thing she saw before she fainted was Liam reaching out to grab her before she hit the floor.

SHE WOKE UP to the sound of knocking.

'Who is it?' Marcy sat up in bed. The leaded windows and apricot-coloured walls told her she was back in her room at the Hayfield. The clock on her bedside table showed it was almost 6 p.m. *Was she sick? What had happened to the day?*

'Room service,' called a voice from outside the door.

Marcy threw on the white bathrobe. *I don't remember ordering anything from room service*, she thought.

'Where would you like me to set this up?' a man asked as she opened the door, wheeling the trolley into the centre of the room.

'I think there's been a mistake,' Marcy said.

The young man quickly checked the bill. 'Room two twelve?'

'Yes, but—'

'Steak, medium rare; baked potato; mashed carrots,' he said, lifting the silver covers from their platters with a dramatic flourish. 'Plus a Caesar salad and some sticky toffee pudding for dessert.'

Marcy was about to protest, but the delicious aroma of the steak plus the very thought of sticky toffee pudding made her reconsider. 'You can set it up right here.' She indicated the side of the bed.

'If you'll just sign this chit,' he told her.

Marcy scribbled her name on the appropriate line, adding a generous tip. *Let's see Peter try to do something about that*, she thought, as the young man headed for the door.

'Enjoy your meal, and have a good night.'

Marcy closed the door after him, then plopped down on the bed and tore into her steak. When was the last time she had eaten?

When was the last time you had something to eat? she heard Liam ask, his face looming above hers. When? Where?

Marks and Spencer, she remembered, the hours she had misplaced suddenly returning to her: Adelaide Road; the garda station; Liam; the mall; losing consciousness; waking up to the sound of Liam's voice: *When was the last time you had something to eat?*

He had escorted her back to her hotel and tucked her into bed. 'Here,' he had told her, handing her a small, white pill. 'Put this under your tongue. It'll help you sleep.'

'I don't need to sleep,' she had argued, her voice weak.

'The hell you don't. Look, I have to go to work. I'll have room service send up something for dinner. In the meantime, get some rest. You don't want to be half-dead when we find your daughter, do you, now? So do us all a favour and take the damn pill.'

'I took the damn pill,' Marcy said now, remembering.

She wolfed down her steak, her baked potato and mashed carrots, her salad and her toffee pudding, then wheeled the trolley into the hall, climbed back into bed, and fell sound asleep.

LIAM'S PHONE CALL woke her up at two the next afternoon.

'Thank God,' he said when she answered on the third ring. 'When you didn't call, I started to worry you'd gone out.'

Marcy looked towards the window. It was pouring with rain outside. She pushed herself into a sitting position. 'I can't seem to keep my eyes open. What kind of pill was that you gave me last night, anyway?'

'Just a Valium.'

'I guess I was exhausted. I've wasted the whole day,' she said.

'You haven't wasted a thing. Have you not seen what's doin' out there?

It's a sign to take a day off and get some rest, Marcy.'

'Doesn't look like I have much choice,' Marcy said.

'I'll swing by on my way to work.'

'No. You don't have to do that.'

'I never do anything I *have* to,' he told her. 'Anyway, I'm off to visit my mum. She's been complainin' she don't see me enough.'

'Didn't you just say you never do anything you *have* to?'

He laughed. 'Guess the rules don't apply to mothers,' he said, before saying goodbye.

Marcy thought of her own mother as she hung up the phone. Certainly, rules of any kind had never applied to her.

She climbed out of bed and stepped into the shower, letting the hot water pour down on her head and wondering, not for the first time, what she could have done differently.

You think too much, Judith had once said, chastising her.

'Don't think,' she told herself now, stepping from the shower and wrapping herself in two luxurious bath towels, then riffling through her bag of recent purchases, selecting the khaki pants and beige T-shirt. She combed her wet hair as she reached for the phone. She read the instructions for making a long-distance call, then punched in Peter's number.

The phone rang four times before voicemail picked it up. 'Hi,' said a woman's peppy voice. 'You've reached Sarah Harris . . .'

'. . . and Peter Taggart.' Peter's voice chimed in.

Sarah continued. 'We're unavailable at the moment.'

'Oh God,' Marcy moaned, remembering that this was the weekend Peter would be visiting their son at the camp where he was a counsellor for the summer. Naturally, Sarah would be beside him, smiling and supportive— the mother Marcy should have been.

'So if you'll leave your name and number and a short message,' Peter said, 'we'll get back to you as soon as we can.'

'Have a wonderful day,' Sarah added, just before the beep.

'I'd love to,' Marcy told them. 'But it seems that someone has cut off my credit, so if the man with the nice smile and straight teeth would be kind enough to straighten this mess out as soon as possible, I'll be generous enough not to put the kibosh on this whole divorce thing as soon as *I* return. With your daughter,' she added for good measure. She slammed down the receiver.

Judith was right. It felt good not to think, to just come out swinging. For about ten seconds. And then it felt like crap.

'God, what have I done?' She groaned. Peter would hit the roof when he heard her message. No way he would restore her credit.

She quickly pressed in another number. 'Please, be home.'

Marcy pictured her sister, back from her morning workout and relaxing with a giant cup of black coffee at her kitchen table.

'Hello?' her sister said now, answering after the first ring.

'Judith, hi.'

'Marcy! Where the hell are you?'

'Still in Ireland. Judith, listen to me. I need your help.'

'All right. What can I do?'

'Peter cancelled my credit cards. I need you to send me a money order, please,' Marcy said. 'Not much. Three thousand dollars should be enough. I wouldn't ask you, but I'm running out of cash . . .'

'Three thousand dollars?' Judith repeated incredulously. 'Are you in some kind of trouble?'

'No. Honestly. Listen, I'll pay you back as soon as I get home.'

'And when will that be?'

'Soon. As soon as I find Devon,' Marcy said, picturing her sister's head drop towards her chest in dismay.

'You said you'd come to terms with that. You told me—'

'She was happy, wasn't she?' Marcy said. 'I mean, it wasn't all misery. There were times when Devon was happy. Weren't there?'

Judith's voice instantly softened. 'Of course there were.'

Marcy thought of the weeks preceding Devon's disappearance, times when her daughter had seemed not only happy but almost serene. Had she already solidified her plans to flee the country? Of course, Judith would argue that people on the verge of suicide were often at peace once they'd decided to end their lives.

'Will you or will you not send me the money?' Marcy pleaded.

'Where do you want it sent?' Judith asked, after a pause.

'Send it to the Hayfield Manor Hotel in Cork.' Marcy grabbed the notepad beside the phone and read Judith the hotel's address.

'I'll go to the bank tomorrow,' Judith said. 'You should have it by Tuesday. Marcy, please—'

'Thank you. I have to go,' Marcy said, before hanging up. She sat for several minutes in silence, her mind blank. Then, accompanied by her new mantra—*Don't think; don't think*—she jumped up, grabbed her new pea jacket and handbag, and headed out of the door.

SHE SAW HIM as soon as she reached the lobby. He was standing, half-hidden, behind a pillar near the grand staircase, and she might have missed him had she not stopped to ask the concierge whether she might borrow an umbrella.

She stopped directly in front of him. 'What are you doing here?' she asked without preamble.

Vic Sorvino raised his eyes to hers, clearly embarrassed at having been discovered. 'Marcy,' he said, the sound of her name on his lips causing her to go immediately weak in the knees.

What is the matter with me, for God's sake? she wondered impatiently. 'What are you doing here?' she asked again.

Vic suddenly looked as confused as she felt. 'I don't know.'

'I don't understand.'

'Neither do I.'

They stood this way for several seconds, Marcy unable to turn away. It wasn't that he was all that much to look at. Liam was far more handsome. There was just something about Vic. Maybe it was the intensity of his blue eyes, the way they latched on to her own, burning into the secrets in her brain. Was that why she was being mean to him? Because she knew that once he *really* saw her, he would run screaming for the nearest exit? As had almost everyone she had ever loved. Her mother. Peter. Devon.

'Have you been following me?' she said. 'Was that you I saw yesterday at the mall?'

'Maybe we should sit down.' He led her towards a nearby sofa, sinking into a velvet seat beside her, taking her hand in his.

'Was that you or not?' she asked again.

'Yes.'

She quickly brought her hand back to her lap. 'Why?'

He shook his head, as if he himself didn't quite believe what he was about to say. 'After I was questioned by the gardai regarding the break-in at your hotel room, I decided to stick around for a few days. I asked Detective Murphy to keep me informed.' Vic shook his head again. 'He called me yesterday, said you were being brought to the station. I went right over, hoping to get a chance to talk to you, convince you that I had nothing to do with the trashing of your room—'

'I never believed it was you,' Marcy said, interrupting.

'Well, thank you for that, anyway.'

'Nobody told me you were there.'

'It doesn't matter,' he continued. 'You left with that young man from the pub, and I decided to follow you. Don't ask me why. I guess I was worried about you. Somebody breaks into your hotel room and trashes your things, that's cause for concern.'

'But not *your* concern.'

Vic sat very still. Then he took a deep breath. 'No, I guess not.' A wry smile tugged at the corners of his mouth. 'OK. I admit I'm dense about these things, but even I see the light eventually.' He rose to his feet. 'I'm sorry. I won't pester you again.'

Vic's eyes wandered towards the lobby's front entrance.

'What is it?' Marcy asked.

'Looks like you have a visitor,' Vic said.

She followed the direction of his gaze to see Liam walk through the front doors, shaking the rain from his shoulders. 'Liam,' she stated, rushing towards him. 'What are you doing here? I thought you were going to see your mother.'

'Decided to come see you first,' he said. Then he kissed her full on the mouth. 'I've got news.'

'What kind of news?' Marcy asked, feeling the imprint of his lips on hers. She glanced towards Vic, knowing he had felt it, too.

But Vic was gone.

ELEVEN

It was almost six in the morning when Marcy finally abandoned the idea of sleep. She had been up all night, tossing and turning, trying to sort through the events of the last twenty-four hours. *Hell, why stop there? How about the last twenty-four years?*

'I've got news,' Liam had announced.

'What kind of news?'

'I drove by the O'Connor house. Don't ask me why.'

'Why?' Marcy asked now, sitting up in bed and staring at the window, her arms wrapped around her bent knees. Sometime in the last few hours, the rain had finally stopped. Was that a sign?

You can stop worrying about me, Devon whispered from the early morning mist outside the window. *I'm fine, Mommy. I'm happy.*

'The lights in the house were all on,' Liam had told her yesterday.

We haven't been happy in such a long time, Peter had said.

'They must have come home early.'

I'm fine, Mommy. I'm happy.

'They're home?'

'So I decided, what the hell,' Liam said. 'I'll just phone them.'

'You phoned the O'Connors? What did you say to them?'

'Well, it was Shannon who answered the phone,' Liam went on. 'Which was perfect. I explained who I was and assured her I wasn't trying to get her in any trouble but that it was very important she listen to me.'

'What did she say?'

'She didn't say anything. She just listened.'

Sit down, girls, the school principal told Marcy and her sister, ushering them inside his brightly lit office. *I'm afraid I have some very bad news.*

'And what did you say?'

'That I knew she'd been out with Jax on Friday night and that he'd given her a pair of earrings—earrings he'd stolen from your hotel room. She got all flustered, said she'd had no idea the earrings had been stolen. She begged me not to go to the gardai.'

Aren't you going to answer that, Marcy?

'I told her that I had good reason to suspect that Jax and Audrey were using her to get to the O'Connor baby . . .'

We've found an overturned canoe . . .

'My God, how did she react to that?'

'Well, naturally, she got very upset . . .'

Has your daughter been depressed lately?

'What did she say?'

'That she was sure I was mistaken. Somehow I managed to convince her. At any rate, she agreed to help us.'

'What?'

'Shannon has agreed to help us find your daughter,' Liam had said, the memory temporarily silencing the other voices in Marcy's head.

'How?' Marcy asked.

'By talking to Audrey, setting up a meeting . . . Except it won't be Shannon who goes to meet her . . .'

'It'll be me,' Marcy had whispered.

'It'll be you,' he repeated.

Marcy pushed herself out of bed now, and walked to the window.

'How soon?' Marcy recalled asking Liam.

'Could be as early as tomorrow.'

Today, Marcy realised, shivering despite her warm pyjamas.

Liam had laughed. 'I told you that things have a way of working out in the end.'

'It's not the end,' she said out loud now.

Devon hadn't drowned.

So this is it? Marcy had asked her husband of almost twenty-five years. *You're really leaving?*

It's better this way, Marcy. You know it is. We'll just end up hating each other if I stay.

Too late, she told him. *I already hate you.*

That's too bad. I was really hoping we could be friends. We still have a son together.

I don't need to be reminded I have a son.

Are you sure of that?

Damn you, Peter, Marcy thought. *Damn you for saying that. Damn you even more for being right.*

Her mind suddenly clearing, she returned to the bed and picked up her phone, quickly punching in the number for Darren's cell phone. It was picked up after three rings, although there was no voice on the other end, only muffled sounds and heavy breathing.

'Hello?' Marcy said. 'Hello, Darren? Darren, are you there?'

'Mom?' a sleepy voice whispered.

'Oh,' Marcy said, realising she had forgotten about the time difference. 'I'm so sorry. Did I wake you?'

She pictured her son huddled beneath the covers of his narrow bed in the old log cabin he shared with the eight ten-year-old boys in his charge, and understood he was keeping his voice purposely low so as not to wake them.

'It's OK,' he told her. Then, with growing panic, 'Is something wrong? Did something happen to Dad? Did he have an accident on his way home?'

'There was no accident,' Marcy assured her son, feeling a pang of jealousy at his concern.

'I don't understand,' Darren said, the last remnants of sleep falling from his voice. 'Why are you calling?'

'I just wanted to talk to you.'

'At one in the morning?'

'I'm really sorry about that. I forgot about the time difference.'

'Time difference? What are you talking about?' Darren asked.

'I'm in Ireland.'

'You're in Ireland?' her son asked, incredulously.

Marcy heard the silent *Are you crazy?* that followed. 'I'm sorry I couldn't be there today,' she told him.

'Why? You never come to Visitors Day.'

'That's not true,' Marcy started to protest, stopping when she realised that it was true. She had always found some excuse not to make the trip to Maine: Devon wasn't feeling well; Devon had been acting up again, refusing to take her meds. 'Anyway, how's the weather up there?' she asked.

'You're asking me about the weather?'

'It rains here almost every day.'

'What the hell are you doing there?' Darren asked. 'Is Aunt Judith with you?'

'No.'

'What's going on, Mom? Are you having a nervous breakdown?'

'What? No, of course not.'

'You're not thinking of doing anything crazy, are you?'

'I'm not thinking of killing myself, Darren.'

'Are you sure? Because it kind of runs in the family.'

'Your sister didn't kill herself.'

'Mom . . .'

'Look, I really should get going; let you get back to sleep.'

There was a second's silence, then, 'Sure,' Darren said.

'I love you,' Marcy said.

'Yeah. Good night, Mom.'

Marcy hung up the phone. So her son couldn't say 'I love you,' even when he feared she was on the verge of suicide. Could she blame him? She hadn't been an active presence in his life in years. Devon had sucked up all her energy, drained her motherly juices dry. And even then, Marcy had managed to fail her. *I'm an awful mother*, she thought.

Oh, please, Judith said impatiently, appearing without warning. *Enough with the self-flagellation. You weren't an awful mother. Do I really have to remind you what a truly awful mother looks like?*

She tried her best, Marcy argued silently.

So did you.

My son hates me. My daughter is . . .

Is what? her sister asked, as clearly as if she were standing right beside her. *Your daughter is what, Marcy?*

What have I done? Marcy wondered. *What am I doing?*

Slowly, Marcy walked to the desk and retrieved her handbag. Then she sank to the carpet and opened it, pulling out the by-now tattered envelope inside and placing the pictures of Devon in a semicircle around the lone picture of her mother.

Then she withdrew the second envelope, unfolded the letter inside it, and began to read.

My beautiful Mommy, she began. *I don't expect you to understand what I'm about to do. Please don't be mad, and understand that this is not a decision I've made lightly. I know how much pain I've caused you. Believe me when I say I have no desire to cause you any more.*

Marcy pictured herself racing down the hall to Devon's bedroom right after the police had left, finding the letter addressed to her that her daughter had placed carefully on her pillow, and pocketing it before Peter could arrive and demand to see it. 'No note?' he had asked, standing ashen-faced in the doorway moments later. 'No,' she had lied, waiting until later when she was alone to open it again. Those first awful lines, lines that seemed to suggest . . .

'No,' Marcy told herself now, as she had told herself then. She forced herself to continue.

These last few years have been a mix of heartache, pain and despair. I know how hard it's been for you. I hope you know how hard it's been for me, too. Sometimes it has taken every ounce of strength I have just to put one foot in front of the other, to make it through each endless day. It's gotten to the point where even saying good morning hurts because I see the hope in your eyes that simple greeting elicits. Then I have to watch that hope die as the day drags on. Each day is worse than the day before. Nights are the worst time of all.

I feel as if I've descended into a bottomless pit of sadness, and there's no way I can climb out. The well is too deep. I feel myself sinking further and further below the surface. I now realise that giving in is the only way out.

I can honestly say I feel better, lighter, more energised than I have in years. I'm actually happy, strange as that must sound. Knowing what I have to do has freed me to remember all the good times we shared: the mornings we spent drawing at the kitchen table, the nights you spent patiently sitting beside my bed, the afternoons we spent curled up together on the sofa watching Sesame Street.

Most of all, I remember our wonderful summers at the cottage, the days spent canoeing, the walks through the woods, the barbecues at sunset. You were always so wise, so patient, so loving. How I wished I could be just like you.

Please forgive the awful things I said to you. You did everything you could. This isn't your fault.

Please know how much I love you.

And know that I'm finally at peace.

Devon.

'Oh God,' Marcy whispered, tears streaming down her face. What did it mean? That her daughter had indeed paddled her canoe into the middle of Georgian Bay and purposely disappeared beneath its frigid surface? That no matter how hard she had tried to convince herself otherwise, nothing could disguise the terrible clarity of Devon's words? Was that why she had refused to show the letter to anyone else? Because then she would have been forced to acknowledge that Devon had taken her own life?

I now realise that giving in is the only way out.

'Oh God,' she said again as the phone beside her bed began to ring. She stared at it without moving. Her daughter was dead. Marcy couldn't deny it any longer. In truth, she had known it all along.

The ringing stopped, only to start up again. Exhausted, Marcy crawled towards the phone and picked it up. 'Hello,' she said.

'Hello, Mommy,' a voice announced curtly. 'I understand you've been looking for me.'

IT WAS ALMOST NOON when Marcy left Hayfield Manor and headed towards St Fin Barre's Cathedral, a short walk away. She had spent the morning in a state of restless anticipation, going over the conversation with her daughter again and again.

'These instructions must be followed to the letter,' Devon had told her in an angry whisper. 'One slip, and I swear you'll never see me again.'

'There won't be any. I promise,' Marcy had said.

Devon had continued. 'Don't tell anyone where you're going. Don't call the police. And not a word to that sexy young boyfriend of yours.'

'What? No. He's not my . . . Devon, please . . .'

'Be in front of St Fin Barre's Cathedral at one o'clock. And remember, we're watching you.'

And then nothing. Their connection had been severed.

Marcy had showered and dressed in her new black trousers and crisp blue-and-white-striped cotton blouse, taking extra time and care with her hair and make-up, wanting to look beautiful for Devon. Now she walked purposefully towards the South Bank, pushing her way through the fog. She had decided to walk rather than take a cab, hoping some fresh air would calm her nerves.

Half an hour later, Marcy finally turned onto Bishop Street, the three giant spires of the French Gothic cathedral rising out of the morning fog. Four large tour buses were parked across the street.

Marcy's eyes shot through the crowds, searching for any sign of Devon. She saw lots of young women, but none with the features that defined her daughter. She checked her watch. It was still early. Devon had told her to be there at one, which was twenty minutes from now. Devon was rarely on time for anything. How many times had she kept Marcy waiting to drive her to school while she dawdled in the bathroom? How many dinner reservations had they forfeited because Devon couldn't decide what to wear?

Marcy understood that Devon's almost pathological tardiness had been due to her insecurity, and was part and parcel of her illness. When Marcy and her daughter were finally reunited, she would make sure Devon got the help she needed. They would find a doctor her daughter liked and trusted; one who would see to it she received the proper dosage of her medication.

Marcy checked her watch again. *Still ten minutes to go*, she thought, wondering if she was waiting in the right spot. *Be in front of St Fin Barre's Cathedral at one o'clock,* Devon had told her.

But the church was enormous, and 'in front' could mean just about anywhere. Was she supposed to stand by the entrance or to either side of the imposing wooden doors? Should she stand close to the building or a comfortable distance away? Would Devon be able to spot her in the middle of all these people?

'Excuse me,' a woman said from somewhere beside her. The accent was distinctly North American.

'Devon?' Marcy said as she turned towards the voice.

'Excuse me,' the woman repeated, 'we're trying to get through.'

'Oh, I'm sorry. I didn't realise . . .'

'Some people are just oblivious,' Marcy heard the woman's male companion mutter as they pushed past.

Marcy felt tears forming behind her eyes. 'Not yet,' she whispered. There was still more than enough time for tears.

'Don't turn around,' a familiar male voice suddenly whispered in her ear. 'Start walking.'

Marcy's breath caught instantly in her lungs. 'Where's Devon?'

'Keep walking straight. You tell anyone where you were going?'

'No. No one.'

'Good. Keep walking. Head towards Sullivan's Quay.'

'Will Devon be there? I just want to see my daughter.'

'You will.'

They walked for several minutes in silence, a thousand thoughts swirling in Marcy's brain. Where was he taking her? Were they really going to see Devon, or was this some sort of trap? A sudden pressure on Marcy's elbow directed her to stop. 'Let me have your phone,' her escort directed. Marcy reached inside her handbag and took out her cell phone. It was pulled from her hand. 'Don't think you'll be needing this any more,' he said, tossing the phone into the nearest trash bin. 'Keep walking.'

'Is all this intrigue really necessary?' Marcy asked as they approached Sullivan's Quay.

'Probably not. But it's kind of fun. Turn left at this next street.'

'Are you really taking me to Devon?'

'What else would I be doin'?' he asked.

'I don't know. What were you doing that afternoon you ran me down with your bicycle?' Marcy spun around on her heel to look the young man directly in the eye.

'Tryin' to get you to mind your own business,' Jax said with a sneer. 'Obviously, it didn't work.'

'Devon *is* my business.'

The boy shrugged. They continued walking for several more streets. 'Get in the car,' he said, stopping suddenly.

'What?'

He reached for the door handle of a small black car parked along the side of the street. 'You want to see your daughter, don't you?'

'Yes. Of course I do.'

He opened the door. 'Then get inside. She's waitin' for you.'

TWELVE

They'd been on the road for almost an hour, Marcy continuing to pepper him with questions, Jax continuing to ignore her, when he finally broke his silence. 'Stop lookin' at me,' he said.

Marcy brought her eyes to her lap. 'Sorry.' She hadn't even realised she was staring. 'Where are we going?' she asked.

'You'll see soon enough.'

Marcy sighed with frustration. *This is ridiculous*, she thought.

She leaned her head against the seat's headrest. They'd left the main road about ten minutes earlier and were now winding their way south along the coastline. Jax was concentrating hard on the road ahead. Rain was now mixing with the fog, making the visibility almost nil.

'How long have you known my daughter?' she ventured to ask, some ten minutes later.

'About a year,' he answered.

'How did you meet?'

'We met at a club called Mulcahy's,' he said.

Marcy suppressed a gasp, wondering if his reference to Mulcahy's had been deliberate, meant to provoke her.

Another lengthy silence.

'Do you mind my asking what your relationship is with my daughter?' Marcy strained to sound casual.

'Are you askin' if we're lovers?' Jax said as they passed a sign announcing they were within twenty kilometres of the town of Skibbereen. 'Is that what you're wantin' to know?'

'Are you?' Marcy asked, a sick sensation in her stomach.

'We were once. Not so much any more.'

'Why is that? Is she with someone else?'

Jax shrugged. 'You'd have to ask Audrey.'

More silence as the small car twisted along the narrow single-lane road. Where the hell was he taking her?

'The day you ran me down with your bicycle,' she said, 'you had to have been following me.'

'You were so pathetic. "Excuse me,"' he said mockingly, raising his voice, '"but do any of you recognise this picture? It's my daughter. Do you recognise her? Can you help me?"' He snickered.

'Who told you to follow me?'

He said nothing.

'Whose idea was it to trash my hotel room? Why did you do those things?' Marcy asked.

He glanced over in her direction. 'We were kinda hopin' it would be enough to convince you to go back home.'

'And stealing my earrings?'

'Oh, that one was my idea,' Jax said. 'Couldn't resist.'

'You gave them to Shannon,' Marcy stated.

'And didn't she look lovely in 'em?' He pulled the car to a sudden stop in the middle of the narrow roadway.

Marcy's first thought was that he was going to kill her and throw her body off one of the surrounding cliffs. She looked frantically out of her side window, seeing nothing but fog. 'Why did you stop? Where are we? Is Devon here?'

Jax burst out laughing. 'Can't quite picture your daughter out gallivantin' with a bunch of sheep. Can you?' He motioned out of the window at the herd of sheep slowly crossing the rural crossroads.

Minutes later, the last of the sheep gone, he threw the car back into gear.

'Is it much further?' Marcy asked. 'I could use a bathroom.'

She had expected to be either ignored or rebuked. Instead, he said, 'There's a place a few kilometres down where we can stop.'

'I'd appreciate it, thank you.'

'I do like to be appreciated. You're welcome.' He laughed.

He was still chuckling when they pulled up in front of an old turquoise-painted pub on the side of the road. 'You got two minutes,' Jax told her. 'Don't do anything stupid.'

Marcy ran for the entrance. Even though the distance was less than six feet from car to pub, she was thoroughly soaked by the time she got inside. The first thing she saw was a roaring fireplace, and she fought the urge to collapse into one of two rickety-looking rocking chairs in front of it.

'Would you just look at you!' a pretty red-haired waitress exclaimed. 'You look frozen. Go stand by the fire, luv. Get warm.'

'Don't have time,' Jax said, coming up behind Marcy and resting a heavy hand on her shoulder. 'Me mum's in need of a toilet,' he announced to the six men gathered at the bar. Marcy winced, then followed the waitress's raised finger towards the washroom at the back of the room. 'I'll have a Guinness,' she heard Jax say.

'Should you be drinking?' Marcy asked, when they were back in the car, the open bottle of beer planted firmly between Jax's sturdy thighs. 'I would have thought the driving's tough enough—'

'Don't think.'

Don't think, she heard Judith say.

'How much longer?' she asked, after another few minutes.

'Not much.' He slowed suddenly and turned down a narrow side road, tossing the now-empty beer bottle into some high grass as he edged the car up the side of a steep cliff.

Even with the wind and the rain, Marcy could hear the waves of the Celtic Sea hitting the rocks below. 'Where are we?' she asked.

'Roaringwater Bay. Good name, eh?'

What was Devon doing in a place called Roaringwater Bay?

She isn't here, Marcy realised with a certitude that almost took her breath away. The boy had never had any intention of taking her to her daughter. In all likelihood, he was spiriting her as far away from Devon as possible. On Devon's instructions? Had this whole elaborate charade been Devon's idea? Was everything? *Does she hate me that much?* Marcy wondered.

Please know how much I love you.

'Did she ever talk about me?' Marcy asked, the question falling from her mouth before she even realised it was forming.

'Audrey?' Jax asked.

'Her name is Devon,' Marcy said, correcting him.

'She's Audrey to me.'

'Did she ever talk about when she was Devon?' Marcy asked.

'Nah. Said there wasn't much to talk about.'

'She never mentioned her father or her aunt?'

'The one who was married six times?' he said.

'Five,' Marcy corrected him absently.

'Said she had a grandma who killed herself.'

'My mother,' Marcy said, as they drove up the side of a steep hill. She saw the outline of an old farmhouse in the distance. Was that where he was taking her?

'Audrey told me about this one time when she was a little girl and you yelled at her for scribblin' on the walls. Said it was her earliest memory. Said she can still hear you screamin'.'

Tears flooded Marcy's eyes.

'You used to yell at her a lot, didn't you, Marcy?' Jax continued, clearly enjoying the sight of Marcy's tears. 'Audrey said you did. She told me you made her take piano lessons and then you'd yell at her when she'd make a mistake.'

So she remembered that, too.

'What's the matter? Cat got your tongue?'

They continued in silence, the farmhouse at the top of the cliff becoming more dilapidated-looking the closer they got. Marcy noted that its windows had been boarded up. No one had lived there for a long time, she realised, as Jax pulled up to the house and stopped the car, although smoke was rising from the chimney.

'Somebody's lit a fire,' he announced, opening his car door.

Immediately, the sound of a baby's cries filled the air, competing with the howling of the wind. Marcy's head shot towards the sound.

'The dulcet tones of Caitlin O'Connor,' Jax said with a laugh.

'She's here?'

'In the flesh.'

'And Devon?'

'Where else would she be?' Jax came around to Marcy's side of the car, opened her door, and grabbed her elbow. 'You can leave your handbag in the car,' he told her. 'You're not gonna need it.'

The old house was dark and smelled of abandonment. Thin streaks of light slithered through the cracks in the thick planks of wood covering the windows, competing with the dull glow radiating from a fireplace in one of the interior rooms. A baby's cries permeated the dank air. Marcy felt Jax's hands pushing her forward.

There was no furniture, nothing to differentiate one room from the next. Just a series of stone walls and dirt-covered floors. 'Follow the screams,' Jax said ominously, as Marcy passed through one doorway and then another, the baby's cries growing louder. 'Duck your head,' Jax said, pushing her into the next room.

The first thing Marcy saw was the shadowy figure of a young woman sitting in a high-backed chair in the middle of an empty room. Next she saw a flash of strawberry-blonde hair. Then the gag in her mouth and the rope wound tightly around her torso, securing her to the chair.

'Oh, my God. Shannon!'

'Shut up,' Jax said, silencing Marcy with another push. Which was when she saw the baby lying in a cardboard box between Shannon's tethered feet and the fireplace.

'Took you long enough,' a voice announced from the shadows.

Marcy's eyes shot towards the sound, her heart pounding, her legs threatening to buckle under her. She saw nothing. 'Devon?' she whispered, the word trampled beneath the baby's piercing cries.

'I was expecting you an hour ago.'

'Yeah, well, have you seen what's doin' out there? Besides, your ma had to make a pit stop,' Jax said with a sneer, and Marcy had to grip the floor with her toes to keep from falling over.

'Devon,' Marcy said, louder this time.

'What's the matter, Mommy?' the voice asked provocatively. 'You don't look very happy to be here.'

Marcy spun around in a helpless circle. 'Where are you?' she pleaded. 'Please, baby, let me see you.'

'I'm not your baby.' The voice was flat, full of familiar disdain.

Marcy's eyes had grown accustomed to the dim light. She could see Shannon more clearly now and noted the almost imperceptible movement of Shannon's feet as they struggled to loosen the rope at her ankles. She read the plea in the girl's eyes as Shannon glanced towards the poker leaning against the stones of the fireplace, then followed those eyes to a door at the opposite end of the room.

'Please, won't you let me see you?' Marcy begged softly, her whole body aching to take her daughter in her arms. Despite the almost surreal tableau in front of her. Despite Devon's part in it.

'You'll see me when I'm ready to be seen.'

'I just want to hold you.'

'I don't think that's a very good idea.'

'Why not? What's going on? What are you mixed up in?'

'Oh, I think you already know the answer to that one. Don't you, Mommy? Understand you gave the gardai quite an earful. Understand they think you're as mad as the proverbial hatter.' She laughed. 'Which fits into our plans rather nicely, actually.'

'What plans?' Marcy saw a shadow flicker on the wall, a shake of long dark hair.

'You want details? You're not going to like them.'

'I think you owe me at least that much.'

'I don't owe you a damn thing.'

'Look,' Jax said impatiently. 'We're wastin' time, Audrey. We've got the money. Let's just shoot 'em and get out of here.'

A muffled scream escaped the gag at Shannon's mouth. She began furiously rocking her chair back and forth, back and forth.

Audrey suddenly emerged from the shadows and walked into the centre of the room, her long dark hair obscuring most of her face, although a gun was clearly visible in her right hand.

'Relax,' she said to Shannon, laying her free hand forcefully on Shannon's shoulder, bringing the girl's rocking to a halt. 'We're not going to shoot you.' She glanced towards Marcy, a spark from the fireplace dancing across her face, illuminating her cruel smile. 'My mother is.'

Marcy gasped and fell back, as if she had been struck. Shannon resumed her frantic struggles with her restraints and the baby continued howling at her feet.

'It's simple, Mommy. You had most of it figured out already. Except your part in it, of course.' Audrey's smile widened. 'The original plan was to kidnap little Caitlin here, hold her for ransom, and make it look as if Shannon was responsible. But then you entered the picture, showing your stupid photographs and telling your sob story to anyone who'd listen, so we had to improvise. We'd been planning this for months, and the last thing we wanted was to draw attention to ourselves just when we were ready to make a move. We tried to distract you, but you're rather single-minded, aren't you, Mommy? Then we thought we'd scare you. Turns out you don't scare easily. Then we realised that you could be our scapegoat. Poor Marcy, undone by grief, fixates on naive Shannon, and when Shannon rebuffs her pathetic attempts at friendship, she goes off the deep end and hires some-one to kidnap her and the baby. Delusional, she kills them both, and then, overwhelmed with guilt and remorse, turns the gun on herself. Meanwhile, her accomplice disappears with the ransom money.'

'That would be me,' Jax said, an audible swagger in his voice.

'Well, not exactly,' Audrey said sweetly, raising the gun in her hand and pointing it directly at Jax's head.

'What the hell are you doin'?' Jax asked, swagger gone.

'It's just so much easier to divide five hundred thousand euros by two than by three, don't you think?' she asked.

Then she pulled the trigger.

Caitlin's screams filled the air as the bullet lifted Jax off his feet and pro-pelled him backwards, his arms shooting up and over his head, his legs extending straight in front of him, blood gushing from his forehead as he crashed to the floor. In the next second, Shannon was hurling herself in Audrey's direction, the chair to which she was tied catching Audrey's hip and knocking them both to the floor, the gun flying from Audrey's hand. Marcy grabbed it just as Audrey was about to, their fingers brushing up against each other, sending shock waves up Marcy's arm, directly to her heart.

'Don't move,' she warned Audrey.

'Could you really shoot me, Mommy?' Audrey asked.

Marcy stared into the young woman's eyes. 'Don't call me Mommy. I don't know who you are, but you're not my daughter.'

'Marcy!' a man shouted.

Marcy didn't have to turn around to know who it was. She had been expecting him. 'Liam,' she said, her head angling towards him while she still kept Audrey firmly in her sights.

'It's OK, Marcy,' Liam said soothingly, emerging from the doorway. 'I've been right on your tail all afternoon. The gardai are on their way. You can give me the gun. It's OK now.'

'Stay back,' she warned, steadying her hand on the weapon.

He laughed. 'Marcy, it's me, Liam. I'm on *your* side.'

'You're not on my side. You planned this whole thing all along.'

How else could Audrey have known about her visits to the garda station, that the gardai had dismissed her as delusional with grief, unless Liam had told her? How else could Jax have known about her mother's suicide and her sister's many marriages? Or that Devon always called her Mommy? All confidences she had shared with Liam. Just as she had told him about her guilt at having yelled at Devon for scribbling on the walls and not practising her piano lessons correctly. Things she had never told anyone else.

'You think this was my idea?' Liam took another step forward. 'Come on, Marcy. Give me the gun.'

'Please, don't make me shoot you.'

'Shoot me? Come on. You're talkin' crazy.'

'Yeah, I'm sure you did a great job of convincing the gardai that I'm nuttier than a jar of cashews.' She laughed, thinking of Judith.

'Marcy, put down the gun. You don't know what you're sayin'.'

It was then that they heard the sound of sirens approaching in the distance. *My God*, Marcy thought, momentarily distracted by the siren's wail. Could she be wrong? Had Liam called the police?

Liam suddenly shot towards her, wresting the gun from her hand and pushing her to the floor. She tripped over Jax's body and rolled towards the fireplace. 'Get the baby,' she heard Liam shout.

Marcy watched Audrey snatch Caitlin and bolt for the back door, Liam right behind her. Struggling to her feet, Marcy grabbed the poker. *What the hell am I going to do with this?* she wondered.

Don't think, she told herself silently.

She raised her arm, heard the whoosh of the poker as it sliced through the air, absorbed the echo of steel impacting on bone as it connected with Liam's back. The gun dropped from his hand as he crumpled to the floor.

Marcy jumped over his unconscious body and grabbed the gun. Outside, the wind snapped at her face as she chased after Audrey. The sirens were getting closer, harmonising with Caitlin's screams. Marcy searched frantically through the fog for Audrey, finally spotting her running down the side of the steep hill. In the distance, she could make out half a dozen police cars making their way up the winding road. 'Audrey,' she shouted. 'Stop! The gardai are here. You can't get away.'

Audrey's response was to edge close to the side of the cliff, the wind causing her long hair to dance wildly around her face, highlighting her superficial resemblance to Devon.

'There's nowhere to go,' Marcy told her.

'One more step and it's bye-bye, baby.' Audrey extended the arm holding Caitlin, dangling the infant over the side of the cliff.

Marcy pictured her mother in the seconds before she took her fatal plunge, imagined her flying through the air to the concrete below. 'Just give her to me, Audrey,' Marcy pleaded. 'That way, at least you'll have a chance of getting away.'

'And what are the odds of that, do you think?' Audrey said. 'Think I can just disappear into thin air? Like your daughter?'

Tears stung Marcy's eyes. 'My daughter didn't disappear,' she said, acknowledging the truth aloud for the first time. 'She's dead.'

'Thought you didn't believe that.'

'I didn't want to believe it.'

'Yeah? Well, I'll tell you what,' Audrey said, as somewhere behind them cars screeched to a halt and doors slammed shut. 'I'll make you a trade— the baby for the gun. What do you say?'

'It's a deal,' Marcy agreed quickly.

'You first,' Audrey directed. 'Toss the gun over here.' She pointed with her free hand to a patch of grass near her feet. 'No funny stuff or I swear the kid takes a very nasty tumble.'

'No funny stuff.' Marcy gently pitched the gun into the tall grass next to Audrey's feet. 'Now give me the baby.'

Audrey stared at Marcy, as if debating her next move. Then she advanced slowly forwards, extending the baby towards Marcy.

Just like my dream, Marcy thought, holding her breath. *Here's the girl you've always wanted,* Devon had said, just before releasing the baby in her arms and letting her fall.

My baby is dead, Marcy thought. *I couldn't save her.*

'She's all yours,' Audrey said now, dropping the crying baby into Marcy's grateful hands.

'Marcy!' a voice shouted, as Vic Sorvino emerged from the fog and ran towards them.

Audrey jumped at the sound of his voice. She lunged towards the gun in the grass, tripping over her feet. Marcy watched helplessly as she over-compensated, stumbling backwards now, arms flailing wildly, and plunged off the side of the steep hill, her screams echoing in the wind, accompanying her into the frigid waves of Roaringwater Bay below.

THIRTEEN

'When did you realise she wasn't your daughter?' Vic was asking, holding on tightly to Marcy's still-shaking hands.

They were sitting in front of the messy desk in Christopher Murphy's office at the garda station. Murphy had just excused himself to confer with Donnelly and Sweeny in another room.

'Not right away,' Marcy answered. 'It was dark in the farmhouse, so when I first saw her, I couldn't be sure. Her hair was the same as Devon's; she looked to be the same height and build, although her voice was different, even when she whispered. But I kept telling myself that her voice could have changed. The usual rationalisations.' She sighed. 'Anyway, at first her hair was hiding most of her face. Then Jax said they should just shoot us and get out of there, and Audrey walked over to Shannon and said, cold as ice, "We're not going to shoot you. My mother is." And suddenly there was this spark from the fireplace that lit up her face. She was smiling, and I heard Peter say, "That girl needs a good set of braces."' Marcy shook her head. 'Devon's teeth were perfect, and this girl's teeth were crooked.' She released a long breath. 'The truth is, I probably knew all along.'

She reached into her handbag and withdrew the envelope containing Devon's photographs and the note her daughter had written, handing it over to Vic. 'You can read it,' she said as Vic gently unfolded the paper. 'I think I knew it was a suicide note all along. I just didn't want to accept it.'

Vic read the letter, then quietly returned it to Marcy's handbag. 'She obviously loved you very much.'

'I loved her, too. But it wasn't enough to save her.'

'I loved my wife. It wasn't enough to save her, either.'

'Your wife had cancer. It's not the same thing.'

'Isn't it? They were both sick. Sick with something they couldn't control,' Vic said. 'You have nothing to feel guilty for, Marcy.'

'Don't I? I told her I was tired of parenting. What kind of mother does that make me?'

'A pretty normal one.'

Marcy thought of the times she had berated Devon for not concentrating on her piano studies, of that awful afternoon when she had hollered at the proud toddler for scribbling on the walls. Except that Devon's note hadn't mentioned those things, Marcy realised. Instead, she had written about all the wonderful times they'd shared, the happy memories of watching TV together, of relaxing at the cottage. She had talked only of love.

'I loved her so much,' Marcy said, crying softly.

'I know you did. And, more importantly, Devon knew it.'

Marcy swiped at her tears as the door opened and Christopher Murphy re-entered the room, followed by Sweeny and Donnelly.

'Apparently, Mr Flaherty has supplied us with a full confession,' Murphy said, plopping down in his swivel chair.

It took Marcy a few seconds to digest what Murphy was saying.

'It seems that Liam's father used to work for the O'Connors' construction company. He was killed in an accident at work some years back and, according to Liam, his family was denied proper compensation. Liam decided to rectify that by kidnapping the O'Connor baby and holding her for ransom. He met Audrey when Jax brought her to Grogan's House one night. Audrey was new in town, in and out of trouble most of her life. Together the three of them hatched this plan to seduce Shannon and kidnap Caitlin, all stuff you pretty much had figured out,' Murphy said, with an admiring nod in Marcy's direction. 'Then you showed up, convinced you'd seen your daughter, and started showing Devon's picture around, and apparently a nosy waitress decided she thought the picture looked like Audrey. Things mushroomed from there.'

'When did they kidnap the baby?' Marcy asked.

'This morning, when Shannon took her for a walk. The ransom demand was made within minutes of her being spirited off. Mr O'Connor had three hours to come up with the money and was warned not to contact us or Caitlin would die.'

Marcy absorbed this information with a nod of her head, still trying to sort out fanciful fiction from hard, cold fact. Liam had been lying to her from the beginning; the only truthful thing he had ever said to her was when he claimed not to recognise Devon's picture. While she flattered herself that he might be genuinely interested in her, his attempts at seduction had been a ruse, calculated to elicit information, to keep her off balance and in line. The times he had urged her to call the police, he had done so not only with the knowledge of how ridiculous she would sound but also to keep suspicion off himself. He hadn't called the O'Connor house last night; he hadn't spoken to Shannon; Shannon had never agreed to get in touch with Audrey. His calls to the hotel last night and this morning had been nothing but a way of checking up on her.

'And now Audrey is dead,' Marcy said out loud.

'I'm afraid so, yes,' Sweeny stated. 'Her body washed up on some rocks near Bear Island about an hour ago.'

'How did you know where to find me?'

'You can thank Mr Sorvino for that,' Colleen Donnelly said.

Marcy looked to Vic for an explanation.

'Check your handbag,' he said. Marcy opened her handbag and began rummaging around inside it. She withdrew her wallet, her passport, the envelope with Devon's pictures and suicide note, a tube of lipstick, a pair of sunglasses, and . . . something else, she realised, her fingers surrounding a small metal object and holding it up. 'What is this? Is this a widget?' she asked accusingly.

'It's a tracking device,' Sweeny explained.

'We planted it in your handbag at Mr Sorvino's rather insistent suggestion,' Murphy said. 'He was convinced you were in danger and was threatening to camp out in our lobby . . .'

'So we decided to humour him,' Sweeny stated. 'We were with you from the moment you left your hotel room this morning.'

The sound of a baby's wails shot through the halls. It was followed by knocking on the door. A woman poked her head inside the room. 'Mr and Mrs O'Connor are waiting in the next room,' Marcy heard her whisper. 'They'd like to see Mrs Taggart.'

Seconds later, the O'Connors were ushered in. Marcy rose to greet them.

'Mrs Taggart, we can't thank you enough,' Mr O'Connor said, striding towards her and furiously pumping her hand.

Mrs O'Connor was standing beside him, her face blotchy from crying, her arms wrapped protectively around her screaming infant. 'I don't seem to know how to comfort her,' she whispered tearfully. 'Shannon says you have quite the way with her. Perhaps you'll share the secrets of your success,' she added shyly.

Marcy smiled, acknowledging the painful truth—that there were no such secrets. 'Sometimes you just get lucky,' she said.

IT WAS DARK by the time Marcy and Vic returned to Hayfield Manor. The intermittent rain had finally stopped; the wind had ceased blowing. According to the taxi driver who drove them to the hotel, tomorrow was expected to be a beautiful day, full of warmth and sunshine. Already it felt more temperate than it had all day, although Marcy was doubtful she would ever feel truly warm again. She was looking forward to a hot meal, followed by a hot bath, then climbing into bed. Tomorrow, she would see what she could do about changing her flight.

'I can't convince you to come to Italy with me?' Vic asked as they lingered in each other's arms beside the hotel's front entrance.

'I'd really love to,' Marcy said, fighting the almost overwhelming urge to lose herself in the comforting passion of his embrace. Except she had been lost for far too long already. 'I just don't think it's a good idea right now. I need time to get my head on straight. I haven't been behaving rationally for almost two years. Since Devon died,' she said, forcing the words from her mouth. 'I need to go home, find a good therapist, make things right with my son. Then maybe, if you're still available . . .'

'I'm available,' Vic said quickly.

Then he kissed her, a gentle kiss she felt lingering on her lips long after they said goodbye. She watched from the doorway as Vic climbed into the waiting taxi and disappeared into the night.

'Marcy?' a voice called from somewhere behind her.

Marcy turned to see a tall, thin woman with blonde hair and well-defined biceps pushing herself off the sofa beside the mahogany staircase and walking towards her. Was it possible?

'Judith? What are you doing here?'

'Did you think I was just going to wait around for you to regain your sanity and come home? I've been sitting here all afternoon. Where have you been? Who was that man?' she said in one breath.

'A friend.'

'You don't have any friends.'

Marcy smiled, drawing her sister into her arms and holding her tight. 'I have you.'

Judith threw her arms around Marcy's neck. 'Yes, you do.'

'You know I love you, don't you?' Marcy asked.

'I love you, too.' Judith pulled slowly out of their embrace. 'What about . . . Did you find . . . Is Devon . . .'

'Devon is dead,' Marcy said, her voice steady. She took a deep breath, released it slowly. 'She killed herself. Just like our mother.'

Tears filled Judith's eyes. 'It wasn't your fault,' she said.

'I know.'

'There was nothing you could have done—for either of them.'

'I know.'

'I'm sorry I wasn't more supportive.'

'You don't have to apologise,' Marcy told her. 'I'm just so glad you're here now.'

'I really do love you, you know.'

'I know.'

'You're sure you're all right?' Judith asked.

Marcy smiled. 'I will be,' she said.

joy **fielding**

Profile

Born:
March 18, 1945, Toronto,
Canada.
Residence:
Toronto and Palm Beach,
Florida.
Family:
Married; two daughters.
Favourite Books:
The Prince of Tides by Pat

Conroy, *Play It As It Lays.*
by Joan Didion.
Favourite TV Shows:
*The Mentalist, Brothers and
Sisters, Dexter.*
Favourite Movie:
*Invasion of the Body
Snatchers.*
Website:
JoyFielding.com

Joy Fielding was not a big reader when she was a child, and only read 'what I was forced to', but she did love to write and found that it came relatively easily to her. She sent her first story to *Jack and Jill* magazine when she was just eight years old, but it was rejected. She also wrote plays that were performed by herself and a group of friends for their captive parents during summer vacations and, at twelve, wrote her first TV script: the story of a twelve-year-old girl who murders her parents, which was also rejected. Undaunted, Joy continued writing all through her teen years and was always the child who was asked to read her compositions out loud in English class. When she graduated from high school, her English teacher told her that she was destined to become a writer, so she majored in English at the University of Toronto.

During her college years, however, Joy caught the acting bug and performed in campus productions. After graduation, she spent several years in Los Angeles, where she appeared in commercials and minor roles—including an episode of *Gunsmoke,* in which she got to kiss Elvis Presley—but she also worked in banks to pay the bills. Eventually, Joy realised that, as her teacher had predicted, writing was her true destiny, and she returned to Toronto, where she became more about writing until it nudged out acting altogether. She wrote her first novel, *The Best of Friends*, at her parents' kitchen table and it was published in 1972. From that moment she has never looked back.

Joy Fielding's years as an actor were to prove beneficial in her writing career. 'Acting taught me drama. The essence of drama is conflict, and to keep readers engaged you always have some sort of conflict going on,' she says. 'Acting taught me how to shape scenes and build tension.'

Joy says she loves writing because she has complete control. 'Nobody does or says anything I don't tell them to—although even this amount of control is illusory, because there comes a point where the characters take over and tell you what they think they should say and do,' she says. 'As a child, I played with cut-out dolls until I was fourteen years old, long past the age when my friends still played with them. I made up elaborate stories with my paper dolls, letting my imagination run wild. That's really all I'm doing today— still playing with my dolls and letting my imagination run loose. Everyone should be so lucky in their chosen profession.'

'You can tell a pretty fantastic tale, but if you populate it with real people feeling real emotions, your readers will follow you anywhere.'

But even if they are figments of her imagination, Joy Fielding says that all her main characters have aspects of her own personality. 'I find that I approach the heroines as if I were a Method actress. I think, How would I react if this were happening to me?' she explains. 'Sometimes I try to take the easy way out by neglecting the characters and concentrating on the plot. This never works and I have to start again. I have to create a history for the characters, figure out who they are, what their backgrounds are, why they act the way they do.' She will even create family trees for her characters, just to keep everything straight.

As for ideas, the author finds them in all sorts of places. She occasionally gets ideas from magazine or newspaper stories. More often, though, something might happen to someone she knows, or to herself, and she recognises the story potential. 'I use whatever I can,' Joy Fielding says. 'Nothing is sacred. I think I'm successful at depicting real women because I understand women, mostly because I understand myself quite well. You can tell a pretty fantastic tale, but if you populate it with real people feeling real emotions, your readers will follow you anywhere.'

Joy still lives in Toronto but has a house in Palm Beach, where she spends as much time as possible. She enjoys working on her golf handicap, playing bridge, and travelling when she has the time. She has been married for more than thirty years to her beloved husband, Warren, and has two daughters, one an actress and the other working behind-the-scenes in the film industry. She is also a new and very devoted grandmother to her grandson, Hayden. 'I am so wildly in love with that little boy, it's ridiculous,' she says. 'Everything he says and does delights me, and I absolutely love spending time with him.'